SOUTH LANARKSHIRE
Leisure & Culture

www.library.southlanarkshire.gov.uk

S̶o̶u̶t̶h̶ ̶L̶a̶n̶a̶r̶k̶s̶h̶i̶r̶e̶ Libraries

This book is to be returned on or
before the last date stamped below
or may be renewed by telephone or
online.

Delivering services for South Lanarkshire

23/3/18		
03/01/19		

COLLINS
CLASSICS

Harper Press
An imprint of HarperCollins*Publishers*
77–85 Fulham Palace Road
Hammersmith
London W6 8JB

This Harper Press paperback edition published 2013

Virginia Woolf asserts the moral right to be identified as the author of this work

A catalogue record for this book is available from the British Library

ISBN: 978-0-00-793440-9

Printed and bound in Great Britain by Clays Ltd, St Ives plc

MIX
Paper from
responsible sources
FSC™ C007454

FSC™ is a non-profit international organisation established to promote the
responsible management of the world's forests. Products carrying the FSC label
are independently certified to assure consumers that they come
from forests that are managed to meet the social, economic and
ecological needs of present and future generations.

Find out more about HarperCollins and the environment at
www.harpercollins.co.uk/green

Life & Times section © HarperCollins*Publishers* Ltd
Gerard Cheshire asserts his moral rights as author of the Life & Times section
Classic Literature: Words and Phrases adapted from
Collins English Dictionary
Typesetting in Kalix by Palimpsest Book Production Limited,
Falkirk, Stirlingshire

South Lanarkshire Library Service	
EK	
C702281896	
Askews & Holts	
CL	£2.50
5507947	

History of Collins

In 1819, millworker William Collins from Glasgow, Scotland, set up a company for printing and publishing pamphlets, sermons, hymn books and prayer books. That company was Collins and was to mark the birth of HarperCollins Publishers as we know it today. The long tradition of Collins dictionary publishing can be traced back to the first dictionary William published in 1824, *Greek and English Lexicon*. Indeed, from 1840 onwards, he began to produce illustrated dictionaries and even obtained a licence to print and publish the Bible.

Soon after, William published the first Collins novel, *Ready Reckoner*; however, it was the time of the Long Depression, where harvests were poor, prices were high, potato crops had failed and violence was erupting in Europe. As a result, many factories across the country were forced to close down and William chose to retire in 1846, partly due to the hardships he was facing.

Aged 30, William's son, William II took over the business. A keen humanitarian with a warm heart and a generous spirit, William II was truly 'Victorian' in his outlook. He introduced new, up-to-date steam presses and published affordable editions of Shakespeare's works and *The Pilgrim's Progress*, making them available to the masses for the first time. A new demand for educational books meant that success came with the publication of travel books, scientific books, encyclopaedias and dictionaries. This demand to be educated led to the later publication of atlases and Collins also held the monopoly on scripture writing at the time.

In the 1860s Collins began to expand and diversify

and the idea of 'books for the millions' was developed. Affordable editions of classical literature were published and in 1903 Collins introduced 10 titles in their Collins Handy Illustrated Pocket Novels. These proved so popular that a few years later this had increased to an output of 50 volumes, selling nearly half a million in their year of publication. In the same year, The Everyman's Library was also instituted, with the idea of publishing an affordable library of the most important classical works, biographies, religious and philosophical treatments, plays, poems, travel and adventure. This series eclipsed all competition at the time and the introduction of paperback books in the 1950s helped to open that market and marked a high point in the industry.

HarperCollins is and has always been a champion of the classics and the current Collins Classics series follows in this tradition – publishing classical literature that is affordable and available to all. Beautifully packaged, highly collectible and intended to be reread and enjoyed at every opportunity.

Life & Times

Mental Health and Creativity

It would be fair to say that Virginia Woolf was an intense and complex personality. Some might describe her as highly imaginative, sensitive and creative, while others might use the words high-maintenance, introspective and obsessive. In truth, she was all of the above, which meant that she was highly regarded as a novelist by many and entirely disregarded by others.

The central sticking point with the latter was that she came from a highly privileged, upper-middle-class background, yet she viewed the world in quite a negative light. Untroubled by the daily pressures of most, her time was spent in deep analysis of life – or rather, her own life and that of her friends and family. Her literature, therefore, could occasionally disconnect with the lay reader, because her concerns could be seen as self-indulgent and focused on a rarified environment to which most people were not privy.

As a human specimen, Woolf was not a very robust figure. She was prone to bouts of depression and breakdown, in part possibly brought on by the lack of any necessity to just get on with activities that were positive for her mental and physical constitution. In the absence of responsibilities to toughen the character, she lived in a world of ever-decreasing circles until, one day, her horizons closed in so tight that she chose suicide as a means of escape. She filled the pockets of her overcoat with pebbles and walked headlong into a river to drown her sorrows, quite literally. Her life was ended by her own thoughts and actions at the age of 59.

Woolf is a classic case of an artist whose creative

expression was bad for their health. Had she abandoned writing in favour of an occupation that took her mind away from her obsessive thoughts, she would undoubtedly have lived a happier and more fulfilled life, but instead she became the author of her own undoing. So, a weighty question remains: was it worth all the pain and suffering? Inevitably those with similar leanings will say *yes*, because they are able to identify with Woolf's desire to commit her thoughts to the written word as a kind of catharsis. Inevitably those who cannot identify will say *no*, because her work offers nothing to which they can relate as they have no need of therapy. It may be that there has never been a more divisive novelist in the history of English literature, and this is probably Woolf's most interesting aspect.

Woolf's main influence on modern literature was her 'stream of consciousness' approach to prose. Her novels were really vehicles for the copious current of thoughts and emotions to flow without parameters. She was an aesthete and intelligentsium, investing all of her mental capacity into understanding and disseminating the minutiae of human nature, human society, human culture and the human condition. Woolf and her set could be seen as looking down on those who chose not to analyse human existence in such microscopic detail, but realistically this was probably the result of insecurities about one's own talent, context and significance. The one thing that is certain about belief systems is that believing things doesn't make them true. This is certainly not to say that Woolf's portfolio has no value – far from it – but that we do well to remember the context of the author. After all, it was precisely because she existed in her particular milieu that she produced her pioneering style of literature. Moreover, had she been born into a more typical, lower-middle or working class background, she would probably not have had the wherewithal to dissect humanity to such a level.

Mrs. Dalloway and To the Lighthouse

Virginia Woolf's prolific patch continued in 1925 and 1927, when she published *Mrs. Dalloway* and then *To the Lighthouse*. In these two novels, she displays the kind of original approach to prose that would forge her reputation as a literary genius. Woolf experimented with innovative approaches to writing that set her apart from her contemporaries by largely abandoning plot in favour of psychological exploration. She made it her mission to delve into the human condition – something most people took so much for granted that they failed to consider its importance.

Of course, this approach didn't make her books easy to read, but the whole point of the method was to challenge literary norms. Just as one needed to apply effort to understand the work of the Cubist artistic movement, which was prevalent at that time, so Woolf published literature with a similar requirement for analysis. She had turned the novel into high art. This wasn't to everyone's taste, but it would inevitably prove very influential. It was a sea change in defining the purpose of the novel, as the author was no longer expected to take the work to the reader. Instead, the reader was expected to do their own work and accept the challenge of interpreting a text's meaning. It was an intellectual workout on offer, rather than an unthinking stroll. Inevitably, this catalysed a division within the realm of the novel, as it divided into the 'literary novel' and the 'commercial novel'. The landscape of fiction publishing had been irreversibly altered by progress, and Woolf was at the forefront of the march to modernity.

The surface plot for *Mrs. Dalloway* is simply that Clarissa Dalloway is preparing to host a party in the evening. But beyond the surface, Woolf explores the thought processes of Mrs. Dalloway as she is prompted to reflect on her life and past events. Central to the novel is reference to the effect of World War I on British society in the post-war years and, in particular, the loss of loved ones and the altering fate of those left behind. The consequences of this included the physical and psychological damage done to those who fought and survived, as well as to those who survived despite never having set foot on the battlefield. It all adds up to an odd juxtaposition of people carrying on their lives, with parties, families and friends, while an unspoken suffering erodes their happiness.

The chronology of *To the Lighthouse* brackets World War I, examining the societal transformation caused by the conflict. The eponymous lighthouse is the summer home of the Ramsay family, on the Isle of Sky, in the Hebrides archipelago, off Scotland. The dynamic of the social environment inevitably changes year after year, but the war causes an abrupt change, due in part to the hiatus, but also due to three deaths – one from old age, one from combat and one from complications in childbirth. The use of the lighthouse is, of course, symbolic as a metaphorical guiding light that leads people to safety in life's travels. Despite the turbulence that life has wrought on the surviving members of the family, they manage to maintain the notion that meeting at the island provides them with a sense of insight and contentment that their world would otherwise lack.

Woolf's general take on society and the individual lives of her characters has an air of the upper-middle class about it, as those are the people seen to throw parties and have holiday homes, but this doesn't detract from the weight of her prose or to remove her meaning from the reaches of other readers. This is because she uses these characters as devices to bring protagonists together in order to investigate the interaction of personality with great skill.

The Bloomsbury Set

Virginia Woolf came from a background of intellectualism,

however, this was largely cemented by her family's relocation from Kensington to Bloomsbury, where she became part of an intellectual elite known as the Bloomsbury Set. Together, they were all goldfish in the same bowl, looking out at the world around them with a similar artistic palette.

The pretentions of her social group actually allowed her to blossom as a writer, because she was given the encouragement and freedom she needed to experiment with her prose. In short, she was allowed to think of herself as an author and she was told what she wanted to hear. This was vitally important to someone with nagging self-doubt, so she developed deep and lasting bonds with those who saw and nurtured her potential. Indeed, she married one of them – Leonard Woolf – and remained devoted to him.

In time, of course, the pretentions of the Bloomsbury Set transcended into success, as they were undoubtedly intelligent, talented and well educated. This process of ascendance was, in part, aided by a number of stunts designed to draw public attention. One stunt in particular has become famous for its daring and humour: the Dreadnought Hoax. This was an elaborate plan to gain egress to the battleship *HMS Dreadnought* for no other reason than to have a good look around. A number of the Bloomsbury Set, including Woolf, disguised themselves as Abyssinian princes. They wore the appropriate garb of robes and turbans, but they also 'blacked-up' and sported fake beards. With escort and interpreter in tow, they boarded a VIP coach and took a train from Paddington to Weymouth, where they were received as genuine royalty with honour guard and allowed to inspect Royal Navy fleet. All the while, they pretended to communicate in a foreign tongue by uttering gibberish furnished with Greek and Latin, which the interpreter duly pretended to understand and translate.

Having returned to London, a photograph of the Bloomsbury Set, still in character, was sent to the *Daily Mirror* newspaper and the hoax was revealed. Not surprisingly, the affair turned into a scandal. The Foreign Office and the Royal Navy were the target of a great deal of finger-pointing, partly in fun and partly in seriousness for allowing such a blatant lapse in national security. The situation wasn't helped by the fact that the Bloomsbury Set were pacifists, which only served to rub salt into the wound. When the Navy high command pushed to have the perpetrators punished, they found themselves powerless to do anything. For one thing, no laws were broken, and secondly the consensus was that they themselves should be punished for allowing themselves to be beguiled by such a lame practical joke.

Needless to say, the Dreadnought Hoax planted the Bloomsbury Set in the public consciousness once and for all, as the oxygen of publicity was theirs to breathe in and enjoy. The hoax occurred on 7 February, 1910. Woolf's first novel was begun the same year, although she did not publish until 1915, by which time she was already a minor celebrity.

Despite her subsequent success, Woolf was never particularly contented, for she had such a troubled soul and indefatigable mind. Today her malady would, doubtless, be described as a bipolar condition, for she oscillated from exuberant mood highs to despairing clinical lows. In the end, she was convinced that she would never come full circle again, so she decided to cut her losses while in the grip of a crushing depression that rendered her unable to see any light at the end of the tunnel. Virginia Woolf died in 1941, leaving behind a highly respected, progressive and considerable canon of essays, critique and novels.

MRS.
DALLOWAY

Mrs. Dalloway

Mrs. Dalloway said she would buy the flowers herself.

For Lucy had her work cut out for her. The doors would be taken off their hinges; Rumpelmayer's men were coming. And then, thought Clarissa Dalloway, what a morning – fresh as if issued to children on a beach.

What a lark! What a plunge! For so it had always seemed to her when, with a little squeak of the hinges, which she could hear now, she had burst open the French windows and plunged at Bourton into the open air. How fresh, how calm, stiller than this of course, the air was in the early morning; like the flap of a wave; the kiss of a wave; chill and sharp and yet (for a girl of eighteen as she then was) solemn, feeling as she did, standing there at the open window, that something awful was about to happen; looking at the flowers, at the trees with the smoke winding off them and the rooks rising, falling; standing and looking until Peter Walsh said, "Musing among the vegetables?" – was that it? – "I prefer men to cauliflowers" – was that it? He must have said it at breakfast one morning when she had gone out on to the terrace – Peter Walsh. He would be back from India one of these days, June or July, she forgot which, for his letters were awfully dull; it was his sayings one remembered; his eyes, his pocket-knife, his smile, his grumpiness and, when millions of things had utterly vanished – how strange it was! – a few sayings like this about cabbages.

She stiffened a little on the kerb, waiting for Durtnall's van to pass. A charming woman, Scrope Purvis thought her (knowing her as one does know people who live next door to one in Westminster); a touch of the bird about her, of the jay, blue-green, light, vivacious, though she was over fifty, and grown very white since her illness. There she perched, never seeing him, waiting to cross, very upright.

For having lived in Westminster – how many years now? over twenty, – one feels even in the midst of the traffic, or waking at night, Clarissa was positive, a particular hush, or solemnity; an indescribable pause; a suspense (but that might be her heart, affected, they said, by influenza) before Big Ben strikes. There! Out it boomed. First a warning, musical; then the hour, irrevocable. The leaden circles dissolved in the air. Such fools we are, she thought, crossing Victoria Street. For Heaven only knows why one loves it so, how one sees it so, making it up, building it round one, tumbling it, creating it every moment afresh; but the veriest frumps, the most dejected of miseries sitting on doorsteps (drink their downfall) do the same; can't be dealt with, she felt positive, by Acts of Parliament for that very reason: they love life. In people's eyes, in the swing, tramp, and trudge; in the bellow and the uproar; the carriages, motor cars, omnibuses, vans, sandwich men shuffling and swinging; brass bands; barrel organs; in the triumph and the jingle and the strange high singing of some aeroplane overhead was what she loved; life; London; this moment of June.

For it was the middle of June. The War was over, except for some one like Mrs. Foxcroft at the Embassy last night eating her heart out because that nice boy was killed and now the old Manor House must go to a cousin; or Lady Bexborough who opened a bazaar, they said, with the telegram in her

hand, John, her favourite, killed; but it was over; thank Heaven
– over. It was June. The King and Queen were at the Palace.
And everywhere, though it was still so early, there was a
beating, a stirring of galloping ponies, tapping of cricket bats;
Lords, Ascot, Ranelagh and all the rest of it; wrapped in the
soft mesh of the grey-blue morning air, which, as the day
wore on, would unwind them, and set down on their lawns
and pitches the bouncing ponies, whose forefeet just struck
the ground and up they sprung, the whirling young men, and
laughing girls in their transparent muslins who, even now,
after dancing all night, were taking their absurd woolly dogs
for a run; and even now, at this hour, discreet old dowagers
were shooting out in their motor cars on errands of mystery;
and the shopkeepers were fidgeting in their windows with
their paste and diamonds, their lovely old sea-green brooches
in eighteenth-century settings to tempt Americans (but one
must economise, not buy things rashly for Elizabeth), and
she, too, loving it as she did with an absurd and faithful
passion, being part of it, since her people were courtiers once
in the time of the Georges, she, too, was going that very night
to kindle and illuminate; to give her party. But how strange,
on entering the Park, the silence; the mist; the hum; the
slow-swimming happy ducks; the pouched birds waddling;
and who should be coming along with his back against the
Government buildings, most appropriately, carrying a despatch
box stamped with the Royal Arms, who but Hugh Whitbread;
her old friend Hugh – the admirable Hugh!

"Good-morning to you, Clarissa!" said Hugh, rather
extravagantly, for they had known each other as children.
"Where are you off to?"

"I love walking in London," said Mrs. Dalloway. "Really,
it's better than walking in the country."

They had just come up – unfortunately – to see doctors.
Other people came to see pictures; go to the opera; take their
daughters out; the Whitbreads came "to see doctors". Times

without number Clarissa had visited Evelyn Whitbread in a nursing home. Was Evelyn ill again? Evelyn was a good deal out of sorts, said Hugh, intimating by a kind of pout or swell of his very well-covered, manly, extremely handsome, perfectly upholstered body (he was almost too well dressed always, but presumably had to be, with his little job at Court) that his wife had some internal ailment, nothing serious, which, as an old friend, Clarissa Dalloway would quite understand without requiring him to specify. Ah yes, she did of course; what a nuisance; and felt very sisterly and oddly conscious at the same time of her hat. Not the right hat for the early morning, was that it? For Hugh always made her feel, as he bustled on, raising his hat rather extravagantly and assuring her that she might be a girl of eighteen, and of course he was coming to her party to-night, Evelyn absolutely insisted, only a little late he might be after the party at the Palace to which he had to take one of Jim's boys, – she always felt a little skimpy beside Hugh; schoolgirlish; but attached to him, partly from having known him always, but she did think him a good sort in his own way, though Richard was nearly driven mad by him, and as for Peter Walsh, he had never to this day forgiven her for liking him.

She could remember scene after scene at Bourton – Peter furious; Hugh not, of course, his match in any way, but still not a positive imbecile as Peter made out; not a mere barber's block. When his old mother wanted him to give up shooting or to take her to Bath he did it, without a word; he was really unselfish, and as for saying, as Peter did, that he had no heart, no brain, nothing but the manners and breeding of an English gentleman, that was only her dear Peter at his worst; and he could be intolerable; he could be impossible; but adorable to walk with on a morning like this.

(June had drawn out every leaf on the trees. The mothers of Pimlico gave suck to their young. Messages were passing from the Fleet to the Admiralty. Arlington Street and Piccadilly seemed to chafe the very air in the Park and lift its leaves hotly, brilliantly, on waves of that divine vitality which Clarissa loved. To dance, to ride, she had adored all that.)

For they might be parted for hundreds of years, she and Peter; she never wrote a letter and his were dry sticks; but suddenly it would come over her. If he were with me now what would he say? – some days, some sights bringing him back to her calmly, without the old bitterness; which perhaps was the reward of having cared for people; they came back in the middle of St. James's Park on a fine morning – indeed they did. But Peter – however beautiful the day might be, and the trees and the grass, and the little girl in pink – Peter never saw a thing of all that. He would put on his spectacles, if she told him to; he would look. It was the state of the world that interested him; Wagner, Pope's poetry, people's characters eternally, and the defects of her own soul. How he scolded her! How they argued! She would marry a Prime Minister and stand at the top of a staircase; the perfect hostess he called her (she had cried over it in her bedroom), she had the makings of the perfect hostess, he said.

So she would still find herself arguing in St. James's Park, still making out that she had been right – and she had too – not to marry him. For in marriage a little licence, a little independence there must be between people living together day in day out in the same house; which Richard gave her, and she him. (Where was he this morning, for instance? Some committee, she never asked what.) But with Peter everything had to be shared; everything gone into. And it was intolerable, and when it came to that scene in the little garden by the fountain, she had to break with him or they would have been destroyed, both of them ruined, she was convinced; though she had borne about with her for years like an arrow sticking in her heart the grief, the anguish; and then the horror of the moment when some one told her at a concert that he had married a woman met on the boat going to India! Never should she forget all that! Cold, heartless, a prude, he called her. Never could she understand how he cared. But those Indian women did presumably – silly, pretty, flimsy nincompoops. And she wasted her pity. For he was quite happy, he assured her – perfectly happy, though he had never done a thing that they talked of; his whole life had been a failure. It made her angry still.

She had reached the Park gates. She stood for a moment, looking at the omnibuses in Piccadilly.

She would not say of any one in the world now that they were this or were that. She felt very young; at the same time unspeakably aged. She sliced like a knife through everything; at the same time was outside, looking on. She had a perpetual sense, as she watched the taxi cabs, of being out, out, far out to sea and alone; she always had the feeling that it was very, very dangerous to live even one day. Not that she thought herself clever, or much out of the ordinary. How she had got through life on the few twigs of knowledge Fräulein Daniels gave them she could not think. She knew nothing; no language, no history; she scarcely read a book now, except memoirs in bed; and yet to her it was absolutely absorbing; all this; the cabs passing; and she would not say of Peter, she would not say of herself, I am this, I am that.

Her only gift was knowing people almost by instinct, she thought, walking on. If you put her in a room with some one, up went her back like a cat's; or she purred. Devonshire House, Bath House, the house with the china cockatoo, she had seen them all lit up once; and remembered Sylvia, Fred, Sally Seton – such hosts of people; and dancing all night; and the waggons plodding past to market; and driving home across the Park. She remembered once throwing a shilling into the Serpentine. But every one remembered; what she loved was this, here, now, in front of her; the fat lady in the cab. Did it matter then, she asked herself, walking towards Bond Street, did it matter that she must inevitably cease completely; all this must go on without her; did she resent it; or did it not become consoling to believe that death ended absolutely? But that somehow in the streets of London, on the ebb and flow of things, here, there, she survived, Peter survived, lived in each other, she being part, she was positive, of the trees at home; of the house there, ugly, rambling all to bits and pieces as it was; part of people she had never met; being laid out like a mist between the people she knew best, who lifted her on their branches as she had seen the trees lift the mist, but it spread ever so far, her life, herself. But what was she dreaming as she looked into Hatchards' shop window? What was she trying to recover? What image of white dawn in the country, as she read in the book spread open:

> Fear no more the heat o' the sun
> Nor the furious winter's rages.

This late age of the world's experience had bred in them all, all men and women, a well of tears. Tears and sorrows; courage and endurance; a perfectly upright and stoical bearing. Think, for example, of the woman she admired most, Lady Bexborough, opening the bazaar.

There were Jorrocks' *Jaunts and Jollities*; there were *Soapy Sponge* and Mrs. Asquith's *Memoirs* and *Big Game Shooting in Nigeria*, all spread open. Ever so many books there were; but none that seemed exactly right to take to Evelyn Whitbread in her nursing home. Nothing that would serve to amuse her and make that indescribably dried-up little woman look, as Clarissa came in, just for a moment cordial; before they settled down for the usual interminable talk of women's ailments. How much she wanted it – that people should look pleased as she came in, Clarissa thought and turned and walked back towards Bond Street, annoyed, because it was silly to have other reasons for doing things. Much rather would she have been one of those people like Richard who did things for themselves, whereas, she thought, waiting to cross, half the time she did things not simply, not for themselves; but to make people think this or that; perfect idiocy she knew (and now the policeman held up his hand) for no one was ever for a second taken in. Oh if she could have had her life over again! she thought, stepping on to the pavement, could have looked even differently!

She would have been, in the first place, dark like Lady Bexborough, with a skin of crumpled leather and beautiful eyes. She would have been, like Lady Bexborough, slow and stately; rather large; interested in politics like a man; with a country house; very dignified, very sincere. Instead of which she had a narrow pea-stick figure; a ridiculous little face, beaked like a bird's. That she held herself well was true; and had nice hands and feet; and dressed well, considering that she spent little. But often now this body she wore (she stopped to look at a Dutch picture), this body, with all its capacities, seemed nothing – nothing at all. She had the oddest sense of being herself invisible; unseen; unknown; there being no more marrying, no more having of children now, but only this astonishing and rather solemn progress with the rest of them, up Bond Street, this being Mrs. Dalloway; not even Clarissa any more; this being Mrs. Richard Dalloway.

Bond Street fascinated her; Bond Street early in the morning in the season; its flags flying; its shops; no splash; no glitter; one roll of tweed in the shop where her father had bought his suits for fifty years; a few pearls; salmon on an iceblock.

"That is all," she said, looking at the fishmonger's. "That is all," she repeated, pausing for a moment at the window of a glove shop where, before the War, you could buy almost perfect gloves. And her old Uncle William used to say a lady is known by her shoes and her gloves. He had turned on his bed one morning in the middle of the War. He had said, "I have had enough." Gloves and shoes; she had a passion for gloves; but her own daughter, her Elizabeth, cared not a straw for either of them.

Not a straw, she thought, going on up Bond Street to a shop where they kept flowers for her when she gave a party. Elizabeth really cared for her dog most of all. The whole house this morning smelt of tar. Still, better poor Grizzle than Miss Kilman; better distemper and tar and all the rest of it than sitting mewed in a stuffy bedroom with a prayer book! Better anything, she was inclined to say. But it might be only a phase, as Richard said, such as all girls go through. It might be falling in love. But why with Miss Kilman? Who had been badly treated of course; one must make allowances for that, and Richard said she was very able, had a really historical mind. Anyhow they were inseparable, and Elizabeth, her own daughter, went to Communion; and how she dressed, how she treated people who came to lunch she did not care a bit, it being her experience that the religious ecstasy made people callous (so did causes); dulled their feelings, for Miss Kilman would do anything for the Russians, starved herself for the Austrians, but in private inflicted positive torture, so insensitive was she, dressed in a green mackintosh coat. Year in year out she wore that coat; she perspired; she was never in the room five minutes without making you feel her superiority, your inferiority; how poor she was; how rich you were; how she lived in a slum without a cushion or a bed or a rug or whatever it might be, all her soul rusted with that grievance sticking in it, her dismissal from school during the War – poor embittered unfortunate creature! For it was not her one hated but the idea of her, which undoubtedly had gathered in to itself a great deal that was not Miss Kilman; had become one of those spectres with which one battles in the night; one of those spectres who stand astride us and suck up half our life-blood, dominators and tyrants; for no doubt with another throw of the dice, had the black been uppermost and not the white, she would have loved Miss Kilman! But not in this world. No.

It rasped her, though, to have stirring about in her this brutal monster! To hear twigs cracking and feel hooves planted down in the depths of that leaf-encumbered forest, the soul; never to be content quite, or quite secure, for at any moment the brute would be stirring, this hatred, which, especially since her illness, had power to make her feel scraped, hurt in her spine; gave her physical pain, and made all pleasure in beauty, in friendship, in being well, in being loved and making her home delightful rock, quiver, and bend as if indeed there were a monster grubbing at the roots, as if the whole panoply of content were nothing but self love! this hatred!

Nonsense, nonsense! she cried to herself, pushing through the swing doors of Mulberry's the florists.

She advanced, light, tall, very upright, to be greeted at once by button-faced Miss Pym, whose hands were always bright red, as if they had been stood in cold water with the flowers.

There were flowers: delphiniums, sweet peas, bunches of lilac; and carnations, masses of carnations. There were roses; there were irises. Ah yes – so she breathed in the earthy garden sweet smell as she stood talking to Miss Pym who owed her help, and thought her kind, for kind she had been years ago; very kind, but she looked older, this year, turning her head from side to side among the irises and roses and nodding tufts of lilac with her eyes half closed, snuffing in, after the street uproar, the delicious scent, the exquisite coolness. And then, opening her eyes, how fresh, like frilled linen clean from a laundry laid in wicker trays, the roses looked; and dark and prim the red carnations, holding their heads up; and all the sweet peas spreading in their bowls, tinged violet, snow white, pale – as if it were the evening and girls in muslin frocks came out to pick sweet peas and roses after the superb summer's day, with its almost blue-black sky, its delphiniums, its carnations, its arum lilies was over; and it was the moment between six and seven when every flower – roses, carnations, irises, lilac – glows; white, violet, red, deep orange; every flower seems to burn by itself, softly, purely in the misty beds; and how she loved the grey white moths spinning in and out, over the cherry pie, over the evening primroses!

And as she began to go with Miss Pym from jar to jar, choosing, nonsense, nonsense, she said to herself, more and more gently, as if this beauty, this scent, this colour, and Miss Pym liking her, trusting her, were a wave which she let flow over her and surmount that hatred, that monster, surmount it all; and it lifted her up and up when – oh! a pistol shot in the street outside!

"Dear, those motor cars," said Miss Pym, going to the window to look, and coming back and smiling apologetically with her hands full of sweet peas, as if those motor cars, those tyres of motor cars, were all *her* fault.

The violent explosion which made Mrs. Dalloway jump and Miss Pym go to the window and apologise came from a motor car which had drawn to the side of the pavement precisely opposite Mulberry's shop window. Passers-by who, of course, stopped and stared, had just time to see a face of the very greatest importance against the dove-grey upholstery, before a male hand drew the blind and there was nothing to be seen except a square of dove grey.

Yet rumours were at once in circulation from the middle of Bond Street to Oxford Street on one side, to Atkinson's scent shop on the other, passing invisibly, inaudibly, like a cloud, swift, veil-like upon hills, falling indeed with something of a cloud's sudden sobriety and stillness upon faces which a second before had been utterly disorderly. But now mystery had brushed them with her wing; they had heard the voice of authority; the spirit of religion was abroad with her eyes bandaged tight and her lips gaping wide. But nobody knew whose face had been seen. Was it the Prince of Wales's, the Queen's, the Prime Minister's? Whose face was it? Nobody knew.

Edgar J. Watkiss, with his roll of lead piping round his

arm, said audibly, humorously of course: "The Proime Minister's kyar."

Septimus Warren Smith, who found himself unable to pass, heard him.

Septimus Warren Smith, aged about thirty, pale-faced, beak-nosed, wearing brown shoes and a shabby overcoat, with hazel eyes which had that look of apprehension in them which makes complete strangers apprehensive too. The world has raised its whip; where will it descend?

Everything had come to a standstill. The throb of the motor engines sounded like a pulse irregularly drumming through an entire body. The sun became extraordinarily hot because the motor car had stopped outside Mulberry's shop window; old ladies on the tops of omnibuses spread their black parasols; here a green, here a red parasol opened with a little pop. Mrs. Dalloway, coming to the window with her arms full of sweet peas, looked out with her little pink face pursed in enquiry. Every one looked at the motor car. Septimus looked. Boys on bicycles sprang off. Traffic accumulated. And there the motor car stood, with drawn blinds, and upon them a curious pattern like a tree, Septimus thought, and this gradual drawing together of everything to one centre before his eyes, as if some horror had come almost to the surface and was about to burst into flames, terrified him. The world wavered and quivered and threatened to burst into flames. It is I who am blocking the way, he thought. Was he not being looked at and pointed at; was he not weighted there, rooted to the pavement, for a purpose? But for what purpose?

"Let us go on, Septimus," said his wife, a little woman, with large eyes in a sallow pointed face; an Italian girl.

But Lucrezia herself could not help looking at the motor car and the tree pattern on the blinds. Was it the Queen in there – the Queen going shopping?

The chauffeur, who had been opening something, turning something, shutting something, got on to the box.

"Come on," said Lucrezia.

But her husband, for they had been married four, five years now, jumped, started, and said, "All right!" angrily, as if she had interrupted him.

People must notice; people must see. People, she thought, looking at the crowd staring at the motor car; the English people, with their children and their horses and their clothes, which she admired in a way; but they were "people" now, because Septimus had said, "I will kill myself"; an awful thing to say. Suppose they had heard him? She looked at the crowd. Help, help! she wanted to cry out to butchers' boys and women. Help! Only last autumn she and Septimus had stood on the Embankment wrapped in the same cloak and, Septimus reading a paper instead of talking, she had snatched it from him and laughed in the old man's face who saw them! But failure one conceals. She must take him away into some park.

"Now we will cross," she said.

She had a right to his arm, though it was without feeling. He would give her, who was so simple, so impulsive, only twenty-four, without friends in England, who had left Italy for his sake, a piece of bone.

The motor car with its blinds drawn and an air of inscrutable reserve proceeded towards Piccadilly, still gazed at, still ruffling the faces on both sides of the street with the same dark breath of veneration whether for Queen, Prince, or Prime Minister nobody knew. The face itself had been seen only once by three people for a few seconds. Even the sex was now in dispute. But there could be no doubt that greatness was seated within; greatness was passing, hidden, down Bond Street, removed only by a hand's-breadth from ordinary people who might now, for the first and last time, be within speaking distance of the majesty of England, of the enduring symbol of the state which will be known to curious antiquaries, sifting the ruins of time, when London is a grass-grown path and all those hurrying along the pavement this Wednesday morning are but bones with a few wedding rings mixed up in their dust and the gold stoppings of innumerable decayed teeth. The face in the motor car will then be known.

It is probably the Queen, thought Mrs. Dalloway, coming out of Mulberry's with her flowers; the Queen. And for a second she wore a look of extreme dignity standing by the flower shop in the sunlight while the car passed at a foot's pace, with its blinds drawn. The Queen going to some hospital; the Queen opening some bazaar, thought Clarissa.

The crush was terrific for the time of day. Lords, Ascot, Hurlingham, what was it? she wondered, for the street was blocked. The British middle classes sitting sideways on the tops of omnibuses with parcels and umbrellas, yes, even furs on a day like this, were, she thought, more ridiculous, more unlike anything there has ever been than one could conceive; and the Queen herself held up; the Queen herself unable to pass. Clarissa was suspended on one side of Brook Street; Sir John Buckhurst, the old Judge on the other, with the car between them (Sir John had laid down the law for years and liked a well-dressed woman) when the chauffeur, leaning ever so slightly, said or showed something to the policeman, who saluted and raised his arm and jerked his head and moved the omnibus to the side and the car passed through. Slowly and very silently it took its way.

Clarissa guessed; Clarissa knew of course; she had seen something white, magical, circular, in the footman's hand, a disc inscribed with a name, – the Queen's, the Prince of Wales's, the Prime Minister's? – which, by force of its own lustre, burnt its way through (Clarissa saw the car diminishing, disappearing), to blaze among candelabras, glittering stars, breasts stiff with oak leaves, Hugh Whitbread and all his colleagues, the gentlemen of England, that night in Buckingham Palace. And Clarissa, too, gave a party. She stiffened a little; so she would stand at the top of her stairs.

The car had gone, but it had left a slight ripple which

flowed through glove shops and hat shops and tailors' shops on both sides of Bond Street. For thirty seconds all heads were inclined the same way – to the window. Choosing a pair of gloves – should they be to the elbow or above it, lemon or pale grey? – ladies stopped; when the sentence was finished something had happened. Something so trifling in single instances that no mathematical instrument, though capable of transmitting shocks in China, could register the vibration; yet in its fulness rather formidable and in its common appeal emotional; for in all the hat shops and tailors' shops strangers looked at each other and thought of the dead; of the flag; of Empire. In a public house in a back street a Colonial insulted the House of Windsor which led to words, broken beer glasses, and a general shindy, which echoed strangely across the way in the ears of girls buying white underlinen threaded with pure white ribbon for their weddings. For the surface agitation of the passing car as it sunk grazed something very profound.

Gliding across Piccadilly, the car turned down St. James's Street. Tall men, men of robust physique, well-dressed men with their tail-coats and their white slips and their hair raked back who, for reasons difficult to discriminate, were standing in the bow window of White's with their hands behind the tails of their coats, looking out, perceived instinctively that greatness was passing, and the pale light of the immortal presence fell upon them as it had fallen upon Clarissa Dalloway. At once they stood even straighter, and removed their hands, and seemed ready to attend their Sovereign, if need be, to the cannon's mouth, as their ancestors had done before them. The white busts and the little tables in the background covered with copies of the *Tatler* and syphons of soda water seemed to approve; seemed to indicate the flowing corn and the manor houses of England; and to return the frail hum of the motor wheels as the walls of a whispering gallery return a single voice expanded and made sonorous by the might of a whole cathedral. Shawled Moll Pratt with her flowers on the pavement wished the dear boy well (it was the Prince of Wales for certain) and would have tossed the price of a pot of beer – a bunch of roses – into St. James's Street out of sheer light-heartedness and contempt of poverty had she not seen the constable's eye upon her, discouraging an old Irishwoman's loyalty. The sentries at St. James's saluted; Queen Alexandra's policeman approved.

A small crowd meanwhile had gathered at the gates of Buckingham Palace. Listlessly, yet confidently, poor people all of them, they waited; looked at the Palace itself with the flag flying; at Victoria, billowing on her mound, admired her shelves of running water, her geraniums; singled out from the motor cars in the Mall first this one, then that; bestowed emotion, vainly, upon commoners out for a drive; recalled their tribute to keep it unspent while this car passed and that; and all the time let rumour accumulate in their veins and thrill the nerves in their thighs at the thought of Royalty looking at them; the Queen bowing; the Prince saluting; at the thought of the heavenly life divinely bestowed upon Kings; of the equerries and deep curtsies; of the Queen's old doll's house; of Princess Mary married to an Englishman, and the Prince – ah! the Prince! who took wonderfully, they said, after old King Edward, but was ever so much slimmer. The Prince lived at St. James's; but he might come along in the morning to visit his mother.

So Sarah Bletchley said with her baby in her arms, tipping her foot up and down as though she were by her own fender in Pimlico, but keeping her eyes on the Mall, while Emily Coates ranged over the Palace windows and thought of the housemaids, the innumerable housemaids, the bedrooms, the innumerable bedrooms. Joined by an elderly gentleman with an Aberdeen terrier, by men without occupation, the crowd increased. Little Mr. Bowley, who had rooms in the Albany and was sealed with wax over the deeper sources of life but could be unsealed suddenly, inappropriately, sentimentally, by this sort of thing – poor women waiting to see the Queen go past – poor women, nice little children, orphans, widows, the War – tut-tut – actually had tears in his eyes. A breeze flaunting ever so warmly down the Mall through the thin trees, past the bronze heroes, lifted some flag flying in the British breast of Mr. Bowley and he raised his hat as the car turned into the Mall and held it high as the car approached; and let the poor mothers of Pimlico press close to him, and stood very upright. The car came on.

Suddenly Mrs. Coates looked up into the sky. The sound of an aeroplane bored ominously into the ears of the crowd. There it was coming over the trees, letting out white smoke from behind, which curled and twisted, actually writing something! making letters in the sky! Every one looked up.

Dropping dead down the aeroplane soared straight up, curved in a loop, raced, sank, rose, and whatever it did, wherever it went, out fluttered behind it a thick ruffled bar of white smoke which curled and wreathed upon the sky in letters. But what letters? A C was it? an E, then an L? Only for a moment did they lie still; then they moved and melted and were rubbed out up in the sky, and the aeroplane shot further away and again, in a fresh space of sky, began writing a K, an E, a Y perhaps?

"Glaxo," said Mrs. Coates in a strained, awe-stricken voice, gazing straight up, and her baby, lying stiff and white in her arms, gazed straight up.

"Kreemo," murmured Mrs. Bletchley, like a sleep-walker. With his hat held out perfectly still in his hand, Mr. Bowley gazed straight up. All down the Mall people were standing and looking up into the sky. As they looked the whole world became perfectly silent, and a flight of gulls crossed the sky, first one gull leading, then another, and in this extraordinary silence and peace, in this pallor, in this purity, bells struck eleven times, the sound fading up there among the gulls.

The aeroplane turned and raced and swooped exactly where it liked, swiftly, freely, like a skater –

"That's an E," said Mrs. Bletchley – or a dancer – "It's toffee," murmured Mr. Bowley – (and the car went in at the gates and nobody looked at it), and shutting off the smoke, away and away it rushed, and the smoke faded and assembled itself round the broad white shapes of the clouds.

It had gone; it was behind the clouds. There was no sound. The clouds to which the letters E, G, or L had attached themselves moved freely, as if destined to cross from West to East on a mission of the greatest importance which would never be revealed, and yet certainly so it was – a mission of the greatest importance. Then suddenly, as a train comes out of a tunnel, the aeroplane rushed out of the clouds again, the sound boring into the ears of all people in the Mall, in the Green Park, in Piccadilly, in Regent Street, in Regent's Park, and the bar of smoke curved behind and it dropped down, and it soared up and wrote one letter after another – but what word was it writing?

Lucrezia Warren Smith, sitting by her husband's side on a seat in Regent's Park in the Broad Walk, looked up.

"Look, look, Septimus!" she cried. For Dr. Holmes had told her to make her husband (who had nothing whatever seriously the matter with him but was a little out of sorts) take an interest in things outside himself.

So, thought Septimus, looking up, they are signalling to me. Not indeed in actual words; that is, he could not read the language yet; but it was plain enough, this beauty, this exquisite beauty, and tears filled his eyes as he looked at the smoke words languishing and melting in the sky and bestowing upon him in their inexhaustible charity and laughing goodness one shape after another of unimaginable beauty and signalling their intention to provide him, for nothing, for ever, for looking merely, with beauty, more beauty! Tears ran down his cheeks.

It was toffee; they were advertising toffee, a nursemaid told Rezia. Together they began to spell t . . . o . . . f . . .

"K . . . R . . ." said the nursemaid, and Septimus heard her say "Kay Arr" close to his ear, deeply, softly, like a mellow organ, but with a roughness in her voice like a grasshopper's, which rasped his spine deliciously and sent running up into his brain waves of sound which, concussing, broke. A marvellous discovery indeed – that the human voice in certain atmospheric conditions (for one must be scientific, above all scientific) can quicken trees into life! Happily Rezia put her hand with a tremendous weight on his knee so that he was weighted down, transfixed, or the excitement of the elm trees rising and falling, rising and falling with all their leaves alight and the colour thinning and thickening from blue to the green of a hollow wave, like plumes on horses' heads, feathers on ladies', so proudly they rose and fell, so superbly, would have sent him mad. But he would not go mad. He would shut his eyes; he would see no more.

But they beckoned; leaves were alive; trees were alive. And the leaves being connected by millions of fibres with his own body, there on the seat, fanned it up and down; when the branch stretched he, too, made that statement. The sparrows fluttering, rising, and falling in jagged fountains were part of the pattern; the white and blue, barred with black branches. Sounds made harmonies with premeditation; the spaces between them were as significant as the sounds. A child cried. Rightly far away a horn sounded. All taken together meant the birth of a new religion –

"Septimus!" said Rezia. He started violently. People must notice.

"I am going to walk to the fountain and back," she said.

For she could stand it no longer. Dr. Holmes might say there was nothing the matter. Far rather would she that he were dead! She could not sit beside him when he stared so and did not see her and made everything terrible; sky and tree, children playing, dragging carts, blowing whistles, falling down; all were terrible. And he would not kill himself; and she could tell no one. "Septimus has been working too hard" – that was all she could say, to her own mother. To love makes one solitary, she thought. She could tell nobody, not even Septimus now, and looking back, she saw him sitting in his shabby overcoat alone, on the seat, hunched up, staring. And it was cowardly for a man to say he would kill himself, but Septimus had fought; he was brave; he was not Septimus now. She put on her lace collar. She put on her new hat and he never noticed; and he was happy without her. Nothing could make her happy without him! Nothing! He was selfish. So men are. For he was not ill. Dr. Holmes said there was nothing the matter with him. She spread her hand before her. Look! Her wedding ring slipped – she had grown so thin. It was she who suffered – but she had nobody to tell.

Far was Italy and the white houses and the room where her sister sat making hats, and the streets crowded every evening with people walking, laughing out loud, not half alive like people here, huddled up in Bath chairs, looking at a few ugly flowers stuck in pots!

"For you should see the Milan gardens," she said aloud. But to whom?

There was nobody. Her words faded. So a rocket fades. Its sparks, having grazed their way into the night, surrender to it, dark descends, pours over the outlines of houses and towers; bleak hill-sides soften and fall in. But though they are gone, the night is full of them; robbed of colour, blank of windows, they exist more ponderously, give out what the frank daylight fails to transmit – the trouble and suspense of things conglomerated there in the darkness; huddled together in the darkness; reft of the relief which dawn brings when, washing the walls white and grey, spotting each window-pane, lifting the mist from the fields, showing the red-brown cows peacefully grazing, all is once more decked out to the eye; exists again. I am alone; I am alone! she cried, by the fountain in Regent's Park (staring at the Indian and his cross), as perhaps at midnight, when all boundaries are lost, the country reverts to its ancient shape, as the Romans saw it, lying cloudy, when they landed, and the hills had no names and rivers wound they knew not where – such was her darkness; when suddenly, as if a shelf were shot forth and she stood on it, she said how she was his wife, married years ago in Milan, his wife, and would never, never tell that he was mad! Turning, the shelf fell; down, down she dropped. For he was gone, she thought – gone, as he threatened, to kill himself – to throw himself under a cart! But no; there he was; still sitting alone on the seat, in his shabby overcoat, his legs crossed, staring, talking aloud.

Men must not cut down trees. There is a God. (He noted such revelations on the backs of envelopes.) Change the world. No one kills from hatred. Make it known (he wrote it down). He waited. He listened. A sparrow perched on the railing opposite chirped Septimus, Septimus, four or five times over and went on, drawing its notes out, to sing freshly and piercingly in Greek words how there is no crime and, joined by another sparrow, they sang in voices prolonged and piercing in Greek words, from trees in the meadow of life beyond a river where the dead walk, how there is no death.

There was his hand; there the dead. White things were assembling behind the railings opposite. But he dared not look. Evans was behind the railings!

"What are you saying?" said Rezia suddenly, sitting down by him.

Interrupted again! She was always interrupting.

Away from people – they must get away from people, he said (jumping up), right away over there, where there were chairs beneath a tree and the long slope of the park dipped like a length of green stuff with a ceiling cloth of blue and pink smoke high above, and there was a rampart of far irregular houses, hazed in smoke, the traffic hummed in a circle, and on the right, dun-coloured animals stretched long necks over the Zoo palings, barking, howling. There they sat down under a tree.

"Look," she implored him, pointing at a little troop of boys carrying cricket stumps, and one shuffled, spun round on his heel and shuffled, as if he were acting a clown at the music hall.

"Look," she implored him, for Dr. Holmes had told her to make him notice real things, go to a music hall, play cricket – that was the very game, Dr. Holmes said, a nice out-of-door game, the very game for her husband.

"Look," she repeated.

Look the unseen bade him, the voice which now communicated with him who was the greatest of mankind, Septimus, lately taken from life to death, the Lord who had come to renew society, who lay like a coverlet, a snow blanket smitten only by the sun, for ever unwasted, suffering for ever, the scapegoat, the eternal sufferer, but he did not want it, he moaned, putting from him with a wave of his hand that eternal suffering, that eternal loneliness.

"Look," she repeated, for he must not talk aloud to himself out of doors.

"Oh look," she implored him. But what was there to look at? A few sheep. That was all.

The way to Regent's Park Tube Station – could they tell her the way to Regent's Park Tube Station – Maisie Johnson wanted to know. She was only up from Edinburgh two days ago.

"Not this way – over there!" Rezia exclaimed, waving her aside, lest she should see Septimus.

Both seemed queer, Maisie Johnson thought. Everything seemed very queer. In London for the first time, come to take up a post at her uncle's in Leadenhall Street, and now walking through Regent's Park in the morning, this couple on the chairs gave her quite a turn; the young woman seeming foreign, the man looking queer; so that should she be very old she would still remember and make it jangle again among her memories how she had walked through Regent's Park on a fine summer's morning fifty years ago. For she was only nineteen and had got her way at last, to come to London; and now how queer it was, this couple she had asked the way of, and the girl started and jerked her hand, and the man – he seemed awfully odd; quarrelling, perhaps; parting for ever, perhaps; something was up, she knew; and now all these people (for she returned to the Broad Walk), the stone basins, the prim flowers, the old men and women, invalids most of them in Bath chairs – all seemed, after Edinburgh, so queer. And Maisie Johnson, as she joined that gently trudging, vaguely gazing, breeze-kissed company – squirrels perching and preening, sparrow fountains fluttering for crumbs, dogs busy with the railings, busy with each other, while the soft warm air washed over them and lent to the fixed unsurprised gaze with which they received life something whimsical and mollified – Maisie Johnson positively felt she must cry Oh! (for that young man on the seat had given her quite a turn. Something was up, she knew).

Horror! horror! she wanted to cry. (She had left her people; they had warned her what would happen.)

Why hadn't she stayed at home? she cried, twisting the knob of the iron railing.

That girl, thought Mrs. Dempster (who saved crusts for the squirrels and often ate her lunch in Regent's Park), don't know a thing yet; and really it seemed to her better to be a little stout, a little slack, a little moderate in one's expectations. Percy drank. Well, better to have a son, thought Mrs. Dempster. She had had a hard time of it, and couldn't help smiling at a girl like that. You'll get married, for you're pretty enough, thought Mrs. Dempster. Get married, she thought, and then you'll know. Oh, the cooks, and so on. Every man has his ways.

But whether I'd have chosen quite like that if I could have known, thought Mrs. Dempster, and could not help wishing to whisper a word to Maisie Johnson; to feel on the creased pouch of her worn old face the kiss of pity. For it's been a hard life, thought Mrs. Dempster. What hadn't she given to it? Roses; figure; her feet too. (She drew the knobbed lumps beneath her skirt.)

Roses, she thought sardonically. All trash, m'dear. For really, what with eating, drinking, and mating, the bad days and good, life had been no mere matter of roses, and what was more, let me tell you, Carrie Dempster had no wish to change her lot with any woman's in Kentish Town! But, she implored, pity. Pity, for the loss of roses. Pity she asked of Maisie Johnson, standing by the hyacinth beds.

Ah, but that aeroplane! Hadn't Mrs. Dempster always longed to see foreign parts? She had a nephew, a missionary. It soared and shot. She always went on the sea at Margate, not out o' sight of land, but she had no patience with women who were afraid of water. It swept and fell. Her stomach was in her mouth. Up again. There's a fine young feller aboard of it, Mrs. Dempster wagered, and away and away it went, fast and fading, away and away the aeroplane shot; soaring over Greenwich and all the masts; over the little island of grey churches, St. Paul's and the rest, till, on either side of London, fields spread out and dark brown woods where adventurous thrushes, hopping boldly, glancing quickly, snatched the snail and tapped him on a stone, once, twice, thrice.

Away and away the aeroplane shot, till it was nothing but a bright spark; an aspiration; a concentration; a symbol (so it seemed to Mr. Bentley, vigorously rolling his strip of turf at Greenwich) of man's soul; of his determination, thought Mr. Bentley, sweeping round the cedar tree, to get outside his body, beyond his house, by means of thought, Einstein, speculation, mathematics, the Mendelian theory – away the aeroplane shot.

Then, while a seedy-looking nondescript man carrying a leather bag stood on the steps of St. Paul's Cathedral, and hesitated, for within was what balm, how great a welcome, how many tombs with banners waving over them, tokens of victories not over armies, but over, he thought, that plaguy spirit of truth seeking which leaves me at present without a situation, and more than that, the cathedral offers company, he thought, invites you to membership of a society; great men belong to it; martyrs have died for it; why not enter in, he thought, put this leather bag stuffed with pamphlets before an altar, a cross, the symbol of something which has soared beyond seeking and questing and knocking of words together and has become all spirit, disembodied, ghostly – why not enter in? he thought and while he hesitated out flew the aeroplane over Ludgate Circus.

It was strange; it was still. Not a sound was to be heard above the traffic. Unguided it seemed; sped of its own free will. And now, curving up and up, straight up, like something mounting in ecstasy, in pure delight, out from behind poured white smoke looping, writing a T, an O, an F.

"What are they looking at?" said Clarissa Dalloway to the maid who opened the door.

The hall of the house was cool as a vault. Mrs. Dalloway raised her hand to her eyes, and, as the maid shut the door to, and she heard the swish of Lucy's skirts, she felt like a nun who has left the world and feels fold around her the familiar veils and the response to old devotions. The cook whistled in the kitchen. She heard the click of the typewriter. It was her life, and, bending her head over the hall table, she bowed beneath the influence, felt blessed and purified, saying to herself, as she took the pad with the telephone message on it, how moments like this are buds on the tree of life, flowers of darkness they are, she thought (as if some lovely rose had blossomed for her eyes only); not for a moment did she believe in God; but all the more, she thought, taking up the pad, must one repay in daily life to servants, yes, to dogs and canaries, above all to Richard her husband, who was the foundation of it – of the gay sounds, of the green lights, of the cook even whistling, for Mrs. Walker was Irish and whistled all day long – one must pay back from this secret deposit of exquisite moments, she thought, lifting the pad, while Lucy stood by her, trying to explain how

"Mr. Dalloway, ma'am—"

Clarissa read on the telephone pad, "Lady Bruton wishes to know if Mr. Dalloway will lunch with her to-day.—

"Mr. Dalloway, ma'am, told me to tell you he would be lunching out."

"Dear!" said Clarissa, and Lucy shared as she meant her to her disappointment (but not the pang); felt the concord between them; took the hint; thought how the gentry love; gilded her own future with calm; and, taking Mrs. Dalloway's parasol, handled it like a sacred weapon which a Goddess, having acquitted herself honourably in the field of battle, sheds, and placed it in the umbrella stand.

"Fear no more," said Clarissa. Fear no more the heat o' the sun; for the shock of Lady Bruton asking Richard to lunch without her made the moment in which she had stood shiver, as a plant on the river-bed feels the shock of a passing oar and shivers: so she rocked: so she shivered.

Millicent Bruton, whose lunch parties were said to be extraordinarily amusing, had not asked her. No vulgar jealousy could separate her from Richard. But she feared time itself, and read on Lady Bruton's face, as if it had been a dial cut in impassive stone, the dwindling of life; how year by year her share was sliced; how little the margin that remained was capable any longer of stretching, of absorbing, as in the youthful years, the colours, salts, tones of existence, so that she filled the room she entered, and felt often as she stood hesitating one moment on the threshold of her drawing-room, an exquisite suspense, such as might stay a diver before plunging while the sea darkens and brightens beneath him, and the waves which threaten to break, but only gently split their surface, roll and conceal and encrust as they just turn over the weeds with pearl.

She put the pad on the hall table. She began to go slowly upstairs, with her hand on the banisters, as if she had left a party, where now this friend now that had flashed back her face, her voice; had shut the door and gone out and stood alone, a single figure against the appalling night, or rather, to be accurate, against the stare of this matter-of-fact June morning; soft with the glow of rose petals for some, she knew, and felt it, as she paused by the open staircase window which let in blinds flapping, dogs barking, let in, she thought, feeling herself suddenly shrivelled, aged, breastless, the grinding, blowing, flowering of the day, out of doors, out of the window, out of her body and brain which now failed, since Lady Bruton, whose lunch parties were said to be extraordinarily amusing, had not asked her.

Like a nun withdrawing, or a child exploring a tower, she went, upstairs, paused at the window, came to the bathroom. There was the green linoleum and a tap dripping. There was an emptiness about the heart of life; an attic room. Women must put off their rich apparel. At mid-day they must disrobe. She pierced the pin-cushion and laid her feathered yellow hat on the bed. The sheets were clean, tight stretched in a broad white band from side to side. Narrower and narrower would her bed be. The candle was half burnt down and she had read deep in Baron Marbot's *Memoirs*. She had read late at night of the retreat from Moscow. For the House sat so long that Richard insisted, after her illness, that she must sleep undisturbed. And really she preferred to read of the retreat from Moscow. He knew it. So the room was an attic; the bed narrow; and lying there reading, for she slept badly, she could not dispel a virginity preserved through childbirth which clung to her like a sheet. Lovely in girlhood, suddenly there came a moment – for example on the river beneath the woods at Clieveden – when, through some contraction of this cold spirit, she had failed him. And then at Constantinople, and again and again. She could see what she lacked. It was not beauty; it was not mind. It was something central which permeated; something warm which broke up surfaces and rippled the cold contact of man and woman, or of women together. For *that* she could dimly perceive. She resented it, had a scruple picked up Heaven knows where, or, as she felt, sent by Nature (who is invariably wise); yet she could not resist sometimes yielding to the charm of a woman, not a girl, of a woman confessing, as to her they often did, some scrape, some folly. And whether it was pity, or their beauty, or that she was older, or some accident – like a faint scent, or a violin next door (so strange is the power of sounds at certain moments), she did undoubtedly then feel what men felt. Only for a moment; but it was enough. It was a sudden revelation, a tinge like a blush which one tried to check and then, as it spread, one yielded to its expansion, and rushed to the farthest verge and there quivered and felt the world come closer, swollen with some astonishing significance, some pressure of rapture, which split its thin skin and gushed and poured with an extraordinary alleviation over the cracks and sores. Then, for that moment, she had seen an illumination; a match burning in a crocus; an inner meaning almost expressed. But the close withdrew; the hard softened. It was over – the moment. Against such moments (with women too) there contrasted (as she laid her hat down) the bed and Baron Marbot and the candle half-burnt. Lying awake, the floor creaked; the lit house was suddenly darkened, and if she raised her head she could just hear the click of the handle released as gently as possible by Richard, who slipped upstairs in his socks and then, as often as not, dropped his hot-water bottle and swore! How she laughed!

But this question of love (she thought, putting her coat away), this falling in love with women. Take Sally Seton; her relation in the old days with Sally Seton. Had not that, after all, been love?

She sat on the floor – that was her first impression of Sally – she sat on the floor with her arms round her knees, smoking a cigarette. Where could it have been? The Mannings'? The Kinloch-Joneses'? At some party (where, she could not be certain), for she had a distinct recollection of saying to the man she was with, "Who is *that*?" And he had told her, and said that Sally's parents did not get on (how that shocked her – that one's parents should quarrel!). But all that evening she could not take her eyes off Sally. It was an extraordinary beauty of the kind she most admired, dark, large-eyed, with that quality which, since she hadn't got it herself, she always envied – a sort of abandonment, as if she could say anything, do anything; a quality much commoner in foreigners than in Englishwomen. Sally always said she had French blood in her veins, an ancestor had been with Marie Antoinette, had his head cut off, left a ruby ring. Perhaps that summer she came to stay at Bourton, walking in quite unexpectedly without a penny in her pocket, one night after dinner, and upsetting poor Aunt Helena to such an extent that she never forgave her. There had been some awful quarrel at home. She literally hadn't a penny that night when she came to them – had pawned a brooch to come down. She had rushed off in a passion. They sat up till all hours of the night talking. Sally it was who made her feel, for the first time, how sheltered the life at Bourton was. She knew nothing about sex – nothing about social problems. She had once seen an old man who had dropped dead in a field – she had seen cows just after their calves were born. But Aunt Helena never liked discussion of anything (when Sally gave her William Morris, it had to be wrapped in brown paper). There they sat, hour after hour, talking in her bedroom at the top of the house, talking about life, how they were to reform the world. They meant to found a society to abolish private property, and actually had a letter written, though not sent out. The ideas were Sally's, of course – but very soon she was just as excited – read Plato in bed before breakfast; read Morris; read Shelley by the hour.

Sally's power was amazing, her gift, her personality. There was her way with flowers, for instance. At Bourton they always had stiff little vases all the way down the table. Sally went out, picked hollyhocks, dahlias – all sorts of flowers that had never been seen together – cut their heads off, and made them swim on the top of water in bowls. The effect was extraordinary – coming in to dinner in the sunset. (Of course Aunt Helena thought it wicked to treat flowers like that.) Then she forgot her sponge, and ran along the passage naked. That grim old housemaid, Ellen Atkins, went about grumbling "Suppose any of the gentlemen had seen?" Indeed she did shock people. She was untidy, Papa said.

The strange thing, on looking back, was the purity, the integrity, of her feeling for Sally. It was not like one's feeling for a man. It was completely disinterested, and besides, it had a quality which could only exist between women, between women just grown up. It was protective, on her side; sprang from a sense of being in league together, a presentiment of something that was bound to part them (they spoke of marriage always as a catastrophe), which led to this chivalry, this protective feeling which was much more on her side than Sally's. For in those days she was completely reckless; did the most idiotic things out of bravado; bicycled round the parapet on the terrace; smoked cigars. Absurd, she was – very absurd. But the charm was overpowering, to her at least, so that she could remember standing in her bedroom at the top of the house holding the hot-water can in her hands and saying aloud, "She is beneath this roof. . . . She is beneath this roof!"

No, the words meant absolutely nothing to her now. She

could not even get an echo of her old emotion. But she could remember going cold with excitement, and doing her hair in a kind of ecstasy (now the old feeling began to come back to her, as she took out her hairpins, laid them on the dressing-table, began to do her hair), with the rooks flaunting up and down in the pink evening light, and dressing, and going downstairs, and feeling as she crossed the hall "if it were now to die 'twere now to be most happy". That was her feeling – Othello's feeling, and she felt it, she was convinced, as strongly as Shakespeare meant Othello to feel it, all because she was coming down to dinner in a white frock to meet Sally Seton!

She was wearing pink gauze – was that possible? She *seemed*, anyhow, all light, glowing, like some bird or air ball that has flown in, attached itself for a moment to a bramble. But nothing is so strange when one is in love (and what was this except being in love?) as the complete indifference of other people. Aunt Helena just wandered off after dinner; Papa read the paper. Peter Walsh might have been there, and old Miss Cummings; Joseph Breitkopf certainly was, for he came every summer, poor old man, for weeks and weeks, and pretended to read German with her, but really played the piano and sang Brahms without any voice.

All this was only a background for Sally. She stood by the fireplace talking, in that beautiful voice which made everything she said sound like a caress, to Papa, who had begun to be attracted rather against his will (he never got over lending her one of his books and finding it soaked on the terrace), when suddenly she said, "What a shame to sit indoors!" and they all went out on to the terrace and walked up and down. Peter Walsh and Joseph Breitkopf went on about Wagner. She and Sally fell a little behind. Then came the most exquisite moment of her whole life passing a stone urn with flowers in it. Sally stopped; picked a flower; kissed her on the lips. The whole world might have turned upside down! The others disappeared; there she was alone with Sally. And she felt that she had been given a present, wrapped up, and told just to keep it, not to look at it – a diamond, something infinitely precious, wrapped up, which, as they walked (up and down, up and down), she uncovered, or the radiance burnt through, the revelation, the religious feeling! – when old Joseph and Peter faced them:

"Star-gazing?" said Peter.

It was like running one's face against a granite wall in the darkness! It was shocking; it was horrible!

Not for herself. She felt only how Sally was being mauled already, maltreated; she felt his hostility; his jealousy; his determination to break into their companionship. All this she saw as one sees a landscape in a flash of lightning – and Sally (never had she admired her so much!) gallantly taking her way unvanquished. She laughed. She made old Joseph tell her the names of the stars, which he liked doing very seriously. She stood there: she listened. She heard the names of the stars.

"Oh this horror!" she said to herself, as if she had known all along that something would interrupt, would embitter her moment of happiness.

Yet how much she owed to Peter Walsh later. Always when she thought of him she thought of their quarrels for some reason – because she wanted his good opinion so much, perhaps. She owed him words: "sentimental", "civilised"; they started up every day of her life as if he guarded her. A book was sentimental; an attitude to life sentimental. "Sentimental", perhaps she was to be thinking of the past. What would he think, she wondered, when he came back?

That she had grown older? Would he say that, or would she see him thinking when he came back, that she had grown older? It was true. Since her illness she had turned almost white.

Laying her brooch on the table, she had a sudden spasm, as if, while she mused, the icy claws had had the chance to fix in her. She was not old yet. She had just broken into her fifty-second year. Months and months of it were still untouched. June, July, August! Each still remained almost whole, and, as if to catch the falling drop, Clarissa (crossing to the dressing-table) plunged into the very heart of the moment, transfixed it, there – the moment of this June morning on which was the pressure of all the other mornings, seeing the glass, the dressing-table, and all the bottles afresh, collecting the whole of her at one point (as she looked into the glass), seeing the delicate pink face of the woman who was that very night to give a party; of Clarissa Dalloway; of herself.

How many million times she had seen her face, and always with the same imperceptible contraction! She pursed her lips when she looked in the glass. It was to give her face point. That was her self – pointed; dartlike; definite. That was her self when some effort, some call on her to be her self, drew the parts together, she alone knew how different, how incompatible and composed so for the world only into one centre, one diamond, one woman who sat in her drawing-room and made a meeting-point, a radiancy no doubt in some dull lives, a refuge for the lonely to come to, perhaps; she had helped young people, who were grateful to her; had tried to be the same always, never showing a sign of all the other sides of her – faults, jealousies, vanities, suspicions, like this of Lady Bruton not asking her to lunch; which, she thought (combing her hair finally), is utterly base! Now, where was her dress?

Her evening dresses hung in the cupboard. Clarissa, plunging her hand into the softness, gently detached the green dress and carried it to the window. She had torn it. Some one had trod on the skirt. She had felt it give at the Embassy party at the top among the folds. By artificial light the green shone, but lost its colour now in the sun. She would mend it. Her maids had too much to do. She would wear it to-night. She would take her silks, her scissors, her – what was it? – her thimble, of course, down into the drawing-room, for she must also write, and see that things generally were more or less in order.

Strange, she thought, pausing on the landing, and assembling that diamond shape, that single person, strange how a mistress knows the very moment, the very temper of her house! Faint sounds rose in spirals up the well of the stairs; the swish of a mop; tapping; knocking; a loudness when the front door opened; a voice repeating a message in the basement; the chink of silver on a tray; clean silver for the party. All was for the party.

(And Lucy, coming into the drawing-room with her tray held out, put the giant candlesticks on the mantelpiece, the silver casket in the middle, turned the crystal dolphin towards the clock. They would come; they would stand; they would talk in the mincing tones which she could imitate, ladies and gentlemen. Of all, her mistress was loveliest – mistress of silver, of linen, of china, for the sun, the silver, doors off their hinges, Rumpelmayer's men, gave her a sense, as she laid the paper-knife on the inlaid table, of something achieved. Behold! Behold! she said, speaking to her old friends in the baker's shop, where she had first seen service at Caterham, prying into the glass. She was Lady Angela, attending Princess Mary, when in came Mrs. Dalloway.)

"Oh Lucy," she said, "the silver does look nice!"

"And how," she said, turning the crystal dolphin to stand straight, "how did you enjoy the play last night?" "Oh, they had to go before the end!" she said. "They had to be back at ten!" she said. "So they don't know what happened," she said. "That does seem hard luck," she said (for her servants stayed later, if they asked her). "That does seem rather a shame," she said, taking the old bald-looking cushion in the middle of the sofa and putting it in Lucy's arms, and giving her a little push, and crying:

"Take it away! Give it to Mrs. Walker with my compliments! Take it away!" she cried.

And Lucy stopped at the drawing-room door, holding the cushion, and said, very shyly, turning a little pink, couldn't she help to mend that dress?

But, said Mrs. Dalloway, she had enough on her hands already, quite enough of her own to do without that.

"But, thank you, Lucy, oh, thank you," said Mrs. Dalloway, and thank you, thank you, she went on saying (sitting down on the sofa with her dress over her knees, her scissors, her silks), thank you, thank you, she went on saying in gratitude to her servants generally for helping her to be like this, to be what she wanted, gentle, generous-hearted. Her servants liked her. And then this dress of hers – where was the tear? and now her needle to be threaded. This was a favourite dress, one of Sally Parker's, the last almost she ever made, alas, for Sally had now retired, lived at Ealing, and if ever I have a moment, thought Clarissa (but never would she have a moment any more), I shall go and see her at Ealing. For she was a character, thought Clarissa, a real artist. She thought of little out-of-the-way things; yet her dresses were never queer. You could wear them at Hatfield; at Buckingham Palace. She had worn them at Hatfield; at Buckingham Palace.

Quiet descended on her, calm, content, as her needle, drawing the silk smoothly to its gentle pause, collected the green folds together and attached them, very lightly, to the belt. So on a summer's day waves collect, overbalance, and fall; collect and fall; and the whole world seems to be saying "that is all" more and more ponderously, until even the heart in the body which lies in the sun on the beach says too, That is all. Fear no more, says the heart. Fear no more, says the heart, committing its burden to some sea, which sighs collectively for all sorrows, and renews, begins, collects, lets fall. And the body alone listens to the passing bee; the wave breaking; the dog barking, far away barking and barking.

"Heavens, the front-door bell!" exclaimed Clarissa, staying her needle. Roused, she listened.

"Mrs. Dalloway will see me," said the elderly man in the hall. "Oh yes, she will see *me*," he repeated, putting Lucy aside very benevolently, and running upstairs ever so quickly. "Yes, yes, yes," he muttered as he ran upstairs. "She will see me. After five years in India, Clarissa will see me."

"Who can – what can," asked Mrs. Dalloway (thinking it was outrageous to be interrupted at eleven o'clock on the morning of the day she was giving a party), hearing a step on the stairs. She heard a hand upon the door. She made to hide her dress, like a virgin protecting chastity, respecting privacy. Now the brass knob slipped. Now the door opened, and in came – for a single second she could not remember what he was called! so surprised she was to see him, so glad, so shy, so utterly taken aback to have Peter Walsh come to her unexpectedly in the morning! (She had not read his letter.)

"And how are you?" said Peter Walsh, positively trembling; taking both her hands; kissing both her hands. She's grown older, he thought, sitting down. I shan't tell her anything about it, he thought, for she's grown older. She's looking at me, he thought, a sudden embarrassment coming over him, though he had kissed her hands. Putting his hand into his pocket, he took out a large pocket-knife and half opened the blade.

Exactly the same, thought Clarissa; the same queer look; the same check suit; a little out of the straight his face is, a little thinner, dryer, perhaps, but he looks awfully well, and just the same.

"How heavenly it is to see you again!" she exclaimed. He had his knife out. That's so like him, she thought.

He had only reached town last night, he said; would have to go down into the country at once; and how was everything, how was everybody – Richard? Elizabeth?

"And what's all this?" he said, tilting his pen-knife towards her green dress.

He's very well dressed, thought Clarissa; yet he always criticises *me*.

Here she is mending her dress; mending her dress as usual, he thought; here she's been sitting all the time I've been in India; mending her dress; playing about; going to parties; running to the House and back and all that, he thought, growing more and more irritated, more and more agitated, for there's nothing in the world so bad for some women as marriage, he thought; and politics; and having a Conservative husband, like the admirable Richard. So it is, so it is, he thought, shutting his knife with a snap.

"Richard's very well. Richard's at a Committee," said Clarissa.

And she opened her scissors, and said, did he mind her just finishing what she was doing to her dress, for they had a party that night?

"Which I shan't ask you to," she said. "My dear Peter!" she said.

But it was delicious to hear her say that – my dear Peter! Indeed, it was all so delicious – the silver, the chairs; all so delicious!

Why wouldn't she ask him to her party? he asked.

Now of course, thought Clarissa, he's enchanting! perfectly enchanting! Now I remember how impossible it was ever to make up my mind – and why did I make up my mind – not to marry him, she wondered, that awful summer?

"But it's so extraordinary that you should have come this morning!" she cried, putting her hands, one on top of another, down on her dress.

"Do you remember," she said, "how the blinds used to flap at Bourton?"

"They did," he said; and he remembered breakfasting alone, very awkwardly, with her father; who had died; and he had not written to Clarissa. But he had never got on well with old Parry, that querulous, weak-kneed old man, Clarissa's father, Justin Parry.

"I often wish I'd got on better with your father," he said.

"But he never liked any one who – our friends," said Clarissa; and could have bitten her tongue for thus reminding Peter that he had wanted to marry her.

Of course I did, thought Peter; it almost broke my heart too, he thought; and was overcome with his own grief, which rose like a moon looked at from a terrace, ghastly beautiful with light from the sunken day. I was more unhappy than I've ever been since, he thought. And as if in truth he were sitting there on the terrace he edged a little towards Clarissa; put his hand out; raised it; let it fall. There above them it hung, that moon. She too seemed to be sitting with him on the terrace, in the moonlight.

"Herbert has it now," she said. "I never go there now," she said.

Then, just as happens on a terrace in the moonlight, when one person begins to feel ashamed that he is already bored, and yet as the other sits silent, very quiet, sadly looking at the moon, does not like to speak, moves his foot, clears his throat, notices some iron scroll on a table leg, stirs a leaf, but says nothing – so Peter Walsh did now. For why go back like this to the past? he thought. Why make him think of it again? Why make him suffer, when she had tortured him so infernally? Why?

"Do you remember the lake?" she said, in an abrupt voice, under the pressure of an emotion which caught her heart, made the muscles of her throat stiff, and contracted her lips in a spasm as she said "lake". For she was a child, throwing bread to the ducks, between her parents, and at the same time a grown woman coming to her parents who stood by the lake, holding her life in her arms which, as she neared them, grew larger and larger in her arms, until it became a whole life, a complete life, which she put down by them and said, "This is what I have made of it! This!" And what had she made of it? What, indeed? sitting there sewing this morning with Peter.

She looked at Peter Walsh; her look, passing through all that time and that emotion, reached him doubtfully; settled on him tearfully; and rose and fluttered away, as a bird touches a branch and rises and flutters away. Quite simply she wiped her eyes.

"Yes," said Peter. "Yes, yes, yes," he said, as if she drew up to the surface something which positively hurt him as it rose. Stop! Stop! he wanted to cry. For he was not old; his life was not over; not by any means. He was only just past fifty. Shall I tell her, he thought, or not? He would like to make a clean breast of it all. But she is too cold, he thought; sewing, with her scissors; Daisy would look ordinary beside Clarissa. And she would think me a failure, which I am in their sense, he thought; in the Dalloways' sense. Oh yes, he had no doubt about that; he was a failure, compared with all this – the inlaid table, the mounted paper-knife, the dolphin and the candle-sticks, the chair-covers and the old valuable English tinted prints – he was a failure! I detest the smugness of the whole affair, he thought; Richard's doing, not Clarissa's; save that she married him. (Here Lucy came into the room, carrying silver, more silver, but charming, slender, graceful she looked, he thought, as she stooped to put it down.) And this has been going on all the time! he thought; week after week; Clarissa's life; while I – he thought; and at once everything seemed to radiate from him; journeys; rides; quarrels; adventures; bridge parties; love affairs; work; work, work! and he took out his knife quite openly – his old horn-handled knife which Clarissa could swear he had had these thirty years – and clenched his fist upon it.

What an extraordinary habit that was, Clarissa thought; always playing with a knife. Always making one feel, too, frivolous; empty-minded; a mere silly chatterbox, as he used. But I too, she thought, and, taking up her needle, summoned, like a Queen whose guards have fallen asleep and left her unprotected (she had been quite taken aback by this visit – it had upset her) so that any one can stroll in and have a look at her where she lies with the brambles curving over her, summoned to her help the things she did; the things she liked; her husband; Elizabeth; her self, in short, which Peter hardly knew now, all to come about her and beat off the enemy.

"Well, and what's happened to you?" she said. So before a battle begins, the horses paw the ground; toss their heads; the light shines on their flanks; their necks curve. So Peter Walsh and Clarissa, sitting side by side on the blue sofa, challenged each other. His powers chafed and tossed in him. He assembled from different quarters all sorts of things; praise; his career at Oxford; his marriage, which she knew nothing whatever about; how he had loved; and altogether done his job.

"Millions of things!" he exclaimed, and, urged by the assembly of powers which were now charging this way and that and giving him the feeling at once frightening and extremely exhilarating of being rushed through the air on the shoulders of people he could no longer see, he raised his hands to his forehead.

Clarissa sat very upright; drew in her breath.

"I am in love," he said, not to her however, but to some one raised up in the dark so that you could not touch her but must lay your garland down on the grass in the dark.

"In love," he repeated, now speaking rather dryly to Clarissa Dalloway; "in love with a girl in India." He had deposited his garland. Clarissa could make what she would of it.

"In love!" she said. That he at his age should be sucked under in his little bow-tie by that monster! And there's no flesh on his neck; his hands are red; and he's six months older than I am! her eye flashed back to her; but in her heart she felt, all the same, he is in love. He has that, she felt; he is in love.

But the indomitable egotism which for ever rides down

the hosts opposed to it, the river which says on, on, on; even though, it admits, there may be no goal for us whatever, still on, on; this indomitable egotism charged her cheeks with colour; made her look very young; very pink; very bright-eyed as she sat with her dress upon her knee, and her needle held to the end of green silk, trembling a little. He was in love! Not with her. With some younger woman, of course.

"And who is she?" she asked.

Now this statue must be brought from its height and set down between them.

"A married woman, unfortunately," he said; "the wife of a Major in the Indian Army."

And with a curious ironical sweetness he smiled as he placed her in this ridiculous way before Clarissa.

(All the same, he is in love, thought Clarissa.)

"She has," he continued, very reasonably, "two small children; a boy and a girl; and I have come over to see my lawyers about the divorce."

There they are! he thought. Do what you like with them, Clarissa! There they are! And second by second it seemed to him that the wife of the Major in the Indian Army (his Daisy) and her two small children became more and more lovely as Clarissa looked at them; as if he had set light to a grey pellet on a plate and there had risen up a lovely tree in the brisk sea-salted air of their intimacy (for in some ways no one understood him, felt with him, as Clarissa did) – their exquisite intimacy.

She flattered him; she fooled him, thought Clarissa; shaping the woman, the wife of the Major in the Indian Army, with three strokes of a knife. What a waste! What a folly! All his life long Peter had been fooled like that; first getting sent down from Oxford; next marrying the girl on the boat going out to India; now the wife of a Major in the Indian Army – thank Heaven she had refused to marry him! Still, he was in love; her old friend, her dear Peter, he was in love.

"But what are you going to do?" she asked him. Oh the lawyers and solicitors, Messrs. Hooper and Grateley of Lincoln's Inn, they were going to do it, he said. And he actually pared his nails with his pocket-knife.

For Heaven's sake, leave your knife alone! she cried to herself in irrepressible irritation; it was his silly unconventionality, his weakness; his lack of the ghost of a notion what any one else was feeling that annoyed her, had always annoyed her; and now at his age, how silly!

I know all that, Peter thought; I know what I'm up against, he thought, running his finger along the blade of his knife, Clarissa and Dalloway and all the rest of them; but I'll show Clarissa – and then to his utter surprise, suddenly thrown by those uncontrollable forces thrown through the air, he burst into tears; wept; wept without the least shame, sitting on the sofa, the tears running down his cheeks.

And Clarissa had leant forward, taken his hand, drawn him to her, kissed him, – actually had felt his face on hers before she could down the brandishing of silver-flashing plumes like pampas grass in a tropic gale in her breast, which, subsiding, left her holding his hand, patting his knee, and feeling as she sat back extraordinarily at her ease with him and light-hearted, all in a clap it came over her. If I had married him, this gaiety would have been mine all day!

It was all over for her. The sheet was stretched and the bed narrow. She had gone up into the tower alone and left them blackberrying in the sun. The door had shut, and there among the dust of fallen plaster and the litter of birds' nests how distant the view had looked, and the sounds came thin and chill (once on Leith Hill, she remembered), and Richard, Richard! she cried, as a sleeper in the night starts and stretches a hand in the dark for help. Lunching with Lady Bruton, it came back to her. He has left me; I am alone for ever, she thought, folding her hands upon her knee.

Peter Walsh had got up and crossed to the window and

stood with his back to her, flicking a bandanna handkerchief from side to side. Masterly and dry and desolate he looked, his thin shoulder-blades lifting his coat slightly; blowing his nose violently. Take me with you, Clarissa thought impulsively, as if he were starting directly upon some great voyage; and then, next moment, it was as if the five acts of a play that had been very exciting and moving were now over and she had lived a lifetime in them and had run away, had lived with Peter, and it was now over.

Now it was time to move, and, as a woman gathers her things together, her cloak, her gloves, her opera-glasses, and gets up to go out of the theatre into the street, she rose from the sofa and went to Peter.

And it was awfully strange, he thought, how she still had the power, as she came tinkling, rustling, still had the power as she came across the room, to make the moon, which he detested, rise at Bourton on the terrace in the summer sky.

"Tell me," he said, seizing her by the shoulders. "Are you happy, Clarissa? Does Richard—"

The door opened.

"Here is my Elizabeth," said Clarissa, emotionally, histrionically, perhaps.

"How d'y do?" said Elizabeth coming forward.

The sound of Big Ben striking the half-hour struck out between them with extraordinary vigour, as if a young man, strong, indifferent, inconsiderate, were swinging dumb-bells this way and that.

"Hullo, Elizabeth!" cried Peter, stuffing his handkerchief into his pocket, going quickly to her, saying "Good-bye, Clarissa" without looking at her, leaving the room quickly, and running downstairs and opening the hall door.

"Peter! Peter!" cried Clarissa, following him out on to the landing. "My party to-night! Remember my party to-night!" she cried, having to raise her voice against the roar of the open air, and, overwhelmed by the traffic and the sound of all the clocks striking, her voice crying "Remember my party tonight!" sounded frail and thin and very far away as Peter Walsh shut the door.

Remember my party, remember my party, said Peter Walsh as he stepped down the street, speaking to himself rhythmically, in time with the flow of the sound, the direct downright sound of Big Ben striking the half-hour. (The leaden circles dissolved in the air.) Oh these parties, he thought; Clarissa's parties. Why does she give these parties? he thought. Not that he blamed her or this effigy of a man in a tail-coat with a carnation in his button-hole coming towards him. Only one person in the world could be as he was, in love. And there he was, this fortunate man, himself, reflected in the plate-glass window of a motor-car manufacturer in Victoria Street. All India lay behind him; plains, mountains; epidemics of cholera; a district twice as big as Ireland; decisions he had come to alone – he, Peter Walsh; who was now really for the first time in his life, in love. Clarissa had grown hard, he thought; and a trifle sentimental into the bargain, he suspected, looking at the great motor-cars capable of doing – how many miles on how many gallons? For he had a turn for mechanics; had invented a plough in his district, had ordered wheel-barrows from England, but the coolies wouldn't use them, all of which Clarissa knew nothing whatever about.

The way she said "Here is my Elizabeth!" – that annoyed him. Why not "Here's Elizabeth" simply? It was insincere. And Elizabeth didn't like it either. (Still the last tremors of the great booming voice shook the air round him; the half-hour; still early; only half-past eleven still.) For he understood young people; he liked them. There was always something cold in Clarissa, he thought. She had always, even as a girl, a sort of timidity, which in middle age becomes conventionality, and then it's all up, it's all up, he thought, looking rather drearily into the glassy depths, and wondering whether by calling at that hour he had annoyed her; overcome with shame suddenly at having been a fool; wept; been emotional; told her everything, as usual, as usual.

As a cloud crosses the sun, silence falls on London; and falls on the mind. Effort ceases. Time flaps on the mast. There we stop; there we stand. Rigid, the skeleton of habit alone upholds the human frame. Where there is nothing, Peter Walsh said to himself; feeling hollowed out, utterly empty within. Clarissa refused me, he thought. He stood there thinking, Clarissa refused me.

Ah, said St. Margaret's, like a hostess who comes into her drawing-room on the very stroke of the hour and finds her guests there already. I am not late. No, it is precisely half-past eleven, she says. Yet, though she is perfectly right, her voice, being the voice of the hostess, is reluctant to inflict its individuality. Some grief for the past holds it back; some concern for the present. It is half-past eleven, she says, and the sound of St. Margaret's glides into the recesses of the heart and buries itself in ring after ring of sound, like something alive which wants to confide itself, to disperse itself, to be, with a tremor of delight, at rest – like Clarissa herself, thought Peter Walsh, coming downstairs on the stroke of the hour in white. It is Clarissa herself, he thought, with a deep emotion, and an extraordinarily clear, yet puzzling, recollection of her, as if this bell had come into the room years ago, where they sat at some moment of great intimacy, and had gone from one to the other and had left, like a bee with honey, laden with the moment. But what room? What moment? And why had he been so profoundly happy when the clock was striking? Then, as the sound of St. Margaret's languished, he thought, She has been ill, and the sound expressed languor and suffering. It was her heart, he remembered; and the sudden loudness of the final stroke tolled for death that surprised in the midst of life, Clarissa falling where she stood, in her drawing-room. No! No! he cried. She is not dead! I am not old, he cried, and marched up Whitehall, as if there rolled down to him, vigorous, unending, his future.

He was not old, or set, or dried in the least. As for caring what they said of him – the Dalloways, the Whitbreads, and their set, he cared not a straw – not a straw (though it was true he would have, some time or other, to see whether Richard couldn't help him to some job). Striding, staring, he glared at the statue of the Duke of Cambridge. He had been sent down from Oxford – true. He had been a Socialist, in some sense a failure – true. Still the future of civilisation lies, he thought, in the hands of young men like that; of young men such as he was, thirty years ago; with their love of abstract principles; getting books sent out to them all the way from London to a peak in the Himalayas; reading science; reading philosophy. The future lies in the hands of young men like that, he thought.

A patter like the patter of leaves in a wood came from behind, and with it a rustling, regular thudding sound, which as it overtook him drummed his thoughts, strict in step, up Whitehall, without his doing. Boys in uniform, carrying guns, marched with their eyes ahead of them, marched, their arms stiff, and on their faces an expression like the letters of a legend written round the base of a statue praising duty, gratitude, fidelity, love of England.

It is, thought Peter Walsh, beginning to keep step with them, a very fine training. But they did not look robust. They were weedy for the most part, boys of sixteen, who might, to-morrow, stand behind bowls of rice, cakes of soap on counters. Now they wore on them unmixed with sensual pleasure or daily preoccupations the solemnity of the wreath which they had fetched from Finsbury Pavement to the empty tomb. They had taken their vow. The traffic respected it; vans were stopped.

I can't keep up with them, Peter Walsh thought, as they marched up Whitehall, and sure enough, on they marched, past him, past every one, in their steady way, as if one will worked legs and arms uniformly, and life, with its varieties, its irreticences, had been laid under a pavement of monuments and wreaths and drugged into a stiff yet staring corpse by discipline. One had to respect it; one might laugh; but one had to respect it, he thought. There they go, thought Peter Walsh, pausing at the edge of the pavement; and all the exalted statues, Nelson, Gordon, Havelock, the black, the spectacular images of great soldiers stood looking ahead of them, as if they too had made the same renunciation (Peter Walsh felt he, too, had made it, the great renunciation), trampled under the same temptations, and achieved at length a marble stare. But the stare Peter Walsh did not want for himself in the least; though he could respect it in others. He could respect it in boys. They don't know the troubles of the flesh yet, he thought, as the marching boys disappeared in the direction of the Strand – all that I've been through, he thought, crossing the road, and standing under Gordon's statue, Gordon whom as a boy he had worshipped; Gordon standing lonely with one leg raised and his arms crossed, – poor Gordon, he thought.

And just because nobody yet knew he was in London, except Clarissa, and the earth, after the voyage, still seemed an island to him, the strangeness of standing alone, alive, unknown, at half-past eleven in Trafalgar Square overcame him. What is it? Where am I? And why, after all, does one do it? he thought, the divorce seeming all moonshine. And down his mind went flat as a marsh, and three great emotions bowled over him; understanding; a vast philanthropy; and finally, as if the result of the others, an irrepressible, exquisite delight; as if inside his brain by another hand strings were pulled, shutters moved, and he, having nothing to do with it, yet stood at the opening of endless avenues, down which if he chose he might wander. He had not felt so young for years.

He had escaped! was utterly free – as happens in the downfall of habit when the mind, like an unguarded flame, bows and bends and seems about to blow from its holding. I haven't felt so young for years! thought Peter, escaping (only of course for an hour or so) from being precisely what he was, and feeling like a child who runs out of doors, and sees, as he runs, his old nurse waving at the wrong window. But she's extraordinarily attractive, he thought, as, walking across Trafalgar Square in the direction of the Haymarket, came a young woman who, as she passed Gordon's statue, seemed, Peter Walsh thought (susceptible as he was), to shed veil after veil, until she became the very woman he had always had in mind; young, but stately; merry, but discreet; black, but enchanting.

Straightening himself and stealthily fingering his pocket-knife he started after her to follow this woman, this excitement, which seemed even with its back turned to shed on him a light which connected them, which singled him out, as if the random uproar of the traffic had whispered through hollowed hands his name, not Peter, but his private name which he called himself in his own thoughts. "You," she said, only "you", saying it with her white gloves and her shoulders. Then the thin long cloak which the wind stirred as she walked past Dent's shop in Cockspur Street blew out with an enveloping kindness, a mournful tenderness, as of arms that would open and take the tired –

But she's not married; she's young; quite young, thought Peter, the red carnation he had seen her wear as she came across Trafalgar Square burning again in his eyes and making her lips red. But she waited at the kerbstone. There was a dignity about her. She was not worldly, like Clarissa; not rich, like Clarissa. Was she, he wondered as she moved, respectable? Witty, with a lizard's flickering tongue, he thought (for one must invent, must allow oneself a little diversion), a cool waiting wit, a darting wit; not noisy.

She moved; she crossed; he followed her. To embarrass her was the last thing he wished. Still if she stopped he would say "Come and have an ice," he would say, and she would answer, perfectly simply, "Oh yes."

But other people got between them in the street, obstructing him, blotting her out. He pursued; she changed. There was colour in her cheeks; mockery in her eyes; he was an adventurer, reckless, he thought, swift, daring, indeed (landed as he was last night from India) a romantic buccaneer, careless of all these damned proprieties, yellow dressing-gowns, pipes, fishing-rods, in the shop windows; and respectability and evening parties and spruce old men wearing white slips beneath their waistcoats. He was a buccaneer. On and on she went, across Piccadilly, and up Regent Street, ahead of him, her cloak, her gloves, her shoulders combining with the fringes and the laces and the feather boas in the windows to make the spirit of finery and whimsy which dwindled out of the shops on to the pavement, as the light of a lamp goes wavering at night over hedges in the darkness.

Laughing and delightful, she had crossed Oxford Street and Great Portland Street and turned down one of the little streets, and now, and now, the great moment was approaching, for now she slackened, opened her bag, and with one look in his direction, but not at him, one look that bade farewell, summed up the whole situation and dismissed it triumphantly, for ever, had fitted her key, opened the door, and gone! Clarissa's voice saying, remember my party, remember my party, sang in his ears. The house was one of those flat red houses with hanging flower-baskets of vague impropriety. It was over.

Well, I've had my fun; I've had it, he thought, looking up at the swinging baskets of pale geraniums. And it was smashed to atoms – his fun, for it was half made up, as he knew very well; invented, this escapade with the girl; made up, as one makes up the better part of life, he thought – making oneself up; making her up; creating an exquisite amusement, and something more. But odd it was, and quite true; all this one could never share – it smashed to atoms.

He turned; went up the street, thinking to find some-where to sit, till it was time for Lincoln's Inn – for Messrs. Hooper and Grateley. Where should he go? No matter. Up the street, then, towards Regent's Park. His boots on the pavement struck out "no matter"; for it was early, still very early.

It was a splendid morning too. Like the pulse of a perfect heart, life struck straight through the streets. There was no fumbling – no hesitation. Sweeping and swerving, accurately, punctually, noiselessly, there, precisely at the right instant, the motor-car stopped at the door. The girl, silk-stockinged, feathered, evanescent, but not to him particularly attractive (for he had had his fling), alighted. Admirable butlers, tawny chow dogs, halls laid in black and white lozenges with white blinds blowing, Peter saw through the opened door and approved of. A splendid achievement in its own way, after all, London; the season; civilisation. Coming as he did from a respectable Anglo-Indian family which for at least three gener-ations had administered the affairs of a continent (it's strange, he thought, what a sentiment I have about that, disliking India, and empire, and army as he did), there were moments when civilisation, even of this sort, seemed dear to him as a personal possession; moments of pride in England; in butlers; chow dogs; girls in their security. Ridiculous enough, still there it is, he thought. And the doctors and men of business and capable women all going about their business, punctual, alert, robust, seemed to him wholly admirable, good fellows, to whom one would entrust one's life, companions in the art of living, who would see one through. What with one thing and another, the show was really very tolerable; and he would sit down in the shade and smoke.

There was Regent's Park. Yes. As a child he had walked in Regent's Park – odd, he thought, how the thought of child-hood keeps coming back to me – the result of seeing Clarissa, perhaps; for women live much more in the past than we do, he thought. They attach themselves to places; and their fathers

– a woman's always proud of her father. Bourton was a nice place, a very nice place, but I could never get on with the old man, he thought. There was quite a scene one night – an argument about something or other, what, he could not remember. Politics presumably.

Yes, he remembered Regent's Park; the long straight walk; the little house where one bought air-balls to the left; an absurd statue with an inscription somewhere or other. He looked for an empty seat. He did not want to be bothered (feeling a little drowsy as he did) by people asking him the time. An elderly grey nurse, with a baby asleep in its perambulator – that was the best he could do for himself; sit down at the far end of the seat by that nurse.

She's a queer-looking girl, he thought, suddenly remembering Elizabeth as she came into the room and stood by her mother. Grown big; quite grown-up, not exactly pretty; handsome rather; and she can't be more than eighteen. Probably she doesn't get on with Clarissa. "There's my Elizabeth" – that sort of thing – why not "Here's Elizabeth" simply? – trying to make out, like most mothers, that things are what they're not. She trusts to her charm too much, he thought. She overdoes it.

The rich benignant cigar smoke eddied coolly down his throat; he puffed it out again in rings which breasted the air bravely for a moment; blue, circular – I shall try and get a word alone with Elizabeth to-night, he thought – then began to wobble into hour-glass shapes and taper away; odd shapes they take, he thought. Suddenly he closed his eyes, raised his hand with an effort, and threw away the heavy end of his cigar. A great brush swept smooth across his mind, sweeping across it moving branches, children's voices, the shuffle of feet, and people passing, and humming traffic, rising and falling traffic. Down, down he sank into the plumes and feathers of sleep, sank, and was muffled over.

* * *

The grey nurse resumed her knitting as Peter Walsh, on the hot seat beside her, began snoring. In her grey dress, moving her hands indefatigably yet quietly, she seemed like the champion of the rights of sleepers, like one of those spectral presences which rise in twilight in woods made of sky and branches. The solitary traveller, haunter of lanes, disturber of ferns, and devastator of great hemlock plants, looking up suddenly, sees the giant figure at the end of the ride.

By conviction an atheist perhaps, he is taken by surprise with moments of extraordinary exaltation. Nothing exists outside us except a state of mind, he thinks; a desire for solace, for relief, for something outside these miserable pigmies, these feeble, these ugly, these craven men and women. But if he can conceive of her, then in some sort she exists, he thinks, and advancing down the path with his eyes upon sky and branches he rapidly endows them with womanhood; sees with amazement how grave they become; how majestically, as the breeze stirs them, they dispense with a dark flutter of the leaves charity, comprehension, absolution, and then, flinging themselves suddenly aloft, confound the piety of their aspect with a wild carouse.

Such are the visions which proffer great cornucopias full of fruit to the solitary traveller, or murmur in his ear like sirens lolloping away on the green sea waves, or are dashed in his face like bunches of roses, or rise to the surface like pale faces which fishermen flounder through floods to embrace.

Such are the visions which ceaselessly float up, pace beside, put their faces in front of, the actual thing; often overpowering the solitary traveller and taking away from him the sense of the earth, the wish to return, and giving him for substitute a general peace, as if (so he thinks as he advances down the forest ride) all this fever of living were simplicity itself; and myriads of things merged in one thing; and this figure, made of sky and branches as it is, had risen from the troubled sea (he is elderly, past fifty now) as a shape might be sucked up out of the waves to shower down from her magnificent hands compassion, comprehension, absolution. So, he thinks, may I never go back to the lamplight; to the sitting-room; never finish my book; never knock out my pipe; never ring for Mrs. Turner to clear away; rather let me walk straight on to this great figure, who will, with a toss of her head, mount me on her streamers and let me blow to nothingness with the rest.

Such are the visions. The solitary traveller is soon beyond the wood; and there, coming to the door with shaded eyes, possibly to look for his return, with hands raised, with white apron blowing, is an elderly woman who seems (so powerful is this infirmity) to seek, over the desert, a lost son; to search for a rider destroyed; to be the figure of the mother whose sons have been killed in the battles of the world. So, as the solitary traveller advances down the village street where the women stand knitting and the men dig in the garden, the evening seems ominous; the figures still; as if some august fate, known to them, awaited without fear, were about to sweep them into complete annihilation.

Indoors among ordinary things, the cupboard, the table, the window-sill with its geraniums, suddenly the outline of the landlady, bending to remove the cloth, becomes soft with light, an adorable emblem which only the recollection of cold human contacts forbids us to embrace. She takes the marmalade; she shuts it in the cupboard.

"There is nothing more to-night, sir?"

But to whom does the solitary traveller make reply?

So the elderly nurse knitted over the sleeping baby in Regent's Park. So Peter Walsh snored.

He woke with extreme suddenness, saying to himself, "The death of the soul."

"Lord, Lord!" he said to himself out loud, stretching and opening his eyes. "The death of the soul." The words attached themselves to some scene, to some room, to some past he had been dreaming of. It became clearer; the scene, the room, the past he had been dreaming of.

It was at Bourton that summer, early in the 'nineties, when he was so passionately in love with Clarissa. There were a great many people there, laughing and talking, sitting round a table after tea, and the room was bathed in yellow light and full of cigarette smoke. They were talking about a man who had married his housemaid, one of the neighbouring squires, he had forgotten his name. He had married his housemaid, and she had been brought to Bourton to call – an awful visit it had been. She was absurdly overdressed, "like a cockatoo," Clarissa had said, imitating her, and she never stopped talking. On and on she went, on and on. Clarissa imitated her. Then somebody said – Sally Seton it was – did it make any real difference to one's feelings to know that before they'd married she had had a baby? (In those days, in mixed company, it was a bold thing to say.) He could see Clarissa now, turning bright pink; somehow contracting; and saying, "Oh, I shall never be able to speak to her again!" Whereupon the whole party sitting round the tea-table seemed to wobble. It was very uncomfortable.

He hadn't blamed her for minding the fact, since in those days a girl brought up as she was knew nothing, but it was her manner that annoyed him; timid; hard; arrogant; prudish. "The death of the soul." He had said that instinctively, ticketing the moment as he used to do – the death of her soul.

Every one wobbled; every one seemed to bow, as she spoke, and then to stand up different. He could see Sally Seton, like a child who has been in mischief, leaning forward, rather flushed, wanting to talk, but afraid, and Clarissa did frighten people. (She was Clarissa's greatest friend, always about the place, an attractive creature, handsome, dark, with the reputation in those days of great daring, and he used to give her cigars, which she smoked in her bedroom, and she had either been engaged to somebody or quarrelled with her family, and old Parry disliked them both equally, which was a great bond.) Then Clarissa, still with an air of being offended with them all, got up, made some excuse, and went off, alone. As she opened the door, in came that great shaggy dog which ran after sheep. She flung herself upon him, went into raptures. It was as if she said to Peter – it was all aimed at him, he knew – "I know you thought me absurd about that woman just now; but see how extraordinarily sympathetic I am; see how I love my Rob!"

They had always this queer power of communicating without words. She knew directly he criticised her. Then she would do something quite obvious to defend herself, like this fuss with the dog – but it never took him in, he always saw through Clarissa. Not that he said anything, of course; just sat looking glum. It was the way their quarrels often began.

She shut the door. At once he became extremely depressed. It all seemed useless – going on being in love; going on quarrelling; going on making it up, and he wandered off alone, among outhouses, stables, looking at the horses. (The place was quite a humble one; the Parrys were never very well off; but there were always grooms and stable-boys about – Clarissa loved riding – and an old coachman – what was his name? – an old nurse, old Moody, old Goody, some such name they called her, whom one was taken to visit in a little room with lots of photographs, lots of bird-cages.)

It was an awful evening! He grew more and more gloomy, not about that only; about everything. And he couldn't see her; couldn't explain to her; couldn't have it out. There were always people about – she'd go on as if nothing had happened. That was the devilish part of her – this coldness, this wooden-ness, something very profound in her, which he had felt again this morning talking to her; an impenetrability. Yet Heaven knows he loved her. She had some queer power of fiddling on one's nerves, turning one's nerves to fiddle-strings, yes.

He had gone in to dinner rather late, from some idiotic idea of making himself felt, and had sat down by old Miss Parry – Aunt Helena – Mr. Parry's sister, who was supposed to preside. There she sat in her white Cashmere shawl, with her head against the window – a formidable old lady, but kind to him, for he had found her some rare flower, and she was a great botanist, marching off in thick boots with a black tin collecting box slung between her shoulders. He sat down beside her, and couldn't speak. Everything seemed to race past him; he just sat there, eating. And then half-way through dinner he made himself look across at Clarissa for the first time. She was talking to a young man on her right. He had a sudden revelation. "She will marry that man," he said to himself. He didn't even know his name.

For of course it was that afternoon, that very afternoon, that Dalloway had come over; and Clarissa called him "Wickham"; that was the beginning of it all. Somebody had brought him over; and Clarissa got his name wrong. She introduced him to everybody as Wickham. At last he said "My name is Dalloway!" – that was his first view of Richard – a fair young man, rather awkward, sitting on a deck-chair, and blurting out "My name is Dalloway!" Sally got hold of it; always after that she called him "My name is Dalloway!"

He was a prey to revelations at that time. This one – that she would marry Dalloway – was blinding – overwhelming at the moment. There was a sort of – how could he put it? – a sort of ease in her manner to him; something maternal; something gentle. They were talking about politics. All through dinner he tried to hear what they were saying.

Afterwards he could remember standing by old Miss Parry's chair in the drawing-room. Clarissa came up, with her perfect manners, like a real hostess, and wanted to introduce him to some one – spoke as if they had never met before, which enraged him. Yet even then he admired her for it. He admired her courage; her social instinct: he admired her power of carrying things through. "The perfect hostess," he said to her, whereupon she winced all over. But he meant her to feel it. He would have done anything to hurt her, after seeing her with Dalloway. So she left him. And he had a feeling that they were all gathered together in a conspiracy against him – laughing and talking – behind his back. There he stood by Miss Parry's chair as though he had been cut out of wood, talking about wild flowers. Never, never had he suffered so infernally! He must have forgotten even to pretend to listen; at last he woke up; he saw Miss Parry looking rather disturbed, rather indignant, with her prominent eyes fixed. He almost cried out that he couldn't attend because he was in Hell! People began going out of the room. He heard them talking about fetching cloaks; about its being cold on the water, and so on. They were going boating on the lake by moonlight – one of Sally's mad ideas. He could hear her describing the moon. And they all went out. He was left quite alone.

"Don't you want to go with them?" said Aunt Helena – old Miss Parry! – she had guessed. And he turned round and there was Clarissa again. She had come back to fetch him. He was overcome by her generosity – her goodness.

"Come along," she said. "They're waiting."

He had never felt so happy in the whole of his life! Without a word they made it up. The walked down to the lake. He had twenty minutes of perfect happiness. Her voice, her laugh, her dress (something floating, white, crimson), her spirit, her adventurousness; she made them all disembark and explore the island; she startled a hen; she laughed; she sang. And all the time, he knew perfectly well, Dalloway was falling in love with her; she was falling in love with Dalloway; but it didn't seem to matter. Nothing mattered. They sat on the ground and talked – he and Clarissa. They went in and out of each other's minds without any effort. And then in a second it was over. He said to himself as they were getting into the boat, "She will marry that man," dully, without any resentment; but it was an obvious thing. Dalloway would marry Clarissa.

Dalloway rowed them in. He said nothing. But somehow as they watched him start, jumping on to his bicycle to ride twenty miles through the woods, wobbling off down the drive, waving his hand and disappearing, he obviously did feel, instinctively, tremendously, strongly, all that; the night; the romance; Clarissa. He deserved to have her.

For himself, he was absurd. His demands upon Clarissa (he could see it now) were absurd. He asked impossible things. He made terrible scenes. She would have accepted him still, perhaps, if he had been less absurd. Sally thought so. She wrote him all that summer long letters; how they had talked of him; how she had praised him, how Clarissa burst into tears! It was an extraordinary summer – all letters, scenes, telegrams – arriving at Bourton early in the morning, hanging about till the servants were up; appalling *tête-à-têtes* with old Mr. Parry at breakfast; Aunt Helena formidable but kind; Sally sweeping him off for talks in the vegetable garden; Clarissa in bed with headaches.

The final scene, the terrible scene which he believed had mattered more than anything in the whole of his life (it might be an exaggeration – but still, so it did seem now), happened at three o'clock in the afternoon of a very hot day. It was a trifle that led up to it – Sally at lunch saying something about Dalloway, and calling him "My name is Dalloway"; whereupon Clarissa suddenly stiffened, coloured, in a way she had, and rapped out sharply, "We've had enough of that feeble joke." That was all; but for him it was as if she had said, "I'm only amusing myself with you; I've an understanding with Richard Dalloway." So he took it. He had not slept for nights. "It's got to be finished one way or the other," he said to himself. He sent a note to her by Sally asking her to meet him by the fountain at three. "Something very important has happened," he scribbled at the end of it.

The fountain was in the middle of a little shrubbery, far from the house, with shrubs and trees all round it. There she came, even before the time, and they stood with the fountain between them, the spout (it was broken) dribbling water incessantly. How sights fix themselves upon the mind! For example, the vivid green moss.

She did not move. "Tell me the truth, tell me the truth," he kept on saying. He felt as if his forehead would burst. She seemed contracted, petrified. She did not move. "Tell me the truth," he repeated, when suddenly that old man Breitkopf popped his head in carrying the *Times*; stared at them; gaped; and went away. They neither of them moved. "Tell me the truth," he repeated. He felt that he was grinding against something physically hard; she was unyielding. She was like iron, like flint, rigid up the backbone. And when she said, "It's no use. It's no use. This is the end" – after he had spoken for hours, it seemed, with the tears running down his cheeks – it was as if she had hit him in the face. She turned, she left him, she went away.

"Clarissa!" he cried. "Clarissa!" But she never came back. It was over. He went away that night. He never saw her again.

It was awful, he cried, awful, awful!

Still, the sun was hot. Still, one got over things. Still, life had a way of adding day to day. Still, he thought, yawning and beginning to take notice – Regent's Park had changed very little since he was a boy, except for the squirrels – still, presumably there were compensations – when little Elise Mitchell, who had been picking up pebbles to add to the pebble collection which she and her brother were making on the nursery mantelpiece, plumped her handful down on the nurse's knee and scudded off again full tilt into a lady's legs. Peter Walsh laughed out.

But Lucrezia Warren Smith was saying to herself, It's

wicked; why should I suffer? she was asking, as she walked down the broad path. No; I can't stand it any longer, she was saying, having left Septimus, who wasn't Septimus any longer, to say hard, cruel, wicked things, to talk to himself, to talk to a dead man, on the seat over there; when the child ran full tilt into her, fell flat, and burst out crying.

That was comforting rather. She stood her upright, dusted her frock, kissed her.

But for herself she had done nothing wrong; she had loved Septimus; she had been happy; she had had a beautiful home, and there her sister lived still, making hats. Why should *she* suffer?

The child ran straight back to its nurse, and Rezia saw her scolded, comforted, taken up by the nurse who put down her knitting, and the kind-looking man gave her his watch to blow open to comfort her – but why should *she* be exposed? Why not left in Milan? Why tortured? Why?

Slightly waved by tears the broad path, the nurse, the man in grey, the perambulator, rose and fell before her eyes. To be rocked by this malignant torturer was her lot. But why? She was like a bird sheltering under the thin hollow of a leaf, who blinks at the sun when the leaf moves; starts at the crack of a dry twig. She was exposed; she was surrounded by the enormous trees, vast clouds of an indifferent world, exposed; tortured; and why should she suffer? Why?

She frowned; she stamped her foot. She must go back again to Septimus since it was almost time for them to be going to Sir William Bradshaw. She must go back and tell him, go back to him sitting there on the green chair under the tree, talking to himself, or to that dead man Evans, whom she had only seen once for a moment in the shop. He had seemed a nice quiet man; a great friend of Septimus's, and he had been killed in the War. But such things happen to every one. Every one has friends who were killed in the War. Every one gives up something when they marry. She had given up her home. She had come to live here, in this awful city. But Septimus let himself think about horrible things, as she could too, if she tried. He had grown stranger and stranger. He said people were talking behind the bedroom walls. Mrs. Filmer thought it odd. He saw things too – he had seen an old woman's head in the middle of a fern. Yet he could be happy when he chose. They went to Hampton Court on top of a bus, and they were perfectly happy. All the little red and yellow flowers were out on the grass, like floating lamps, he said, and talked and chattered and laughed, making up stories. Suddenly he said, "Now we will kill ourselves," when they were standing by the river, and he looked at it with a look which she had seen in his eyes when a train went by, or an omnibus – a look as if something fascinated him; and she felt he was going from her and she caught him by the arm. But going home he was perfectly quiet – perfectly reasonable. He would argue with her about killing themselves; and explain how wicked people were; how he could see them making up lies as they passed in the street. He knew all their thoughts, he said; he knew everything. He knew the meaning of the world, he said.

Then when they got back he could hardly walk. He lay on the sofa and made her hold his hand to prevent him from falling down, down, he cried, into the flames! and saw faces laughing at him, calling him horrible disgusting names, from the walls, and hands pointing round the screen. Yet they were quite alone. But he began to talk aloud, answering people, arguing, laughing, crying, getting very excited and making her write things down. Perfect nonsense it was; about death; about Miss Isabel Pole. She could stand it no longer. She would go back.

She was close to him now, could see him staring at the sky, muttering, clasping his hands. Yet Dr. Holmes said there was nothing the matter with him. What, then, had happened – why had he gone, then, why, when she sat by him, did he start, frown at her, move away, and point at her hand, take her hand, look at it terrified?

Was it that she had taken off her wedding ring? "My hand has grown so thin," she said; "I have put it in my purse," she told him.

He dropped her hand. Their marriage was over, he thought, with agony, with relief. The rope was cut; he mounted; he was free, as it was decreed that he, Septimus, the lord of men, should be free; alone (since his wife had thrown away her wedding ring; since she had left him), he, Septimus, was alone, called forth in advance of the mass of men to hear the truth, to learn the meaning, which now at last, after all the toils of civilisation – Greeks, Romans, Shakespeare, Darwin, and now himself – was to be given whole to. . . . "To whom?" he asked aloud, "To the Prime Minister," the voices which rustled above his head replied. The supreme secret must be told to the Cabinet; first, that trees are alive; next, there is no crime; next, love, universal love, he muttered, gasping, trembling, painfully drawing out these profound truths which needed, so deep were they, so difficult, an immense effort to speak out, but the world was entirely changed by them for ever.

No crime; love; he repeated, fumbling for his card and pencil, when a Skye terrier snuffed his trousers and he started in an agony of fear. It was turning into a man! He could not watch it happen! It was horrible, terrible to see a dog become a man! At once the dog trotted away.

Heaven was divinely merciful, infinitely benignant. It spared him, pardoned his weakness. But what was the scientific explanation (for one must be scientific above all things)? Why could he see through bodies, see into the future, when dogs will become men? It was the heat wave presumably, operating upon a brain made sensitive by eons of evolution. Scientifically speaking, the flesh was melted off the world. His body was macerated until only the nerve fibres were left. It was spread like a veil upon a rock.

He lay back in his chair, exhausted but upheld. He lay resting, waiting, before he again interpreted, with effort, with agony, to mankind. He lay very high, on the back of the world. The earth thrilled beneath him. Red flowers grew through his flesh; their stiff leaves rustled by his head. Music began clanging against the rocks up here. It is a motor horn down in the street, he muttered; but up here it cannoned from rock to rock, divided, met in shocks of sound which rose in smooth columns (that music should be visible was a discovery) and became an anthem, an anthem twined round now by a shepherd boy's piping (That's an old man playing a penny whistle by the public-house, he muttered) which, as the boy stood still, came bubbling from his pipe, and then, as he climbed higher, made its exquisite plaint while the traffic passed beneath. This boy's elegy is played among the traffic, thought Septimus. Now he withdraws up into the snows, and roses hang about him – the thick red roses which grow on my bedroom wall, he reminded himself. The music stopped. He has his penny, he reasoned it out, and has gone on to the next public-house.

But he himself remained high on his rock, like a drowned sailor on a rock. I leant over the edge of the boat and fell down, he thought. I went under the sea. I have been dead and yet am now alive, but let me rest still, he begged (he was talking to himself again – it was awful, awful!); and as, before waking, the voices of birds and the sounds of wheels chime and chatter in a queer harmony, grow louder and louder, and the sleeper feels himself drawing to the shores of life, so he felt himself drawing towards life, the sun growing hotter, cries sounding louder, something tremendous about to happen.

He had only to open his eyes; but a weight was on them; a fear. He strained; he pushed; he looked; he saw Regent's Park before him. Long streamers of sunlight fawned at his feet. The trees waved, brandished. We welcome, the world seemed to say; we accept; we create. Beauty, the world seemed to say. And as if to prove it (scientifically) wherever he looked, at the houses, at the railings, at the antelopes stretching over the palings, beauty sprang instantly. To watch a leaf quivering in the rush of air was an exquisite joy. Up in the sky swallows swooping, swerving, flinging themselves in and out, round and round, yet always with perfect control as if elastics held them; and the flies rising and falling; and the sun spotting now this leaf, now that, in mockery, dazzling it with soft gold in pure good temper; and now and again some chime (it might be a motor horn) tinkling divinely on the grass stalks – all of this, calm and reasonable as it was, made out of ordinary things as it was, was the truth now; beauty, that was the truth now. Beauty was everywhere.

"It is time," said Rezia.

The word "time" split its husk; poured its riches over him; and from his lips fell like shells, like shavings from a plane, without his making them, hard, white, imperishable, words, and flew to attach themselves to their places in an ode to Time; an immortal ode to Time. He sang. Evans answered from behind the tree. The dead were in Thessaly, Evans sang, among the orchids. There they waited till the War was over, and now the dead, now Evans himself –

"For God's sake don't come!" Septimus cried out. For he could not look upon the dead.

But the branches parted. A man in grey was actually walking towards them. It was Evans! But no mud was on him; no wounds; he was not changed. I must tell the whole world, Septimus cried, raising his hand (as the dead man in the grey suit came nearer), raising his hand like some colossal figure who has lamented the fate of man for ages in the desert alone with his hands pressed to his forehead, furrows of despair on his cheeks, and now sees light on the desert's edge which broadens and strikes the iron-black figure (and Septimus half rose from his chair), and with legions of men prostrate behind him he, the giant mourner, receives for one moment on his face the whole –

"But I am so unhappy, Septimus," said Rezia, trying to make him sit down.

The millions lamented; for ages they had sorrowed. He would turn round, he would tell them in a few moments, only a few moments more, of this relief, of this joy, of this astonishing revelation –

"The time, Septimus," Rezia repeated. "What is the time?"

He was talking, he was starting, this man must notice him. He was looking at them.

"I will tell you the time," said Septimus, very slowly, very drowsily, smiling mysteriously at the dead man in the grey suit. As he sat smiling, the quarter struck – the quarter to twelve.

And that is being young, Peter Walsh thought as he passed them. To be having an awful scene – the poor girl looked absolutely desperate – in the middle of the morning. But what was it about, he wondered; what had the young man in the overcoat been saying to her to make her look like that; what awful fix had they got themselves into, both to look so desperate as that on a fine summer morning? The amusing thing about coming back to England, after five years, was the way it made, anyhow the first days, things stand out as if one had never seen them before; lovers squabbling under a tree; the domestic family life of the parks. Never had he seen London look so enchanting – the softness of the distances; the richness; the greenness; the civilisation, after India, he thought, strolling across the grass.

This susceptibility to impressions had been his undoing, no doubt. Still at his age he had, like a boy or a girl even, these alternations of mood; good days, bad days, for no reason whatever, happiness from a pretty face, downright misery at the sight of a frump. After India of course one fell in love with every woman one met. There was a freshness about them; even the poorest dressed better than five years ago surely; and to his eye the fashions had never been so becoming; the long black cloaks; the slimness; the elegance; and then the delicious and apparently universal habit of paint. Every woman, even the most respectable, had roses blooming under glass; lips cut with a knife; curls of Indian ink; there was design, art, everywhere; a change of some sort had undoubtedly taken place. What did the young people think about? Peter Walsh asked himself.

Those five years – 1918 to 1923 – had been, he suspected, somehow very important. People looked different. Newspapers seemed different. Now, for instance, there was a man writing quite openly in one of the respectable weeklies about waterclosets. That you couldn't have done ten years ago – written quite openly about water-closets in a respectable weekly. And then this taking out a stick of rouge, or a powder-puff, and making up in public. On board ship coming home there were lots of young men and girls – Betty and Bertie he remembered in particular – carrying on quite openly; the old mother sitting and watching them with her knitting, cool as a cucumber. The girl would stand still and powder her nose in front of every one. And they weren't engaged; just having a good time; no feelings hurt on either side. As hard as nails she was – Betty Whatshername – but a thorough good sort. She would make a very good wife at thirty – she would marry when it suited her to marry; marry some rich man and live in a large house near Manchester.

Who was it now who had done that? Peter Walsh asked himself, turning into the Broad Walk – married a rich man and lived in a large house near Manchester? Somebody who had written him a long, gushing letter quite lately about "blue hydrangeas". It was seeing blue hydrangeas that made her think of him and the old days – Sally Seton, of course! It was Sally Seton – the last person in the world one would have expected to marry a rich man and live in a large house near Manchester, the wild, the daring, the romantic Sally!

But of all that ancient lot, Clarissa's friends – Whitbreads, Kindersleys, Cunninghams, Kinloch-Joneses – Sally was probably the best. She tried to get hold of things by the right end anyhow. She saw through Hugh Whitbread anyhow – the admirable Hugh – when Clarissa and the rest were at his feet.

"The Whitbreads?" he could hear her saying. "Who are the Whitbreads? Coal merchants. Respectable tradespeople."

Hugh she detested for some reason. He thought of nothing but his own appearance, she said. He ought to have been a Duke. He would be certain to marry one of the Royal Princesses. And of course Hugh had the most extraordinary, the most natural, the most sublime respect for the British aristocracy of any human being he had ever come across. Even Clarissa had to own that. Oh, but he was such a dear, so unselfish, gave up shooting to please his old mother – remembered his aunts' birthdays, and so on.

Sally, to do her justice, saw through all that. One of the things he remembered best was an argument one Sunday morning at Bourton about women's rights (that antediluvian topic), when Sally suddenly lost her temper, flared up, and told Hugh that he represented all that was most detestable in British middle-class life. She told him that she considered him responsible for the state of "those poor girls in Piccadilly" Hugh, the perfect gentleman, poor Hugh! – never did a man look more horrified! She did it on purpose, she said afterwards (for they used to get together in the vegetable garden and compare notes). "He's read nothing, thought nothing, felt nothing," he could hear her saying in that very emphatic voice which carried so much farther than she knew. The stable boys had more life in them than Hugh, she said. He was a perfect specimen of the public school type, she said. No country but England could have produced him. She was really spiteful, for some reason; had some grudge against him. Something had happened – he forgot what – in the smoking-room. He had insulted her – kissed her? Incredible! Nobody believed a word against Hugh, of course. Who could? Kissing Sally in the smoking-room! If it had been some Honourable Edith or Lady Violet, perhaps; but not that ragamuffin Sally without a penny to her name, and a father or a mother gambling at Monte Carlo. For of all the people he had ever met Hugh was the greatest snob – the most obsequious – no, he didn't cringe exactly. He was too much of a prig for that. A first-rate valet was the obvious comparison – somebody who walked behind carrying suit cases; could be trusted to send telegrams – indispensable to hostesses. And he'd found his job – married his Honourable Evelyn; got some little post at Court, looked after the King's cellars, polished the Imperial shoe-buckles, went about in knee-breeches and lace ruffles. How remorseless life is! A little job at Court!

He had married this lady, the Honourable Evelyn, and they lived hereabouts, so he thought (looking at the pompous houses overlooking the Park), for he had lunched there once in a house which had, like all Hugh's possessions, something that no other house could possibly have – linen cupboards it might have been. You had to go and look at them – you had to spend a great deal of time always admiring whatever it was – linen cupboards, pillow-cases, old oak furniture, pictures, which Hugh had picked up for an old song. But Mrs. Hugh sometimes gave the show away. She was one of those obscure mouse-like little women who admire big men. She was almost negligible. Then suddenly she would say something quite unexpected – something sharp. She had the relics of the grand manner, perhaps. The steam coal was a little too strong for her – it made the atmosphere thick. And so there they lived, with their linen cupboards and their old masters and their pillow-cases fringed with real lace, at the rate of five or ten thousand a year presumably, while he, who was two years older than Hugh, cadged for a job.

At fifty-three he had to come and ask them to put him into some secretary's office, to find him some usher's job teaching little boys Latin, at the beck and call of some mandarin in an office, something that brought in five hundred a year; for if he married Daisy, even with his pension, they could never do on less. Whitbread could do it presumably; or Dalloway. He didn't mind what he asked Dalloway. He was a thorough good sort; a bit limited; a bit thick in the head; yes; but a thorough good sort. Whatever he took up he did in the same matter-of-fact sensible way; without a touch of imagination, without a spark of brilliancy, but with the inexplicable niceness of his type. He ought to have been a country gentleman – he was wasted on politics. He was at his best out of doors, with horses and dogs – how good he was, for instance, when that great shaggy dog of Clarissa's got caught in a trap and had its paw half torn off, and Clarissa turned faint and Dalloway did the whole thing; bandaged, made splints; told Clarissa not to be a fool. That was what she liked him for, perhaps – that was what she needed. "Now, my dear, don't be a fool. Hold this – fetch that," all the time talking to the dog as if it were a human being.

But how could she swallow all that stuff about poetry? How could she let him hold forth about Shakespeare? Seriously and solemnly Richard Dalloway got on his hind legs and said that no decent man ought to read Shakespeare's sonnets because it was like listening at keyholes (besides, the relationship was not one that he approved). No decent man ought to let his wife visit a deceased wife's sister. Incredible! The only thing to do was to pelt him with sugared almonds – it was at dinner. But Clarissa sucked it all in; thought it so honest of him; so independent of him; Heaven knows if she didn't think him the most original mind she'd ever met!

That was one of the bonds between Sally and himself. There was a garden where they used to walk, a walled-in place, with rose-bushes and giant cauliflowers – he could remember Sally tearing off a rose, stopping to exclaim at the beauty of the cabbage leaves in the moonlight (it was extraordinary how vividly it all came back to him, things he hadn't thought of for years), while she implored him, half laughing of course, to carry off Clarissa, to save her from the Hughs and the Dalloways and all the other "perfect gentlemen" who would "stifle her soul" (she wrote reams of poetry in those days), make a mere hostess of her, encourage her world-liness. But one must do Clarissa justice. She wasn't going to marry Hugh anyhow. She had a perfectly clear notion of what she wanted. Her emotions were all on the surface. Beneath, she was very shrewd – a far better judge of character than Sally, for instance, and with it all, purely feminine; with that extraordinary gift, that woman's gift, of making a world of her own wherever she happened to be. She came into a room; she stood, as he had often seen her, in a doorway with lots of people round her. But it was Clarissa one remembered. Not that she was striking; not beautiful at all; there was nothing picturesque about her; she never said anything specially clever; there she was, however; there she was.

No, no, no! He was not in love with her any more! He only felt, after seeing her that morning, among her scissors and silks, making ready for the party, unable to get away from the thought of her; she kept coming back and back like a sleeper jolting against him in a railway carriage; which was not being in love, of course; it was thinking of her, criticising her, starting again, after thirty years, trying to explain her. The obvious thing to say of her was that she was worldly; cared too much for rank and society and getting on in the world – which was true in a sense; she had admitted it to him. (You could always get her to own up if you took the trouble; she was honest.) What she would say was that she hated frumps, fogies, failures, like himself presumably; thought people had no right to slouch about with their hands in their pockets; must do something, be something; and these great swells, these Duchesses, these hoary old Countesses one met in her drawing-room, unspeakably remote as he felt them to be from anything that mattered a straw, stood for something real to her. Lady Bexborough, she said once, held herself upright (so did Clarissa herself; she never lounged in any sense of the word; she was straight as a dart, a little rigid in fact). She said they had a kind of courage which the older she grew the more she respected. In all this there was a great deal of Dalloway, of course; a great deal of the public-spirited, British Empire, tariff-reform, governing-class spirit, which had grown on her, as it tends to do. With twice his wits, she had to see things through his eyes – one of the tragedies of married life. With a mind of her own, she must always be quoting Richard – as if one couldn't know to a tittle what Richard thought by reading the *Morning Post* of a morning! These parties, for example, were all for him, or for her idea of him (to do Richard justice he would have been happier farming in Norfolk). She made her drawing-room a sort of meeting-place; she had a genius for it. Over and over again he had seen her take some raw youth, twist him, turn him, wake him up; set him going. Infinite numbers of dull people conglomerated round her, of course. But odd unexpected people turned up; an artist some- times; sometimes a writer; queer fish in that atmosphere. And behind it all was that network of visiting, leaving cards, being kind to people; running about with bunches of flowers, little presents; So-and-so was going to France – must have an air- cushion; a real drain on her strength; all that interminable traffic that women of her sort keep up; but she did it genuinely, from a natural instinct.

Oddly enough, she was one of the most thorough-going sceptics he had ever met, and possibly (this was a theory he used to make up to account for her, so transparent in some ways, so inscrutable in others), possibly she said to herself, As we are a doomed race, chained to a sinking ship (her favourite reading as a girl was Huxley and Tyndall, and they were fond of these nautical metaphors), as the whole thing is a bad joke, let us, at any rate, do our part; mitigate the sufferings of our fellow-prisoners (Huxley again); decorate the dungeon with flowers and air-cushions; be as decent as we possibly can. Those ruffians, the Gods, shan't have it all their own way – her notion being that the Gods, who never lost a chance of hurting, thwarting and spoiling human lives, were seriously put out if, all the same, you behaved like a lady. That phase came directly after Sylvia's death – that horrible affair. To see your own sister killed by a falling tree (all Justin Parry's fault – all his carelessness) before your very eyes, a girl too on the verge of life, the most gifted of them, Clarissa always said, was enough to turn one bitter. Later she wasn't so positive, perhaps; she thought there were no Gods; no one was to blame; and so she evolved this atheist's religion of doing good for the sake of goodness.

And of course she enjoyed life immensely. It was her nature to enjoy (though, goodness only knows, she had her reserves; it was a mere sketch, he often felt, that even he, after all these years, could make of Clarissa). Anyhow there was no bitterness in her; none of that sense of moral virtue which is so repulsive in good women. She enjoyed practically everything. If you walked with her in Hyde Park, now it was a bed of tulips, now a child in a perambulator, now some absurd little drama she made up on the spur of the moment. (Very likely she would have talked to those lovers, if she had thought them unhappy.) She had a sense of comedy that was really exquisite, but she needed people, always people, to bring it out, with the inevitable result that she frittered her time away, lunching, dining, giving these incessant parties of hers, talking nonsense, saying things she didn't mean, blunting the edge of her mind, losing her discrimination. There she would sit at the head of the table taking infinite pains with some old buffer who might be useful to Dalloway – they knew the most appalling bores in Europe – or in came Elizabeth and every thing must give way to *her*. She was at a High School, at the inarticulate stage last time he was over, a

round-eyed, pale-faced girl, with nothing of her mother in
her, a silent, stolid creature, who took it all as a matter of
course, let her mother make a fuss of her, and then said "May
I go now?" like a child of four; going off, Clarissa explained,
with that mixture of amusement and pride which Dalloway
himself seemed to rouse in her, to play hockey. And now
Elizabeth was "out", presumably; thought him an old fogy,
laughed at her mother's friends. Ah well, so be it. The compensation of growing old, Peter Walsh thought, coming out of
Regent's Park, and holding his hat in hand, was simply this;
that the passions remain as strong as ever, but one has gained
– at last! – the power which adds the supreme flavour to
existence – the power of taking hold of experience, of turning
it round, slowly, in the light.

A terrible confession it was (he put his hat on again),
but now at the age of fifty-three, one scarcely needed people
any more. Life itself, every moment of it, every drop of it,
here, this instant, now, in the sun, in Regent's Park, was
enough. Too much, indeed. A whole lifetime was too short
to bring out, now that one had acquired the power, the full
flavour; to extract every ounce of pleasure, every shade of
meaning; which both were so much more solid than they used
to be, so much less personal. It was impossible that he should
ever suffer again as Clarissa had made him suffer. For hours
at a time (pray God that one might say these things without
being overheard!), for hours and days he never thought of
Daisy.

Could it be that he was in love with her, then, remembering the misery, the torture, the extraordinary passion of
those days? It was a different thing altogether – a much
pleasanter thing – the truth being, of course, that now *she*
was in love with *him*. And that perhaps was the reason why,
when the ship actually sailed, he felt an extraordinary relief,
wanted nothing so much as to be alone; was annoyed to
find all her little attentions – cigars, notes, a rug for the

voyage – in his cabin. Every one if they were honest would say the same; one doesn't want people after fifty; one doesn't want to go on telling women they are pretty; that's what most men of fifty would say, Peter Walsh thought, if they were honest.

But then these astonishing accesses of emotion – bursting into tears this morning, what was all that about? What could Clarissa have thought of him? thought him a fool presumably, not for the first time. It was jealousy that was at the bottom of it – jealousy which survives every other passion of mankind, Peter Walsh thought, holding his pocket-knife at arm's length. She had been meeting Major Orde, Daisy said in her last letter; said it on purpose, he knew; said it to make him jealous; he could see her wrinkling her forehead as she wrote, wondering what she could say to hurt him; and yet it made no difference; he was furious! All this pother of coming to England and seeing lawyers wasn't to marry her, but to prevent her from marrying anybody else. That was what tortured him, that was what came over him when he saw Clarissa so calm, so cold, so intent on her dress or whatever it was; realising what she might have spared him, what she had reduced him to – a whimpering, snivelling old ass. But women, he thought, shutting his pocket-knife, don't know what passion is. They don't know the meaning of it to men. Clarissa was as cold as an icicle. There she would sit on the sofa by his side, let him take her hand, give him one kiss on the cheek – Here he was at the crossing.

A sound interrupted him; a frail quivering sound, a voice bubbling up without direction, vigour, beginning or end, running weakly and shrilly and with an absence of all human meaning into

ee um fah um so
foo swee too eem oo –

the voice of no age or sex, the voice of an ancient spring spouting from the earth; which issued, just opposite Regent's Park Tube Station, from a tall quivering shape, like a funnel, like a rusty pump, like a wind-beaten tree for ever barren of leaves which lets the wind run up and down its branches singing

ee um fah um so
foo swee too eem oo,

and rocks and creaks and moans in the eternal breeze.

Through all ages – when the pavement was grass, when it was swamp, through the age of tusk and mammoth, through the age of silent sunrise – the battered woman – for she wore a skirt – with her right hand exposed, her left clutching at her side, stood singing of love – love which has lasted a million years, she sang, love which prevails, and millions of years ago, her lover, who had been dead these centuries, had walked, she crooned, with her in May; but in the course of ages, long as summer days, and flaming, she remembered, with nothing but red asters, he had gone; death's enormous sickle had swept those tremendous hills, and when at last she laid her hoary and immensely aged head on the earth, now become a mere cinder of ice, she implored the Gods to lay by her side a bunch of purple heather, there on her high burial place which the last rays of the last sun caressed; for then the pageant of the universe would be over.

As the ancient song bubbled up opposite Regent's Park Tube Station, still the earth seemed green and flowery; still, though it issued from so rude a mouth, a mere hole in the earth, muddy too, matted with root fibres and tangled grasses, still the old bubbling burbling song, soaking through the knotted roots of infinite ages, and skeletons and treasure, streamed away in rivulets over the pavement and all along the Marylebone Road, and down towards Euston, fertilising, leaving a damp stain.

Still remembering how once in some primeval May she had walked with her lover, this rusty pump, this battered old woman with one hand exposed for coppers, the other clutching her side, would still be there in ten million years, remembering how once she had walked in May, where the sea flows now, with whom it did not matter – he was a man, oh yes, a man who had loved her. But the passage of ages had blurred the clarity of that ancient May day; the bright petalled flowers were hoar and silver frosted; and she no longer saw, when she implored him (as she did now quite clearly) "look in my eyes with thy sweet eyes intently," she no longer saw brown eyes, black whiskers or sunburnt face, but only a looming shape, a shadow shape, to which, with the bird-like freshness of the very aged, she still twittered "give me your hand and let me press it gently" (Peter Walsh couldn't help giving the poor creature a coin as he stepped into his taxi), "and if some one should see, what matter they?" she demanded; and her fist clutched at her side, and she smiled, pocketing her shilling, and all peering inquisitive eyes seemed blotted out, and the passing generations – the pavement was crowded with bustling middle-class people – vanished, like leaves, to be trodden under, to be soaked and steeped and made mould of by that eternal spring –

　　　　　ee um fah um so
　　　　　foo swee too eem oo.

"Poor old woman," said Rezia Warren Smith.

Oh poor old wretch! she said, waiting to cross.

Suppose it was a wet night? Suppose one's father, or somebody who had known one in better days had happened to pass, and saw one standing there in the gutter? And where did she sleep at night?

Cheerfully, almost gaily, the invincible thread of sound wound up into the air like the smoke from a cottage chimney, winding up clean beech trees and issuing in a tuft of blue smoke among the topmost leaves. "And if some one should see, what matter they?"

Since she was so unhappy, for weeks and weeks now, Rezia had given meanings to things that happened, almost felt sometimes that she must stop people in the street, if they looked good, kind people, just to say to them "I am unhappy"; and this old woman singing in the street "if some one should see, what matter they?" made her suddenly quite sure that everything was going to be right. They were going to Sir William Bradshaw; she thought his name sounded nice; he would cure Septimus at once. And then there was a brewer's cart, and the grey horses had upright bristles of straw in their tails; there were newspaper placards. It was a silly, silly dream, being unhappy.

So they crossed, Mr. and Mrs. Septimus Warren Smith, and was there, after all, anything to draw attention to them, anything to make a passer-by suspect here is a young man who carries in him the greatest message in the world, and is, moreover, the happiest man in the world, and the most miserable? Perhaps they walked more slowly than other people, and there was something hesitating, trailing, in the man's walk, but what more natural for a clerk, who has not been in the West End on a weekday at this hour for years, than to keep looking at the sky, looking at this, that and the other, as if Portland Place were a room he had come into when the family are away, the chandeliers being hung in holland bags, and the caretaker, as she lets in long shafts of dusty light upon deserted, queer-looking arm-chairs, lifting one corner of the long blinds, explains to the visitors what a wonderful place it is; how wonderful, but at the same time, he thinks, as he looks at chairs and tables, how strange.

To look at, he might have been a clerk, but of the better sort; for he wore brown boots; his hands were educated; so, too, his profile – his angular, big-nosed, intelligent, sensitive profile; but not his lips altogether, for they were loose; and his eyes (as eyes tend to be), eyes merely; hazel, large; so that he was, on the whole, a border case, neither one thing nor the other; might end with a house at Purley and a motor car, or continue renting apartments in back streets all his life; one of those half-educated, self-educated men whose education is all learnt from books borrowed from public libraries, read in the evening after the day's work, on the advice of well-known authors consulted by letter.

As for the other experiences, the solitary ones, which people go through alone, in their bedrooms, in their offices, walking the fields and the streets of London, he had them; had left home, a mere boy, because of his mother; she lied; because he came down to tea for the fiftieth time with his hands unwashed; because he could see no future for a poet in Stroud; and so, making a confidante of his little sister, had gone to London leaving an absurd note behind him, such as great men have written, and the world has read later when the story of their struggles has become famous.

London has swallowed up many millions of young men called Smith; thought nothing of fantastic Christian names like Septimus with which their parents have thought to distinguish them. Lodging off the Euston Road, there were experiences, again experiences, such as change a face in two years from a pink innocent oval to a face lean, contracted, hostile. But of all this what could the most observant of friends have said except what a gardener says when he opens the conservatory door in the morning and finds a new blossom on his plant: – It has flowered; flowered from vanity, ambition, idealism, passion, loneliness, courage, laziness, the usual seeds, which all muddled up (in a room off the Euston Road), made him shy, and stammering, made him anxious to improve himself, made him fall in love with Miss Isabel Pole, lecturing in the Waterloo Road upon Shakespeare.

Was he not like Keats? she asked; and reflected how she

might give him a taste of *Antony and Cleopatra* and the rest; lent him books; wrote him scraps of letters; and lit in him such a fire as burns only once in a lifetime, without heat, flickering a red-gold flame infinitely ethereal and insubstantial over Miss Pole; *Antony and Cleopatra*; and the Waterloo Road. He thought her beautiful, believed her impeccably wise; dreamed of her, wrote poems to her, which, ignoring the subject, she corrected in red ink; he saw her, one summer evening, walking in a green dress in a square. "It has flowered," the gardener might have said, had he opened the door; had he come in, that is to say, any night about this time, and found him writing; found him tearing up his writing; found him finishing a masterpiece at three o'clock in the morning and running out to pace the streets, and visiting churches, and fasting one day, drinking another, devouring Shakespeare, Darwin, *The History of Civilisation*, and Bernard Shaw.

Something was up, Mr. Brewer knew; Mr. Brewer, managing clerk at Sibleys and Arrowsmiths, auctioneers, valuers, land and estate agents; something was up, he thought, and, being paternal with his young men, and thinking very highly of Smith's abilities, and prophesying that he would, in ten or fifteen years, succeed to the leather arm-chair in the inner room under the skylight with the deed-boxes round him, "if he keeps his health," said Mr. Brewer, and that was the danger – he looked weakly; advised football, invited him to supper and was seeing his way to consider recommending a rise of salary, when something happened which threw out many of Mr. Brewer's calculations, took away his ablest young fellows, and eventually, so prying and insidious were the fingers of the European War, smashed a plaster cast of Ceres, ploughed a hole in the geranium beds, and utterly ruined the cook's nerves at Mr. Brewer's establishment at Muswell Hill.

Septimus was one of the first to volunteer. He went to France to save an England which consisted almost entirely of Shakespeare's plays and Miss Isabel Pole in a green dress walking in a square. There in the trenches the change which Mr. Brewer desired when he advised football was produced instantly; he developed manliness; he was promoted; he drew the attention, indeed the affection of his officer, Evans by name. It was a case of two dogs playing on a hearth-rug; one worrying a paper screw, snarling, snapping, giving a pinch, now and then, at the old dog's ear; the other lying somnolent, blinking at the fire, raising a paw, turning and growling good-temperedly. They had to be together, share with each other, fight with each other, quarrel with each other. But when Evans (Rezia, who had only seen him once, called him "a quiet man", a sturdy red-haired man, undemonstrative in the company of women), when Evans was killed, just before the Armistice, in Italy, Septimus, far from showing any emotion or recognising that here was the end of a friendship, congratulated himself upon feeling very little and very reason-ably. The War had taught him. It was sublime. He had gone through the whole show, friendship, European War, death, had won promotion, was still under thirty and was bound to survive. He was right there. The last shells missed him. He watched them explode with indifference. When peace came he was in Milan, billeted in the house of an innkeeper with a courtyard, flowers in tubs, little tables in the open, daughters making hats, and to Lucrezia, the younger daughter, he became engaged one evening when the panic was on him – that he could not feel.

For now that it was all over, truce signed, and the dead buried, he had, especially in the evening, these sudden thun-derclaps of fear. He could not feel. As he opened the door of the room where the Italian girls sat making hats, he could see them; could hear them; they were rubbing wires among coloured beads in saucers; they were turning buckram shapes this way and that; the table was all strewn with feathers, spangles, silks, ribbons; scissors were rapping on the table; but something failed him; he could not feel. Still, scissors rapping, girls laughing, hats being made protected him; he was assured of safety; he had a refuge. But he could not sit there all night. There were moments of waking in the early morning. The bed was falling; he was falling. Oh for the scissors and the lamplight and the buckram shapes! He asked Lucrezia to marry him, the younger of the two, the gay, the frivolous, with those little artist's fingers that she would hold up and say "It is all in them." Silk, feathers, what not, were alive to them.

"It is the hat that matters most," she would say, when they walked out together. Every hat that passed, she would examine; and the cloak and the dress and the way the woman held herself. Ill-dressing, over-dressing she stigmatised, not savagely, rather with impatient movements of the hands, like those of a painter who puts from him some obvious well-meant glaring imposture; and then, generously, but always critically, she would welcome a shop-girl who had turned her little bit of stuff gallantly, or praise, wholly, with enthusiastic and professional understanding, a French lady descending from her carriage, in chinchilla, robes, pearls.

"Beautiful!" she would murmur, nudging Septimus, that he might see. But beauty was behind a pane of glass. Even taste (Rezia liked ices, chocolates, sweet things) had no relish to him. He put down his cup on the little marble table. He looked at people outside; happy they seemed, collecting in the middle of the street, shouting, laughing, squabbling over nothing. But he could not taste, he could not feel. In the tea-shop among the tables and the chattering waiters the appalling fear came over him – he could not feel. He could reason; he could read, Dante for example, quite easily ("Septimus, do put down your book," said Rezia, gently shutting the *Inferno*), he could add up his bill; his brain was perfect; it must be the fault of the world then – that he could not feel.

"The English are so silent," Rezia said. She liked it, she

said. She respected these Englishmen, and wanted to see London, and the English horses, and the tailor-made suits, and could remember hearing how wonderful the shops were, from an aunt who had married and lived in Soho.

It might be possible, Septimus thought, looking at England from the train window, as they left Newhaven; it might be possible that the world itself is without meaning.

At the office they advanced him to a post of considerable responsibility. They were proud of him; he had won crosses. "You have done your duty; it is up to us –" began Mr. Brewer; and could not finish, so pleasurable was his emotion. They took admirable lodgings off the Tottenham Court Road.

Here he opened Shakespeare once more. That boy's business of the intoxication of language – *Antony and Cleopatra* – had shrivelled utterly. How Shakespeare loathed humanity – the putting on of clothes, the getting of children, the sordidity of the mouth and the belly! This was now revealed to Septimus; the message hidden in the beauty of words. The secret signal which one generation passes, under disguise, to the next is loathing, hatred, despair. Dante the same. Aeschylus (translated) the same. There Rezia sat at the table trimming hats. She trimmed hats for Mrs. Filmer's friends; she trimmed hats by the hour. She looked pale, mysterious, like a lily, drowned, under water, he thought.

"The English are so serious," she would say, putting her arms round Septimus, her cheek against his.

Love between man and woman was repulsive to Shakespeare. The business of copulation was filth to him before the end. But, Rezia said, she must have children. They had been married five years.

They went to the Tower together; to the Victoria and Albert Museum; stood in the crowd to see the King open Parliament. And there were the shops – hat shops, dress shops, shops with leather bags in the window, where she would stand staring. But she must have a boy.

She must have a son like Septimus, she said. But nobody could be like Septimus; so gentle; so serious; so clever. Could she not read Shakespeare too? Was Shakespeare a difficult author? she asked.

One cannot bring children into a world like this. One cannot perpetuate suffering, or increase the breed of these lustful animals, who have no lasting emotions, but only whims and vanities, eddying them now this way, now that.

He watched her snip, shape, as one watches a bird hop, flit in the grass, without daring to move a finger. For the truth is (let her ignore it) that human beings have neither kindness, nor faith, nor charity beyond what serves to increase the pleasure of the moment. They hunt in packs. Their packs scour the desert and vanish screaming into the wilderness. They desert the fallen. They are plastered over with grimaces. There was Brewer at the office, with his waxed moustache, coral tie-pin, white slip, and pleasurable emotions – all coldness and clamminess within, – his geraniums ruined in the War – his cook's nerves destroyed; or Amelia Whatshername, handing round cups of tea punctually at five – a leering, sneering obscene little harpy; and the Toms and Berties in their starched shirt fronts oozing thick drops of vice. They never saw him drawing pictures of them naked at their antics in his notebook. In the street, vans roared past him; brutality blared out on placards; men were trapped in mines; women burnt alive; and once a maimed file of lunatics being exercised or displayed for the diversion of the populace (who laughed aloud) ambled and nodded and grinned past him, in the Tottenham Court Road, each half apologetically, yet triumphantly, inflicting his hopeless woe. And would *he* go mad?

At tea Rezia told him that Mrs. Filmer's daughter was expecting a baby. *She* could not grow old and have no children! She was very lonely, she was very unhappy! She cried for the first time since they were married. Far away he heard her sobbing; he heard it accurately, he noticed it distinctly; he compared it to a piston thumping. But he felt nothing.

His wife was crying, and he felt nothing; only each time she sobbed in this profound, this silent, this hopeless way, he descended another step into the pit.

At last, with a melodramatic gesture which he assumed mechanically and with complete consciousness of its insincerity, he dropped his head on his hands. Now he had surrendered; now other people must help him. People must be sent for. He gave in.

Nothing could rouse him. Rezia put him to bed. She sent for a doctor – Mrs. Filmer's Dr. Holmes. Dr. Holmes examined him. There was nothing whatever the matter, said Dr. Holmes. Oh, what a relief! What a kind man, what a good man! thought Rezia. When he felt like that he went to the Music Hall, said Dr. Holmes. He took a day off with his wife and played golf. Why not try two tabloids of bromide dissolved in a glass of water at bedtime? These old Bloomsbury houses, said Dr. Holmes, tapping the wall, are often full of very fine panelling, which the landlords have the folly to paper over. Only the other day, visiting a patient, Sir Somebody Something, in Bedford Square –

So there was no excuse; nothing whatever the matter, except the sin for which human nature had condemned him to death; that he did not feel. He had not cared when Evans was killed; that was worst; but all the other crimes raised their heads and shook their fingers and jeered and sneered over the rail of the bed in the early hours of the morning at the prostrate body which lay realising its degradation; how he had married his wife without loving her; had lied to her; seduced her; outraged Miss Isabel Pole, and was so pocked and marked with vice that women shuddered when they saw him in the street. The verdict of human nature on such a wretch was death.

Dr. Holmes came again. Large, fresh-coloured, handsome,

flicking his boots, looking in the glass, he brushed it all aside – headaches, sleeplessness, fears, dreams – nerve symptoms and nothing more, he said. If Dr. Holmes found himself even half a pound below eleven stone six, he asked his wife for another plate of porridge at breakfast. (Rezia would learn to cook porridge.) But, he continued, health is largely a matter in our own control. Throw yourself into outside interests; take up some hobby. He opened Shakespeare – *Antony and Cleopatra;* pushed Shakespeare aside. Some hobby, said Dr. Holmes, for did he not owe his own excellent health (and he worked as hard as any man in London) to the fact that he could always switch off from his patients on to old furniture? And what a very pretty comb, if he might say so, Mrs. Warren Smith was wearing!

When the damned fool came again, Septimus refused to see him. Did he indeed? said Dr. Holmes, smiling agreeably. Really he had to give that charming little lady, Mrs. Smith, a friendly push before he could get past her into her husband's bedroom.

"So you're in a funk," he said agreeably, sitting down by his patient's side. He had actually talked of killing himself to his wife, quite a girl, a foreigner, wasn't she? Didn't that give her a very odd idea of English husbands? Didn't one owe perhaps a duty to one's wife? Wouldn't it be better to do something instead of lying in bed? For he had had forty years' experience behind him; and Septimus could take Dr. Holmes's word for it – there was nothing whatever the matter with him. And next time Dr. Holmes came he hoped to find Smith out of bed and not making that charming little lady his wife anxious about him.

Human nature, in short, was on him – the repulsive brute, with the blood-red nostrils. Holmes was on him. Dr. Holmes came quite regularly every day. Once you stumble, Septimus wrote on the back of a postcard, human nature is on you. Holmes is on you. Their only chance was to escape, without letting Holmes know; to Italy – anywhere, anywhere, away from Dr. Holmes.

But Rezia could not understand him. Dr. Holmes was such a kind man. He was so interested in Septimus. He only wanted to help them, she said. He had four little children and he had asked her to tea, she told Septimus.

So he was deserted. The whole world was clamouring: Kill yourself, kill yourself, for our sakes. But why should he kill himself for their sakes? Food was pleasant; the sun hot; and this killing oneself, how does one set about it, with a table knife, uglily, with floods of blood, – by sucking a gaspipe? He was too weak; he could scarcely raise his hand. Besides, now that he was quite alone, condemned, deserted, as those who are about to die are alone, there was a luxury in it, an isolation full of sublimity; a freedom which the attached can never know. Holmes had won of course; the brute with the red nostrils had won. But even Holmes himself could not touch this last relic straying on the edge of the world, this outcast, who gazed back at the inhabited regions, who lay, like a drowned sailor, on the shore of the world.

It was at that moment (Rezia had gone shopping) that the great revelation took place. A voice spoke from behind the screen. Evans was speaking. The dead were with him.

"Evans, Evans!" he cried.

Mr. Smith was talking aloud to himself, Agnes the servant girl cried to Mrs. Filmer in the kitchen. "Evans, Evans!" he had said as she brought in the tray. She jumped, she did. She scuttled downstairs.

And Rezia came in, with her flowers, and walked across the room, and put the roses in a vase, upon which the sun struck directly, and it went laughing, leaping round the room.

She had had to buy the roses, Rezia said, from a poor man in the street. But they were almost dead already, she said, arranging the roses.

So there was a man outside; Evans presumably; and the

roses, which Rezia said were half dead, had been picked by him in the fields of Greece. "Communication is health; communication is happiness, communication" he muttered.

"What are you saying, Septimus?" Rezia asked, wild with terror, for he was talking to himself.

She sent Agnes running for Dr. Holmes. Her husband, she said, was mad. He scarcely knew her.

"You brute! You brute!" cried Septimus, seeing human nature, that is Dr. Holmes, enter the room.

"Now what's all this about," said Dr. Holmes in the most amiable way in the world. "Talking nonsense to frighten your wife?" But he would give him something to make him sleep. And if they were rich people, said Dr. Holmes, looking ironically round the room, by all means let them go to Harley Street; if they had no confidence in him, said Dr. Holmes, looking not quite so kind.

It was precisely twelve o'clock; twelve by Big Ben; whose stroke was wafted over the northern part of London; blent with that of other clocks, mixed in a thin ethereal way with the clouds and wisps of smoke, and died up there among the seagulls – twelve o'clock struck as Clarissa Dalloway laid her green dress on her bed, and the Warren Smiths walked down Harley Street. Twelve was the hour of their appointment. Probably, Rezia thought, that was Sir William Bradshaw's house with the grey motor car in front of it. (The leaden circles dissolved in the air.)

Indeed it was – Sir William Bradshaw's motor car; low, powerful, grey with plain initials interlocked on the panel, as if the pomps of heraldry were incongruous, this man being the ghostly helper, the priest of science; and, as the motor car was grey, so to match its sober suavity, grey furs, silver grey rugs were heaped in it, to keep her ladyship warm while she waited. For often Sir William would travel sixty miles or more down into the country to visit the rich, the afflicted, who could afford the very large fee which Sir William very properly charged for his advice. Her ladyship waited with the rugs about her knees an hour or more, leaning back, thinking sometimes of the patient, sometimes, excusably, of the wall of gold, mounting minute by minute while she waited; the wall of gold that was mounting between them and all shifts and anxieties (she had borne them bravely; they had had their struggles) until she felt wedged on a calm ocean, where only spice winds blow; respected, admired, envied, with scarcely anything left to wish for, though she regretted her stoutness; large dinner-parties every Thursday night to the profession; an occasional bazaar to be opened; Royalty greeted; too little time, alas, with her husband, whose work grew and grew; a boy doing well at Eton; she would have liked a daughter too; interests she had, however, in plenty; child welfare; the after-care of the epileptic, and photography, so that if there was a church building, or a church decaying, she bribed the sexton, got the key and took photographs, which were scarcely to be distinguished from the work of professionals, while she waited.

Sir William himself was no longer young. He had worked very hard; he had won his position by sheer ability (being the son of a shopkeeper); loved his profession; made a fine figure-head at ceremonies and spoke well – all of which had by the time he was knighted given him a heavy look, a weary look (the stream of patients being so incessant, the responsibilities and privileges of his profession so onerous), which weariness, together with his grey hairs, increased the extraordinary distinction of his presence and gave him the reputation (of the utmost importance in dealing with nerve cases) not merely of lightning skill and almost infallible accuracy in diagnosis, but of sympathy; tact; understanding of the human soul. He could see the first moment they came into the room (the Warren Smiths they were called); he was certain directly he saw the man; it was a case of extreme gravity. It was a case of complete breakdown – complete physical and nervous breakdown, with every symptom in an advanced stage, he ascertained in two or three minutes (writing answers to questions, murmured discreetly, on a pink card).

How long had Dr. Holmes been attending him?

Six weeks.

Prescribed a little bromide? Said there was nothing the matter? Ah yes (those general practitioners! thought Sir William. It took half his time to undo their blunders. Some were irreparable).

"You served with great distinction in the War?"

The patient repeated the word "war" interrogatively.

He was attaching meanings to words of a symbolical kind. A serious symptom to be noted on the card.

"The War?" the patient asked. The European War – that little shindy of schoolboys with gunpowder? Had he served with distinction? He really forgot. In the War itself he had failed.

"Yes, he served with the greatest distinction," Rezia assured the doctor; "he was promoted."

"And they have the very highest opinion of you at your office?" Sir William murmured, glancing at Mr. Brewer's very generously worded letter. "So that you have nothing to worry you, no financial anxiety, nothing?"

He had committed an appalling crime and been condemned to death by human nature.

"I have – I have," he began, "committed a crime –"

"He has done nothing wrong whatever," Rezia assured the doctor. If Mr. Smith would wait, said Sir William, he would speak to Mrs. Smith in the next room. Her husband was very seriously ill, Sir William said. Did he threaten to kill himself?

Oh, he did, she cried. But he did not mean it, she said. Of course not. It was merely a question of rest, said Sir William; of rest, rest, rest; a long rest in bed. There was a delightful home down in the country where her husband would be perfectly looked after. Away from her? she asked. Unfortunately, yes; the people we care for most are not good for us when we are ill. But he was not mad, was he? Sir Walter said he never spoke of "madness"; he called it not having a sense of proportion. But her husband did not like doctors. He would refuse to go there. Shortly and kindly Sir William explained to her the state of the case. He had threatened to kill himself. There was no alternative. It was a question of law. He would lie in bed in a beautiful house in the country. The nurses were admirable. Sir William would visit him once a week. If Mrs. Warren Smith was quite sure she had no more questions to ask – he never hurried his patients – they would return to her husband. She had nothing more to ask – not of Sir William.

So they returned to the most exalted of mankind; the criminal who faced his judges; the victim exposed on the heights; the fugitive; the drowned sailor; the poet of the immortal ode; the Lord who had gone from life to death; to Septimus Warren Smith, who sat in the arm-chair under the skylight staring at a photograph of Lady Bradshaw in Court dress, muttering messages about beauty.

"We have had our little talk," said Sir William.

"He says you are very, very ill," Rezia cried.

"We have been arranging that you should go into a home," said Sir William.

"One of Holmes's homes?" sneered Septimus.

The fellow made a distasteful impression. For there was in Sir William, whose father had been a tradesman, a natural respect for breeding and clothing, which shabbiness nettled; again, more profoundly, there was in Sir William, who had never had time for reading, a grudge, deeply buried, against cultivated people who came into his room and intimated that doctors, whose profession is a constant strain upon all the highest faculties, are not educated men.

"One of *my* homes, Mr. Warren Smith," he said, "where we will teach you to rest."

And there was just one thing more.

He was quite certain that when Mr. Warren Smith was well he was the last man in the world to frighten his wife. But he had talked of killing himself.

"We all have our moments of depression," said Sir William.

Once you fall, Septimus repeated to himself, human nature is on you. Holmes and Bradshaw are on you. They scour the desert. They fly screaming into the wilderness. The rack and the thumbscrew are applied. Human nature is remorseless.

"Impulses come upon him sometimes?" Sir William asked, with his pencil on a pink card.

That was his own affair, said Septimus.

"Nobody lives for himself alone," said Sir William, glancing at the photograph of his wife in Court dress.

"And you have a brilliant career before you," said Sir William. There was Mr. Brewer's letter on the table. "An exceptionally brilliant career."

But if he confessed? If he communicated? Would they let him off then, Holmes and Bradshaw?

"I – I –" he stammered.

But what was his crime? He could not remember it.

"Yes?" Sir William encouraged him. (But it was growing late.)

Love, trees, there is no crime – what was his message? He could not remember it.

"I – I –" Septimus stammered.

"Try to think as little about yourself as possible," said Sir William kindly. Really, he was not fit to be about.

Was there anything else they wished to ask him? Sir William would make all arrangements (he murmured to Rezia) and he would let her know between five and six that evening.

"Trust everything to me," he said, and dismissed them.

Never, never had Rezia felt such agony in her life! She

had asked for help and been deserted! He had failed them! Sir William Bradshaw was not a nice man.

The upkeep of that motor car alone must cost him quite a lot, said Septimus, when they got out into the street.

She clung to his arm. They had been deserted.

But what more did she want?

To his patients he gave three-quarters of an hour; and if in this exacting science which has to do with what, after all, we know nothing about – the nervous system, the human brain – a doctor loses his sense of proportion, as a doctor he fails. Health we must have; and health is proportion; so that when a man comes into your room and says he is Christ (a common delusion), and has a message, as they mostly have, and threatens, as they often do, to kill himself, you invoke proportion; order rest in bed; rest in solitude; silence and rest; rest without friends, without books, without messages; six months' rest; until a man who went in weighing seven stone six comes out weighing twelve.

Proportion, divine proportion, Sir William's goddess, was acquired by Sir William walking hospitals, catching salmon, begetting one son in Harley Street by Lady Bradshaw, who caught salmon herself and took photographs scarcely to be distinguished from the work of professionals. Worshipping proportion, Sir William not only prospered himself but made England prosper, secluded her lunatics, forbade childbirth, penalised despair, made it impossible for the unfit to propagate their views until they, too, shared his sense of proportion – his, if they were men, Lady Bradshaw's if they were women (she embroidered, knitted, spent four nights out of seven at home with her son), so that not only did his colleagues respect him, his subordinates fear him, but the friends and relations of his patients felt for him the keenest gratitude for insisting that these prophetic Christs and Christesses, who prophesied the end of the world, or the advent of God, should drink milk in bed, as Sir William ordered; Sir William with his thirty years' experience of these kinds of cases, and his infallible instinct, this is madness, this sense; in fact, his sense of proportion.

But Proportion has a sister, less smiling, more formidable, a Goddess even now engaged – in the heat and sands of India, the mud and swamp of Africa, the purlieus of London, wherever in short the climate or the devil tempts men to fall from the true belief which is her own – is even now engaged in dashing down shrines, smashing idols, and setting up in their place her own stern countenance. Conversion is her name and she feasts on the wills of the weakly, loving to impress, to impose, adoring her own features stamped on the face of the populace. At Hyde Park Corner on a tub she stands preaching; shrouds herself in white and walks penitentially disguised as brotherly love through factories and parliaments; offers help, but desires power; smites out of her way roughly the dissentient, or dissatisfied; bestows her blessing on those who, looking upward, catch submissively from her eyes the light of their own. This lady too (Rezia Warren Smith divined it) had her dwelling in Sir William's heart, though concealed, as she mostly is, under some plausible disguise; some venerable name; love, duty, self-sacrifice. How he would work – how toil to raise funds, propagate reforms, initiate institutions! But Conversion, fastidious Goddess, loves blood better than brick, and feasts most subtly on the human will. For example, Lady Bradshaw. Fifteen years ago she had gone under. It was nothing you could put your finger on; there had been no scene, no snap; only the slow sinking, waterlogged, of her will into his. Sweet was her smile, swift her submission; dinner in Harley Street, numbering eight or nine courses, feeding ten or fifteen guests of the professional classes, was smooth and urbane. Only as the evening wore on a very slight dulness, or uneasiness perhaps, a nervous twitch, fumble, stumble and confusion indicated, what it was really painful to believe – that the poor lady lied. Once, long ago, she had caught salmon freely: now, quick to minister to the craving which lit her husband's eye so oilily for dominion, for power, she cramped, squeezed, pared, pruned, drew back, peeped through; so that without knowing precisely what made the evening disagreeable, and caused this pressure on the top of the head (which might well be imputed to the professional conversation, or the fatigue of a great doctor whose life, Lady Bradshaw said, "is not his own but his patient's"), disagreeable it was: so that guests, when the clock struck ten, breathed in the air of Harley Street even with rapture; which relief, however, was denied to his patients.

There in the grey room, with the pictures on the wall, and the valuable furniture, under the ground glass skylight, they learnt the extent of their transgressions; huddled up in arm-chairs, they watched him go through, for their benefit, a curious exercise with the arms, which he shot out, brought sharply back to his hip, to prove (if the patient was obstinate) that Sir William was master of his own actions, which the patient was not. There some weakly broke down; sobbed, submitted; others, inspired by Heaven knows what intemperate madness, called Sir William to his face a damnable humbug; questioned, even more impiously, life itself. Why live? they demanded. Sir William replied that life was good. Certainly Lady Bradshaw in ostrich feathers hung over the mantelpiece, and as for his income it was quite twelve thousand a year. But to us, they protested, life has given no such bounty. He acquiesced. They lacked a sense of proportion. And perhaps, after all, there is no God? He shrugged his shoulders. In short, this living or not living is an affair of our own? But there they were mistaken. Sir William had a friend in Surrey where they taught, what Sir William frankly admitted was a difficult art – a sense of proportion. There were, moreover, family affection; honour; courage; and a brilliant career. All of these had in Sir William a resolute champion. If they failed, he had to support him police and the good of society, which, he remarked very quietly, would take care, down in Surrey, that these unsocial impulses, bred more than anything by the lack of good blood, were held in control. And then stole out from her hiding-place and mounted her throne that Goddess whose lust is to override opposition, to stamp indelibly in the sanctuaries of others the image of herself. Naked, defenceless, the exhausted, the friendless received the impress of Sir William's will. He swooped; he devoured. He shut people up. It was this combination of decision and humanity that endeared Sir William so greatly to the relations of his victims.

But Rezia Warren Smith cried, walking down Harley Street, that she did not like that man.

Shredding and slicing, dividing and subdividing, the clocks of Harley Street nibbled at the June day, counselled submission, upheld authority, and pointed out in chorus the supreme advantages of a sense of proportion, until the mound of time was so far diminished that a commerical clock, suspended above a shop in Oxford Street, announced, genially and fraternally, as if it were a pleasure to Messrs. Rigby and Lowndes to give the information gratis, that it was half-past one.

Looking up, it appeared that each letter of their names stood for one of the hours; subconsciously one was grateful to Rigby and Lowndes for giving one time ratified by Greenwich; and this gratitude (so Hugh Whitbread ruminated, dallying there in front of the shop window) naturally took the form later of buying off Rigby and Lowndes socks or shoes. So he ruminated. It was his habit. He did not go deeply. He brushed surfaces; the dead languages, the living, life in Constantinople, Paris, Rome; riding, shooting, tennis, it had been once. The malicious asserted that he now kept guard at Buckingham Palace, dressed in silk stockings and knee-breeches, over what nobody knew. But he did it extremely efficiently. He had been afloat on the cream of English society for fifty-one years. He had known Prime Ministers. His affections were understood to be deep. And if it were true that he had not taken part in any of the great movements of the time or held important office, one or two humble reforms stood to his credit; an improvement in public shelters was one; the protection of owls in Norfolk another; servant girls had reason to be grateful to him; and his name at the end of letters to the *Times*, asking for funds, appealing to the public to protect, to preserve, to clear up litter, to abate smoke, and stamp out immorality in parks, commanded respect.

A magnificent figure he cut too, pausing for a moment (as the sound of the half-hour died away) to look critically, magisterially, at socks and shoes; impeccable, substantial, as if he beheld the world from a certain eminence, and dressed to match; but realised the obligations which size, wealth, health entail, and observed punctiliously even when not absolutely necessary, little courtesies, old-fashioned ceremonies which gave a quality to his manner, something to imitate, something to remember him by, for he would never lunch, for example, with Lady Bruton, whom he had known these twenty years, without bringing her in his outstretched hand a bunch of carnations and asking Miss Brush, Lady Bruton's secretary, after her brother in South Africa, which, for some reason, Miss Brush, deficient though she was in every attribute of female charm, so much resented that she said "Thank you, he's doing very well in South Africa," when, for half-a-dozen years, he had been doing badly in Portsmouth.

Lady Bruton herself preferred Richard Dalloway, who arrived at the same moment. Indeed they met on the doorstep.

Lady Bruton preferred Richard Dalloway of course. He was made of much finer material. But she wouldn't let them run down her poor dear Hugh. She could never forget his kindness – he had been really remarkably kind – she forgot precisely upon what occasion. But he had been – remarkably kind.

Anyhow, the difference between one man and another does not amount to much. She had never seen the sense of cutting people up, as Clarissa Dalloway did – cutting them up and sticking them together again; not at any rate when one was sixty-two. She took Hugh's carnations with her angular grim smile. There was nobody else coming, she said. She had got them there on false pretences, to help her out of a difficulty – "But let us eat first," she said.

And so there began a soundless and exquisite passing to and fro through swing doors of aproned white-capped maids, handmaidens not of necessity, but adepts in a mystery or grand deception practised by hostesses in Mayfair from one-thirty to two, when, with a wave of the hand, the traffic ceases, and there rises instead this profound illusion in the first place about the food – how it is not paid for; and then that the table spreads itself voluntarily with glass and silver, little mats, saucers of red fruit; films of brown cream mask turbot; in casseroles severed chickens swim; coloured, undo-mestic, the fire burns; and with the wine and the coffee (not paid for) rise jocund visions before musing eyes; gently specu-lative eyes; eyes to whom life appears musical, mysterious; eyes now kindled to observe genially the beauty of the red carnations which Lady Bruton (whose movements were always angular) had laid beside her plate, so that Hugh Whitbread, feeling at peace with the entire universe and at the same time completely sure of his standing, said, resting his fork: "Wouldn't they look charming against your lace?"

Miss Brush resented this familiarity intensely. She thought him an underbred fellow. She made Lady Bruton laugh.

Lady Bruton raised the carnations, holding them rather stiffly with much the same attitude with which the General held the scroll in the picture behind her; she remained fixed, tranced. Which was she now, the General's great-grand-daughter? great-great-grand-daughter? Richard Dalloway asked himself. Sir Roderick, Sir Miles, Sir Talbot – that was it. It was remarkable how in that family the likeness persisted in the women. She should have been a general of dragoons herself. And Richard would have served under her, cheerfully; he had the greatest respect for her; he cherished these romantic views about well-set-up old women of pedigree, and would have liked, in his good-humoured way, to bring some young hot-heads of his acquaintance to lunch with her; as if a type like hers could be bred of amiable tea-drinking enthusiasts! He knew her country. He knew her people. There was a vine, still bearing, which either Lovelace or Herrick – she never read a word of poetry herself, but so the story ran – had sat under. Better wait to put before them the question that bothered her (about making an appeal to the public; if so, in what terms and so on), better wait until they have had their coffee, Lady Bruton thought; and so laid the carnations down beside her plate.

"How's Clarissa?" she asked abruptly.

Clarissa always said that Lady Bruton did not like her. Indeed, Lady Bruton had the reputation of being more interested in politics than people; of talking like a man; of having had a finger in some notorious intrigue of the eighties, which was now beginning to be mentioned in memoirs. Certainly there was an alcove in her drawing-room, and a table in that alcove, and a photograph upon that table of General Sir Talbot Moore, now deceased, who had written there (one evening in the eighties) in Lady Bruton's presence, with her cognisance, perhaps advice, a telegram ordering the British troops to advance upon an historical occasion. (She kept the pen and told the story.) Thus, when she said in her offhand way "How's Clarissa?" husbands had difficulty in persuading their wives and indeed, however devoted, were secretly doubtful themselves, of her interest in women who often got in their husbands' way, prevented them from accepting posts abroad, and had to be taken to the seaside in the middle of the session to recover from influenza. Nevertheless her inquiry, "How's Clarissa?" was known by women infallibly to be a signal from a well-wisher, from an almost silent companion, whose utterances (half a dozen perhaps in the course of a lifetime) signified recognition of some feminine comradeship which went beneath masculine lunch parties and united Lady Bruton and Mrs. Dalloway, who seldom met, and appeared when they did meet indifferent and even hostile, in a singular bond.

"I met Clarissa in the Park this morning," said Hugh Whitbread, diving into the casserole, anxious to pay himself this little tribute, for he had only to come to London and he met everybody at once; but greedy, one of the greediest men she had ever known, Milly Brush thought, who observed men with unflinching rectitude, and was capable of everlasting devotion, to her own sex in particular, being knobbed, scraped, angular, and entirely without feminine charm.

"D'you know who's in town?" said Lady Bruton suddenly bethinking her. "Our old friend, Peter Walsh."

They all smiled. Peter Walsh! And Mr. Dalloway was genuinely glad, Milly Brush thought; and Mr. Whitbread thought only of his chicken.

Peter Walsh! All three, Lady Bruton, Hugh Whitbread, and Richard Dalloway, remembered the same thing – how passionately Peter had been in love; been rejected; gone to India; come a cropper; made a mess of things; and Richard Dalloway had a very great liking for the dear old fellow too. Milly Brush saw that; saw a depth in the brown of his eyes; saw him hesitate; consider; which interested her, as Mr. Dalloway always interested her, for what was he thinking she wondered, about Peter Walsh?

That Peter Walsh had been in love with Clarissa; that he would go back directly after lunch and find Clarissa; that he would tell her, in so many words, that he loved her. Yes, he would say that.

Milly Brush once might almost have fallen in love with these silences; and Mr. Dalloway was always so dependable; such a gentleman too. Now, being forty, Lady Bruton had only to nod, or turn her head a little abruptly, and Milly Brush took the signal, however deeply she might be sunk in these reflections of a detached spirit, of an uncorrupted soul whom life could not bamboozle, because life had not offered her a trinket of the slightest value; not a curl, smile, lip, cheek, nose; nothing whatever; Lady Bruton had only to nod, and Perkins was instructed to quicken the coffee.

"Yes; Peter Walsh has come back," said Lady Bruton. It was vaguely flattering to them all. He had come back, battered, unsuccessful, to their secure shores. But to help him, they reflected, was impossible; there was some flaw in his character. Hugh Whitbread said one might of course mention his name to So-and-so. He wrinkled lugubriously, consequentially, at the thought of the letters he would write to the heads of Government offices about "my old friend, Peter Walsh," and so on. But it wouldn't lead to anything – not to anything permanent, because of his character.

"In trouble with some woman," said Lady Bruton. They had all guessed that *that* was at the bottom of it.

"However," said Lady Bruton, anxious to leave the subject, "we shall hear the whole story from Peter himself."

(The coffee was very slow in coming.)

"The address?" murmured Hugh Whitbread; and there was at once a ripple in the grey tide of service which washed round Lady Bruton day in, day out, collecting, intercepting, enveloping her in a fine tissue which broke concussions, mitigated interruptions, and spread round the house in Brook Street a fine net where things lodged and were picked out accurately, instantly, by grey-haired Perkins, who had been with Lady Bruton these thirty years and now wrote down the address, handed it to Mr. Whitbread, who took out his pocket-book, raised his eyebrows, and slipping it in among documents of the highest importance, said that he would get Evelyn to ask him to lunch.

(They were waiting to bring the coffee until Mr. Whitbread had finished.)

Hugh was very slow, Lady Bruton thought. He was getting fat, she noticed. Richard always kept himself in the pink of condition. She was getting impatient, the whole of her being was setting positively, undeniably, domineeringly brushing aside all this unnecessary trifling (Peter Walsh and his affairs) upon that subject which engaged her attention, and not merely her attention, but that fibre which was the ramrod of her soul, that essential part of her without which Millicent Bruton would not have been Millicent Bruton; that project for emigrating young people of both sexes born of respectable parents and setting them up with a fair prospect of doing well in Canada. She exaggerated. She had perhaps lost her sense of proportion. Emigration was not to others the obvious remedy, the sublime conception. It was not to them (not to Hugh, or Richard, or even to devoted Miss Brush) the liberator of the pent egotism, which a strong martial woman, well nourished, well descended, of direct impulses, downright feelings, and little introspective power (broad and simple – why could not every one be broad and simple? she asked) feels rise within her, once youth is past, and must eject upon some object – it may be Emigration, it may be Emancipation; but whatever it be, this object round which the essence of her soul is daily secreted becomes inevitably prismatic, lustrous, half looking-glass, half precious stone; now carefully hidden in case people should sneer at it; now proudly displayed. Emigration had become, in short, largely Lady Bruton.

But she had to write. And one letter to the *Times*, she used to say to Miss Brush, cost her more than to organise an expedition to South Africa (which she had done in the war). After a morning's battle beginning, tearing up, beginning again, she used to feel the futility of her own womanhood as she felt it on no other occasion, and would turn gratefully to the thought of Hugh Whitbread who possessed – no one could doubt it – the art of writing letters to the *Times*.

A being so differently constituted from herself, with such a command of language; able to put things as editors liked them put; had passions which one could not call simply greed. Lady Bruton often suspended judgement upon men in deference to the mysterious accord in which they, but no woman, stood to the laws of the universe; knew how to put things; knew what was said; so that if Richard advised her, and Hugh wrote for her, she was sure of being somehow right. So she let Hugh eat his soufflé; asked after poor Evelyn; waited until they were smoking, and then said,

"Milly, would you fetch the papers?"

And Miss Brush went out, came back; laid papers on the table; and Hugh produced his fountain pen; his silver fountain pen, which had done twenty years' service, he said, unscrewing the cap. It was still in perfect order; he had shown it to the makers; there was no reason, they said, why it should ever wear out; which was somehow to Hugh's credit, and to the credit of the sentiments which his pen expressed (so Richard Dalloway felt) as Hugh began carefully writing capital letters with rings round them in the margin, and thus marvellously reduced Lady Bruton's tangles to sense, to grammar such as the editor of the *Times*, Lady Bruton felt, watching the marvellous transformation, must respect. Hugh was slow. Hugh was pertinacious. Richard said one must take risks. Hugh proposed modifications in deference to people's feelings, which, he said rather tartly when Richard laughed, "had to be considered," and read out "how, therefore, we are of opinion that the times are ripe . . . the superfluous youth of our ever-increasing population . . . what we owe to the dead . . ." which Richard thought all stuffing and bunkum, but no harm in it, of course, and Hugh went on drafting sentiments in alphabetical order of the highest nobility, brushing the cigar ash from his waist-coat, and summing up now and then the progress they had made until, finally, he read out the draft of a letter which Lady Bruton felt certain was a masterpiece. Could her own meaning sound like that?

Hugh could not guarantee that the editor would put it in; but he would be meeting somebody at luncheon.

Whereupon Lady Bruton, who seldom did a graceful thing, stuffed all Hugh's carnations into the front of her dress, and flinging her hands out called him "My Prime Minister!" What she would have done without them both she did not know. They rose. And Richard Dalloway strolled off as usual to have a look at the General's portrait, because he meant, whenever he had a moment of leisure, to write a history of Lady Bruton's family.

And Millicent Bruton was very proud of her family. But they could wait, they could wait, she said, looking at the picture; meaning that her family, of military men, administrators, admirals, had been men of action, who had done their duty; and Richard's first duty was to his country, but it was a fine face, she said; and all the papers were ready for Richard down at Aldmixton whenever the time came; the Labour Government she meant. "Ah, the news from India!" she cried.

And then, as they stood in the hall taking yellow gloves from the bowl on the malachite table and Hugh was offering Miss Brush with quite unnecessary courtesy some discarded ticket or other compliment, which she loathed from the depths of her heart and blushed brick red, Richard turned to Lady Bruton, with his hat in his hand, and said, "We shall see you at our party to-night?" whereupon Lady Bruton resumed the magnificence which letter-writing had shattered. She might come; or she might not come. Clarissa had wonderful energy. Parties terrified Lady Bruton. But then, she was getting old. So she intimated, standing at her doorway; handsome; very erect; while her chow stretched behind her, and Miss Brush disappeared into the background with her hands full of papers.

And Lady Bruton went ponderously, majestically, up to her room, lay, one arm extended, on the sofa. She sighed, she snored, not that she was asleep, only drowsy and heavy, drowsy and heavy, like a field of clover in the sunshine this hot June day, with the bees going round and about and the yellow butterflies. Always she went back to those fields down in Devonshire, where she had jumped the brooks on Patty, her pony, with Mortimer and Tom, her brothers. And there were the dogs; there were the rats; there were her father and mother on the lawn under the trees, with the tea-things out, and the beds of dahlias, the hollyhocks, the pampas grass; and they, little wretches, always up to some mischief! stealing back through the shrubbery, so as not to be seen, all bedraggled from some roguery. What old nurse used to say about her frocks!

Ah dear, she remembered – it was Wednesday in Brook Street. Those kind good fellows, Richard Dalloway, Hugh Whitbread, had gone this hot day through the streets whose growl came up to her lying on the sofa. Power was hers, position, income. She had lived in the forefront of her time. She had had good friends; known the ablest men of her day. Murmuring London flowed up to her, and her hand, lying on the sofa back, curled upon some imaginary baton such as her grandfathers might have held, holding which she seemed, drowsy and heavy, to be commanding battalions marching to Canada, and those good fellows walking across London, that territory of theirs, that little bit of carpet, Mayfair.

And they went further and further from her, being attached to her by a thin thread (since they had lunched with her) which would stretch and stretch, get thinner and thinner as they walked across London; as if one's friends were attached to one's body, after lunching with them, by a thin thread, which (as she dozed there) became hazy with the sound of bells, striking the hour or ringing to service, as a single spider's thread is blotted with rain-drops, and, burdened, sags down. So she slept.

And Richard Dalloway and Hugh Whitbread hesitated at the corner of Conduit Street at the very moment that Millicent Bruton, lying on the sofa, let the thread snap; snored. Contrary winds buffeted at the street corner. They looked in at a shop window; they did not wish to buy or to talk but to part, only with contrary winds buffeting the street corner, with some sort of lapse in the tides of the body, two forces meeting in a swirl, morning and afternoon, they paused. Some newspaper placard went up in the air, gallantly, like a kite at first, then paused, swooped, fluttered; and a lady's veil hung. Yellow awnings trembled. The speed of the morning traffic slackened, and single carts rattled carelessly down half-empty streets. In Norfolk, of which Richard Dalloway was half thinking, a soft warm wind blew back the petals; confused the waters; ruffled the flowering grasses. Haymakers, who had pitched beneath hedges to sleep away the morning toil, parted curtains of green blades; moved trembling globes of cow parsley to see the sky; the blue, the steadfast, the blazing summer sky.

Aware that he was looking at a silver two-handled Jacobean mug, and that Hugh Whitbread admired condescendingly, with airs of connoisseurship, a Spanish necklace which he thought of asking the price of in case Evelyn might like it – still Richard was torpid; could not think or move. Life had thrown up this wreckage; shop windows full of coloured paste, and one stood stark with the lethargy of the old, stiff with the rigidity of the old, looking in. Evelyn Whitbread might like to buy this Spanish necklace – so she might. Yawn he must. Hugh was going into the shop.

"Right you are!" said Richard, following.

Goodness knows he didn't want to go buying necklaces with Hugh. But there are tides in the body. Morning meets afternoon. Borne like a frail shallop on deep, deep floods, Lady Bruton's great-grandfather and his memoir and his campaigns in North America were whelmed and sunk. And Millicent Bruton too. She went under. Richard didn't care a straw what became of Emigration; about that letter, whether the editor put it in or not. The necklace hung stretched between Hugh's admirable fingers. Let him give it to a girl, if he must buy jewels – any girl, any girl in the street. For the worthlessness of this life did strike Richard pretty forcibly – buying necklaces for Evelyn. If he had a boy he'd have said, Work, work. But he had his Elizabeth; he adored his Elizabeth.

"I should like to see Mr. Dubonnet," said Hugh in his curt worldly way. It appeared that this Dubonnet had the measurements of Mrs. Whitbread's neck, or, more strangely still, knew her views upon Spanish jewellery and the extent of her possessions in that line (which Hugh could not remember). All of which seemed to Richard Dalloway awfully odd. For he never gave Clarissa presents, except a bracelet two or three years ago, which had not been a success. She never wore it. It pained him to remember that she never wore it. And as a single spider's thread after wavering here and there attaches itself to the point of a leaf, so Richard's mind, recovering from its lethargy, set now on his wife, Clarissa, whom Peter Walsh had loved so passionately; and Richard had had a sudden vision of her there at luncheon; of himself and Clarissa; of their life together; and he drew the tray of old jewels towards him, and taking up first this brooch, then that ring, "How much is that?" he asked, but doubted his own taste. He wanted to open the drawing-room door and come in holding out something; a present for Clarissa. Only what? But Hugh was on his legs again. He was unspeakably pompous. Really, after dealing here for thirty-five years he was not going to be put off by a mere boy who did not know his business. For Dubonnet, it seemed, was out, and Hugh would not buy anything until Mr. Dubonnet chose to be in;

at which the youth flushed and bowed his correct little bow.
It was all perfectly correct. And yet Richard couldn't have
said that to save his life! Why these people stood that damned
insolence he could not conceive. Hugh was becoming an
intolerable ass. Richard Dalloway could not stand more than
an hour of his society. And, flicking his bowler hat by way of
farewell, Richard turned at the corner of Conduit Street eager,
yes, very eager, to travel that spider's thread of attachment
between himself and Clarissa; he would go straight to her, in
Westminster.

But he wanted to come in holding something. Flowers?
Yes, flowers, since he did not trust his taste in gold; any
number of flowers, roses, orchids, to celebrate what was,
reckoning things as you will, an event; this feeling about her
when they spoke of Peter Walsh at luncheon; and they never
spoke of it; not for years had they spoken of it; which, he
thought, grasping his red and white roses together (a vast
bunch in tissue paper), is the greatest mistake in the world.
The time comes when it can't be said; one's too shy to say it,
he thought, pocketing his sixpence or two of change, setting
off with his great bunch held against his body to Westminster
to say straight out in so many words (whatever she might
think of him), holding out his flowers, "I love you." Why
not? Really it was a miracle thinking of the war, and thousands of poor chaps, with all their lives before them, shovelled
together, already half forgotten; it was a miracle. Here he was
walking across London to say to Clarissa in so many words
that he loved her. Which one never does say, he thought.
Partly one's lazy; partly one's shy. And Clarissa – it was difficult to think of her; except in starts, as at luncheon, when
he saw her quite distinctly; their whole life. He stopped at
the crossing; and repeated – being simple by nature, and
undebauched, because he had tramped, and shot; being
pertinacious and dogged, having championed the down-
trodden and followed his instincts in the House of Commons;

being preserved in his simplicity yet at the same time grown rather speechless, rather stiff – he repeated that it was a miracle, that he should have married Clarissa; a miracle – his life had been a miracle, he thought; hesitating to cross. But it did make his blood boil to see little creatures of five or six crossing Piccadilly alone. The police ought to have stopped the traffic at once. He had no illusions about the London police. Indeed, he was collecting evidence of their malpractices; and those costermongers, not allowed to stand their barrows in the streets; and prostitutes, good Lord, the fault wasn't in them, nor in young men either, but in our detestable social system and so forth; all of which he considered, could be seen considering, grey, dogged, dapper, clean, as he walked across the Park to tell his wife that he loved her.

For he would say it in so many words, when he came into the room. Because it is a thousand pities never to say what one feels, he thought, crossing the Green Park and observing with pleasure how in the shade of the trees whole families, poor families, were sprawling; children kicking up their legs; sucking milk; paper bags thrown about, which could easily be picked up (if people objected) by one of those fat gentlemen in livery; for he was of opinion that every park, and every square, during the summer months should be open to children (the grass of the park flushed and faded, lighting up the poor mothers of Westminster and their crawling babies, as if a yellow lamp were moved beneath). But what could be done for female vagrants like that poor creature, stretched on her elbow (as if she had flung herself on the earth, rid of all ties, to observe curiously, to speculate boldly, to consider the whys and the wherefores, impudent, loose-lipped, humorous), he did not know. Bearing his flowers like a weapon, Richard Dalloway approached her; intent he passed her; still there was time for a spark between them – she laughed at the sight of him, he smiled good-humouredly, considering the problem of the female vagrant; not that they would ever speak. But he would tell Clarissa that he loved her, in so many words. He had, once upon a time, been jealous of Peter Walsh; jealous of him and Clarissa. But she had often said to him that she had been right not to marry Peter Walsh; which, knowing Clarissa, was obviously true; she wanted support. Not that she was weak; but she wanted support.

As for Buckingham Palace (like an old prima donna facing the audience all in white) you can't deny it a certain dignity, he considered, nor despise what does, after all, stand to millions of people (a little crowd was waiting at the gate to see the King drive out) for a symbol, absurd though it is; a child with a box of bricks could have done better, he thought; looking at the memorial to Queen Victoria (whom he could remember in her horn spectacles driving through Kensington), its white mound, its billowing motherliness; but he liked being ruled by the descendant of Horsa; he liked continuity; and the sense of handing on the traditions of the past. It was a great age in which to have lived. Indeed, his own life was a miracle; let him make no mistake about it; here he was, in the prime of life, walking to his house in Westminster to tell Clarissa that he loved her. Happiness is this, he thought.

It is this, he said, as he entered Dean's Yard. Big Ben was beginning to strike, first the warning, musical; then the hour, irrevocable. Lunch parties waste the entire afternoon, he thought, approaching his door.

The sound of Big Ben flooded Clarissa's drawing-room, where she sat, ever so annoyed, at her writing-table; worried; annoyed. It was perfectly true that she had not asked Ellie Henderson to her party; but she had done it on purpose. Now Mrs. Marsham wrote: "She had told Ellie Henderson she would ask Clarissa – Ellie so much wanted to come."

But why should she invite all the dull women in London to her parties? Why should Mrs. Marsham interfere? And there was Elizabeth closeted all this time with Doris Kilman. Anything more nauseating she could not conceive. Prayer at this hour with that woman. And the sound of the bell flooded the room with its melancholy wave; which receded, and gathered itself together to fall once more, when she heard, distractingly, something fumbling, something scratching at the door. Who at this hour? Three, good Heavens! Three already! For with overpowering directness and dignity the clock struck three; and she heard nothing else; but the door handle slipped round and in came Richard! What a surprise! In came Richard, holding out flowers. She had failed him, once at Constantinople; and Lady Bruton, whose lunch parties were said to be extraordinarily amusing, had not asked her. He was holding out flowers – roses, red and white roses. (But he could not bring himself to say he loved her; not in so many words.)

But how lovely, she said, taking his flowers. She understood; she understood without his speaking; his Clarissa. She put them in vases on the mantelpiece. How lovely they looked! she said. And was it amusing, she asked? Had Lady Bruton asked after her? Peter Walsh was back. Mrs. Marsham had written. Must she ask Ellie Henderson? That woman Kilman was upstairs.

"But let us sit down for five minutes," said Richard.

It all looked so empty. All the chairs were against the wall. What had they been doing? Oh, it was for the party; no, he had not forgotten the party. Peter Walsh was back. Oh yes; she had had him. And he was going to get a divorce; and he was in love with some woman out there. And he hadn't changed in the slightest. There she was, mending her dress. . . .

"Thinking of Bourton," she said.

"Hugh was at lunch," said Richard. She had met him too! Well, he was getting absolutely intolerable. Buying Evelyn necklaces; fatter than ever; an intolerable ass.

"And it came over me 'I might have married you'," she said, thinking of Peter sitting there in his little bow-tie; with that knife, opening it, shutting it. "Just as he always was, you know."

They were talking about him at lunch, said Richard. (But he could not tell her he loved her. He held her hand. Happiness is this, he thought.) They had been writing a letter to the *Times* for Millicent Bruton. That was about all Hugh was fit for.

"And our dear Miss Kilman?" he asked. Clarissa thought the roses absolutely lovely; first bunched together; now of their own accord starting apart.

"Kilman arrives just as we've done lunch," she said. "Elizabeth turns pink. They shut themselves up. I suppose they're praying."

Lord! He didn't like it; but these things pass over if you let them.

"In a mackintosh with an umbrella," said Clarissa.

He had not said "I love you"; but he held her hand. Happiness is this, is this, he thought.

"But why should I ask all the dull women in London to my parties?" said Clarissa. And if Mrs. Marsham gave a party, did *she* invite her guests?

"Poor Ellie Henderson," said Richard – it was a very odd thing how much Clarissa minded about her parties, he thought.

But Richard had no notion of the look of a room. However – what was he going to say?

If she worried about these parties he would not let her give them. Did she wish she had married Peter? But he must go.

He must be off, he said, getting up. But he stood for a moment as if he were about to say something; and she wondered what? Why? There were the roses.

"Some Committee?" she asked, as he opened the door.

"Armenians," he said; or perhaps it was "Albanians."

And there is a dignity in people; a solitude; even between husband and wife a gulf; and that one must respect, thought Clarissa, watching him open the door; for one would not part with it oneself or take it, against his will, from one's husband, without losing one's independence, one's self-respect – something, after all, priceless.

He returned with a pillow and a quilt.

"An hour's complete rest after luncheon," he said. And he went.

How like him! He would go on saying "An hour's complete rest after luncheon" to the end of time, because a doctor had ordered it once. It was like him to take what doctors said literally; part of his adorable, divine simplicity, which no one had to the same extent; which made him go and do the thing while she and Peter frittered their time away bickering. He was already half-way to the House of Commons, to his Armenians, his Albanians, having settled her on the sofa, looking at his roses. And people would say, "Clarissa Dalloway is spoilt." She cared much more for her roses than for the Armenians. Hunted out of existence, maimed, frozen, the victims of cruelty and injustice (she had heard Richard say so over and over again) – no, she could feel nothing for the Albanians, or was it the Armenians? but she loved her roses (didn't that help the Armenians?) – the only flowers she could bear to see cut. But Richard was already at the House of Commons; at his Committee, having settled all her difficulties. But no; alas, that was not true. He did not see the reasons against asking Ellie Henderson. She would do it, of course, as he wished it. Since he had brought the pillows, she would lie down. . . . But – but – why did she suddenly feel, for no reason that she could discover, desperately unhappy? As a person who has dropped some grain of pearl or diamond into the grass and parts the tall blades very carefully, this way and that, and searches here and there vainly, and at last spies it there at the roots, so she went through one thing and another; no, it was not Sally Seton saying that Richard would never be in the Cabinet because he had a second-class brain (it came back to her); no, she did not mind that; nor was it to do with

Elizabeth either and Doris Kilman; those were facts. It was a feeling, some unpleasant feeling, earlier in the day perhaps; something that Peter had said, combined with some depression of her own, in her bedroom, taking off her hat; and what Richard had said had added to it, but what had he said? There were his roses. Her parties! That was it! Her parties! Both of them criticised her very unfairly, laughed at her very unjustly, for her parties. That was it! That was it!

Well, how was she going to defend herself? Now that she knew what it was, she felt perfectly happy. They thought, or Peter at any rate thought, that she enjoyed imposing herself; liked to have famous people about her; great names; was simply a snob in short. Well, Peter might think so. Richard merely thought it foolish of her to like excitement when she knew it was bad for her heart. It was childish, he thought. And both were quite wrong. What she liked was simply life.

"That's what I do it for," she said, speaking aloud, to life.

Since she was lying on the sofa, cloistered, exempt, the presence of this thing which she felt to be so obvious became physically existent; with robes of sound from the street, sunny, with hot breath, whispering, blowing out the blinds. But suppose Peter said to her, "Yes, yes, but your parties – what's the sense of your parties?" all she could say was (and nobody could be expected to understand): They're an offering; which sounded horribly vague. But who was Peter to make out that life was all plain sailing? – Peter always in love, always in love with the wrong woman? What's your love? she might say to him. And she knew his answer; how it is the most important thing in the world and no woman could possibly understand it. Very well. But could any man understand what she meant either? about life? She could not imagine Peter or Richard taking the trouble to give a party for no reason whatever.

But to go deeper, beneath what people said (and these judgements, how superficial, how fragmentary they are!) in her own mind now, what did it mean to her, this thing she called life? Oh, it was very queer. Here was So-and-so in South Kensington; some one up in Bayswater; and somebody else, say, in Mayfair. And she felt quite continuously a sense of their existence; and she felt what a waste; and she felt what a pity; and she felt if only they could be brought together; so she did it. And it was an offering; to combine, to create; but to whom?

An offering for the sake of offering, perhaps. Anyhow, it was her gift. Nothing else had she of the slightest importance; could not think, write, even play the piano. She muddled Armenians and Turks; loved success; hated discomfort; must be liked; talked oceans of nonsense: and to this day, ask her what the Equator was, and she did not know.

All the same, that one day should follow another; Wednesday, Thursday, Friday, Saturday; that one should wake up in the morning; see the sky; walk in the park; meet Hugh Whitbread; then suddenly in came Peter; then these roses; it was enough. After that, how unbelievable death was! – that it must end; and no one in the whole world would know how she had loved it all; how, every instant . . .

The door opened. Elizabeth knew that her mother was resting. She came in very quietly. She stood perfectly still. Was it that some Mongol had been wrecked on the coast of Norfolk (as Mrs. Hilbery said), had mixed with the Dalloway ladies, perhaps a hundred years ago? For the Dalloways, in general, were fair-haired; blue-eyed; Elizabeth, on the contrary, was dark; had Chinese eyes in a pale face; an Oriental mystery; was gentle, considerate, still. As a child, she had had a perfect sense of humour; but now at seventeen, why, Clarissa could not in the least understand, she had become very serious; like a hyacinth sheathed in glossy green, with buds just tinted, a hyacinth which has had no sun.

She stood quite still and looked at her mother; but the door was ajar, and outside the door was Miss Kilman, as

Clarissa knew; Miss Kilman in her mackintosh, listening to whatever they said.

Yes, Miss Kilman stood on the landing, and wore a mackintosh; but had her reasons. First, it was cheap; second, she was over forty; and did not, after all, dress to please. She was poor, moreover; degradingly poor. Otherwise she would not be taking jobs from people like the Dalloways; from rich people, who liked to be kind. Mr. Dalloway, to do him justice, had been kind. But Mrs. Dalloway had not. She had been merely condescending. She came from the most worthless of all classes – the rich, with a smattering of culture. They had expensive things everywhere; pictures, carpets, lots of servants. She considered that she had a perfect right to anything that the Dalloways did for her.

She had been cheated. Yes, the word was no exaggeration, for surely a girl has a right to some kind of happiness? And she had never been happy, what with being so clumsy and so poor. And then, just as she might have had a chance at Miss Dolby's school, the war came; and she had never been able to tell lies. Miss Dolby thought she would be happier with people who shared her views about the Germans. She had had to go. It was true that the family was of German origin; spelt the name Kiehlman in the eighteenth century; but her brother had been killed. They turned her out because she would not pretend that the Germans were all villains – when she had German friends, when the only happy days of her life had been spent in Germany! And after all, she could read history. She had had to take whatever she could get. Mr. Dalloway had come across her working for the Friends. He had allowed her (and that was really generous of him) to teach his daughter history. Also she did a little Extension lecturing and so on. Then Our Lord had come to her (and here she always bowed her head). She had seen the light two years and three months ago. Now she did not envy women like Clarissa Dalloway; she pitied them.

She pitied and despised them from the bottom of her heart, as she stood on the soft carpet, looking at the old engraving of a little girl with a muff. With all this luxury going on, what hope was there for a better state of things? Instead of lying on a sofa – "My mother is resting," Elizabeth had said – she should have been in a factory; behind a counter; Mrs. Dalloway and all the other fine ladies!

Bitter and burning, Miss Kilman had turned into a church two years three months ago. She had heard the Rev. Edward Whittaker preach; the boys sing; had seen the solemn lights descend, and whether it was the music, or the voices (she herself when alone in the evening found comfort in a violin; but the sound was excruciating; she had no ear), the hot and turbulent feelings which boiled and surged in her had been assuaged as she sat there, and she had wept copiously, and gone to call on Mr. Whittaker at his private house in Kensington. It was the hand of God, he said. The Lord had shown her the way. So now, whenever the hot and painful feelings boiled within her, this hatred of Mrs. Dalloway, this grudge against the world, she thought of God. She thought of Mr. Whittaker. Rage was succeeded by calm. A sweet savour filled her veins, her lips parted, and, standing formidable upon the landing in her mackintosh, she looked with steady and sinister serenity at Mrs. Dalloway, who came out with her daughter.

Elizabeth said she had forgotten her gloves. That was because Miss Kilman and her mother hated each other. She could not bear to see them together. She ran upstairs to find her gloves.

But Miss Kilman did not hate Mrs. Dalloway. Turning her large gooseberry-coloured eyes upon Clarissa, observing her small pink face, her delicate body, her air of freshness and fashion, Miss Kilman felt, Fool! Simpleton! You who have known neither sorrow nor pleasure; who have trifled your life away! And there rose in her an overmastering desire to overcome her; to unmask her. If she could have felled her it would have eased her. But it was not the body; it was the soul and its mockery that she wished to subdue; make feel her mastery. If only she could make her weep; could ruin her; humiliate her; bring her to her knees crying, You are right! But this was God's will, not Miss Kilman's. It was to be a religious victory. So she glared; so she glowered.

Clarissa was really shocked. This a Christian – this woman! This woman had taken her daughter from her! She in touch with invisible presences! Heavy, ugly, commonplace, without kindness or grace, she know the meaning of life!

"You are taking Elizabeth to the Stores?" Mrs. Dalloway said.

Miss Kilman said she was. They stood there. Miss Kilman was not going to make herself agreeable. She had always earned her living. Her knowledge of modern history was thorough in the extreme. She did out of her meagre income set aside so much for causes she believed in; whereas this woman did nothing, believed nothing; brought up her daughter – but here was Elizabeth, rather out of breath, the beautiful girl.

So they were going to the Stores. Odd it was, as Miss Kilman stood there (and stand she did, with the power and taciturnity of some prehistoric monster armoured for primeval warfare), how, second by second, the idea of her diminished, how hatred (which was for ideas, not people) crumbled, how she lost her malignity, her size, became second by second merely Miss Kilman, in a mackintosh, whom Heaven knows Clarissa would have liked to help.

At this dwindling of the monster, Clarissa laughed. Saying good-bye, she laughed.

Off they went together, Miss Kilman and Elizabeth, downstairs.

With a sudden impulse, with a violent anguish, for this woman was taking her daughter from her, Clarissa leant over the banisters and cried out, "Remember the party! Remember our party to-night!"

But Elizabeth had already opened the front door; there was a van passing; she did not answer.

Love and religion! thought Clarissa, going back into the drawing-room, tingling all over. How detestable, how detestable they are! For now that the body of Miss Kilman was not before her, it overwhelmed her – the idea. The cruellest things in the world, she thought, seeing them clumsy, hot, domineering, hypocritical, eavesdropping, jealous, infinitely cruel and unscrupulous, dressed in a mackintosh coat, on the landing; love and religion. Had she ever tried to convert any one herself? Did she not wish everybody merely to be themselves? And she watched out of the window the old lady opposite climbing upstairs. Let her climb upstairs if she wanted to; let her stop; then let her, as Clarissa had often seen her, gain her bedroom, part her curtains, and disappear again into the background. Somehow one respected that – that old woman looking out of the window, quite unconscious that she was being watched. There was something solemn in it – but love and religion would destroy that, whatever it was, the privacy of the soul. The odious Kilman would destroy it. Yet it was a sight that made her want to cry.

Love destroyed too. Everything that was fine, everything that was true went. Take Peter Walsh now. There was a man, charming, clever, with ideas about everything. If you wanted to know about Pope, say, or Addison, or just to talk nonsense, what people were like, what things meant, Peter knew better than any one. It was Peter who had helped her; Peter who had lent her books. But look at the women he loved – vulgar, trivial, commonplace. Think of Peter in love – he came to see her after all these years, and what did he talk about? Himself. Horrible passion! she thought. Degrading passion! she thought, thinking of Kilman and her Elizabeth walking to the Army and Navy Stores.

Big Ben struck the half-hour.

How extraordinary it was, strange, yes, touching to see the old lady (they had been neighbours ever so many years) move away from the window, as if she were attached to that sound, that string. Gigantic as it was, it had something to do with her. Down, down, into the midst of ordinary things the finger fell making the moment solemn. She was forced, so Clarissa imagined, by that sound, to move, to go – but where? Clarissa tried to follow her as she turned and disappeared, and could still just see her white cap moving at the back of the bedroom. She was still there moving about at the other end of the room. Why creeds and prayers and mackintoshes? When, thought Clarissa, that's the miracle, that's the mystery; that old lady, she meant, whom she could see going from chest of drawers to dressing-table. She could still see her. And the supreme mystery which Kilman might say she had solved, or Peter might say he had solved, but Clarissa didn't believe either of them had the ghost of an idea of solving, was simply this: here was one room; there another. Did religion solve that, or love?

Love – but here the other clock, the clock which always struck two minutes after Big Ben, came shuffling in with its lap full of odds and ends, which it dumped down as if Big Ben were all very well with his majesty laying down the law, so solemn, so just, but she must remember all sorts of little things besides – Mrs. Marsham, Ellie Henderson, glasses for ices – all sorts of little things came flooding and lapping and dancing in on the wake of that solemn stroke which lay flat like a bar of gold on the sea. Mrs. Marsham, Ellie Henderson, glasses for ices. She must telephone now at once.

Volubly, troublously, the late clock sounded, coming in on the wake of Big Ben, with its lap full of trifles. Beaten up, broken up by the assault of carriages, the brutality of vans, the eager advance of myriads of angular men, of flaunting women, the domes and spires of offices and hospitals, the last relics of this lap full of odds and ends seemed to break, like the spray of an exhausted wave, upon the body of Miss Kilman standing still in the street for a moment to mutter "It is the flesh."

It was the flesh that she must control. Clarissa Dalloway had insulted her. That she expected. But she had not triumphed; she had not mastered the flesh. Ugly, clumsy, Clarissa Dalloway had laughed at her for being that; and had revived the fleshly desires, for she minded looking as she did beside Clarissa. Nor could she talk as she did. But why wish to resemble her? Why? She despised Mrs. Dalloway from the bottom of her heart. She was not serious. She was not good. Her life was a tissue of vanity and deceit. Yet Doris Kilman had been overcome. She had, as a matter of fact, very nearly burst into tears when Clarissa Dalloway laughed at her. "It is the flesh, it is the flesh," she muttered (it being her habit to talk aloud), trying to subdue this turbulent and painful feeling as she walked down Victoria Street. She prayed to God. She could not help being ugly; she could not afford to buy pretty clothes. Clarissa Dalloway had laughed – but she would concentrate her mind upon something else until she had reached the pillar-box. At any rate she had got Elizabeth. But she would think of something else; she would think of Russia; until she reached the pillar-box.

How nice it must be, she said, in the country, struggling, as Mr. Whittaker had told her, with that violent grudge against the world which had scorned her, sneered at her, cast her off; beginning with this indignity – the infliction of her unlovable body which people could not bear to see. Do her hair as she might, her forehead remained like an egg, bald, white. No clothes suited her. She might buy anything. And for a woman, of course, that meant never meeting the opposite sex. Never would she come first with any one. Sometimes lately it had seemed to her that, except for Elizabeth, her food was all that she lived for; her comforts; her dinner, her tea; her hot-water bottle at night. But one must fight; vanquish; have faith in God. Mr. Whittaker had said she was there for a purpose. But no one knew the agony! He said, pointing to the crucifix, that God knew. But why should she have to suffer when other women, like Clarissa Dalloway, escaped? Knowledge comes through suffering, said Mr. Whittaker.

She had passed the pillar-box, and Elizabeth had turned into the cool brown tobacco department of the Army and Navy Stores while she was still muttering to herself what Mr. Whittaker had said about knowledge coming through suffering and the flesh. "The flesh," she muttered.

What department did she want? Elizabeth interrupted her.

"Petticoats," she said abruptly, and stalked straight on to the lift.

Up they went. Elizabeth guided her this way and that; guided her in her abstraction as if she had been a great child, an unwieldy battleship. There were the petticoats, brown, decorous, striped, frivolous, solid, flimsy; and she chose, in her abstraction, portentously, and the girl serving thought her mad.

Elizabeth rather wondered, as they did up the parcel, what Miss Kilman was thinking. They must have their tea, said Miss Kilman, rousing, collecting herself. They had their tea.

Elizabeth rather wondered whether Miss Kilman could be hungry. It was her way of eating, eating with intensity, then looking, again and again, at the plate of sugared cakes on the table next them; then, when a lady and a child sat down and the child took the cake, could Miss Kilman really mind it? Yes, Miss Kilman did mind it. She had wanted that cake – the pink one. The pleasure of eating was almost the only pure pleasure left her, and then to be baffled even in that!

When people are happy they have a reserve, she had told Elizabeth, upon which to draw, whereas she was like a wheel without a tyre (she was fond of such metaphors), jolted by every pebble – so she would say staying on after the lesson, standing by the fire-place with her bag of books, her "satchel", she called it, on a Tuesday morning, after the lesson was over. And she talked too about the war. After all, there were people who did not think the English invariably right. There were books. There were meetings. There were other points of view. Would Elizabeth like to come with her to listen to So-and-so (a most extraordinary-looking old man)? Then Miss Kilman took her to some church in Kensington and they had tea with a clergyman. She had lent her books. Law, medicine, politics, all professions are open to women of your generation, said Miss Kilman. But for herself, her career was absolutely ruined, and was it her fault? Good gracious, said Elizabeth, no.

And her mother would come calling to say that a hamper had come from Bourton and would Miss Kilman like some flowers? To Miss Kilman she was always very, very nice, but Miss Kilman squashed the flowers all in a bunch, and hadn't any small talk, and what interested Miss Kilman bored her mother, and Miss Kilman and she were terrible together; and Miss Kilman swelled and looked very plain, but Miss Kilman was frightfully clever. Elizabeth had never thought about the poor. They lived with everything they wanted, – her mother had breakfast in bed every day; Lucy carried it up; and she liked old women because they were Duchesses, and being descended from some Lord. But Miss Kilman said (one of those Tuesday mornings when the lesson was over), "My grandfather kept an oil and colour shop in Kensington." Miss Kilman was quite different from any one she knew; she made one feel so small.

Miss Kilman took another cup of tea. Elizabeth, with her oriental bearing, her inscrutable mystery, sat perfectly upright; no, she did not want anything more. She looked for her gloves – her white gloves. They were under the table. Ah, but she must not go! Miss Kilman could not let her go! This youth, that was so beautiful; this girl, whom she genuinely loved! Her large hand opened and shut on the table.

But perhaps it was a little flat somehow, Elizabeth felt. And really she would like to go.

"But," said Miss Kilman, "I've not quite finished yet."

Of course, then, Elizabeth would wait. But it was rather stuffy in here.

"Are you going to the party to-night?" Miss Kilman said. Elizabeth supposed she was going; her mother wanted her to go. She must not let parties absorb her, Miss Kilman said, fingering the last two inches of a chocolate éclair.

She did not much like parties, Elizabeth said. Miss Kilman opened her mouth, slightly projected her chin, and swallowed down the last inches of the chocolate éclair, then wiped her fingers, and washed the tea round in her cup.

She was about to split asunder, she felt. The agony was so terrific. If she could grasp her, if she could clasp her, if she could make her hers absolutely and for ever and then die; that was all she wanted. But to sit here, unable to think of anything to say; to see Elizabeth turning against her; to be felt repulsive even by her – it was too much; she could not stand it. The thick fingers curled inwards.

"I never go to parties," said Miss Kilman, just to keep Elizabeth from going. "People don't ask me to parties" – and she knew as she said it that it was this egotism that was her undoing; Mr. Whittaker had warned her; but she could not help it. She had suffered so horribly. "Why should they ask me?" she said. "I'm plain, I'm unhappy." She knew it was idiotic. But it was all those people passing – people with parcels who despised her – who made her say it. However, she was Doris Kilman. She had her degree. She was a woman who had made her way in the world. Her knowledge of modern history was more than respectable.

"I don't pity myself" she said. "I pity" – she meant to

say "your mother," but no, she could not, not to Elizabeth. "I pity other people," she said, "more."

Like some dumb creature who has been brought up to a gate for an unknown purpose, and stands there longing to gallop away, Elizabeth Dalloway sat silent. Was Miss Kilman going to say anything more?

"Don't quite forget me," said Doris Kilman; her voice quivered. Right away to the end of the field the dumb creature galloped in terror.

The great hand opened and shut.

Elizabeth turned her head. The waitress came. One had to pay at the desk, Elizabeth said, and went off, drawing out, so Miss Kilman felt, the very entrails of her body, stretching them as she crossed the room, and then, with a final twist, bowing her head very politely, she went.

She had gone. Miss Kilman sat at the marble table among the éclairs, stricken once, twice, thrice by shocks of suffering. She had gone. Mrs. Dalloway had triumphed. Elizabeth had gone. Beauty had gone, youth had gone.

So she sat. She got up, blundered off among the little tables, rocking slightly from side to side, and somebody came after her with her petticoat, and she lost her way, and was hemmed in by trunks specially prepared for taking to India; next got among the accouchement sets and baby linen; through all the commodities of the world, perishable and permanent, hams, drugs, flowers, stationery, variously smelling, now sweet, now sour, she lurched; saw herself thus lurching with her hat askew, very red in the face, full length in a looking-glass; and at last came out into the street.

The tower of Westminster Cathedral rose in front of her, the habitation of God. In the midst of the traffic, there was the habitation of God. Doggedly she set off with her parcel to that other sanctuary, the Abbey, where, raising her hands in a tent before her face, she sat beside those driven into shelter too; the variously assorted worshippers, now divested of social rank, almost of sex, as they raised their hands before their faces; but once they removed them, instantly reverent, middle-class, English men and women, some of them desirous of seeing the wax works.

But Miss Kilman held her tent before her face. Now she was deserted; now rejoined. New worshippers came in from the street to replace the strollers, and still, as people gazed round and shuffled past the tomb of the Unknown Warrior, still she barred her eyes with her fingers and tried in this double darkness, for the light in the Abbey was bodiless, to aspire above the vanities, the desires, the commodities, to rid herself both of hatred and of love. Her hands twitched. She seemed to struggle. Yet to others God was accessible and the path to Him smooth. Mr. Fletcher, retired, of the Treasury, Mrs. Gorham, widow of the famous K.C., approached Him simply, and having done their praying, leant back, enjoyed the music (the organ pealed sweetly), and saw Miss Kilman at the end of the row, praying, praying, and, being still on the threshold of their underworld, thought of her sympathetically as a soul haunting the same territory; a soul cut out of immaterial substance; not a woman, a soul.

But Mr. Fletcher had to go. He had to pass her, and being himself neat as a new pin, could not help being a little distressed by the poor lady's disorder; her hair down; her parcel on the floor. She did not at once let him pass. But, as he stood gazing about him, at the white marbles, grey window panes, and accumulated treasures (for he was extremely proud of the Abbey), her largeness, robustness, and power as she sat there shifting her knees from time to time (it was so rough the approach to her God – so tough her desires) impressed him, as they had impressed Mrs. Dalloway (she could not get the thought of her out of her mind that afternoon), the Rev. Edward Whittaker, and Elizabeth too.

And Elizabeth waited in Victoria Street for an omnibus. It was so nice to be out of doors. She thought perhaps she need not go home just yet. It was so nice to be out in the air. So she would get on to an omnibus. And already, even as she stood there, in her very well-cut clothes, it was beginning. . . . People were beginning to compare her to poplar trees, early dawn, hyacinths, fawns, running water, and garden lilies; and it made her life a burden to her, for she so much preferred being left alone to do what she liked in the country, but they would compare her to lilies, and she had to go to parties, and London was so dreary compared with being alone in the country with her father and the dogs.

Buses swooped, settled, were off – garish caravans, glistening with red and yellow varnish. But which should she get on to? She had no preferences. Of course, she would not push her way. She inclined to be passive. It was expression she needed, but her eyes were fine, Chinese, oriental, and, as her mother said, with such nice shoulders and holding herself so straight, she was always charming to look at; and lately, in the evening especially, when she was interested, for she never seemed excited, she looked almost beautiful, very stately, very serene. What could she be thinking? Every man fell in love with her, and she was really awfully bored. For it was beginning. Her mother could see that – the compliments were beginning. That she did not care more about it – for instance for her clothes – sometimes worried Clarissa, but perhaps it was as well with all those puppies and guinea pigs about having distemper, and it gave her a charm. And now there was this odd friendship with Miss Kilman. Well, thought Clarissa about three o'clock in the morning, reading Baron Marbot for she could not sleep, it proves she has a heart.

Suddenly Elizabeth stepped forward and most competently boarded the omnibus, in front of everybody. She took a seat on top. The impetuous creature – a pirate – started forward, sprang away; she had to hold the rail to steady herself, for a pirate it was, reckless, unscrupulous, bearing down ruthlessly, circumventing dangerously, boldly snatching a passenger, or ignoring a passenger, squeezing eel-like and arrogant in between, and then rushing insolently, all sails spread, up Whitehall. And did Elizabeth give one thought to poor Miss Kilman who loved her without jealousy, to whom she had been a fawn in the open, a moon in a glade? She was delighted to be free. The fresh air was so delicious. It had been so stuffy in the Army and Navy Stores. And now it was like riding, to be rushing up Whitehall; and to each movement of the omnibus the beautiful body in the fawn-coloured coat responded freely like a rider, like the figure-head of a ship, for the breeze slightly disarrayed her; the heat gave her cheeks the pallor of white painted wood; and her fine eyes, having no eyes to meet, gazed ahead, blank, bright, with the staring incredible innocence of sculpture.

It was always talking about her own sufferings that made Miss Kilman so difficult. And was she right? If it was being on committees and giving up hours and hours every day (she hardly ever saw him in London) that helped the poor, her father did that, goodness knows – if that was what Miss Kilman meant about being a Christian; but it was so difficult to say. Oh, she would like to go a little further. Another penny was it to the Strand? Here was another penny, then. She would go up the Strand.

She liked people who were ill. And every profession is open to the women of your generation, said Miss Kilman. So she might be a doctor. She might be a farmer. Animals are often ill. She might own a thousand acres and have people under her. She would go and see them in their cottages. This was Somerset House. One might be a very good farmer – and that, strangely enough, though Miss Kilman had her share in it, was almost entirely due to Somerset House. It looked so splendid, so serious, that great grey building. And she liked the feeling of people working. She liked those churches, like shapes of grey paper, breasting the stream of the Strand. It was quite different here from Westminster, she thought, getting off at Chancery Lane. It was so serious; it was so busy. In short, she would like to have a profession. She would become a doctor, a farmer, possibly go into Parliament if she found it necessary, all because of the Strand.

The feet of those people busy about their activities, hands putting stone to stone, minds eternally occupied not with trivial chatterings (comparing women to poplars – which was rather exciting, of course, but very silly), but with thoughts of ships, of business, of law, of administration, and with it all so stately (she was in the Temple), gay (there was a river), pious (there was the Church), made her quite determined, whatever her mother might say, to become either a farmer or a doctor. But she was, of course, rather lazy.

And it was much better to say nothing about it. It seemed so silly. It was the sort of thing that did sometimes happen, when one was alone – buildings without architects' names, crowds of people coming back from the city having more power than single clergymen in Kensington, than any of the books Miss Kilman had lent her, to stimulate what lay slumbrous, clumsy, and shy on the mind's sandy floor, to break surface, as a child suddenly stretches its arms; it was just that, perhaps, a sigh, a stretch of the arms, an impulse, a revelation, which has its effects for ever, and then down again it went to the sandy floor. She must go home. She must dress for dinner. But what was the time? – where was a clock?

She looked up Fleet Street. She walked just a little way towards St. Paul's, shyly, like some one penetrating on tiptoe, exploring a strange house by night with a candle, on edge lest the owner should suddenly fling wide his bedroom door and ask her business, nor did she dare wander off into queer alleys, tempting by-streets, any more than in a strange house open doors which might be bedroom doors, or sitting-room doors, or lead straight to the larder. For no Dalloways came down the Strand daily; she was a pioneer, a stray, venturing, trusting.

In many ways, her mother felt, she was extremely

immature, like a child still, attracted to dolls, to old slippers; a perfect baby; and that was charming. But then, of course, there was in the Dalloway family the tradition of public service. Abbesses, principles, head mistresses, dignitaries, in the republic of women – without being brilliant, any of them, they were that. She penetrated a little further in the direction of St. Paul's. She liked the geniality, sisterhood, motherhood, brotherhood of this uproar. It seemed to her good. The noise was tremendous; and suddenly there were trumpets (the unemployed) blaring, rattling about in the uproar; military music; as if people were marching; yet had they been dying – had some woman breathed her last, and whoever was watching, opening the window of the room where she had just brought off that act of supreme dignity, looked down on Fleet Street, that uproar, that military music would have come triumphing up to him, consolatory, indifferent.

It was not conscious. There was no recognition in it of one's fortune, or fate, and for that very reason even to those dazed with watching for the last shivers of consciousness on the faces of the dying, consoling. Forgetfulness in people might wound, their ingratitude corrode, but this voice, pouring endlessly, year in, year out, would take whatever it might be; this vow; this van; this life; this procession, would wrap them all about and carry them on, as in the rough stream of a glacier the ice holds a splinter of bone, a blue petal, some oak trees, and rolls them on.

But it was later than she thought. Her mother would not like her to be wandering off alone like this. She turned back down the Strand.

A puff of wind (in spite of the heat, there was quite a wind) blew a thin black veil over the sun and over the Strand. The faces faded; the omnibuses suddenly lost their glow. For although the clouds were of mountainous white so that one could fancy hacking hard chips off with a hatchet, with broad golden slopes, lawns of celestial pleasure gardens, on their flanks, and had all the appearance of settled habitations assembled for the conference of gods above the world, there was a perpetual movement among them. Signs were interchanged, when, as if to fulfil some scheme arranged already, now a summit dwindled, now a whole block of pyramidal size which had kept its station inalterably advanced into the midst or gravely led the procession to fresh anchorage. Fixed though they seemed at their posts, at rest in perfect unanimity, nothing could be fresher, freer, more sensitive superficially than the snow-white or gold-kindled surface; to change, to go, to dismantle the solemn assemblage was immediately possible; and in spite of the grave fixity, the accumulated robustness and solidity, now they struck light to the earth, now darkness.

Calmly and competently, Elizabeth Dalloway mounted the Westminster omnibus.

Going and coming, beckoning, signalling, so the light and shadow, which now made the wall grey, now the bananas bright yellow, now made the Strand grey, now made the omnibuses bright yellow, seemed to Septimus Warren Smith lying on the sofa in the sitting-room; watching the watery gold glow and fade with the astonishing sensibility of some live creature on the roses, on the wall-paper. Outside the trees dragged their leaves like nets through the depths of the air; the sound of water was in the room, and through the waves came the voices of birds singing. Every power poured its treasures on his head, and his hand lay there on the back of the sofa, as he had seen his hand lie when he was bathing, floating, on the top of the waves, while far away on shore he heard dogs barking and barking far away. Fear no more, says the heart in the body; fear no more.

He was not afraid. At every moment Nature signified by some laughing hint like that gold spot which went round the wall – there, there, there – her determination to show, by brandishing her plumes, shaking her tresses, flinging her mantle this way and that, beautifully, always beautifully, and standing close up to breathe through her hollowed hands Shakespeare's words, her meaning.

Rezia, sitting at the table twisting a hat in her hands, watched him; saw him smiling. He was happy then. But she could not bear to see him smiling. It was not marriage; it was not being one's husband to look strange like that, always to be starting, laughing, sitting hour after hour silent, or clutching her and telling her to write. The table drawer was full of those writings; about war; about Shakespeare; about great discoveries; how there is no death. Lately he had become excited suddenly for no reason (and both Dr. Holmes and Sir William Bradshaw said excitement was the worst thing for him), and waved his hands and cried out that he knew the truth! He knew everything! That man, his friend who was killed, Evans, had come, he said. He was singing behind the screen. She wrote it down just as he spoke it. Some things were very beautiful; others sheer nonsense. And he was always stopping in the middle, changing his mind; wanting to add something; hearing something new; listening with his hand up. But she heard nothing.

And once they found the girl who did the room reading one of these papers in fits of laughter. It was a dreadful pity. For that made Septimus cry out about human cruelty – how they tear each other to pieces. The fallen, he said, they tear to pieces. "Holmes is on us," he would say, and he would invent stories about Holmes; Holmes eating porridge; Holmes reading Shakespeare – making himself roar with laughter or rage, for Dr. Holmes seemed to stand for something horrible to him. "Human nature", he called him. Then there were the visions. He was drowned, he used to say, and lying on a cliff with the gulls screaming over him. He would look over the edge of the sofa down into the sea. Or he was hearing music. Really it was only a barrel organ or some man crying in the street. But "Lovely!" he used to cry, and the tears would run down his cheeks, which was to her the most dreadful thing of all, to see a man like Septimus, who had fought, who was brave, crying. And he would lie listening until suddenly he would cry that he was falling down, down into the flames! Actually she would look for flames, it was so vivid. But there was nothing. They were alone in the room. It was a dream, she would tell him, and so quiet him at last, but sometimes she was frightened too. She sighed as she sat sewing.

Her sigh was tender and enchanting, like the wind outside a wood in the evening. Now she put down her scissors; now she turned to take something from the table. A little stir, a little crinkling, a little tapping built up something on the table there, where she sat sewing. Through his eyelashes he could see her blurred outline; her little black body; her face and hands; her turning movements at the table, as she took up a reel, or looked (she was apt to lose things) for her silk. She was making a hat for Mrs. Filmer's married daughter, whose name was – he had forgotten her name.

"What is the name of Mrs. Filmer's married daughter?" he asked.

"Mrs. Peters," said Rezia. She was afraid it was too small, she said, holding it before her. Mrs. Peters was a big woman; but she did not like her. It was only because Mrs. Filmer had been so good to them – "She gave me grapes this morning," she said – that Rezia wanted to do something to show that they were grateful. She had come into the room the other evening and found Mrs. Peters, who thought they were out, playing the gramophone.

"Was it true?" he asked. She was playing the gramophone? Yes; she had told him about it at the time; she had found Mrs. Peters playing the gramophone.

He began, very cautiously, to open his eyes, to see whether a gramophone was really there. But real things – real things were too exciting. He must be cautious. He would not go mad. First he looked at the fashion papers on the lower shelf, then gradually at the gramophone with the green trumpet. Nothing could be more exact. And so, gathering courage, he looked at the sideboard; the plate of bananas; the engraving of Queen Victoria and the Prince Consort; at the mantelpiece, with the jar of roses. None of these things moved. All were still; all were real.

"She is a woman with a spiteful tongue," said Rezia.

"What does Mr. Peters do?" Septimus asked.

"Ah," said Rezia, trying to remember. She thought Mrs. Filmer had said that he travelled for some company. "Just now he is in Hull," she said.

"Just now!" She said with her Italian accent. She said that herself. He shaded his eyes so that he might see only a little of her face at a time, first the chin, then the nose, then the forehead, in case it were deformed, or had some terrible mark on it. But no, there she was, perfectly natural, sewing, with the pursed lips that women have, the set, the melancholy expression, when sewing. But there was nothing terrible about it, he assured himself, looking a second time, a third time at her face, her hands, for what was frightening or disgusting in her as she sat there in broad daylight, sewing? Mrs. Peters had a spiteful tongue. Mr. Peters was in Hull. Why then rage and prophesy? Why fly scourged and outcast? Why be made to tremble and sob by the clouds? Why seek truths and deliver messages when Rezia sat sticking pins into the front of her dress, and Mr. Peters was in Hull? Miracles, revelations, agonies, loneliness, falling through the sea, down, down into the flames, all were burnt out, for he had a sense, as he watched Rezia trimming the straw hat for Mrs. Peters, of a coverlet of flowers.

"It's too small for Mrs. Peters," said Septimus.

For the first time for days he was speaking as he used to do! Of course it was – absurdly small, she said. But Mrs. Peters had chosen it.

He took it out of her hands. He said it was an organ grinder's monkey's hat.

How it rejoiced her, that! Not for weeks had they laughed like this together, poking fun privately like married people. What she meant was that if Mrs. Filmer had come in, or Mrs. Peters or anybody, they would not have understood what she and Septimus were laughing at.

"There," she said, pinning a rose to one side of the hat. Never had she felt so happy! Never in her life!

But that was still more ridiculous, Septimus said. Now the poor woman looked like a pig at a fair. (Nobody ever made her laugh as Septimus did.)

What had she got in her work-box? She had ribbons and beads, tassels, artificial flowers. She tumbled them out on the table. He began putting odd colours together – for though he had no fingers, could not even do up a parcel, he had a wonderful eye, and often he was right, sometimes absurd, of course, but sometimes wonderfully right.

"She shall have a beautiful hat!" he murmured, taking up this and that, Rezia kneeling by his side, looking over his shoulder. Now it was finished – that is to say the design; she must stitch it together. But she must be very, very careful, he said, to keep it just as he had made it.

So she sewed. When she sewed, he thought, she made a sound like a kettle on the hob; bubbling, murmuring, always busy, her strong little pointed fingers pinching and poking; her needle flashing straight. The sun might go in and out, on the tassels, on the wall-paper, but he would wait, he thought, stretching out his feet, looking at his ringed sock at the end of the sofa; he would wait in this warm place, this pocket of still air, which one comes on at the edge of a wood sometimes in the evening, when, because of a fall in the ground, or some arrangement of the trees (one must be scientific above all, scientific), warmth lingers, and the air buffets the cheek like the wing of a bird.

"There it is," said Rezia, twirling Mrs. Peters' hat on the tips of her fingers. "That'll do for the moment. Later . . ." her sentence bubbled away drip, drip, drip, like a contented tap left running.

It was wonderful. Never had he done anything which made him feel so proud. It was so real, it was so substantial, Mrs. Peters' hat.

"Just look at it," he said.

Yes, it would always make her happy to see that hat. He had become himself then, he had laughed then. They had been alone together. Always she would like that hat.

He told her to try it on.

"But I must look so queer!" she cried, running over to the glass and looking first this side, then that. Then she snatched it off again, for there was a tap at the door. Could it be Sir William Bradshaw? Had he sent already?

No! it was only the small girl with the evening paper.

What always happened, then happened – what happened every night of their lives. The small girl sucked her thumb at the door; Rezia went down on her knees; Rezia cooed and kissed; Rezia got a bag of sweets out of the table drawer. For so it always happened. First one thing, then another. So she built it up, first one thing and then another. Dancing, skipping, round and round the room they went. He took the paper. Surrey was all out, he read. There was a heat wave. Rezia repeated: Surrey was all out. There was a heat wave, making it part of the game she was playing with Mrs. Filmer's grandchild, both of them laughing, chattering at the same time, at their game. He was very tired. He was very happy. He would sleep. He shut his eyes. But directly he saw nothing the sounds of the game became fainter and stranger and sounded like the cries of people seeking and not finding, and passing further and further away. They had lost him!

He started up in terror. What did he see? The plate of bananas on the sideboard. Nobody was there (Rezia had taken the child to its mother; it was bedtime). That was it: to be alone for ever. That was the doom pronounced in Milan when he came into the room and saw them cutting out buckram shapes with their scissors; to be alone for ever.

He was alone with the sideboard and the bananas. He was alone, exposed on this bleak eminence, stretched out – but not on a hill-top; not on a crag; on Mrs. Filmer's sitting-room sofa. As for the visions, the faces, the voices of the dead, where were they? There was a screen in front of him, with black bulrushes and blue swallows. Where he had once seen mountains, where he had seen faces, where he had seen beauty, there was a screen.

"Evans!" he cried. There was no answer. A mouse had squeaked, or a curtain rustled. Those were the voices of the dead. The screen, the coal-scuttle, the sideboard remained to him. Let him then face the screen, the coal-scuttle and the sideboard . . . but Rezia burst into the room chattering.

Some letter had come. Everybody's plans were changed. Mrs. Filmer would not be able to go to Brighton after all. There was no time to let Mrs. Williams know, and really Rezia thought it very, very annoying, when she caught sight of the hat and thought . . . perhaps . . . she . . . might just make a little. . . . Her voice died out in contented melody.

"Ah, damn!" she cried (it was a joke of theirs, her swearing); the needle had broken. Hat, child, Brighton, needle. She built it up; first one thing, then another, she built it up, sewing.

She wanted him to say whether by moving the rose she had improved the hat. She sat on the end of the sofa.

They were perfectly happy now, she said suddenly, putting the hat down. For she could say anything to him now. She could say whatever came into her head. That was almost the first thing she had felt about him, that night in the café when he had come in with his English friends. He had come in, rather shyly, looking round him, and his hat had fallen when he hung it up. That she could remember. She knew he was English, though not one of the large Englishmen her sister admired, for he was always thin; but he had a beautiful fresh colour; and with his big nose, his bright eyes, his way of sitting a little hunched made her think, she had often told him, of a young hawk, that first evening she saw him, when they were playing dominoes, and he had come in – of a young hawk; but with her he was always very gentle. She had never seen him wild or drunk, only suffering sometimes through this terrible war, but even so, when she came in, he would put it all away. Anything, anything in the whole world, any little bother with her work, anything that struck her to say she would tell him, and he understood at once. Her own family even were not the same. Being older than she was and being so clever – how serious he was, wanting her to read Shakespeare before she could even read a child's story in English! – being so much more experienced, he could help her. And she, too, could help him.

But this hat now. And then (it was getting late) Sir William Bradshaw.

She held her hands to her head, waiting for him to say did he like the hat or not, and as she sat there, waiting, looking down, he could feel her mind, like a bird, falling from branch to branch, and always alighting, quite rightly; he could follow her mind, as she sat there in one of those loose lax poses that came to her naturally, and, if he should say anything, at once she smiled, like a bird alighting with all its claws firm upon the bough.

But he remembered. Bradshaw said, "The people we are most fond of are not good for us when we are ill." Bradshaw said he must be taught to rest. Bradshaw said they must be separated.

"Must", "must", why "must"? What power had Bradshaw over him? "What right has Bradshaw to say 'must' to me?" he demanded.

"It is because you talked of killing yourself," said Rezia. (Mercifully, she could now say anything to Septimus.)

So he was in their power! Holmes and Bradshaw were on him! The brute with the red nostrils was snuffing into every secret place! "Must" it could say! Where were his papers? the things he had written?

She brought him his papers, the things he had written, things she had written for him. She tumbled them out on to the sofa. They looked at them together. Diagrams, designs, little men and women brandishing sticks for arms, with wings – were they? – on their backs; circles traced round shillings and sixpences – the suns and stars; zigzagging precipices with mountaineers ascending roped together, exactly like knives and forks; sea pieces with little faces laughing out of what might perhaps be waves: the map of the world. Burn them! he cried. Now for his writings; how the dead sing behind rhododendron bushes; odes to Time; conversations with Shakespeare; Evans, Evans, Evans – his messages from the dead; do not cut down trees; tell the Prime Minister. Universal love: the meaning of the world. Burn them! he cried.

But Rezia laid her hands on them. Some were very beautiful, she thought. She would tie them up (for she had no envelope) with a piece of silk.

Even if they took him, she said, she would go with him. They could not separate them against their wills, she said.

Shuffling the edges straight, she did up the papers, and tied the parcel almost without looking, sitting close, sitting beside him, he thought, as if all her petals were about her. She was a flowering tree; and through her branches looked out the face of a lawgiver, who had reached a sanctuary where she feared no one; not Holmes; not Bradshaw; a miracle, a triumph, the last and greatest. Staggering he saw her mount the appalling staircase, laden with Holmes and Bradshaw, men who never weighed less than eleven stone six, who sent their wives to court, men who made ten thousand a year and talked of proportion; who differed in their verdicts (for Holmes said one thing, Bradshaw another), yet judges they were; who mixed the vision and the sideboard; saw nothing clear, yet ruled, yet inflicted. Over them she triumphed.

"There!" she said. The papers were tied up. No one should get at them. She would put them away.

And, she said, nothing should separate them. She sat down beside him and called him by the name of that hawk or crow which being malicious and a great destroyer of crops was precisely like him. No one could separate them, she said.

Then she got up to go into the bedroom to pack their things, but hearing voices downstairs and thinking that Dr. Holmes had perhaps called, ran down to prevent him coming up.

Septimus could hear her talking to Holmes on the staircase.

"My dear lady, I have come as a friend," Holmes was saying.

"No. I will not allow you to see my husband," she said.

He could see her, like a little hen, with her wings spread barring his passage. But Holmes persevered.

"My dear lady, allow me . . ." Holmes said, putting her aside (Holmes was a powerfully built man).

Holmes was coming upstairs. Holmes would burst open the door. Holmes would say, "In a funk, eh?" Holmes would get him. But no; not Holmes; not Bradshaw. Getting up rather unsteadily, hopping indeed from foot to foot, he considered Mrs. Filmer's nice clean bread knife with "Bread" carved on the handle. Ah, but one mustn't spoil that. The gas fire? But it was too late now. Holmes was coming. Razors he might have got, but Rezia, who always did that sort of thing, had packed them. There remained only the window, the large Bloomsbury lodging-house window; the tiresome, the troublesome, and rather melodramatic business of opening the window and throwing himself out. It was their idea of tragedy, not his or Rezia's (for she was with him). Holmes and Bradshaw liked that sort of thing. (He sat on the sill.) But he would wait till the very last moment. He did not want to die. Life was good. The sun hot. Only human beings? Coming down the staircase opposite an old man stopped and stared at him. Holmes was at the door. "I'll give it you!" he cried, and flung himself vigorously, violently down on to Mrs. Filmer's area railings.

"The coward!" cried Dr. Holmes, bursting the door open. Rezia ran to the window, she saw; she understood. Dr. Holmes and Mrs. Filmer collided with each other. Mrs. Filmer flapped her apron and made her hide her eyes in the bedroom. There was a great deal of running up and down stairs. Dr. Holmes came in – white as a sheet, shaking all over, with a glass in his hand. She must be brave and drink something, he said (What was it? Something sweet), for her husband was horribly mangled, would not recover consciousness, she must not see him, must be spared as much as possible, would have the inquest to go through, poor young woman. Who could have foretold it? A sudden impulse, no one was in the least to blame (he told Mrs. Filmer). And why the devil he did it, Dr. Holmes could not conceive.

It seemed to her as she drank the sweet stuff that she was opening long windows, stepping out into some garden. But where? The clock was striking – one, two, three: how sensible the sound was; compared with all this thumping and whispering; like Septimus himself. She was falling asleep. But the clock went on striking, four, five, six and Mrs. Filmer waving her apron (they wouldn't bring the body in here, would they?) seemed part of that garden; or a flag. She had once seen a flag slowly rippling out from a mast when she stayed with her aunt at Venice. Men killed in battle were thus saluted, and Septimus had been through the War. Of her memories, most were happy.

She put on her hat, and ran through cornfields – where could it have been? – on to some hill, somewhere near the sea, for there were ships, gulls, butterflies; they sat on a cliff. In

London, too, there they sat, and, half dreaming, came to her through the bedroom door, rain falling, whisperings, stirrings among dry corn, the caress of the sea, as it seemed to her, hollowing them in its arched shell and murmuring to her laid on shore, strewn she felt, like flying flowers over some tomb.

"He is dead," she said, smiling at the poor old woman who guarded her with her honest light-blue eyes fixed on the door. (They wouldn't bring him in here, would they?) But Mrs. Filmer pooh-poohed. Oh no, oh no! They were carrying him away now. Ought she not to be told? Married people ought to be together, Mrs. Filmer thought. But they must do as the doctor said.

"Let her sleep," said Dr. Holmes, feeling her pulse. She saw the large outline of his body dark against the window. So that was Dr. Holmes.

One of the triumphs of civilisation, Peter Walsh thought. It is one of the triumphs of civilisation, as the light high bell of the ambulance sounded. Swiftly, cleanly, the ambulance sped to the hospital, having picked up instantly, humanely, some poor devil; some one hit on the head, struck down by disease, knocked over perhaps a minute or so ago at one of these cross-ings, as might happen to oneself. That was civilisation. It struck him coming back from the East – the efficiency, the organisa-tion, the communal spirit of London. Every cart or carriage of its own accord drew aside to let the ambulance pass. Perhaps it was morbid; or was it not touching rather, the respect which they showed this ambulance with its victim inside – busy men hurrying home, yet instantly bethinking them as it passed of some wife; or presumably how easily it might have been them there, stretched on a shelf with a doctor and a nurse. . . . Ah, but thinking became morbid, sentimental, directly one began conjuring up doctors, dead bodies; a little glow of pleasure, a sort of lust, too, over the visual impression warned one not to go on with that sort of thing any more – fatal to art, fatal to friendship. True. And yet, thought Peter Walsh, as the ambulance turned the corner, though the light high bell could be heard down the next street and still farther as it crossed the Tottenham Court Road, chiming constantly, it is the privilege of loneliness; in privacy one may do as one chooses. One might weep if no one saw. It had been his undoing – this susceptibility – in Anglo-Indian society; not weeping at the right time, or laughing either. I have that in me, he thought, standing by the pillar-box, which could now dissolve in tears. Why, heaven knows. Beauty of some sort probably, and the weight of the day, which, beginning with that visit to Clarissa, had exhausted him with its heat, its intensity, and the drip, drip of one impression after another down into that cellar where they stood, deep, dark, and no one would ever know. Partly for that reason, its secrecy, complete and inviolable, he had found life like an unknown garden, full of turns and corners, surprising, yes; really it took one's breath away, these moments; there coming to him by the pillar-box opposite the British Museum one of them, a moment, in which things came together; this ambulance; and life and death. It was as if he were sucked up to some very high roof by that rush of emotion, and the rest of him, like a white shell-sprinkled beach, left bare. It had been his undoing in Anglo-Indian society – this susceptibility.

Clarissa once, going on top of an omnibus with him somewhere, Clarissa superficially at least, so easily moved, now in despair, now in the best of spirits, all aquiver in those days and such good company, spotting queer little scenes, names, people from the top of a bus, for they used to explore London and bring back bags full of treasures from the Caledonian market – Clarissa had a theory in those days – they had heaps of theories, always theories, as young people have. It was to explain the feeling they had of dissatisfaction; not knowing people; not being known. For how could they know each other? You met every day; then not for six months, or years. It was unsatisfactory, they agreed, how little one knew people. But she said, sitting on the bus going up Shaftesbury Avenue, she felt herself everywhere; not "here, here, here"; and she tapped the back of the seat; but everywhere. She waved her hand, going up Shaftesbury Avenue. She was all that. So that to know her, or any one, one must seek out the people who completed them; even the places. Odd affinities she had with people she had never spoken to, some woman in the street, some man behind a counter – even trees, or barns. It ended in a transcendental theory which, with her horror of death, allowed her to believe, or say that she believed (for all her scepticism), that since our apparitions, the part of us which appears, are so momentary compared with the other, the unseen part of us, which spreads wide, the unseen might survive, be recovered somehow attached to this person or that, or even haunting certain places, after death . . . perhaps – perhaps.

Looking back over that long friendship of almost thirty years her theory worked to this extent. Brief, broken, often painful as their actual meetings had been, what with his absences and interruptions (this morning, for instance, in came Elizabeth, like a long-legged colt, handsome, dumb, just as he was beginning to talk to Clarissa), the effect of them on his life was immeasurable. There was a mystery about it. You were given a sharp, acute, uncomfortable grain – the actual meeting; horribly painful as often as not; yet in absence, in the most unlikely places, it would flower out, open, shed its scent, let you touch, taste, look about you, get the whole feel of it and understanding, after years of lying lost. Thus she had come to him; on board ship; in the Himalayas; suggested by the oddest things (so Sally Seton, generous, enthusiastic goose! thought of *him* when she saw blue hydrangeas). She had influenced him more than any person he had ever known. And always in this way coming before him without his wishing it, cool, lady-like, critical; or ravishing, romantic, recalling some field or

English harvest. He saw her most often in the country, not in London. One scene after another at Bourton. . . .

He had reached his hotel. His crossed the hall, with its mounds of reddish chairs and sofas, its spike-leaved, withered-looking plants. He got his key off the hook. The young lady handed him some letters. He went upstairs – he saw her most often at Bourton, in the late summer, when he stayed there for a week, or fortnight even, as people did in those days. First on top of some hill there she would stand, hands clapped to her hair, her cloak blowing out, pointing, crying to them – she saw the Severn beneath. Or in a wood, making the kettle boil – very ineffective with her fingers; the smoke curtseying, blowing in their faces; her little pink face showing through; begging water from an old woman in a cottage, who came to the door to watch them go. They walked always; the others drove. She was bored driving, disliked all animals, except that dog. They tramped miles along roads. She would break off to get her bearings, pilot him back across country; and all the time they argued, discussed poetry, discussed people, discussed politics (she was a Radical then); never noticing a thing except when she stopped, cried out at a view or a tree, and made him look with her; and so on again, through stubble fields, she walking ahead, with a flower for her aunt, never tired of walking for all her delicacy; to drop down on Bourton in the dusk. Then, after dinner, old Breitkopf would open the piano and sing without any voice, and they would lie sunk in arm-chairs, trying not to laugh, but always breaking down and laughing, laughing – laughing at nothing. Breitkopf was supposed not to see. And then in the morning, flirting up and down like a wagtail in front of the house. . . .

Oh it was a letter from her! This blue envelope; that was her hand. And he would have to read it. Here was another of those meetings, bound to be painful! To read her letter needed the devil of an effort. How heavenly it was to see him. She must tell him that. That was all.

But it upset him. It annoyed him. He wished she hadn't written it. Coming on top of his thoughts, it was like a nudge in the ribs. Why couldn't she let him be? After all, she had married Dalloway, and lived with him in perfect happiness all these years.

These hotels are not consoling places. Far from it. Any number of people had hung up their hats on those pegs. Even the flies, if you thought of it, had settled on other people's noses. As for the cleanliness which hit him in the face, it wasn't cleanliness, so much as bareness, frigidity; a thing that had to be. Some arid matron made her rounds at dawn sniffing, peering, causing blue-nosed maids to scour, for all the world as if the next visitor were a joint of meat to be served on a perfectly clean platter. For sleep, one bed; for sitting in, one arm-chair; for cleaning one's teeth and shaving one's chin, one tumbler, one looking-glass. Books, letters, dressing-gown, slipped about on the impersonality of the horse-hair like incongruous impertinences. And it was Clarissa's letter that made him see all this. "Heavenly to see you!" She must say so! He folded the paper; pushed it away; nothing would induce him to read it again!

To get that letter to him by six o'clock she must have sat down and written it directly after he left her; stamped it; sent somebody to the post. It was, as people say, very like her. She was upset by his visit. She had felt a great deal; had for a moment, when she kissed his hand, regretted, envied him even, remembered possibly (for he saw her look it) something he had said – how they would change the world if she married him perhaps; whereas, it was this; it was middle age; it was mediocrity; then forced herself with her indomitable vitality to put all that aside, there being in her a thread of life which for toughness, endurance, power to overcome obstacles, and carry her triumphantly through he had never known the like of. Yes; but there would come a reaction directly he left the room. She would be frightfully sorry for him; she would think what in the world she could do to give him pleasure (short always of the one thing), and he could see her with the tears running down her cheeks going to her writing-table and dashing off that one line which he was to find greeting him. . . . "Heavenly to see you!" And she meant it.

Peter Walsh had now unlaced his boots.

But it would not have been a success, their marriage. The other thing, after all, came so much more naturally.

It was odd; it was true; lots of people felt it. Peter Walsh, who had done just respectably, filled the usual posts adequately, was liked, but thought a little cranky, gave himself airs – it was odd that *he* should have had, especially now that his hair was grey, a contented look; a look of having reserves. It was this that made him attractive to women, who liked the sense that he was not altogether manly. There was something unusual about him, or something behind him. It might be that he was bookish – never came to see you without taking up the book on the table (he was now reading, with his boot-laces trailing on the floor); or that he was a gentleman, which showed itself in the way he knocked the ashes out of his pipe, and in his manners of course to women. For it was very charming and quite ridiculous how easily some girl without a grain of sense could twist him round her finger. But at her own risk. That is to say, though he might be ever so easy, and indeed with his gaiety and good-breeding fascinating to be with, it was only up to a point. She said something – no, no; he saw through that. He wouldn't stand that – no, no. Then he could shout and rock and hold his sides together over some joke with men. He was the best judge of cooking in India. He was a man. But not the sort of man one had to respect – which was a mercy; not like Major Simmons, for instance; not in the least like that, Daisy thought, when in spite of her two small children, she used to compare them.

He pulled off his boots. He emptied his pockets. Out came with his pocket-knife a snapshot of Daisy on the verandah; Daisy all in white, with a fox-terrier on her knee; very charming, very dark; the best he had ever seen of her. It did come, after all, so naturally; so much more naturally than Clarissa. No fuss. No bother. No finicking and fidgeting. All plain sailing. And the dark, adorably pretty girl on the verandah exclaimed (he could hear her). Of course, of course she would give him everything! she cried (she had no sense of discretion), everything he wanted! she cried, running to meet him, whoever might be looking. And she was only twenty-four. And she had two children. Well, well!

Well indeed he had got himself into a mess at his age. And it came over him when he woke in the night pretty forcibly. Suppose they did marry? For him it would be all very well, but what about her? Mrs. Burgess, a good sort and no chatterbox, in whom he had confided, thought this absence of his in England, ostensibly to see lawyers, might serve to make Daisy reconsider, think what it meant. It was a question of her position, Mrs. Burgess said; the social barrier; giving up her children. She'd be a widow with a past one of these days, draggling about in the suburbs, or more likely, indiscriminate (you know, she said, what such women get like, with too much paint). But Peter Walsh pooh-poohed all that. He didn't mean to die yet. Anyhow, she must settle for herself; judge for herself, he thought, padding about the room in his socks, smoothing out his dress-shirt, for he might go to Clarissa's party, or he might go to one of the Halls, or he might settle in and read an absorbing book written by a man he used to know at Oxford. And if he did retire, that's what he'd do – write books. He would go to Oxford and poke about in the Bodleian. Vainly the dark, adorably pretty girl ran to the end of the terrace; vainly waved her hand; vainly cried she didn't care a straw what people said. There he was, the man she thought the world of, the perfect gentleman, the fascinating, the distinguished (and his age made not the least difference to her), padding about a room in an hotel in Bloomsbury, shaving, washing, continuing, as he took up cans, put down razors, to poke about in the Bodleian, and get at the truth about one or two little matters that interested him. And he would have a chat with whoever it might be, and so come to disregard more and more precise hours for lunch and miss engagements; and when Daisy asked him, as she would, for a kiss, a scene, fail to come up to the scratch (though he was genuinely devoted to her) – in short it might be happier, as Mrs. Burgess said, that she should forget him, or merely remember him as he was in August 1922, like a figure standing at the cross roads at dusk, which grows more and more remote as the dog-cart spins away, carrying her securely fastened to the back seat, though her arms are outstretched, and as she sees the figure dwindle and disappear, still she cries out how she would do anything in the world, anything, anything, anything. . . .

He never knew what people thought. It became more and more difficult for him to concentrate. He became absorbed; he became busied with his own concerns; now surly, now gay; dependent on women, absent-minded, moody, less and less able (so he thought as he shaved) to understand why Clarissa couldn't simply find them a lodging and be nice to Daisy; introduce her. And then he could just – just do what? Just haunt and hover (he was at the moment actually engaged in sorting out various keys, papers), swoop and taste, be alone, in short, sufficient to himself; and yet nobody of course was more dependent upon others (he buttoned his waistcoat); it had been his undoing. He could not keep out of smoking-rooms, liked colonels, liked golf, liked bridge, and above all women's society, and the fineness of their companionship, and their faithfulness and audacity and greatness in loving which, though it had its drawbacks, seemed to him (and the dark, adorably pretty face was on top of the envelopes) so wholly admirable, so splendid a flower to grow on the crest of human life, and yet he could not come up to the scratch, being always apt to see round things (Clarissa had sapped something in him permanently), and to tire very easily of mute devotion and to want variety in love, though it would make him furious if Daisy loved anybody else, furious! for he was jealous, uncontrollably jealous by temperament. He suffered tortures! But where was his knife; his watch; his seals, his note-case, and Clarissa's letter which he would not read again but liked to think of, and Daisy's photograph? And now for dinner.

They were eating.

Sitting at little tables round vases, dressed or not dressed, with their shawls and bags laid beside them, with their air of false composure, for they were not used to so many courses at dinner; and confidence, for they were able to pay for it; and strain, for they had been running about London all day shopping, sightseeing; and their natural curiosity, for they looked round and up as the nice-looking gentleman in horn-rimmed spectacles came in; and their good nature, for they would have been glad to do any little service, such as lend a time-table or impart useful information; and their desire, pulsing in them, tugging at them subterraneously, somehow to establish connections if it were only a birthplace (Liverpool, for example), in common or friends of the same name; with their furtive glances, odd silences, and sudden withdrawals into family jocularity and isolation; there they sat eating dinner when Mr. Walsh came in and took his seat at a little table by the curtain.

It was not that he said anything, for being solitary he could only address himself to the waiter; it was his way of looking at the menu, of pointing his forefinger to a particular wine, of hitching himself up to the table, of addressing himself seriously, not gluttonously to dinner, that won him their respect; which, having to remain unexpressed for the greater part of the meal, flared up at the table where the Morrises sat when Mr. Walsh was heard to say at the end of the meal, "Bartlett pears." Why he should have spoken so moderately yet firmly, with the air of a disciplinarian well within his rights which are founded upon justice, neither young Charles Morris, nor old Charles, neither Miss Elaine nor Mrs. Morris knew. But when he said, "Bartlett pears," sitting alone at his table, they felt that he counted on their support in some lawful demand; was champion of a cause which immediately became their own, so that their eyes met his eyes sympathetically, and when they all reached the smoking-room simultaneously, a little talk between them became inevitable.

It was not very profound – only to the effect that London was crowded; had changed in thirty years; that Mr. Morris preferred Liverpool; that Mrs. Morris had been to the Westminster flower-show, and that they had all seen the Prince of Wales. Yet, thought Peter Walsh, no family in the world can compare with the Morrises; none whatever; and their relations to each other are perfect, and they don't care a hang for the upper classes, and they like what they like, and Elaine is training for the family business, and the boy has won a scholarship at Leeds, and the old lady (who is about his own age) has three more children at home; and they have two motor cars, but Mr. Morris still mends the boots on Sunday: it is superb, it is absolutely superb, thought Peter Walsh, swaying a little backwards and forwards with his liqueur glass in his hand among the hairy red chairs and ash-trays, feeling very well pleased with himself, for the Morrises liked him. Yes, they liked a man who said "Bartlett pears." They liked him, he felt.

He would go to Clarissa's party. (The Morrises moved off; but they would meet again.) He would go to Clarissa's party, because he wanted to ask Richard what they were doing in India – the conservative duffers. And what's being acted? And music. . . . Oh yes, and mere gossip.

For this is the truth about our soul, he thought, our self, who fish-like inhabits deep seas and plies among obscurities threading her way between the boles of giant weeds, over sun-flickered spaces and on and on into gloom, cold, deep, inscrutable; suddenly she shoots to the surface and sports on the wind-wrinkled waves; that is, has a positive need to brush, scrape, kindle herself, gossiping. What did the Government mean – Richard Dalloway would know – to do about India?

Since it was a very hot night and the paper boys went by with placards proclaiming in huge red letters that there was a heatwave, wicker chairs were placed on the hotel steps and there, sipping, smoking, detached gentlemen sat. Peter Walsh sat there. One might fancy that day, the London day, was just beginning. Like a woman who had slipped off her print dress and white apron to array herself in blue and pearls, the day changed, put off stuff, took gauze, changed to evening, and with the same sigh of exhilaration that a woman breathes, tumbling petticoats on the floor, it too shed dust, heat, colour; the traffic thinned; motor cars, tinkling, darting, succeeded the lumber of vans; and here and there among the thick foliage of the squares an intense light hung. I resign, the evening seemed to say, as it paled and faded above the battlements and prominences, moulded, pointed, of hotel, flat, and block of shops, I fade, she was beginning, I disappear, but London would have none of it, and rushed her bayonets into the sky, pinioned her, constrained her to partnership in her revelry.

For the great revolution of Mr. Willett's summer time had taken place since Peter Walsh's last visit to England. The prolonged evening was new to him. It was inspiriting, rather. For as the young people went by with their despatch-boxes, awfully glad to be free, proud too, dumbly, of stepping this famous pavement, joy of a kind, cheap, tinselly, if you like, but all the same rapture, flushed their faces. They dressed well too; pink stockings; pretty shoes. They would now have two hours at the pictures. It sharpened, it refined them, the yellow-blue evening light; and on the leaves in the square shone lurid, livid – they looked as if dipped in sea water – the foliage of a submerged city. He was astonished by the beauty; it was encouraging too, for where the returned Anglo-Indian sat by rights (he knew crowds of them) in the Oriental Club biliously summing up the ruin of the world, here was he, as young as ever; envying young people their summer time and the rest of it, and more than suspecting from the words of a girl, from a housemaid's laughter – intangible things you couldn't lay your hands on – that shift in the whole pyramidal accumulation which in his youth had seemed immovable. On top of them it had pressed; weighed them down, the women especially, like those flowers Clarissa's Aunt Helena used to press between sheets of grey blotting-paper with Littré's dictionary on top, sitting under the lamp after dinner. She was dead now. He had heard of her, from Clarissa, losing the sight of one eye. It seemed so fitting – one of nature's masterpieces – that old Miss Parry should turn to glass. She would die like some bird in a frost gripping her perch. She belonged to a different age, but being so entire, so complete, would always stand up on the horizon, stone-white, eminent, like a lighthouse marking some past stage on this adventurous, long, long voyage, this interminable – (he felt for a copper to buy a paper and read about Surrey and Yorkshire; he had held out that copper millions of times – Surrey was all out once more) – this interminable life. But cricket was no mere game. Cricket was important. He could never help reading about cricket. He read the scores in the stop press first, then how it was a hot day; then about a murder case. Having done things millions of times enriched them, though it might be said to take the surface off. The past enriched, and experience, and having cared for one or two people, and so having acquired the power which the young lack, of cutting short, doing what one likes, not caring a rap what people say and coming and going without any very great expectations (he left his paper on the table and moved off), which however (and he looked for his hat and coat) was not altogether true of him, not to-night, for here he was starting to go to a party, at his age, with the belief upon him that he was about to have an experience. But what?

Beauty anyhow. Not the crude beauty of the eye. It was

not beauty pure and simple – Bedford Place leading into Russell Square. It was straightness and emptiness of course; the symmetry of a corridor; but it was also windows lit up, a piano, a gramophone sounding; a sense of pleasure-making hidden, but now and again emerging when, through the uncurtained window, the window left open, one saw parties sitting over tables, young people slowly circling, conversations between men and women, maids idly looking out (a strange comment theirs, when work was done), stockings drying on top ledges, a parrot, a few plants. Absorbing, mysterious, of infinite richness, this life. And in the large square where the cabs shot and swerved so quick, there were loitering couples, dallying, embracing, shrunk up under the shower of a tree; that was moving; so silent, so absorbed, that one passed, discreetly, timidly, as if in the presence of some sacred cere-mony to interrupt which would have been impious. That was interesting. And so on into the flare and glare.

His light overcoat blew open, he stepped with indescrib-able idiosyncrasy, leant a little forward, tripped, with his hands behind his back and his eyes still a little hawk-like; he tripped through London, towards Westminster, observing.

Was everybody dining out, then? Doors were being opened here by a footman to let issuc a high-stepping old dame, in buckled shoes, with three purple ostrich feathers in her hair. Doors were being opened for ladies wrapped like mummies in shawls with bright flowers on them, ladies with bare heads. And in respectable quarters with stucco pillars through small front gardens, lightly swathed, with combs in their hair (having run up to see the children), women came; men waited for them, with their coats blowing open, and the motor started. Everybody was going out. What with these doors being opened, and the descent and the start, it seemed as if the whole of London were embarking in little boats moored to the bank, tossing on the waters, as if the whole place were floating off in carnival. And Whitehall was skated over, silver beaten as it was, skated over by spiders, and there was a sense of midges round the arc lamps; it was so hot that people stood about talking. And here in Westminster was a retired Judge, presumably, sitting four square at his house door dressed all in white. An Anglo-Indian presumably.

And here a shindy of brawling women, drunken women; here only a policeman and looming houses, high houses, domed houses, churches, parliaments, and the hoot of a steamer on the river, a hollow misty cry. But it was her street, this, Clarissa's; cabs were rushing round the corner, like water round the piers of a bridge, drawn together, it seemed to him because they bore people going to her party, Clarissa's party.

The cold stream of visual impressions failed him now as if the eye were a cup that overflowed and let the rest run down its china walls unrecorded. The brain must wake now. The body must contract now, entering the house, the lighted house, where the door stood open, where the motor cars were standing, and bright women descending: the soul must brave itself to endure. He opened the big blade of his pocket-knife.

Lucy came running full tilt downstairs, having just nipped in to the drawing-room to smooth a cover, to straighten a chair, to pause a moment and feel whoever came in must think how clean, how bright, how beautifully cared for, when they saw the beautiful silver, the brass fire-irons, the new chair-covers, and the curtains of yellow chintz: she appraised each; heard a roar of voices; people already coming up from dinner; she must fly!

The Prime Minister was coming, Agnes said: so she had heard them say in the dining-room, she said, coming in with a tray of glasses. Did it matter, did it matter in the least, one Prime Minister more or less? It made no difference at this hour of the night to Mrs. Walker among the plates, saucepans, cullenders, frying-pans, chicken in aspic, ice-cream freezers, pared crusts of bread, lemons, soup tureens, and pudding basins which, however hard they washed up in the scullery, seemed to be all on top of her, on the kitchen table, on chairs, while the fire blared and roared, the electric lights glared, and still supper had to be laid. All she felt was, one Prime Minister more or less made not a scrap of difference to Mrs. Walker.

The ladies were going upstairs already, said Lucy; the ladies were going up, one by one, Mrs. Dalloway walking last and almost always sending back some message to the kitchen, "My love to Mrs. Walker," that was it one night. Next morning they would go over the dishes – the soup, the salmon; the salmon, Mrs. Walker knew, as usual underdone, for she always got nervous about the pudding and left it to Jenny; so it happened, the salmon was always underdone. But some lady with fair hair and silver ornaments had said, Lucy said, about the entrée, was it really made at home? But it was the salmon that bothered Mrs. Walker, as she spun the plates round and round, and pushed in dampers and pulled out dampers; and there came a burst of laughter from the dining-room; a voice speaking; then another burst of laughter – the gentlemen enjoying themselves when the ladies had gone. The tokay, said Lucy running in. Mr. Dalloway had sent for the tokay, from the Emperor's cellars, the Imperial Tokay.

It was borne through the kitchen. Over her shoulder Lucy reported how Miss Elizabeth looked quite lovely; she couldn't take her eyes off her; in her pink dress, wearing the necklace Mr. Dalloway had given her. Jenny must remember the dog, Miss Elizabeth's fox-terrier, which, since it bit, had to be shut up and might, Elizabeth thought, want something. Jenny must remember the dog. But Jenny was not going upstairs with all those people about. There was a motor at the door already! There was a ring at the bell – and the gentlemen still in the dining-room, drinking tokay!

There, they were going upstairs; that was the first to come, and now they would come faster and faster, so that Mrs. Parkinson (hired for parties) would leave the hall door ajar, and the hall would be full of gentlemen waiting (they stood waiting, sleeking down their hair) while the ladies took their cloaks off in the room along the passage; where Mrs. Barnet helped them, old Ellen Barnet, who had been with the family for forty years, and came every summer to help the ladies, and remembered mothers when they were girls, and though very unassuming did shake hands; said "milady" very respectfully, yet had a humorous way with her, looking at the young ladies, and ever so tactfully helping Lady Lovejoy, who had some trouble with her underbodice. And they could not help feeling, Lady Lovejoy and Miss Alice, that some little privilege in the matter of brush and comb was awarded them having known Mrs. Barnet – "thirty years, milady," Mrs. Barnet supplied her. Young ladies did not use rouge, said Lady Lovejoy, when they stayed at Bourton in the old days. And Miss Alice did not need rouge, said Mrs. Barnet, looking at her fondly. There Mrs. Barnet would sit, in the cloakroom, patting down the furs, smoothing out the Spanish shawls, tidying the dressing-table, and knowing perfectly well, in spite of the furs and the embroideries, which were nice ladies, which were not. The dear old body, said Lady Lovejoy, mounting the stairs, Clarissa's old nurse.

And then Lady Lovejoy stiffened. "Lady and Miss Lovejoy," she said to Mr. Wilkins (hired for parties). He had an admirable manner, as he bent and straightened himself, bent and straightened himself and announced with perfect impartiality "Lady and Miss Lovejoy . . . Sir John and Lady Needham . . . Miss Weld . . . Mr. Walsh." His manner was admirable; his family life must be irreproachable, except that it seemed impossible that a being with greenish lips and shaven cheeks could ever have blundered into the nuisance of children.

"How delightful to see you!" said Clarissa. She said it to every one. How delightful to see you! She was at her worst – effusive, insincere. It was a great mistake to have come. He should have stayed at home and read his book, thought Peter

Walsh; should have gone to a music hall; he should have stayed at home, for he knew no one.

Oh dear, it was going to be a failure; a complete failure, Clarissa felt it in her bones as dear old Lord Lexham stood there apologising for his wife who had caught cold at the Buckingham Palace garden party. She could see Peter out of the tail of her eye, criticising her, there, in that corner. Why, after all, did she do these things? Why seek pinnacles and stand drenched in fire? Might it consume her anyhow! Burn her to cinders! Better anything, better brandish one's torch and hurl it to earth than taper and dwindle away like some Ellie Henderson! It was extraordinary how Peter put her into these states just by coming and standing in a corner. He made her see herself; exaggerate. It was idiotic. But why did he come, then, merely to criticise? Why always take, never give? Why not risk one's one little point of view? There he was wandering off, and she must speak to him. But she would not get the chance. Life was that – humiliation, renunciation. What Lord Lexham was saying was that his wife would not wear her furs at the garden party because "my dear, you ladies are all alike" – Lady Lexham being seventy-five at least! It was delicious, how they petted each other, that old couple. She did like old Lord Lexham. She did think it mattered, her party, and it made her feel quite sick to know that it was all going wrong, all falling flat. Anything, any explosion, any horror was better than people wandering aimlessly, standing in a bunch at a corner like Ellie Henderson, not even caring to hold themselves upright.

Gently the yellow curtain with all the birds of Paradise blew out and it seemed as if there were a flight of wings into the room, right out, then sucked back. (For the windows were open.) Was it draughty, Ellie Henderson wondered? She was subject to chills. But it did not matter that she should come down sneezing to-morrow; it was the girls with their naked shoulders she thought of, being trained to think of others by an old father, an invalid, late vicar of Bourton, but he was dead now; and her chills never went to her chest, never. It was the girls she thought of, the young girls with their bare shoulders, she herself having always been a wisp of a creature, with her thin hair and meagre profile; though now, past fifty, there was beginning to shine through some mild beam, something purified into distinction by years of self-abnegation but obscured again, perpetually, by her distressing gentility, her panic fear, which arose from three hundred pounds income, and her weaponless state (she could not earn a penny) and it made her timid, and more and more disqualified year by year to meet well-dressed people who did this sort of thing every night of the season, merely telling their maids "I'll wear so and so," whereas Ellie Henderson ran out nervously and bought cheap pink flowers, half-a-dozen, and then threw a shawl over her old black dress. For her invitation to Clarissa's party had come at the last moment. She was not quite happy about it. She had a sort of feeling that Clarissa had not meant to ask her this year.

Why should she? There was no reason really, except that they had always known each other. Indeed, they were cousins. But naturally they had rather drifted apart, Clarissa being so sought after. It was an event to her, going to a party. It was quite a treat just to see the lovely clothes. Wasn't that Elizabeth, grown up, with her hair done in the fashionable way, in the pink dress? Yet she could not be more than seventeen. She was very, very handsome. But girls when they first came out didn't seem to wear white as they used. (She must remember everything to tell Edith.) Girls wore straight frocks, perfectly tight, with skirts well above the ankles. It was not becoming, she thought.

So, with her weak eyesight, Ellie Henderson craned rather forward, and it wasn't so much she who minded not having any one to talk to (she hardly knew anybody there), for she felt that they were all such interesting people to watch;

politicians presumably; Richard Dalloway's friends; but it was Richard himself who felt that he could not let the poor creature go on standing there all the evening by herself.

"Well, Ellie, and how's the world treating *you*?" he said in his genial way, and Ellie Henderson, getting nervous and flushing and feeling that it was extraordinarily nice of him to come and talk to her, said that many people really felt the heat more than the cold.

"Yes, they do," said Richard Dalloway. "Yes."

But what more did one say?

"Hullo, Richard," said somebody, taking him by the elbow, and, good Lord, there was old Peter, old Peter Walsh. He was delighted to see him – ever so pleased to see him! He hadn't changed a bit. And off they went together walking right across the room, giving each other little pats, as if they hadn't met for a long time, Ellie Henderson thought, watching them go, certain she knew that man's face. A tall man, middle aged, rather fine eyes, dark, wearing spectacles, with a look of John Burrows. Edith would be sure to know.

The curtain with its flight of birds of Paradise blew out again. And Clarissa saw – she saw Ralph Lyon beat it back, and go on talking. So it wasn't a failure after all! it was going to be all right now – her party. It had begun. It had started. But it was still touch and go. She must stand there for the present. People seemed to come in a rush.

"Colonel and Mrs. Garrod . . . Mr. Hugh Whitbread . . . Mr. Bowley . . . Mrs. Hilbery . . . Lady Mary Maddox . . . Mr. Quin . . ." intoned Wilkins. She had six or seven words with each, and they went on, they went into the rooms; into something now, not nothing, since Ralph Lyon had beat back the curtain.

And yet for her own part, it was too much of an effort. She was not enjoying it. It was too much like being – just anybody, standing there; anybody could do it; yet this anybody she did a little admire, couldn't help feeling that she had, anyhow, made this happen, that it marked a stage, this post that she felt herself to have become, for oddly enough she had quite forgotten what she looked like, but felt herself a stake driven in at the top of her stairs. Every time she gave a party she had this feeling of being something not herself, and that every one was unreal in one way; much more real in another. It was, she thought, partly their clothes, partly being taken out of their ordinary ways, partly the background; it was possible to say things you couldn't say anyhow else, things that needed an effort; possible to go much deeper. But not for her; not yet anyhow.

"How delightful to see you!" she said. Dear old Sir Harry! He would know every one.

And what was so odd about it was the sense one had as they came up the stairs one after another, Mrs. Mount and Celia, Herbert Ainsty, Mrs. Dakers – oh, and Lady Bruton!

"How awfully good of you to come!" she said, and she meant it – it was odd how standing there one felt them going on, going on, some quite old, some . . .

What name? Lady Rosseter? But who on earth was Lady Rosseter?

"Clarissa!" That voice! It was Sally Seton! Sally Seton! after all these years! She loomed through a mist. For she hadn't looked like *that*, Sally Seton, when Clarissa grasped the hot-water can. To think of her under this roof, under this roof! Not like that!

All on top of each other, embarrassed, laughing, words tumbled out – passing through London; heard from Clara Haydon; what a chance of seeing you! So I thrust myself in – without an invitation. . . .

One might put down the hot-water can quite compos-edly. The lustre had left her. Yet it was extraordinary to see her again, older, happier, less lovely. They kissed each other, first this cheek, then that, by the drawing-room door, and Clarissa turned, with Sally's hand in hers, and saw her rooms full, heard the roar of voices, saw the candlesticks, the blowing curtains, and the roses which Richard had given her.

"I have five enormous boys," said Sally.

She had the simplest egotism, the most open desire to be thought first always, and Clarissa loved her for being still like that. "I can't believe it!" she cried, kindling all over with pleasure at the thought of the past.

But alas, Wilkins; Wilkins wanted her; Wilkins was emitting in a voice of commanding authority, as if the whole company must be admonished and the hostess reclaimed from frivolity, one name:

"The Prime Minister," said Peter Walsh.

The Prime Minister? Was it really? Ellie Henderson marvelled. What a thing to tell Edith!

One couldn't laugh at him. He looked so ordinary. You might have stood him behind a counter and bought biscuits – poor chap, all rigged up in gold lace. And to be fair, as he went his rounds, first with Clarissa, then with Richard escorting him, he did it very well. He tried to look somebody. It was amusing to watch. Nobody looked at him. They just went on talking, yet it was perfectly plain that they all knew, felt to the marrow of their bones, this majesty passing; this symbol of what they all stood for, English society. Old Lady Bruton, and she looked very fine too, very stalwart in her lace, swam up, and they withdrew into a little room which at once became spied upon, guarded, and a sort of stir and rustle rippled through every one openly: the Prime Minister!

Lord, lord, the snobbery of the English! thought Peter Walsh, standing in the corner. How they loved dressing up in gold lace and doing homage! There! That must be – by Jove it was – Hugh Whitbread, snuffing round the precincts of the great, grown rather fatter, rather whiter, the admirable Hugh!

He looked always as if he were on duty, thought Peter, a privileged but secretive being, hoarding secrets which he would die to defend, though it was only some little piece of tittle-tattle dropped by a court footman which would be in all the papers tomorrow. Such were his rattles, his baubles, in playing with which he had grown white, come to the verge of old age, enjoying the respect and affection of all who had the privilege of knowing this type of the English public school man. Inevitably one made up things like that about Hugh; that was his style; the style of those admirable letters which Peter had read thousands of miles across the sea in the *Times*, and had thanked God he was out of that pernicious hubble-bubble if it were only to hear baboons chatter and coolies beat their wives. An olive-skinned youth from one of the Universities stood obsequiously by. Him he would patronise, initiate, teach how to get on. For he liked nothing better than doing kindnesses, making the hearts of old ladies palpitate with the joy of being thought of in their age, their affliction, thinking themselves quite forgotten, yet here was dear Hugh driving up and spending an hour talking of the past, remembering trifles, praising the home-made cake, though Hugh might eat cake with a Duchess any day of his life, and, to look at him, probably did spend a good deal of time in that agreeable occupation. The All-judging, the All-merciful, might excuse. Peter Walsh had no mercy. Villains there must be, and, God knows, the rascals who get hanged for battering the brains of a girl out in a train do less harm on the whole than Hugh Whitbread and his kindness! Look at him now, on tiptoe, dancing forward, bowing and scraping, as the Prime Minister and Lady Bruton emerged, intimating for all the world to see that he was privileged to say something, something private, to Lady Bruton as she passed. She stopped. She wagged her fine old head. She was thanking him presumably for some piece of servility. She had her toadies, minor officials in Government offices who ran about putting through little jobs on her behalf, in return for which she gave them luncheon. But she derived from the eighteenth century. She was all right.

And now Clarissa escorted her Prime Minister down the

room, prancing, sparkling, with the stateliness of her grey hair. She wore ear-rings, and a silver-green mermaid's dress. Lolloping on the waves and braiding her tresses she seemed, having that gift still; to be; to exist; to sum it all up in the moment as she passed; turned, caught her scarf in some other woman's dress, unhitched it, laughed, all with the most perfect ease and air of a creature floating in its element. But age had brushed her; even as a mermaid might behold in her glass the setting sun on some very clear evening over the waves. There was a breath of tenderness; her severity, her prudery, her woodenness were all warmed through now, and she had about her as she said good-bye to the thick gold-laced man who was doing his best, and good luck to him, to look important, an inexpressible dignity; an exquisite cordiality; as if she wished the whole world well, and must now, being on the very verge and rim of things, take her leave. So she made him think. (But he was not in love.)

Indeed, Clarissa felt, the Prime Minister had been good to come. And, walking down the room with him, with Sally there and Peter there and Richard very pleased, with all those people rather inclined, perhaps, to envy, she had felt that intoxication of the moment, that dilatation of the nerves of the heart itself till it seemed to quiver, steeped, upright; – yes, but after all it was what other people felt, that; for, though she loved it and felt it tingle and sting, still these semblances, these triumphs (dear old Peter, for example, thinking her so brilliant), had a hollowness; at arm's length they were, not in the heart; and it might be that she was growing old, but they satisfied her no longer as they used; and suddenly, as she saw the Prime Minister go down the stairs, the gilt rim of the Sir Joshua picture of the little girl with a muff brought back Kilman with a rush; Kilman her enemy. That was satisfying; that was real. Ah, how she hated her – hot, hypocritical, corrupt; with all that power; Elizabeth's seducer; the woman who had crept in to steal and defile (Richard would say, What nonsense!). She hated her: she loved her. It was enemies one wanted, not friends – not Mrs. Durrant and Clara, Sir William and Lady Bradshaw, Miss Truelock and Eleanor Gibson (whom she saw coming upstairs). They must find her if they wanted her. She was for the party!

There was her old friend Sir Harry.

"Dear Sir Harry!" she said, going up to the fine old fellow who had produced more bad pictures than any other two Academicians in the whole of St. John's Wood (they were always of cattle, standing in sunset pools absorbing moisture, or signifying, for he had a certain range of gesture, by the raising of one foreleg and the toss of the antlers, "the Approach of the Stranger" – all his activities, dining out, racing, were founded on cattle standing, absorbing moisture in sunset pools).

"What are you laughing at?" she asked him. For Willie Titcomb and Sir Harry and Herbert Ainsty were all laughing. But no. Sir Harry could not tell Clarissa Dalloway (much though he liked her; of her type he thought her perfect, and threatened to paint her) his stories of the music hall stage. He chaffed her about her party. He missed his brandy. These circles, he said, were above him. But he liked her; respected her, in spite of her damnable, difficult, upper-class refinement, which made it impossible to ask Clarissa Dalloway to sit on his knee. And up came that wandering will-o'-the-wisp, that vagous phosphorescence, old Mrs. Hilbery, stretching her hands to the blaze of his laughter (about the Duke and the Lady), which, as she heard it across the room, seemed to reassure her on a point which sometimes bothered her if she woke early in the morning and did not like to call her maid for a cup of tea: how it is certain we must die.

"They won't tell us their stories," said Clarissa.

"Dear Clarissa!" exclaimed Mrs. Hilbery. She looked to-night, she said, so like her mother as she first saw her walking in a garden in a grey hat.

And really Clarissa's eyes filled with tears. Her mother, walking in a garden! But alas, she must go.

For there was Professor Brierly, who lectured on Milton, talking to little Jim Hutton (who was unable even for a party like this to compass both tie and waistcoat or make his hair lie flat), and even at this distance they were quarrelling, she could see. For Professor Brierly was a very queer fish. With all those degrees, honours, lectureships between him and the scribblers, he suspected instantly an atmosphere not favourable to his queer compound; his prodigious learning and timidity; his wintry charm without cordiality; his innocence blent with snobbery; he quivered if made conscious, by a lady's unkempt hair, a youth's boots, of an underworld, very creditable doubtless, of rebels, of ardent young people; of would-be geniuses, and intimated with a little toss of the head, with a sniff – Humph! – the value of moderation; of some slight training in the classics in order to appreciate Milton. Professor Brierly (Clarissa could see) wasn't hitting it off with little Jim Hutton (who wore red socks, his black being at the laundry) about Milton. She interrupted.

She said she loved Bach. So did Hutton. That was the bond between them, and Hutton (a very bad poet) always felt that Mrs. Dalloway was far the best of the great ladies who took an interest in art. It was odd how strict she was. About music she was purely impersonal. She was rather a prig. But how charming to look at! She made her house so nice, if it weren't for her Professors. Clarissa had half a mind to snatch him off and set him down at the piano in the back room. For he played divinely.

"But the noise!" she said. "The noise!"

"The sign of a successful party." Nodding urbanely, the Professor stepped delicately off.

"He knows everything in the whole world about Milton," said Clarissa.

"Does he indeed?" said Hutton, who would imitate the

Professor throughout Hampstead: the Professor on Milton; the Professor on moderation; the Professor stepping delicately off.

But she must speak to that couple, said Clarissa, Lord Gayton and Nancy Blow.

Not that *they* added perceptibly to the noise of the party. They were not talking (perceptibly) as they stood side by side by the yellow curtains. They would soon be off elsewhere, together; and never had very much to say in any circumstances. They looked; that was all. That was enough. They looked so clean, so sound, she with an apricot bloom of powder and paint, but he scrubbed, rinsed, with the eyes of a bird, so that no ball could pass him or stroke surprise him. He struck, he leapt, accurately, on the spot. Ponies' mouths quivered at the end of his reins. He had his honours, ancestral monuments, banners hanging in the church at home. He had his duties; his tenants; a mother and sisters; had been all day at Lords, and that was what they were talking about – cricket, cousins, the movies – when Mrs. Dalloway came up. Lord Gayton liked her most awfully. So did Miss Blow. She had such charming manners.

"It is angelic – it is delicious of you to have come!" she said. She loved Lords; she loved youth, and Nancy, dressed at enormous expense by the greatest artists in Paris, stood there looking as if her body had merely put forth, of its own accord, a green frill.

"I had meant to have dancing," said Clarissa.

For the young people could not talk. And why should they? Shout, embrace, swing, be up at dawn; carry sugar to ponies; kiss and caress the snouts of adorable chows; and then, all tingling and streaming, plunge and swim. But the enormous resources of the English language, the power it bestows, after all, of communicating feelings (at their age, she and Peter would have been arguing all the evening), was not for them. They would solidify young. They would be good beyond measure to the people on the estate, but alone, perhaps, rather dull.

"What a pity!" she said. "I had hoped to have dancing."

It was so extraordinarily nice of them to have come! But talk of dancing! The rooms were packed.

There was old Aunt Helena in her shawl. Alas, she must leave them – Lord Gayton and Nancy Blow. There was old Miss Parry, her aunt.

For Miss Helena Parry was not dead: Miss Parry was alive. She was past eighty. She ascended staircases slowly with a stick. She was placed in a chair (Richard had seen to it). People who had known Burma in the 'seventies were always led up to her. Where had Peter got to? They used to be such friends. For at the mention of India, or even Ceylon, her eyes (only one was glass) slowly deepened, became blue, beheld, not human beings – she had no tender memories, no proud illusions about Viceroys, Generals, Mutinies – it was orchids she saw, and mountain passes, and herself carried on the backs of coolies in the 'sixties over solitary peaks; or descending to uproot orchids (startling blossoms, never beheld before) which she painted in water-colour; an indomitable Englishwoman, fretful if disturbed by the war, say, which dropped a bomb at her very door, from her deep meditation over orchids and her own figure journeying in the 'sixties in India – but here was Peter.

"Come and talk to Aunt Helena about Burma," said Clarissa.

And yet he had not had a word with her all the evening!

"We will talk later," said Clarissa, leading him up to Aunt Helena, in her white shawl, with her stick.

"Peter Walsh," said Clarissa.

That meant nothing.

Clarissa had asked her. It was tiring; it was noisy; but Clarissa had asked her. So she had come. It was a pity that they lived in London – Richard and Clarissa. If only for Clarissa's health it would have been better to live in the country. But Clarissa had always been fond of society.

"He has been in Burma," said Clarissa.

Ah! She could not resist recalling what Charles Darwin had said about her little book on the orchids of Burma.

(Clarissa must speak to Lady Bruton.)

No doubt it was forgotten now, her book on the orchids of Burma, but it went into three editions before 1870, she told Peter. She remembered him now. He had been at Bourton (and he had left her, Peter Walsh remembered, without a word in the drawing-room that night when Clarissa had asked him to come boating).

"Richard so much enjoyed his lunch party," said Clarissa to Lady Bruton.

"Richard was the greatest possible help," Lady Bruton replied. "He helped me to write a letter. And how are you?"

"Oh, perfectly well!" said Clarissa. (Lady Bruton detested illness in the wives of politicians.)

"And there's Peter Walsh!" said Lady Bruton (for she could never think of anything to say to Clarissa; though she liked her. She had lots of fine qualities; but they had nothing in common – she and Clarissa. It might have been better if Richard had married a woman with less charm, who would have helped him more in his work. He had lost his chance of the Cabinet). "There's Peter Walsh!" she said, shaking hands with that agreeable sinner, that very able fellow who should have made a name for himself but hadn't (always in difficulties with women), and, of course, old Miss Parry. Wonderful old lady!

Lady Bruton stood by Miss Parry's chair, a spectral grenadier, draped in black, inviting Peter Walsh to lunch; cordial; but without small talk, remembering nothing whatever about the flora or fauna of India. She had been there, of course; had stayed with three Viceroys; thought some of the Indian civilians uncommonly fine fellows; but what a tragedy it was – the state of India! The Prime Minister had just been telling her (old Miss Parry, huddled up in her shawl, did not care what the Prime Minister had just been telling her), and Lady Bruton would like to have Peter Walsh's opinion, he being fresh from the centre, and she would get Sir Sampson to meet him, for really it prevented her from sleeping at night, the folly of it, the wickedness she might say, being a soldier's daughter. She was an old woman now, not good for much. But her house, her servants, her good friend Milly Brush – did he remember her? – were all there only asking to be used if – if they could be of help, in short. For she never spoke of England, but this isle of men, this dear, dear land, was in her blood (without reading Shakespeare), and if ever a woman could have worn the helmet and shot the arrow, could have led troops to attack, ruled with indomitable justice barbarian hordes and lain under a shield noseless in a church, or made a green grass mound on some primeval hillside, that woman was Millicent Bruton. Debarred by her sex, and some truancy, too, of the logical faculty (she found it impossible to write a letter to the *Times*), she had the thought of Empire always at hand, and had acquired from her association with that armoured goddess her ramrod bearing, her robustness of demeanour, so that one could not figure her even in death parted from the earth or roaming territories over which, in some spiritual shape, the Union Jack had ceased to fly. To be not English even among the dead – no, no! Impossible!

But was it Lady Bruton (whom she used to know)? Was it Peter Walsh grown grey? Lady Rosseter asked herself (who had been Sally Seton). It was old Miss Parry certainly – the old aunt who used to be so cross when she stayed at Bourton. Never should she forget running along the passage naked, and being sent for by Miss Parry! And Clarissa! Oh Clarissa! Sally caught her by the arm.

Clarissa stopped beside them.

"But I can't stay," she said. "I shall come later. Wait," she said, looking at Peter and Sally. They must wait, she meant, until all these people had gone.

"I shall come back," she said, looking at her old friends, Sally and Peter, who were shaking hands, and Sally, remembering the past no doubt, was laughing.

But her voice was wrung of its old ravishing richness; her eyes not aglow as they used to be, when she smoked cigars, when she ran down the passage to fetch her sponge bag without a stitch of clothing on her, and Ellen Atkins asked, What if the gentlemen had met her? But everybody forgave her. She stole a chicken from the larder because she was hungry in the night; she smoked cigars in her bedroom; she left a priceless book in the punt. But everybody adored her (except perhaps Papa). It was her warmth; her vitality – she would paint, she would write. Old women in the village never to this day forgot to ask after "your friend in the red cloak who seemed so bright". She accused Hugh Whitbread, of all people (and there he was, her old friend Hugh, talking to the Portuguese Ambassador), of kissing her in the smoking-room to punish her for saying that women should have votes. Vulgar men did, she said. And Clarissa remembered having to persuade her not to denounce him at family prayers – which she was capable of doing with her daring, her recklessness, her melodramatic love of being the centre of everything and creating scenes, and it was bound, Clarissa used to think, to end in some awful tragedy; her death; her martyrdom; instead of which she had married, quite unexpectedly, a bald man with a large buttonhole who owned, it was said, cotton mills at Manchester. And she had five boys!

She and Peter had settled down together. They were talking: it seemed so familiar – that they should be talking. They would discuss the past. With the two of them (more even than with Richard) she shared her past; the garden; the trees; old Joseph Breitkopf singing Brahms without any voice; the drawing-room wallpaper; the smell of the mats. A part of this Sally must always be; Peter must always be. But she must leave them. There were the Bradshaws, whom she disliked. She must go up to Lady Bradshaw (in grey and silver, balancing like a sea-lion at the edge of its tank, barking for invitations, Duchesses, the typical successful man's wife), she must go up to Lady Bradshaw and say . . .

But Lady Bradshaw anticipated her.

"We are shockingly late, dear Mrs. Dalloway; we hardly dared to come in," she said.

And Sir William, who looked very distinguished, with his grey hair and blue eyes, said yes; they had not been able to resist the temptation. He was talking to Richard about that Bill probably, which they wanted to get through the Commons. Why did the sight of him, talking to Richard, curl her up? He looked what he was, a great doctor. A man absolutely at the head of his profession, very powerful, rather worn. For think what cases came before him – people in the uttermost depths of misery; people on the verge of insanity; husbands and wives. He had to decide questions of appalling difficulty. Yet – what she felt was, one wouldn't like Sir William to see one unhappy. No; not that man.

"How is your son at Eton?" she asked Lady Bradshaw.

He had just missed his eleven, said Lady Bradshaw, because of the mumps. His father minded even more than he did, she thought, "being," she said, "nothing but a great boy himself."

Clarissa looked at Sir William, talking to Richard. He did not look like a boy – not in the least like a boy. She had once gone with some one to ask his advice. He had been perfectly right; extremely sensible. But Heavens – what a relief to get out to the street again! There was some poor wretch sobbing, she remembered, in the waiting-room. But she did not know what it was about Sir William; what exactly she disliked. Only Richard agreed with her, "didn't like his taste, didn't like his smell." But he was extraordinarily able. They were talking about this Bill. Some case Sir William was mentioning, lowering his voice. It had its bearing upon what he was saying about the deferred effects of shell shock. There must be some provision in the Bill.

Sinking her voice, drawing Mrs. Dalloway into the shelter of a common femininity, a common pride in the illustrious qualities of husbands and their sad tendency to overwork, Lady Bradshaw (poor goose – one didn't dislike her) murmured how, "just as we were starting, my husband was called up on the telephone, a very sad case. A young man (that is what Sir William is telling Mr. Dalloway) had killed himself. He had been in the army." Oh! thought Clarissa, in the middle of my party, here's death, she thought.

She went on, into the little room where the Prime Minister had gone with Lady Bruton. Perhaps there was somebody there. But there was nobody. The chairs still kept the impress of the Prime Minister and Lady Bruton, she turned deferentially, he sitting four-square, authoritatively. They had been talking about India. There was nobody. The party's splendour fell to the floor, so strange it was to come in alone in her finery.

What business had the Bradshaws to talk of death at her party? A young man had killed himself. And they talked of it at her party – the Bradshaws talked of death. He had killed himself – but how? Always her body went through it first, when she was told, suddenly, of an accident; her dress flamed, her body burnt. He had thrown himself from a window. Up had flashed the ground; through him, blundering, bruising, went the rusty spikes. There he lay with a thud, thud, thud in his brain, and then a suffocation of blackness. So she saw it. But why had he done it? And the Bradshaws talked of it at her party!

She had once thrown a shilling into the Serpentine, never anything more. But he had flung it away. They went on living (she would have to go back; the rooms were still crowded; people kept on coming). They (all day she had been thinking of Bourton, of Peter, of Sally), they would grow old. A thing there was that mattered; a thing, wreathed about with chatter, defaced, obscured in her own life, let drop every day in corruption, lies, chatter. This he had preserved. Death was defiance. Death was an attempt to communicate; people feeling the impossibility of reaching the centre which, mystically, evaded them; closeness drew apart; rapture faded; one was alone. There was an embrace in death.

But this young man who had killed himself – had he plunged holding his treasure? "If it were now to die, 'twere now to be most happy," she had said to herself once, coming down, in white.

Or there were the poets and thinkers. Suppose he had had that passion, and had gone to Sir William Bradshaw, a great doctor, yet to her obscurely evil, without sex or lust, extremely polite to women, but capable of some indescribable outrage – forcing your soul, that was it – if this young man had gone to him, and Sir William had impressed him, like that, with his power, might he not then have said (indeed she felt it now), Life is made intolerable; they make life intolerable, men like that?

Then (she had felt it only this morning) there was the terror; the overwhelming incapacity, one's parents giving it into one's hands, this life, to be lived to the end, to be walked with serenely; there was in the depths of her heart an awful fear. Even now, quite often if Richard had not been there reading the *Times*, so that she could crouch like a bird and gradually revive, send roaring up that immeasurable delight, rubbing stick to stick, one thing with another, she must have perished. She had escaped. But that young man had killed himself.

Somehow it was her disaster – her disgrace. It was her punishment to see sink and disappear here a man, there a woman, in this profound darkness, and she forced to stand here in her evening dress. She had schemed; she had pilfered. She was never wholly admirable. She had wanted success, – Lady Bexborough and the rest of it. And once she had walked on the terrace at Bourton.

Odd, incredible; she had never been so happy. Nothing could be slow enough; nothing last too long. No pleasure could equal, she thought, straightening the chairs, pushing in one book on the shelf, this having done with the triumphs of youth, lost herself in the process of living, to find it, with a shock of delight, as the sun rose, as the day sank. Many a time had she gone, at Bourton when they were all talking, to look at the sky; or seen it between people's shoulders at dinner; seen it in London when she could not sleep. She walked to the window.

It held, foolish as the idea was, something of her own in it, this country sky, this sky above Westminster. She parted the curtains; she looked. Oh, but how surprising! – in the room opposite the old lady stared straight at her! She was going to bed. And the sky. It will be a solemn sky, she had thought, it will be a dusky sky, turning away its cheek in beauty. But there it was – ashen, pale, raced over quickly by tapering vast clouds. It was new to her. The wind must have risen. She was going to bed, in the room opposite. It was fascinating to watch her, moving about, that old lady, crossing the room, coming to the window. Could she see her? It was fascinating, with people still laughing and shouting in the drawing-room, to watch that old woman, quite quietly, going to bed alone. She pulled the blind now. The clock began striking. The young man had killed himself; but she did not pity him; with the clock striking the hour, one, two, three, she did not pity him, with all this going on. There! the old lady had put out her light! The whole house was dark now with this going on, she repeated, and the words came to her, fear no more the heat of the sun. She must go back to them. But what an extraordinary night! She felt somehow very like him – the young man who had killed himself. She felt glad that he had done it; thrown it away while they went on living. The clock was striking. The leaden circles dissolved in the air. But she must go back. She must assemble. She must find Sally and Peter. And she came in from the little room.

"But where is Clarissa?" said Peter. He was sitting on the sofa with Sally. (After all these years he really could not call her "Lady Rosseter".) "Where's the woman gone to?" he asked. "Where's Clarissa?"

Sally supposed, and so did Peter for the matter of that, that there were people of importance, politicians, whom neither of them knew unless by sight in the picture papers, whom Clarissa had to be nice to, had to talk to. She was with them. Yet there was Richard Dalloway not in the Cabinet. He hadn't been a success? Sally supposed. For herself, she scarcely ever read the papers. She sometimes saw his name mentioned. But then – well, she lived a very solitary life, in the wilds, Clarissa would say, among great merchants, great manufacturers, men, after all, who did things. She had done things too!

"I have five sons!" she told him.

Lord, lord, what a change had come over her! The softness of motherhood; its egotism too. Last time they met, Peter remembered, had been among the cauliflowers in the moonlight, the leaves "like rough bronze" she had said, with her literary turn; and she had picked a rose. She had marched him up and down that awful night, after the scene by the fountain; he was to catch the midnight train. Heavens, he had wept!

That was his old trick, opening a pocket-knife, thought Sally, always opening and shutting a knife when he got excited. They had been very, very intimate, she and Peter Walsh, when he was in love with Clarissa, and there was that dreadful, ridiculous scene over Richard Dalloway at lunch. She had called Richard "Wickham". Why not call Richard "Wickham"? Clarissa had flared up! and indeed they had never seen each other since, she and Clarissa, not more than half-a-dozen times perhaps in the last ten years. And Peter Walsh had gone off to India, and she had heard vaguely that he had made an unhappy marriage, and she didn't know whether he had any children, and she couldn't ask him, for he had changed. He was rather shrivelled-looking, but kinder, she felt, and she had a real affection for him, for he was connected with her youth, and she still had a little Emily Brontë he had given her, and he was to write, surely? In those days he was to write.

"Have you written?" she asked him, spreading her hand, her firm and shapely hand, on her knee in a way he recalled.

"Not a word!" said Peter Walsh, and she laughed.

She was still attractive, still a personage, Sally Seton. But who was this Rosseter? He wore two camellias on his wedding day – that was all Peter knew of him. "They have myriads of servants, miles of conservatories," Clarissa wrote; something like that. Sally owned it with a shout of laughter.

"Yes, I have ten thousand a year" – whether before the tax was paid or after, she couldn't remember, for her husband, "whom you must meet," she said, "whom you would like," she said, did all that for her.

And Sally used to be in rags and tatters. She had pawned her great-grandfather's ring which Marie Antoinette had given him – had he got it right? – to come to Bourton.

Oh yes, Sally remembered; she had it still, a ruby ring which Marie Antoinette had given her great-grandfather. She never had a penny to her name in those days, and going to Bourton always meant some frightful pinch. But going to Bourton had meant so much to her – had kept her sane, she believed, so unhappy had she been at home. But that was all a thing of the past – all over now, she said. And Mr. Parry was dead; and Miss Parry was still alive. Never had he had such a shock in his life! said Peter. He had been quite certain she was dead. And the marriage had been, Sally supposed, a success? And that very handsome, very self-possessed young woman was Elizabeth, over there, by the curtains, in pink.

(She was like a poplar, she was like a river, she was like a hyacinth, Willie Titcomb was thinking. Oh how much nicer to be in the country and do what she liked! She could hear her poor dog howling, Elizabeth was certain.) She was not a bit like Clarissa, Peter Walsh said.

"Oh, Clarissa!" said Sally.

What Sally felt was simply this. She had owed Clarissa an enormous amount. They had been friends, not acquaintances, friends, and she still saw Clarissa all in white going about the house with her hands full of flowers – to this day tobacco plants made her think of Bourton. But – did Peter understand? – she lacked something. Lacked what was it? She had charm; she had extraordinary charm. But to be frank (and she felt that Peter was an old friend, a real friend – did absence matter? Did distance matter? She had often wanted to write to him, but torn it up, yet felt he understood, for people understand without things being said, as one realises growing old, and old she was, had been that afternoon to see her sons at Eton, where they had the mumps), to be quite frank, then, how could Clarissa have done it? – married Richard Dalloway? a sportsman, a man who cared only for dogs. Literally, when he came into the room he smelt of the stables. And then all this? She waved her hand.

Hugh Whitbread it was, strolling past in his white waistcoat, dim, fat, blind, past everything he looked, except self-esteem and comfort.

"He's not going to recognise *us*," said Sally, and really she hadn't the courage – so that was Hugh! The admirable Hugh!

"And what does he do?" she asked Peter.

He blacked the King's boots or counted bottles at Windsor, Peter told her. Peter kept his sharp tongue still! But Sally must be frank, Peter said. That kiss now, Hugh's.

On the lips, she assured him, in the smoking-room one evening. She went straight to Clarissa in a rage. Hugh didn't do such things! Clarissa said, the admirable Hugh! Hugh's socks were without exception the most beautiful she had ever seen – and now his evening dress. Perfect! And had he children?

"Everybody in the room has six sons at Eton," Peter told her, except himself. He, thank God, had none. No sons, no daughters, no wife. Well, he didn't seem to mind, said Sally. He looked younger, she thought, than any of them.

But it had been a silly thing to do, in many ways, Peter said, to marry like that; "a perfect goose she was," he said, but, he said, "we had a splendid time of it." But how could that be? Sally wondered; what did he mean? and how odd it was to know him and yet not know a single thing that had happened to him. And did he say it out of pride? Very likely, for after all it must be galling for him (though he was an oddity, a sort of sprite, not at all an ordinary man), it must be lonely at his age to have no home, nowhere to go to. But he must stay with them for weeks and weeks. Of course he would; he would love to stay with them, and that was how it came out. All these years the Dalloways had never been once. Time after time they had asked them. Clarissa (for it was Clarissa of course) would not come. For, said Sally, Clarissa was at heart a snob – one had to admit it, a snob. And it was that that was between them, she was convinced. Clarissa thought she had married beneath her, her husband being – she was proud of it – a miner's son. Every penny they had he had earned. As a little boy (her voice trembled) he had carried great sacks.

(And so she would go on, Peter felt, hour after hour; the miner's son; people thought she had married beneath her; her five sons; and what was the other thing – plants, hydrangeas, syringas, very, very rare hybiscus lilies that never grow north of the Suez Canal, but she, with one gardener in a suburb near Manchester, had beds of them, positively beds! Now all that Clarissa had escaped, unmaternal as she was.)

A snob was she? Yes, in many ways. Where was she, all this time? It was getting late.

"Yet," said Sally, "when I heard Clarissa was giving a party, I felt I couldn't *not* come – must see her again` (and I'm staying in Victoria Street, practically next door). So I just came without an invitation. But," she whispered, "tell me, do. Who is this?"

It was Mrs. Hilbery, looking for the door. For how late it was getting! And, she murmured, as the night grew later, as people went, one found old friends; quiet nooks and corners; and the loveliest views. Did they know, she asked, that they were surrounded by an enchanted garden? Lights and trees and wonderful gleaming lakes and the sky. Just a few fairy lamps, Clarissa Dalloway had said, in the back garden! But she was a magician! It was a park. . . . And she didn't know their names, but friends she knew they were, friends without names, songs without words, always the best. But there were so many doors, such unexpected places, she could not find her way.

"Old Mrs. Hilbery," said Peter; but who was that? That lady standing by the curtain all the evening, without speaking? He knew her face; connected her with Bourton. Surely she used to cut up underclothes at the large table in the window? Davidson, was that her name?

"Oh, that is Ellie Henderson," said Sally. Clarissa was really very hard on her. She was a cousin, very poor. Clarissa *was* hard on people.

She was rather, said Peter. Yet, said Sally, in her emotional way, with a rush of that enthusiasm which Peter used to love her for, yet dreaded a little now, so effusive she might become – how generous to her friends Clarissa was! And what a rare quality one found it, and how sometimes at night or on Christmas Day, when she counted up her blessings, she put that friendship first. They were young; that was it. Clarissa was pure-hearted; that was it. Peter would think her sentimental. So she was. For she had come to feel that it was the only thing worth saying – what one felt. Cleverness was silly. One must say simply what one felt.

"But I do not know," said Peter Walsh, "what I feel."

Poor Peter, thought Sally. Why did not Clarissa come and talk to them? That was what he was longing for. She knew it. All the time he was thinking only of Clarissa, and was fidgeting with his knife.

He had not found life simple, Peter said. His relations with Clarissa had not been simple. It had spoilt his life, he said.

(They had been so intimate – he and Sally Seton, it was absurd not to say it.) One could not be in love twice, he said. And what could she say? Still, it is better to have loved (but he would think her sentimental – he used to be so sharp). He must come and stay with them in Manchester. That is all very true, he said. All very true. He would love to come and stay with them, directly he had done what he had to do in London.

And Clarissa had cared for him more than she had ever cared for Richard, Sally was positive of that.

"No, no, no!" said Peter (Sally should not have said that – she went too far). That good fellow – there he was at the end of the room, holding forth, the same as ever, dear old Richard. Who was he talking to? Sally asked, that very distinguished-looking man? Living in the wilds as she did, she had an insatiable curiosity to know who people were. But Peter did not know. He did not like his looks, he said, probably a Cabinet Minister. Of them all, Richard seemed to him the best, he said – the most disinterested.

"But what has he done?" Sally asked. Public work, she supposed. And were they happy together? Sally asked (she herself was extremely happy); for, she admitted, she knew nothing about them, only jumped to conclusions, as one does, for what can one know even of the people one lives with every day? she asked. Are we not all prisoners? She had read a wonderful play about a man who scratched on the wall of his cell, and she had felt that was true of life – one scratched on the wall. Despairing of human relationships (people were so difficult), she often went into her garden and got from her flowers a peace which men and women never gave her. But no; he did not like cabbages; he preferred human beings, Peter said. Indeed, the young are beautiful, Sally said, watching Elizabeth cross the room. How unlike Clarissa at her age! Could he make anything of her? She would not open her lips. Not much, not yet, Peter admitted. She was like a lily, Sally said, a lily by the side of a pool. But Peter did not agree that we know nothing. We know everything, he said; at least he did.

But these two, Sally whispered, these two coming now (and really she must go, if Clarissa did not come soon), this distinguished-looking man and his rather common-looking wife who had been talking to Richard – what could one know about people like that?

"That they're damnable humbugs," said Peter, looking at them casually. He made Sally laugh.

But Sir William Bradshaw stopped at the door to look at a picture. He looked in the corner for the engraver's name. His wife looked too. Sir William Bradshaw was so interested in art.

When one was young, said Peter, one was too much excited to know people. Now that one was old, fifty-three to be precise (Sally was fifty-five, in body, she said, but her heart was like a girl's of twenty); now that one was mature then, said Peter, one could watch, one could understand, and one did not lose the power of feeling, he said. No, that is true, said Sally. She felt more deeply, more passionately, every year. It increased, he said, alas, perhaps, but one should be glad of it – it went on increasing in his experience. There was some one in India. He would like to tell Sally about her. He would like Sally to know her. She was married, he said. She had two small children. They must all come to Manchester, said Sally – he must promise before they left.

"There's Elizabeth," he said, "she feels not half what we feel, not yet." "But," said Sally, watching Elizabeth go to her father, "one can see they are devoted to each other." She could feel it by the way Elizabeth went to her father.

For her father had been looking at her, as he stood talking to the Bradshaws, and he had thought to himself, Who is that lovely girl? And suddenly he realised that it was his Elizabeth, and he had not recognised her, she looked so lovely in her pink frock! Elizabeth had felt him looking at her as she talked to Willie Titcomb. So she went to him and they stood together, now that the party was almost over, looking at the people going, and the rooms getting emptier and emptier, with things scattered on the floor. Even Ellie Henderson was going, nearly last of all, though no one had spoken to her, but she had wanted to see everything, to tell Edith. And Richard and Elizabeth were rather glad it was over, but Richard was proud of his daughter. And he had not meant to tell her, but he could not help telling her. He had looked at her, he said, and he had wondered, Who is that lovely girl? and it was his daughter! That did make her happy. But her poor dog was howling.

"Richard has improved. You are right," said Sally. "I shall go and talk to him. I shall say good-night. What does the brain matter," said Lady Rosseter, getting up, "compared with the heart?"

"I will come," said Peter, but he sat on for a moment. What is this terror? what is this ecstasy? he thought to himself. What is it that fills me with extraordinary excitement?

It is Clarissa, he said.

For there she was.

THE END

CLASSIC LITERATURE: WORDS AND PHRASES
adapted from the *Collins English Dictionary*

Accoucheur NOUN a male midwife or doctor ❑ *I think my sister must have had some general idea that I was a young offender whom an Accoucheur Policemen had taken up (on my birthday) and delivered over to her* (*Great Expectations* by Charles Dickens)

addled ADJ confused and unable to think properly ❑ *But she counted and counted till she got that addled* (*The Adventures of Huckleberry Finn* by Mark Twain)

admiration NOUN amazement or wonder ❑ *lifting up his hands and eyes by way of admiration* (*Gulliver's Travels* by Jonathan Swift)

afeard ADJ afeard means afraid ❑ *shake it–and don't be afeard* (*The Adventures of Huckleberry Finn* by Mark Twain)

affected VERB affected means followed ❑ *Hadst thou affected sweet divinity* (*Doctor Faustus 5.2* by Christopher Marlowe)

aground ADV when a boat runs aground, it touches the ground in a shallow part of the water and gets stuck ❑ *what kep' you?–boat get aground?* (*The Adventures of Huckleberry Finn* by Mark Twain)

ague NOUN a fever in which the patient has alternate hot and cold shivering fits ❑ *his exposure to the wet and cold had brought on fever and ague* (*Oliver Twist* by Charles Dickens)

alchemy ADJ false or worthless ❑ *all wealth alchemy* (*The Sun Rising* by John Donne)

all alike PHRASE the same all the time ❑ *Love, all alike* (*The Sun Rising* by John Donne)

alow and aloft PHRASE alow means in the lower part or bottom, and aloft means on the top, so alow and aloft means on the top and in the bottom or throughout ❑ *Someone's turned the chest out alow and aloft* (*Treasure Island* by Robert Louis Stevenson)

ambuscade NOUN ambuscade is not a proper word. Tom means an ambush, which is when a group of people attack their enemies, after hiding and waiting for them ❑ *and so we would lie in ambuscade, as he called it* (*The Adventures of Huckleberry Finn* by Mark Twain)

amiable ADJ likeable or pleasant ❑ *Such amiable qualities must speak for themselves* (*Pride and Prejudice* by Jane Austen)

amulet NOUN an amulet is a charm thought to drive away evil spirits. ❑ *uttered phrases at once occult and familiar, like the amulet worn on the heart* (*Silas Marner* by George Eliot)

amusement NOUN here amusement means a strange and disturbing puzzle ❑ *this was an amusement the other way* (*Robinson Crusoe* by Daniel Defoe)

ancient NOUN an ancient was the flag displayed on a ship to show which country it belongs to. It is also called the ensign ❑ *her ancient and pendants out* (*Robinson Crusoe* by Daniel Defoe)

antic ADJ here antic means horrible or grotesque ❑ *armed and dressed after a very antic manner* (*Gulliver's Travels* by Jonathan Swift)

antics NOUN antics is an old word meaning clowns, or people who do silly things to make other people laugh ❑ *And point like antics at his triple crown* (*Doctor Faustus 3.2* by Christopher Marlowe)

appanage NOUN an appanage is a living

allowance ❏ *As if loveliness were not the special prerogative of woman–her legitimate appanage and heritage!* (*Jane Eyre* by Charlotte Brontë)

appended VERB appended means attached or added to ❏ *and these words appended* (*Treasure Island* by Robert Louis Stevenson)

approver NOUN an approver is someone who gives evidence against someone he used to work with ❏ *Mr. Noah Claypole: receiving a free pardon from the Crown in consequence of being admitted approver against Fagin* (*Oliver Twist* by Charles Dickens)

areas NOUN the areas is the space, below street level, in front of the basement of a house ❏ *The Dodger had a vicious propensity, too, of pulling the caps from the heads of small boys and tossing them down areas* (*Oliver Twist* by Charles Dickens)

argument NOUN theme or important idea or subject which runs through a piece of writing ❏ *Thrice needful to the argument which now* (*The Prelude* by William Wordsworth)

artificially ADV artfully or cleverly ❏ *and he with a sharp flint sharpened very artificially* (*Gulliver's Travels* by Jonathan Swift)

artist NOUN here artist means a skilled workman ❏ *This man was a most ingenious artist* (*Gulliver's Travels* by Jonathan Swift)

assizes NOUN assizes were regular court sessions which a visiting judge was in charge of ❏ *you shall hang at the next assizes* (*Treasure Island* by Robert Louis Stevenson)

attraction NOUN gravitation, or Newton's theory of gravitation ❏ *he predicted the same fate to attraction* (*Gulliver's Travels* by Jonathan Swift)

aver VERB to aver is to claim something strongly ❏ *for Jem Rodney, the mole catcher, averred that one evening as he was returning homeward* (*Silas Marner* by George Eliot)

baby NOUN here baby means doll, which is a child's toy that looks like a small person ❏ *and skilful dressing her baby* (*Gulliver's Travels* by Jonathan Swift)

bagatelle NOUN bagatelle is a game rather like billiards and pool ❏ *Breakfast had been ordered at a pleasant little tavern, a mile or so away upon the rising ground beyond the green; and there was a bagatelle board in the room, in case we should desire to unbend our minds after the solemnity.* (*Great Expectations* by Charles Dickens)

bah EXCLAM Bah is an exclamation of frustration or anger ❏ *"Bah," said Scrooge.* (*A Christmas Carol* by Charles Dickens)

bairn NOUN a northern word for child ❏ *Who has taught you those fine words, my bairn?* (*Wuthering Heights* by Emily Brontë)

bait VERB to bait means to stop on a journey to take refreshment ❏ *So, when they stopped to bait the horse, and ate and drank and enjoyed themselves, I could touch nothing that they touched, but kept my fast unbroken.* (*David Copperfield* by Charles Dickens)

balustrade NOUN a balustrade is a row of vertical columns that form railings ❏ *but I mean to say you might have got a hearse up that staircase, and taken it broadwise, with the splinter-bar towards the wall, and the door towards the balustrades: and done it easy* (*A Christmas Carol* by Charles Dickens)

bandbox NOUN a large lightweight box for carrying bonnets or hats ❏ *I am glad I bought my bonnet, if it is only for the fun of having another bandbox* (*Pride and Prejudice* by Jane Austen)

barren NOUN a barren here is a stretch or expanse of barren land ❏ *a line of upright stones, continued the* *length of the barren* (*Wuthering Heights* by Emily Brontë)

basin NOUN a basin was a cup without a handle ❑ *who is drinking his tea out of a basin* (*Wuthering Heights* by Emily Brontë)

battalia NOUN the order of battle ❑ *till I saw part of his army in battalia* (*Gulliver's Travels* by Jonathan Swift)

battery NOUN a Battery is a fort or a place where guns are positioned ❑ *You bring the lot to me, at that old Battery over yonder* (*Great Expectations* by Charles Dickens)

battledore and shuttlecock NOUN The game battledore and shuttlecock was an early version of the game now known as badminton. The aim of the early game was simply to keep the shuttlecock from hitting the ground. ❑ *Battledore and shuttlecock's a wery good game vhen you an't the shuttlecock and two lawyers the battledores, in which case it gets too excitin' to be pleasant* (*Pickwick Papers* by Charles Dickens)

beadle NOUN a beadle was a local official who had power over the poor ❑ *But these impertinences were speedily checked by the evidence of the surgeon, and the testimony of the beadle* (*Oliver Twist* by Charles Dickens)

bearings NOUN the bearings of a place are the measurements or directions that are used to find or locate it ❑ *the bearings of the island* (*Treasure Island* by Robert Louis Stevenson)

beaufet NOUN a beaufet was a sideboard ❑ *and sweet-cake from the beaufet* (*Emma* by Jane Austen)

beck NOUN a beck is a small stream ❑ *a beck which follows the bend of the glen* (*Wuthering Heights* by Emily Brontë)

bedight VERB decorated ❑ *and bedight with Christmas holly stuck into the top.* (*A Christmas Carol* by Charles Dickens)

Bedlam NOUN Bedlam was a lunatic asylum in London which had statues carved by Caius Gabriel Cibber at its entrance ❑ *Bedlam, and those carved maniacs at the gates* (*The Prelude* by William Wordsworth)

beeves NOUN oxen or castrated bulls which are animals used for pulling vehicles or carrying things ❑ *to deliver in every morning six beeves* (*Gulliver's Travels* by Jonathan Swift)

begot VERB created or caused ❑ *Begot in thee* (*On His Mistress* by John Donne)

behoof NOUN behoof means benefit ❑ *"Yes, young man," said he, releasing the handle of the article in question, retiring a step or two from my table, and speaking for the behoof of the landlord and waiter at the door* (*Great Expectations* by Charles Dickens)

berth NOUN a berth is a bed on a boat ❑ *this is the berth for me* (*Treasure Island* by Robert Louis Stevenson)

bevers NOUN a bever was a snack, or small portion of food, eaten between main meals ❑ *that buys me thirty meals a day and ten bevers* (*Doctor Faustus 2.1* by Christopher Marlowe)

bilge water NOUN the bilge is the widest part of a ship's bottom, and the bilge water is the dirty water that collects there ❑ *no gush of bilge-water had turned it to fetid puddle* (*Jane Eyre* by Charlotte Brontë)

bills NOUN bills is an old term meaning prescription. A prescription is the piece of paper on which your doctor writes an order for medicine and which you give to a chemist to get the medicine ❑ *Are not thy bills hung up as monuments* (*Doctor Faustus 1.1* by Christopher Marlowe)

black cap NOUN a judge wore a black cap when he was about to sentence a prisoner to death ❑ *The judge assumed the black cap, and the* *prisoner still stood with the same air and gesture. (Oliver Twist* by Charles Dickens)

boot-jack NOUN a wooden device to help take boots off ❏ *The speaker appeared to throw a boot-jack, or some such article, at the person he addressed (Oliver Twist* by Charles Dickens)

booty NOUN booty means treasure or prizes ❏ *would be inclined to give up their booty in payment of the dead man's debts (Treasure Island* by Robert Louis Stevenson)

Bow Street runner PHRASE Bow Street runners were the first British police force, set up by the author Henry Fielding in the eighteenth century ❏ *as would have convinced a judge or a Bow Street runner (Treasure Island* by Robert Louis Stevenson)

brawn NOUN brawn is a dish of meat which is set in jelly ❏ *Heaped up upon the floor, to form a kind of throne, were turkeys, geese, game, poultry, brawn, great joints of meat, sucking-pigs (A Christmas Carol* by Charles Dickens)

bray VERB when a donkey brays, it makes a loud, harsh sound ❏ *and she doesn't bray like a jackass (The Adventures of Huckleberry Finn* by Mark Twain)

break VERB in order to train a horse you first have to break it ❏ *"If a high-mettled creature like this," said he, "can't be broken by fair means, she will never be good for anything" (Black Beauty* by Anna Sewell)

bullyragging VERB bullyragging is an old word which means bullying. To bullyrag someone is to threaten or force someone to do something they don't want to do ❏ *and a lot of loafers bullyragging him for sport (The Adventures of Huckleberry Finn* by Mark Twain)

but PREP except for (this) ❏ *but this, all pleasures fancies be (The Good-Morrow* by John Donne)

by hand PHRASE by hand was a common expression of the time meaning that baby had been fed either using a spoon or a bottle rather than by breast-feeding ❏ *My sister, Mrs. Joe Gargery, was more than twenty years older than I, and had established a great reputation with herself . . . because she had bought me up 'by hand' (Great Expectations* by Charles Dickens)

bye-spots NOUN bye-spots are lonely places ❏ *and bye-spots of tales rich with indigenous produce (The Prelude* by William Wordsworth)

calico NOUN calico is plain white fabric made from cotton ❏ *There was two old dirty calico dresses (The Adventures of Huckleberry Finn* by Mark Twain)

camp-fever NOUN camp-fever was another word for the disease typhus ❏ *during a severe camp-fever (Emma* by Jane Austen)

cant NOUN cant is insincere or empty talk ❏ *"Man," said the Ghost, "if man you be in heart, not adamant, forbear that wicked cant until you have discovered What the surplus is, and Where it is." (A Christmas Carol* by Charles Dickens)

canty ADJ canty means lively, full of life ❏ *My mother lived til eighty, a canty dame to the last (Wuthering Heights* by Emily Brontë)

canvas VERB to canvas is to discuss ❏ *We think so very differently on this point Mr Knightley, that there can be no use in canvassing it (Emma* by Jane Austen)

capital ADJ capital means excellent or extremely good ❏ *for it's capital, so shady, light, and big (Little Women* by Louisa May Alcott)

capstan NOUN a capstan is a device used on a ship to lift sails and anchors ❏ *capstans going, ships going out to sea, and unintelligible sea creatures roaring curses over the bulwarks at respondent lightermen (Great Expectations* by Charles Dickens)

case-bottle NOUN a square bottle designed to fit with others into a case ❑ *The spirit being set before him in a huge case-bottle, which had originally come out of some ship's locker* (*The Old Curiosity Shop* by Charles Dickens)

casement NOUN casement is a word meaning window. The teacher in *Nicholas Nickleby* misspells window showing what a bad teacher he is ❑ *W-i-n, win, d-e-r, der, winder, a casement.* (*Nicholas Nickleby* by Charles Dickens)

cataleptic ADJ a cataleptic fit is one in which the victim goes into a trancelike state and remains still for a long time ❑ *It was at this point in their history that Silas's cataleptic fit occurred during the prayer-meeting* (*Silas Marner* by George Eliot)

cauldron NOUN a cauldron is a large cooking pot made of metal ❑ *stirring a large cauldron which seemed to be full of soup* (*Alice's Adventures in Wonderland* by Lewis Carroll)

cephalic ADJ cephalic means to do with the head ❑ *with ink composed of a cephalic tincture* (*Gulliver's Travels* by Jonathan Swift)

chaise and four NOUN a closed four-wheel carriage pulled by four horses ❑ *he came down on Monday in a chaise and four to see the place* (*Pride and Prejudice* by Jane Austen)

chamberlain NOUN the main servant in a household ❑ *In those times a bed was always to be got there at any hour of the night, and the chamberlain, letting me in at his ready wicket, lighted the candle next in order on his shelf* (*Great Expectations* by Charles Dickens)

characters NOUN distinguishing marks ❑ *Impressed upon all forms the characters* (*The Prelude* by William Wordsworth)

chary ADJ cautious ❑ *I should have been chary of discussing my guardian too freely even with her* (*Great Expectations* by Charles Dickens)

cherishes VERB here cherishes means cheers or brightens ❑ *some philosophic song of Truth that cherishes our daily life* (*The Prelude* by William Wordsworth)

chickens' meat PHRASE chickens' meat is an old term which means chickens' feed or food ❑ *I had shook a bag of chickens' meat out in that place* (*Robinson Crusoe* by Daniel Defoe)

chimeras NOUN a chimera is an unrealistic idea or a wish which is unlikely to be fulfilled ❑ *with many other wild impossible chimeras* (*Gulliver's Travels* by Jonathan Swift)

chines NOUN chine is a cut of meat that includes part or all of the backbone of the animal ❑ *and they found hams and chines uncut* (*Silas Marner* by George Eliot)

chits NOUN chits is a slang word which means girls ❑ *I hate affected, niminy-piminy chits!* (*Little Women* by Louisa May Alcott)

chopped VERB chopped means come suddenly or accidentally ❑ *if I had chopped upon them* (*Robinson Crusoe* by Daniel Defoe)

chute NOUN a narrow channel ❑ *One morning about day-break, I found a canoe and crossed over a chute to the main shore* (*The Adventures of Huckleberry Finn* by Mark Twain)

circumspection NOUN careful observation of events and circumstances; caution ❑ *I honour your circumspection* (*Pride and Prejudice* by Jane Austen)

clambered VERB clambered means to climb somewhere with difficulty, usually using your hands and your feet ❑ *he clambered up and down stairs* (*Treasure Island* by Robert Louis Stevenson)

clime NOUN climate ❑ *no season knows nor clime* (*The Sun Rising* by John Donne)

clinched VERB clenched ❏ *the tops whereof I could but just reach with my fist clinched* (*Gulliver's Travels* by Jonathan Swift)

close chair NOUN a close chair is a sedan chair, which is an covered chair which has room for one person. The sedan chair is carried on two poles by two men, one in front and one behind ❏ *persuaded even the Empress herself to let me hold her in her close chair* (*Gulliver's Travels* by Jonathan Swift)

clown NOUN clown here means peasant or person who lives off the land ❏ *In ancient days by emperor and clown* (*Ode on a Nightingale* by John Keats)

coalheaver NOUN a coalheaver loaded coal onto ships using a spade ❏ *Good, strong, wholesome medicine, as was given with great success to two Irish labourers and a coalheaver* (*Oliver Twist* by Charles Dickens)

coal-whippers NOUN men who worked at docks using machines to load coal onto ships ❏ *here, were colliers by the score and score, with the coal-whippers plunging off stages on deck* (*Great Expectations* by Charles Dickens)

cobweb NOUN a cobweb is the net which a spider makes for catching insects ❏ *the walls and ceilings were all hung round with cobwebs* (*Gulliver's Travels* by Jonathan Swift)

coddling VERB coddling means to treat someone too kindly or protect them too much ❏ *and I've been coddling the fellow as if I'd been his grandmother* (*Little Women* by Louisa May Alcott)

coil NOUN coil means noise or fuss or disturbance ❏ *What a coil is there?* (*Doctor Faustus 4.7* by Christopher Marlowe)

collared VERB to collar something is a slang term which means to capture. In this sentence, it means he stole it [the money] ❏ *he collared it* (*The Adventures of Huckleberry Finn* by Mark Twain)

colling VERB colling is an old word which means to embrace and kiss ❏ *and no clasping and colling at all* (*Tess of the D'Urbervilles* by Thomas Hardy)

colloquies NOUN colloquy is a formal conversation or dialogue ❏ *Such colloquies have occupied many a pair of pale-faced weavers* (*Silas Marner* by George Eliot)

comfit NOUN sugar-covered pieces of fruit or nut eaten as sweets ❏ *and pulled out a box of comfits* (*Alice's Adventures in Wonderland* by Lewis Carroll)

coming out VERB when a girl came out in society it meant she was of marriageable age. In order to 'come out' girls were expecting to attend balls and other parties during a season ❏ *The younger girls formed hopes of coming out a year or two sooner than they might otherwise have done* (*Pride and Prejudice* by Jane Austen)

commit VERB commit means arrest or stop ❏ *Commit the rascals* (*Doctor Faustus 4.7* by Christopher Marlowe)

commodious ADJ commodious means convenient ❏ *the most commodious and effectual ways* (*Gulliver's Travels* by Jonathan Swift)

commons NOUN commons is an old term meaning food shared with others ❏ *his pauper assistants ranged themselves behind him; the gruel was served out; and a long grace was said over the short commons.* (*Oliver Twist* by Charles Dickens)

complacency NOUN here complacency means a desire to please others. To-day complacency means feeling pleased with oneself without good reason. ❏ *Twas thy power that raised the first complacency in me* (*The Prelude* by William Wordsworth)

complaisance NOUN complaisance was eagerness to please ❏ *we cannot wonder at his complaisance* (*Pride and Prejudice* by Jane Austen)

complaisant ADJ complaisant means polite ❑ *extremely cheerful and complaisant to their guest* (*Gulliver's Travels* by Jonathan Swift)

conning VERB conning means learning by heart ❑ *Or conning more* (*The Prelude* by William Wordsworth)

consequent NOUN consequence ❑ *as avarice is the necessary consequent of old age* (*Gulliver's Travels* by Jonathan Swift)

consorts NOUN concerts ❑ *The King, who delighted in music, had frequent consorts at Court* (*Gulliver's Travels* by Jonathan Swift)

conversible ADJ conversible meant easy to talk to, companionable ❑ *He can be a conversible companion* (*Pride and Prejudice* by Jane Austen)

copper NOUN a copper is a large pot that can be heated directly over a fire ❑ *He gazed in stupefied astonishment on the small rebel for some seconds, and then clung for support to the copper* (*Oliver Twist* by Charles Dickens)

copper-stick NOUN a copper-stick is the long piece of wood used to stir washing in the copper (or boiler) which was usually the biggest cooking pot in the house ❑ *It was Christmas Eve, and I had to stir the pudding for next day, with a copper-stick, from seven to eight by the Dutch clock* (*Great Expectations* by Charles Dickens)

counting-house NOUN a counting-house is a place where accountants work ❑ *Once upon a time—of all the good days in the year, on Christmas Eve—old Scrooge sat busy in his counting-house* (*A Christmas Carol* by Charles Dickens)

courtier NOUN a courtier is someone who attends the king or queen—a member of the court ❑ *next the ten courtiers;* (*Alice's Adventures in Wonderland* by Lewis Carroll)

covies NOUN covies were flocks of partridges ❑ *and will save all of the best covies for you* (*Pride and Prejudice* by Jane Austen)

cowed VERB cowed means frightened or intimidated ❑ *it cowed me more than the pain* (*Treasure Island* by Robert Louis Stevenson)

cozened VERB cozened means tricked or deceived ❑ *Do you remember, sir, how you cozened me* (*Doctor Faustus 4.7* by Christopher Marlowe)

cravats NOUN a cravat is a folded cloth that a man wears wrapped around his neck as a decorative item of clothing ❑ *we'd 'a' slept in our cravats to-night* (*The Adventures of Huckleberry Finn* by Mark Twain)

crock and dirt PHRASE crock and dirt is an old expression meaning soot and dirt ❑ *and the mare catching cold at the door, and the boy grimed with crock and dirt* (*Great Expectations* by Charles Dickens)

crockery NOUN here crockery means pottery ❑ *By one of the parrots was a cat made of crockery* (*The Adventures of Huckleberry Finn* by Mark Twain)

crooked sixpence PHRASE it was considered unlucky to have a bent sixpence ❑ *You've got the beauty, you see, and I've got the luck, so you must keep me by you for your crooked sixpence* (*Silas Marner* by George Eliot)

croquet NOUN croquet is a traditional English summer game in which players try to hit wooden balls through hoops ❑ *and once she remembered trying to box her own ears for having cheated herself in a game of croquet* (*Alice's Adventures in Wonderland* by Lewis Carroll)

cross PREP across ❑ *The two great streets, which run cross and divide it into four quarters* (*Gulliver's Travels* by Jonathan Swift)

culpable ADJ if you are culpable for something it means you are to blame ❑ *deep are the sorrows that spring from false ideas for which no*

man is culpable. (*Silas Marner* by George Eliot)

cultured ADJ cultivated ❑ *Nor less when spring had warmed the cultured Vale* (*The Prelude* by William Wordsworth)

cupidity NOUN cupidity is greed ❑ *These people hated me with the hatred of cupidity and disappointment.* (*Great Expectations* by Charles Dickens)

curricle NOUN an open two-wheeled carriage with one seat for the driver and space for a single passenger ❑ *and they saw a lady and a gentleman in a curricle* (*Pride and Prejudice* by Jane Austen)

cynosure NOUN a cynosure is something that strongly attracts attention or admiration ❑ *Then I thought of Eliza and Georgiana; I beheld one the cynosure of a ballroom, the other the inmate of a convent cell* (*Jane Eyre* by Charlotte Brontë)

dalliance NOUN someone's dalliance with something is a brief involvement with it ❑ *nor sporting in the dalliance of love* (*Doctor Faustus Chorus* by Christopher Marlowe)

darkling ADV darkling is an archaic way of saying in the dark ❑ *Darkling I listen* (*Ode on a Nightingale* by John Keats)

delf-case NOUN a sideboard for holding dishes and crockery ❑ *at the pewter dishes and delf-case* (*Wuthering Heights* by Emily Brontë)

determined ■ VERB here determined means ended ❑ *and be out of vogue when that was determined* (*Gulliver's Travels* by Jonathan Swift) ■ VERB determined can mean to have been learned or found especially by investigation or experience ❑ *All the sensitive feelings it wounded so cruelly, all the shame and misery it kept alive within my breast, became more poignant as I thought of this; and I determined that the life was unendurable* (*David Copperfield* by Charles Dickens)

Deuce NOUN a slang term for the Devil ❑ *Ah, I dare say I did. Deuce take me, he added suddenly, I know I did. I find I am not quite unscrewed yet.* (*Great Expectations* by Charles Dickens)

diabolical ADJ diabolical means devilish or evil ❑ *and with a thousand diabolical expressions* (*Treasure Island* by Robert Louis Stevenson)

direction NOUN here direction means address ❑ *Elizabeth was not surprised at it, as Jane had written the direction remarkably ill* (*Pride and Prejudice* by Jane Austen)

discover VERB to make known or announce ❑ *the Emperor would discover the secret while I was out of his power* (*Gulliver's Travels* by Jonathan Swift)

dissemble VERB hide or conceal ❑ *Dissemble nothing* (*On His Mistress* by John Donne)

dissolve VERB dissolve here means to release from life, to die ❑ *Fade far away, dissolve, and quite forget* (*Ode on a Nightingale* by John Keats)

distrain VERB to distrain is to seize the property of someone who is in debt in compensation for the money owed ❑ *for he's threatening to distrain for it* (*Silas Marner* by George Eliot)

Divan NOUN a Divan was originally a Turkish council of state—the name was transferred to the couches they sat on and is used to mean this in English ❑ *Mr Brass applauded this picture very much, and the bed being soft and comfortable, Mr Quilp determined to use it, both as a sleeping place by night and as a kind of Divan by day.* (*The Old Curiosity Shop* by Charles Dickens)

divorcement NOUN separation ❑ *By all pains which want and divorcement hath* (*On His Mistress* by John Donne)

dog in the manger, PHRASE this phrase describes someone who prevents you from enjoying something that they themselves have no need for ❏ *You are a dog in the manger, Cathy, and desire no one to be loved but yourself* (*Wuthering Heights* by Emily Brontë)

dolorifuge NOUN dolorifuge is a word which Thomas Hardy invented. It means pain-killer or comfort ❏ *as a species of dolorifuge* (*Tess of the D'Urbervilles* by Thomas Hardy)

dome NOUN building ❏ *that river and that mouldering dome* (*The Prelude* by William Wordsworth)

domestic NOUN here domestic means a person's management of the house ❏ *to give some account of my domestic* (*Gulliver's Travels* by Jonathan Swift)

dunce NOUN a dunce is another word for idiot ❏ *Do you take me for a dunce? Go on?* (*Alice's Adventures in Wonderland* by Lewis Carroll)

Ecod EXCLAM a slang exclamation meaning 'oh God!' ❏ *"Ecod," replied Wemmick, shaking his head, "that's not my trade."* (*Great Expectations* by Charles Dickens)

egg-hot NOUN an egg-hot (see also 'flip' and 'negus') was a hot drink made from beer and eggs, sweetened with nutmeg ❏ *She fainted when she saw me return, and made a little jug of egg-hot afterwards to console us while we talked it over.* (*David Copperfield* by Charles Dickens)

encores NOUN an encore is a short extra performance at the end of a longer one, which the entertainer gives because the audience has enthusiastically asked for it ❏ *we want a little something to answer encores with, anyway* (*The Adventures of Huckleberry Finn* by Mark Twain)

equipage NOUN an elegant and impressive carriage ❏ *and besides, the equipage did not answer to any of their neighbours* (*Pride and Prejudice* by Jane Austen)

exordium NOUN an exordium is the opening part of a speech ❏ *"Now,*

Handel," as if it were the grave beginning of a portentous business exordium, he had suddenly given up that tone (*Great Expectations* by Charles Dickens)

expect VERB here expect means to wait for ❏ *to expect his farther commands* (*Gulliver's Travels* by Jonathan Swift)

familiars NOUN familiars means spirits or devils who come to someone when they are called ❏ *I'll turn all the lice about thee into familiars* (*Doctor Faustus 1.4* by Christopher Marlowe)

fantods NOUN a fantod is a person who fidgets or can't stop moving nervously ❏ *It most give me the fantods* (*The Adventures of Huckleberry Finn* by Mark Twain)

farthing NOUN a farthing is an old unit of British currency which was worth a quarter of a penny ❏ *Not a farthing less. A great many back-payments are included in it, I assure you.* (*A Christmas Carol* by Charles Dickens)

farthingale NOUN a hoop worn under a skirt to extend it ❏ *A bell with an old voice–which I dare say in its time had often said to the house, Here is the green farthingale* (*Great Expectations* by Charles Dickens)

favours NOUN here favours is an old word which means ribbons ❏ *A group of humble mourners entered the gate: wearing white favours* (*Oliver Twist* by Charles Dickens)

feigned VERB pretend or pretending ❏ *not my feigned page* (*On His Mistress* by John Donne)

fence ◼ NOUN a fence is someone who receives and sells stolen goods ❏ *What are you up to? Ill-treating the boys, you covetous, avaricious, in-sa-ti-a-ble old fence?* (*Oliver Twist* by Charles Dickens) ◼ NOUN defence or protection ❏ *but honesty hath no fence against superior cunning* (*Gulliver's Travels* by Jonathan Swift)

fess ADJ fess is an old word which means pleased or proud ❑ *You'll be fess enough, my poppet* (*Tess of the D'Urbervilles* by Thomas Hardy)

fettered ADJ fettered means bound in chains or chained ❑ *"You are fettered," said Scrooge, trembling. "Tell me why?"* (*A Christmas Carol* by Charles Dickens)

fidges VERB fidges means fidgets, which is to keep moving your hands slightly because you are nervous or excited ❑ *Look, Jim, how my fingers fidges* (*Treasure Island* by Robert Louis Stevenson)

finger-post NOUN a finger-post is a sign-post showing the direction to different places ❑ *"The gallows," continued Fagin, "the gallows, my dear, is an ugly finger-post, which points out a very short and sharp turning that has stopped many a bold fellow's career on the broad highway."* (*Oliver Twist* by Charles Dickens)

fire-irons NOUN fire-irons are tools kept by the side of the fire to either cook with or look after the fire ❑ *the fire-irons came first* (*Alice's Adventures in Wonderland* by Lewis Carroll)

fire-plug NOUN a fire-plug is another word for a fire hydrant ❑ *The pony looked with great attention into a fire-plug, which was near him, and appeared to be quite absorbed in contemplating it* (*The Old Curiosity Shop* by Charles Dickens)

flank NOUN flank is the side of an animal ❑ *And all her silken flanks with garlands dressed* (*Ode on a Grecian Urn* by John Keats)

flip NOUN a flip is a drink made from warmed ale, sugar, spice and beaten egg ❑ *The events of the day, in combination with the twins, if not with the flip, had made Mrs. Micawber hysterical, and she shed tears as she replied* (*David Copperfield* by Charles Dickens)

flit VERB flit means to move quickly ❑ *and if he had meant to flit to Thrushcross Grange* (*Wuthering Heights* by Emily Brontë)

floorcloth NOUN a floorcloth was a hard-wearing piece of canvas used instead of carpet ❑ *This avenging phantom was ordered to be on duty at eight on Tuesday morning in the hall (it was two feet square, as charged for floorcloth)* (*Great Expectations* by Charles Dickens)

fly-driver NOUN a fly-driver is a carriage drawn by a single horse ❑ *The fly-drivers, among whom I inquired next, were equally jocose and equally disrespectful* (*David Copperfield* by Charles Dickens)

fob NOUN a small pocket in which a watch is kept ❑ *"Certain," replied the man, drawing a gold watch from his fob* (*Oliver Twist* by Charles Dickens)

folly NOUN folly means foolishness or stupidity ❑ *the folly of beginning a work* (*Robinson Crusoe* by Daniel Defoe)

fond ADJ fond means foolish ❑ *Fond worldling* (*Doctor Faustus 5.2* by Christopher Marlowe)

fondness NOUN silly or foolish affection ❑ *They have no fondness for their colts or foals* (*Gulliver's Travels* by Jonathan Swift)

for his fancy PHRASE for his fancy means for his liking or as he wanted ❑ *and as I did not obey quick enough for his fancy* (*Treasure Island* by Robert Louis Stevenson)

forlorn ADJ lost or very upset ❑ *you are from that day forlorn* (*Gulliver's Travels* by Jonathan Swift)

foster-sister NOUN a foster-sister was someone brought up by the same nurse or in the same household ❑ *I had been his foster-sister* (*Wuthering Heights* by Emily Brontë)

fox-fire NOUN fox-fire is a weak glow that is given off by decaying, rotten wood ❑ *what we must have was a lot of them rotten chunks that's called fox-fire* (*The*

Adventures of Huckleberry Finn by Mark Twain)

frozen sea PHRASE the Arctic Ocean ❑ *into the frozen sea* (*Gulliver's Travels* by Jonathan Swift)

gainsay VERB to gainsay something is to say it isn't true or to deny it ❑ *"So she had," cried Scrooge. "You're right. I'll not gainsay it, Spirit. God forbid!"* (*A Christmas Carol* by Charles Dickens)

gaiters NOUN gaiters were leggings made of a cloth or piece of leather which covered the leg from the knee to the ankle ❑ *Mr Knightley was hard at work upon the lower buttons of his thick leather gaiters* (*Emma* by Jane Austen)

galluses NOUN galluses is an old spelling of gallows, and here means suspenders. Suspenders are straps worn over someone's shoulders and fastened to their trousers to prevent the trousers falling down ❑ *and home-knit galluses* (*The Adventures of Huckleberry Finn* by Mark Twain)

galoot NOUN a sailor but also a clumsy person ❑ *and maybe a galoot on it chopping* (*The Adventures of Huckleberry Finn* by Mark Twain)

gayest ADJ gayest means the most lively and bright or merry ❑ *Beth played her gayest march* (*Little Women* by Louisa May Alcott)

gem NOUN here gem means jewellery ❑ *the mountain shook off turf and flower, had only heath for raiment and crag for gem* (*Jane Eyre* by Charlotte Brontë)

giddy ADJ giddy means dizzy ❑ *and I wish you wouldn't keep appearing and vanishing so suddenly; you make one quite giddy.* (*Alice's Adventures in Wonderland* by Lewis Carroll)

gig NOUN a light two-wheeled carriage ❑ *when a gig drove up to the garden gate: out of which there jumped a fat gentleman* (*Oliver Twist* by Charles Dickens)

gladsome ADJ gladsome is an old word meaning glad or happy ❑ *Nobody ever stopped him in the street to say, with gladsome looks* (*A Christmas Carol* by Charles Dickens)

glen NOUN a glen is a small valley; the word is used commonly in Scotland ❑ *a beck which follows the bend of the glen* (*Wuthering Heights* by Emily Brontë)

gravelled VERB gravelled is an old term which means to baffle or defeat someone ❑ *Gravelled the pastors of the German Church* (*Doctor Faustus 1.1* by Christopher Marlowe)

grinder NOUN a grinder was a private tutor ❑ *but that when he had had the happiness of marrying Mrs Pocket very early in his life, he had impaired his prospects and taken up the calling of a Grinder* (*Great Expectations* by Charles Dickens)

gruel NOUN gruel is a thin, watery cornmeal or oatmeal soup ❑ *and the little saucepan of gruel (Scrooge had a cold in his head) upon the hob.* (*A Christmas Carol* by Charles Dickens)

guinea, half a NOUN half a guinea was ten shillings and sixpence ❑ *but lay out half a guinea at Ford's* (*Emma* by Jane Austen)

gull VERB gull is an old term which means to fool or deceive someone ❑ *Hush, I'll gull him supernaturally* (*Doctor Faustus 3.4* by Christopher Marlowe)

gunnel NOUN the gunnel, or gunwale, is the upper edge of a boat's side ❑ *But he put his foot on the gunnel and rocked her* (*The Adventures of Huckleberry Finn* by Mark Twain)

gunwale NOUN the side of a ship ❑ *He dipped his hand in the water over the boat's gunwale* (*Great Expectations* by Charles Dickens)

Gytrash NOUN a Gytrash is an omen of misfortune to the superstitious, usually taking the form of a hound ❑ *I remembered certain of Bessie's tales, wherein figured a*

North-of-England spirit, called a 'Gytrash' (Jane Eyre by Charlotte Brontë)

hackney-cabriolet NOUN a two-wheeled carriage with four seats for hire and pulled by a horse ❑ *A hackney-cabriolet was in waiting; with the same vehemence which she had exhibited in addressing Oliver, the girl pulled him in with her, and drew the curtains close. (Oliver Twist* by Charles Dickens)

hackney-coach NOUN a four-wheeled horse-drawn vehicle for hire ❑ *The twilight was beginning to close in, when Mr. Brownlow alighted from a hackney-coach at his own door, and knocked softly. (Oliver Twist* by Charles Dickens)

haggler NOUN a haggler is someone who travels from place to place selling small goods and items ❑ *when I be plain Jack Durbeyfield, the haggler (Tess of the D'Urbervilles* by Thomas Hardy)

halter NOUN a halter is a rope or strap used to lead an animal or to tie it up ❑ *I had of course long been used to a halter and a headstall (Black Beauty* by Anna Sewell)

hamlet NOUN a hamlet is a small village or a group of houses in the countryside ❑ *down from the hamlet (Treasure Island* by Robert Louis Stevenson)

hand-barrow NOUN a hand-barrow is a device for carrying heavy objects. It is like a wheelbarrow except that it has handles, rather than wheels, for moving the barrow ❑ *his sea chest following behind him in a hand-barrow (Treasure Island* by Robert Louis Stevenson)

handspike NOUN a handspike was a stick which was used as a lever ❑ *a bit of stick like a handspike (Treasure Island* by Robert Louis Stevenson)

haply ADV haply means by chance or perhaps ❑ *And haply the Queen-Moon is on her throne (Ode on a Nightingale* by John Keats)

harem NOUN the harem was the part of the house where the women lived ❑ *mostly they hang round the harem (The Adventures of Huckleberry Finn* by Mark Twain)

hautboys NOUN hautboys are oboes ❑ *sausages and puddings resembling flutes and hautboys (Gulliver's Travels* by Jonathan Swift)

hawker NOUN a hawker is someone who sells goods to people as he travels rather than from a fixed place like a shop ❑ *to buy some stockings from a hawker (Treasure Island* by Robert Louis Stevenson)

hawser NOUN a hawser is a rope used to tie up or tow a ship or boat ❑ *Again among the tiers of shipping, in and out, avoiding rusty chain-cables, frayed hempen hawsers (Great Expectations* by Charles Dickens)

headstall NOUN the headstall is the part of the bridle or halter that goes around a horse's head ❑ *I had of course long been used to a halter and a headstall (Black Beauty* by Anna Sewell)

hearken VERB hearken means to listen ❑ *though we sometimes stopped to lay hold of each other and hearken (Treasure Island* by Robert Louis Stevenson)

heartless ADJ here heartless means without heart or dejected ❑ *I am not heartless (The Prelude* by William Wordsworth)

hebdomadal ADJ hebdomadal means weekly ❑ *It was the hebdomadal treat to which we all looked forward from Sabbath to Sabbath (Jane Eyre* by Charlotte Brontë)

highwaymen NOUN highwaymen were people who stopped travellers and robbed them ❑ *We are high-waymen (The Adventures of Huckleberry Finn* by Mark Twain)

hinds NOUN hinds means farm hands, or people who work on a farm ❑ *He called his hinds about him (Gulliver's Travels* by Jonathan Swift)

histrionic ADJ if you refer to some-one's behaviour as histrionic, you are being critical of it because it is dramatic and exaggerated ❑ *But the histrionic muse is the darling* (*The Adventures of Huckleberry Finn* by Mark Twain)

hogs NOUN hogs is another word for pigs ❑ *Tom called the hogs 'ingots'* (*The Adventures of Huckleberry Finn* by Mark Twain)

horrors NOUN the horrors are a fit, called delirium tremens, which is caused by drinking too much alcohol ❑ *I'll have the horrors* (*Treasure Island* by Robert Louis Stevenson)

huffy ADJ huffy means to be obviously annoyed or offended about some-thing ❑ *They will feel that more than angry speeches or huffy actions* (*Little Women* by Louisa May Alcott)

hulks NOUN hulks were prison-ships ❑ *The miserable companion of thieves and ruffians, the fallen outcast of low haunts, the associate of the scourings of the jails and hulks* (*Oliver Twist* by Charles Dickens)

humbug NOUN humbug means nonsense or rubbish ❑ *"Bah," said Scrooge. "Humbug!"* (*A Christmas Carol* by Charles Dickens)

humours NOUN it was believed that there were four fluids in the body called humours which decided the temperament of a person depending on how much of each fluid was present ❑ *other peccant humours* (*Gulliver's Travels* by Jonathan Swift)

husbandry NOUN husbandry is farming animals ❑ *bad husbandry were plentifully anointing their wheels* (*Silas Marner* by George Eliot)

huswife NOUN a huswife was a small sewing kit ❑ *but I had put my huswife on it* (*Emma* by Jane Austen)

ideal ADJ ideal in this context means imaginary ❑ *I discovered the yell was not ideal* (*Wuthering Heights* by Emily Brontë)

If our two PHRASE if both our ❑ *If our two loves be one* (*The Good-Morrow* by John Donne)

ignis-fatuus NOUN ignis-fatuus is the light given out by burning marsh gases, which lead careless travellers into danger ❑ *it is madness in all women to let a secret love kindle within them, which, if unreturned and unknown, must devour the life that feeds it; and, if discovered and responded to, must lead ignis-fatuus-like, into miry wilds whence there is no extrication.* (*Jane Eyre* by Charlotte Brontë)

imaginations NOUN here imaginations means schemes or plans ❑ *soon drove out those imaginations* (*Gulliver's Travels* by Jonathan Swift)

impressible ADJ impressible means open or impressionable ❑ *for Marner had one of those impressible, self-doubting natures* (*Silas Marner* by George Eliot)

in good intelligence PHRASE friendly with each other ❑ *that these two persons were in good intelligence with each other* (*Gulliver's Travels* by Jonathan Swift)

inanity NOUN inanity is silliness or dull stupidity ❑ *Do we not wile away moments of inanity* (*Silas Marner* by George Eliot)

incivility NOUN incivility means rude-ness or impoliteness ❑ *if it's only for a piece of incivility like to-night's* (*Treasure Island* by Robert Louis Stevenson)

indigenae NOUN indigenae means natives or people from that area ❑ *an exotic that the surly indigenae will not recognise for kin* (*Wuthering Heights* by Emily Brontë)

indocible ADJ unteachable ❑ *so they were the most restive and indocible* (*Gulliver's Travels* by Jonathan Swift)

ingenuity NOUN inventiveness ❑ *entreated me to give him something as an encouragement to ingenuity* (*Gulliver's Travels* by Jonathan Swift)

ingots NOUN an ingot is a lump of a valuable metal like gold, usually shaped like a brick ❑ *Tom called the hogs 'ingots' (The Adventures of Huckleberry Finn* by Mark Twain)

inkstand NOUN an inkstand is a pot which was put on a desk to contain either ink or pencils and pens ❑ *throwing an inkstand at the Lizard as she spoke (Alice's Adventures in Wonderland* by Lewis Carroll)

inordinate ADJ without order. To-day inordinate means 'excessive'. ❑ *Though yet untutored and inordinate (The Prelude* by William Wordsworth)

intellectuals NOUN here intellectuals means the minds (of the workmen) ❑ *those instructions they give being too refined for the intellectuals of their workmen (Gulliver's Travels* by Jonathan Swift)

interview NOUN meeting ❑ *By our first strange and fatal interview (On His Mistress* by John Donne)

jacks NOUN jacks are rods for turning a spit over a fire ❑ *It was a small bit of pork suspended from the kettle hanger by a string passed through a large door key, in a way known to primitive housekeepers unpossessed of jacks (Silas Marner* by George Eliot)

jews-harp NOUN a jews-harp is a small, metal, musical instrument that is played by the mouth ❑ *A jews-harp's plenty good enough for a rat (The Adventures of Huckleberry Finn* by Mark Twain)

jorum NOUN a large bowl ❑ *while Miss Skiffins brewed such a jorum of tea, that the pig in the back premises became strongly excited (Great Expectations* by Charles Dickens)

jostled VERB jostled means bumped or pushed by someone or some people ❑ *being jostled himself into the kennel (Gulliver's Travels* by Jonathan Swift)

keepsake NOUN a keepsake is a gift which reminds someone of an

event or of the person who gave it to them. ❑ *books and ornaments they had in their boudoirs at home: keepsakes that different relations had presented to them (Jane Eyre* by Charlotte Brontë)

kenned VERB kenned means knew ❑ *though little kenned the lamplighter that he had any company but Christmas! (A Christmas Carol* by Charles Dickens)

kennel NOUN kennel means gutter, which is the edge of a road next to the pavement, where rain water collects and flows away ❑ *being jostled himself into the kennel (Gulliver's Travels* by Jonathan Swift)

knock-knee ADJ knock-knee means slanted, at an angle. ❑ *LOT 1 was marked in whitewashed knock-knee letters on the brewhouse (Great Expectations* by Charles Dickens)

ladylike ADJ to be ladylike is to behave in a polite, dignified and graceful way ❑ *No, winking isn't ladylike (Little Women* by Louisa May Alcott)

lapse NOUN flow ❑ *Stealing with silent lapse to join the brook (The Prelude* by William Wordsworth)

larry NOUN larry is an old word which means commotion or noisy celebration ❑ *That was all a part of the larry! (Tess of the D'Urbervilles* by Thomas Hardy)

laths NOUN laths are strips of wood ❑ *The panels shrunk, the windows cracked; fragments of plaster fell out of the ceiling, and the naked laths were shown instead (A Christmas Carol* by Charles Dickens)

leer NOUN a leer is an unpleasant smile ❑ *with a kind of leer (Treasure Island* by Robert Louis Stevenson)

lenitives NOUN these are different kinds of drugs or medicines: lenitives and palliatives were pain relievers; aperitives were laxatives; abstersives caused vomiting; corrosives destroyed human tissue; restringents caused constipation;

cephalalgics stopped headaches; icterics were used as medicine for jaundice; apophlegmatics were cough medicine, and acoustics were cures for the loss of hearing ❑ *lenitives, aperitives, abstersives, corrosives, restringents, palliatives, laxatives, cephalalgics, icterics, apophlegmatics, acoustics* (*Gulliver's Travels* by Jonathan Swift)

lest CONJ in case. If you do something lest something (usually) unpleasant happens you do it to try to prevent it happening ❑ *She went in without knocking, and hurried upstairs, in great fear lest she should meet the real Mary Ann* (*Alice's Adventures in Wonderland* by Lewis Carroll)

levee NOUN a levee is an old term for a meeting held in the morning, shortly after the person holding the meeting has got out of bed ❑ *I used to attend the King's levee once or twice a week* (*Gulliver's Travels* by Jonathan Swift)

life-preserver NOUN a club which had lead inside it to make it heavier and therefore more dangerous ❑ *and with no more suspicious articles displayed to view than two or three heavy bludgeons which stood in a corner, and a 'life-preserver' that hung over the chimney-piece.* (*Oliver Twist* by Charles Dickens)

lighterman NOUN a lighterman is another word for sailor ❑ *in and out, hammers going in ship-builders' yards, saws going at timber, clashing engines going at things unknown, pumps going in leaky ships, capstans going, ships going out to sea, and unintelligible sea creatures roaring curses over the bulwarks at respondent lightermen* (*Great Expectations* by Charles Dickens)

livery NOUN servants often wore a uniform known as a livery ❑ *suddenly a footman in livery came running out of the wood* (*Alice's Adventures in Wonderland* by Lewis Carroll)

livid ADJ livid means pale or ash coloured. Livid also means very angry ❑ *a dirty, livid white* (*Treasure Island* by Robert Louis Stevenson)

lottery-tickets NOUN a popular card game ❑ *and Mrs. Philips protested that they would have a nice comfortable noisy game of lottery tickets* (*Pride and Prejudice* by Jane Austen)

lower and upper world PHRASE the earth and the heavens are the lower and upper worlds ❑ *the changes in the lower and upper world* (*Gulliver's Travels* by Jonathan Swift)

lustres NOUN lustres are chandeliers. A chandelier is a large, decorative frame which holds light bulbs or candles and hangs from the ceiling ❑ *the lustres, lights, the carving and the guilding* (*The Prelude* by William Wordsworth)

lynched VERB killed without a criminal trial by a crowd of people ❑ *He'll never know how nigh he come to getting lynched* (*The Adventures of Huckleberry Finn* by Mark Twain)

malingering VERB if someone is malingering they are pretending to be ill to avoid working ❑ *And you stand there malingering* (*Treasure Island* by Robert Louis Stevenson)

managing PHRASE treating with consideration ❑ *to think the honour of my own kind not worth managing* (*Gulliver's Travels* by Jonathan Swift)

manhood PHRASE manhood means human nature ❑ *concerning the nature of manhood* (*Gulliver's Travels* by Jonathan Swift)

man-trap NOUN a man-trap is a set of steel jaws that snap shut when trodden on and trap a person's leg ❑ *"Don't go to him," I called out of the window, "he's an assassin! A man-trap!"* (*Oliver Twist* by Charles Dickens)

maps NOUN charts of the night sky ❑

Let maps to others, worlds on worlds have shown (*The Good-Morrow* by John Donne)

mark VERB look at or notice ❑ *Mark but this flea, and mark in this* (*The Flea* by John Donne)

maroons NOUN A maroon is someone who has been left in a place which it is difficult for them to escape from, like a small island ❑ *if schooners, islands, and maroons* (*Treasure Island* by Robert Louis Stevenson)

mast NOUN here mast means the fruit of forest trees ❑ *a quantity of acorns, dates, chestnuts, and other mast* (*Gulliver's Travels* by Jonathan Swift)

mate VERB defeat ❑ *Where Mars did mate the warlike Carthigens* (*Doctor Faustus Chorus* by Christopher Marlowe)

mealy ADJ Mealy when used to describe a face meant pallid, pale or colourless ❑ *I only know two sorts of boys. Mealy boys, and beef-faced boys* (*Oliver Twist* by Charles Dickens)

middling ADV fairly or moderately ❑ *she worked me middling hard for about an hour* (*The Adventures of Huckleberry Finn* by Mark Twain)

mill NOUN a mill, or treadmill, was a device for hard labour or punishment in prison ❑ *Was you never on the mill?* (*Oliver Twist* by Charles Dickens)

milliner's shop NOUN a milliner's sold fabrics, clothing, lace and accessories; as time went on they specialized more and more in hats ❑ *to pay their duty to their aunt and to a milliner's shop just over the way* (*Pride and Prejudice* by Jane Austen)

minching un' munching PHRASE how people in the north of England used to describe the way people from the south speak ❑ *Minching un' munching!* (*Wuthering Heights* by Emily Brontë)

mine NOUN gold ❑ *Whether both*

th'Indias of spice and mine (*The Sun Rising* by John Donne)

mire NOUN mud ❑ *Tis my fate to be always ground into the mire under the iron heel of oppression* (*The Adventures of Huckleberry Finn* by Mark Twain)

miscellany NOUN a miscellany is a collection of many different kinds of things ❑ *under that, the miscellany began* (*Treasure Island* by Robert Louis Stevenson)

mistarshers NOUN mistarshers means moustache, which is the hair that grows on a man's upper lip ❑ *when he put his hand up to his mistarshers* (*Tess of the D'Urbervilles* by Thomas Hardy)

morrow NOUN here good-morrow means tomorrow and a new and better life ❑ *And now good-morrow to our waking souls* (*The Good-Morrow* by John Donne)

mortification NOUN mortification is an old word for gangrene which is when part of the body decays or 'dies' because of disease ❑ *Yes, it was a mortification–that was it* (*The Adventures of Huckleberry Finn* by Mark Twain)

mought VERB mought is an old spelling of might ❑ *what you mought call me? You mought call me captain* (*Treasure Island* by Robert Louis Stevenson)

move VERB move me not means do not make me angry ❑ *Move me not, Faustus* (*Doctor Faustus 2.1* by Christopher Marlowe)

muffin-cap NOUN a muffin-cap is a flat cap made from wool ❑ *the old one, remained stationary in the muffin-cap and leathers* (*Oliver Twist* by Charles Dickens)

mulatter NOUN a mulatter was another word for mulatto, which is a person with parents who are from different races ❑ *a mulatter, most as white as a white man* (*The Adventures of Huckleberry Finn* by Mark Twain)

mummery NOUN mummery is an old

word that meant meaningless (or pretentious) ceremony ❏ *When they were all gone, and when Trabb and his men—but not his boy: I looked for him—had crammed their mummery into bags, and were gone too, the house felt wholesomer.* (*Great Expectations* by Charles Dickens)

nap NOUN the nap is the woolly surface on a new item of clothing. Here the surface has been worn away so it looks bare ❏ *like an old hat with the nap rubbed off* (*The Adventures of Huckleberry Finn* by Mark Twain)

natural ■ NOUN a natural is a person born with learning difficulties ❏ *though he had been left to his particular care by their deceased father, who thought him almost a natural.* (*David Copperfield* by Charles Dickens) ■ ADJ natural meant illegitimate ❏ *Harriet Smith was the natural daughter of somebody* (*Emma* by Jane Austen)

navigator NOUN a navigator was originally someone employed to dig canals. It is the origin of the word 'navvy' meaning a labourer ❏ *She ascertained from me in a few words what it was all about, comforted Dora, and gradually convinced her that I was not a labourer—from my manner of stating the case I believe Dora concluded that I was a navigator, and went balancing myself up and down a plank all day with a wheelbarrow—and so brought us together in peace.* (*David Copperfield* by Charles Dickens)

necromancy NOUN necromancy means a kind of magic where the magician speaks to spirits or ghosts to find out what will happen in the future ❏ *He surfeits upon cursed necromancy* (*Doctor Faustus chorus* by Christopher Marlowe)

negus NOUN a negus is a hot drink made from sweetened wine and water ❏ *He sat placidly perusing the newspaper, with his little head on one side, and a glass of warm*

sherry negus at his elbow. (*David Copperfield* by Charles Dickens)

nice ADJ discriminating. Able to make good judgements or choices ❏ *consequently a claim to be nice* (*Emma* by Jane Austen)

nigh ADV nigh means near ❏ *He'll never know how nigh he come to getting lynched* (*The Adventures of Huckleberry Finn* by Mark Twain)

nimbleness NOUN nimbleness means being able to move very quickly or skilfully ❏ *and with incredible accuracy and nimbleness* (*Treasure Island* by Robert Louis Stevenson)

noggin NOUN a noggin is a small mug or a wooden cup ❏ *you'll bring me one noggin of rum* (*Treasure Island* by Robert Louis Stevenson)

none ADJ neither ❏ *none can die* (*The Good-Morrow* by John Donne)

notices NOUN observations ❏ *Arch are his notices* (*The Prelude* by William Wordsworth)

occiput NOUN occiput means the back of the head ❏ *saw off the occiput of each couple* (*Gulliver's Travels* by Jonathan Swift)

officiously ADV kindly ❏ *the governess who attended Glumdalclitch very officiously lifted me up* (*Gulliver's Travels* by Jonathan Swift)

old salt PHRASE old salt is a slang term for an experienced sailor ❏ *a 'true sea-dog', and a 'real old salt'* (*Treasure Island* by Robert Louis Stevenson)

or ere PHRASE before ❏ *or ere the Hall was built* (*The Prelude* by William Wordsworth)

ostler NOUN one who looks after horses at an inn ❏ *The bill paid, and the waiter remembered, and the ostler not forgotten, and the chambermaid taken into consideration* (*Great Expectations* by Charles Dickens)

ostry NOUN an ostry is an old word for a pub or hotel ❏ *lest I send you into the ostry with a vengeance*

(*Doctor Faustus 2.2* by Christopher Marlowe)

outrunning the constable PHRASE outrunning the constable meant spending more than you earn ❑ *but I shall by this means be able to check your bills and to pull you up if I find you outrunning the constable.* (*Great Expectations* by Charles Dickens)

over ADV across ❑ *It is in length six yards, and in the thickest part at least three yards over* (*Gulliver's Travels* by Jonathan Swift)

over the broomstick PHRASE this is a phrase meaning 'getting married without a formal ceremony' ❑ *They both led tramping lives, and this woman in Gerrard-street here, had been married very young, over the broomstick (as we say), to a tramping man, and was a perfect fury in point of jealousy.* (*Great Expectations* by Charles Dickens)

own VERB own means to admit or to acknowledge ❑ *It's my old girl that advises. She has the head. But I never own to it before her. Discipline must be maintained* (*Bleak House* by Charles Dickens)

page NOUN here page means a boy employed to run errands ❑ *not my feigned page* (*On His Mistress* by John Donne)

paid pretty dear PHRASE paid pretty dear means paid a high price or suffered quite a lot ❑ *I paid pretty dear for my monthly fourpenny piece* (*Treasure Island* by Robert Louis Stevenson)

pannikins NOUN pannikins were small tin cups ❑ *of lifting light glasses and cups to his lips, as if they were clumsy pannikins* (*Great Expectations* by Charles Dickens)

pards NOUN pards are leopards ❑ *Not charioted by Bacchus and his pards* (*Ode on a Nightingale* by John Keats)

parlour boarder NOUN a pupil who lived with the family ❑ *and somebody had lately raised her from the condition of scholar to parlour boarder* (*Emma* by Jane Austen)

particular, a London PHRASE London in Victorian times and up to the 1950s was famous for having very dense fog–which was a combination of real fog and the smog of pollution from factories ❑ *This is a London particular . . . A fog, miss* (*Bleak House* by Charles Dickens)

patten NOUN pattens were wooden soles which were fixed to shoes by straps to protect the shoes in wet weather ❑ *carrying a basket like the Great Seal of England in plaited straw, a pair of pattens, a spare shawl, and an umbrella, though it was a fine bright day* (*Great Expectations* by Charles Dickens)

paviour NOUN a paviour was a labourer who worked on the street pavement ❑ *the paviour his pickaxe* (*Oliver Twist* by Charles Dickens)

peccant ADJ peccant means unhealthy ❑ *other peccant humours* (*Gulliver's Travels* by Jonathan Swift)

penetralium NOUN penetralium is a word used to describe the inner rooms of the house ❑ *and I had no desire to aggravate his impatience previous to inspecting the penetralium* (*Wuthering Heights* by Emily Brontë)

pensive ADV pensive means deep in thought or thinking seriously about something ❑ *and she was leaning pensive on a tomb-stone on her right elbow* (*The Adventures of Huckleberry Finn* by Mark Twain)

penury NOUN penury is the state of being extremely poor ❑ *Distress, if not penury, loomed in the distance* (*Tess of the D'Urbervilles* by Thomas Hardy)

perspective NOUN telescope ❑ *a pocket perspective* (*Gulliver's Travels* by Jonathan Swift)

phaeton NOUN a phaeton was an open carriage for four people ❑ *often condescends to drive by my humble abode in her little phaeton and ponies* (*Pride and Prejudice* by Jane Austen)

phantasm NOUN a phantasm is an illusion, something that is not real. It is sometimes used to mean ghost ❑ *Experience had bred no fancies in him that could raise the phantasm of appetite* (*Silas Marner* by George Eliot)

physic NOUN here physic means medicine ❑ *there I studied physic two years and seven months* (*Gulliver's Travels* by Jonathan Swift)

pinioned VERB to pinion is to hold both arms so that a person cannot move them ❑ *But the relentless Ghost pinioned him in both his arms, and forced him to observe what happened next.* (*A Christmas Carol* by Charles Dickens)

piquet NOUN piquet was a popular card game in the C18th ❑ *Mr Hurst and Mr Bingley were at piquet* (*Pride and Prejudice* by Jane Austen)

plaister NOUN a plaister is a piece of cloth on which an apothecary (or pharmacist) would spread ointment. The cloth is then applied to wounds or bruises to treat them ❑ *Then, she gave the knife a final smart wipe on the edge of the plaister, and then sawed a very thick round off the loaf: which she finally, before separating from the loaf, hewed into two halves, of which Joe got one, and I the other.* (*Great Expectations* by Charles Dickens)

plantations NOUN here plantations means colonies, which are countries controlled by a more powerful country ❑ *besides our plantations in America* (*Gulliver's Travels* by Jonathan Swift)

plastic ADJ here plastic is an old term meaning shaping or a power that was forming ❑ *A plastic power abode with me* (*The Prelude* by William Wordsworth)

players NOUN actors ❑ *of players which upon the world's stage be* (*On His Mistress* by John Donne)

plump ADV all at once, suddenly ❑ *But it took a bit of time to get it well round, the change come so uncommon plump, didn't it?* (*Great Expectations* by Charles Dickens)

plundered VERB to plunder is to rob or steal from ❑ *These crosses stand for the names of ships or towns that they sank or plundered* (*Treasure Island* by Robert Louis Stevenson)

pommel ■ VERB to pommel someone is to hit them repeatedly with your fists ❑ *hug him round the neck, pommel his back, and kick his legs in irrepressible affection!* (*A Christmas Carol* by Charles Dickens) ■ NOUN a pommel is the part of a saddle that rises up at the front ❑ *He had his gun across his pommel* (*The Adventures of Huckleberry Finn* by Mark Twain)

poor's rates NOUN poor's rates were property taxes which were used to support the poor ❑ *"Oh!" replied the undertaker; "why, you know, Mr. Bumble, I pay a good deal towards the poor's rates."* (*Oliver Twist* by Charles Dickens)

popular ADJ popular means ruled by the people, or Republican, rather than ruled by a monarch ❑ *With those of Greece compared and popular Rome* (*The Prelude* by William Wordsworth)

porringer NOUN a porringer is a small bowl ❑ *Of this festive composition each boy had one porringer, and no more* (*Oliver Twist* by Charles Dickens)

postboy NOUN a postboy was the driver of a horse-drawn carriage ❑ *He spoke to a postboy who was dozing under the gateway* (*Oliver Twist* by Charles Dickens)

post-chaise NOUN a fast carriage for two or four passengers ❑ *Looking round, he saw that it was a post-chaise, driven at great speed* (*Oliver Twist* by Charles Dickens)

postern NOUN a small gate usually at the back of a building ❑ *The little servant happening to be entering the fortress with two hot rolls, I passed through the postern and crossed the* *drawbridge, in her company* (*Great Expectations* by Charles Dickens)

pottle NOUN a pottle was a small basket ❏ *He had a paper-bag under each arm and a pottle of strawberries in one hand . . .* (*Great Expectations* by Charles Dickens)

pounce NOUN pounce is a fine powder used to prevent ink spreading on untreated paper ❏ *in that grim atmosphere of pounce and parchment, red-tape, dusty wafers, inkjars, brief and draft paper, law reports, writs, declarations, and bills of costs* (*David Copperfield* by Charles Dickens)

pox NOUN pox means sexually transmitted diseases like syphilis ❏ *how the pox in all its consequences and denominations* (*Gulliver's Travels* by Jonathan Swift)

prelibation NOUN prelibation means a foretaste of or an example of something to come ❏ *A prelibation to the mower's scythe* (*The Prelude* by William Wordsworth)

prentice NOUN an apprentice ❏ *and Joe, sitting on an old gun, had told me that when I was 'prentice to him regularly bound, we would have such Larks there!* (*Great Expectations* by Charles Dickens)

presently ADV immediately ❏ *I presently knew what they meant* (*Gulliver's Travels* by Jonathan Swift)

pumpion NOUN pumpkin ❏ *for it was almost as large as a small pumpion* (*Gulliver's Travels* by Jonathan Swift)

punctual ADJ kept in one place ❏ *was not a punctual presence, but a spirit* (*The Prelude* by William Wordsworth)

quadrille ■ NOUN a quadrille is a dance invented in France which is usually performed by four couples ❏ *However, Mr Swiveller had Miss Sophy's hand for the first quadrille (country-dances being low, were utterly proscribed)* (*The Old Curiosity Shop* by Charles Dickens) ■ NOUN quadrille was a card game for four people ❏ *to make up her pool of quadrille in the evening* (*Pride and Prejudice* by Jane Austen)

quality NOUN gentry or upper-class people ❏ *if you are with the quality* (*The Adventures of Huckleberry Finn* by Mark Twain)

quick parts PHRASE quick-witted ❏ *Mr Bennet was so odd a mixture of quick parts* (*Pride and Prejudice* by Jane Austen)

quid NOUN a quid is something chewed or kept in the mouth, like a piece of tobacco ❏ *rolling his quid* (*Treasure Island* by Robert Louis Stevenson)

quit VERB quit means to avenge or to make even ❏ *But Faustus's death shall quit my infamy* (*Doctor Faustus 4.3* by Christopher Marlowe)

rags NOUN divisions ❏ *Nor hours, days, months, which are the rags of time* (*The Sun Rising* by John Donne)

raiment NOUN raiment means clothing ❏ *the mountain shook off turf and flower, had only heath for raiment and crag for gem* (*Jane Eyre* by Charlotte Brontë)

rain cats and dogs PHRASE an expression meaning rain heavily. The origin of the expression is unclear ❏ *But it'll perhaps rain cats and dogs to-morrow* (*Silas Marner* by George Eliot)

raised Cain PHRASE raised Cain means caused a lot of trouble. Cain is a character in the Bible who killed his brother Abel ❏ *and every time he got drunk he raised Cain around town* (*The Adventures of Huckleberry Finn* by Mark Twain)

rambling ADJ rambling means confused and not very clear ❏ *my head began to be filled very early with rambling thoughts* (*Robinson Crusoe* by Daniel Defoe)

raree-show NOUN a raree-show is an old term for a peep-show or a fairground entertainment ❑ *A raree-show is here, with children gathered round* (*The Prelude* by William Wordsworth)

recusants NOUN people who resisted authority ❑ *hardy recusants* (*The Prelude* by William Wordsworth)

redounding VERB eddying. An eddy is a movement in water or air which goes round and round instead of flowing in one direction ❑ *mists and steam-like fogs redounding everywhere* (*The Prelude* by William Wordsworth)

redundant ADJ here redundant means overflowing but Wordsworth also uses it to mean excessively large or too big ❑ *A tempest, a redundant energy* (*The Prelude* by William Wordsworth)

reflex NOUN reflex is a shortened version of reflexion, which is an alternative spelling of reflection ❑ *To cut across the reflex of a star* (*The Prelude* by William Wordsworth)

Reformatory NOUN a prison for young offenders/criminals ❑ *Even when I was taken to have a new suit of clothes, the tailor had orders to make them like a kind of Reformatory, and on no account to let me have the free use of my limbs.* (*Great Expectations* by Charles Dickens)

remorse NOUN pity or compassion ❑ *by that remorse* (*On His Mistress* by John Donne)

render VERB in this context render means give. ❑ *and Sarah could render no reason that would be sanctioned by the feeling of the community.* (*Silas Marner* by George Eliot)

repeater NOUN a repeater was a watch that chimed the last hour when a button was pressed–as a result it was useful in the dark ❑ *And his watch is a gold repeater, and worth a hundred pound if it's worth a penny.* (*Great Expectations* by Charles Dickens)

repugnance NOUN repugnance means a strong dislike of something or someone ❑ *overcoming a strong repugnance* (*Treasure Island* by Robert Louis Stevenson)

reverence NOUN reverence means bow. When you bow to someone, you briefly bend your body towards them as a formal way of showing them respect ❑ *made my reverence* (*Gulliver's Travels* by Jonathan Swift)

reverie NOUN a reverie is a daydream ❑ *I can guess the subject of your reverie* (*Pride and Prejudice* by Jane Austen)

revival NOUN a religious meeting held in public ❑ *well I'd ben a-running' a little temperance revival thar' bout a week* (*The Adventures of Huckleberry Finn* by Mark Twain)

revolt VERB revolt means turn back or stop your present course of action and go back to what you were doing before ❑ *Revolt, or I'll in piecemeal tear thy flesh* (*Doctor Faustus 5.1* by Christopher Marlowe)

rheumatics/rheumatism NOUN rheumatics [rheumatism] is an illness that makes your joints or muscles stiff and painful ❑ *a new cure for the rheumatics* (*Treasure Island* by Robert Louis Stevenson)

riddance NOUN riddance is usually used in the form good riddance which you say when you are pleased that something has gone or been left behind ❑ *I'd better go into the house, and die and be a riddance* (*David Copperfield* by Charles Dickens)

rimy ADJ rimy is an adjective which means covered in ice or frost ❑ *It was a rimy morning, and very damp* (*Great Expectations* by Charles Dickens)

riper ADJ riper means more mature or older ❑ *At riper years to Wittenberg he went* (*Doctor Faustus chorus* by Christopher Marlowe)

rubber NOUN a set of games in whist or backgammon ❑ *her father was sure of his rubber* (*Emma* by Jane Austen)

ruffian NOUN a ruffian is a person who behaves violently ❑ *and when the ruffian had told him* (*Treasure Island* by Robert Louis Stevenson)

sadness NOUN sadness is an old term meaning seriousness ❑ *But I prithee tell me, in good sadness* (*Doctor Faustus 2.2* by Christopher Marlowe)

sailed before the mast PHRASE this phrase meant someone who did not look like a sailor ❑ *he had none of the appearance of a man that sailed before the mast* (*Treasure Island* by Robert Louis Stevenson)

scabbard NOUN a scabbard is the covering for a sword or dagger ❑ *Girded round its middle was an antique scabbard; but no sword was in it, and the ancient sheath was eaten up with rust* (*A Christmas Carol* by Charles Dickens)

schooners NOUN A schooner is a fast, medium-sized sailing ship ❑ *if schooners, islands, and maroons* (*Treasure Island* by Robert Louis Stevenson)

science NOUN learning or knowledge ❑ *Even Science, too, at hand* (*The Prelude* by William Wordsworth)

scrouge VERB to scrouge means to squeeze or to crowd ❑ *to scrouge in and get a sight* (*The Adventures of Huckleberry Finn* by Mark Twain)

scrutore NOUN a scrutore, or escritoire, was a writing table ❑ *set me gently on my feet upon the scrutore* (*Gulliver's Travels* by Jonathan Swift)

scutcheon/escutcheon NOUN an escutcheon is a shield with a coat of arms, or the symbols of a family name, engraved on it ❑ *On the scutcheon we'll have a bend* (*The Adventures of Huckleberry Finn* by Mark Twain)

sea-dog PHRASE sea-dog is a slang term for an experienced sailor or pirate ❑ *a 'true sea-dog', and a 'real old salt,'* (*Treasure Island* by Robert Louis Stevenson)

see the lions PHRASE to see the lions was to go and see the sights of London. Originally the phrase referred to the menagerie in the Tower of London and later in Regent's Park ❑ *We will go and see the lions for an hour or two—it's something to have a fresh fellow like you to show them to, Copperfield* (*David Copperfield* by Charles Dickens)

self-conceit NOUN self-conceit is an old term which means having too high an opinion of oneself, or deceiving yourself ❑ *Till swollen with cunning, of a self-conceit* (*Doctor Faustus chorus* by Christopher Marlowe)

seneschal NOUN a steward ❑ *where a grey-headed seneschal sings a funny chorus with a funnier body of vassals* (*Oliver Twist* by Charles Dickens)

sensible ADJ if you were sensible of something you are aware or conscious of something ❑ *If my children are silly I must hope to be always sensible of it* (*Pride and Prejudice* by Jane Austen)

sessions NOUN court cases were heard at specific times of the year called sessions ❑ *He lay in prison very ill, during the whole interval between his committal for trial, and the coming round of the Sessions.* (*Great Expectations* by Charles Dickens)

shabby ADJ shabby places look old and in bad condition ❑ *a little bit of a shabby village named Pikesville* (*The Adventures of Huckleberry Finn* by Mark Twain)

shay-cart NOUN a shay-cart was a small cart drawn by one horse ❑ *"I were at the Bargemen t'other night, Pip;" whenever he subsided into affection, he called me Pip, and whenever he relapsed into politeness he called me Sir; "when there come up in his shay-cart Pumblechook."* (*Great Expectations* by Charles Dickens)

shilling NOUN a shilling is an old unit

of currency. There were twenty shillings in every British pound ❑ *"Ten shillings too much," said the gentleman in the white waistcoat.* (*Oliver Twist* by Charles Dickens)

shines NOUN tricks or games ❑ *well, it would make a cow laugh to see the shines that old idiot cut* (*The Adventures of Huckleberry Finn* by Mark Twain)

shirking VERB shirking means not doing what you are meant to be doing, or evading your duties ❑ *some of you shirking lubbers* (*Treasure Island* by Robert Louis Stevenson)

shiver my timbers PHRASE shiver my timbers is an expression which was used by sailors and pirates to express surprise ❑ *why, shiver my timbers, if I hadn't forgotten my score!* (*Treasure Island* by Robert Louis Stevenson)

shoe-roses NOUN shoe-roses were roses made from ribbons which were stuck on to shoes as decoration ❑ *the very shoe-roses for Netherfield were got by proxy* (*Pride and Prejudice* by Jane Austen)

singular ADJ singular means very great and remarkable or strange ❑ *"Singular dream," he says* (*The Adventures of Huckleberry Finn* by Mark Twain)

sire NOUN sire is an old word which means lord or master or elder ❑ *She also defied her sire* (*Little Women* by Louisa May Alcott)

sixpence NOUN a sixpence was half of a shilling ❑ *if she had only a shilling in the world, she would be very lilkely to give away sixpence of it* (*Emma* by Jane Austen)

slavey NOUN the word slavey was used when there was only one servant in a house or boarding-house–so she had to perform all the duties of a larger staff ❑ *Two distinct knocks, sir, will produce the slavey at any time* (*The Old Curiosity Shop* by Charles Dickens)

slender ADJ weak ❑ *In slender accents*

of sweet verse (*The Prelude* by William Wordsworth)

slop-shops NOUN slop-shops were shops where cheap ready-made clothes were sold. They mainly sold clothes to sailors ❑ *Accordingly, I took the jacket off, that I might learn to do without it; and carrying it under my arm, began a tour of inspection of the various slop-shops.* (*David Copperfield* by Charles Dickens)

sluggard NOUN a lazy person ❑ *"Stand up and repeat 'Tis the voice of the sluggard,'" said the Gryphon.* (*Alice's Adventures in Wonderland* by Lewis Carroll)

smallpox NOUN smallpox is a serious infectious disease ❑ *by telling the men we had smallpox aboard* (*The Adventures of Huckleberry Finn* by Mark Twain)

smalls NOUN smalls are short trousers ❑ *It is difficult for a large-headed, small-eyed youth, of lumbering make and heavy countenance, to look dignified under any circumstances; but it is more especially so, when superadded to these personal attractions are a red nose and yellow smalls* (*Oliver Twist* by Charles Dickens)

sneeze-box NOUN a box for snuff was called a sneeze-box because sniffing snuff makes the user sneeze ❑ *To think of Jack Dawkins — lummy Jack — the Dodger — the Artful Dodger — going abroad for a common twopenny-halfpenny sneeze-box!* (*Oliver Twist* by Charles Dickens)

snorted VERB slept ❑ *Or snorted we in the Seven Sleepers' den?* (*The Good-Morrow* by John Donne)

snuff NOUN snuff is tobacco in powder form which is taken by sniffing ❑ *as he thrust his thumb and fore-finger into the proffered snuff-box of the undertaker: which was an ingenious little model of a patent coffin.* (*Oliver Twist* by Charles Dickens)

soliloquized VERB to soliloquize is

when an actor in a play speaks to himself or herself rather than to another actor ❑ *"A new servitude! There is something in that," I soliloquized (mentally, be it understood; I did not talk aloud) (Jane Eyre* by Charlotte Brontë)

sough NOUN a sough is a drain or a ditch ❑ *as you may have noticed the sough that runs from the marshes (Wuthering Heights* by Emily Brontë)

spirits NOUN a spirit is the nonphysical part of a person which is believed to remain alive after their death ❑ *that I might raise up spirits when I please (Doctor Faustus 1.5* by Christopher Marlowe)

spleen ■ NOUN here spleen means a type of sadness or depression which was thought to only affect the wealthy ❑ *yet here I could plainly discover the true seeds of spleen (Gulliver's Travels* by Jonathan Swift) ■ NOUN irritability and low spirits ❑ *Adieu to disappointment and spleen (Pride and Prejudice* by Jane Austen)

spondulicks NOUN spondulicks is a slang word which means money ❑ *not for all his spondulicks and as much more on top of it (The Adventures of Huckleberry Finn* by Mark Twain)

stalled of VERB to be stalled of something is to be bored with it ❑ *I'm stalled of doing naught (Wuthering Heights* by Emily Brontë)

stanchion NOUN a stanchion is a pole or bar that stands upright and is used as a building support ❑ *and slid down a stanchion (The Adventures of Huckleberry Finn* by Mark Twain)

stang NOUN stang is another word for pole which was an old measurement ❑ *These fields were intermingled with woods of half a stang (Gulliver's Travels* by Jonathan Swift)

starlings NOUN a starling is a wall built around the pillars that support a bridge to protect the pillars ❑ *There were states of the tide when, having been down the river, I could not get back through the eddy-chafed arches and starlings of old London Bridge (Great Expectations* by Charles Dickens)

startings NOUN twitching or night-time movements of the body ❑ *with midnight's startings (On His Mistress* by John Donne)

stomacher NOUN a panel at the front of a dress ❑ *but send her aunt the pattern of a stomacher (Emma* by Jane Austen)

stoop VERB swoop ❑ *Once a kite hovering over the garden made a stoop at me (Gulliver's Travels* by Jonathan Swift)

succedaneum NOUN a succedaneum is a substitute ❑ *But as a succedaneum (The Prelude* by William Wordsworth)

suet NOUN a hard animal fat used in cooking ❑ *and your jaws are too weak For anything tougher than suet (Alice's Adventures in Wonderland* by Lewis Carroll)

sultry ADJ sultry weather is hot and damp. Here sultry means unpleasant or risky ❑ *for it was getting pretty sultry for us (The Adventures of Huckleberry Finn* by Mark Twain)

summerset NOUN summerset is an old spelling of somersault. If someone does a somersault, they turn over completely in the air ❑ *I have seen him do the summerset (Gulliver's Travels* by Jonathan Swift)

supper NOUN supper was a light meal taken late in the evening. The main meal was dinner which was eaten at four or five in the afternoon ❑ *and the supper table was all set out (Emma* by Jane Austen)

surfeits VERB to surfeit in something is to have far too much of it, or to overindulge in it to an unhealthy degree ❑ *He surfeits upon cursed necromancy (Doctor Faustus chorus* by Christopher Marlowe)

surtout NOUN a surtout is a long close-fitting overcoat ❑ *He wore a long* *black surtout reaching nearly to his ankles* (*The Old Curiosity Shop* by Charles Dickens)

swath NOUN swath is the width of corn cut by a scythe ❑ *while thy hook Spares the next swath* (*Ode to Autumn* by John Keats)

sylvan ADJ sylvan means belonging to the woods ❑ *Sylvan historian* (*Ode on a Grecian Urn* by John Keats)

taction NOUN taction means touch. This means that the people had to be touched on the mouth or the ears to get their attention ❑ *without being roused by some external taction upon the organs of speech and hearing* (*Gulliver's Travels* by Jonathan Swift)

Tag and Rag and Bobtail PHRASE the riff-raff, or lower classes. Used in an insulting way ❑ *"No," said he; "not till it got about that there was no protection on the premises, and it come to be considered dangerous, with convicts and Tag and Rag and Bobtail going up and down."* (*Great Expectations* by Charles Dickens)

tallow NOUN tallow is hard animal fat that is used to make candles and soap ❑ *and a lot of tallow candles* (*The Adventures of Huckleberry Finn* by Mark Twain)

tan VERB to tan means to beat or whip ❑ *and if I catch you about that school I'll tan you good* (*The Adventures of Huckleberry Finn* by Mark Twain)

tanyard NOUN the tanyard is part of a tannery, which is a place where leather is made from animal skins ❑ *hid in the old tanyard* (*The Adventures of Huckleberry Finn* by Mark Twain)

tarry ADJ tarry means the colour of tar or black ❑ *his tarry pig-tail* (*Treasure Island* by Robert Louis Stevenson)

thereof PHRASE from there ❑ *By all desires which thereof did ensue* (*On His Mistress* by John Donne)

thick with, be PHRASE if you are "thick with someone" you are very close, sharing secrets–it is often used to describe people who are planning something secret ❑ *Hasn't he been thick with Mr Heathcliff lately?* (*Wuthering Heights* by Emily Brontë)

thimble NOUN a thimble is a small cover used to protect the finger while sewing ❑ *The paper had been sealed in several places by a thimble* (*Treasure Island* by Robert Louis Stevenson)

thirtover ADJ thirtover is an old word which means obstinate or that someone is very determined to do want they want and can not be persuaded to do something in another way ❑ *I have been living on in a thirtover, lackadaisical way* (*Tess of the D'Urbervilles* by Thomas Hardy)

timbrel NOUN timbrel is a tambourine ❑ *What pipes and timbrels?* (*Ode on a Grecian Urn* by John Keats)

tin NOUN tin is slang for money/cash ❑ *Then the plain question is, an't it a pity that this state of things should continue, and how much better would it be for the old gentleman to hand over a reasonable amount of tin, and make it all right and comfortable* (*The Old Curiosity Shop* by Charles Dickens)

tincture NOUN a tincture is a medicine made with alcohol and a small amount of a drug ❑ *with ink composed of a cephalic tincture* (*Gulliver's Travels* by Jonathan Swift)

tithe NOUN a tithe is a tax paid to the church ❑ *and held farms which, speaking from a spiritual point of view, paid highly-desirable tithes* (*Silas Marner* by George Eliot)

towardly ADJ a towardly child is dutiful or obedient ❑ *and a towardly child* (*Gulliver's Travels* by Jonathan Swift)

toys NOUN trifles are things which are considered to have little importance, value, or significance ❑ *purchase my* *life from them bysome bracelets, glass rings, and other toys* (*Gulliver's Travels* by Jonathan Swift)

tract NOUN a tract is a religious pamphlet or leaflet ❑ *and Joe Harper got a hymn-book and a tract* (*The Adventures of Huckleberry Finn* by Mark Twain)

train-oil NOUN train-oil is oil from whale blubber ❑ *The train-oil and gunpowder were shoved out of sight in a minute* (*Wuthering Heights* by Emily Brontë)

tribulation NOUN tribulation means the suffering or difficulty you experience in a particular situation ❑ *Amy was learning this distinction through much tribulation* (*Little Women* by Louisa May Alcott)

trivet NOUN a trivet is a three-legged stand for resting a pot or kettle ❑ *a pocket-knife in his right; and a pewter pot on the trivet* (*Oliver Twist* by Charles Dickens)

trot line NOUN a trot line is a fishing line to which a row of smaller fishing lines are attached ❑ *when he got along I was hard at it taking up a trot line* (*The Adventures of Huckleberry Finn* by Mark Twain)

troth NOUN oath or pledge ❑ *I wonder, by my troth* (*The Good-Morrow* by John Donne)

truckle NOUN a truckle bedstead is a bed that is on wheels and can be slid under another bed to save space ❑ *It rose under my hand, and the door yielded. Looking in, I saw a lighted candle on a table, a bench, and a mattress on a truckle bedstead.* (*Great Expectations* by Charles Dickens)

trump NOUN a trump is a good, reliable person who can be trusted ❑ *This lad Hawkins is a trump, I perceive* (*Treasure Island* by Robert Louis Stevenson)

tucker NOUN a tucker is a frilly lace collar which is worn around the neck ❑ *Whereat Scrooge's niece's sister—the plump one with the lace*

tucker: not the one with the roses—blushed. (*A Christmas Carol* by Charles Dickens)

tureen NOUN a large bowl with a lid from which soup or vegetables are served ❑ *Waiting in a hot tureen!* (*Alice's Adventures in Wonderland* by Lewis Carroll)

turnkey NOUN a prison officer; jailer ❑ *As we came out of the prison through the lodge, I found that the great importance of my guardian was appreciated by the turnkeys, no less than by those whom they held in charge.* (*Great Expectations* by Charles Dickens)

turnpike NOUN the upkeep of many roads of the time was paid for by tolls (fees) collected at posts along the road. There was a gate to prevent people travelling further along the road until the toll had been paid. ❑ *Traddles, whom I have taken up by appointment at the turnpike, presents a dazzling combination of cream colour and light blue; and both he and Mr. Dick have a general effect about them of being all gloves.* (*David Copperfield* by Charles Dickens)

twas PHRASE it was ❑ *twas but a dream of thee* (*The Good-Morrow* by John Donne)

tyrannized VERB tyrannized means bullied or forced to do things against their will ❑ *for people would soon cease coming there to be tyrannized over and put down* (*Treasure Island* by Robert Louis Stevenson)

'un NOUN 'un is a slang term for one– usually used to refer to a person ❑ *She's been thinking the old 'un* (*David Copperfield* by Charles Dickens)

undistinguished ADJ undiscriminating or incapable of making a distinction between good and bad things ❑ *their undistinguished appetite to devour everything* (*Gulliver's Travels* by Jonathan Swift)

use NOUN habit ❑ *Though use make you apt to kill me* (*The Flea* by John Donne)

vacant ADJ vacant usually means empty, but here Wordsworth uses it to mean carefree ❑ *To vacant musing, unreproved neglect* (*The Prelude* by William Wordsworth)

valetudinarian NOUN one too concerned with his or her own health. ❑ *for having been a valetudinarian all his life* (*Emma* by Jane Austen)

vamp VERB vamp means to walk or tramp to somewhere ❑ *Well, vamp on to Marlott, will 'ee* (*Tess of the D'Urbervilles* by Thomas Hardy)

vapours NOUN the vapours is an old term which means unpleasant and strange thoughts, which make the person feel nervous and unhappy ❑ *and my head was full of vapours* (*Robinson Crusoe* by Daniel Defoe)

vegetables NOUN here vegetables means plants ❑ *the other vegetables are in the same proportion* (*Gulliver's Travels* by Jonathan Swift)

venturesome ADJ if you are venturesome you are willing to take risks ❑ *he must be either hopelessly stupid or a venturesome fool* (*Wuthering Heights* by Emily Brontë)

verily ADV verily means really or truly ❑ *though I believe verily* (*Robinson Crusoe* by Daniel Defoe)

vicinage NOUN vicinage is an area or the residents of an area ❑ *and to his thought the whole vicinage was haunted by her.* (*Silas Marner* by George Eliot)

victuals NOUN victuals means food ❑ *grumble a little over the victuals* (*The Adventures of Huckleberry Finn* by Mark Twain)

vintage NOUN vintage in this context means wine ❑ *Oh, for a draught of vintage!* (*Ode on a Nightingale* by John Keats)

virtual ADJ here virtual means powerful or strong ❑ *had virtual faith* (*The Prelude* by William Wordsworth)

vittles NOUN vittles is a slang word which means food ❑ *There never was such a woman for givin' away vittles and drink* (*Little Women* by Louisa May Alcott)

voided straight PHRASE voided straight is an old expression which means emptied immediately ❑ *see the rooms be voided straight* (*Doctor Faustus 4.1* by Christopher Marlowe)

wainscot NOUN wainscot is wood panel lining in a room so wainscoted means a room lined with wooden panels ❑ *in the dark wainscoted parlor* (*Silas Marner* by George Eliot)

walking the plank PHRASE walking the plank was a punishment in which a prisoner would be made to walk along a plank on the side of the ship and fall into the sea, where they would be abandoned ❑ *about hanging, and walking the plank* (*Treasure Island* by Robert Louis Stevenson)

want VERB want means to be lacking or short of ❑ *The next thing wanted was to get the picture framed* (*Emma* by Jane Austen)

wanting ADJ wanting means lacking or missing ❑ *wanting two fingers of the left hand* (*Treasure Island* by Robert Louis Stevenson)

wanting, I was not PHRASE I was not wanting means I did not fail ❑ *I was not wanting to lay a foundation of religious knowledge in his mind* (*Robinson Crusoe* by Daniel Defoe)

ward NOUN a ward is, usually, a child who has been put under the protection of the court or a guardian for his or her protection ❑ *I call the Wards in Jarndyce. The are caged up with all the others.* (*Bleak House* by Charles Dickens)

waylay VERB to waylay someone is to lie in wait for them or to intercept them ❑ *I must go up the road and waylay him* (*The Adventures of Huckleberry Finn* by Mark Twain)

weazen NOUN weazen is a slang word for throat. It actually means shrivelled ❑ *You with a uncle too! Why, I knowed you at Gargery's when you was so small a wolf that I could have took your weazen betwixt this finger and thumb and chucked you away dead* (*Great Expectations* by Charles Dickens)

wery ■ ADV very ❑ *Be wery careful o' vidders all your life* (*Pickwick Papers* by Charles Dickens) ■ *See* wibrated

wherry NOUN wherry is a small swift rowing boat for one person ❑ *It was flood tide when Daniel Quilp sat himself down in the wherry to cross to the opposite shore.* (*The Old Curiosity Shop* by Charles Dickens)

whether PREP whether means which of the two in this example ❑ *we came in full view of a great island or continent (for we knew not whether)* (*Gulliver's Travels* by Jonathan Swift)

whetstone NOUN a whetstone is a stone used to sharpen knives and other tools ❑ *I dropped pap's whetstone there too* (*The Adventures of Huckleberry Finn* by Mark Twain)

wibrated VERB in Dickens's use of the English language 'w' often replaces 'v' when he is reporting speech. So here 'wibrated' means 'vibrated'. In *Pickwick Papers* a judge asks Sam Weller (who constantly confuses the two letters) 'Do you spell it with a "v" or a "w"?' to which Weller replies 'That depends upon the taste and fancy of the speller, my Lord' ❑ *There are strings . . . in the human heart that had better not be wibrated* (*Barnaby Rudge* by Charles Dickens)

wicket NOUN a wicket is a little door in a larger entrance ❑ *Having rested here, for a minute or so, to collect a good burst of sobs and an imposing show of tears and terror, he knocked loudly at the wicket* (*Oliver Twist* by Charles Dickens)

without CONJ without means unless ❑ *You don't know about me, without you have read a book by the name of The Adventures of Tom Sawyer* (*The Adventures of Huckleberry Finn* by Mark Twain)

wittles ■ NOUN vittles is a slang word which means food ❑ *I live on broken wittles–and I sleep on the coals* (*David Copperfield* by Charles Dickens) ■ *See* wibrated

woo VERB courts or forms a proper relationship with ❑ *before it woo* (*The Flea* by John Donne)

words, to have PHRASE if you have words with someone you have a disagreement or an argument ❑ *I do not want to have words with a young thing like you.* (*Black Beauty* by Anna Sewell)

workhouse NOUN workhouses were places where the homeless were given food and a place to live in return for doing very hard work ❑ *And the Union workhouses? demanded Scrooge. Are they still in operation?* (*A Christmas Carol* by Charles Dickens)

yawl NOUN a yawl is a small boat kept on a bigger boat for short trips. Yawl is also the name for a small fishing boat ❑ *She sent out her yawl, and we went aboard* (*The Adventures of Huckleberry Finn* by Mark Twain)

yeomanry NOUN the yeomanry was a collective term for the middle classes involved in agriculture ❑ *The yeomanry are precisely the order of people with whom I feel I can have nothing to do* (*Emma* by Jane Austen)

yonder ADV yonder means over there ❑ *all in the same second we seem to hear low voices in yonder!* (*The Adventures of Huckleberry Finn* by Mark Twain)

Prologue
Chorjah, Afghanistan

Things are hidden beneath the surface in Afghanistan. The ubiquitous dust covers everything, concealing friends and enemies alike and if you swept it away, you would find the remains of a bombed-out clinic, landmines or bodies. They all looked the same. The monochrome landscape hid the shifting patterns of alliances where danger lived side by side with refuge. Where nothing is what it seems.

I could see the dust eddying up ahead and I slowed down. There was no point in hurrying; the battle was over and the settling sand covered the inevitable bodies like a shroud merging into the featureless background. Yet another blameless village, with little left standing after yet another battle. Blameless? I'd given up seeking blame; the loyalties and motives of these people changed like the sands that surrounded them and were as difficult to pin down.

I pulled into the village and skidded to a halt in front of what looked like the village well. I turned to Ali; we'd both been assigned to this sector. 'What do you think?' He turned to the interpreter in the back seat who simply shrugged. We looked around at the by-now-familiar desolation. Everything was brown: from the rocky hills surrounding the village to the mud walls of the huts – even the sky was cast brown from the dust blowing across the valley. It was like an old sepia print from a previous century and little had changed in that time. I pulled my neck scarf up across my mouth, but it made little difference. The dust got everywhere, even into the spirit – particularly into the spirit.

This was what defeat looked like. Defeat not just for our forces, but for the entire country. There weren't any winners here – even containment was precarious. As the dust settled, we looked at the torn scraps of clothing scattered around us, some still attached to the remains of body parts that had been blasted across the street. In a doorway a medic knelt by a casualty, bandaging his leg. I walked over to him. The boy couldn't have been more than eleven, an age when he should have been out in the fields, protected from care, but here was advanced to the equal of a man. There was no sign of growth on his smooth brown chin.

I looked questioningly at the doctor who shook his head. There was little more he could do until the back-up ambulances got here. I watched as he walked back to a long, low building off the main square. I assume that this was the clinic – such as it was – but I heard a smashing sound inside and ran across to the entrance. Although we'd been told that the village was cleared of local fighters, I wasn't going to take any chances so I went down onto my knees and crawled in through the doorway with my gun over my shoulder.

It was dark inside and I waited for my eyes to adjust. I couldn't see the doctor but across the room a man was running his gun butt along the shelves and smashing the medicines onto the floor. The advance guard couldn't be sure that they'd cleared the village and it might have been another cock-up, but this was different. The villagers had been through enough without having their clinic trashed. I watched for a moment as the fighter started on another shelf and then I stood up and shouted to him to get his hands in the air. 'And I mean high in the air, as high as you can reach.'

I kept my back against the wall and edged sideways into the room. The Taliban fighter opposite had stopped and was looking at me nervously – I could see in his eyes that he was weighing up the chances of turning his gun on me. For a moment, I wished he'd try it but as I went over to him, he dropped the gun and raised his hands. I was damned if I was going to let him get away with it and swung the butt of my gun against his jaw and he fell to his knees.

The shelves were now almost empty with the broken glass lying everywhere. These were medicines that could save lives and all this bastard wanted to do was destroy them. I kicked out at him and sent him sprawling over the broken glass. He was still holding onto his gun so I stood on his hand and leaned down into his face. I felt as much sympathy for him as I would a cockroach – shooting was too good for him.

I put his gun into my waistband and pulled him up by his collar and he offered no resistance as I punched him with my elbow and then kneed him savagely in his balls. I could see him gag with pain but still he said nothing – if he thought he was being a hero I could show him how wrong he was.

I knew there was still fight left in him – he was waiting for me to make a mistake, but I wasn't going to give him the opportunity. He went limp and, taken unawares I pulled at him, only for him to jump up and pull free. I crouched and circled him. I was angry and I wanted him to know it. 'Those medicines mean nothing to you, do they? And these people are nothing to you. What little they have, you take away.'

I don't know whether he understood. He smiled and spat out one of his teeth. 'Western medicine,' he grunted and at that, I lunged forward and kicked at his heels until he went down again. I jumped on him and dragged him to his feet and punched him again and again until there was no fight left in him. And still I hit him. I pushed him against the wall and smashed his face against it. Blood spurted out of his eye socket but through my eyes I could only see a red mist.

'That's enough. Let him go!' Ali had his arm around my neck and was pulling me away. 'You've done enough. You're going to kill him.'

There was the familiar pounding in my ears. I didn't really care if I killed him. In fact, I wanted to kill him. I started to wrestle with Ali but suddenly realised that it was pointless. We had a prisoner – we might even get some useful information out of him but killing him would achieve nothing, however much I wanted it.

I relaxed my grip and he slid down onto the floor. 'Okay, okay. I've stopped now. Get him out of here before I start again.' Ali let go of me and pulled out some cable ties to secure the prisoner – not that he looked much of a danger anymore but I really didn't care. I looked across the room as the doctor came in. 'Everything under control?' he asked cheerily. 'I was thinking of giving you some help but you seemed to be managing on your own.' He looked down at the prisoner who was groaning on the floor. 'I suppose I'd better patch him up. You made a pretty thorough job of him, didn't you?'

'Did you see him smash those medicines?' I asked. 'As though the village doesn't have enough problems.'

The doctor shook his head. 'It's not just the soldiers we're fighting. That kid out there has signs of malaria on top of his wounds. They've peddled these drugs which are manufactured in some shed in Kabul using little more than talcum powder. Only another way of fighting battles.'

I left him and went back outside, putting on my sunglasses against the glare. Ali went off to the east. I beckoned over my interpreter and he followed me across to the west where the alleyway into the centre of the village became narrower the further in we got.

We moved slowly, the pathway was blocked in places by the rubble of destroyed houses. We saw few signs of life – it was only the women who were left after such a bombardment and most of them didn't want to show their faces to our soldiers. Many were simply mourning the loss of their menfolk – husbands and sons only a few years older than the injured boy lying by the wall.

As we walked past an open doorway, we saw a woman inside and stopped. The interpreter started talking to her, but after a while he turned to me to say that she had nothing to tell us. This was our job; to try to find out who had attacked them; whether they knew any of the soldiers or could tell us anything about where they came from or where they went to.

We were clearing up after the fighting, but it had to be done. The extremes of intelligence were apparent here: on the one hand, billions of dollars of high-tech equipment, satellite surveillance, vast banks of subterranean computers searching for clues, monitoring mobile phones and the Internet; against that, on the ground, the Stone-Age technology of a few people like me and Ali trying to talk to people who didn't want to talk to you, who held you responsible for the war that had been unleashed on them and who saw no friends, only enemies.

We came to an opening in the alleyway; a space with a couple of makeshift football posts propped up at either end. Opposite, on the other side of the pitch, I heard the woman before I saw her. She was prostrate over a boy and her body shuddered with racking sobs. Her son – it must have been her son – was lying in a mangled heap, half propped against the wall. I pulled out my mirror from inside my tunic and held it out to see what was around the corner. I thought I saw someone suddenly disappear down towards where Ali was coming through. There was nothing I could do to help until I'd made sure the place was safe.

Looking back towards the woman, I saw movement in an adjacent doorway. I crouched and lay flat with my rifle pointing towards it. As I watched, a figure edged his way out into the open. He was carrying a Kalashnikov but it didn't seem to be giving him much confidence and I could sense his indecision. Finally he decided to make a run for it. I aimed carefully – I didn't want to hit him – and loosed off a couple of rounds and watched as he scrambled for cover and disappeared from view behind the crumbling houses. At least he now felt as unsafe here as I did.

I stood up and kept my rifle ready when I heard someone else behind me, and it wasn't the interpreter. I waited and Ali finally came up. 'I heard shooting,' he said and looked across to the body on the other side. 'Jesus, did you have to do that?'

I shook my head – there didn't seem any point saying anything. Looking around, I couldn't see anyone else, but I pressed myself against the houses surrounding the football pitch and started to manoeuvre myself closer to the woman. The advance party was supposed to have neutralised the village and made it safe, but they couldn't be sure. No one knew what safe meant in this place where acting out God's will was supposed to be the salvation, but to me was the only the eternal sentence.

Ali followed me as I worked my way to where the twisted body lay. He was a boy, barely older than the one I'd first seen lying against the wall. I bent down and checked his pulse, but there was nothing. I swallowed the familiar bile that rose in my throat. Could I ever get used to a place where peace was so fleeting? Ali stared down at the boy. 'How old is he?' he asked and then turned to me. 'Why did you have to shoot him? You can see he's not even got a weapon.'

I looked up at him. 'It wasn't me,' but as I said it, I realised how weak it sounded. But dammit, he was only my partner – I wasn't answerable to him. I started to explain but thought better of it. He'd have forgotten this by the time we got back.

I gestured to the interpreter to speak to the woman, but it was sometime before he could get any response. He finally managed to persuade her into her house and gestured us inside. I held up my hand to stop him and waited by the doorway, indicating that he should stand on the other side. If this was a trap, then it was my responsibility to spring it without injury. I took off my sunglasses and crouched low and rolled inside, bringing my rifle up ready to fire, but apart from the woman, there was no one else there.

I rose slowly to my feet and called out to Ali and the interpreter. I could now see the woman more clearly. She was young – perhaps in her early thirties although women aged quicker here and it was difficult to tell behind her copious robes. She had stopped crying and appeared calm, but I could see the emptiness in her dark eyes. How often had she imagined this fate for her son and now that it had happened what did she have left to live for? The interpreter said something to her but she appeared not to hear and just stared across the room. He tried again and hesitantly, she turned and started to tell him what had happened.

'She says her son was only thirteen, he was too young to be caught up in this… "murder" she called it. His name is Shamir.'

Hearing the name, the woman wailed again and rocked backwards and forwards. I wished the doctor could be here to give her a sedative, but we had to see this through and could only wait until her sobs subsided. Eventually she started again, but in a low voice that we could hardly hear and I turned to the interpreter.

'She was born in this village,' he translated, 'but she managed to get sent to a local college after the Taliban were driven out by the Americans.' He paused to let her catch up. 'But it lasted less than a year until she was forced back here. She says she learnt a little about the world outside and doesn't understand why she's forced into a life she didn't choose.'

'Is she married?' I asked.

'Of course.' He didn't even need to ask. I could see the small beds lining the walls and wondered how many children she'd had. She started talking again. 'She says she recognised one of the young men. He used to live here in the village before going away.'

'Does he have a name?' I asked, although even as I said it I realised that a name probably wouldn't get us far.

I waited for the translation. 'She has a name, but there's also a photograph.'

This was something else, perhaps a breakthrough. 'How can she have a photograph?'

I waited again for the reply and he paused before translating the answer. When he finally did, it was clear he was now struggling to control himself. 'The boy outside,' he paused before starting again. 'The boy outside, her son, he was shot in the back as he was trying to get to safety. But she says he'd taken a photograph on his phone.'

No one said anything for a few moments. What was there to say? A thirteen-year-old boy, on the threshold of manhood, had been killed in sight of his mother. Another death anonymous to the rest of the world but at the centre of hers.

There was little I could do. 'Does she have someone who can come over and stay with her? We can't leave her like this.' As I said it, I realised that she had started talking again and as I watched her I could see a look of resolve cross her face.

The interpreter listened for a while before turning to us. 'She wants you to do something for her. She wants you to find her eldest son and tell him about Shamir. She hasn't heard anything from him and thinks he might have left Afghanistan as a refugee a few years ago. She thinks he might be in England. His name is Sayed Alam. She has a picture for you.'

I was aware that she was looking inside a large bag and then she looked up and held out a photograph and waited for an answer. What could I say? What were the chances of finding someone in a place that had no structure and no laws? I took the photo. 'This is Sayed?' I asked. She nodded – it didn't need translating, and I mumbled something about doing what I could. Rarely have I ever felt so useless in the face of such grief, but I had to go on. 'About the other boy? You say she has another photo?' The least I could do was to offer some kind of reassurance that I would help, however hopeless it seemed.

The interpreter spoke to the woman for a few moments then turned back to me. 'Before the fighting started she could see her son talking to this man. She watched as he took out a phone and took a photograph of them together.' I waited for the woman to say more. 'When the first attack took place the son rushed back but dropped his phone. It's still out there.'

I left them and walked outside to where the body lay, and Ali followed. One of the boy's legs stuck out at an unnatural angle and I could see the edge of a phone underneath it. I picked it up and turned it on and immediately I could see the boy as he'd been in life, a few moments before, smiling at the camera held by the young man next to him. I handed it to Ali who nodded sombrely as he looked at it. He still wasn't saying anything but this wasn't the time to talk about it. I turned and saw that the woman had followed me out and was looking down at the picture on the phone. She collapsed to the floor and wailed, helpless in her grief.

'Does he have a name?' I asked the interpreter. "The other boy?'

'Jafar Nazim. She says he must have been about twenty-one. He was a nice boy, but they got hold of him and turned him into a fighter.'

'Doesn't she hold us responsible for Shamir's death?'

'I think she would but she's probably beyond that now.'

'Ask her again. Ask her why she's telling us this.'

The interpreter repeated what she said in flat tones. 'Until now he'd managed to keep out of the fighting but Jafar always brought trouble with him. If it hadn't been for him, her son would have been left alone. He would have still been alive. People here are dead even as they're born which is why she's so happy her eldest son got out. At least he should be safe. She says she's given up taking sides – there's so little to choose between any of them. She wants it all to end so they can bring up their families in peace.'

I looked again at the photograph. They were good-looking boys – the older one particularly so and he was out there somewhere. I clicked on "share" and sent the photo to my own email address. I'd leave the boy's phone inside for her to find later.

I looked down at her. Her sobs were getting quieter. 'She's giving us the name of this Jafar Nazim in return for our help in finding her boy somewhere in Europe possibly even in a refugee camp.' I turned to Ali. 'What do you think?'

'This is your call. This is your responsibility.' He turned and walked off.

I watched him go with surprise. My responsibility? I was responsible for this?

'Find her boy,' the interpreter repeated. 'You're from England – you can find him if he's there.' That was a very big "if" but I didn't say anything. 'She says if you find Jafar Nazim then try to get him to stop. He can't come back to the village, but he has to be shown that killing isn't the way.'

'Ask her how I can find him.'

'He has family in the next village. Ask for Amina – she's his aunt. She says she'll know where you can find him.' He waited for her to finish. 'But she says that's for you, she's not interested in Jafar. It's her son she wants you to find. Her son Sayed. Find him, she says.'

I looked at her plaintive, tear-streaked face. In a few months I'd be back in England. I could leave, but she never could. Perhaps after all I could trace her son. Records were kept of refugees – after a fashion – and it wasn't impossible that I'd be able to find out something. 'How long ago did Sayed leave?'

'She says it must have been about two years ago. He left the village as soon as he could. The local schoolteacher taught him some English and he worked at it whenever he could. He wanted to act as an interpreter and went off to see your army. He came back a couple of times but after that she didn't hear anything until a few months ago when someone told her he'd gone to Europe as a refugee. She thinks with his English it must have been to Britain.'

We left them and headed back to base, but the depth of her grief stayed with me. Ali was particularly subdued. I tried to get him talking but he ignored me and concentrated on the bleak landscape around us.

Chapter One

I managed to track down Jafar Nazim before the end of my tour of duty in Afghanistan. I'd visited his aunt and asked for her help, but she was extremely doubtful that there was anything she could do but agreed to contact me if he turned up in the village. When he did, I took my interpreter and drove to meet him but by that time, it was clear that he was a hardened fighter and nothing I could say dissuaded him from thinking of me as an infidel and a sworn enemy of Islam. I even showed him the photograph of him with his dead friend but nothing would move him. In retrospect I think it was only because he felt safe in his aunt's house that he didn't have a gun trained on me when I met him. Killing had become an automatic reflex for him and I was probably lucky to get out of there alive. But now that I was back in the UK with time on my hands, I started to honour my promise to his mother and look for Sayed.

Despite the huge number of refugees finding their way to Europe, records of varying quality had been kept and since Sayed had at least some English, I thought his mother was probably right in thinking that he'd been sent to the UK. The majority of Afghan refugees live in London and through the local refugee community organisation I finally located him living with another Afghan family. He'd enrolled at a local college and by all accounts he was assimilating well. I tracked him down on the phone but first I wanted him to contact his mother. After that we could meet. I managed to set up a Skype connection with the Chorjah village headman and sent on the message that Sayed was safe and well. It wasn't much but at least I'd made a small contribution to one family in that beleaguered country.

Most of the 10,000 Afghan refugees in England live in introverted communities in north and west London – in contrast to those from the Indian subcontinent who make their way to the east of London. But their communities are as close, and many are built around the local mosque and they were sometimes a very useful source of intelligence. I therefore had mixed motives when I visited Sayed in Harrow a few weeks later.

Walking through the streets, the pungent smells of eastern Asia enveloped me and I almost felt myself back in Afghanistan. I'd arranged to meet in the local park and when I got there I could see that someone was already sitting at the end of one of the benches. I stopped a while and brought out the old photograph his mother had given me – he was clearly recognisable. A young man in a public park – what could be more harmless? Sayed wasn't physically imposing, he was quite slight and normally no one would have looked at him twice – no one, that is, who hadn't spent time with him.

After a few minutes in his company it was as though he'd cast a spell over you and not for the first time I was thankful that he was on our side – or least so I hoped. I sat at the other end of the bench and pulled out the photograph his mother had given me, hoping that he would recognise it. 'She wants to hear from you,' I told him. 'She knows you're alive and well here in London, but she wants to speak to you.' I held out a piece of paper. 'I have the number of the village headman here. He has a mobile so you can arrange it through him.' The phone with his brother's photograph on it would have long-since expired.

He took the paper and glanced at it before putting it in his pocket. He said something I didn't catch. 'Was she well?' he repeated.

'It's been very difficult for her. Your village was badly damaged.' I needed to decide whether to tell him about his brother, because I didn't want him to associate me with bad news. His mother would tell him soon enough. 'How is life treating you here?'

He said nothing for a while.

'I thought I could train as a doctor,' he said eventually. 'Allah knows how many doctors are needed back home, but I didn't have the basic qualifications, so they suggested I take a degree in Pharmacy and I've been enjoying it – I only have a year to go now and then perhaps I can return and help. I want to try to put something back.'

I told him how the Taliban had targeted the clinic in Chorjah and he snorted. 'Yes – they call it "Western Medicine" as though it was the work of the devil. The truth is they want people to be kept in poverty and illness to make them easier to control.'

I was taken aback by his fierceness but also encouraged by it. 'And how are things otherwise? What about the family you're staying with?'

'It's okay. They're very religious and don't really approve of my attitude, but they don't force themselves upon me. I spend the evenings on my studies and in the mornings I work in a café to pay the rent. I suppose I should say that things are okay.'

'Your English is very good.' This wasn't flattery.

'Thank you. I was already quite fluent before I got here.'

'And your mosque?' I had to ask this. 'Have they made you welcome?'

Another pause. 'I suppose they have.' He finally turned to look at me and I saw that his photographs didn't do him justice. He had the most piercing brown eyes and held my gaze with an air of steady self-confidence. 'So tell me why you're really here?'

I was taken aback for a moment. Was I really that easy to read? 'I told you. I promised your mother that I would contact you and hand over that phone number.'

'There's always something more,' he said, looking at me steadily. 'With you people there's always something more.'

'It's up to you,' I said guardedly. 'If you feel you can help us then we'd appreciate it, but it really is up to you. You've been around the army in Afghanistan. You must have some idea how things work. We can't afford to miss any opportunity to get intelligence.'

'You want me to spy for you.' He didn't say it as a question and he didn't seem to be in the least embarrassed.

'If you want to put it that way.' There was no point in dressing this up. He obviously knew his mind. 'You're part of the community here, you could keep your ear to the ground and let us know if there's anything suspicious.'

'When you say "community" you mean Muslim community. Why don't you just say so?'

I sighed inwardly. 'Yes. You know I do and you know why.' Despite my reservations, I thought I'd take a chance by telling him about his brother, hoping that it might help me get his confidence. 'There's something I didn't tell you. It's about your brother.' Immediately I could see his face cloud over as though he knew what I was going to say. 'In the attack on your village, he was shot. I'm afraid he was killed.'

I waited to see the reaction, but Sayed just stared at me. I pulled out my phone and scrolled through the photographs until I found the one I had copied. I held the phone out to him and he took it and looked at it for a long time. I could see his eyes water, but he still said nothing.

'He looks happy here,' he said finally. 'You say this was taken just before he was killed?' I nodded. 'That's something, I suppose. The other boy is Jafar. He was only a few years older than me, but he couldn't wait to join the fighters. Do you know what happened to him?'

'I traced him through his aunt.' At least I could show that I was involved. 'She arranged a meeting, but it was a waste of time. He would have killed me if he could.'

'That was Jafar. Always destined for a martyr's death. Another wasted life. I should have realised that the war would catch up with my brother eventually.'

'If you feel that way, why don't you try to help us?' I said. 'You don't have to decide anything now.' I took a card out of my pocket. 'My office and my mobile numbers.' I held it out to him and he hesitated before putting it in his pocket. 'Young men your age are being indoctrinated here in London and are being sent out to kill. Is it so unreasonable to try to stop them?'

Sayed looked around him. In the corner was a playground and the screams of the children carried across the park. 'As you say, I don't have to decide anything now.' He stood up and held out his hand. 'Thank you for the message from my mother. I haven't spoken to her for a long time. She's already lost one son so I must try and make up for it.'

I watched as he left the park. There was something about him that struck a chord with me. He'd had to learn independence at an early age – as I had. There was an inner strength there, someone who'd worked out for himself what he thought was important. Someone who lived by his own values and was little affected by outside pressures. It was an independence that I recognised but it meant I couldn't tell whether I would ever hear from him again.

I'd been spending most of my time up in London where I'd been given a grace-and-favour apartment while I was on secondment to Whitehall. I'd enjoyed rubbing shoulders with the other agencies I was supposed to be working with and, while it beat my last tour in Afghanistan, the trouble was that I wasn't so sure about the pinstriped role. After a while though, I thought I was starting to get the hang of it and was beginning to understand the nuances of mandarin-speak.

I was back in my flat later that evening, struggling with a new recipe on the flat's tiny electric hob. At the critical moment when I had to stir hard to stop the sauce from curdling, there was a hammering on the door. I was very tempted to ignore it – I wasn't expecting anyone, so it was probably a neighbour wanting to borrow some milk. Except I didn't have any neighbours.

Reluctantly, I turned off the stove and went over and opened the door. As I did so, two men pushed past me, while a third grabbed my arm and bent it up high behind my back. Instinctively I turned with the force of his attack and pulled him towards me until he lost his balance and I was able to get my other arm around his neck and pull down. The man grunted before loosening his grip and I kicked him hard on his shin and managed to grab him and ram his head into the doorframe until he fell unconscious. I turned to face the other two, my vision distorted by the familiar rush of blood to my head. I looked around for something I could use – taking out one of them might be possible without a weapon, but not all three.

'Okay, you've had your fun,' one of the men said, pulling out his wallet and showing me his identification. 'Damian Webster, Military Police Investigation Department. Let's all cool it, shall we?' He turned to his partner. 'See if he's okay. We might need an ambulance.'

I stepped to one side to let him through. The man on the floor was starting to come around, so I guessed he'd be okay. 'Let's see that identification again.' I took it with a shaking hand, the adrenaline still coursing through my veins. I inspected it carefully but it seemed to be genuine. 'So what's all this about? Why couldn't you make an appointment like any normal person?'

'What? And give you time to hide the evidence?'

'Evidence? What are you talking about?'

'We need to search the flat.' He turned to his partner. 'How is he?'

The other man was struggling to his feet.

'I think he'll survive. Though he'll have a hell of a headache.' He looked across at me. 'That's a nasty temper, you've got. You could have killed him.'

I shrugged. 'Then don't barge in like that. Have you got a warrant?'

'Don't need one. It's government property so you have no rights over it. Now are you going to co-operate or is it going to get even nastier?'

'What are you looking for?' As I said it I realised how feeble it sounded – I would find out soon enough what this was all about. 'Help yourself. If you find anything valuable I'll let you have a share of it.' I glanced across at the man I'd attacked and could see that he wasn't going to be needing an ambulance. Perhaps I was slipping – they don't usually get up so fast.

My dinner was ruined so I sat at the table and waited for them to finish, and it didn't take long. Webster had gone straight into the bedroom and now came back out with a handful of files. He didn't need to tell me that they were exactly where he'd been told they would be. I'd been around long enough to recognise when evidence had been planted.

Webster brought the files over to the table and spread them out in front of me. 'These belong to you?' he asked. 'All marked Top Secret – Not to be Taken Out.' Of course he'd added that last bit. Top Secret files are never to be taken out which is why they're secret. I said nothing and tried desperately to think how they might have got there. They'd obviously been planted by someone, but I couldn't think who. This was a Court Martial offence staring me in the face. Someone wanted me out and I had no idea who.

Webster picked up the files and put them in his briefcase. 'Anything to say?' he asked and I shook my head. 'Thought not.' He turned to the others – the man I'd attacked was still looking very unsteady, but he was at least walking. 'Are we all set? We've got what we came for.' He turned back to me. 'I think this is a matter for Headquarters.'

*****

The Old Priory at Chicksands in Bedfordshire has been there since the *Doomsday Book* recorded it nearly 900 years ago. It was appropriated at the start of the Second World War when it was used as a decoding centre for the Enigma transmissions and these days it's the headquarters of DISC – the Defence Intelligence and Security Services, otherwise known as the British Army Intelligence Corps, of which I was an officer, and about to find out for how much longer I would remain one.

The parklands, stretching down to the banks of the River Flit, are magnificent and trees were in full leaf as Ali and I wandered down to the riverbank, but this time we barely noticed them.

Idly, Ali picked up a stone and attempted to skim it across the water, but it tripped over itself and sank with barely a ripple. 'Don't give up the day job,' I said and chose my own stone more carefully. 'One, two, three, four,' I counted before it stalled. 'You know there are world championships at skimming?' I said inconsequentially. 'Held at some disused slate quarry up in Scotland. Think about it. What sort of person takes leave from their work and goes all the way up to some remote island in Scotland to see if they can skim stones further than anyone else? D'you think skimming along the surface is a sort of metaphor for life?' I thought about that. 'Can't see how.' I tried again but this time it only managed three jumps before joining the others on the riverbed. 'Why do you think they're doing this?' I asked, not for the first time. Ali shrugged and tried another stone, this time with more success. 'See that? Six!' 'Perhaps you should go up to Scotland for training,' I said. 'It'd look good on your résumé – qualified stone-skimmer.' Ali ignored me and said, also not for the first time, 'I'm not surprised they didn't believe you.' 'It's a pretty easy way of getting rid of someone, isn't it? Everyone takes files home – you just have to wait 'til you know someone's taken some files and call out the guard. Now, watch this.' I'd found a stone that looked perfect and flicked it across the water. 'Note the wrist action coupled with the follow-through,' I said as I counted. 'Ten! There you are. Try beating that.' But there was no time. Ali's phone rang and we were called back.

Hence the tribunal. There wasn't much I could do to prevent it. I could have told them that I had no idea how the files had found their way into my flat, but Ali told me not to. He was representing me as my "officer friend" and said that they'd find this so far-fetched that there was no chance they'd believe me. 'Tell them it was an oversight,' he said, adding that no less than a former Sea Lord and security minister had once been caught taking out classified papers. They only found out when he saw them plastered over the pages of *The Mail on Sunday* – apparently he'd dropped them while walking a friend's dog. So I told them what Ali had suggested and it turned out that he was right. I had to admit that he'd done a good job and had shown a commanding presence in the court. He was classically tall, dark and handsome and this had obviously impressed the judges. There was something about Ali that seemed to show an inner certainty, though where it came from I had no idea.

'It looks as though they bought it,' he said after the judges had filed out and we gathered up our papers. "Resignation with honour" was the verdict – whatever honour is in these circumstances. The clowns who'd planted the files hadn't shown any. Leaving the makeshift courtroom, we passed back through the gothic splendour of the priory's entrance hall into the daylight and headed across the park towards our quarters in the accommodation block.

'I thought it was going pear-shaped when they started to read out your previous history,' Ali said. 'Quite colourful, wasn't it? Insubordination, fights, arguing with superior officers…. There was a particularly juicy case when you attacked a lance corporal…'

'He withdrew his complaint,' I said. 'He dropped it when he realised how he'd look if it came to court.'

'Not before you'd broken his arm, it seems.'

'That was the way he fell, but I would have been happy to have done it myself. The villagers in Chorjah didn't need corrupt soldiers looting what little they had. We were there to liberate them, not their belongings,' I said it with some feeling – no one can remain unchanged after seeing the hardship that was part of their daily lives.

'However it was, it didn't sound good being read out like that. Attacking one of the investigating officers in your flat didn't do you any favours either. Don't forget I've seen you in action when you decided to take matters into your own hands. You can be very dangerous at times.'

'Me? A pussycat. But there are some causes worth fighting for inside and outside the army.'

'It'll be outside from now on,' Ali said tersely and followed me into the room I'd been allocated. 'You've been lucky,' he said.

'It could easily have been a dishonourable discharge. In fact I'm surprised it wasn't. I often saw files lying about in your flat.'

'Files, perhaps, but not "Top Secret" ones. Anyone could break into my quarters.'

'I still think you were lucky. I don't think they wanted the publicity of a full hearing. Sweeping things under the carpet is their speciality and they've got a pretty big carpet. But you'll have to resign your commission.'

'It doesn't make sense. Someone had to have access to the files to take them out and that's a pretty restricted number of people. It shouldn't be too difficult to find out.' I shrugged. 'Not that there's any point now. It'd be too late and I can't see what good it would do.' I hesitated. 'Perhaps you could look into it for me?'

'Me?' Ali said in surprise. 'How do you expect me to go about that?'

'You could make some enquiries, look at the logs and things like that. Christ, Ali, you're supposed to be an intelligence officer. You can find a way.'

'That's if someone really planted the files on you.'

'What do you mean *if*? You still don't believe me?'

'Yes, of course. I only meant … well, never mind.'

'But you'll look into it?'

'Alright, I'll look into it, but right now I've got to sort out my papers. I'll see you back in London.'

'As a civilian?'

Ali looked a bit embarrassed. 'I suppose,' he said rather weakly, but then added, 'something will come up.' It didn't sound to me as though he was convinced.

After he'd left, I walked to the window and looked across the park. After so many years in the army, it felt like an amputation. They say that when a limb is cut off you can still feel it and the army still felt a part of me and on balance they'd looked after me well. I suppose I had to admit that they'd even seen things in me that I was unaware of, for which I suppose I had to be grateful, but choices weren't something they were strong on. Everything had been laid out for me and I followed, like a greyhound chasing a mechanical hare but now it was time to go offpiste. I was on my own.

I'd been in the army since I was a teenager and although from time to time I'd had itchy feet, I hadn't really thought of a life on the outside. I suppose that's not quite true; I *had* thought about it, just as people dream of winning the lottery, but it'd only led to flights of daydreaming which left me with a smile on my face but no real idea of what else I might actually be suited for. I had been good at what I did.

I walked out into the park and looked back at the priory where I'd undergone my initial training. I wondered that mine was nothing compared to some of the dramas it must have seen in its history. Perhaps this was the way it should be, the army just a preparation for the rest of my life. I could feel angry about it, that they'd thrown out someone who had served them well, but what was the point in looking backwards? I phoned for a taxi to take me to the station and packed my few things while waiting.

It was a slow train back into London and to my small flat off the Strand. I changed out of my uniform and habit made me fold it in its creases before hanging it up. Creases! Perhaps the most useless thing ever invented although my life might now be measured in terms of life pre-creases and after creases – PC and AC.

I looked around my cramped room which still didn't look much like a home even after all these months. I'd have to find somewhere else to live. I had a bit of money put by, so I could survive for a time while I took stock. "Taking stock" – I wondered about that. I don't think I'd ever taken stock in my life – I'd been single-minded in the army, working towards the next level with little interest in looking around me and I'd done pretty well. Would I be like the recidivist released from prison who promptly steals again in order to be sent back behind the familiar bars? A hermit crab scrambling into someone else's shell? That was for later, in the meantime self-pity wasn't my style.

Chapter Two

I still had my security pass and hoping that they might not have cancelled it already, the next day I headed back to my office off Whitehall where I'd been working as a liaison officer for the past nine months.

I slipped my card through the scanner but the door remained firmly shut. I pulled out my phone and called Joan, the office administrator. Typical of her to withdraw my pass so quickly – hastening the departing to prove a point. I was never sure where I was with Joan. She liked order; everything inside the box with no loose ends and no ambiguity and I didn't fit anywhere in that. But I didn't think she wanted me out.

Joan buzzed me through and I went upstairs to the office where she kept guard behind a walnut desk that she'd probably inherited from Lord Palmerston – they'd both been there long enough. 'James,' she said mockingly, 'the happy warrior is returning to the scene of his crime? I always thought you'd get caught one day.'

I let that pass and sat down at her desk which started emitting growling noises. I'd forgotten Ruffles, her Scottie dog which guarded her rather ineffectually from somewhere underneath. My ankles had had run-ins with him before. 'Oh come on, Joan,' I said, 'don't pretend you're not going to miss me.'

'Just as I miss the flu after it's gone,' she said rather unkindly.

'I suppose I should be flattered that you only think of me as a bout of flu. It could have been worse – what about appendicitis or even botulism?'

'Only because I didn't think of them. You know I've always wondered whether you'd last.'

'What do you mean?'

'After such a rapid rise from the ranks, I wondered whether you could keep it up. It could be only up or down. People like you never stay still.'

'So you think I'm like Icarus? Flying too close to the sun and falling to earth?'

'Something like that. You were never bothered about fitting in, were you? Not interested in making alliances, you carried on your own sweet way without regard for anyone else.'

'That's a bit extreme, isn't it? It was a job and I did it. That's all. What other people thought was up to them. What counted to me was whether the job was done well and I've been pretty successful so far.'

'As you say – so far. And now it's all over. If you'd tried harder to get people on your side this would never have happened. You'd still be with us.'

I knew Joan was right, but I wasn't going to admit it. Ali had often told me the same thing.

I shook my head. 'Too many people in the department regard someone like me who's come up through the ranks as second class. Not out of the top drawer and no idea how to pass the port. The way some of them looked at me in the officers' mess – thinking that a working-class officer didn't belong.'

'Only a few of them are like that. Anyway, you're not alone. Ali's family are immigrants. You can hardly call him upper class.'

'His father's a leading surgeon, he went to a minor public school and they live in a mansion in Kensington. Hardly working class.'

Joan laughed. 'That's what I mean. You've got a chip on your shoulder but won't admit it. You think of your colleagues as opponents.'

'Some of them were. They thought they had a divine right to be here without having to work at it. I had to fight hard to get where I am.'

'And where's that? You've thrown it all away now.'

'I didn't throw it away – someone did it for me. And you talk as though my life is over. It's only just beginning.'

'I hope so, for your sake. Anyway, you're right, I will miss you. You always managed to cheer the place up. Any idea of what you're going to do?'

'Security, I suppose. With the world as it is there's always a demand for trained security specialists. What about that company that provided guards for ships going past Somalia? The pirates attacked and they all jumped overboard to escape? Interesting business model.'

Joan hesitated. 'I checked the file register. To make sure.'

I was amazed, this was another new side to Joan. 'Did you find anything? Anyone who took them out over that time?'

'No, nothing. You didn't sign it out and you didn't sign it back in.' Joan sniffed – she was quite a sniffer. 'I don't know how you managed to take it out without signing the register, but the last entry is a few days before you…' She stopped as if she suddenly realised that she was about to launch herself into dangerous waters.

'Before I what? You mean, before my flat was raided? After that I couldn't sign them back in, could I? Because by then those goons had them.'

'All I'm saying is that the file register doesn't tell you anything and I can't help thinking that if you'd taken them out, then you would have signed for them.'

'I didn't sign for them, because I didn't take them out,' I said. I even patted her dog before I stood up and went down the corridor to what I now had to call my old office. Before doing so I put my head into my colleague James's office; he and I went way back – he'd even been to my wedding – so the least I could do was say goodbye and he might even want to thank me for opening the way for a possible promotion. It certainly gave him a motive.

James looked up from his computer screen. 'Philip. I know I'm in a minority around here but I'm really sorry about what's happened.' He even said it as though he meant it and knowing him, he probably did, potential promotion notwithstanding.

'Think of it as a rebirth,' I said. 'A whole new future awaits. A blank canvas ready for me to daub on.'

'I think you should consider yourself lucky that you got away with resignation. Not a stain on your character, as they say.'

'A bit of a dirty mark, though.'

'Nothing that won't wash out. It could have been worse, they could have accused you of spying.'

'On the strength of a single file? I don't think so – with my background it's not very likely – Ali would make a better suspect. Anyway, it didn't contain information of any use to an enemy. It was only marked "Top Secret" to keep it away from Whitehall's prying eyes. I sometimes wonder who the biggest enemy is: Isis, Al Qaeda or the government. I suppose I won't have to worry about that sort of thing anymore. It'll feel strange.'

'The first thing you'll have to do,' said James, 'is find somewhere to live and I've been making some enquiries and think I can help. A friend of mine might have somewhere you can stay on a temporary basis while he's posted overseas. He can meet you this evening if you want.'

'What sort of place is it? And where?'

'It's a bit special. Can we meet in Wapping this evening?'

'Wapping? It's not one of those yuppie flats, is it? That's not quite my style.'

'No, it's suitably bohemian even for you.'

I left him and went back to my office. There wasn't much I needed to take – there wasn't much I was allowed to take. I'd got an old bag and was putting my few personal possessions into it. It wasn't something to be hurried because each had its own memories. I was zipping up my bag when I saw a note stuck onto my computer keyboard. It said simply "Phone Sayed."

'Why hasn't anyone told me about this?' I said out loud, but of course there was no one there. I started to go back to Joan's office, but thought better of it. There wasn't much point. I sat down and thought what I should do. It was some time since I'd last met him. A routine meeting to show him that I was still around. I'd had to hand in my service phone so he hadn't been able to contact me through that and phoning the office was probably a last resort which might mean that he might finally have something for me. It was all too late – I'd have to hand this over to Ali and let him follow it up but then I realised I couldn't let this go. I thought back to the village where I'd met Sayed's mother and remembered Ali's coldness. I could always pass this onto him afterwards but for the moment I had to find out what Sayed wanted. I took out my personal phone and sent him a message saying that I'd meet him in the usual place the following morning. I stood up and picked up my bag and left my office for the last time.

I can't say that Wapping, in London's East End, is my normal stamping ground, although I'd sailed out of St Katharine Docks a couple of times, but James wouldn't say anything more about it and I was intrigued by his secrecy. The Town of Ramsgate is a tiny riverside pub by the Thames downstream from Tower Bridge where you can leave behind the avaricious financiers in the City of London before reaching the even more avaricious financiers of Canary Wharf. It's squeezed between the lovely Georgian buildings surrounding the Wapping Steps and old warehouses now converted into flats. The pub has been there for hundreds of years and it feels it as you sit on the balcony overlooking the muddy Thames below.

'Sorry I'm late.' James arrived rather flushed. 'My friend couldn't come so he's asked me to let you in. He's given me a set of keys.'

We went out along Wapping High Street towards Tower Bridge and then turned into an alley heading towards the river. The alley stopped at the river's edge and a wooden walkway spanned across the river to a rusty pontoon which had several barges moored alongside. James led me to a decrepit-looking boat at the end. 'This is it,' he said. 'The MV *Salacia*.' It was low tide and the old boat was sitting in the mud at a slight angle.

'Christ,' I said. 'Will it float when the tide comes back in or does it just sit in the mud with only its superstructure above the water?' I started across the walkway gingerly. "Gangplank" I suppose it was. 'Have many people been lost going over this?'

'It has seen better days,' James admitted, 'but you can't really beat the location and there's lots of space.' He pulled out the keys and unlocked the door into the saloon.

I had to admit that it was a breathtaking view, with the old warehouses of Butler's Wharf across the river and Tower Bridge and the Shard upstream to the west.

'It's very sought after,' James added.

'Sought after? Does that mean you have to send out a rescue party at high tide to see if there are any survivors?'

I looked around at the mess. 'Did he do a moonlight flit from the bailiffs? It doesn't look as though anyone's lived here for a while.' I gave the barometer a statutory tap in passing and climbed down the companionway steps.

Below was a narrow corridor opening up into a large cabin, with a huge bed in the corner, demonstrating no modesty in its owner. 'How long has he owned it? Did he buy it or was he awarded it as salvage?'

'He's had it a few years and is always meaning to refurbish it, but he says something always gets in the way.'

'Sloth, probably.'

'The deal is that you can live here on a low rent if you agree to do the place up. His posting is due to last a year or two. It's got a steel hull which is sound, so it's only the fittings that need attention.'

'Just the fittings. That's all right then,' I said sarcastically. 'Shouldn't take me longer than ten years.' I looked around. The first thing it needed was a good clean up. In this state you could barely see the wood for the rubbish, but it had potential even if it needed a lot of work. It would take time but it seemed that I had a lot of that right now.

We went out on deck and watched the muddy water swirl past, miniature whirlpools forming in the strong current. There was only one mast left and it had been hinged down over the coach roof, while the two huge wooden leeboards were still fixed to either side of the hull. I jumped up and down on the deck but it felt reasonably firm, although I'd lay odds that it leaked – probably directly above the bed. My sailing experience had given me a little knowledge of boats, although old lumbering great barges were a bit above my pay grade.

'So?' asked James. 'What do you think? It's quite an opportunity.'

'That's one way of describing it, but I'll take her – for better or for worse until dry rot do us part.'

The fact was that I was excited, not just by the extraordinary location of the boat, but that for the first time in my life I would be able to work towards a home of my own. Since I was a young boy I'd lived in places where I'd been sent and after joining the army there'd been little choice over the quarters I'd had to live in. There'd always been a drab uniformity about the places that the army allocated, as though personal taste didn't exist and we were all expected to be the same. I used to read design magazines the way other people read pornography – furtively and worried lest anyone saw me doing it. I was no idealist – I'd done what I had to do in the army and had expected to carry on doing it for some years.

But there are some values which are personal. To give people the security to feel safe in their own homes was just the start. With that security they were finally able to live their own lives and that was what counted more. I'd collected books about the great twentieth-century designers and had often wondered how I could use their ideas in a place of my own. Perhaps this was my chance, however temporary it might be. Perhaps now I could create my own space – it would give me a challenge. But first I had to meet with Sayed Alam.

I was early at the park the following morning. It had been over a month since I'd last arranged a meeting with Sayed and then it had been at my request and he'd been as difficult to read as ever. He'd re-established contact with his mother who was happy that he was so far away from the fighting, but it was difficult to see when he might be able to go back and see her. It was a bit early for the children and the playground was strangely silent. In fact, there were few other people in the park and I hoped that I wasn't too conspicuous in this predominantly Muslim area.

When Sayed arrived he sat down with his back towards me but said nothing. When I asked after his mother, his reply was monosyllabic. I guessed that he was still undecided about helping us and I couldn't really blame him. He'd had a foot in two camps now for some years and it couldn't be easy. In his local community he had to give the impression that he was one of them so he could only regard talking to me as a betrayal – which I suppose it was, although it was difficult to identify exactly who he was betraying.

We were both silent for a while. 'We have discussion classes after Friday prayers,' he started. 'It's something I go to, but my heart isn't really in it. I don't recognise my Allah in their speeches – my Allah is peaceful.'

I didn't say anything. He'd never spoken so personally before – he'd always kept his distance and I realised that he was finding it difficult. Things are straightforward in theory, but become more complicated when you have to deal with them in real life.

'There's someone who comes occasionally to the meetings. He's a little older than I am and he's always been quiet. But there was something about him. When he did speak he talked with such... such belief. It wasn't like any of the others. And I think he's been away, because he seems much more confident since he's been back.'

'So what do you think has happened?'

'There are camps. We've been told about these special camps where they're supposed to teach Koranic studies in detail but I think they're more than that. We're often asked if we want to go, but most of us know it's not for us. I think that's where he's been.'

I'd never seen Sayed so unsure of himself. Usually he was in control, but this time he seemed uncertain and I could only assume that he was having trouble facing the conflict. 'Sayed,' I said, 'tell me straight. Do you think he's been radicalised?'

Sayed hesitated. 'Perhaps not yet,' he said eventually. 'But I think they're working on him.'

'They?' I asked, but it was a rhetorical question. If he knew who *they* were he would have told me. I thought about this. 'Perhaps you could volunteer for one of the courses? Find out what goes on there.'

'It could be dangerous.'

'Not necessarily. You're a Muslim; you're a refugee from Afghanistan. There's no reason for anyone to suspect you. But of course you don't have to do it if you don't want to,' I added hurriedly. 'I'm not putting any pressure on you.'

'All I can say is that I'll think about it.' Sayed stood up. 'I'll think about it and be in touch.'

I had to admit that the timing couldn't really be worse. Here I was being given important information a few days after the intelligence services had told me they could manage without me. I decided I wouldn't tell Sayed just yet about our separation. He was in such an unusually confused state that I thought it would only make matters worse. If he was going to live with himself, it had to be his decision, made without pressure or distraction.

Although I hadn't been planning on moving into the barge so quickly, I decided that at least it would keep me occupied while I tried to work out what to do, but I didn't know how much time I had. My natural reaction to what Sayed had told me was to get Ali and the department involved, but something told me to hold back until I could get a handle on things.

It took me a couple of weeks to get myself sorted out. There were forms to sign, lawyers' representatives to consult, old colleagues to bid farewell. It was worse than my divorce, severing all ties with the family that had almost brought me up.

I decided I didn't need more clutter so I put my meagre belongings into storage along with my old uniforms. This was the new, slimmed-down Philip Hennessey, no ties and floating on hopes. But I wasn't going to succumb to bitterness even though someone had set me up and the powers that be thought it appropriate to cut me loose. Did they really think so little of me? Yes, all right, there was some bitterness, but my shoulders were broad and I'd fight to show them that it was their loss, not mine. Knock me down and see me bounce back.

I found the work on *Salacia* to be therapeutic; it also allowed me to think back over the past few years and put them in some kind of context for the future. It was particularly satisfying to unload all the rubbish I'd cleaned out of her onto one of the Thames-based refuse contractors whose barges ply up and down the river. They came and moored a skip alongside which I filled to overflowing and although things looked a bit bare, at least I could now start to design the layout. It was like sloughing off my previous life and working towards a new one. I ordered in some light ash boards to put up as panelling, which, although not very nautical, made the place much more cheerful.

I also found myself adjusting to the unique routine of the river: its constantly changing tides, the gurgling of the water as it rushed past the hull on the ebb. Slowly, the old girl started to take shape and the physical work was doing me good after my time behind a desk.

It was after I'd been living aboard for a couple of weeks that I had a visitor. I was working down in the bottom of the hull and at first I didn't hear the knocking. Whoever it was didn't give up and eventually I went topside to see who it was. It was a woman, perhaps a bit younger than me. Well and expensively dressed, quite tall and attractive with shoulder-length hair, not quite blonde. She was standing at the foot of the gangway knocking on the hull. 'I'm sorry to disturb you,' she said. She hesitated. 'Could I come aboard?'

'Be my guest,' I replied, putting down the paintbrush I'd been holding.

The tide was low and she obviously had difficulty clambering up the steep gangway. She was wearing a smart trouser suit which appeared to be designed to conceal whatever was causing her limp. I held out my hand to help her up, but she shook her head and pulled herself on deck. Whether it was pride or my paint-covered hands, I couldn't tell. I led her towards the saloon and held open the door for her.

Inside, she sat with some difficulty on the only low chair that wasn't hidden underneath painting materials. 'I'm sorry to come unannounced,' she started. 'But your wife… I mean your ex-wife, Sally, suggested you might be able to help me. She said you had some time on your hands.'

I held up my palms. 'At the moment all I've got on my hands is paint. How did she think I could help?'

'It's about my father. I think he's been murdered.'

Chapter Three

I suppose that's a pretty good way to get my attention. I wiped my hands on a nearby rag. 'Sally suggested you came? What did she want me to do?' It was clear that my visitor was on the verge of tears and comforting distraught strangers was not one of my strengths. 'You'd better come in and tell me about it.' I held open the saloon door and followed her in. I took a toolbox off one of the chairs and asked her to sit.

'I should have rung first, but I needed to explain this face to face.' She inspected the chair and brushed off the dust before sitting.

'You say Sally told you about me. How did you know her?'

'We were at school together.' Seeing that I pulled a face, she added, 'Yes, I know, a private school. Sally told me what you thought of them.'

I shrugged. 'It's not your fault. But you're here now so you might as well tell me about it.' I sat down opposite her and waited for her to begin – I wasn't at all sure I wanted to hear what she had to say – after all, I had my own problems. But then there were worse ways of spending time – it could turn out to be interesting.

'It's about my father. He went into hospital for an operation, but it was routine, there was no way he was expected to die. We were all shocked by it – even the doctors. It was so sudden that no one seems to know exactly what happened. It appears he had a heart attack after the operation and they couldn't revive him.'

'I'm sorry,' I started. 'Look, I don't even know your name.'

'It's Greta. Greta Satchwell.'

'Greta, I'm not a doctor, I don't see how I can help.'

'My father is…' she hesitated. 'He… was a property developer. Greg Satchwell. He was working on a development but it had turned sour. His partners were losing money and they blamed him. They're people who… how can I put it? People with a lot of influence who don't like to be crossed. They're not exactly blue-chip investors. Before they started this development they'd taken out some kind of life insurance on my father. It was to pay off the partnership's loans if anything happened. I think they did something, gave him something. He didn't die naturally.'

I thought about this. Despite her obvious grief, she seemed to be in control and didn't seem the type to be making wild accusations. 'I still don't see how I can help. This should be a matter for the coroner – is there going to be an inquest?'

'I don't know, but I'm the only one who knows that there were people who wanted him dead.'

'Have you been to the police?'

'I got as far as the front desk then I thought how ridiculous it sounded, so I left without seeing anyone. They would simply have fobbed me off with some feeble excuse. I've never got the impression that the police are very interested in crime.'

'It does seem a bit far-fetched.' As I saw the expression on her face, I added quickly, 'Not that it can't happen. But this isn't really my thing. I don't know anything about murder.' That didn't sound right. 'Not private-enterprise murder, that is.'

'Your wife… I mean Sally, said you'd worked in intelligence. She said that you'd recently left the army and that you weren't doing anything else. I can pay you for your time.'

I needed to think about this. I couldn't see that there was really anything I could do, but on the other hand what did I have to lose? This woman, Greta, seemed very self-assured and not short of a few bob – she looked as though she could be interesting if you got to know her. As I looked at her, I saw lines of wafer-thin scars underneath her eyes – perhaps it was related to her limp, but they only added to my interest. I wouldn't be taking advantage and it might lead to something – quite what, I had no idea. And being selfish about it, I might get to spend more time in her company which was an appealing thought. 'Tell me more.'

Greta shifted in her chair and crossed her legs stiffly. She was obviously in some discomfort and I started to help her but she shook her head impatiently as though annoyed with herself. 'He went into a private hospital off Harley Street. It was to have a lesion cut out from his liver. He'd had MRI as well as ultrasound scans which indicated it was unlikely to be malignant, but they wanted to remove it to make sure. It was keyhole surgery, but he needed a general anaesthetic followed by a few hours in intensive care to monitor recovery. The surgeon said it was a straightforward operation and it went well and after a few hours they took him back to his room for overnight recovery.' Until then Greta was showing remarkable self-control, but I could sense this was starting to slip.

'He seemed fine in the evening.' She took a deep breath before continuing, her eyes starting to water. 'They called me early the next morning. He'd... he'd been taken back into intensive care. He'd had some kind of heart attack so they tried to give him emergency bypass surgery. By the time I got there, he was dead.'

She started crying softly and I looked around fruitlessly for a tissue – all I had were dirty rags. 'Did you ask the doctors what had happened?'

It took a while before Greta could speak again. Finally she wiped her eyes. 'I'm sorry,' she said unnecessarily. 'They said they didn't know what had happened. They said there's always a risk in surgery and I should accept it. But they didn't know what I know.'

'About your father's partners, you mean?'

'Yes. They wanted him dead. I'm sure they killed him and that's why I want you to investigate it.' She had mastered her grief. Instead this was some determined lady and I thought that trying to find a murderer might prove easier than trying to say I wouldn't.

'Tell me about the partners,' I said, as much to give me breathing space as anything.

'My father never talked much about them, but he'd worked on other developments with them. They were money men, not developers at all, which was why they needed my father. He'd done well for them in the past.' She reached into her bag and after a few moments' search, brought out a business card which she handed me. "Tribune Investments" it read and a name, "Brendan E. Rogers" with just a phone number, email, and an address in London's W1 district. 'My father told me that the most recent development had hit some problems. The original survey had been botched and the land needed a big clean-up before they could start building. I work for an accountancy company and he showed me the original figures, but extra outlays like that might have destroyed any profit, not to mention the additional costs of delays and finance charges.'

I thought about this before replying. As she said, it wasn't as though I had anything else that was important. But this sounded like a non-starter to me. I'd had some experience of doctors and knew that they could throw up an impenetrable wall. Against that, what had I got to lose? That I wouldn't mind meeting Greta again didn't figure in my decision. 'Okay. Since you're a friend of Sally's, I'll go as far as talking to the hospital and see what they have to say but I'm sure there's a good medical reason for what's happened.' I smiled at her in what I hoped was a reassuring way until I saw the resentment in her eyes and realised that I was merely being patronising. Her quiet force was quite persuasive. 'Okay, okay,' I said, holding up my hands in surrender. 'I'll talk to them and let you know what they say.' It was like the army all over again. I seemed to have lost any free will in her presence and maybe I should have put my tongue back in my mouth. I scrabbled around for a writing pad and handed it to her. 'Write down the names of everyone involved. Perhaps you should start with what you and Sally might know but I don't, so I need all your details, as well as those of your father. And the hospital – I'll need their details as well.'

She took the pad and started writing and while she did so I thought about this some more. I wasn't really a gun for hire. What with the work on the boat, I had deliberately not given myself any time to think of the future. There were probably plenty of security companies out there who would employ me, but I wasn't really yet ready for private enterprise. Perhaps I'd been waiting for some kind of delayed shock to kick in, when I would finally come to accept that my army career was over. Perhaps this was an opportunity being handed to me gift-wrapped, but I wasn't sure that there was much future for an investigator working on his own. These days, things were too complicated.

Greta finished writing her list, handed me the pad and put her hand on the chair and stood up before limping to the windows and looking out over the river. 'Quite a view. My father used to love the river. He visited all the riverside pubs and read up on their history. He was a bit of a romantic, I suppose.' She pointed downriver. 'Over there's The Mayflower. It was one of his favourites.' I could hear her catch her breath but said nothing. 'He was a fine man,' she talked as though she was alone, as though I didn't exist. 'I'm going to miss him so much.' She said nothing more but I could see her shoulders shake. I felt a coward not to go over to her but she seemed to be in her own world and I didn't want to intrude.

Finally, she sniffed hard and turned back to me. 'I'm sorry. It's all happened so suddenly. We were very close.'

'I'll do what I can.' It felt so lame but I didn't know quite what to say. 'I'll help you down the gangplank.'

She shook her head. 'I can manage, thanks. Call me as soon as you have some news.' She held out her hand and I shook it before opening the saloon door for her and following her on deck. I looked on anxiously as she held onto the rope railing on her way down to the pontoon. I watched until she was safely ashore.

Back in the saloon, a slight hint of her perfume remained which made itself felt even over the default smell of paint. Wondering what I was letting myself in for, I phoned my ex-wife. We were still on good terms, each of us recognising that our marriage was simply a mistake that we got out of as soon as we decently could. Since then, while I stayed on in the army, she'd managed to qualify as a doctor which meant that she was sometimes almost impossible to get hold of, so I left my usual message in her mailbox.

I picked up the pad on which Greta had written down the names and contact details. Swearing yet again at the phone company who still hadn't managed to install the Internet, I realised that after this I wasn't going to get any more work done on the boat. I cleaned myself up and took my laptop for a walk down to the nearby café. I thought I could use their Wi-Fi to find out a bit more about the people I was now apparently investigating.

Later that day, I brought a chair up on deck and sat with my notepad looking at the river which was busily minding its own business on its way to the sea. I found there was something calming in the way the water acted as a backdrop, changing with the tides and the weather – disinterested in any human dramas that might unfold around it.

It turned out that Greta's father, Greg, was quite well known as a developer of admittedly third-tier developments. He had an impressive track record, with several laudatory interviews in the trade press. His partners, on the other hand, appeared to have a much lower profile. Indeed, I had found out almost nothing about them beyond their swanky address in the middle of the hedge-fund district in London's Mayfair. I didn't find out much about Greta herself, although I did discover that she had quite a senior position in one of the big accountancy firms.

The hospital, on the other hand, had pages devoted to it, or rather its parent company did – IHG was a huge multinational which appeared to have health interests around the globe. It seemed that there was a lot of money in illness and these were the institutional shamans of the twenty-first century.

I'd put in a call to the hospital's general manager and engaged in a game of telephone snooker as the calls went back and forth. Ever since some Australian journalists managed to get through to a ward by pretending they were royalty (and a pretty poor pretence it was) hospitals were wary about who phoned them. By using a thinly-veiled threat about the sudden and inexplicable death of Gregory Satchwell, I had finally managed to make an appointment for the following day with their general manager, David Evans. The doctor, on the other hand, hadn't returned my calls.

As if she knew I was thinking about her, at that moment my phone bleeped. I picked it up and checked the caller ID. 'Sally,' I said, without waiting to hear her talk. 'How is the medical business? Are you winning?'

'If you only knew,' she replied testily. 'Did Greta find you out on your raft?'

'It's not a raft.' Considering the effort I had put in, I rather resented her levity. 'It's soon to be a luxury river cruiser.'

'Yeah, James told me about it. He said you'd set up a standing order to the nearby rescue services, as a sort of payment in advance.' Sally always had an amusing look on life. Amusing to her, that is.

'You'll have to come and see for yourself,' I replied austerely.

'Only if you have spare lifejackets.' She laughed, not very nicely, I thought.

The badinage had gone far enough. 'Tell me about Greta,' I asked. 'Why did you think I could help? I don't know anything about her father's illness.'

'I couldn't think of anyone else,' Sally said – not exactly flatteringly. 'Anyway, it'll do you good to get out into the real world for a change.'

'Since when have I not been in the real world? Who do you think has been helping to keep you safe from terrorism? There hasn't been a single terrorist attack while I've been on watch.' (Although there had been several attempted ones that we'd prevented.)

'Didn't James Bond work for the other lot? I meant the real world that the rest of us live in.' She stopped suddenly and her voice became serious. 'Greta's not a fool, you know. If she thinks something's not right, then there's probably something in it. Certainly something worth looking into and it's not as if you're overburdened with work.'

I let that one pass. 'Is there any reason to think she's right in thinking that Greg Satchwell was murdered? Couldn't it have been from natural causes?'

'It could, but the operation was fairly routine. It was only laparoscopy – keyhole surgery, that is, so there wasn't major trauma. On the other hand late fifties can sometimes be a dangerous age for a man.'

'I'm seeing the hospital manager tomorrow. Is there anything specific I should ask?'

'See if they'd done an electrocardiogram at any stage. That should have given them advance warning of any problems. And see if there was a blood test.'

'So you don't think this might be a wild goose chase?'

'It might be, but as I say, I trust Greta. I've known her a long time.'

'Yes, since school. She told me.' Was there a note of bitterness in my voice?

'Let me know what happens,' Sally said, and then she was gone, even before I had time to arrange for her to come and see my new home.

By this time, it was getting darker and I stayed a while as the lights along the river grew brighter. I felt a strange and rather exhilarating sense of freedom and wondered whether this was what Sally called the real world. I didn't have layers of superior officers above me and I could choose what I wanted to do, not that my range of choices was exactly large, but still. How much of what people did came about as a result of accidents? Some event, tiny in itself, like the fluttering of a butterfly's wings, but enough to send a life off in a completely different direction?

In Harley Street the next day, I could take my pick of hospitals – I couldn't work out how they could fit so many of them into such a tight space. As for doctors, I was spoiled for choice – there were long rows of brass nameplates outside each of the Georgian town houses. Most of them specialised in diseases of the rich. Couriers on bicycles, going the wrong way up a one-way street, weaved in and out of the pedestrians, carrying urgent blood supplies and perhaps even spare body parts.

When I eventually found the hospital, I wondered if it was the right place – it certainly didn't feel anything like a hospital. The double doors were manned by someone who looked like a visiting admiral, complete with waistcoat and brass buttons – I wondered whether I had to tip him on my way in.

The reception area looked like the lobby of the United Nations, with women dressed from head to toe in black, escorted by contrasting young men in casual jeans and Armani leather jackets.

I was shown up to a characterless office – in an effort not to look like a hospital, these places seemed to specialise in bland interiors whose motif was clearly beige. The veneers were of an indeterminate light wood and even the floor-to-ceiling slatted blinds were beige – the blind leading the bland, I thought. Although I'd asked Greta to confirm her authority for him to speak to me, David Evans was as bland as the décor and very uncommunicative. He would only confirm the basic facts. 'Mr Satchwell came in for a relatively routine operation which, as far as anyone could tell, had been successful and that it was only later, during the early morning, that he had deteriorated.' Evans shook his head sadly. 'These things happen and we're truly sorry when they do, but it's not our fault.'

'I'm not saying it was, but there must be a reason for his relapse. So far, no one has given his daughter any explanation.'

'You'll have to speak to the doctors about that,' Evans said with practised evasion. 'My job here is to make the hospital run smoothly. The patients are the responsibility of the medical staff.'

'Surely their security is your responsibility?'

'Security, yes, and you'll find that we take it very seriously. All visitors have to sign in and we have CCTV cameras throughout the hospital which are monitored permanently by our security staff.'

My pulse quickened at the mention of surveillance cameras. 'Can I look at the recordings for that evening?'

Evans was clearly about to say no, but stopped himself while he thought about it. 'I don't see why not,' he said finally. 'If only because it will reassure you that nothing untoward happened here.'

He stood up. 'I'll take you to our security office and show you the cameras on the way.'

I followed him out of his office and along the corridor where he pointed out the cameras at both ends, as well as two covering the nurses' station. 'As I said, all visitors have to sign in and we can also record them down in reception and then follow them around.' He turned to a door near the end of the corridor and opened it, allowing me to go ahead of him.

A man was sitting in front of a bank of TV monitors and, seeing the general manager, he stood up and looked at me expectantly. 'Bob, this is Philip Hennessey,' Evans said. 'This is Bob Tyler, our acting head of security.' I shook Tyler's outstretched hand. 'Mr Hennessey is helping Mr Satchwell's daughter come to terms with her father's death.' *I suppose that's one way of putting it*, I thought.

Bob Tyler was in his mid to late fifties but was someone who clearly looked after himself.

'I said we'd give him what help we could,' continued Evans, 'so that he can see that there was nothing… suspicious about it.' He hesitated over the word "suspicious", as though it had a nasty taste. 'Perhaps you could show him the recordings from the cameras?' It was clear he'd now finished with me – not that there was much else I could get out of him. Being allowed to look at the video recordings was more than I thought I'd get.

Bob pointed to one of the screens. 'That's the corridor outside what was Mr Satchwell's room, number 315.' So Bob had already looked into it and knew the room number. As though reading my mind, he added, 'Whenever there are sudden deaths we have to produce a report about the general circumstances. We don't comment on the medical aspect, but we like people to know that we are aware of the circumstances.'

So they can hush it up, I thought uncharitably.

Bob pulled out a disc for the previous week's recordings and showed me how to cue it to the time that Greg Satchwell returned from his few hours in intensive care. After that I pushed it to fast forward and made a note of how many people came into his room.

By the time I got to midnight I had a total of eight visits, but of those the night nurse had entered five times, Greta once, followed shortly afterwards by a doctor who was obviously bringing Greta up to date.

After she'd left, there was quite a long gap before the doctor returned. I noted the times and went back and played each visit more slowly. On the face of it, it was a perfectly normal evening in a private hospital, quiet and calm. But why would a doctor make a second call so late at night? What could he find out that he didn't already know?

On a hunch, I asked for the disc for the reception area and Bob cued it to ten minutes before the doctor was seen for the second time on the corridor above. Sure enough, it showed someone entering and signing in. He was wearing street clothes – what looked like a sports jacket, rather than the white coat he was wearing when he appeared later up on the third floor. I looked more closely at the screen and realised that this wasn't the doctor coming back but someone entirely different. Bob, who'd been watching the videos over my shoulder, was starting to look concerned by what I was finding. He suggested we look at the third-floor reception area and after a few minutes the stranger could be seen coming out from the lift and approaching the nurses' station.

This time he'd acquired the white coat, although I couldn't tell where he'd picked it up from or where he had found the stethoscope he had around his neck. He started talking to the nurses who handed him some records which he examined before handing them back and heading for Greg Satchwell's room. I wondered why the nurses hadn't questioned him but realised that the stethoscope was his badge of authority.

I turned to Bob. 'Can you print out a face shot from this, and also from the recording when he originally signed in?' Bob re-cued the video and zoomed into the face and pressed the "print screen" button. 'And the recordings?' I asked. 'Can I get a copy?'

'Absolutely not,' he said without hesitation. 'I've gone too far with this already.' He handed me the printouts. 'You can't tell anyone where you got these from, or my job's on the line.

I'm letting you have them on condition you tell me if you find out anything, I might need some support.'

'Thanks for your help.' I folded the printouts into my pocket. As an afterthought, I asked him if he'd been working at the hospital long.

'Only a few months,' he replied. 'When the previous security manager left they transferred me temporarily from one of their other, smaller, hospitals.'

'How many do they have?'

'In London? Six here but dozens more around the country.'

'Do you think they'll offer you the job permanently?' I asked.

'Huh? No, not at my age. They'll probably bring in some kid and put him over my head. Roll on retirement,' he added.

I wondered what it must be like only to have retirement to look forward to – all those empty days. I thanked Bob for his help and assured him that I'd keep in touch, even though I had no intention of doing so. He'd certainly been more helpful than I had expected – perhaps that's why he was only acting head of security. I thought about it on my way back to Wapping, unsure of what to do next. Certainly it was odd that a different doctor should make a call so late at night, but wasn't it a jump too far to go from that to murder?

But at least I had something concrete to investigate, and on my way back I ducked into an Internet café and scanned the photo into my phone. I emailed it to Greta and asked her to phone me as soon as she got it. I thought it was now time to follow it up from the other end and find out more about Tribune Investments, but that wasn't going to be easy.

I hadn't been back long before Greta phoned. She sounded excited and slightly breathless. 'That man, who is he? I've seen him before. He works at Tribune Investments.'

Chapter Four

It appeared that Greta might have been right about her father's death after all, but recognising the man in the printout wasn't going to get us very far. Without independent corroboration of the link with Tribune Investments they could simply deny it and there wouldn't be anything we could do. I scrolled through my contact list – over the years I'd used an odd-job man to help with my various removals and do-it-yourself fit-outs – Paul was a man with a van, but I thought he might be able to help. It rang for a long time but didn't go to voicemail, so I assumed he would answer in due course. When he finally did, it was clear that I'd woken him.

Paul was not an early riser, nor did he snap into immediate consciousness when he finally did rise – although I use the word "rise" loosely, since from what I knew of him he was generally horizontal for a considerable time after waking.

When I was finally confident that he was vaguely compos mentis, I explained that I wanted him to wait outside the Tribune offices and photograph whoever went in or out. I emailed the scanned picture from the hospital saying that he should phone me immediately if he saw the man anywhere.

'A stakeout,' he said. 'How exciting!' At least that seemed to wake him.

Of course, he was quite wrong. A stakeout is almost terminally boring which was why I wasn't going to do it myself, and anyway, Greta was paying for it. If the suspect really did work at Tribune then I might not have long to wait and if Paul got a photo of him entering or leaving Tribune's premises, it would be pretty damning evidence.

Next, I looked up the number of Greg Satchwell's doctor that Greta had left on the pad. This time the phone was answered by a secretary. I explained who I was and she replied that Professor West had been told by Greta Satchwell to expect my call. Professor? Greta hadn't told me that bit – he must have been from a teaching hospital. The secretary confirmed this when she made an appointment for me the following morning at an NHS hospital in London's West End.

I noted down directions and wondered about the life of consultants who bridged the gap between public and private medicine, keeping a foot in both camps. Perhaps in their view the one was subsidising the other. There wasn't much more I could do now, so I climbed into my overalls and got back to work on the boat.

Arriving at the hospital the next day, I felt a bit like Theseus in the labyrinth, and wished I had an Ariadne to leave a thread for me to follow. The place was a contortion of corridors, cul-de-sacs, and no-entry zones – it certainly couldn't be mistaken for the private clinics around Harley Street and this one even smelled like a hospital. Finally, I managed to find the professor's office, but it had taken so long that I was running late when I arrived. The secretary looked pointedly at the wall clock.

'I know, I know,' I apologised. That's why hospital appointments always tell you to come fifteen minutes early, to give you time to get lost.

The professor was quite a short man, with a little goatee beard. To be honest, I wasn't that keen on short men with goatee beards, but I tried not to hold that against him.

'Greta has told me about her concerns,' he said. He had a clipped, rather self-conscious way of talking, a bit schoolmasterly, but then he was a professor. 'I have to say that I share some of these concerns and I'm glad that someone is looking into it for her.'

I nodded in acknowledgement but was surprised that he appeared sympathetic – sympathy isn't something usually expressed by doctors, even when they felt it. 'Can you tell me more about your concerns? From a medical point of view of course?'

The professor steepled his fingers. If there's one thing I like less than a short man with a goatee beard, it's a short man with a goatee beard who steepled his fingers. It was a sign that I was about to receive a lecture, but to be fair, that's why I was there. 'As far as I was concerned it was straightforward. The removal of a lesion by laparoscopy, I've done it hundreds of times.'

'And there was nothing about this that made it any different?'

'Nothing. It was entirely straightforward. After the procedure, he was kept in ICU for a few hours. Intensive care is a precaution in case there are reactions to the procedure or the drugs. But in Mr Satchwell's case there were none.'

Afterwards, I went in to see him when his daughter, Greta, arrived and I explained that everything had gone well and the sample had been sent off for a biopsy, although I doubted that this was really necessary, but it was a precaution we always take in these circumstances. I checked his notes with the night nurse and they indicated nothing out of the ordinary.'

'You didn't go back again later?'

He looked surprised. 'No. There was no reason to. Everything looked normal.'

'When did you realise that there were complications?'

'I'm not sure I would describe them as "complications",' he replied, rather pedantically. 'I don't think there was any relationship between my procedure and what happened next.'

You would say that, wouldn't you? I thought. 'But when did you hear that he had relapsed?' I repeated.

'I got a call from the duty doctor early the next morning. He asked me if there was anything about the operation that he should know – it was as though he was accusing me. I told him there wasn't. He told me that they were trying an emergency bypass, but he said he wasn't hopeful.' West paused. 'In the end I suppose his prognosis was right. It appeared that Mr Satchwell never regained consciousness.'

'So what do you think happened?'

'I've given this some thought,' the professor replied guardedly. 'It could have been related to the anticoagulant we used. There's always a trade-off for patients who take anti-coagulants for their heart condition balanced against the need for blood clotting during an operation.'

'And was Mr Satchwell taking anticoagulants? Did he have a heart condition prior to this?'

'I think it was more of a precaution than a condition. We'd changed his prescription some days before the operation, to minimise the time between stopping it for the laparoscopy, and then starting it again afterwards. When carrying out surgery, you don't want uncontrolled bleeding so we stop the anticoagulants beforehand. All this is perfectly routine,' he added, as though I was questioning his clinical judgement.

'But clotting is a risk? I understand that if he had previously diagnosed coronary disease, anything that promoted clotting could be dangerous.' I mentally thanked my Internet session on Wikipedia for providing me with a rudimentary medical knowledge.

'Theoretically, yes. But most unlikely to have any effect in such a short timescale.'

'But you're sure that the ultimate cause of death was a heart attack?' So far he had not committed himself.

The professor was silent for a few moments. 'The duty doctor said there was no doubt, but that doesn't explain the cause. It could have been a natural event, that his time was up, if you like.'

'But you don't think so? Had he had an ECG beforehand, or any blood tests for cardiac markers?' This time it was my ex-wife I thanked for her input.

'No, we didn't see the need. I told you his heart condition appeared only very minor.'

'Enough to kill him.' I couldn't help myself but I was getting annoyed by the professor's rather smug evasions.

As though sensing my frustration, the professor suddenly seemed to change tack. 'You must understand, I wasn't there when he had the seizure that killed him. As I told you, when I left him late the previous night he seemed fine. I didn't get back to the hospital until after he'd died, so there was nothing I could do. I was told it was a heart attack, so I had to accept it.'

'So you did go back that morning?'

'Yes, of course, he was my patient.' West turned and looked out of the window for quite a long time before speaking again. 'I don't want you to get the wrong idea. The hospital is always going to say that it was natural causes. They don't want to admit that anything could have gone wrong, but it's different for me. I have a professional responsibility, but I have a personal one as well and I think that something's not right here. I've had some concerns about this hospital and had been thinking of changing.'

'Concerns about the hospital? What sort of concerns?'

'It's got a big multinational behind it which means they have almost unlimited resources. If there's any possibility of someone making a mistake – even a minor one that's obvious to everyone, they clam up and go into denial. It's not the right way to run a hospital – you have to be aware of the risks and be open about them. It took them years before they even recognised that infections could be carried by their own medical staff.'

I thought the professor was being remarkably complacent. 'You put up with this? You work with these people even though you knew about their cover-ups?'

'I didn't know for sure,' he said defensively. 'It was part of their culture.'

'A culture that allows a university professor – a public figure – to be employed to treat patients privately for a healthy fee?'

'I'm not going to argue with you. These are the conditions we have to work under. I didn't make the rules.'

'From what you say there don't appear to be many rules. Who benefits most from your relationship with IHG? Them, for having a professor on their notepaper, or you for the fees you can charge?'

'I don't have to put up with this,' he snapped. 'Who are you, anyway? Coming in here and making accusations?'

'I thought it was you who was making accusations, Professor. I'm just asking questions and you've already said enough for me to report you to the BMA. Tell me what else you know about this hospital.'

He looked down at his phone and I could tell he was debating whether to call security to have me thrown out but he hesitated. He looked back up at me. 'You should be aware that they swim in a murky pool. The largest hospital group in the US was forced to pay a record fine – nearly a billion dollars, which they settled for falsifying invoices. They also paid doctors backhanders for referring their patients to their hospitals.'

'Are you suggesting that they might have had a hand in Greg Satchwell's death?'

'Not directly, no...' He hesitated and I waited for him to steeple his fingers again, but the fight seemed to have left him. 'I'm saying that things aren't always as they appear.'

'And that seems to apply to you as well, Professor.' I stood up. 'Thank you for your time.'

As I navigated my way through the corridors out to fresh air, I thought things hadn't turned out quite as I expected. Perhaps I was naïve but it hadn't occurred to me that private hospitals could operate fraudulently. Equally, I hadn't realised how big these organisations were, given that they also owned scores of hospitals throughout America where most were private. Perhaps there was an internal conspiracy within IHG to cover up all unexplained deaths? Before speaking to Professor West I would have thought such a thing impossible, but now I was not so sure. Private healthcare was a massive business, even in the UK and, as Professor West had said, where there's money there's often corruption.

It seemed even more likely that Greta's suspicions might be based upon reality, which made me look at things in a different light. If even his doctor was concerned about the sudden death then this didn't look like the waste of time I thought it was. I decided that since I was quite close by, I would go across to the Tribune offices and see if Paul had taken up station yet. Despite his apparent waywardness, he was fairly reliable.

I worried about the "fairly" but I needn't have. In fact it was difficult to miss him. He's tall and gangling, and was wearing threadbare jeans and a leather flying jacket that looked as though it had been through a world war and ended up on the losing side. But it wasn't that that attracted attention, more the fact that he was standing two doors down from the Tribune front door and making no effort to look occupied. He saw me coming and I signalled to him. 'You're supposed to look unobtrusive,' I said. 'You look like an overgrown kid waiting to see if Santa Claus is going to come down the chimney. Have you seen anything yet?'

Paul started to pout and I had to stop myself from laughing. Clearly he'd rather fancied his role as a super-sleuth. 'Give me a chance,' he said plaintively. 'I've only been here an hour.'

I realised I had a decision to make. Either I could go back and wait on the boat on the off chance that Paul could identify the suspect, or I could barge in and wave the photograph at the reception desk and see if anyone was prepared to talk to me. Action against inaction? I hadn't spent all those years in army intelligence for nothing. Their motto was: if in doubt, don't. Wait until your intel has built up a picture of the situation before doing anything. Was this why I was no longer serving? Waiting wasn't really my style and anyway, what did I have to lose? If they threw me out, I could still come back if Paul discovered anything. I decided to chance it. Directing Paul to wait in a slightly less obvious place, I checked that I still had the photographs in my pocket and headed up the steps to brandish it.

They buzzed me through the front door into a large reception area. There was no hint of blandness here. Quite the opposite – it looked as though I was walking through some of the pages of my books on design. Among the artwork on the walls, a large, bright Lichtenstein print dominated the room, at least I assume it was a print otherwise it would have been worth as much as the building. The furniture, what there was of it, was minimalist Bauhaus, pieces that I coveted but had no hope of affording. Someone clearly had taste, taste backed up by deep pockets. If this was a front, it was a damned impressive one. The receptionist, who would rate as employee of the year if she was as efficient as she was attractive, was looking at me expectantly and I decided to start at the top. 'I wanted to see Mr Rogers. Is he free?' She asked if I had an appointment, knowing full well that I didn't. She was about to give me the brush off and she was clearly as practised at giving it as I was at taking it, although generally it's been from women more in my league. I interrupted her before she could get into her stride. 'If he's here, tell him it's about Greg Satchwell. I'm investigating his death.'

That almost penetrated her poise – obviously the name meant something to her because instead of calling security, she asked me to take a seat. I watched as instead of phoning she turned to her computer and typed a message on her keyboard, that way I wouldn't know what she was saying about me, although I could probably guess.

After several minutes, it seemed that she had got her answer. 'Mr Rogers says he can give you five minutes. If you'll come this way?'

I followed her upstairs in the lift and she led me to what must have been the *piano nobile*, the main first-floor reception room when the house was first built in the late seventeenth century. Again, the décor was contemporary, with matching Eames chairs and ottomans in front of the fireplace. There were more pictures on the wall, and a huge pair of Warhol screen prints of flowers faced the full-height windows looking onto the street.

Brendan Rogers was sitting at a large rosewood conference table, with papers scattered around him. He looked up and nodded at the receptionist. 'Thank you, Moira,' he said, dismissing her. Turning to me he said, 'Mr Hennessey, is it?' He indicated one of the cane chairs across the table which looked like an original Marcel Breuer. 'Have a seat. You said it was about Greg Satchwell?'

Greta hadn't told me much about Rogers but this was a man who exuded calm and authority in equal quantities – clearly a man accustomed to having his own way. He was quite heavyset, wearing a charcoal double-breasted suit. His complexion was dark but his heavy beard was smooth – his five o'clock shadow probably appeared sometime around midday, suggesting that he probably shaved more than once a day. All in all, I thought, a man careful of his appearance. I sat where he indicated. 'Yes. His daughter, Greta, has asked me to look into it.'

'Look into it?' Rogers repeated. 'So that's your man who's been waiting outside in the street watching our front door?'

Ouch! That was below the belt, I thought, but tried to pretend that it hadn't hurt. 'I understand that you were a partner in his latest development?'

'My company was, yes. We'd done several projects together quite successfully.'

'But this one wasn't a success, was it?'

Rogers paused, as though anticipating where this was going. 'We've learned to take these things in our stride,' he said finally. 'We can still come out ahead.'

'Is it true that you had taken out insurance on Mr Satchwell's life?' I decided to go with the direct approach.

'Key Man insurance? Yes. That was quite normal; we take it out on all our top staff and on the important people we work with. Key men in fact – the clue's in the name. They are important to us and we need to look after them.'

'And you are aware that Mr Satchwell died suddenly from an unknown cause?'

'We knew he died suddenly, but we didn't think the cause was unknown. I understood it was a heart attack.'

'So you'll collect on the insurance?'

Rogers laughed. 'Ah, I see where this is going. You suspect we had something to do with his death?' He shook his head. 'You're way off track. We wanted him alive more than most. Sure, we'll get the insurance pay-out but that might not even cover the costs we're facing getting his development back on its legs. It's certainly not a motive for a killing. I'm not quite sure what kind of operation you think this is, though you have quite some nerve walking in here off the street and accusing us of murder.'

'I'm not accusing anyone.' I realised I was in danger of getting thrown out before I could learn anything. 'I'm trying to find out what happened.' I thought it time to shake his complacency and took out the photograph, smoothed it down and placed it in front of him. 'This man was seen entering the hospital shortly before midnight. After going through reception, he put on a white coat pretending to be a doctor. He then went upstairs and into room 315 and a few hours later Greg Satchwell was dead when none of the doctors expected it. That's what I mean about dying from an unknown cause.' I waited a beat before delivering my coup de grâce. 'Greta Satchwell says she's seen this man here in your offices.'

Rogers continued looking at the photograph before raising his eyes to meet mine. He said nothing for a while and then picked up the phone and punched in a number. 'Warren, could you come in here for a moment?' He put down the phone and then turned to me. 'Perhaps you should have done your homework before charging in here.' He said nothing further and in a few moments the door was opened and the man in my photograph walked in. 'Mr Hennessey, meet Warren Bidwell, our security consultant.'

I tried to remain impassive as though this sort of thing happened to me all the time, but it was like having your ace of spades trumped by the two of diamonds. After my interview with Professor West and now this, I was starting to feel way out of my depth, but just because Brendan Rogers was admitting that this Bidwell character worked for them, it didn't mean that he wasn't involved.

'Mr Hennessey here thinks you had something to do with Greg Satchwell's sudden death. He's seen the video camera recording showing you went to his hospital room a few hours before Satchwell died.'

'That's what you pay me for, guv.' My "suspect" didn't seem in the least bothered at being found out. 'I always keep tabs on the company's partners, especially when there's a lot of money at stake.'

'After eleven o'clock at night?' I asked disbelievingly.

'It's the best time. No doctors around, only the night staff, while the security people are probably snoozing in front of their video displays. The nurses were happy to show me the patient's records and talk about the operation. If it had been any other time they would have been too busy.'

'Mr Hennessey,' Brendan Rogers interrupted, 'Greta has obviously not told you very much about our operation. We are very,' he tapped the table to emphasise his point, 'very careful. We don't just insure our partners' lives, we investigate them thoroughly and monitor them as long as we are working together. We don't like surprises. If a partner goes into hospital for an operation, we like to check it out and make sure that we've been told the truth. Our Key Man insurance covers hospitalisation as well as death so we need to make sure of the facts before we put in a claim. It wouldn't have been the first time that a partner tried to mislead us. Warren here was able to confirm that the operation was routine. As I told you, we take every precaution possible and so I can assure you that we had nothing whatsoever to do with Greg Satchwell's premature death.' He looked at me as though expecting a response, but I could think of nothing to say.

'In fact,' he went on, 'I liked Greg; I liked him a lot. He was the same sort of man as I am. He was self-reliant and could see through problems clearly and didn't like wasting time.' Rogers said this looking at me pointedly. 'Greg was on his way to turning his development around in spite of the problems they'd had. There was no way I wanted him dead – I wanted him very much alive.'

Rogers paused for a moment. 'In fact,' he continued, 'perhaps I could spare Warren here to give you some help in looking into this.'

That took me aback. Another meeting that wasn't exactly turning out as I had suspected. 'I'll bear that in mind,' I said lamely. 'It's early days yet.'

Rogers stood up, but didn't offer his hand. 'Bear it in mind.' He gestured to Warren to show me out. 'And your colleague outside, take him with you.'

Chapter Five

I'd phoned Greta and asked her to meet me back at the barge. I thought that if I was going to destroy her theories about her father, then it should be to her face. First, I had to tell Paul that his career as a private eye was going to be short-lived – I didn't have the heart to tell him that he'd been rumbled. He seemed disappointed, although whether this was because he wasn't going to be making any money or because he had rather fancied himself as a super-sleuth, I couldn't tell. He said he didn't have anything better to do, and since he hadn't seen my new home, we went back to Wapping.

'I'd get this fixed, if I were you, before someone falls in,' Paul said as he clambered up the gangplank. He looked around and nodded approvingly. 'Neat. You could give some good parties here, though you'd have to have a lifeguard on duty and make sure that all the guests could swim. You could give them water-wings as they get on board.' I took him into the saloon, which I admit still wasn't looking at its best. 'Have you had a break-in?' he asked sarcastically. 'You know I could help you with this. Get it sorted in no time.'

'Can't afford you. Besides, it's good therapy. Keeps my mind off my future, assuming I have one. Don't touch that.' Paul was playing with the boat controls while making "broom-broom" noises. 'It's not a racing car,' I said. 'I've got someone coming to look at the engines next week. I've no idea whether they work or not – I haven't dared to try them out.'

'Not much danger of you making a moonlight flit then, unless you go downriver with the tide. So how come you've got time for this investigation business? What happened to the army?' I hadn't had the courage to tell him that I'd been thrown out – which was what it was, despite the "honourable resignation" label. I explained that I'd had enough and wanted to try something else. Perhaps that wasn't too far from the truth.

'Is this your client now?' Paul was looking across the pontoon where Greta was heading for the boat. We watched anxiously as she pulled herself up the gangplank holding hard onto the handrail.

When she came on deck, I introduced her to Paul and explained that I'd asked him to keep watch on the Tribune offices that morning. I held open the saloon door and we followed her in. I cleared the chair again and this time she sat without checking. I turned to Paul and suggested that he might have better things to do elsewhere, which of course he didn't, but he took the hint and left us alone.

'I joined Paul there,' I said. 'Since you recognised the person at the hospital, there didn't seem much point in delaying. I managed to speak to Brendan Rogers.'

Greta looked surprised. 'He agreed to see you?'

'I said it was about your father's death so he couldn't really refuse.'

'And the man in the photograph, did he admit that he worked for them?'

'He did better than that, he introduced me to him. His name's Warren Bidwell and he's their security consultant.'

'So they didn't try to hide it then?'

'Not at all, but they said he was only checking out your father's operation. It seems they're a suspicious lot, Tribune.'

'Lots of people, including me, are suspicious of *them*,' said Greta. 'They're the sort of people who breed suspicion. I'm not sure how my father ever joined up with them and although I often asked him, he was always quite evasive. I suppose given where their money comes from, suspicion is a way of life.'

'He didn't end up with a decapitated horse at the end of his bed, so I suppose they must have trusted one another up to a point. So where *does* the money come from?'

'As I told you the other day, it's very unclear. The only thing I know is that it doesn't come from here but from overseas. They don't list a single UK investor and most of the investors they do list are anonymous corporations in the Cayman Islands or some such.'

'Presumably your father checked them out, and you said that he'd done previous work with them, so he at least must have thought they were above board.'

'He and Brendan Rogers seemed to get along well together and he'd made them quite a lot of money in the past. What did you think of them?'

I shrugged. 'They've got some pretty fancy offices for a start, and if they're not short of money, they're not short of good taste either. Walls covered with Warhols and Lichtensteins – they even had a couple of Richard Hamiltons. But I can't see how they would risk anything illegal if the source of their money is suspect. It would bring them too much attention and that's probably the last thing they want. I'm almost sorry to say this, but I don't think they had anything to do with your father's death.'

'What about the life insurance? Did they tell you about that?'

'Key Man insurance? Yes. They explained that it was routine. They take out insurance on all their partners but they said it wasn't enough to cover any losses. They also said that your father had managed to turn the project around and there might not be any.'

'That's not what my father was telling me just before he died. Mind you, it would be typical of him to exaggerate the problems so he could take all the more credit if he managed to sort it out.'

'Why don't we go and have a look ourselves? See what's happening to it – could you arrange that?'

'I suppose I could.' She shook her hair out of her eyes in an almost coquettish gesture but it was clearly something she did without thinking. 'I haven't had much time to think about it, but as far as I know my father left me everything so I suppose the development company is mine now. I had a sort of paralysis and couldn't really face up to anything. I did check with the staff in his office and they told me they'd had to put construction on hold while they checked the legal situation with Tribune Investments. But it seemed that everything was under control so they carried on, but I'm really not sure that it's worth continuing with. Perhaps I should cut our losses and sell it on.'

'Let's take a look first. You could come with me and see for yourself. We could go there in the morning.'

The development was on a brownfield site in Camden, north London. It had once been an old piano factory, but that had been back in the days when people were taught piano as a matter of course. These days it was only a privileged few and piano-making in the UK was now almost defunct. We found the site office in a large cabin in one corner and introduced ourselves to the site agent, who had been told to expect us. He already knew Greta who introduced us. 'Charlie Atwell. He's worked with my father on and off for years.' His fluorescent hi-vis jacket only partly concealed his gut which was hanging over his waistband. He must have been pushing sixty, although his deeply lined face might have been deceptive. Certainly he looked as though he'd had a hard physical life.

'And a better boss you couldn't hope for,' he said, shaking my hand. 'It's a great loss.' He sighed. 'Not that we always saw eye to eye. We've had some right old barneys over the years, but it was never personal. He always listened to his people. Sure, he made the final decision, but he listened and you can't say that about many people these days. He didn't come the big "I am" – didn't need to, he owned the company so it was his loss if it went wrong.'

'And did it?' I asked. 'Go wrong, I mean?'

'This one's certainly had its moments. It's not often that someone was able to put one over on Greg, but they managed it here. The agent didn't tell him about the soil condition and the first surveyor missed it. It's delayed us months.'

'But you're back working now?'

'I'll show you. Here,' he said holding out hard hats for us both. 'You'd better put these on.'

I took mine and looked around the site. Two huge drilling machines, rather like giant corkscrews, were being set up.

'We've excavated the contaminated top soil already,' Atwell said. 'The drilling machines had already been delivered to site so they've been sitting around doing nothing but racking up bills. Then,' he hesitated, looking at Greta, 'after your father died we had to stop again while they sorted out the financing. But, we're up and running again and we'll start piling in the morning.'

We followed him along the scaffolding boards that ran around the site. Wooden pegs marked out the limits of the construction and the varying levels. We watched as the workmen moved the machines into position, but it was impossible to work out where they were going to be building.

'London clay,' Atwell said. 'Our worst enemy. We've had to put in these deep piled foundations and then support the concrete foundation beams off the top of them. In a building up the road cracks started appearing within a few months of moving in. Sad, really,' he said. 'It was an old people's home so they had to move everybody out and pull the building down and then rebuild it. I imagine a few lawyers got rich on that one. Here, I'll show you the plans.'

Inside the office, he pulled out a set of drawings from a plan chest. It was a fairly typical residential development with shops and offices on the ground floor and flats above. The building was set around a courtyard in the centre, which the plans showed as landscaped with a small pond. 'That's a swimming pond,' Charlie said. 'They're all the rage these days. Entirely natural, no heating, just plants and pond animals to keep the water clean.'

'Quite a smart address for a newt.' I couldn't guess who would be more surprised when they came across each other, the swimmer or the newts and I wondered how long it would be before they gave up on it and filled it in and paved it over. Charlie showed us some typical flat layouts and then told us how much they were asking for them. 'You have to be joking. Are the walls lined with gold leaf?'

Charlie ignored this. 'There's such a demand for flats, especially in Camden. Industrial units are being bought up, pulled down and rebuilt as housing. Lord knows where the people are going to find jobs. The people who used to work in places like this have been forced out.' Charlie turned to Greta. 'Your father's investors went through the figures and realised that the delays could be turned to their advantage because rising prices might mean they could put them up. In fact, with prices rising as fast as they are, there might be more money in leaving them empty until they level off. That's what happened in the early seventies. I was working for Wimpey at the time. Office rents were going up so fast that the owners made more money keeping their buildings empty. Remember Centrepoint? Empty for years after they'd built it. "Unacceptable face of capitalism" it was called. Ironic that it gave its name to a charity for the homeless.'

'So even with all the delays, you think you could still come out ahead?' Greta asked.

'I'm not the money man, but from what I gathered it'll still manage to wash its face. Greg seemed to have a golden touch that didn't desert him even... even...' His voice trailed off. 'We'll miss him,' Charlie added finally. He looked around the site. 'He used to love it on site. Any excuse and he'd come by and have a chat. I think it was his personal touch that made him successful. He was very open with everyone and treated them all the same whoever they were. I remember one time when the police came, all puffed up, he had them eating out of his hands in no time.'

'What police?'

'Someone walking past had seen him injecting himself and thought he was a junkie, so they called the police.'

'Injecting himself? Why? What was he–?'

'I didn't tell you,' Greta interrupted. 'My father was diabetic.'

I was too astonished to reply. *That's rather an important detail you've kept from me*, I thought and wondered if there was anything else I hadn't been told.

After that bombshell, we stayed a while looking around the site, while Charlie pointed out some of the more innovative features of the development. 'The sort of detail Greg brought to the project to make his developments special,' was how he explained it.

We took a taxi back to the West End and Greta's office. 'That should satisfy you that Tribune didn't want your father dead,' I said. 'The project wasn't losing money, even if it wasn't going to make as much as they hoped.'

'There's still the life insurance.' Greta clearly didn't want to give up on her pet theory without a fight.

'I really don't think an organisation like Tribune Investments is going to have people killed for their life insurance. They'd be better off burglarising Hatton Garden diamond vaults than risking themselves in anything as extreme as murder. Think about it for a moment and you'll realise how far-fetched it was. I agreed to look into it for you and speak to the hospital and I've done more than that.'

Greta was staring out of the taxi window. 'But I'm sure that something happened,' she said finally. 'There was no way he should have died like that, so suddenly. What can I do now?' she asked, showing an unusual helplessness.

I like to think my training has made me pretty tough and I don't allow much to get to me, except for an attractive woman, that is, especially one on the verge of tears. Does it every time. 'Okay, okay, I'll give it one last shot but it really will be the last. Incidentally, where did your father live?'

'St John's Wood, north of Regent's Park. In a mansion block not far from Lord's cricket ground. He was a member and used to watch the cricket quite often.'

'And have you still got it? I mean, is it still as he left it?' There wouldn't be much point looking around an empty flat.

'I haven't even begun to think about it yet,' Greta said. 'It's still too early. I took his things back from the hospital and left them there and I haven't been back since.'

'Why don't I meet you there later and we can go through his things together? See if there's anything that looks unusual. It's not likely, but it might be worth a try.' She gave me the address of her father's flat and we arranged to meet there during her lunchtime. She asked me not to be late since she didn't want to be there on her own.

By now the taxi had stopped outside Greta's office; she worked for one of those large accountancy firms identified only by their initials which meant they weren't really identified at all, since they all sounded interchangeable with each other and with advertising agencies. Gentleman that I am, I allowed her to pay and then took the Underground back to the barge to do a couple of hours' work before our meeting.

It was on the way back that I saw a face looking at me in the next compartment. It was a fleeting glance before he turned away, but I realised I'd seen him before, though I couldn't remember where. London is a big city and you don't see the same person twice in different places at different times. Not unless he's following you, that is. From what Brendan Rogers had told me, this was probably one of Tribune's "precautions" though what they thought they would learn by following me I had no idea. As I got back to the boat I wondered whether, if I saw him again, I should offer him a paintbrush and ask him to help. He was going to be very bored otherwise.

By the time I got to St John's Wood later that day, Greta was already there, pacing the pavement anxiously. I hadn't noticed whether I was still being followed, but I thought it best not to look around too often. If my tail thought that I'd noticed him, then I didn't want him to think that I was acting for his benefit, rather than mine. Equally, I couldn't tell whether Greta was being followed but thought it would upset her if I asked.

She took me up in the lift and unlocked both locks and ushered me inside. There was a musty smell in the flat and I suggested she open the windows to make the place feel less depressing. There was a large living room with full-width sliding windows opening onto a huge terrace. In the distance, I could see the stand of the MCC cricket ground at Lord's, although the pitch itself was hidden.

Pity, I thought, otherwise with a good pair of binoculars and the radio turned on, he could have enjoyed the comfort of test matches from his own home.

I followed Greta into one of the bedrooms which had obviously been fitted out as an office. Using another of her keys, she unlocked the bureau in the corner and then the filing cabinets next to it. Most of the cabinets were almost empty. 'He only kept personal files here,' Greta explained. 'All the papers relating to his developments were kept in the office.'

I went through them without any idea of what I might be looking for. There were albums of photographs of his developments in one drawer, and correspondence with the Inland Revenue in another. I read some of the letters, but they were all routine and none indicated any possible problems. I sat down at the bureau, which was a fine piece of period furniture and probably worth a good few thousand. The pigeon holes contained old postcards, along with cheque stubs going back decades. Greg Satchwell appeared to be someone who didn't like throwing things away.

'Did he live alone?' I asked Greta, suddenly aware of how little I knew about her father.

'He had on-and-off lady friends, but nothing permanent. No one who'd taken up occupation.'

'And your mother?'

'She died a few years ago. We used to live in a house quite close by, but my father moved here after she died. I'd already got a flat of my own so he didn't want to be rattling around in a big house where everything was a reminder of her. Also, a flat meant fewer ties. If he wanted to go away he only had to shut the front door and leave, but a house meant there was too much that needed looking after.'

'Did he have any help?'

'There was a woman who came in a couple of times a week to tidy and clean, but otherwise he looked after himself. He was out somewhere most evenings so he didn't cook much. Although, actually, he was quite a good cook,' she added.

'He kept the place tidy.'

'Yes. He didn't like mess. I think he was rather relieved when I moved into my own flat, because my room was always a tip.'

I shut the bureau and stood up. 'I don't know what we're looking for, but as far as I can tell, it's not here. Let's try his bedroom.'

Greta led me back through the living room to the master bedroom which shared the same full-width windows onto the terrace. The room was as tidy as all the others, except for a couple of plastic carrier bags thrown onto the bed. I checked the bedside table and then went into the walk-in cupboard. All his suits were hanging neatly, some in the plastic covers they'd come back in from the cleaners. 'What's on the bed?'

'Just his possessions from the hospital,' Greta said. 'I threw everything from his bedside table into those bags. I haven't looked at them but I can't imagine there's anything interesting there.'

I tipped the contents of both bags onto the bed. There was his wristwatch, a couple of magazines and a paperback. A dressing gown, some tissues and his medication. 'You brought his medicines back?' I asked Greta.

'As I said, I brought everything here. I put them all in the bags.'

I spread out the medicines over the bed cover. Apart from the specialist medicines there was his anticoagulant, Oxaban, which he'd been taking for his heart, as well as the insulin for his diabetes. I picked them up and shook them. There were still plenty of anticoagulants left as well as insulin cartridges. I put them down on the bed and started going through them. The Oxaban bottle looked a bit odd and as I inspected the label it came unstuck and fell off, which I thought was strange. I looked at it more carefully and there was something about it that suggested it wasn't the original label.

I picked up the insulin container. 'This label's been stuck on top of an older one. Look.' I pushed my thumbnail under the top label and started to peel it back. 'The label underneath appears to be in Greek. As far as I can make out, the use-by date on it was two years ago.' It was marked with the hospital's details. 'Didn't he take his own medication with him?'

'No, he had to use theirs. He went in for a pre-assessment a couple of weeks beforehand and they prescribed new medication. They told him they needed to keep control of what the patient was being given.'

I looked at the Oxaban again. According to Professor West he prescribed this in preference to the normal anti-coagulant so it didn't conflict with the operation. But if he'd spent two weeks on a medicine that had been relabelled and might be out-of-date like the insulin, then it must have made him vulnerable.

I inspected the labels more closely. 'Out-of-date insulin could have contributed to his death,' I said, 'but I need to find out about this Oxaban.' I looked at Greta. 'I think we need to follow this up. I'll have to trace these back and find out where they came from.' Finally it seemed to me I had a definite lead, even if it wasn't the one Greta had given me.

Chapter Six

We wrapped the medicines carefully and locked the flat. From Greta's initial fears that her father might have been murdered by his associates, we seemed to have moved to something much more complicated. 'Perhaps I should go back to the hospital and see if this wipes the self-satisfied smile from the general manager's face,' I said.

'I can't see him giving you any information. He'll shut up like a clam if he knows there's any suggestion of the hospital being at fault.'

'Yes, but the security consultant might help, but I think we should find out more about this Oxaban first.'

'Sally might be able to give us some medical background. Phone her and see if we could meet this evening.' I pulled out my phone and dialled her number. As usual it went straight to voicemail so I left a message and for good measure sent her a text, saying that we'd be expecting her on the boat this evening. I didn't want to give her a choice, so I added that it was urgent.

This time I left Greta to take a taxi back to her office. I decided to walk across the park to Regent's Park Underground Station and see if the quiet open space stimulated my thinking. I didn't know much about drugs but knew that some still had their full active ingredients many months, sometimes even years after their labelled sell-by date, but I didn't know if insulin was one of them. And if the insulin cartridges were faulty, then it begged the question whether the anticoagulant was what it said on the tin. We needed to trace the supply route, but this was turning into something that I hadn't bargained for.

But now I had something to follow up and I wasn't going to let it go. I dismissed the idea of passing it onto the police – I couldn't see them getting very far. The hospital would bring down the shutters and simply deny everything. Both Professor West and Bob Tyler had made that very clear. Acting alone, I might have better luck in looking at what went on behind the scenes. If I could meet Sally then she might be able to help me with the medical side of things. At that moment I had no idea how significant the relabelled medicines were.

My thoughts were interrupted by my mobile trilling its annoying sound at me. How often had I decided to change the ringtone but forgotten to do anything about it? It was a message from Sayed asking for a meeting. It was his usual terse communication and gave nothing away about whether it was urgent or not but I realised that I couldn't carry on keeping Sayed to myself. I didn't think I'd ever live it down if there was any fundamentalist activity and it emerged that I'd told no one.

I thought it was safer asking Sayed to meet me on the river, rather than in his park as before. There were too many people there who might be interested in an Afghan meeting a white man in the park. I sent him detailed instructions about how to find *Salacia* and asked him to meet me there at around five pm which should give him plenty of time.

But I realised that it was decision time as I sat on a bench by the boating lake, watching the families enjoying the sunshine and the groups of people on the rowing boats who were apparently trying to re-enact the sinking of the *Bismarck*. Judging by the amount of water spraying around they were doing quite a good job of it, while the ducks were doing their best to keep away from the hostilities.

On our second meeting, I'd finally found the courage to tell Sayed that I no longer worked for military intelligence and that I had to hand his case over to someone else, but he'd been quite adamant that if I did so, it would be the last we heard from him. I couldn't quite work out why he had so much apparent faith in me but then I thought that given his unsettled history he might regard me as one of the few constant threads running through his difficult life.

As I considered it further, I realised that I really didn't have much of a choice. I couldn't keep Sayed to myself and the most obvious person to share him with was Ali, but I'd not forgotten the way he'd behaved in the Afghan village and his accusations that I'd shot Sayed's brother. If he still believed that, it might make things difficult. But he came from a Muslim family – even if he denied being religious himself – so Sayed might feel more relaxed with him.

I decided that I'd have to risk it – apart from anything else, I didn't know who I could bring in. Strictly speaking this was not a matter for military intelligence but should have been passed over to our Thames House co-ordinators at MI5. Since I'd mainly worked overseas, I'd had more to do with MI6, but this was a domestic matter. I realised that I'd been staring at my blank phone for some time and shook myself out of my indecisiveness and scrolled through to Ali's number and dialled it.

He answered on the second ring as though waiting for the call. When I asked him to meet me on the river, he told me that he'd got an important meeting. 'Cancel it.' This was more important than anything else he might be doing. 'Cancel and meet me and a private informer on the barge.'

'Private informer?' he spluttered. 'You're not supposed to have private informers. You know they have to be registered.'

If he was expecting me to argue, he was disappointed because he must have realised without my saying it that I was no longer bound to his rules. 'Is that agreed then?' I repeated. 'Five o'clock at the barge. Oh… and come alone.' I knew he wouldn't appreciate that last comment, but I hung up before he could say anything. I knew he wouldn't be able to resist coming to find out what the Big Mystery was.

Sayed arrived early, saying he'd left himself enough time to find the place. 'This is pretty cool,' he said as he stood on the pontoon looking at the boat. He was even speaking like a native and I admired the effort that had gone into it. I gestured him to come up and moved aside to let him go into the saloon ahead of me.

He walked to the windows and looked out. 'Wow, what a view. How long have you lived here?'

'A few months. Ever since I left the army. Tea?' I asked and Sayed, still looking around, simply nodded. I fiddled in the galley and handed him a mug and took one myself and sat down. 'So how's it going?'

'Okay,' he said, sitting down opposite me. 'It's going okay. I'm getting good marks on my pharmacy course and will finish it soon. Then I'm thinking of going back home. They need me there.'

'And did you decide to enrol in the Koranic classes?' I thought I should get to the point before Ali arrived. 'Incidentally, you didn't tell me the name of the person you were concerned about.'

'Khazim, Khazim Ali. He's a model pupil – too perfect in fact. He carries this sort of aura around with him. The imams call it holy, I call it smug and self-satisfied but people don't seem to see in me the same dedication that they see in him. There's a group within a group that I wasn't invited to join. Khazim always stays on after the class. I waited behind once to see what happened and he didn't leave until nearly two hours later.'

At that moment, I could see Ali walking along the pontoon and I went to the door to let him in. 'This better be good,' he said as he clambered up the gangway. 'I had to cancel a meeting with the head of the department.'

'Who's this?' Sayed had stood up and was looking across at Ali. He turned to me. 'I told you I only wanted to deal with you.'

'Take it easy,' I said and let Ali go in ahead of me. 'Sit down, Sayed, and I'll explain. Ali's a former colleague. I haven't told him anything about you, but he used to work with me in intelligence and he was there in Afghanistan when we met your mother.' Sayed was staring at me. 'I told you that I'm not in the army anymore, but Ali is and he can probably be of more help.'

Ali was looking puzzled. 'Ali, this is Sayed.' Ali came in and approached Sayed and held out his hand. Sayed looked up at Ali before turning and looking fiercely at me but I pretended I hadn't noticed and continued my explanation. 'I managed to trace Sayed here in London and we've been in touch on and off since I got back.'

Sayed's hostility was obviously affecting Ali who stepped back and sat down next to me. 'This is a security matter,' I continued. 'Sayed thinks some of the people at his mosque are being radicalised and he said he might look into it for me. I suggested he attended the same Koranic classes so he could observe this person more closely.' But I could see that I wasn't making much impression on Sayed who was heading out of the saloon.

He stopped at the doorway and turned. 'I'm sorry. I don't want to become a code number in an intelligence operation. I'm only here because you helped put me in touch with my mother.'

'Ali was there too,' I protested, but it seemed to make little impression on him. 'Wait a moment and think about it. It was both of us in your village – we were together. We saw your brother, Shamir, and had the photograph of him and Jafar. We were a team.'

I reached inside my jacket and pulled out the photo and held it out to Sayed. 'This is your brother Shamir?' I looked across at Ali before adding, 'We were both there when he was shot.'

Sayed took the photograph and looked at it without saying anything. It was as though he was transported back to a different world in a different time in a different continent. 'That's Jafar with him,' he said eventually. 'Always the fighter.'

'Sayed.' I sensed that he might listen to us. 'Ali can help you. He has more contacts.' I glanced across to Ali who was looking intently at Sayed and I risked playing the race card. 'He's a Muslim so he understands your background better than I do and wants to help. Why don't you come back inside and we can talk about it? It's still up to you what you do, I'm not putting any pressure on you.'

Sayed finally came in and sat down. 'You were in Chorjah when he was killed? How did it happen?'

Ali looked across at me again before replying. 'I'm sure Philip told you. There was an attack on your village. We didn't get there until afterwards.'

'But you say you were there when he was killed?'

I didn't like where this was going and thought it was time to take over. 'It must have been a sniper. We didn't see him. But I haven't asked why Shamir was there in the first place. Why hadn't he left as you did?'

'He couldn't. If you look at the photo again you'll see he's leaning against Jafar. Shamir was crippled when he was young. It was polio – several of the kids caught it but Shamir was the worst.'

'Weren't you inoculated against it?' I asked without thinking.

'It was when the Taliban came. I told you they shut down the little clinic saying it was the work of the West and they wouldn't have anything to do with it. By the time the clinic reopened again it was too late.' Sayed picked up the photo and looked at it again before handing it back to Ali. 'I have a copy and look at it when I call home.'

'How is your mother?' I asked.

'As well as we could hope for,' Sayed said. 'They have some sort of peace now, so things are a bit better.'

'Ali might be able to help you get back to visit,' I said. 'He might get you a ride on one of his transport planes that's always going out there.'

'They're not mine,' Ali said before appearing to realise how negative it sounded. 'But I could always see what I could do,' he added, rather grudgingly, I thought.

'But you'll keep an eye on this Khazim for us?' I said and turned to Ali. 'Sayed thinks that he's been groomed for some kind of project.'

'A tip worth knowing,' said Ali. 'It's one of the first lessons they teach us. Sometimes a mark on their forehead means that they're preparing something. Look out for that because it means they've been praying hard to build up confidence and forcing their forehead down onto the floor. MI5 has foiled several plots because the agent has noticed marks.'

Sayed nodded and stood up. 'I'll remember that. I'll be in touch if I find out anything else,' and without saying goodbye, he jumped off the boat and walked down the pontoon.

I watched him go before turning to Ali. 'What do you think?' I asked, although I could see that I wasn't going to like the answer.

'You've been in touch with him all the time you've been back here in the UK?' he asked and I could see that he was quite angry. 'You should have told me about him – I needed to know. Are there any rules that you think apply to you? You have such a high opinion of yourself that you think you don't need anyone's help, you can manage everything on your own. How I ever thought of you as a friend I don't know – it took me too long to see you for what you were.'

'And what am I? I'm the same person I've always been – I think it's you who's changed.'

'And why are you calling me a Muslim? I told you I've got no religion. I renounced all that a long time ago. I don't like to be labelled like that.'

'But you still have the same heritage. I thought it was something Sayed could relate to.'

'So how long have you been seeing him on your own? You're supposed to register and share informants.'

'But I *am* sharing it,' I protested. 'I asked you here because I wanted you to know about it.'

'This isn't a matter for military intelligence. This should be handled by MI5. They've got all the personnel and experience at this sort of thing. Instead you're handling it like an amateur – which is what you are. You're on the outside now.'

Ouch, that was a bit mean, if true. 'You saw him, Ali. He won't deal with anyone else – he nearly walked out when he saw you. Don't ask me why, but he won't. And anyway, he hasn't any concrete information. At the moment it's only suspicions. If it turns out that he's really onto something then we can call in the experts. And in the meantime, you know about it so that makes it semi-official.'

'That's a pretty good indication of what you think counts as official. Nothing that anyone else would recognise.' He stood up. 'Okay, I'll register it with them, and monitor the situation, but it's not going to make you very popular.' He paused, and I wasn't looking forward to what he had to add. 'This boy, Sayed, how do you think you're helping him? It's your guilty conscience, trying to make amends for what happened out there.'

'And what did happen out there? Nothing happened.' I really didn't know how to get through to him. 'I don't have a guilty conscience. I'm helping him because it's the right thing to do and he's helping me for the same reason. Not everything can be reduced to desiccated policies and strategies. Some things we do simply because they are right.'

Ali shrugged. 'That was your job: to follow policies and strategies, but of course you didn't think that was enough.'

'We were doing the right thing, Ali,' I said. 'It might not have been pretty but we were doing it for the right reasons.'

He stared at me before heading out of the saloon and I could see that it was pointless saying any more. 'Ali, before you storm off, did you manage to look into those files?'

He stopped in the doorway. 'Files?' he said blankly.

'Yes. You said you were going to look into who planted them.'

If anything he looked even more annoyed. 'I made some enquiries but as far as I could find out it all seems to have been a mistake.'

'A mistake? It cost me my career.'

'I know but there's nothing I can do. It was all a bit messy.'

Messy was one way of putting it, I thought, although I could think of several other suitable words.

As I watched him go, I wondered about our friendship. He hadn't been the same person since our tour in Afghanistan. You could never tell with him; sometimes he would act like a high priest, above all mortal concerns, but at other times he saw things quite differently and appeared to show little regard for rules if he thought they were simply obstacles. Perhaps because of his Asian background he'd always had a different way of looking at things that I had found refreshing, but now I wasn't so sure.

I went back inside and put in a desultory hour's working, but it did little to relieve my depression at the way things had changed between us.

Chapter Seven

When she arrived, Greta was wearing her usual trouser suit and waved away my attempt to help her on board. I showed her into the saloon and opened a bottle of wine. This was the first time she had been able to relax with me, but now she seemed surprisingly reticent – even shy. She was obviously still grieving – she told me how close she'd been to her father who certainly wasn't of an age to die.

'I'm sorry,' she said after a while. 'I'm not normally like this but I'm still finding it hard to deal with. It was a routine operation.'

'I can understand the shock.' As I said it I realised how feeble it sounded. 'I promise I'll get to the bottom of it.' Although I felt much less confident than I sounded.

I tried pointing out the various sights along the river but her listless attention wandered so I was glad when Sally finally arrived and Greta immediately perked up. In the same way, and despite our divorce, Sally often managed to lift my spirits.

Unlike Greta, Sally was pint-sized, with close-cropped dark hair, but she made up in personality what she lacked in size and people crossed her at their peril. As her determination to qualify as a doctor had demonstrated, once she'd made up her mind about something that was it.

Recognising that her usual levity would be out of place, she refrained from making any more sarcastic comments about my boat, though I had no doubt that she would be saving them up for a later date. I poured out the wine and brought some chairs up on deck. I thought we might as well make ourselves comfortable while I brought Sally up to date with my various researches, ending with the false label stuck over the insulin cartridges.

I took them out of the evidence bag I'd put them in and handed them to her.

'I looked it up before coming,' she said, putting them on the table next to her. 'The insulin is obviously for his diabetes, and insulin is particularly susceptible to degradation. The active ingredients fade very quickly, in a matter of months, so if the original expiration date on this batch was correct, then it would have lost its usefulness long before. I'm not sure if you realise how serious this is – relabelling drugs like this is criminal. Thanks,' she said, taking the glass from me. 'I needed this after the day I've had.'

'The start of the slippery slope,' I said – she'd often had a go at me for my alcohol consumption, so I couldn't let it pass.

Sally ignored me as she downed a good measure of her wine. 'Have you heard of the MHRA? The Medicines and Healthcare Regulatory Agency? They're the government body that oversees all aspects of pharmaceuticals. They licence drugs and manufacturers, they monitor clinic trials and investigate counterfeit medications. I think you should call them in; they're the experts in this sort of thing.'

I explained my fears about the hospital clamming up and repeated what I'd been told by the professor and Bob Tyler. 'I've arranged to see Tyler again tomorrow, although I've no idea whether he's going to stonewall me, or whether he's prepared to help. He seemed pretty genuine and didn't hold back his criticism of some of the hospital's policies. Apparently, they're currently advertising for a new head of security without letting him apply, so that hasn't helped. But tell us about the other medication – what about this Oxaban?'

Sally picked up the second medicine. 'Oxaban is an anticoagulant, a Factor Xa inhibitor. It's an alternative to Warfarin which is given to thin the blood and stop it clotting, so there's less chance of thrombosis – of an artery getting blocked. If patients have CHD, that's coronary heart disease, then they're put on anticoagulants to prevent heart attacks. But if the patient needs an operation then the last thing they want is for the blood to be so thin that it doesn't clot, so they either stop the anticoagulant a few days before the surgical procedure, or replace it with a specialist anticoagulant a couple of weeks beforehand. This Oxaban is one of a number available. They then start the normal anticoagulant shortly afterwards.'

'And are they subject to degradation like insulin?'

'Some of them are, yes. The active ingredients of Warfarin, for example, and other vitamin K antagonists, have only a short life so it's vital that their expiration date is followed exactly.' She looked more closely at the label, turning it around. 'Although we can see clearly that the insulin cartridges have been relabelled, there's no evidence that this has.'

'No, but it's possible, isn't it? Tell us about the heart attack. Could that have been caused by taking medications beyond their expiration date?'

'The heart attack,' Sally repeated thoughtfully. 'I haven't seen his notes, so I can't comment in any detail, but if he was taking something like Oxaban, then he must have had a pre-existing CHD – not uncommon in a man of his age.'

'But what caused the heart attack?' I repeated.

'That's assuming that it *was* a heart attack and I have no reason to think it wasn't, so there could have been a number of causes. He was diabetic, which meant he was more at risk…'

'But could the wrongly-labelled medicines have caused it?' I interrupted impatiently.

Sally gave me a look as if to say "calm down". 'I was coming to that. All we know from Professor West is that the operation on your father's liver went well and that following a few hours observation in ICU – intensive care – his recovery was considered satisfactory and he was moved back to his room. And then it was some hours later – about ten hours, I think – that his monitor was showing irregular heart function and the nursing staff called in the duty doctor. From what you say, they didn't have time to carry out an ECG or take a blood sample but it was clearly a heart attack so they paged their cardiologist while they prepared him for the operating theatre. When the cardiologist arrived, they started an emergency bypass operation, but it was too late.' Sally looked across at Greta who was sobbing quietly at this cold recitation of the facts. 'I'm sorry, Greta,' Sally said. 'Perhaps Philip and I should talk this over between us?'

'No.' Greta took a deep breath and managed to compose herself a little. 'I have to hear this. Carry on, please.'

I sensed that we were moving away from the main points. 'So what do you think caused the heart attack?' I repeated. 'Could it have been the out-of-date insulin or the anticoagulants?'

'It could have been either, or both together, but whether they caused it is another matter. If his insulin was ineffective then he could have suffered hypoglycaemia – a form of shock reaction which can lead to a coma. In turn this could have produced heart palpitations. If the anticoagulants weren't effective then there might have been internal bleeding following the operation that could eventually have led to a heart attack.'

'Will there be an autopsy?' asked Greta.

'That's up to the coroner,' Sally said. 'It's quite likely, given that the death was unexpected, but I don't think it's likely to show very much. They'll do blood tests, but we already know that the insulin must have been ineffective.'

'But there's something suspect about this Oxaban,' I said. 'Could we get it analysed – find out what it really is?'

'We could and I think we should, but it might not lead us anywhere. We'd still need to go back and find out where it came from. At least someone should and I still think we need to bring in the MHRA. Even if Greta's father wasn't killed by these medications, other people might be.' Sally paused for a moment and put the bottle down. 'Do you know anything about counterfeit pharmaceuticals?'

'It wasn't really my field,' I replied. 'I was more concerned with who had how many tanks and who had the anti-tank missiles to fight them. A bit different from this sort of thing.

But anyone who has email is bombarded with offers for Internet medications – Viagra mostly. I've always wondered how anyone buying them could know whether they were fake or not.'

'Much of what is sold online is,' Sally said. 'The websites are virtually untraceable and who's going to complain anyway? And who are they going to complain to? It must be the easiest money ever made – set up a website, take the money and send them a variant of lactose powder in return. I've only read the occasional article in the *BMJ* – the *British Medical Journal*. Given the cost of some pharmaceuticals today, there's a lot of money to be made by faking them. Take Oxaban: there was another blood thinner, Heparin, made in China but sold in the USA. It turned out to be contaminated and nearly a hundred people died before they found the cause and withdrew it. That's one of the problems, you have to identify a common cause before you can isolate what's causing it and that often involves a lot of luck to find it.

'The trouble is that everyone knows about the so-called lifestyle drugs like Viagra, so even if they find out they're fakes, they don't think it's very serious. It's a bit like buying a fake Rolex. If you know you're paying less than they're worth then it's obvious there's something funny about it. And with fake Viagra it can often work by a psychosomatic placebo effect: it's effective because you think it is.' Sally picked up the insulin cartridges again. 'I think we could be looking at something that goes much deeper.'

We were all silent for a moment, taking sips of our wine. 'That was the plot of *The Third Man*,' I said, as the memory slowly dawned on me. 'The Orson Welles character, Harry Lime, was stealing penicillin and watering it down. It was set immediately after the end of the war and it probably went on in real life. Penicillin was very expensive back then.'

'Adulterated antibiotics can present some of the worst cases,' Sally said. 'My agency does a lot of work in Africa helping some of the immunisation programmes and these drugs are causing major problems. There's already growing resistance to them, and if antibiotics are being manufactured with reduced active ingredients, then that only increases the problem.

'Some agencies estimate that tens of thousands of lives are lost because of watered-down antimalarials. Malaria is one of the biggest killers in Africa and there are numerous charities working on self-immunisation, where they don't have so much control over the supply of the drugs. It makes it almost impossible to ascertain whether some of these programmes are effective or not.'

'How do these drugs get distributed?' I asked. 'It's funny, I've never really thought about it before, they're just sort of there. You take a prescription to the chemist and they hand it over. I suppose because there's no competition. We don't ask what they are, we follow the doctor's prescription, pay the standard NHS rate and take them away. I suppose if we had to pay the real price then we might start looking at what was the best.'

'Many of the drugs are generic,' Sally said. 'That is they're out of patent, or were never in patent in the first place. Anyone can make them and they're much cheaper. As for competition, you should see the number of drug company reps we get calling at the surgery. It's been a bit better since they introduced a new code of practice a couple of years ago, but I can tell you the competition is fierce out there. Unless you're a monopoly supplier of a drug in-patent, you've got to fight it out on the open market and the worldwide market is huge.'

'So who organises the vaccination programmes?' I asked. 'Is it the UN?'

'It can be one of a number of aid agencies but they're usually overseen by the WHO – the World Health Organization, usually in association with UNICEF, because it affects principally the children. There's a really big programme being planned now for East Africa. Instead of relying on people to come to a few vaccination centres, they're trying to set up units in most of the villages with the vaccinations being delivered directly to them.'

'But doesn't that increase the risk of counterfeits getting into the supply chain?' I asked. 'There wouldn't be any centralised control.'

'It's a trade-off,' Sally said. 'Previous centralised programmes often failed because they didn't have the reach and missed out swathes of the rural population. And also localised corruption doesn't help. We'll see.'

I thought about this. 'Perhaps I should admit that I have a sort of personal interest.'

Sally looked surprised. 'What kind of personal interest?'

'I told you about my mother?'

'How could I forget? It must be something you have to live with every day. But you said you didn't know anything about what exactly happened.'

I turned to Greta. 'My mother committed suicide when I was eight – nearly nine. You understand things differently at that age. They told me about my mother's death but it wasn't until some years later that I learnt what had happened. They hid it from me at the time, but when I was old enough I went back to find out what happened. I discovered that she'd committed suicide.' I'd told Sally about the suicide, but not the reasons behind it, but now I wanted Greta to know the details – to show that I had at least some idea of what she was going through.

Greta was staring at me in shock. 'That must have been devastating.'

'She was suffering from depression and she did kill herself, but it wasn't really her fault.'

'Fault?' Greta said. 'That's a strange word to use. How could it have been her fault?'

'She was on a mixture of antidepressants but I've since discovered that in some cases they can actually increase the risk of suicide, rather than reduce it.'

'That's why we're told to be careful when prescribing them,' Sally said. 'It seems that some psychotropic drugs can have that effect. Especially in larger doses.'

I nodded. 'It seems they didn't know that at the time. The pharmaceutical companies were peddling their antidepressants in ever increasing quantities without proper trials on the effects.

I managed to get a transcript of the inquest and from the reports I read, it seemed that her doctor prescribed these antidepressants without realising that she sort of got sucked into a vicious cycle. From what I could tell, it seems she was taking drugs hoping they would help, but instead they led her to kill herself.'

'Philip, I'm so sorry,' Greta said and I wasn't sure I could handle the pity in her eyes.

'Why didn't you tell me this before?' Sally asked. 'When did you find this out?'

'Just before we got married, but I didn't want to say anything in case… you know, in case…'

'You mean in case it changed the way I thought about you?'

'I always thought you were judging me. Looking out for signs of the effect my upbringing might have had on me. It was bad enough you knowing that my mother had killed herself without adding to your anxiety by telling you that it was avoidable.'

'Philip, that's not true. I wasn't *judging* you, but with your childhood it would have been surprising if it had left you unscathed.'

'People always assume that because I was brought up in institutions that it was difficult and I suppose it was in many ways. But I tried not to bear a grudge although many of the kids did. We had talks from various worthy people who came and told us that we were in control of our future and that background wasn't important. Complete nonsense, of course, and I still get angry at what happened to my parents – angry at the life together that was taken away from us. It's caused a few problems over the years – it sort of builds up, raising the pressure until I explode. Most of the time I manage to control it, but not always. When I discovered the truth about my mother, about what had really killed her, I nearly went off the rails.'

I said nothing, remembering my stunned reaction when I learnt about my mother's prescriptions and wondering what she must have been going through right at the end. My memories of her were of a sort of hazy, undefined warmth – a warmth that was never really replaced. Finding out about the effect of her medication had at least given me the consolation of knowing that she hadn't intended her own death. She hadn't meant to leave me alone. 'I still can't understand why it happened the way it did, but thinking about it makes it worse so the only way I can live with myself is if I put it behind me.'

'As long as you could do what you wanted.' Sally said. 'I often wondered why you went into the army. It didn't strike me as a place for an individualist but then I realised it gave you a structure and a platform and you made the best of it.'

'It didn't make me easy to live with, did it?'

Sally smiled. 'I wasn't easy to live with either. We were both looking for someone who would complement us; instead we got someone who competed with us. We were both too preoccupied with our work – we would have made good colleagues, but we made lousy spouses.'

She held up her glass and I got up and poured out some more wine and eventually the conversation moved on. It was the first time that Greta had seen Sally since her father's death and they swapped reminiscences about him, but when this moved onto their school days, I thought it was time to intervene. 'You've both hung up your hockey sticks long since. Leave them where they belong, gathering dust in an attic.'

'Don't listen to him, Greta,' said Sally. 'Philip's always had a chip on his shoulder about anyone who went to a private school.'

'So would you, if you'd been brought up in an orphanage,' I replied. 'The only thing it has in common with your school was that it was residential. Apart from that, it couldn't have been more different. Your school had bars on the outside to keep people out, mine had them on the inside to keep us in.'

'You haven't done too badly out of it,' Sally said. 'You did well in the army – first in your year when you passed out, as I remember.'

'I was always good at passing out,' I said. 'And things look so very different when you wake up in the morning.'

'Facetiousness, like sarcasm, is the lowest form of wit,' Sally said, rather archly, I thought.

'You always told me that I was the lowest form of wit.'

'And I was right. If you hadn't tried to pretend everything was a joke – even things you really cared about – then perhaps we'd still be married.' She paused. 'On second thoughts, perhaps not. We're too different.'

'You're too much of an idealist, tilting at windmills trying to tend to all the world's ills. After Afghanistan, I've had enough of trying to help people I don't know and who aren't grateful for it anyway. Someone else can do that now.'

'I know you better than that. You try not to show it, but underneath you care as much as I do.'

'If you say so.' I knew better than to argue with her. 'But if there are people out there manufacturing counterfeit drugs, the damage they do could be massive.'

'Deadly. And it's still happening. It's difficult to control in the less developed countries but my agency is trying.'

'I'd certainly never have the patience to be a doctor. I'd feel too helpless much of the time.'

'At least we're agreed on that, but you might be able to find out where these drugs came from.'

'That's only if you're still prepared to see it through,' Greta interjected. 'I'm still willing to pay for your time.'

Greta and Sally were both looking at me expectantly.

'I always want to see things through,' I said.

Chapter Eight

It wasn't until sometime later that evening that they left. It had done Greta good to be with us and she appeared much more cheerful than when she arrived. Sally finally agreed that I should keep my appointment with Bob Tyler at the hospital so the next morning I was back at Harley Street. I announced myself at reception and remembered the way to Bob's office upstairs. I knocked and went straight in. Bob was talking to one of his staff and held up his hand. 'Just a second,' he said. When he'd finished his conversation, he turned back to me. 'So what can I do for you now?' His colleague nodded as he passed me and shut the door behind him.

I fished inside my bag and brought out the two evidence envelopes and put them in front of him. 'These were found with Greg Satchwell's other medications.'

'So?' he said. Clearly he was forcing me to make the running.

'Look at them carefully.'

He took the bags and held them up one by one. 'Can I take them out?' he asked.

I nodded. They'd been through so many hands that a few more wouldn't make any difference.

He pulled out the insulin phial and turned it around frowning. He stopped as he saw the edge of the label where it had been partly pulled off. 'What's this?'

'You can see for yourself. The label's been stuck over another one. It's out of date.'

He examined it more carefully, and pulled at the edge of the overlapping label until it started to peel off. 'Is this Greek underneath? It looks like it.' He put the phial down and took out the Oxaban. 'What about this one?'

'It's got the same supplier's name as the insulin but it didn't look as though it was the original label so it's got to be suspect. We think it might be counterfeit.'

'We?' he repeated. 'And who exactly is "we"?'

'Greta Satchwell and me. Does it matter who? You can see for yourself.'

'So what do you want me to do about it?'

I sighed in frustration. He'd already told me he wanted to help and now he was trying to stonewall me. Clearly someone had got to him and warned him off, so I thought I'd give it to him straight. 'You realise that this could blow your hospital apart if it became known that you were providing counterfeit drugs to patients. Think of the headlines – it wouldn't only be in this country, either. This would echo around the world, especially in America with all the problems they've had with your major competitor. Professor West told me about that. "The largest fraud settlement in history" wasn't it? Nearly a billion dollars it cost them. Think how much it'll cost your group if this became public. Treating people with phoney drugs, with no active ingredients – I can see the headlines now.'

'How do you know they have no active ingredients?' he asked but I think after my little speech he was stalling for time.

'Because insulin degrades after a few months.' I pointed to the packet of phials. 'That stuff is useless and could have killed your patient. In fact, it's almost certain that it's already killed someone, if not Greg Satchwell. There could be dozens of people we don't know anything about who've died because of this.'

Bob Tyler stared at me and then picked up the phone.

'I wouldn't do that,' I continued. 'Until we find out what's happened, the fewer people who know about this the better.'

He paused with the phone in his hands. Eventually he nodded. 'So what do you want me to do?' he said, replacing the handset.

I think he was beginning to realise how serious things were.

'The first thing to do is to find out where these came from,' I said.

'That shouldn't be too difficult.' He pulled his computer keyboard towards him. 'We keep records of all patient prescriptions.' After a few moments he pulled out a page as it emerged from his printer and turned back to me. 'We'll have to go downstairs to the basement to check the drugs registry. All drugs delivered to us are listed and their origin checked for just such a situation. Counterfeit pharmaceuticals are everybody's nightmare so we keep strict records of where everything comes from, with batch numbers and sometimes even electronic tags.'

I followed him down the stairs into a basement, past humming radiotherapy suites and into a room harshly lit by neon fluorescents. There wasn't much doubt how important the people who worked in this office were regarded.

Tyler nodded at the staff as he walked in and a woman came over. 'Lisa, this is Philip Hennessey. He's… he's helping us with a stock problem. Can you find the record for this consignment?' He handed her the printout.

Lisa went straight to a shelf of lever-arch files and, checking along the row for the correct dates she pulled one out and rifled through it.

'These are doubled up,' Bob explained. 'In addition to the computer prescription, we file a hard copy which is referenced back to the original batch number of the supplier's delivery to us.'

Lisa wrote down the delivery note number and Bob went over to a nearby computer terminal and keyed in his password. He went through various menus until he found what he was looking for and printed it out. He handed the delivery note to me.

'Holden Healthcare,' I said, reading the heading. 'Do you do much business with them?'

'I thought it probably was them. They supply most of our pharmaceuticals.'

'So if we can show that they're the source of these adulterated drugs, then it could put your hospital in the clear.'

He didn't say anything for a while, before shaking his head. 'I don't think so.'

'Why not? If you demonstrate that you knew nothing about it and bought them in good faith then how can you be held responsible?'

'IHG owns Holden Healthcare. They're in the same group as this hospital.'

Perhaps I should have known that a hospital chain as big as this wouldn't pass up the profits to be made wholesaling drugs, but then this wasn't my field of expertise, although I seemed to be learning fast.

We were back in Bob Tyler's office and he was looking up the hospital's records for Holden Healthcare. 'I'd say, looking at these figures, about eighty percent of the drugs we buy come from Holden,' he said. 'The rest come from a variety of sources – most from wholesalers but some even come direct from the manufacturer.'

'So where do the wholesalers get them from?'

'It's a very fragmented market. There are hundreds, probably thousands of companies selling pharmaceuticals and they source their supplies from all over. I think we should go to Holden Healthcare and ask them. They would want to know if this batch has been relabelled.'

'Not if they did it themselves.' I said it without thinking. 'No, forget that. It doesn't seem very likely that they had anything to do with this, but even so let's play it safe – we don't want to alert them that we're investigating them. I don't think they'd give us any answers, anyway.'

'I suppose I could go up there and say that I'm carrying out a routine audit and see where it leads.'

'If you're going, then I'm coming with you. I want to see their set-up for myself. Tell them that I'm a consultant and leave it at that. Whereabouts are they, anyway?'

'They've got several depots.' He picked up the delivery note and read it again. 'This comes from Northampton. That's an hour or so up the M1.'

I didn't bother to tell him I knew where Northampton was. Instead, I reached over and picked up his handset and held it out to him. 'Call them now. Make an appointment for tomorrow. We can't afford to hang about.' Once again he hesitated before taking the telephone. I could almost read what was going through his mind from the expression on his face. But, finally, he must have realised that he had little choice and had to appear to help me if only to delay matters. Perhaps even to bring in his bosses.

'And if you want to keep your job, I wouldn't talk to anyone about this,' I added. 'From what I've seen of your general manager, the first thing he'd do if he heard about this would be to send you on indefinite gardening leave. He'd see you as a danger to him and big corporations like IHG probably have lots of practice in cover-ups.'

Once again, I could see his mind working and finally accepting what I had to say. He dialled an internal number. 'Lisa? Who's our contact at Holden Healthcare?' he asked, and wrote down the name she gave him. He pulled the delivery note towards him and dialled the number and turned on the speakerphone.

I listened as he got put through to the Holden rep who appeared surprised at the apparent urgency of the request. Tyler handled him well and didn't give anything away or invent any story that might trip us up later. Finally, he hung up, having made the appointment for the following morning.

'You didn't say anything about me,' I said. 'You didn't tell them there'd be two of us.'

'As you said, there was no need. You can come along as long as you don't say anything and let me do the talking.'

Fat chance, I thought, though I nodded sagely, as though in agreement.

On my way back, I tried to make some sense of what Bob Tyler had told me, but the situation was getting complicated by these interconnecting threads. I'd researched the US hospital group that I'd told Bob Tyler about and it was all there on a website. I couldn't understand how fraud on such a large scale was even possible, let alone apparently undetectable. From what I'd read, I couldn't tell whether it had been calculated criminal action that had led the hospital to defraud people, or whether it was simply naivety – just thinking that they wouldn't get caught. Now, faced with the involvement of another multinational hospital group, I couldn't tell what I was getting involved in. I could only guess that the stakes were probably high.

Bob Tyler gave me a lift the next morning in his rather elderly but well-maintained BMW which still seemed a source of great pride to him. For a change, there were only two sets of roadworks on our way up the M1 motorway and we reached Northampton in good time. Apart from the remnants of the old shoe companies, it's a town devoted to warehousing and huge new sheds were being erected right up to the edge of the motorway.

We followed the signs to one of the older industrial estates and pulled up outside an anonymous building surrounded by a high wire fence. On the surface at least their security seemed quite impressive, as our details were noted at the gatehouse and our photographs taken and inserted into security passes before we were allowed to drive across to the reception area.

Instead of the hospital's normal rep, we were met by Colin Farrow, the sales manager, sharply dressed as befits a salesman. He took us up to a first floor office which overlooked the car park on one side and the warehouse floor on the other, where rows of racking stretched into the distance. I could see that the glass was armour plated with an alarm sensor running around its perimeter. More security.

'So how can we help you?' asked Colin after arranging coffee. 'We were intrigued at the urgency, so perhaps you could tell us why it couldn't wait.'

'I discovered that our quality control system hasn't been followed and we're required to have regular meetings with our suppliers and this one's overdue.'

I thought Bob Tyler's lying was quite smooth. We'd agreed that at this first meeting we would sound them out and not tell them anything about the switched labels.

'So why is the hospital's security manager involved?' Farrow seemed quite on the ball and I wondered if he suspected something was amiss. 'Why isn't it Lisa? – Isn't she the person we normally deal with?'

'I happened to be free and fancied a drive,' replied Tyler. I thought that was pushing it – not since it first opened has anyone ever fancied a drive up the M1. 'Also, since Mr Hennessey was due to be visiting us today, I thought it would be useful for us both to learn a bit about our suppliers and how they operate. Mr Hennessey is a management consultant and I thought it would kill two birds with one stone if he came along and saw the supply chain at first hand.'

'Yes,' I said. 'I'm interested in the way you source your stock – the sort of suppliers you have. Also, the distribution side – how you store the drugs and how the flow of orders works and what happens once you've received them.'

Farrow looked at me for a moment before replying. 'We like to think of ourselves as a one-stop shop.' He pointed to an information chart on the wall. 'You can see it here. We're aiming to be a single point of call where our customers can get the majority of their requirements.' He turned to Bob. 'Your own hospitals, for example, take most of their day-to-day requirements from us. There are some more specialised drugs that they get from elsewhere, but we try to be able to provide them with most of what they need.'

'And what about the ordering process?' I asked. 'How does that work?'

'We've taken a leaf out of the automotive industry and linked our computer systems with our key customers,' he said finally. Even if he thought this was a charade he had clearly decided to go along with it until he could find out what it was really about. 'It's like a just-in-time system but perhaps not quite as sophisticated. We've installed our programs and databases on the hospitals' computers and new orders are sent directly online. It's like any other stock control system except that the storage conditions and shelf life of each drug can be different, so it ensures that when replacements are ordered each batch is well within its use-by date. Most drugs have a long shelf life, but if they don't it can be critical.'

'And what happens when you receive the order?' I asked.

'The computer matches up all orders received during the day and prints out a picking list – that's a list that is taken into the warehouse and each item is put into a single delivery.'

'Can we see how that works?'

Once again, Farrow hesitated fleetingly. 'I don't see why not,' he said, although I couldn't tell whether his teeth were gritted or not.

'Fine,' I said. 'But can I use your facilities first? It's the coffee…' I added lamely.

'At the end of the corridor on the right,' said Farrow.

I got up and left the room, shutting the door carefully behind me. I was surprised, given their obvious suspicions, that they didn't accompany me. Towards the end of the corridor was a staff noticeboard. Checking that I wasn't being watched, I looked through it quickly, but there seemed to be only the usual announcements, plus the warning of a fire drill at the end of the week. There didn't seem much of importance but I took out my phone and photographed it just the same. You never know.

When I returned, Colin took us downstairs and punched a code into the combination lock and led us into the warehouse. 'It's carefully temperature-controlled,' he said, turning back to us. 'Exactly fifteen degrees, night and day.' He pointed towards an enclosure with what looked like a huge fridge door. 'Over there we keep the pharmaceuticals that need to be refrigerated. They have a different stocking policy to the rest.'

'You mean like Father Christmas?' I said, immediately aware that it wasn't one of my best.

Colin Farrow ignored me and led us past the racking through to a separate, partitioned-off part of the factory. He took us into a small office. 'You have to put on protective covering before going in here,' he said, handing us plastic bonnets, gloves and overalls. 'It's to protect the stock, not you.'

Attired a bit like Grayson Perry, we emerged into a huge space where several large machines were lined up, their compressed air lines hissing and sucking as the packaging capsules were fed into them like a belt of machine-gun cartridges.

'This is our re-batching area,' Farrow had to raise his voice above the noise. 'Over there you can see the consignments that we've brought in. Normally they're loose but sometimes they're already packaged so we have to strip out the packaging to relabel them.'

Clearly I was missing something here. 'You repackage them?' I asked in disbelief. 'Is that legal? You mean you're capable of relabelling your drugs on an industrial scale?'

Colin Farrow laughed. 'I can see you don't know much about pharmaceuticals.'

'That's why I'm here,' I said, trying to hide my frustration since this was the last thing I expected to see. 'Why are you repacking them?'

'It's called parallel trading. Although we're supposed to operate in a single market, every European country has different prices for its pharmaceuticals. They're either set by the market or, in countries like the UK, they're set by the NHS purchasing departments. The pharmaceutical companies themselves sell into each market at the best price they can achieve, but there's a huge variation. One of the reasons for wholesalers like us is that we can source the drugs in the cheapest market places and sell into the most expensive.'

'But why do you have to relabel them?' I asked dumbly.

'There's not much point in sending out instructions written in Greek, is there?' It seemed to me that he was enjoying making me look an idiot. 'Also, there are different regulatory notes that we have to put in, depending upon the market. I told you, the pharmaceutical market isn't just huge, it's very, very complicated. We're only a tiny part of it.'

'What happens if the original label shows that the medicines are past or near their sell-by dates?'

'They wouldn't,' Farrow replied. 'We only buy in drugs that have a commercially viable shelf life. There wouldn't be any point buying them in, repackaging them and finding we have to destroy them because they're out of date.'

'So, what you're doing here – relabelling drugs – that's a normal part of the distribution process?' I asked, hiding my disbelief.

'Absolutely. It happens everywhere, in every country, although I often wonder if there isn't a better way.'

'So once the drugs have been relabelled to conform to UK regulations you can put them into your stock system?' This was Bob Tyler, who'd been very quiet until then, whether it was because he was enjoying my discomfort or whether because he also was learning about it, I couldn't tell.

'That's right,' Farrow said. 'Much of the value-added here is in the repackaging which needs a licence, but the second part is acting as wholesaler which is back in the section we came into.'

We followed him back across the factory floor where he approached a worker who held what looked like a bar-code scanner and was pushing a trolley divided into separate compartments. The trolley had a computer screen fixed to the handles. 'All the orders we received yesterday have been separated into individual picking lists and given to the team here on the floor who go round collecting all the items for despatch later today. The list has a barcode against each item which he scans and then he scans the code on the shelf here to ensure that the two match. That automatically deducts the quantity from the stock list and he puts it here in the trolley.'

'How does he know where to find everything?' I asked.

'The barcode on the list gives the aisle number,' Colin replied. 'Also, the list is automatically arranged so the operative moves around in the most efficient way. We're working on introducing robots, to replace the people – funnily enough it's not as difficult as you might think.'

'Impressive. Can you tell where everything comes from?' I asked.

'Of course.' Colin obviously found the question slightly insulting. 'I'll show you.' He took the scanner and pressed a few buttons and then ran it across the barcode on the shelf and then pointed to the screen on the trolley. 'This displays the history of the batch, in this case from two suppliers. I'm afraid I can't tell you more, but this one has a long shelf life so it isn't time critical. From the menu I can also list everyone who's received deliveries of this, but that's also commercially confidential I'm afraid.'

'Can we see the refrigerated items?'

'It's too cold unless you have proper clothing, but the set-up's the same.'

Colin continued with the tour but I listened with only half an ear. A plan was starting to form in my head and I laid it out to Bob Tyler on the drive back. If we could use the scanner and trolley unobserved for a few minutes we could check back on where both the insulin and the Oxaban came from without alerting them.

'And exactly how are you proposing to get back into the offices?' he asked. 'You saw the security.'

'Didn't you notice I left my briefcase behind? That's our excuse for going back.'

'A pretty thin one, if you ask me. They'll probably have opened it by now and gone through everything inside. Anyway, even if we managed to get back in, how are you going to get into the warehouse?'

'They won't get into my briefcase because it's a special design and as for getting into the warehouse, I noted down the number he keyed in. I don't want you to think I'm being smug or anything but I'm supposed to be an expert in getting into places where people are trying to keep me out. First though, we've got to get Lisa to order some more insulin and Oxaban, then we tell them we want to pick up the briefcase on our way to see another supplier. It's got to be this Friday, just before their fire practice.'

Chapter Nine

'Interesting case,' Colin Farrow said, handing it to me when we returned a couple of days later. 'Where did you get it?' He would have been surprised if he knew but I certainly wasn't going to tell him.

'I inherited it from an uncle,' I said blandly. 'It's got quite a history. I'm really sorry to take up your time again, especially since you were so helpful the other day. I checked with Lisa in the office and she said that she'd just placed an order with you so I wondered while we're here if I could see how it looks when it's printed out here as a picking list. It would help to give me a better picture of how it all works.'

If Colin thought I had any ulterior motives, he probably couldn't work out what they might be. 'I don't see why not,' he said. 'It's already on the shop floor but I can print out a copy.' He went over to his computer and hit some keys and then waited by the laser printer for the paperwork to emerge.

I took the printouts and scanned through them. 'Impressive,' I said. 'And they'll be delivered in the morning?'

'Our standard delivery is forty-eight hours. But we can do faster if required. It's a pretty smooth operation.'

I continued asking Colin some questions while watching the clock for my cue. As before, coffee was brought up and, checking my watch, I again asked if I could use the "facilities" and hoped he'd got me marked down as having a weak bladder.

'You'll have to be quick. We've got a fire practice in a few minutes.'

I left the room but instead of going along the corridor, I headed down the stairs and went inside the downstairs toilets and crouched on the pan in one of the cubicles, leaving the door ajar. I was sweating under the two layers of thermal underwear I'd put on but I didn't have to wait long until the fire alarm went off and I could hear people clattering down the stairs and along the corridor. Someone came in to check the toilets but they obviously just looked at the unlocked doors and didn't look any further. When it was quiet outside, I risked going out and looking around. I could see no one so I headed back to the door into the warehouse.

I keyed in the number I'd memorised and put my head around the door. I could see staff ambling towards the fire exits at the far end of the warehouse, their backs towards me and apparently in no hurry to finish the drill. I walked quickly towards the refrigerated area, putting on the cotton gloves I'd kept in my pockets. As I approached the insulated unit, I saw the door handle turn and I ran and hid behind the racking just as the door opened. This was starting to feel like some of my earlier training and I made an effort to control my breathing as I watched the man close the door carefully and follow the others towards the rear fire exit. I waited in case he turned back and when he disappeared around the racking at the far end of the warehouse, I let myself into the refrigerated area. Fortunately I found the trolley inside and grabbed it, but my breathing was still creating clouds of condensation in the cold.

All I had to do now was to find out how the scanner worked. I'd watched as Colin Farrow had done it, but part of the keyboard had been covered, although I could see that he was working through a series of menus on the scanner screen. I took out the picking list Colin had printed out and picked up the scanner and followed the sub-menu until it read "Customer". I scanned the barcode and then went backwards in the menu and after several cul-de-sacs I finally came across another screen which asked: "Location?" I hit "Enter" and looked at the screen on the trolley handle but nothing happened. I tried various other key combinations until I saw the screen come up with "Ais: K. Bay: 47".

I pushed the trolley across the central divide until I came to the aisle marked "K". I turned left, but saw the bay numbers were counting down from thirty-six. I turned the trolley around and headed the other way and stopped at Bay 47. There they were, the boxes of insulin. I scanned the label on the shelf and once again I followed the sub-menus until I found "Supplier" and again I hit "Enter". The screen on the trolley came up with pages of dates and deliveries by which time I was starting to shiver in the cold. I brought out my phone and tried to keep it still as I photographed each page.

By this time I was starting to get the hang of the system, so I tried looking for the history which would tell me exactly when the batch of insulin had been delivered to the hospital as well as who else had been sent a delivery from the same batch. Once again, pages of despatches came up on the trolley screen and I didn't know if I had time to copy them all, but I photographed the history of deliveries up to the most recent, just the previous week.

I was starting to get really cold and was shivering uncontrollably. I couldn't hear anything inside the insulated walls, so I went back through the door and looked back towards the fire escape. I could hear the low hum of people talking, but there was no sign of them returning. I jumped up and down to try to warm up before going back to Bay 47 and reached behind the stack of boxes and pulled out one from the back. Taking out my penknife, I cut through the cellophane wrapping and carefully opened the end of the box, and pulled out one of the packages which I put in my pocket. I toyed with the idea of trying to enter a false withdrawal on the scanner but it would take too long even if I could work out how to do it.

Taking a big risk, I then scanned in the next item on the picking list, the Oxaban, and navigated the menu until it told me "Ais: Q. Bay: 41". I drove the trolley canting on two wheels like a rally driver until I located the shelf and forced my numb fingers to follow the menu. They would be returning any moment so I didn't have time to do anything except photograph the suppliers' details. I then pushed the trolley to where I found it and headed for the exit. They were already coming in through the open fire exit but fortunately they were still taking their time so I shut the door quickly and ran towards the aisle closest to the wall. If I could go around to the back of the warehouse I could come up to them from behind as they returned from their muster station.

Judging that the person holding the clipboard was the last to come back in, I skirted around behind him towards the open fire door, and then turned and called out to him. He turned in some confusion. 'I'm really sorry,' I said, before he could say anything himself. 'I'm a visitor and I was caught, er… I was in the toilet when the alarm went off. I followed a group out, but was too embarrassed… I mean… I sort of hid, not knowing qu… quite what to do.' The cold was making my stuttering sound quite realistic. 'I was visiting Colin Farrow. I don't suppose you could take me there, could you?' It was clear that he couldn't work out where I'd come from, but fortunately it wasn't really his concern and he took me through the warehouse and back up to the sales office. I found Bob and Colin sitting together in a rather strained silence.

'Where have you been?' Colin asked as soon as he saw me. 'You weren't in the toilet when the fire alarm went off.'

'I'm terribly sorry,' I said. 'The upstairs toilet was occupied so I went to the downstairs one and then followed people out and didn't quite know what to do and sort of got mislaid.'

'Mislaid, eh? I suppose that's one way of putting it. Have you seen everything you want?'

I couldn't tell whether he was being sarcastic or not, so I played it dumb. 'Yes, thanks very much. It's all been very interesting, but the fire drill has made us late and we'd better get a move on and get out of your hair.' I nudged Bob and we headed for the door. In the corridor, I stopped. 'I forgot my briefcase.'

Colin Farrow went back into his office and came out with my case which he handed me.

'I don't want to leave it behind a second time, do I?'

Later, in the car, Bob chose to share with me various bits of his mind, none of which was particularly flattering. I heard him out – I suppose I deserved it. While he embellished his opinions the second time around, I scrolled through the pictures on my phone. Finally, when he took a breath so he could start all over again, I interrupted. 'We've got what we were looking for. The name of the supplier. It's Tau Pharmaceuticals, in Mombasa, Kenya.'

I pulled out the insulin and Oxaban that I'd taken from the shelves. 'I've got this as well. We can see whether it matches up with the medicines Greg Satchwell was given.'

'How the hell did you get those? If my bosses at IHG find out about this then that's my job down the drain. They'll crucify me when they learn that I brought you in.'

'Either they know what's going on at Holden or they don't, and if they don't, then they needn't find out. Your hospital is pretty low down the food chain when it comes to the IHG's management. The company's so big there could easily be some kind of rogue outfit working a fiddle on the side. It could even be Holden. I didn't trust that Colin Farrow. He was far too suspicious – especially since as far as he knew we were on the same side. But where's the profit? How do they benefit from selling out-of-date or even counterfeit drugs? I can't see it. Perhaps he's got a business going on the side that IHG don't know about.'

Bob shook his head. 'I don't see how he could get away with that, not with all the controls the company has in place. So what are we supposed to do now?'

'Good question. You'll have to let me think about it.' I might have traced the supply line back a few paces, but like Bob, it wasn't clear where this was going to get us. This was leading me away from my starting point, which was looking into Greta's father's death. But whatever was going on at IHG needed investigation although I couldn't see how that could be done. In any event, I didn't think that Greta would be prepared to let matters drop even if I told her that there wasn't anything more I could do. She certainly wouldn't be happy to wait for the coroner to look into it. At least I'd been able to show that her initial fears were groundless.

As I rehearsed the arguments in my head, all I heard was Greta's urging me to continue. Wasn't I the one with connections in the intelligence world? There was something clearly not right with IHG and although it was difficult to see what I could do, it had to be worth a try.

As we neared the end of the M1 motorway, I decided I'd call James at the Whitehall office to see if we could meet up. I thought he was still on my side and he'd been working in Whitehall longer than me and had always seemed to master the intricacies of those "inter-departmental meetings" that I always found so baffling. I think it was genetic – I always thought the best way forwards was forwards, but most people in Whitehall seemed to think progress could only be achieved by going sideways. It was as though they wanted to display a superior intelligence by presenting a distorted picture of reality that they alone could understand. Anyway, we arranged to meet at the pub we used to go to, underneath the arches by Charing Cross Station. I didn't tell him what it was about; I told him that I needed his help, to which he replied, "Again?" Predictably, I thought.

James was already waiting for me when I arrived. He bought me a drink and we went to our usual alcove where we couldn't be overheard. I hadn't seen him since he'd handed me the keys at Wapping. He'd been abroad for a few days on some project and was unusually reticent when I tried to ask him about it.

'So how's the good ship *Salacia*?' he asked, putting the beer glass in front of me. 'Still afloat?'

'Only at high tide. She's continuing to show promise. Let's hope she keeps it. I really owe you for finding it for me.' I raised my glass in a mock toast. 'So, how have you managed without me?' I asked.

'With difficulty, I suspect, but I haven't been in the office that much, so I don't really know. Have you made any progress looking into the mislaid files?'

'The last thing they were was *mis*-laid. They were very much *laid*. Laid down in my flat. Ali said he was looking into it.'

I decided to get to the point. 'Do you know anyone in the Medicines and Healthcare Regulatory Agency?'

'The MHRA? No, I don't think so. Why?'

'Sally – my ex – showed me some pharmaceuticals that appear to have been relabelled and asked if I could look into it. She added that since I didn't have anything else to do it might keep me off the streets.' Just the sort of cutting remark that James knew Sally would make. 'What do you know about them?'

James thought for a moment. 'A government agency, supposed to be responsible for the safety of drugs in the UK. But I have heard criticism; that they're not proactive, but they say they're short-staffed and their remit is so wide they can't cover it all. They recently had a big success in a raid organised as part of an Interpol operation. Huge haul of fake drugs – worth over £15 million apparently, but their inspectors are a bit too thin on the ground to be able to do much more than react to reports sent to them. They're also accused of being too close to the drug companies, but I suppose that's always going to be a problem if you work so closely with an industry. They want to encourage best practice first, so enforcement comes some way behind.'

I took the evidence bag out of my pocket and passed it to him. 'I've put it in the bag to protect it, but you can see the label clearly. You can see it's been stuck over the top of another one – an older one.'

James took it. 'Jesus! Where did this come from? Is this why you're asking about the MHRA?'

'It's a long story. Sally told me that these were prescribed to someone at an IHG hospital, so I made some enquiries and managed to trace them back to the original manufacturer, but I need help to take it further. I thought about going to the MHRA direct but they'd take it away and I'd never hear another word. If you can arrange a meeting then I might be able to stay involved. I've still got my security clearance, haven't I?'

'As far as I know, but this isn't exactly your field, so why the interest?'

'As I said, I want to see this through.' I wasn't going to tell him about Greta Satchwell yet.

James sighed. 'I suppose I'll have to see what I can do – do you want to let me have the medicines to show them? It might whet their appetite.'

'No, they'll hold onto them and I won't see them again. Just tell them about it, that should be enough, and afterwards you could come and see me back at Wapping. You could even lend a hand with a paintbrush.'

It felt strange going back to Wapping without our usual discussion of the office affairs, although I didn't miss the internal office politics which always struck me as a diversion from our real job.

When I got back on board, I phoned Greta. I'd had an idea that we might take some time out from the investigation, as I supposed I must now call it, and get to know one another better. I was nervous about asking her, but I chanced it and asked if she wanted to come around for dinner. *Salacia's* galley was far from ready, but I thought that after the electric hob in the Whitehall flat, I could probably manage something half-way edible. I was a bit old fashioned about my cooking; I didn't believe in lots of equipment, just good quality ingredients, competently assembled.

I was relieved when Greta didn't hesitate and told me she'd be around later. Meanwhile, I discovered that a phone line had finally been installed so I had Internet connection on board and I thought I'd do some research into the pharmaceutical business and counterfeits in particular. It didn't prove to be very easy, partly because the distribution chain was so complex but partly also because it turned out that what one rich country called a counterfeit drug, another, poorer, country called an affordable one.

While I was struggling with understanding this, James phoned. He'd set up a meeting at the MHRA's offices in the morning. 'I had to stretch the truth,' he said, 'and give the impression that you were still connected with us, so don't let on otherwise.'

'I'll wear my Whitehall suit and tie – that should impress them. Did they give any indication that they already knew about this – that perhaps they were already investigating IHG?'

'I didn't tell them much, that you'd found out something which we thought would be of interest to them and that we'd appreciate their seeing us and letting us know what they think. I should warn you, that you're not going to be alone. Our friends at Six have declared an interest and want to get involved.'

'MI6 – how did they find out about it?'

'Apparently, MHRA aren't the only ones interested in counterfeit drugs. For some reason, Six is as well, so they had no choice but to ask them along, although I bet they did it through gritted teeth – people don't like calling in SIS – they tend to lose control when they're involved. Bloke by the name of Ken Maxwell. Do you know him?'

'I haven't had much to do with them. Have you met him before?'

'He was out in Afghanistan when I was there. Looking into opium distribution. Apparently, he's a narcotics specialist.'

'Narcotics? What's the connection?'

'No idea, but we'll likely find out tomorrow.'

'You're going to be there? Haven't you got better things to do?'

'Not if Six is interested. It'll be a great opportunity to look over their shoulder.'

I rang off, feeling the return of a familiar excitement. The situation seemed to be escalating and I realised that I was in danger of getting elbowed to one side. But at least, for the moment, I still had a foot in the door.

Greta was due shortly and Wapping isn't well stocked with shops, just the local offshoots of the big supermarkets selling, apart from the range of frozen and ready-cooked meals, an extraordinary range of sweets, crisps and other snacks. What I called "food" occupied only a small area at the back. There wasn't time to go anywhere else so I did my best and managed to find some pre-packed fillet steak and picked up some onions and mushrooms.

I could drum up a beef stroganoff, which didn't take long to make but was interesting and different.

Back on the boat, I started to clear up the saloon, stuffing the tools and paint into a cupboard. I ran the vacuum cleaner over the floor and what passed for furniture, before going down to the galley and getting everything ready and laying it out so it would be quick to cook when Greta arrived.

I was finishing my preparation when the ship's bell rang, loud enough for my neighbours to go topside to see if they had visitors. I wiped my hands and adjusted the cutlery on the makeshift dining table before going up the companionway to let Greta in. She was looking stunning; a bright red dress with a black leather belt hung loosely around her waist. Little aquamarine earrings just the right size not to be too flashy. She walked around inspecting the saloon. 'How are you getting on with it?' she asked.

'The boat? I haven't had much time the past few days, you've been keeping me pretty busy. Drink?'

'Gin and tonic, if you have it.'

'No boat is complete if it can't serve gin and tonic,' I said with some relief. The only spirits I had were that or whisky. I mixed the drinks and we sat down. 'Here's to your father.' I raised my glass. 'I'm sorry I never knew him.'

Greta sipped her drink and pulled a face. 'You certainly make them strong, don't you? Yes, here's to my father. I think you would have liked him. He was a bit like you, got straight to the point, didn't like faffing around.'

'Impatient, you mean? I'm not sure that's an advantage, it can get you into trouble.'

'Tell me about what forced you out of the army. Sally didn't say much about it.'

'There's not much to tell. They said I'd been taking home classified files, which was only partly true. I only took home ones which weren't high security, but somehow they managed to find some marked "Top Secret".'

'You must have been in the army quite a time?'

'It seemed like forever – over ten years. I joined up when I was a teenager. After the orphanage, it was pretty much the same thing, swapping one kind of institution for another.'

'But you did well?'

'I suppose so. I joined up in the ranks, but they obviously saw something in me that I didn't see. Eventually they sent me to staff college and gave me a commission at the end of it.'

'Sally told me that you graduated top of the class?'

I laughed. 'It was a very bad year and I was lucky. I wish she wouldn't go around talking about me.'

'I wouldn't have met you if she hadn't. It's good that you're still friends – it doesn't often happen like that.'

'We've worked hard at it – harder than we ever worked on our brief marriage. It's easier when there's a distance between you. There's more respect and you don't take each other so much for granted. I think we knew the marriage was a mistake almost from the start. We were both looking for some kind of security and saw something in each other that wasn't actually there. That impatience of mine didn't help, it rubbed her up the wrong way. You can't be impatient if you want to qualify as a doctor, let alone if you want to practise as one.' I finished my drink. 'Come on, let's eat.'

Greta followed me downstairs and I took the bottle of wine that I'd opened to allow it to breathe and poured her a glass. She sat watching me cook. 'You seem to know your way around a recipe. What is it?'

'Beef stroganoff.' I turned up the gas on the frying pan. The saffron rice was bubbling happily. 'It's really a cheating recipe; it's easy to make but looks difficult.' I spooned the rice into a dish and took it to the table, and served up the strips of beef onto plates with the mushroom and cream sauce and handed one to her. I topped up her glass and poured one for myself.

'Looks good. You obviously enjoy cooking.'

'You've got to if you live on your own. Actually, I cooked even when I was married – Sally was a terrible cook.'

'A new man?'

'Recycled, I'm afraid. But that's enough. Tell me about yourself.'

'I told you almost all there was to know at my father's flat. Brought up in some privilege, I suppose. St John's Wood, private school, comfortable red-brick university. Graduate traineeship with an international accountant. Everything went my way apart from the accident. I suppose Sally told you about that.'

Sally had mentioned Greta a few times but she'd told me nothing about an accident. 'No,' I said. 'What happened?'

'A car crash when I was fourteen. A kid driving a stolen car. I was in hospital for nearly six months, and you can see it's left me with one leg slightly shorter than the other.'

'Greta. That's terrible.' I didn't know quite what else to say.

'I was very sporty up until then, but all that ended. It took me ages after I'd got back to school before I could adjust. I'd lost all my confidence and Sally sort of took me under her wing and helped me build it up. Not that I'm that confident now – I still find it hard to open up to people.'

'Many people aren't worth opening up to. It's better that way around rather than wear your heart on your sleeve and get it damaged. What about your mother?'

'She died a couple of years ago. My father took it very badly and I don't think I gave him the support he needed, but it was a difficult time for me, just as I was branching out on my own. Now he's gone, I reproach myself every day that I wasn't more helpful. I thought he'd buried himself in his work, but I don't think he ever got over it.'

'We go through life accumulating "might-have-beens", although you seem to have more than most. The longer you live, the more there are. It's that butterfly again, flapping its wings and causing all sorts of problems. I wonder if it knows all the trouble it's caused.' I got up and went over to the stove and picked up the frying pan. 'More?'

'Please, it's delicious. No, really, you should give me the recipe and I'll try it myself sometime.'

'I got it from a recipe book I found in a second-hand bookshop. *Où Est Le Garlic?* – the title sort of grabbed me – by Len Deighton. I didn't realise he wrote cookery books.'

'I didn't realise you were the sort of person who trawled through bookshops looking for cookbooks. I would never have guessed.'

'I don't "trawl" through them. I happened to be in one.' I gave her some more rice and beef and then helped myself to what was left and sat down. 'I've found out where the medicines came from.' I poured us out some more wine. 'Kenya.' I didn't tell her how I'd found this out. 'I'm seeing the Medicines and Healthcare Regulatory Agency tomorrow. They investigate counterfeit drugs. I'm hoping they'll take over – they've obviously got more resources to look into it.'

'I don't want you to give up. We have to follow this through.'

'Let's see what the MHRA say first, shall we? We can decide what to do later.'

We talked on into the evening, both relaxed in each other's company. Chastely, I called a taxi to take her back to her flat in Marylebone.

Chapter Ten

I was at the MHRA offices early the next morning and was shown up to a large conference room overlooking Victoria Station. I'd always found it a good idea to arrive early; that way you could hear what people were saying about the others before they arrived. It also stopped them talking about you.

I was met by a tall, rather languorous man who introduced himself: 'Ed Carpenter, MHRA investigator. Take a seat.' He gestured towards the table and I sat down facing him. We chatted inconsequentially about mutual acquaintances until the others arrived in a group. Ed introduced them.

'James of course you know and this is Ken Maxwell, from SIS across the river.' The MI6 officer, in contrast to the others, was casually dressed in chinos and an open-neck shirt. He simply nodded at me impassively and sat down at the end of the table next to James. I wondered again who'd brought them in and what interest they had in counterfeit drugs.

Ed Carpenter sat down at the head of the table and I took out the evidence bag containing the drugs and handed it to him. 'There's the relabelled Oxaban and the out-of-date insulin.'

He looked at them carefully and then handed it across to the SIS agent. 'And these both came from an IHG hospital?' Ed asked.

I nodded. 'They were supplied to the hospital by a company called Holden Healthcare which is an IHG subsidiary.'

Ed Carpenter looked puzzled. 'How did you manage to find all this out?'

'I've been making my own enquiries. A patient at the hospital died unexpectedly and we found these amongst his things.'

'We?'

'Yes, his daughter and me. She thought her father's death was suspicious and asked me to help her.' I explained the background, leading up to discovering the drugs that the hospital had given him. I glossed over our visit to the Holden operation, but took some pleasure in playing my trump card. 'It's manufactured by Tau Pharmaceuticals in Kenya.'

Ed looked up quickly. 'Tau? How do you know that?'

I took a deep breath; this was the hook I wanted to catch them with. 'The IHG security manager, Bob Tyler, took me up to Northampton to visit the Holden unit up there.'

'And they told you who their supplier was?' The MHRA man clearly wasn't going to believe that.

'Not exactly I made… er… shall we say discreet enquiries.'

'You mean you blagged your way in,' offered James – typical of him.

'I took photographs.' I ignored him and handed across the prints I'd had made earlier.

'Can I see those?' It was the first time the SIS man had said anything. He examined the enlargements I'd made and simply nodded and handed them back to Ed.

Ed took back the pictures. 'So, what do you think, Ken?'

'It's a good lead,' Maxwell said. 'But if it's really from Kenya, I'm not sure that it would be of much interest to us, unless, of course, Al-Shabaab is involved, although they don't usually operate that far south. It's certainly worth following up.'

'Okay.' Carpenter placed the prints into a folder with an air of finality. 'I think we can take it from here. Thanks for bringing this along. We'll start our own enquiries.'

I was starting to lose the initiative. 'But you don't know where to look,' I said quickly, having expected this brush-off. 'I can take you there and show you exactly the place where they're stored.' I could see him hesitate. 'I'm handing you this on a plate.'

Ed Carpenter thought about this. 'Let me check it out first, see if we've got any reference to these drugs. They should be on our database somewhere, along with a licence. I'll look it up and come back to you.' He stood up, and held out his hand again. 'Thanks for coming in. We'll talk shortly.'

So I was being dismissed, but I'd done what I could.

I left with James and took a taxi back to his office.

'What do you think?' I asked.

'He must be tempted. It can't be every day that someone offers to take them directly to a counterfeit drug supplier – especially one owned by IHG. This could cause them major problems – even bigger than the Volkswagen scandal.'

'You think there might be an innocent explanation? That Holden and IHG know nothing about this?'

'If Ed Carpenter finds the evidence sitting on their shelves then they're not going to be able to explain it away very easily.'

'That's why I think they're likely to agree to an inspection. It could be quite a coup for him.'

I left James outside his offices and went back to Wapping on the Underground. I couldn't tell Greta much until I'd heard from Ed Carpenter, but I didn't have long to wait.

He called as I was opening up the barge. 'We'll go with your suggestion,' he said brusquely. 'I'll pick you up outside our offices at six-thirty tomorrow morning.' And then he hung up. It was clear he wasn't very happy about it, but then no one likes an outsider muscling in on their job. It's called "NIH" – Not Invented Here. I would be there on sufferance – but at least I'd be there.

Ed was much more friendly the next day when he picked me up. He sounded almost cheerful. His home was in south London and he'd managed a clear drive thanks to the early start. We headed out north once again.

'What do you know about counterfeit medicines?' he asked as we settled down on the motorway.

I said I'd spent some time on the Internet but nothing more.

'It's very complicated,' he said. 'Most people have only heard of the big companies, GlaxoSmithKline or AstraZeneca, but there are thousands of them out there and many thousands more wholesalers and distributors. In addition, some groups like IHG have their own distributors and even generic manufacturing companies, while different countries use different purchasing patterns. The NHS in the UK tries to negotiate centrally for their drugs. It all makes it very difficult to follow the supply route and see if the drugs are certified.

'What makes it even more difficult is parallel trading. Do you know about that?' he asked and I told him that I'd seen the repackaging at Holden. 'Wholesalers buy them where they're cheap – Greece, for example, and then sell them in Germany or the UK where they're the most expensive. Parallel trading means that the medicines you pick up at your local pharmacy can have gone through over half a dozen different distributors.'

'How much of a problem is caused by counterfeits?' I asked.

'No one really knows, but ten years ago the World Health Organisation reckoned it was $32 billion so it must be bigger than that now. The market for pharmaceuticals is over a trillion dollars so a counterfeit rate of five percent is still a huge figure and research shows that many markets have failure rates much higher than this. It's also a trade that attracts almost no publicity. Obviously the drug companies themselves do what they can to prevent it, but it's not in their interests to give it much publicity since it only creates uncertainty and doubt. The fact is that many hundreds of people in the west die from fake or adulterated drugs but it's very difficult to prove. That's why we decided that we couldn't afford to miss this inspection. Usually all we have is the fake drug which doesn't get us far and it's not often that we can question the supplier and trace the product back to its manufacturer.' He paused and looked in his rear-view mirror. 'Shit! Look at that! Does he think he can just push me out of the way?'

I turned and looked backwards at a souped-up Ford that was tailgating us, flashing his headlights. I turned back and checked the speedometer. 'You're already doing eighty. He'll probably be picked up by the speed cameras up ahead.'

A gap opened up in the middle lane and we pulled over to allow the Ford to pass, which he did with a blaring of horns.

'Stupid idiot,' Ed said. 'I was telling you about counterfeiting, but the problem doesn't stop there. Some drugs have been stolen from warehouses and relabelled, others are past their active life and have been re-dated – like yours. But by far the main problems are in the developing countries such as Africa where large-scale immunisation programmes can be undermined by counterfeits. Take malaria for example: if a counterfeit has less than the right amount of active ingredients then far from helping it can actually cause harm because the low dose only serves to build up resistance, which is counterproductive.' He paused again, before adding: 'People always talk about the problem with narcotics – you say the word "drugs" and that's what they think of, but counterfeit, mislabelled or out-of-date drugs are actually far more of a problem but we don't hear much about them. They certainly kill more people. The public don't know anything about fake drugs, but they're killers and on a massive scale – few people understand how big the problem really is.'

'So what do you think about this manufacturer in Kenya, Tau Pharmaceuticals? Did you find out anything about them?'

'They're quite a big player – "Tau" is Tswana for "lion" and I think that's how they like to be seen. East Africa is a base for quite a few pharmaceutical companies, often with Indian connections. It's one of the routes used for smuggling. Across the Indian Ocean to places like Zanzibar, which is a free port and a pretty lawless sort of place at the best of times. From there, shipments are broken up into smaller consignments which are easier to handle and which are moved up and down the coast by small sailing ships. I think the Mombasa address is simply a warehouse, not a manufacturer which is probably back in India.'

'So this Ken Maxwell, why is SIS interested?'

'Until recently the main source of counterfeits was from India or China and it's ironic because that's the main source of the genuine drugs as well. But now some terrorist groups have discovered that faking drugs is an easy way of making money. SIS thinks that ISIS might have set up small-scale manufacturing plants in the parts of the Middle East under their control and is sending them south to Africa, although they could just as easily set up a wholesaling organisation there or bring them in from India or China.'

By this time we'd reached the motorway turn-off and Ed pulled over into the slip road.

'How are we going to handle this?' I asked.

'We have the authority to make unannounced inspections, so I'll say I wanted to see their cold-storage facility.'

'What about me?'

'They've seen you before with the IHG guy, so perhaps they'll think you're a whistle-blower. Whatever they think probably isn't going to be complimentary if you turn up with me.'

Only the security staff were on duty when we arrived as it was too early for the office workers. The night-time guards opened up and allowed us to wait in the reception area. At just before eight o'clock, Colin Farrow walked in and did a perfect double-take as he saw me. 'You...' he started, and his face flushed. He was obviously about to say something when he saw Ed and immediately recognised that he was looking at trouble.

Ed stood up and held out his identification. 'MHRA. We want to check some of your stock.'

Farrow inspected the identification and then looked at his watch. 'A bit early, isn't it?' he asked, as though we were offering him a double whisky for breakfast.

'You know what they say,' was Ed's response. 'Can we go straight through?'

'Can I get you a coffee or something, so you can tell me what this is all about? I can't start the day without a coffee. I've got to go to my office to drop off my case.'

'Later perhaps, when we've looked around. We'll wait for you down here,' Ed said.

After Farrow had gone upstairs, he turned to me. 'You can see why we don't announce our visits. Just think what they might get up to with a little notice.'

'Did you bring coats with you?' Farrow asked as he returned. 'We keep parkas for visitors – it's through here.' He opened the door of a changing room where there was a rack of quilts in different sizes. 'Help yourself,' he said opening a locker and pulling out a coat.

Ed and I chose from the rack and put on the jackets as we followed Farrow out and into the warehouse. 'Is it just the refrigerated area you want to see?' Farrow asked.

'For the moment. We might have a more general look around later.'

We followed him across the warehouse to the cold area, where Farrow opened the door and led us through. Immediately our breath condensed in clouds. 'Is there anything in particular you're looking for?' he asked, shivering slightly.

I'd told Ed to look at rows "K" and "Q" but he didn't make it that obvious. 'We want to check the temperatures and the use-by dates to make sure that the storage conditions are right,' he said and wandered on ahead apparently randomly. I followed, checking the aisle numbers and when we reached "K" we turned into it, with Colin Farrow following. Ed was looking to his right and left until he stopped suddenly. Ahead of us were rows of empty shelves. 'What's happening here?'

Was it my imagination, or was there a ghost of a smile hovering around Farrow's lips? 'We've been clearing out-of-date stock.'

'Where's it gone?' asked Ed.

'I'll have to check the records but we're getting it incinerated in accordance with our licence.'

Ed nodded and headed off again, and I could tell he was now aiming for the second aisle. I followed him but couldn't recognise the bays from my earlier visit when I could barely keep my hands still from shivering. He turned in at "Q" and made his way down to Bay 40, adjacent to the place they had stored the Oxaban. This time, he looked across to me. It was empty.

I was feeling a bit subdued the next morning as I went out to get something for lunch. Ed Carpenter had taken the fiasco at

Holden Healthcare philosophically, but said that without any direct evidence there wasn't much else he or the MHRA could do. Every time I thought I was making some progress it seemed I was knocked back to first base. It was time I started thinking about my own future and give up any further investigations. I was obviously absorbed in my own thoughts when I suddenly became aware of a car stopped ahead. The driver leant over and opened the passenger door, blocking my path. I looked in and saw that it was the spook from MI6. I got in without waiting to be told. It was clear he wanted to take me for a ride and whatever he had to say was preferable to milk and eggs.

'Ken Maxwell, isn't it?' I asked in a friendly sort of way. 'I wasn't expecting to see you again.' He didn't say anything but put the car in gear and drove off engaging the clutch with a jerk. I didn't speak for a while either. He'd come to the point eventually. I turned and saw him looking closely into the rear-view mirror. 'Expecting company?' I asked and started to turn around.

'Don't look back,' he said tersely and made a sudden left turn into a narrow street leading away from the river. On the A13, he headed east before turning off at Silvertown, heading for Victoria Dock.

He parked on double yellow lines in front of the Excel exhibition centre. He got out and walked across to the dockside opposite the old Spillers flour depository and I followed him and we sat down on a bench overlooking the water. There was no show at the exhibition hall and the wide, open concourse in front was almost deserted. Anyone following us had nowhere to hide.

Nonetheless, I looked around to make sure and then sat down next to him. 'That was melodramatic. Was it really necessary?'

'We're not taking any chances. That boat of yours is pretty conspicuous and easy to stake out.'

'I suppose it's not as though there's a basement exit for me to slip out through, but why should you think anyone's watching me?'

'We heard what happened yesterday at Holden Healthcare. It seems they were forewarned about the visit.'

'Possibly. But they knew what we were looking for, because we raised the second order deliberately, so they could have checked it and found the problem themselves. I've been thinking about it, and it could have been an accident, a duff load of medicines somehow contaminating the rest. I would have thought the controls here are too tight for them to risk passing off counterfeits on a regular basis so that seems the most likely explanation. What bothers me is Colin Farrow. He seemed to be too suspicious for someone who didn't have something to hide.'

'Perhaps he's the suspicious type?' Maxwell looked around again to make sure we were alone. 'I've found that most of the drug companies are pretty paranoid.'

'Perhaps, but even on our first visit his whole manner suggested that he was waiting for us to find something. It's as though he knew there was something to be found. Still, I suppose you can't condemn someone for being suspicious. Anyway, why all this drama?'

'Ed told me that without any evidence the MHRA can't take it any further. They don't have the resources and there's so little to go on.'

'There's Tau Pharmaceuticals – that's a lead.'

'Yes, but it's in Africa. They're not going to send someone there. They say that if Holden knew about the faulty drugs, then after their inspection found nothing they're not likely to do it again if they think there could be another inspection.'

'So what brings you out here to kidnap me?'

'It's not a kidnap, just a friendly meeting. I've made some enquiries about Tau. It's part of the Bakaar family holdings. The son, Jamaal Bakaar is based in Mombasa and has fingers in a host of pies, not all of them halal. He holds himself out as a devout Muslim, but his values seem to be rather flexible.'

'And what about his pharmaceutical business? Is it big?'

'It is by Kenyan standards, but Tau is mainly a wholesaler. As far as we can tell, they do some small scale manufacturing, but our information is a bit out of date so we need to get confirmation of that. He has distribution agreements with some of the major companies, so they must think he's on the level.'

'Unless it's because they haven't caught him out yet. But I suppose they don't have much choice about who they do business with. They probably have to deal with things as they find them – they must have a canteen of long spoons.'

'It isn't easy in East Africa. Business relies on contacts and family connections. Many people have burnt their fingers trying to bypass the established companies. But they're established for a reason.'

'So who are his major suppliers – pharmaceutical suppliers, that is?'

'Tau is the East African subsidiary of the Bakaar group who have a manufacturing facility outside Mumbai in India.'

'And you think they might be the source of the fakes?'

'That's what we're hoping you'll find out for us.'

'What? How can I find out about them?' I couldn't see where this was leading.

'You've got the perfect cover to follow this up. There's no connection with MI6. You've been dismissed from the service and are clearly on your own.'

'Resigned, not dismissed,' I said almost automatically, my mind following the consequences of what Ken Maxwell was saying.

'Dismissed, resigned, it makes no difference. It's all the same to people on the outside. If they looked into it they'd see someone who was on a fast track for promotion suddenly leaving after a disciplinary hearing. If we'd wanted your help on this we could have asked for a transfer, or a secondment. Whatever the real situation might be, to anyone making enquiries, you've left the army under a bit of a cloud so no one would make any connection with us.'

'Unless, of course, you engineered the whole thing, which you couldn't have because you didn't know anything about this until I found out about Tau Pharmaceuticals.'

'Yes, well, we have a lead and we need to follow it up.'

'*We've* got the lead?' I repeated.

'Okay, okay, you've got the lead, which makes your position even better. You did it without us and now we want you to help us follow it up. It isn't as if you've got a lot else on.'

'Everyone goes around thinking I don't have anything better to do except to be available for them. I do have my own life to lead.'

'I'm sure you've got a hundred pressing matters jostling for your time, but we think there might be a connection between Jamaal Bakaar and Al-Shabaab and if we have a lead into them, then it's a matter of national security. Something you were working on yourself until a short while ago. We think this is a situation we can take advantage of.'

'Take advantage of the situation, or of me?'

Maxwell said nothing for a while. 'Extraordinary place this,' he said, looking around. 'It's difficult to imagine that these were once working docks. Even more difficult to realise that this was once the centre of an empire.'

'You didn't bring me here to give me a history lesson. I don't understand this… this situation. How can you take advantage of it? What is this "situation" anyway?'

'I've discussed it with my colleagues, and we think that if you're prepared to follow it up, we could give you covert support. We can have people on the ground who can advise and help.'

'When you say "follow it up" what exactly do you mean?' I didn't see why I should make this easy for him. If he wanted my help then he could spell it out.

'You could go and call on Bakaar Pharmaceuticals for us.'

'What? In Mumbai? You want me to go to India?'

'To start with.'

'To start with! What's that supposed to mean?'

'The MHRA think it's quite likely that the counterfeits might be manufactured elsewhere.'

'If they *are* counterfeits.'

'That's what we hope you can find out. But the trail starts with Tau and Jamaal Bakaar in Mombasa and leads directly across the Indian Ocean to Bakaar in Mumbai.'

'So you don't want me to go to Mombasa?'

Ken nodded. 'As I say, there's little actual manufacturing in Kenya. It's Mumbai where virtually all the drugs come from. So, what do you think?'

'I think it's crazy. I don't know anything about pharmaceuticals. I don't know anything about East Africa, or India and my knowledge of Al-Shabaab is probably out of date.'

'You don't have to worry about Al-Shabaab. If you can demonstrate their involvement then we can take over. It would be too dangerous for you on your own. But you could do the initial spadework – find out where these drugs come from. The MHRA will give you a basic course in counterfeit detection. There's a lab they use that you can visit and they can show you how to use some portable equipment.'

'So I pitch up in Mumbai one day and start making enquiries? Just like that?'

'We thought you could say you were representing a pharmaceutical wholesaler. That would give you a cover story which would get you into these companies so you could sniff around.'

'Sniff around? Is that what you call it?'

'If Bakaar's subsidiary, Tau, is working with terrorists knowingly or not knowingly, then we need to investigate. You've heard what Ed Carpenter told you about the counterfeit market. If they're involved in any scale, the money to be made could be huge. And that goes into their coffers to allow them to buy bigger and better arms – even missiles.'

'If that's an appeal to my patriotism, you can forget it. I've already done my bit for Queen and country in Afghanistan. Can you drive me back now? I still need to buy my milk and eggs.'

'Think about it,' Ken Maxwell said. 'We want you to go and make out that you're a potential customer who's asking about their pharmaceuticals. You'll have no link with us and nothing can be traced back to us. We'll even pay your expenses.' He stood up and I followed him back to the car, which, miraculously, hadn't been ticketed. 'Let us know,' he said and got in the car and drove off.

Chapter Eleven

Later that evening, I finally got around to telling Greta what had been happening. We were sitting out on the aft deck of the barge and it was getting to be quite a habit – at least I hoped it was. I was making things out to be somewhat more heroic than they actually were. She seemed quite impressed until I got to my latest visit to Holden and the empty shelves.

'So they must be part of it?' she said. 'Surely that's an admission of guilt?'

I sighed. 'If only it were. But we've got no proof. They said they were clearing out old stock so how can we prove otherwise? In any event, they probably *were* and that's not illegal.'

'But you know where it came from and who manufactured it.'

'And what can I do with that information?' I wasn't going to tell her about my morning with the SIS. 'Ed Carpenter of the MHRA was very nice about it, but he explained that without evidence there was nothing they could do. They weren't going to start an investigation only on the evidence of a couple of dodgy drugs. There wasn't much I could say to that – I had to agree with him, so we're back to first base.'

Greta thought about that. 'Couldn't you follow it up? Go out there, I mean, to Mumbai. See what you could find out?'

'What? India? Why is everybody trying to get me out of the country?'

'Who else has asked you?'

I realised that I'd said too much. 'No one. It was a suggestion made in passing from the MHRA. They said they'd help me with analysing equipment. But you're not seriously suggesting I go to Mumbai? That's crazy.'

'I could pay.' Greta was sounding desperate. 'I could make it worth your while. I can't stop now.'

'I told you I couldn't achieve very much on my own. And even if I could, what would be the benefit?' I couldn't bring myself to say that it wouldn't bring her father back, but the words hung in the air.

'From what you say people are dying out there every day because of fake or sub-standard drugs. We can't walk away and ignore it.'

'The Crusades ended a thousand years ago, we're not going to bring them back now.'

'Sarcasm doesn't help,' Greta said tersely. 'You're not prepared to leave it there, are you? Aren't there any other agencies you could get involved?'

Much as I wanted to see this through, I felt I was getting boxed in and I wasn't sure that I could keep my independence. 'There might be.' I said it reluctantly. 'I've spoken to some of the intelligence agencies and they might be able to help, but it's still such a long shot.'

'Perhaps there might be someone else who could help. I had a meeting with Brendan Rogers of Tribune Investments. I had to go over the Camden development with him and he told me how sorry he was about my father. I think he realised that for a while I'd thought he had something to do with it, so it was a bit embarrassing, but he said that they'd always got on really well together and that if I wanted any help in finding out what happened, then I should just ask him.'

'Perhaps,' I said warily, 'but it's difficult to see what he can do.'

'There's no harm in asking. They've got lots of contacts.'

'Many of them dubious,' I replied rather cattily. 'But you're assuming that I can carry on with this. We're facing a brick wall after the fiasco at Holden and now the MHRA have backed out, there's nothing I can do on my own.'

But that night, after she'd left, when I sat aimlessly watching the water go past, I realised that I'd find it impossible to walk away from this – I'd got my teeth into the chase. Then, remembering what Greta had said and thinking back to my conversation with Ken Maxwell, I thought that perhaps Brendan Rogers could help us after all.

Tribune's offices looked, if anything, even more opulent on my second visit. Was that a new Warhol they'd acquired since I was there last? I looked closely but saw it was only a print, which was letting the side down a bit, even if it was signed.

I was shown upstairs to Rogers' office. He was sitting behind his desk and I took the chair he indicated opposite. Once again, I noted Rogers' aura of uneasy calm – a volcano whose lava was bubbling below the surface – somebody who could be a forceful enemy, but a useful friend.

'I hear you've crossed us off your list of suspects,' he said, coming straight to the point. 'Not that I blame Greta for her suspicions. I would probably have felt the same in her situation. I think she was casting around for someone to blame and we happened to be the nearest target – it's understandable. You're still not sure of the actual cause of death?'

'Not until we get the autopsy results and the medicines analysed,' I said. 'But Greta told you about his medications – the out-of-date insulin and relabelled Oxaban?'

'She did, although I'm told that you're not sure about the Oxaban – that you're going to get it analysed. She said that you'd called in the government drugs agency and they mounted a dawn raid on the wholesaler.'

'The MHRA, yes, but it wasn't as dramatic as a dawn raid – it was all very low key, but I think they were expecting us and they removed anything incriminating.'

'So you think IHG or Holden Healthcare might be involved?'

'I don't know. Without any evidence, they'll probably shrug it off and explain away the problems with Greg Satchwell's drugs as simply an aberration – a rogue contamination which they say happens from time to time.'

'So how can Tribune Investments help?. I told Greta we'd do what we could – within reason of course.' He picked up the phone and pressed a button. 'We'd better get Warren Bidwell up here; this is more his thing than mine. I understand that you've just left the army?' he said while we waited. 'Greta said you were in intelligence?'

'Military intelligence, it's not the same thing. These days we leave the spying to our civilian brothers.'

'So why did you leave?'

'Differences of opinion, I suppose.' I certainly wasn't going to give him the full details. 'Perhaps it was time to try something else.'

'And is this investigation the "something else"?'

I wasn't going to be drawn. 'We'll see,' is all I said before Warren Bidwell came into the room.

'Warren – you remember Philip Hennessey?'

'Of course.' Warren, sitting on the chair next to me, shook my hand. 'Brendan has told me a bit about this, so how can we help?'

'I'd like you to help me set up a dummy company.' I then explained my plan. 'Holden – that's the IHG wholesaler – explained away the drugs as being an aberration, so we asked them who the supplier was and they gave us the name of one of the leading European parallel traders. They explained that they were probably bought in Greece and that's where the relabelling occurred, although an out-of-date batch must have found its way in somehow.'

'So?'

'I found out who actually supplied these drugs and it wasn't who they said it was. By the time they'd cleared out their shelves and deleted the computer records, the MHRA didn't have anything left to go on.'

'But if they went as far as doctoring their records, then surely IHG must be involved in the counterfeiting?' Warren asked.

'Again, not necessarily. It could be another case of parallel trading and all they're trying to conceal is that the supplier didn't have EU certification. It's a big jump from there to deliberately sourcing fakes.'

'How did you find out where they actually came from?'

'Let's say I went undercover.' I didn't add that it was under the cover of two layers of thermal underwear. I handed them the prints I'd made for the MHRA.

Rogers looked at them and then handed them to Warren. 'Mombasa. I didn't know they manufactured drugs in Kenya.'

'The MHRA don't think they do, they think it's just a wholesaler and that the actual manufacturer is a company in Mumbai,' I replied. 'Greta wants me to follow this up. People are dying because of counterfeit or out-of-date drugs and she thinks she owes it to her father to do something about it. She says she stands to inherit his estate and the money would be tainted unless she did something with it. But if I do go out there I need a cover story that holds water. That's why I want you to set up a company for me. From what I understand, it's something you do quite often with your other partners. You could announce that you're looking into a new partnership in pharmaceutical distribution. In fact, from what I've seen, there's so much money in it that I'm surprised you haven't done it already.'

Brendan Rogers smiled. 'Perhaps,' he said to Warren. 'Perhaps it might work. After all, it's effectively only a feasibility study that you're proposing, you're not going to be doing any trading. What I don't understand though, is what's in it for you? What's your real interest in this?'

'I told you, I'm doing it to help Greta. And I can't leave it. This needs investigating.' Obviously I couldn't tell him anything about the involvement of SIS.

'And you're even prepared to go traipsing around the world on what will probably turn out to be a waste of time?'

'I don't think it will be. I'll say that I'm looking into the feasibility of setting up a new pharmaceuticals' wholesaling business and if I've got a believable backstory then I don't see why manufacturers wouldn't make me welcome. Other wholesalers, too.

It's not as though there's much of a commitment. All we need to say is that I'm trying to see if there's a viable business. A research trip, but I need to establish that the business behind me is a serious player. People need to see that there's some muscle behind the venture.'

'What do you think, Warren?' Rogers asked Bidwell.

'We could certainly help.' Warren laughed. 'Especially if we didn't actually have to do anything.' He hesitated. 'But it's not really our style to advertise our involvement. We've always kept in the background.' He turned to me. 'We call it the Google test. If you Google us and can't find anything then that's how we like it and want to keep it.'

'What about one of your associated companies?' I asked. 'One that people can Google if they want to check up on me?'

'There's Orion,' Warren said looking at Rogers. 'They might be amenable to this. They might even be interested to see if there's a market there for themselves.' Warren turned back to me. 'They're a specialist chemical company, so it's the right sort of area. It wouldn't commit them to anything. We might not even need to start up a dummy company; they could say they were retaining a consultant.' He thought for a moment. 'But you'd have to act the part. You can't walk in and pretend to know what you're talking about. You'd have to *know* what you're talking about.'

I sighed. '*Appear* to know at least. I'm having to go back to school.' This was something Ken Maxwell had insisted upon. 'The MHRA have arranged a session with one of their investigation laboratories. I'm going there for a briefing in the morning.'

'But this lead you're following up,' Rogers said. 'Greta says that the insulin was out of date but you don't have the analysis of this Oxaban.'

'Not yet. But we're taking it with us to get it analysed at the laboratory. Since it came from the same supplier as the insulin, it's quite likely that there's something wrong with it, but we'll see.'

'Okay,' said Rogers. 'I'll let you know what Orion say.'

This time we were heading north on the old A1 in Ed Carpenter's BMW. The laboratory was in Welwyn Garden City, about twenty miles north of London and Ed had decided to come with me as a sort of refresher course. I had to admit feeling a bit nervous; I'd only done a few years of chemistry at school and didn't exactly distinguish myself. Ed's satnav guided us to the company's entrance and we were met at reception by a woman who introduced herself as one of the analytical chemists. Libby Anderson was an elegant-looking woman, probably in her late forties, but her white coat concealed a trim figure which suggested that she kept in shape. She kitted us out with our own white coats and gave us safety glasses.

But the laboratory we were shown into was like nothing I remembered. Instead of the stained wooden work surfaces with test-tube racks and Bunsen burners, the place was spotless. 'Most of our analysis is automated these days,' she explained pointing to the rows of space-age-looking machines. The atmosphere here felt more like a church, with hushed voices of the staff and the low hum of the machines and the flickering of computer screens. 'I understand you're particularly interested in pharmaceutical analysis,' Libby continued. 'We're one of a number of laboratories which are accredited by the MHRA to provide independent testing and analysis.

'Most pharmaceutical companies have their own in-house labs, but they need independent corroboration so we're sent random samples of each batch. We have the details of the original constituents programmed into the machines and the analysis compares each batch with the control.' She led us across to one of the machines. 'The standard technique is GC.' She looked at me expectantly, hoping to see signs of recognition which I was unfortunately unable to provide.

'Gas chromatography,' she added as though it was obvious. 'It's our basic analytical tool. It's analogous to distillation where each chemical has a different boiling point, so as the temperature is raised each individual chemical evaporates successively giving us a spectrum where we can identify each constituent. These machines use inert gases to move the constituents through a column, like the refractory in a whisky distillery which detects each component part. When I first started we had to read them off a rolling graph paper, with a needle spiking as it detected each component. Nowadays, it's automatic and we can see it here on the computer screen.'

Ed and I peered over her shoulder at the screen but the chemical formulae were beyond me. 'You don't have to worry about those,' she said, as though reading my mind. 'We pre-programme the machine with the name of each of the compounds so you only have to call up the name; so it's aspirin, rather than acetylsalicylic acid.' We followed her to the next machine.

'This is a Raman spectrometer. It's sort of like a prism: we send a laser beam into the compound and the light is scattered in different ways by the different molecules so once again we can tell what the constituent parts are.'

She moved over to a desk and picked up what looked like an oversized mobile phone. 'And this incredible piece of equipment is a Truscan which uses the same principles of spectroscopy, but, as you can see, in a highly miniaturised form. We're testing it here against its big brother and the results are remarkable. You can point it at the compound and it'll check against its database and come up with a pass or fail. You don't even need to unwrap them; it'll work through the packaging. It's revolutionised the detection of counterfeit pharmaceuticals.'

She took us over to another workbench and let us try it on several of the sample compounds they had. That something so small could identify fakes seemed to me more like magic than science. 'You said you had something you wanted us to check?' Libby said. 'Some samples of Oxaban and some insulin, wasn't it? Let's put it through the GC machine first.'

I took out the evidence bag and handed it to her, along with the Oxaban I'd taken from Holden Healthcare. I followed her across the lab where she took out a capsule and placed it into a stainless-steel container which she pushed into a slot. Moving across to the computer screen, she scrolled through the various anticoagulants until she came to Oxaban, and entered that and started the machine. 'I'll turn on the running display so you can watch it working. Along the bottom here is the control – you can see the spikes corresponding to each compound, while this along the top is our sample which should mirror the control.'

We watched as the line stayed flat until it suddenly spiked before running flat again. 'There you go. It's matching the control, but do you see the spike isn't as high?'

When the test came to an end, Libby took the second sample of Oxaban and put that in the machine and repeated the process. 'Shall we try the insulin now?' she asked and took out the sample and re-programmed the machine. When she had finished she printed out the three read-outs and spread them on a nearby table.

'Taking the insulin first, it's the identical chemical make-up so it hasn't been adulterated in any way, but the active ingredients are way down, which is what you'd expect if it's out-of-date stock which it appears to be from the label underneath.'

'What about the Oxaban?'

'They're certainly both Oxaban. Or rather they used to be. Like the insulin, you can see that nearly all the peaks correspond, but are not as high. That means that although they contain the right active ingredients, they're not in sufficient quantity – it's only showing about twenty-five percent of what it should be. That could be as a result of it being out-of-date, but you can also see some peaks which aren't on the control graph. That can't be a result of natural degradation over time; it has to mean they've deliberately used an inert compound to dilute it.'

'So you think both fakes?' I asked.

'I wouldn't call them fakes,' she said. 'Fakes don't usually have any active ingredients at all. I'd call this counterfeit because, although they do have the correct elements, they're not there in sufficient strength.'

'Does that mean it wouldn't work?'

She laughed. 'I'm only a chemist. You'd have to ask a pharmacist, although it stands to reason that at only twenty-five percent strength, it's not going to do much good.' As she handed the Oxaban back to me, she added, 'We'll email the official report through later. I'll show you how to use the Truscan now and we can repeat this to see how it checks out.'

We spent the rest of the morning going through the various drug classifications and more detailed instructions on how to programme the Truscan, before heading back to London. I thought that smartphones were the latest in miniaturised technology, but the analytical equipment she had shown me far surpassed it. If only they were cheap enough to send out to all vaccination stations then perhaps counterfeit drugs would never get through.

'So that seems to corroborate the fact that Greg Satchwell's Oxaban came from the same batch as we found at Holden Healthcare,' I said to Ed on the drive back.

'Looks that way. Though we're going to have some difficulty with the evidence now they've cleared out their shelves. It would be your word against theirs that your sample came from them. Even if you could prove it, they could say you obtained it illegally and they'd probably be right.'

I looked out of the windows at the passing countryside. Greta wasn't going to like this. First she comes to me thinking her father had been killed by business associates and now it appeared that it was probably the subsidiary of a huge American hospital group. But Ed was right, we wouldn't be able to prove it. 'She'll be devastated when I tell her,' I said. 'She'll want to show that someone was responsible.'

Ed sighed. 'All we can do is follow it up and try to discover the original source of the drugs and prevent it happening to someone else and I think that's something for MI6, rather than us.'

Chapter Twelve

Back at Wapping, the unfinished jobs around *Salacia* greeted me with what I thought was silent reproach. True, the place was looking much better than when I'd first moved in but there was still so much to do if I was going to keep my bargain with her absentee owner.

I'd arranged to join Greta the next day at her father's weekend cottage on the south coast. Sally, unusually, had found some free time and was going to drive me down. First I had to run my clothes through the nearby launderette which was a chore that always left me depressed. It wasn't so much the fact that this was where life's losers could be found – I didn't think this at all. What depressed me was the way so many of the regulars were able to sit in front of the machines without doing anything. I suppose it was about as entertaining as daytime television.

Sally picked me up in her red Mazda sports car. She already had the hood down, which I wasn't so sure about if you're going to drive through south London, but she was obviously relieved that she'd managed to bring another week to a conclusion without doing any harm, and was cheerful company on the way down.

I was looking forward to seeing Greta's place. She'd told me about it before and it sounded idyllic. Although not quite on the foreshore of Chichester harbour, it enjoyed an uninterrupted view across a field to the water's edge with a footpath that took you to a small hard where the locals launched their dinghies. I remembered the place from when I used to race cruisers on Hayling Island but I'd never been on this side before – and I don't think inadvertently running aground counted.

Greta seemed more relaxed than I'd known her and more outgoing. Obviously she was coming to terms with her father's death, although she still wanted to know what I'd found out about the medication he'd been taking, even though there wasn't much new I wanted to tell her.

It was a glorious late spring day and we made arrangements for a waterside table at the local pub where we could watch the parked cars being submerged by the incoming tide. It was here that King Canute was supposed to have shown his courtiers that he couldn't turn back the tide and his example was being followed by a number of tourists and we enjoyed the floor show enacted in front of us.

'The best one,' Greta said, 'was when a dog was trapped in a car with the water rising and this parking warden took off his trousers and waded into the water in his underpants. The crowd was roaring him on and gave a great cheer when he took the dog and brought it back to the beach.'

'That must be the only time a parking warden has been popular,' I said. 'What happened to the car?'

'It was only a Citroën 2CV, so it didn't make much difference.'

We were served our lunch and I braced myself to tell them about the results of my visit to the Welwyn laboratory. The circumstances didn't seem ideal but they had to know. 'I'm afraid I've got the test results for your father's medication,' I said. 'It confirmed that the insulin was out of date as we suspected.'

Greta stared at me without saying anything. Sally reached across and took her hand. 'And the Oxaban?'

I hesitated, knowing how distressing this would be. 'It had only twenty-five percent of active ingredients and contained some impurities. I'm afraid the view was that it was probably counterfeit.'

'Counterfeit?' Sally cried out involuntarily. 'It couldn't be counterfeit. We're not a third world country. This was prescribed by a leading hospital.'

I watched Greta whose face looked as though a cloud had passed over it; she seemed to stare fixedly at nothing until a tear coursed slowly down her cheek. Sally squeezed her hand but Greta didn't seem to notice. I cursed myself for not breaking it more gently and tried to think of something encouraging but realised there was nothing. The sound of the people around us appeared to be silenced as though we existed in a separate world.

'So he was killed after all?' Greta whispered as though talking to the Gods.

I couldn't answer this and looked across at Sally – she was the only one who could.

'Not necessarily,' she said warily. 'But without effective insulin and an anticoagulant, it would certainly have put him at much greater risk during the surgery.'

'So they *did* kill him?' Greta repeated, although it wasn't clear who she meant by "they". 'I knew it must have been something. He wouldn't have left me like that...' She petered out and Sally and I looked at each other, helpless at the raw and irrational grief.

'We don't know that for sure,' Sally said but it was unclear whether Greta was listening.

Greta turned to me. 'You have to do something.' A light glistened in her damp eyes. 'You have to find them. Whatever it takes.' What could I say to that? The MHRA and the security services agreed we'd reached a dead end – we simply didn't have enough to go on. I could tell them about Tau but where would that get us? I shrugged uneasily.

'There must be something you could do.' Greta repeated and turned to Sally. 'Tell him. Tell him he's got to follow this up.'

Sally turned back to me. 'How far did you get?'

I told them about tracing the drugs back to Tau Pharmaceuticals in Kenya but said the trail grew cold after that.

'Can't you organise a raid on their premises, or something?' Sally asked.

I shook my head. 'We don't have enough to justify a raid even if we had the authority to organise one. In any event, Tau doesn't manufacture drugs themselves so whatever we found wouldn't get us far. We have to discover who is making these counterfeits and I'm afraid we're no nearer that.'

'I don't understand you,' Greta said so loudly that people started to look at us. 'You've tracked these adulterated drugs from Harley Street to Kenya, but you say you're no nearer finding out the truth?'

Ouch, I thought, *that hurt*. 'I didn't quite say that. I said we still don't know who's making the fakes so it's difficult to see where to go next.'

'You said that this company, Tau Pharmaceuticals, was supplied by an Indian company, Bakaar. Why can't you investigate them? The fakes must be coming from them.'

'We know that there's fake Oxaban being made, we know it's associated with Tau and we know Tau are supplied by Bakaar, but they're only one supplier amongst dozens. I suppose we might be able to follow that trail.'

'What's stopping you?' Greta said. 'Why don't you go back to your friends in intelligence and tell them people are being killed by these fake drugs? Tell them they have to do something.'

'Kenya seems to be the main destination. It's where a lot of the fake drugs end up and it's not just people who are dying but whole communities.'

'It's always the poor countries that suffer,' Sally said. 'My charity does a lot of work in East Africa. We set up micro-financing units which have been very successful.'

'Mainly with the women,' Greta said bitterly. 'Why is it always the women who have to make the running?' I couldn't tell whether this was aimed at me.

'Nearly all our successful case studies have been of women,' Sally continued. 'The men are too easily tempted by other things, while the women generally stay dedicated. Setting up new little businesses like that is becoming increasingly necessary with the problem of terrorism and its disastrous effect on the tourist industry. Visitor numbers are down – in some places by nearly half – and there's no sign of containing the terrorism anytime soon.' Sally turned to me. 'Do you know anything about Al-Shabaab?'

I thought about this and decided that there wasn't anything secret about the little I did know. 'It was another classic case of people ignoring problems unless it affected them directly. When ships started being taken by Somali pirates then finally the world's security forces did something about it. Somalia was lawless and no multinational had any interests there, so there wasn't anything that could be done by land forces and nobody was interested anyway. But the pirates were making fortunes: millions in ransoming shipping so Al-Shabaab organised them and used the money to fund their terrorism. More recently they've looked further south towards Kenya and have carried out numerous horrendous attacks. Al-Shabaab is well equipped and heavily armed but it's difficult to see what their strategic objective is. They're not going to be able to undermine the entire Kenyan state so I suppose it's the usual murder and mayhem. Their only strategic objective is to keep Kenya as near a subsistence economy as possible. If they could, they'd bomb everyone back to the Stone Age and then step in to fill the gap that's left. Fortunately, Kenya has too many friends in the West to let this happen but it doesn't stop them trying.'

'Poor Kenya,' Sally said. 'As soon as they sort out one problem they're hit with another. When we were preparing reports about Islamic terrorism one of the features we looked at was the effect that poverty had. The better off the people were the more they felt they had a stake in their society and the less easy it was for fundamentalists to influence them.'

'That's why Al-Shabaab wants to do as much damage as possible. They don't care about poverty – they positively welcome it.'

'And do everything they can to ensure it,' Greta added.

'And fundamental to creating wealth is increasing life expectancy,' Sally took over the subject – after all she knew much more about it than I did. 'Studies show that if people can expect their babies to survive childhood then they reduce the size of their families. And if you couple that with improvements in agricultural production societies become more stable. And one of the keys to that is reducing diseases – particularly childhood diseases and Kenya, along with most of East Africa is making huge strides in achieving this.'

'Wouldn't that be an obvious target for Al-Shabaab?' Greta asked. 'Given what you say about the relationship with development and health, wouldn't they attack any programme designed to improve health?'

'I think they're always on the lookout for new targets,' I said. 'The other day you mentioned a big vaccination programme. Has anything moved with that?'

'Apparently, it's imminent,' Sally said. 'My agency isn't directly involved but our partners have been gearing up for this for some time. It's under the umbrella of the WHO but involves all the local charities. It's one of the largest programmes there's been. Tens of millions of pounds.'

I suppose it was my ingrained suspicious nature that made me sit up at this piece of news. I had learnt quickly that where there were contracts for pharmaceuticals up for grabs there were counterfeits ready to fulfil them. 'Do you know anything more about it?'

'I think I mentioned that they're trying a new approach by delivering the vaccines directly to the villages.' Sally considered this for a moment. 'It's covering the whole of East Africa so the possibility of introducing fakes must be enormous.'

'And what would be the result if substandard counterfeits were delivered instead?' I asked.

'I suppose that without proper protection all the targeted recipients could be at risk. In the worst case, it could even lead to thousands of preventable deaths. But it could take some years before anyone noticed.'

Greta turned to me and it was clear that she was now on a mission.

'Okay, okay.' I said. 'I get the message. I'll go back to Ken Maxwell and see what I can do. See if I can arrange to go to

Mumbai and follow it up from there, but whoever's making these fake drugs seems to be covering their tracks pretty well.' I looked around at the empty plates. 'Now, do you want anything else? I'll go and order it.'

I went in and got some more drinks, but as I was about to go back out I heard Sally talking, and I stopped and listened. At first I couldn't hear properly as a crowd outside started to leave, but then I heard her say. 'He tries to hide it, and most of the time it's fine, but there's a part of him that you can't reach and I never discovered what it was. He has this terrible temper and it's as though he's trying to take out his problem childhood on everyone else. He used to frighten me at times.'

'Did he ever…?' Greta didn't finish.

'Hit me? No, no. Nothing like that. But it was like living on the slopes of a volcano, you never knew if it was going to erupt and whether you'd be covered by the fall out. It wasn't easy.'

'Did you discuss it with him?'

'I tried. I suggested some sort of counselling, but he said that counselling was for wimps and started to get angry that I'd even mentioned it so I had to drop it. In the end there was too much that I was supposed to ignore that I gave up. At times he was so… so dangerous really. I think it was only the army that channelled his aggression, It always seemed such a waste that he couldn't adapt.'

I flushed and held the glass so tightly that I was about to break it. I recognised the throbbing starting in my head and thought about walking off, but I didn't have a car. I knew I had a temper but I didn't think it had affected our marriage. I thought we'd grown out of it and found incompatibility in each other's dedication to their work but to find out that I was at fault was shattering. I stood with the glasses in my hand in a state of indecision but I realised that I couldn't abandon them but would have to pretend I hadn't heard anything. I would have to grit my teeth and carry on and try to work it out afterwards.

They saw me coming and obviously changed the subject but as I put the glasses down on the table, I saw that my hand was shaking and hoped they wouldn't notice. Sally looked up at me. 'We were wondering whether you were missing the army,' she said smoothly. 'It must be quite a wrench for you after all that time.'

I sat down and tried to draw a breath, I could still feel my heart pounding and I forced myself to relax. 'I haven't had much time to miss it,' I said eventually. 'In the past few weeks, I've spent more time with the security services than I ever did when I was in the army. But unlike you I don't want to spend my life trying to put right the world's ills.'

'Cynic,' Greta said. 'You were doing valuable work in the army.'

'It didn't always feel like it,' I said. 'Trying to make a difference in a country where normal standards don't seem to apply and where people would say one thing to your face and quite another to their neighbours. Most of them didn't seem to want our help so I don't know why we bothered.'

'But you did,' Sally said. 'You cared about your work, I know you did, so why keep up this pretence? Greta might not be able to see through it, but I can.'

I wondered how such a view squared with what I'd heard her say about me just before, but my work in the army had been important to me whatever anybody else thought. 'Perhaps. I suppose both of us were preoccupied with our work with little time left over for the other. A recipe for a divorce, I would think.'

'Which duly came.' Sally didn't sound too upset about it. Perhaps after what I'd heard she thought she was well out of it.

'Are you seeing anyone else?' I regretted it as soon as I said it but then I wasn't feeling at my most tactful.

Sally gave me that quick look that I recognised as a danger sign. This was none of my business. 'No time,' she said instead. 'What about you?' She suddenly blushed as she looked across at Greta. I always liked that about her; one minute the doctor in control, the next blushing like a schoolgirl. She used to get so angry when I teased her about it, but this time I decided to ignore it. As if to cover her embarrassment, she looked at her watch.

'I've got to get back. I've got a huge stack of reports to read.' She stood up and took her car keys out of her bag. 'Thanks for lunch. Enjoy yourselves,' she said and left us alone.

We watched her go without saying anything.

'So why *did* you two split up?' Greta asked after a while.

I turned to look at her. The sunlight was slanting across her face, revealing hardly visible thin veins of scarring, presumably from her accident. But rather than detract, it only added to her attraction. I suddenly realised that I was staring, but in view of what I'd heard Sally say, it wasn't a question I was keen to answer. 'What was that?' I asked. 'Sorry, I was elsewhere. You want to know why we split up? As always, a variety of reasons. Partly it was her work. Sally's an unremitting idealist. I tried to tell her that she couldn't change the world single-handedly, but she thought she could.' I stood up and went to the bar to pay.

When I got back, Greta was gathering her things.

'A walk along the seafront?' I suggested.

The tide was still in and the mud flats were covered and there were only the fields stretching down to the water's edge. Greta had spent her childhood holidays here and played "Swallows and Amazons", messing around in a succession of sailing dinghies. This was something I had in common with her since I'd sailed often at the other side of the harbour.

'So when were you here before?'

'The home I was in used to organise trips out here. One of the sailing clubs provided the dinghies and we'd race each other around the harbour. I sort of got hooked and went on to sail bigger boats after I'd joined the army. We had quite a team. We even won things.'

'Can I ask something?' Greta hesitated. 'Why were you in the orphanage? What happened to your father?'

'I don't mind you asking. I got over it a long time ago. I never knew my father. Never even knew what happened to him.

It was just me and my mother. But then she died and there wasn't anyone else.'

'And you said it was suicide? That must be difficult to live with.'

'But it wasn't her fault. It was the medication she was given I'm sure she didn't mean to leave me alone.' I shrugged. 'By the time I found out, I was already settled in the army, so that provided some kind of reassurance. It had a structure.' I started walking again. 'Come on, let's talk about something cheerful for a change.' I'd need more time to consider what I'd overheard and I wasn't going to raise it with Greta.

Chapter Thirteen

Lots of people say they don't like Mumbai. Too many people, too many beggars, too much pollution. There was certainly a murky pall hanging over the city when I arrived, but as for the people, that's what makes it India and without the incessant bustle of its millions it'd be like the Sahara without the sand. I'd booked a small hotel in the downtown area, off a side street near the grand Taj Mahal Palace Hotel. It was an anonymous sort of place, one you wouldn't really notice unless you were looking for it, which suited me fine.

When I'd last visited India, it had taken me a while to work out what side of the road people were supposed to be driving on, so the prospect of hiring a car didn't fill me with great enthusiasm. I would have preferred to get someone more accustomed to the local driving habits, which seemed to require more the skills of a toreador, but I needed flexibility, so I reserved a car before I left London. I was flying out over the weekend and had arranged to visit the Bakaar facility outside Mumbai the Monday after I arrived and thought that I'd need to do a bit of sniffing around afterwards. Fortunately, my Indian visa was still valid which saved a great deal of bureaucracy – something the Indians had inherited from the British and elevated into an art form.

I'd been pushing on an open door when I'd reported to Ken Maxwell. He'd been frustrated at his inability to follow things through within his agency and when I told him what Sally had told me about the vaccination programme he was able to confirm this through the MHRA. He realised what was at stake and made immediate arrangements for me to go out to Mumbai and for one of his staff to meet me out there.

The SIS contact in Mumbai – Ranish – came around to the hotel later that day and I explained about the imminent vaccination programme and why we needed to check up on the Bakaar facility. I couldn't see where else they could be coming from and he briefed me on the extended Bakaar family. Like all dynasties in India, they'd had their share of arguments and press speculation, but the family's head, Ajmal Bakaar, now a grandfather of six, ruled his empire with a pretty firm hand. His various sons ran different parts of the business and it was his youngest son, Jamaal, who ran the company's operations in East India. They were one of the most prominent in India's Muslim business circles and pharmaceuticals was only one of their divisions, which included engineering and mining. They were still active amongst the Mumbai Muslims and supported numerous Islamic charities. There was no suggestion that Ajmal Bakaar had cut corners on his way to the top, but in Indian business that didn't necessarily mean much. After giving me a recommendation for a restaurant that evening, Ranish arranged to meet me at my hotel the next morning.

It was just as well he did, since I doubt that I would have been able to find my way without his directions. Bakaar Pharmaceuticals Mumbai division was in an industrial estate near the docks and it was a large complex, I guessed about the size of Holden Healthcare's and built only ten years previously but already showing its age. There were several other businesses on the estate with premises of a similar period, as well as a few older units around the site. Despite the high-tech nature of its production, Bakaar's industrial estate had a rather run-down feel, with grass verges overgrown and empty lots abandoned to squatters. It wasn't the sort of place that inspired confidence. I dropped off Ranish and left him investigating the estate while I drove into their car park and went in for my appointment.

I was taken around by their general manager, Ahmed Bashara, who turned out to be a cousin of Ajmal Bakaar – they were clearly keeping nepotism in the family. His English was nearly perfect, as it is with so many Indian businessmen, and despite the state of the premises, the manufacturing facility he took me around was quite impressive, with rows of machines pumping out pharmaceuticals of a bewildering variety. My cover from Orion seemed to hold up well and I was starting to recognise some of the machines, or at least some of the processes.

My guide was clearly enthusiastic at the prospect of gaining a new customer. 'We're shipping to the UK every week through the docks at Jawaharlal Nehru Port, a few miles west of here. Holden Healthcare is one of the biggest customers but then they have the IHG account. There's room for an intermediate size of operation – one that can reach the smaller pharmacies. A lot of Indians go to the local market to buy their medicines which makes distribution difficult, so we have to use wholesalers even for sales on our own doorstep.'

'So you do distribute locally?'

'Yes, but it's a small part of our business and we have to use specialist distributors.'

'What about East Africa? I understand you've got facilities there?'

'In Kenya, yes, outside Mombasa. It's run by one of Ajmal Bakaar's sons but we don't manufacture there, it's only a distributor.'

'Is one of them Tau Pharmaceuticals? Do you supply them direct from here in Mumbai?' I asked.

'Oh yes,' he said. 'Regularly. In fact, we've got a shipment going out at the end of the week. But the main drugs we send them are probably antimalarials and Aids treatments.'

'You make those here?'

'Yes, of course. We're set up to supply much of what they sell in Kenya. These machines are very versatile.' The pride in his voice was unmistakeable and from what I had seen probably justified.

'But I've read that you have serious problems with counterfeiters in the local markets?' I thought I'd risk the direct approach.

'It's what people in the West think of when they think of India and it annoys me. It's prejudice. They haven't seen this sort of operation – we may not have the most modern equipment, but we can match what the West has. We don't need to counterfeit the drugs when we can make them to this sort of standard. I admit that the research behind these drugs is mostly Western, but they wouldn't license us to make these pharmaceuticals if we couldn't do it, and we can produce the same quality but also cheaper than they can. We export back to the West anyway and we're starting to catch up on the R&D side – Indian chemists are starting to match the best in the world. Certainly we have problems in the local markets – that's where many people have to buy their drugs, but then a lot of what they buy is based upon faith rather than science.'

'As you say, if people could see your operation here, it would shake up a few assumptions.' I could see nothing wrong with flattery. 'What about your anticoagulants? Oxaban, for example?'

'Yes, we're licensed to make Oxaban, it's one of a range we make here and in Kolkata. Sells very well around the world. Is that something you would be interested in buying?'

'Possibly,' I said guardedly. 'It's early days yet. When is your next scheduled manufacture? Perhaps I could come and watch it?'

'There won't be much to see that's different from this. We run it pretty regularly, at least once a week – we use that machine over there. Let me check the schedule.' He went over to a stand attached to the machine and flipped through the pages. 'As I said, it's pretty regular. We're running it again tomorrow – it's part of the consignment to Mombasa going out in a couple of days. You'd be welcome to come back but, as I say, it'll look pretty much the same.'

'Thanks for the invitation – I'll certainly think about that.' I looked around the factory. 'What about your quality control procedures? Do you carry out analysis here?'

'I'll take you through to our laboratories,' he said and I followed him through into a long room which reminded me of the labs in Welwyn. 'Our facilities here are about the same age as the machinery out there,' he continued. 'They're pretty standard analytical techniques. We're contracted to provide them to our licensors as part of our agreements and so we take random samples of each batch to ensure conformity. You mentioned Oxaban – we keep details of every manufacturing run over there in those filing cupboards, backed up by computer files that we email to the licensor. We do the same for all the drugs we make under licence.' He led me past the work benches, manned by white-coated technicians, stopping occasionally to boast about some improvements they'd made to the analysis procedures.

'But I'd be interested to see more of the logistics,' I said. 'It must be difficult to move things around in a country this size.'

'We have our main facility in Kolkata, in the east. It's cheaper to move stuff around by sea than by road – it doesn't take much longer either. Let me show you the despatch area.'

We left the laboratories and I followed him across the factory floor to a heavily insulated partition that closed off part of the building. It looked like the area I'd visited at Holden Healthcare.

'Through there is the cold area,' he continued. 'About a quarter of our products has to be stored in cold rooms. We can manufacture at room temperature, we just have to move it through for storage. We use refrigerated containers for shipping, but on this side we can ship them normally.'

We followed the partition past racks of cartons to the loading area, where trucks were lined up in bays being loaded. This was the area I was really interested in. 'Do you use your own transport?' I asked, although I could see there was a variety of liveries displayed on the sides of the trucks.

'No, it's not economic. We subcontract all our logistics to various companies, some local, some national. Although we arrange despatch of refrigerated consignments from here, we haven't got the space to store the bulk of our products so we arrange collections every day. The transport companies make up the containers for us and then take them through to the docks for shipment – Europe or East Africa. The US shipments are manufactured in Kolkata.'

'What about Afghanistan? Do you send much there?'

'Not as much as East Africa, but it's a growing market. It seems the Taliban don't agree with Western medicine, so it's a bit of a struggle to get it into liberated areas.'

'What about this big vaccination programme that's coming up? I understand it's one of the biggest for East Africa.'

Ahmed paused to think. 'A vaccination programme, you say. No, I don't think I know about that. We'd normally supply such a programme from here in Mumbai but it's the sort of thing that Jamaal Bakaar usually deals with, but he hasn't told me anything about it.'

I thought that odd. If this programme was as big as I'd been told then surely Ahmed would have been involved in the tendering process. After all, it would be his factory that would be making the drugs. I decided to let it pass. 'What about shift work? Do you work around the clock?'

'Not on a regular basis. When we've had production problems and are running behind our schedule, or when we have an unusually large order to get out, but normally it's two shifts between seven in the morning and six in the evening. If we're running a night shift there's a separate team that comes in – they're often moonlighting from some of the other pharmaceutical companies around here. We won't be operating all the machines, only those we need in order to catch up on the backlog.'

I thought I'd seen enough. It didn't seem to me that they were manufacturing counterfeits in this facility, but I wasn't going to find out unless I had access to the product and I didn't see how I could get a sample. If I asked him for one I'd probably be out on my ear. I thanked him and explained that I was visiting a number of companies in the region and that I'd report back to my bosses at Orion. I wanted to get back to the car and check out some of the transport companies but I told him I'd think about coming back to see the Oxaban being manufactured. It might even give me an opportunity to get hold of a sample.

Ranish was nowhere to be seen when I got back, so I drove slowly out of the car park looking around to see where he'd got to.

He had my mobile phone number so I pulled off outside the estate and waited.

After a few minutes, he opened the car door and got in. 'There's another pharmaceutical manufacturer on the estate. It's in one of the older units and it's quite small. Perhaps we should have a look at that?'

'I don't think so, not without knowing more about them first. I think they'd be a bit suspicious if we went and knocked on their door unannounced. But it's the supply chain we need to follow up now, so I think we need to check the transport companies they use.'

'There's a place where we could wait. If you pull in around the corner behind that tree, you can see Bakaar's loading bays but you'll be concealed. As far as I can tell the bays this side are despatch, so we don't have to worry about deliveries.'

'Okay, but why don't you go over to the other company and track the despatches over there, while I do it here? We could get an idea of which transport companies collect from this estate.' I checked my mobile. 'There's a strong signal here so we can keep in touch, but I think we've got a long wait ahead of us.'

It was past midnight when we finally got back to the hotel. I was still suffering from jet lag and could barely keep awake and simply tumbled into my bed without even eating anything.

I struggled to wake up the following morning, still unable to reset my body's time clock. Ranish had taken away the lists we had made of transport companies and was researching them from his office – wherever that was. I decided that I'd do some investigation in Mumbai itself – I thought there was a good chance of counterfeit drugs being sold somewhere in such a big city, so I headed for Crawford Market, the largest in Mumbai and a brisk walk from my hotel.

By the time I got there, I'd passed half a dozen pharmacies of varying sizes, from ramshackle street-corner operations, to wide-fronted, gleaming shops, clearly aiming at the more upmarket of Mumbai's residents. I'd asked for Oxaban in each of them and found that half offered me a generic equivalent. At the market itself, I realised that language was going to be a problem, so I backtracked to the last pharmacy which had stocked it and asked them to write down the word for Oxaban in both Hindi and Marathi. Perhaps I should have waited until Ranish was with me.

Crawford Market is huge and sells everything from bananas to parrots. As with all Indian markets, the stalls are competitively arranged to attract attention from their neighbours by using the most brilliant of colours. The place was thronged with people, mainly locals, but quite a few tourists were obstructing the flow by taking photographs on their mobile phones. The noise was deafening, echoing around the halls, while on display was a bewildering range of products unfamiliar to westerners including many stalls offering patent medicines. These were clearly selling only to locals and I couldn't identify much of what they were selling but at each I showed them the translation I'd been given. Most of them looked at me blankly, but a few nodded and brought out the medicines from under the counter. My main concern was how I would ever find them again, so I made a note of the stall numbers – when I could find them – and noted the locations with the GPS on my phone.

I could have spent the entire day there; the range of goods on offer was extraordinary and the sights, but above all the smells, were so peculiarly Indian and made even more exotic because I had little idea what many of the items on display were. Snake skins, desiccated lizards, poached ivory trinkets and mysterious-looking plants crowded on rickety wooden tables. The stallholders were friendly and laughed at my inability to speak their language. Many managed some English and helped me find more of the medicine sellers than I would be able to locate on my own. Even so, to judge by much of what they told me, Western medicine appeared to offer inferior cures to those of tradition.

Back in my hotel, I spread my haul across the table and brought out the Truscan, making a careful list of what I'd bought and where. I analysed each one with disappointing results – all passed the tests, which I thought was unusual. There was one more pharmacy near the hotel that had been shut when I went past, so I thought I had nothing to lose by going back.

This was a shop for Mumbai's masses. It had a tiny glass frontage that was so dirty I could barely see through it and the entrance was in an alleyway down the side which had been shut when I first went past it. This time it was open and I went through into the shop which had boxes lying everywhere.

The man behind the counter must have been approaching seventy, and had a wizened face with skin like parchment. I asked if he spoke English, but he simply smiled and shook his head. I handed over my paper with Oxaban written on it, and he looked at it thoughtfully for a moment as if trying to remember where he'd put it.

Eventually, his face brightened and he turned and went deep into the further recesses of the shop, finally emerging with a very dusty pack of Oxaban which he placed on the counter with a flourish.

I thanked him as best I could and took it back to my room and tested it with the Truscan. Finally, a result! It showed less than twenty-five percent of the proper active ingredients – the same as the sample from Greg Satchwell's flat. The correlation was so close it could even be from the same batch.

I realised that there was no point in going back to the shop without Ranish to translate so I pulled out my phone and called him. It took him a while to answer but when he finally did so he said he'd made little progress. I told him about my discovery and he said he'd be back with me within the hour.

When he got back to the hotel, I briefed him on my progress and took him back to the grubby shop near the hotel. 'What we don't know,' I told him on the way, 'is whether the reduction in active ingredient in the Oxaban is because it's past its sell-by date, or whether it's been deliberately manufactured that way to save costs.' I paused to think about it. 'Perhaps it doesn't make any difference. It was passed off as something it wasn't and far from helping patients, it would probably cause them harm. Anyway, if we're able to track down the distributor we might find out which it was.'

We stopped outside the shop. 'Tell him that I'm researching for a UK company and ask for the names of his suppliers. He's got no reason to hide it.'

We went in and it soon became clear that the old man didn't want to co-operate. Even though I didn't understand exactly what was being said, I could tell from his attitude that he was very suspicious about our motives and wasn't giving much away.

'Try money,' I said finally.

A little can go a long way in India and Ranish brought out his wallet and put some notes down on the counter. The old man looked at them for a moment as if deciding whether it was enough. He then reached under the counter and pulled out a huge book which looked like a Dickensian ledger. He opened it and turned it around so Ranish could read it.

He flicked through the pages quickly. 'These are dating back years,' he said. 'What exactly am I supposed to be looking for?'

'Ask about the Oxaban,' I said. 'Can he show you who it came from?'

Ranish discussed this with the man who took the book back and turned through the pages until he stopped and passed it back to Ranish. 'Here it is,' he said, running his finger down the columns. 'I hate to say this, but it's supplied by Bakaar, from here in Mumbai.'

I took a moment to consider this. 'It can't be,' I said finally. 'Bakaar took us around their factory yesterday. They wouldn't have done that if they were making counterfeits. We saw their quality control systems and they couldn't have faked a set-up like that; there's got to be another explanation. Assuming the drugs were at full strength when they left Bakaar, by the time they got here, to this shop, the active ingredients had somehow dropped by three quarters.' I looked again at the old man who couldn't have had anything to do with this. 'Ask him who delivers it,' I said.

I waited until Ranish had translated the question and I heard the answer but instead of translating, Ranish went silent.

'What is it?' I asked. 'Did he say the company's called Comar?'

Ranish finally turned to me. 'Yes. Comar Transport. That's one of the companies I saw yesterday at Bakaar's. It's one of the transport firms they use.'

'If they're being supplied by Bakaar then wouldn't they make the delivery?'

'Not necessarily,' Ranish said. 'I looked at Comar's website back in the office, and it seems that their speciality is international forwarding. It doesn't make sense that they should be making local deliveries – least of all here in Mumbai's market which is usually supplied by rickshaw.'

'Bashara told me they have a separate division. A separate contract with Bakaar for Mumbai customers. They said it was only a small part of their sales so it wasn't very significant.'

'Perhaps, but it wasn't mentioned on the Comar website. I wonder why they're keeping quiet about it.'

'If they do have a local service then they could introduce other people's drugs into the supply chain and pass them off as Bakaar's. Comar looks promising.'

Chapter Fourteen

I was getting increasingly anxious about the impending East African vaccination programme so back at the hotel, I phoned Ken Maxwell at MI6. We agreed that the UK office of the FDA were probably in a better position to monitor it than Sally, and he told me that an announcement would be made in the next week about the successful bidder, which didn't leave much time for us to locate the source of the counterfeits. It was frustrating to feel so close to the likely source, but unable to discover where they were being made.

Ranish was waiting for me downstairs, and we went into the bar and ordered a couple of Kingfisher beers. I told him that the vaccination programme was about to start any time and that we were up against it.

'It would explain where they're coming from,' I said when we'd sat down. 'They infiltrate the genuine supply chain with counterfeits. That could be how the fake Oxaban arrived at Holden Healthcare – it slipped through. Perhaps there was a mix-up in the Bakaar facility in Mombasa.'

'But that would mean that Bakaar is a part of this and I don't see that. If they wanted to counterfeit drugs they could do it easily and they certainly wouldn't show people around their facilities if they were.'

'Not necessarily.' I picked up my bottle and poured some beer into my glass. 'Whatever's going on, it seems likely that Comar's involved somewhere along the line.' I drank some of the beer before continuing. 'We've identified the fake drugs in a pharmacy supplied by them and they're the common denominator between that and Bakaar Pharmaceuticals. It could make the perfect cover. Have you ever heard of them?'

'Comar? Only what I found out on the web. Their warehousing facility is in Bhiwandi, between Bakaar's facility and central Mumbai. There are lots of companies opening up distribution centres there including pharmaceutical distributors.'

'I suppose the best place to hide a distribution centre is in the middle of other distribution centres. But we can't turn up and knock on their door; we don't even know what we're looking for yet.'

'This might help when we find it.' Ranish brought out a device from his pocket and put it on the table in front of me. 'It's a GPS satellite tracker. We can track anything anywhere around the world with this.'

I picked it up. It was about the size of a matchbox, but finished in a matt black. 'So that's what you people get up to – and you've invented one that actually works? But it won't be able to transmit a position inside a shipping container, will it?'

'No, but we can pick up the signal as soon as it's unloaded. It's magnetic as well.' Ranish took it from me and held it close to his steel watch strap. It jumped out of his hand and stuck firmly to his wrist. 'All we have to do now,' he said, pulling it off with some difficulty, 'is find the shipment we need to track.'

'Ahmed Bashara told me they're running a consignment of Oxaban to East Africa the day after tomorrow. Perhaps if we looked into Comar's operation we might find a way of smuggling that into the shipment.'

Ranish frowned. 'I don't see how.'

'Don't be so negative. Let's go back to Bhiwandi this afternoon when the drivers clock off. See if one of them can help us.'

Yet again, we headed north from Mumbai to the developing businesses in Bhiwandi.

Comar Logistics, to give it its proper name, was a ramshackle affair compared with the gleaming new industrial units which surrounded it. It had obviously been there for some years but didn't seem to be sharing the economic boom enjoyed by its neighbours which included a new centre for Jaguar Land Rover and a massive 560,000 square-foot DHL facility. There were about a dozen trucks lined up alongside the rows of loading bays.

'I don't see how we're going to get inside,' I said. 'My cover as a pharmaceutical wholesaler isn't going to carry much weight with a transport company.'

'I don't know about that. You could say that Bakaar's general manager, Ahmed Bashara, suggested you visit them on your way back from seeing them. There's no secret that they work together.'

'We don't know whether they're delivering or collecting. They might be employed by someone else who has nothing to do with Bakaar.'

'I told you, their trucks were in the despatch bays. They were collecting, not delivering.'

'It'll look a bit suspicious. Just walking in off the streets?'

'You're English. Indians aren't often surprised by what the English do. We think most of you are eccentric. We often wonder how you ever managed to get an empire.'

'It might explain why we lost it. No, that's not going to work. If they're involved they'd be immediately suspicious about a westerner turning up on their doorstep and asking about Bakaar.' Even though Ranish was probably right and that many people in Asia thought that most Europeans – particularly the British – were a spanner short of a toolkit, it would be too risky. 'Let's wait and see,' I went on. 'See if we can talk to one of their drivers. I'll move the car out of sight.'

I found a place where we could watch Comar's entrance and the trucks arriving and departing.

After about an hour, we watched as a truck pulled in and reversed into one of the loading bays. The driver got out and went inside and about fifteen minutes later we saw him come out of the front entrance; he'd changed out of his uniform and appeared to be heading home. 'You go and speak to him,' I told Ranish. 'I'll follow behind. Tell him you've got a proposition for him. Do you think more bribery will work?'

'Sure, why not?' Ranish got out of the car. 'Have you any idea how little these drivers earn?'

I watched Ranish come up behind the driver and walk in step with him. I stayed where I was until they turned around a corner and went out of sight. Cautiously, I followed and again waited as they headed towards the centre of Bhiwandi.

Eventually, I saw Ranish stop and turn back towards me. I leant over and opened the door for him as he slipped into his seat. 'Well? How did it go?'

'He said he didn't want to talk to me on the street. He told me to come by his house later. He gave me the address.'

We decided to kill time by taking a further look around the estate which was still being developed as a centre of distribution for the Mumbai area.

After about an hour, we thought we'd left it long enough and Ranish got out his mobile phone map and directed me to the address the driver had given him. We headed into the centre of Bhiwandi and the streets got narrower, and there were more and more people milling around on the pavements. Some of the women were carrying tall baskets on their heads showing amazing balance while others were holding umbrellas to shade them from the evening sun. The air was smoky with the exhaust of the motorcycles thronging the street and the road was becoming too congested for me to drive much further.

'Stop here.' Ranish looked up from his phone. 'He told me he lived above that mobile phone shop. Park over there and we can go up together.'

'No. You'll have to go in there alone. It would excite too much attention if he saw a westerner was involved. We've got to keep this as low-key as we can.'

'What do you want me to ask him? How much should we offer?'

'I'll leave that up to you. You know the value of money here better than I do. Ask him specifically about consignments picked up from Bakaar. Find out whether the trucks pick up from anywhere either before or afterwards. I'll wait here.'

In the event, I went for a short walk and examined the extraordinary range of shops that lined the dusty street and found it almost as colourful as the Crawford Street market. I looked across and saw Ranish come out. He looked both ways and then headed for the car. I caught up with him and unlocked the door and we got in. 'So?' I asked.

'He told me he doesn't do the Bakaar collections. Their speciality is international groupage. They collect from their customers and consolidate the consignments into containers which they take to the docks.'

'What about the Oxaban delivery to our friend back in Mumbai? Did you ask him about that?'

'He simply repeated that all their work was international. He didn't know anything about Comar making local deliveries. I asked about East Africa and he said that there's a regular driver who makes the daily collections from Bakaar.'

'Does he pick up from anywhere else at the same time?'

'He didn't know, but he said that when all the collections are brought back to the warehouse, they're broken down by destination and held over until the consignment is complete and then they're taken to the docks the next day.'

'So Bakaar's next pick-up for Africa is tomorrow. Does he know what time the driver leaves?'

'It seems the first shift starts at six in the morning.'

'That must mean that Comar operates a night shift.'

'Must do. They'd have to if they're to get the containers packed for despatch in the morning.'

'So you have an early start. How are you going to know which truck you should follow?'

'He told me he would phone me and give me the registration number.'

'Oh, the power of money. Is there nothing it won't buy?'

'You can afford to be cynical,' Ranish said with a note of bitterness. 'You don't have to live off Indian wages.'

Ouch! I thought. 'Sorry but I don't imagine you do too badly yourself, working for SIS.'

'It's not something I advertise,' Ranish said. 'My wife thinks I'm an accountant.'

'And I'm sure with your training you'd be very good at cooking the books.' I looked at my watch. 'With reasonable traffic we'll be back at the hotel not too late. I'll drop you off on the way back but I'll stay here tomorrow and wait for you to call in.'

'You're not coming with me?'

'No, I'd be too noticeable. You follow the truck and let me know what happens.'

The next day dragged by. It was frustrating not to be involved, knowing that somewhere nearby there could be a factory sending out potentially lethal medicines. To kill time, I put in a call to Ali to see if he'd heard anything from Sayed. He was about to go into a meeting and couldn't really talk, but as far as I could make out Sayed still thought that something was being planned, but didn't yet know what. He told me he'd reported the contact to MI5 who were prepared for me to continue to liaise with him – for the moment at least.

I finally met up with Ranish in the hotel bar later that afternoon, and the bartender brought out two Kingfishers without being asked. Perhaps it was because of the tip I'd left him the previous evening.

Ranish explained that the driver had been as good as his word and had phoned him with the details of which truck to follow and although Ranish reported that it had made three stops before Bakaar and several afterwards, he said that none of them was anything to do with pharmaceuticals – one was a car parts supplier, another an electronics manufacturer and all of them were well known in India.

'So we've got nowhere?' I asked.

'Looks like it. If Comar *are* introducing fake pharmaceuticals into Bakaar's supply lines, then it has to be by another route. They may not be the smartest outfit around, but they're used by some pretty impressive names.'

We drank our beers and considered the situation. It was frustrating that every time I thought we'd got a solid lead, it seemed to melt away.

'Time to use that gizmo of yours,' I said. 'We've established that Bakaar is not the source of the fakes, we've checked out their transport company and can't find anything wrong with them either.'

'We haven't ruled out Comar. Although if they are involved I can't see how they're doing it.'

'We've got to look further along the supply chain but I'm afraid we're running out of time.'

'So what do we do next?' Ranish asked.

'We'll go back to your driver. Wave some more money at him. Tell him they're running some Oxaban tomorrow and see if he can somehow attach your device to the consignment and we follow it from there.'

Ranish shook his head. 'It's one thing asking him about delivery runs, but asking him to interfere with the consignment is something else. He's likely to refuse.'

'Have you got any better ideas?'

'You could do it yourself. Bashara said you could go back to watch the Oxaban manufacture.'

'No. Let's try the driver first.' I checked my watch. 'If we leave now we should get there before it's too late. Let's go and see what he says.'

'Okay, but I think I know what that'll be. It wasn't easy persuading him to give me the information in the first place.'

We finished our beers and Ranish took over the driving and we made it to Bhiwandi in record time.

I waited again in the car outside the mobile phone shop but this time I didn't have to wait so long before Ranish emerged looking grim. 'I managed to persuade him eventually, but he's not happy with it. He said it was one thing telling him about deliveries, but interfering with them could get him sacked without a reference.'

'You told him what to look out for?'

'I think when I landed this job they must have thought I had some brains.'

'Sorry, but it's our only lead. If he screws it up we've got nothing left.'

'Despite his reluctance, he seemed like his head's screwed on. I think he'll manage it okay.' Ranish put the car in gear and drove off. 'All this effort and we end up reliant on one man.'

I looked at my watch for the hundredth time. Ranish had left me in the hotel while he went back to the driver's house to get his report. I'd spent the day researching vaccination programmes around the world. I was interested in what they were doing in Afghanistan where it seemed that the various UN agencies were also planning wide-ranging programmes – there had been so many years where the country had been effectively closed to them that they were making strenuous efforts to catch up. But it seemed there was still a long way to go, particularly in rural areas where it was hard to reach them.

I thought back to Sayed's brother and the unnecessary suffering caused by what were essentially easily preventable diseases. The historical incidence of measles alone was quite horrific but it was clear that considerable progress could be made. But there simply weren't the resources to be able to monitor standards throughout the country and terrorist groups were not interested in increasing the life expectancy. They were only interested in reducing it.

I signalled for another Kingfisher but then thought better of it and decided I'd take a walk outside the hotel.

The opportunity to stretch my legs relaxed me a bit and I almost missed Ranish who was locking his car around the corner.

I caught up with him as he entered the hotel, but he hadn't seen me so I called out to him. He turned and I could see immediately that he was not bringing good news. 'Ranish, what's the matter?'

'Let's go upstairs.' He walked to the lifts without waiting for a reply.

I followed him and after I'd shut the door to my room, I asked him again what had happened.

'I went back to the driver's house.' Ranish sat on the bed and put his head in his hands.

I got a glass of water from the sink and gave it to him. 'What happened?'

Ranish looked up. 'He hadn't got back and his wife told me he shouldn't be long, so I waited with her. We made small talk for a while and then there was a screeching of tyres outside. We rushed out to see him being thrown from the back of a truck.'

'Jesus! What happened to him?'

'He'd been beaten up badly so we got an ambulance. I think he'll survive but it was touch and go.' He managed to drink some of the water. 'I told you it was too risky. We nearly got him killed.'

'We did? How?'

'He had a sign around his neck saying, "YOU NEXT".'

'In English?'

'Yes. And since neither the driver nor his family spoke any English, I can only think it was aimed at us.'

'The poor man. I should have done it myself but it never occurred to me that it would be dangerous. I should have realised who we're up against. What about his family?'

'Distraught, as you'd expect. I don't think they quite understand my involvement. They certainly don't understand why he was attacked.'

'Just as well. You'll have to think of a story to cover this. We can't afford to let this get public. Somehow you're going to have to speak to the police.'

'I'm already on it. I'm going there in the morning.'

'Why would anyone do this? He was only a driver. Why attack him to get at us?'

'And possibly destroy a family in the process. He's going to find it difficult to get another job – assuming he pulls through. We'll have to ask London if they can do something for them. We might have to if we want it kept quiet.'

'So that leaves the crucial question; did he manage to plant the tracker?'

Chapter Fifteen

'We'll have to wait and see,' I said. I was back in London being debriefed by Ken Maxwell who'd also received Ranish's encrypted report. 'Even if he did manage to get the tracker into one of the boxes, if they've been loaded into a container then we won't get a signal until they're unloaded again – presumably in Mombasa?'

'We managed to track it to the vicinity of the Bakaar factory.' Ken Maxwell was staring at his laptop which showed the western half of the Indian Ocean with not very much on it. 'So we know it was working, but when the signal stopped we don't know if that's because it was put into a container, or whether they took it off the driver and smashed it.'

'Are you able to do anything about the driver's family?'

'We're looking into that, but I think probably. According to Ranish, he was effectively working for us at the time so we're responsible.'

'It's certainly raised the stakes and now we're running out of time. We have to do something.' I went over and picked up the computer. 'Full of tricks, I suppose?'

'Plenty,' Ken said, taking it back from me. 'There's nothing more easily infiltrated than laptops, especially when they're connected to the Internet and particularly when it's an open one like yours. But we use it with a satellite phone which links it to a secure network.'

'But it's safe to use anywhere? Encryption courtesy GCHQ?'

'They're the experts. I access their main computer and even an international hacker can't see what I can see. Which,' he added, 'at the moment is not very much.'

'Nearly 3,000 miles from Mumbai to Mombasa, say eighteen knots for a routine freighter. About a week. It'll be days before we know.' I poured myself another coffee then waved the pot at Ken but he shook his head. 'So that's about it.'

I sat down and sipped my drink. 'Unless we manage to get a signal from the tracker we seem to have hit another dead end. As far as we can tell, Bakaar is clean, so where do we look now? I still think Comar's got something to do with it.' I banged the desk in frustration. 'Jesus! Can't we raid these places? We can't sit here and do nothing, we haven't much time left.'

'If we carry out raids and don't find anything then we'll face claims for damages and even if we do, they'll just change the supply route and use another method of delivery. Our best lead is still to wait for the tracker. If we haven't picked up a signal in a few days we'll have to start again and think of another way of tracing the counterfeits.'

Ken snapped his laptop closed and stood up. 'I suppose we can let you get back to your skipper's duties now. There's nothing much more you can do.'

'Hey, not so fast. I can't let it go – I need to follow this through. I can still use the Orion cover story and go back and make some more enquiries in East Africa.'

'For all we know your Orion cover was blown. If they picked up the driver then they must know about Ranish and so it's likely they also know about you.'

'Perhaps, but there's no reason the driver should have known about me. He only ever met Ranish.'

'Given what happened to him it would be pretty dangerous to chance it. You could have been rumbled so if we're going to try again we'd have to use another agent.'

'But I know more about the pharmaceutical supply chain than any of your agents. They won't necessarily know what to look for.' I wasn't going to let him pass this onto someone else after all I'd done. 'I can't leave it. I have to see it through, whether it's with your help or without it.'

'I suppose I could ask, but I don't think that would work. I'll see what they say back at Vauxhall Cross.'

I felt a great sense of anti-climax after I'd shown Ken off the boat and watched him walk away along the pontoon. I'd forgotten how keyed up I became when out in the field. My few days in India had brought back all my training and I realised how much I was missing the action. But there was nothing more I could do, so I tried to resign myself to going back to work on the boat, but at least I'd get to see Greta who was taking me out for dinner that evening. I was looking forward to seeing her again although I wasn't sure quite how much I could tell her about my trip. It would at least take my mind off it and I realised that I was starting to think of her more often.

In the morning, I tried to concentrate on the work schedule on the boat, but my mind wasn't on it. Until we knew whether the tracker had been placed we had no leads to follow up. It seemed that the opposition – whoever they were – had covered their tracks too well.

As I climbed reluctantly into my work clothes, the phone rang. It was Ken but frustratingly he wouldn't tell me why he needed to see me so urgently, but I realised that it must have been important if I was finally being allowed into their inner sanctum at Vauxhall Cross. Most intriguing of all was his curt explanation: 'We've picked up a signal. Zanzibar. I'll tell you more when you get here.'

Ken came down to meet me at reception. 'It seems the driver was able to plant it after all,' he told me as he took me through security and up to a meeting room overlooking the Thames. 'They appear to have offloaded in Zanzibar Island – not on the mainland at Mombasa. They must have sent it airfreight, not by ship.'

I knew Ed Carpenter from the MHRA but not the man or the woman who sat opposite him. 'Sue is from our East African desk,' he explained, 'and Brent Hillman, here, is from the FDA.

The US Food and Drugs Administration Agency,' he added by way of introduction although it would be difficult to mistake Brent for anything other than an American. He was a big, jowly man, with short, gingery hair and a permanent sun tan.

'They keep a watching brief over counterfeit pharmaceuticals,' Ken Maxwell continued, 'especially in Africa, so we thought they'd be interested in this.' He sat down next to them and turned to me. 'As I told you, we've picked up the signal in Zanzibar. Somehow the consignment has been offloaded although the plane manifest said it was for Mombasa. This might be a breakthrough – smuggling is one of Zanzibar's major industries but we've always thought it was narcotics. Now it seems they might've added counterfeiting to their repertoire.'

'So it seems you might be able to help us after all,' Ken continued. 'Our East African agents are still monitoring the Tau facility and the docks in Mombasa, but Brent here thinks your cover could still be useful. The FDA's been pretty active in the region and he thinks they've become too high profile. A newcomer might be able to draw attention away from them and could remain unobserved.'

I looked across to Brent.

'That's right, Phil,' he said in a rasping voice and I cringed at his familiarity. 'Looks like you've turned up something interesting.'

I nodded and turned back to Ken. 'So you want me to go to Zanzibar?'

'I'm afraid we do. Somewhat against my better judgement, however. What do you think, Brent?'

The FDA man sighed as though facing a prospect not of his choosing. 'They told us about your record, kid,' he said and I winced again. Why did he have to lay it on so thick? 'You're army taught, accustomed to working under cover. You can obviously look after yourself and you've had some training in the pharmaceutical business. I suppose it'd be a waste not to use you. But as they say back in the old country, if that's where you want to go, I wouldn't have started from here.'

'Thanks,' I said, although it wasn't the most ringing endorsement I'd ever heard. I turned back to Ken Maxwell. 'Perhaps you should offer me a job?'

'It wouldn't be the first time that someone had transferred.'

Interesting, I thought. 'Do you have anyone else in Zanzibar?'

'Not yet but we're having someone fly across. Dickson Kogo; I'm told he's highly competent.'

'So the plane made an unscheduled stop on its way to Mombasa? How did they manage that?'

'We were hoping you could find that out.' Ken picked up a remote control. 'You'll see,' he said as the blinds closed and a screen came down from the ceiling. 'This is the track we've recorded from Mumbai.' Ken brought up a satellite photo of the western Indian Ocean. 'You can see the signal disappearing as it went into the container in Mumbai and then it appears again here.' He pressed some buttons on his remote control and the picture zoomed into Zanzibar Island.

'There's the container port,' he said pointing towards the centre. 'It's next to the capital, Stone Town, but you can see that the track doesn't start again there. They must have used a ULD airfreight can – that's a lightweight container that fits inside the aircraft hull – and then unloaded the container at the airport – it's not possible to get access to an individual container while it's still on the plane. You can see the track starts again a few miles north and stops.'

He fiddled with some more buttons and the picture zoomed in even closer. 'It's an industrial area – you can see the oil storage tanks in the background – but they appear to have unloaded the container here in this building. He pointed to a long roof close to the beach. 'It seems to be a warehousing facility of some kind. There's an island over a mile opposite – Grave Island. We think that's privately owned.'

'Did the track go there directly,' I asked, 'or did it stop somewhere along the route?'

'No. While it was in the container we didn't get any signal. Only when it was unloaded.'

I looked around the table. 'So what do you want me to do?'

'The same as you did in Mumbai, but with a slight difference,' Ken replied. 'You've still got your cover from Orion. You go in there and say you've heard that you might be able to buy pharmaceuticals on the cheap and see if they bite.'

'Sounds dangerous. After what happened in Mumbai they could be expecting us.'

'I can't see we have any choice. We'll have to take the chance – this is the only lead we've got.'

'We know that Zanzibar is a centre for narcotics.' This was Brent, the FDA man. 'It's got a long history of lawlessness. Hundreds of years, in fact.'

'That's reassuring,' I said.

'But what we're really interested in,' Ken Maxwell took over, 'is to find out whether there's any connection with Islamic groups. They've been spreading down from Somalia through northern Kenya. Zanzibar is nominally part of Tanzania, but it acts as though it's entirely independent. Pemba, the island next door, is even worse – it's East Africa's equivalent of Spain's Costa del Sol. Heads of organised crime have estates out there, knowing that no one can touch them.'

'Sounds charming,' I said. 'If I don't come back are you going to finish off the barge?'

Ken ignored me. 'We've booked you on a flight to Nairobi in the morning, and then a connection onto Zanzibar. Dickson will meet you there. Oh, before you go, Sue will give you some lessons on the secure laptop you're taking with you.'

Sue stood up and I nodded a general goodbye to the table and followed her out along the corridor into an office, which was little more than a corridor leading to a small internal balcony. On the table were a laptop and a cable leading outside to what looked like an early brick-like mobile phone. 'It needs a clear view of the sky to get a signal. Links to the geo-stationary satellites, but operates at a much faster speed than an ordinary satphone. Also, it can only be hacked by another computer using our software, so look after it.'

She opened the laptop and booted it up and plugged the phone into the USB port. 'Email works in the normal way and we've programmed in contact details here at Vauxhall Cross. Video conferencing works like Skype.' Sue showed me which drop-down menus to choose from. 'And this is a new app that you'll probably need.' She clicked on an icon on the desktop and a map of the world appeared. 'It's a bit like Google Earth, but it's in real time. You zoom into the area you're interested in and you can see the picture's changing to a live satellite image.' She held out the mouse to me. 'Try it.'

I moved the cursor over Zanzibar Island and clicked on the zoom button. The picture jerked as the image lagged behind the cursor movement, but it grew bigger until finally I could see the same view that Ken had brought up on his screen. 'Grave Island, wasn't it?' I asked, moved the cursor across to the oil storage tanks opposite and then zoomed in further to see an aircraft container parked outside a long building. 'Amazing. Why didn't we use this before?'

'Because it's not possible to track individual containers on ships, let alone planes,' Sue said. 'Also, there's a slight drawback because it needs light so it doesn't work at night.' She took back the mouse. 'It does have a tracking function, however.' She zoomed out until a ship appeared on the screen and then clicked on it. 'It'll track that ship now. It's a bit like an optical radar.'

'So what happens at night?'

'It'll lose the target but can extrapolate the future position based on the speed and heading. It's really very simple.'

'If you happen to have a constellation of satellites handy.'

Following Sayed's phone call, I checked with Ali but he told me that he wouldn't be able to make it and told me to go ahead without him. For a change, I decided that I'd go up to North London to meet Sayed, instead of asking him down to Wapping. In a funny sort of way, I hoped that he wouldn't have anything of importance to tell me because I wasn't sure how I'd be able to handle it, but there was no point worrying about it until it happened.

The melting pot of that area of London had seen countless immigrant communities established, but not without a cost of social division. Walking through the streets, I could see graffiti tags indicating the presence of rival gangs. I'd forgotten exactly where the park was where I'd met Sayed and took out my phone to check, but as I turned the corner I realised this was a mistake.

Facing me was a group of youths. 'Nice phone, mister,' one of them said, approaching me with his hand outstretched. 'D'you want to hand it over?'

This was the last thing I needed. I took a step backwards and slipped the phone into my pocket. They didn't like that and spread out. I turned with my back against the garden wall which would at least provide some protection.

'Don't get involved,' I said. 'It's not worth it over a phone.' I realised how stupid it sounded, since common sense told me to hand it over, but I was damned if I would. If they wanted a fight, I'd give them one.

'It's an iPhone, right?' the boy said. 'Cost a lot?' He was clearly taunting me, but I said nothing and watched them carefully. The others seemed to be waiting for a sign from the leader, so I should take him out first. It was then that he brought out the knife.

I couldn't believe that he intended to knife me for an iPhone. I thought about trying to dial the police with the phone in my pocket, but that would leave me vulnerable with only one free hand. I realised that I should probably hand it over, but I felt the familiar drumming in my temple as the adrenaline coursed through my veins. The boy took a step towards me, which was his mistake, he was now in reach. But I had to make sure that the others didn't jump me.

'Thank God you're here!' I shouted, waving at an imaginary person behind them. Obvious, but it seemed to work. The others turned around to see who I was calling to, but the boy with the knife showed why he was the leader and only hesitated fractionally.

But it was enough. I feinted a punch with my left hand, hoping he would think I was a southpaw.

As he went to parry it, I twisted around and grabbed his wrist. He fought back, and he was strong. He still had the knife in his hand and was trying to kick me. I yanked his arm forward and got two hands on his wrist and flipped it backwards. He gasped, but turned into me, still hanging onto the knife.

I glanced up at his friends who were clearly intending to join in. I had to finish this in the next few seconds. I stamped on his foot with my heel, and chopped at the nerve centre at the side of his wrist which should have left him without feeling in his arm. He didn't seem to notice and his grip on the knife was to be as strong as ever. We pulled apart and he faced up to me. 'Get him boys,' he shouted and lunged forward. As he thrust forward I pulled his arm and twisted it around until I had my other arm around his neck. I dragged him backwards and in his effort to keep his balance he relaxed his grip on the knife which fell to the floor. I kicked again at the back of his legs and as he fell to the floor I reached down and picked up the knife. I kneeled over him and put the knife to his throat and looked up at the others. 'Stay where you are, or I'll kill him. To make sure they understood I grabbed his hair and pulled his head up so I had a better angle for the knife.

One of the boys started forward and I cut into his friend's neck where I knew it wouldn't be fatal. The boy stopped and I could see in his face that he wasn't prepared for such violence. All he knew was that everyone else had given up. The boy on the floor was still struggling but I tightened my grip around his neck and pulled him to his feet so we were both facing the rest of his gang. They were clearly undecided, but the blood trickling from his neck made them hesitate.

'You wanted a fight,' I said. 'So watch this.' I spun the boy around and landed two heavy punches to his gut. He gasped and fell forward and I hit him on the side of his face. I could barely see him as the red mist almost covered my eyes. I hit him again with a punch to the kidneys and could feel that all resistance had gone out of him but this still wasn't enough. I threw the knife over my shoulder into a garden behind me and hit him again on the side of his face. His head spun around with a sickened crack and I steadied him up for what should have been his final moment.

'Stop! Stop!' It took a moment before I was aware of someone shouting at me. I'd forgotten the other boys and through the red haze, I could see that they'd gone, but still someone was shouting at me and I became aware that I knew the voice from somewhere. 'Stop,' he said again. 'You'll kill him. He's finished, let him go.'

Slowly I looked around but at first my vision was blurred. Eventually I recognised Sayed standing next to me and shouting. I let go of the boy who fell to the floor. I shook my head to try to clear it and looked down at the apparently lifeless boy who'd attacked me.

Sayed kneeled down next to him and took his pulse. 'He's still alive,' he said, 'but I think we need an ambulance.' He brought out his phone and looked behind me and gave the name of the street. 'He might have internal injuries so we need to be careful,' he said, but there was still a lot of blood on the boy's neck. He took out a tissue and examined it more closely. 'No, it's only superficial. At least his pulse is steady,' he said holding the boy's wrist. 'I think he should be okay.' He turned and looked up at me. 'What the hell happened here?'

I looked down at my hands which were still shaking. I realised what would have happened if he hadn't turned up, but I didn't want to admit it. I hadn't started it. 'The boy got what was coming to him,' I said, but as I said it I realised that again I'd gone too far. Much too far. 'He tried to steal my phone,' but I realised that this wasn't enough reason for him to lie unconscious on the floor. 'He had a knife,' I added.

After the ambulance came and took the boy away, I followed Sayed back up the street and recognised the park up ahead. We walked together in silence and we crossed the road and sat on our usual bench.

'That's what they teach you in the army is it?'

I didn't reply. I'd shown weakness and didn't see how I could recover from it, but Sayed didn't seem to notice. 'He had a knife, you say?'

I nodded.

'You were lucky.'

I was slowly coming to my senses and realised that if he thought it was luck I wasn't going to tell him otherwise. I took a grip on myself and tried to change the subject and asked him how he'd been.

It clearly took him an effort to respond – he'd obviously been shaken at what he'd seen but then I was pretty shaken myself. 'Are you alright?' I asked.

It took him a while before he relaxed and finally told me about his recent trip back home to Afghanistan. It seemed that Ali had managed to get Sayed a seat on a plane after all, so that meant he was quite well disposed towards our service. 'Things have improved so much,' he said. 'They're still far from perfect, but at least people are now able to have some kind of normal life. They've even managed to rebuild the clinic and have restarted the vaccination programmes so people shouldn't have to suffer like my brother did.'

Perhaps we managed to do some good after all, I thought, as he carried on telling me about his visit – he was becoming quite animated – and I didn't try to interrupt – he'd get around to telling me what he'd wanted to tell me in his own time.

'Anyway,' he said finally. 'Thanks for arranging the seat on the plane. I couldn't have got there without it.'

'Don't thank me. It was Ali. He can't come, but I'll pass on your thanks.' I hesitated, I still didn't want Sayed to think I was pushing him. 'And your mother? How is she?'

'She's doing well, although things are never going to be the same for her. She was very happy that you'd managed to track me down and arrange the visit. It's created quite a lot of goodwill out there.'

'Are you still wanting to go back when your course is finished?'

'I think so. There's so much to do out there. The international agencies are getting better at organising their vaccination programmes and there's a huge amount of charitable money floating around to push them forward. It's a really exciting time to be involved.'

'There's a lot of fakes around as well. That's the sort of difference you can make, to ensure that the drugs you administer are real.'

Chapter Sixteen

It was late at night when I finally arrived at Unguja, Zanzibar's international airport. A reservation had been made for me at the Africa House Hotel which had once been the English Club. It had recently been restored to its former magnificence – a level of luxury that the British colonial masters had probably created to remind the locals who was in charge. But those days were long gone and Zanzibar's turbulent history continued without much effort spent in achieving a national consensus.

It lost its nominal independence when it joined Tanganyika to form a self-governing part of the Republic of Tanzania, but that only served to exacerbate tensions on the islands. Since then conflict between the factions had simmered close to the surface, occasionally threatening to break out into civil war. Coupled with its position out in the Indian Ocean off the East African coast, it was an ideal base for smuggling – particularly from India. The encroaching Somalian pirate activity further up the coast only made the atmosphere even more febrile.

I'd been told to wait at the hotel until the local man from Mombasa, Dickson Kogo, made contact so I went straight there, checked in and went up to my room. Following the warnings from my controllers, I took out a scanner and checked the room for bugs. I couldn't see why anyone was expecting me, but it was a routine precaution.

The next morning I woke early and decided to investigate the town. Zanzibar had been an important trading post for hundreds of years and the ancient carved doorways betrayed their Arab influence. The rising sun threw long, intricate shadows onto the narrow streets which were busy even at this time and the balconies nearly closed over me, forming an arch of intricate wooden trellis work.

Many of the men wore white *kofia* caps on their heads, often with startlingly white full-length robes and although a few of the women were almost completely covered by sombre black *chadors*, in contrast many others had the confidence to wear brightly coloured headscarves. The main trade had been in slaves – a business the Europeans took over with alacrity when they arrived. Some slaves were even taken overland to Africa's west coast before being shipped off to the Caribbean sugar estates, or the American cotton plantations of the Deep South. One of the old slave markets was now a moving monument to this trade and I stayed there awhile before heading back to the hotel.

I was finishing breakfast in my room when there was a light tapping at my door. 'Dickson,' I said. 'I was told to expect you. But they gave me a password just in case.'

Dickson laughed. 'Grave Island.' He walked past me onto the balcony. 'You can't quite see it from here, it's around the docks there, but you've got a great view over the ocean.' He sat on one of the metal chairs. 'The islands over there are kept as nature reserves. It's one of the few things the political parties can agree on.'

I glanced across at the low-lying islands surrounded by a skirt of white sand. I hadn't come to admire the view but had to agree it was a pretty stunning place. I turned back to Dickson. 'Have you been able to locate the warehouse?'

'It's a company called Ansaar Enterprises,' Dickson replied. 'A few miles north of here, set back from the main road.'

'Muslim owned?'

'Everyone in Zanzibar is Muslim.'

'Have you seen anything? Any indication of what they're doing?'

'I've been watching. They've got the container on a trailer outside. That must have been delivered from the airport and they've been unloading it into the warehouse, but from the road you can't see what's going on at the back.'

'You haven't seen anything going in or out?'

'I can see the masts of the boats, but unless we can watch from the sea, we can't tell what's happening.'

I went over to my bag and pulled out the satellite printout and put it down on the table. 'We know that the most recent consignment has been delivered and unloaded here because of the tracker, but we needed to get in there somehow and find out what else they've got stored. This could be a major distribution centre.'

'If it is then it would be dangerous for you to go anywhere near it. Especially after what happened in Mombasa. I heard someone nearly got killed there, so it makes sense to go carefully.'

'Yes, but we've got no choice. We have to get in there. My guess is that the switch is being orchestrated by the transport company, so if I say they sent me then that should get me in.' Dickson said something I didn't quite catch. 'What was that? Did you say, "straws in the wind"?' Dickson shrugged. 'Oh. Never mind,' I said. 'Let's get on with it. Wait for me downstairs. I'll make everything secure here and then you can show me the layout.'

We headed out of town and, as Dickson had said, it was only a few miles before he turned off down a dusty, unmade track and parked. I followed as he got out and pushed his way into the bushes. He stopped at a small clearing. 'It's over there,' he said, pointing towards the coast.

I crouched and peered through the branches. Above the foreshore was a long, low ramshackle building with a corrugated iron roof. In front of it, the container they'd unloaded at the airport was still on its trailer with its door folded back, although the tractor that had brought it had left. The door into the warehouse was half open but I couldn't see inside because of shadows. But there were boxes on the ground and it was clear they were unloading. Despite the dilapidated condition of the building, I could see that the doors and windows were barred and secure. Floodlights and infrared cameras were positioned around the compound, looking incongruous against the apparent neglect of the building they were monitoring.

As I watched, someone came out pulling a pallet of boxes which he set down and proceeded to load into the container. 'See that?' I said. 'They're loading *and* unloading. They must be rearranging the consignment to be taken onto Mombasa.'

'You think the container's going to be sent to Kenya?'

'Where else would it go? It's supposed to be a direct shipment – from the Bakaar factory in Mumbai, to the Tau distribution centre outside Mombasa. But it looks as though they're rearranging the contents en route.'

'But what about the tracker?' Dickson asked. 'Isn't that still sending a signal from inside the warehouse?'

'The Oxaban consignment? Yes, so we know it's been unloaded. But we still don't know whether it's full strength or a counterfeit. It looks as though they're breaking up the contents and sorting through them before sending them on.'

'The container's still outside so I guess they're intending to put back what they don't want and send it onto Mombasa as shown on the manifest.'

'There've got to be fakes in that container, otherwise what's the point of taking it off the plane here in Zanzibar? Somehow the fakes must be mixed up with the real pharmaceuticals.' I thought about this. 'It's got to be Comar. Otherwise I don't see how they're doing it.'

'The fakes are sent in the same consignment and then the fakes are removed here in Zanzibar and the real ones put back.'

'So what do they do with the fakes? We know that the container's heading for Bakaar's distributor in Mombasa, so we need to find out where they're sending the stuff they've taken off.'

Dickson suddenly grabbed my arm. 'Wait. There, look.' He pointed out to sea where a boat was approaching the beach, but all I could see was the sail being dropped. 'I bet they're loading up from the other side. It makes sense. It's a perfect place to break up shipments and distribute them along the coast.'

'But in a sailing boat?'

'A dhow,' he corrected me. 'With the steady winds they have around here, it's as fast as a motorboat. You'd be amazed at the way the skippers handle them – almost everything along this coast is carried by dhow.'

It was a frustrating wait but nearly an hour later, we saw the top of the mast move and head off away from us to the north. 'The island over there,' I said, 'is that Grave Island? It must have a perfect view of the front of this place. I was told it was private – do you know who owns it?'

'It's owned by an Italian – a woman. Apparently she's quite some force around here. But she's built a small resort with huts along the beach on the other side, so we could go there if we booked one of the huts.'

'Why Grave Island?'

'The locals know it as Chapwani Island but to the Wabenzies they call it after the war grave site on the island. Twenty-eight British people drowned when their ship was sunk by a German light cruiser in the First World War, and they're buried on Chapwani.'

'Wabenzies?' I repeated.

'Yes, you know, Europeans who drive Mercedes Benzes.'

I shrugged. That went a bit past me. 'How do we get there?' I asked, getting back to the subject in hand.

'By dhow from Stone Town. Apparently the island's being run partly as an eco-resort so we could say we wanted to stay to observe the wildlife. It would give us a good cover story if we go in with binoculars.'

'Okay. We're not going to find out what's going on by standing around here. Let's go back and find ourselves a dhow.'

We headed back to the car.

'I think we'll have to book ourselves in for the night,' Dickson said. 'We could say we want to look at the graves, but they won't be happy if we wander around and then leave without spending any money.'

'I don't mind. Give them a call and make a reservation. We might even treat ourselves to a decent meal.'

We went back to the Africa House and I threw a few things into an overnight bag and we headed for the sea. Stone Town's foreshore doubles as its high street – without worrying about docks or jetties, all the boats simply sail right up the beach to unload their cargo. The car ferries lower their ramps onto the sand and the cars and trucks drive off into the maze of streets that border the sea while tourist touts wait on the beach, surrounding arriving visitors like a swarm of flies.

I'd left Dickson to negotiate with the numerous boatmen who were hanging around until he agreed a price with one and I met him on the beach. He'd left the car in one of the side streets and went back to get the equipment that would qualify us as dedicated observers of the local fauna. He threw the backpack into the dhow and the skipper pushed us off and hoisted a threadbare sail which had more patches than a chessboard. But Dickson was right, it had quite a turn of speed and the shallow draft meant that we were able to get quite close inshore to the island even at half-tide. After that, it was a case of sliding through the muddy coral towards the resort's reception area.

The receptionist checked us in and asked if we wanted to go straight to our rooms but I said that we'd go later.

'So, you're here to see the bats then?' she said.

'Bats?' I repeated dumbly.

'Yes. I assumed that's what you came to look at.'

'Of course,' I said, thoroughly confused. 'Amongst other things. But the bats in particular.' I looked across at Dickson but he clearly had no idea what she was talking about either. 'Is that what most people come to see?' I asked her.

'We've got quite a few different animals on the island,' she said. 'Some people come for the beaches on the south side but most come to see the wildlife.' She made some notes on the computer and then indicated a flower bed where a woman was on her knees weeding. 'That's Ariana. She owns this place.'

We went over and as we approached, the woman saw us and stood up. Even in her work-clothes, she was exceptionally elegant and wasn't in the least embarrassed by being found on her knees in a flowerbed and I suspected that it would take a lot to embarrass her. Dickson had told me that she was a qualified engineer who'd built some of the roads on the island before starting up this small resort. She regarded me with a sort of amused detachment which I found rather disconcerting, but she was all business when I explained warily that we wanted to keep watch over the warehouse opposite.

'Do you know anything about them?' I asked.

'Smugglers cave?' she said. 'There's a lot you have to understand about Zanzibar and that includes knowing when to stop asking questions. It's taken me years to be accepted here and they still think the idea of a woman engineer is almost impossible to believe, but then I can show them the roads I've built here and they can't really argue. But when it comes to one of the island's main industries – smuggling – it's best not to enquire too deeply.'

I thought I should change the subject. 'It's quite a place you have here.'

'We work hard at it. We run it as a sort of co-operative. All the staff have other duties – growing the vegetables, for example. Some of them even make the dresses we sell in the shop.'

'It seems to me to be pretty close to paradise here.'

'Perhaps, but my real daydream is to sail around the world.'

'What? And leave this place?' However much I enjoyed sailing, it didn't seem a good idea to me.

'This will be here when I get back. But it's only fantasy. Occasionally we get yachts passing through and I always make them welcome and ask about their adventures.' She sighed again and I recognised that despite the apparent paradise she had created, few people are ever fully content. 'I suppose that's the nearest I'm ever going to get to my dream.' She looked wistfully out to sea. 'But don't let me keep you, the bats are also at that end of the island.'

I still didn't understand about the bats but before I could ask, Dickson pulled at my sleeve and hefted the backpack onto his shoulder. I followed him out along the seashore towards the small beach we had seen at the tip of the island. 'Christ!' I said. 'Look at that.' I pointed towards an extraordinary animal that was moving along the shore. It must have been nearly a foot across and appeared untroubled by our presence.

'Coconut crab,' Dickson said prodding it with his boot. 'Extraordinary, aren't they? They climb the palm trees and snap off the coconuts, and then come down and open them up with their claws. Some of them can grow to more than six feet across.'

'As long as they don't decide to change their diet and come searching for me in the night. What other surprises does this island hold?'

I watched the huge crab wander off and then Dickson and I headed for the end of the island. Passing a stand of about half a dozen trees near the point, I was surprised at the strength of the wind that had the leaves dancing noisily. At the point, we had a clear view across the narrow passage to the Ansaar warehouse. 'Couldn't be better,' I said. 'A front-row seat.'

We set ourselves down on the edge of a small beach where some bushes allowed us some cover and Dickson took out a notebook and made a note of the time. I pulled out the laptop and satellite phone and set it up with some difficulty and then we settled down to wait.

'Looking across to Zanzibar over there, that's probably the real Grave Island,' I said. 'Their adulterated drugs kill people around the world, but that's where their graves are being dug.'

Dickson nodded, but continued to check the coast. 'Look,' he said suddenly. 'See the boat there?' I picked up my binoculars and we watched as a dhow headed towards the beach. 'It's definitely making for Ansaar,' he said as the crew dropped the sail and poled the dhow up the sand and jumped out. They were obviously expected because the loading door slid open and two men started carrying out boxes. I watched as they loaded the boat – the dhow was deceptively spacious and it was a substantial load they put in, taking well over an hour before the crew pushed the boat out into the water and jumped in. The lateen sail was hoisted and the boat headed out north towards Pemba and the mainland of Kenya.

'If only they carried registration numbers,' Dickson said ruefully.

'They'd probably be faked, like their cargo,' I replied, equally ruefully. I pulled the laptop towards me and opened it up. 'Anyway, I think British Intelligence can do better than that.' I plugged in the satellite phone and checked the signal on my laptop, loaded the tracking program and zoomed in towards Grave Island until I could identify the boat that had left and then set it on automatic tracking.

'Clever.' Dickson had been watching me. 'I've been issued with the same laptop, but it doesn't have that program.'

'Trouble is that it only works during the day. It'll estimate where it might have got to during the night, but it's useless unless it's out at sea on a steady course and speed.'

As the afternoon wore on there had only been one other boat – another collection, but this time the load was much smaller and the dhow headed south towards Dar es Salaam but it was the consignment towards Kenya that interested me. That was where the Bakaar distributor was.

As the sun dropped behind the trees casting a gloom over the water, I gradually became aware of a strange squeaking noise coming from the trees behind us. I turned, but although I could see movement, I couldn't make out what it was – was it my imagination, but were the trees moving? It seemed that they were alive and the squeaking was getting louder. I reached for the binoculars and adjusted them until the picture came into focus. The trees were indeed alive.

I tapped Dickson on the shoulder. 'Look at that.' I pointed at the trees. 'It's the bats.' As I said it, a single bat flew up and flapped around over us until it was joined by others and they headed across the water to the main island. Then dozens more followed them, then hundreds more. There were so many of them that the evening gloom almost turned to darkness while the sky over us was blanketed by a non-stop cloud of black bats.

'Fruit bats,' Dickson said – he was turning out to be quite a useful eco-guide. 'Going off for breakfast. They won't come back again until sunrise.'

It was a truly incredible sight. They had been sleeping on the boughs of the trees – and must have been almost ten deep because they kept coming – it didn't seem possible that so many of them could have been roosting on just a few trees. There were tens of thousands of them and it wasn't until nearly twenty minutes later that the last one fluttered away across the water.

'While they're looking for their breakfast,' I said to Dickson, 'let's go and get our dinner.'

'Quite a place, this Grave Island.' The terrace of our beach hut looked out across to the lights of Stone Town. 'Let's hope we don't get attacked by bats or coconut crabs.'

'Or the antelopes,' Dickson said. 'There're supposed to be antelopes here as well – dwarf antelopes.'

'That's all right then. I think I could handle dwarf antelopes, it's the thought of being suffocated by a swarm of 10,000 bats that troubles me. It's a magnificent view, though; I'd like to come back sometime. Spend some time here. It's very relaxing – if you don't have work to do.' I turned back to my computer and lifted the lid. I'd left the program running but the picture was now dark. I could see where the dhow had been tracked on its way north. It had sailed quite a distance off Pemba Island, and appeared to be heading either for Tanga or the Kenyan border beyond. I plugged the laptop into the resort's rather unreliable electrical supply and checked the signal on the satellite phone and closed the lid. Hopefully, we'd know more in the morning.

Chapter Seventeen

We took the island's boat back to Stone Town and in my hotel room I set up the satellite phone on the balcony. Now that daylight had arrived, I could check the dhow's position. The program couldn't track the boat at night, but before it got too dark it calculated the position as if it continued at the same speed and course. There were three boats in the general vicinity, but only one in almost exactly the right position. This had to be the one and it had made good progress during the night. It had passed Tanga and was clearly heading for somewhere near the Tanzania-Kenya border. We would have a better idea where in a few hours but we needed to find out more about Ansaar.

I turned back to Dickson. 'Somehow we've got to get inside their warehouse. In Mumbai, we tracked a transport company called Comar Logistics. We think the drugs being made by Bakaar Pharmaceuticals are full strength, so the fakes must be introduced into the supply line by Comar. I told you we set up this fake front complete with business cards and real addresses so I could use the same cover here.'

'As you say, they'll be very suspicious.'

'Yes, but I'm hoping the mention of Comar will get me in. If my theory is right then only someone who knows about the fakes would know about Comar.'

'Possibly, though it sounds risky. If you don't pull it off they might realise they've been rumbled and shut down the entire operation and move it somewhere else. We might be burning our boats.'

'Not necessarily. There's always the dhow we're tracking towards the mainland. That's still a strong lead.'

'It's your call,' Dickson said doubtfully.

I thought about that. 'Did you bring a gun?'

'I suppose that means you're not convinced either. The answer's no, not officially.'

'And unofficially?'

'Rarely without one,' Dickson said, with what I thought was a note of conceit but it was reassuring nonetheless.

'I told you, Comar is our trump card, so I'll have to play it.'

'You could fold your hand.'

'And then what? No, it's got to be worth the risk – not that there's much choice.'

'But if it doesn't work they might realise they've been rumbled.'

'I see you always look on the bright side,' I said. 'Have a little faith. I'll take the car and drop you off on the way so you can keep lookout.'

Perhaps I had my army training to blame for being so reckless, but my adrenaline level was rising and anyway, I couldn't see the alternative so I left Dickson keeping watch and drove back onto the main road and then turned into Ansaar's entrance. I turned the car to face out in case I needed a quick getaway and went up and knocked on their front door. It took a while before someone opened it. At first I could barely see, the sun was so bright and he was standing back in the shadow. 'Can I come in?' I asked. 'Do you speak English?'

'A little. What you want?'

'Can I come in and talk about it?'

I could see the man shrug and then stand aside and I stepped inside as he shut the door behind me plunging the room into darkness. I stumbled on the uneven mud floor and could make out another man sitting at a table by a window overlooking the beach. It seemed the perfect place for smuggling. I walked over to the table which had paperwork scattered across it. 'I was told you might be able to help me,' I said, but the man looked up at me without expression. He was quite short and could have done with losing a few pounds, but the most noticeable thing about him was his left hand – his middle fingers were missing above the knuckles. I hoped he hadn't noticed me staring at them and looked away.

'I represent some British interests. We're looking into new ways of distributing pharmaceuticals within Africa – if you understand what I mean. A different type of operation, one that can cut costs but still gives us a good profit.' Despite my heavy hints there was no reaction so it was time to play my trump card. 'I was out in Mumbai and met with Comar Logistics and they suggested that you might be able to help me.' Was it my imagination or did I see a flicker of recognition. 'Can you? Help me, that is?'

No-Fingers finally held out his arm and gestured towards the chair opposite him. 'Comar, you say?' he said in heavily accented English.

'Yes, outside Mumbai.'

'And how you think we can help you?'

'I was told you had access to… to… Let's call them cut-price drugs. Pharmaceuticals,' I corrected myself in case they thought I was talking about narcotics. 'We want to set up a distribution network across in West Africa.'

'And you thought that Ansaar could help?'

'Can you? We can pay in any currency. Any country.'

'What particular… drugs are you looking for?'

'The whole range. Anticoagulants, antimalarials and HIV treatments including antiretrovirals.'

'What sort of quantities?'

'How much can you supply?' I replied, sensing that he might be biting.

He said nothing and I grew increasingly uncomfortable under his gaze. 'Where are you staying?' he asked finally.

'At the Africa House. I arrived last night.' I didn't want to tell him that I'd spent the previous afternoon watching his warehouse.

'So you came straight here?'

'I told you, I came here to see you. To see if you could supply us.'

'It's possible, but you'd have to speak to my boss. He decide. Come back this afternoon. At three. Do you have a business card?'

I took one out, it was the cover that I'd cooked up with Orion, but I hesitated. 'That comes later,' I said as I put it back into my wallet. 'Let's see if we can work together first.'

I stopped to pick up Dickson on my way back to the hotel. 'I think they've bitten,' I told him. 'I'm going back this afternoon. They told me the boss would be there. We might be in.' I put the car in gear and headed back to Stone Town. 'In the meantime, let's find out where our boat has got to.'

Back at the hotel, I pulled out the laptop and took it out onto the balcony and set up the program and waited for it to boot up. The track was still heading a bit north of the Tanzanian-Kenyan borders. 'There's a little island here,' I said, zooming into the chart. 'Wasini Island? About forty-five miles south of Mombasa. Ever heard of it?'

'It rings a bell.' Dickson looked over my shoulder at the computer screen and frowned. 'Shimoni's the village opposite on the mainland, one of the various slave holding points along the East African coast. You can see the jetty used by the ferries, but they won't be unloading in full view of everyone in the village. They must have a place somewhere among the mangroves.'

'We're not going to be able to get there before it reaches the coast and starts unloading. We'll have to send someone down there from your office. It's only fifty miles – it shouldn't take them long.'

Dickson pulled out his mobile phone and pressed a speed dial button. It was answered quickly and he spoke in rapid Swahili of which the only words I recognised were Shimoni and Wasini. He came over to the laptop and zeroed the screen over the dhow which was now about twenty miles off the coast. He read off the co-ordinates and after a while he hung up. 'They're sending someone. They've got satellite surveillance in the office so they'll pick her up on their system and direct him when the boat looks as though it's unloading.'

'Okay. There's nothing much more we can do until this afternoon. Let's go and try out the restaurant.'

'You'd better keep watch from behind the trees,' I said to Dickson as I dropped him off by the muddy track that we'd used that morning. 'Wish me luck – I hope my cover holds.'

I drove on and pulled into Ansaar's entrance and parked again facing out, leaving the keys in the ignition in case Dickson needed to take it. The door opened before I could knock on it and the same man gestured me inside and told me to sit at the table. There was no one else in the room but I could hear talking on the other side of the wall. Presumably that's where they kept the stock.

After a few minutes, the door opened and a tall, dark-skinned man walked in with No-Fingers, the man I'd spoken to in the morning, following at what looked like a respectful distance. I stood up – there was no doubt that this was the boss, his bearing proclaimed a self-confident arrogance. If he'd been dressed in a dishdash and Arab headdress, he would have passed as a tribal chief, such was the way he carried himself. He was slim with deep crease lines in his face and a few days' growth of greying beard. His eyes were dark brown and drilled into me with an alarming intensity. 'My name is Ansaar, this is my business. Sit down.' He took his own place opposite me. 'I understand that you're interested in obtaining pharmaceuticals.' His English was excellent, with a slight American twang.

'*Might* be interested,' I said, not wanting to appear too keen. 'It would depend.'

'These things usually do,' he said without irony. 'What makes you think we can help you?'

'I told him this morning.' I gestured at No-Fingers who was still standing by the window. 'Comar Logistics in Mumbai told me they supply you here in East Africa.'

'But you want to distribute in West Africa?'

'I assumed you'd got the distribution in East Africa all tied up, and it's West Africa where we think we can have the biggest impact – particularly Nigeria.'

'It can be a dangerous place to do business, Nigeria.'

'I think we're up to it.' I brought out the business card I'd cooked up with Orion to be as uninformative as possible. "International Pharmaceuticals" didn't tell them much. I pushed the card over the table and he picked it up and studied it. 'I represent a consortium of businessmen,' I continued, 'British and overseas – we're looking for new opportunities. After Comar told me about your operation, they suggested I come here and see for myself.'

'They did, did they? And what exactly did they want you to see?'

He was clearly not going to make it easy for me. 'As I said this morning, we're interested in a wide range of pharmaceuticals, anything from anticoagulants to antiretrovirals.'

'And you think we can supply them?'

'As I told you, it was Comar's suggestion.'

'And you came alone?'

'No. I left my colleague back at the hotel.'

'This too can be a dangerous place to do business, especially for people who don't know how things work here.' He turned to his assistant. 'Search him,' he said tersely.

I looked across to No-Fingers who gestured for me to stand. I held my arms above my head as he patted me down and seemed almost disappointed that he'd found nothing – perhaps if I'd been armed it would have made my visit more plausible. He pushed me roughly back down onto my chair. I started to protest, but then thought better of it. That could come later. I looked across the table where Ansaar was looking at me steadily, as though trying to make up his mind. Finally, he stood up. 'Okay, this way.'

I stood up and followed him through the door into the warehouse, No-Fingers following close behind. By this time, my eyes had adapted to the darkness and I could see the rows of boxes stacked up to the ceiling. Some were loose but most were on pallets. 'Is this what you're after,' he said gesturing to the piles of boxes. I stopped and inspected one batch which appeared to be labelled in Swahili. Opposite, I could see the closed loading doors which had to be the ones opening onto the beach that we'd watched from Grave Island. I thought I recognised part of the consignment from Bakaar Pharmaceuticals stacked nearby. But I realised that they had stopped and were watching me. It was clear that no one was intending to show me any of their stock and with a dull feeling in my stomach I feared that my approach had failed.

We stopped at the other end of the warehouse, outside what looked like an internal office and he stood aside, gesturing me to enter and I walked in past him but immediately realised that it wasn't an office. The only furniture was a dusty table and two rickety chairs, otherwise it was bare, with no windows. There was a torn poster on the wall with what looked like Arabic script. This was starting to look dangerous.

I looked back and saw that No-Fingers was coming in and I realised that this wasn't going to be my day. I immediately tensed and moved my weight onto the balls of my feet ready for an attack. Ansaar followed No-Fingers into the room as though to watch the entertainment. I stepped back to give myself more space and looked around for any weapons within reach but there was nothing. But I could take them both and waited for them to get closer.

'That's enough.' I looked across and saw a gun aimed at me. However much I'd trained in unarmed combat, I hadn't yet found a way of beating a gun. I assumed it was loaded and held up my hands. 'Sit.' Ansaar was obviously someone of few words. I sat.

It was then that I saw Ansaar was holding a box tape dispenser and was pulling out the brown plastic tape ready to start wrapping, and it looked as though I was going to be the parcel. I stiffened, but hoped they wouldn't notice. Tape wasn't elastic, and if I held my arms away from me then I might be able to get some kind of advantage. No-Fingers took the tape and started wrapping it around me and looked as though he was enjoying it. Meanwhile Ansaar took the other chair and sat opposite me.

'You say it was Comar who told you to come here?'

'Yes. Comar.' At least they hadn't put any tape over my mouth. Not yet at any rate.

The man lit a cigarette and took his time about it, blowing the smoke towards me. 'Would it surprise you to learn that I've never heard of Comar?'

No-Fingers now had me trussed to his satisfaction but I held my arms tightly against the tape while I tried to figure out a response. It seemed that I had miscalculated badly. 'But you must have heard of them. They're the people who airfreighted you that container outside.'

'Ah,' he said, tapping the ash of his cigarette on the floor. 'A shipping company. I'm afraid I don't take notice of details like that.'

'So who *did* send it?' I wasn't going to let on that I knew it was Bakaar Pharmaceuticals.

'You don't seem to know very much. You come blundering in here with some story about representing mysterious backers. So who do you represent?'

'I told you…' A searing pain shot across my shoulder and I saw No-Fingers was holding a rubber cosh and was clearly looking forward to getting in some practice.

'I can see that this might take some time,' the man said, standing up. He looked across at No-Fingers. 'Leave it till later. We'll take him with us.' He turned back to me. 'We're going to get you out of here – in case you're not alone and there's someone else out there. Take you somewhere where no one will find you.'

From what I could tell, this came as a disappointment to No-Fingers who was clearly getting warmed up and he followed the man out, swinging his cosh as though practising for later. They closed the door behind them, but I hadn't heard them lock it – I'd already established that the place was quite secure, so they probably didn't think it necessary. I was finally able to relax my arms and saw the tape bend, giving me some movement in my arms and wrists.

If they were taking me somewhere else – and I didn't think they'd be leaving me here – then it would be impossible to track me. The word "track" suddenly hit me. If I could find the tracking unit from the boxes then it might give me a chance. There had to be some visible sign that it had been inserted *after* the boxes had been sealed. All I had to do was find it and I didn't have much time – they'd be coming back for me soon. They hadn't taped my legs, presumably to make it easier to move me when they left.

I stood up and went to the door but the tape binding my wrists made it impossible to reach the latch. I turned back and pulled the chair over and, by steadying myself against the wall I managed to stand on it and lift the latch.

I put my head around the door and looked cautiously out into the warehouse, but the place was empty. They must have gone back to the front office at the far end. I pushed the door closed behind me and ran over to the centre of the warehouse where I'd seen Bakaar's Oxaban stored. Whoever had unloaded them hadn't troubled to stack them properly – the piles were still on pallets and the top boxes were leaning over precariously. I looked around, there had to be some sort of knife here to cut open the boxes.

The pallet mover was close by the loading doors and I risked moving it and pushing it under the pallet of the pile of Oxaban boxes. I turned them a bit so I could see the labels, but still couldn't see if any had been tampered with. I moved to the first pile and managed to get my hands on one of the lower boxes and turn it around, but as I did so the top boxes toppled over and the entire stack scattered across the floor.

Instinctively I ran across to the other side of the entrance doors and crouched behind another row of stores. The office door was flung open and I saw No-Fingers through a gap in the rows. He came across and stood looking at the boxes over the floor. He looked across to the office at the far end and I congratulated myself on closing the door. He then made a start of stacking the boxes, but after a few moments I saw him shrug and then walk back to the office. I guessed from the look of the way much of their stock had been arranged that it was something that happened quite frequently.

When I heard the office door shut again, I came out and started going through the cases on the floor until I saw a Stanley knife sticking out underneath one of the other boxes. Crouching, I managed to pick it up, but it took several attempts before I was able to cut through the packing tape on my wrists.

Finally free, I was able to reach in and get my hands on the first batch. By this time, I was sweating heavily and my hands were getting slippery. I knelt down and got a finger under the corner of the box and turned it towards me. It toppled onto its side. I hoped that the side of the box I had opened was the right side. Using the Stanley knife, I managed to cut it open and take out a packet and stuff it into my pocket. If I hadn't found the tracker at least I had a sample to analyse.

I looked around frantically, aware that time was running out. I guessed that the fakes must already have been taken out so were probably near the loading doors leading out to the beach on the other side. I went over there and saw another pile of Oxaban boxes. These had to be the ones, although I still couldn't see any signs of the tracker. Clutching the knife, I cut away a piece of the wrapping tape and managed to get a hand in.

I froze at the sound of Ansaar's voice and turned to face him. He was holding up the tracker unit and a look of triumph spread across his face. 'Is this what you're looking for?'

It took me a moment to recover. 'No, it was this.' I held up the knife. I moved slowly towards him, balancing lightly on the balls of my feet, ready for any move. This time, the advantage was with me and I was going to take him down, but he stood his ground with the same triumphant look on his face. I suddenly realised I was too late and started to turn but No-Fingers was behind me. He finally got to use his cosh and I blacked out.

Chapter Eighteen

I regained consciousness slowly. I opened my eyes but everything was still black. I tried to run my hands over my eyes to make sure they were still functioning, but I couldn't move. I tried again and then tried my legs until I realised that I was strapped down; my eyes were open, there was nothing to see.

My head ached fiercely and my shoulder was still throbbing from No-Finger's attentions but there was nothing I could do. I called out, but my voice simply echoed around the empty room. I thought I heard a rushing sound outside – perhaps the sea, but I couldn't be sure – the way my head was feeling I could be in a washing machine on its spin cycle. After a while, I gave up struggling and waited.

I might have blacked out again when the door was suddenly thrown open and a shaft of light hit my eyes. I blinked feebly and turned my head to see No-Fingers walk in, As far as I could see, he had a bucket with a towel over it, but I couldn't be sure.

'I think it's about time we found out who you are and what you're doing her.' I recognised Ansaar's voice but couldn't see where he was. 'It seems a bit foolish to come here on your own. This can be a dangerous place.'

I shook my head to try to get some sensible thoughts. 'I'm not alone,' I managed to say. 'A colleague is following me.'

'And how is he going to find you here?' Ansaar asked. 'No one knows where you are. Now are you going to tell me who you're from?'

'International Pharmaceuticals. I told you, Comar sent me.'

'International Pharmaceuticals,' he repeated. 'Not very informative, is it. And as for Comar, as I told you, I've never heard of them.'

'This is a procedure made popular by our American friends, I think.' I felt the table tilt with my head downwards, and Ansaar came and stood over me. 'Are you going to save us a lot of trouble and mess? Tell us who you're from and get it over with.'

I started to speak, but my throat was too dry. Finally I managed to croak, 'International Pharmaceuticals, I told you. Comar suggested I see you.'

'Yes, I heard all that, but what we want is the truth.' I could see him nod to No-Fingers and a wet towel was thrown over my face and I was in complete darkness – no light filtered through the thick cloth. I realised what was about to happen and tried to take a deep breath but the towel covered my face and I started gagging. I felt, as much as heard, water being poured over my face and I retched instinctively which only made it worse. I struggled for air but only got mouthfuls of water. I tried swallowing but instead I sucked the water into my lungs. My chest heaved in convulsions and I struggled against the shackles holding me down. My body's reflexes took over leaving me with no control as my throat sucked in the water. Bright lights flashed inside my head like an explosion and I realised that in a few more moments I would drown. I tried to fight but there was nothing I could do, and then relief as the towel was taken away and I was able to gulp down some air. I gagged again and was racked with coughing.

'That's the beauty of waterboarding,' Ansaar said, leering at me. 'When you think you're going to die, you remember that relief is in your hands. All you have to do is tell us who sent you and it will all be over. Who was it? Who are you?'

'I told you, International Pharmaceuticals, Comar–' I was cut off by the towel being thrown over my face and once again I was in darkness, which only added to the fear. And don't let anyone tell you they don't feel fear. I was shaking with terror. I tried to snatch a breath but it made little difference as I at first heard the water trickling down the towel from my forehead. They were taking it deliberately slowly so I could sense what was about to happen.

At first it was just a drip, filling up my nose, but then it increased until once again I was gagging with my mouth and throat full of water. I waited to breathe in as long as I could, but I couldn't hold out and sucked the water back down my throat. Was this to be my final ignominious moment? When the retching subsided I felt – almost relief. Let it wash into me, I thought and started to relax and as I looked down at my body from above, I didn't recognise the shuddering and threshing. Now it was all over.

The sudden light in my eyes woke me up and for a moment I'd forgotten where I was. I tried to turn my head, but could see nothing, although the door was still closed and there were voices outside. I tried to shout, but instead I was suddenly seized by coughing and vomited up a shower of water mixed with bloody bile which covered my face. I slowly realised that I was alive but felt so bad that I couldn't help wondering whether the alternative might have been preferable.

I tried moving my arms again but they were still bound firmly and then I heard the door open and turned to see someone walk in.

I blinked hard to clear my eyes. 'Dickson?' I croaked weakly. 'Is that you?' I was incapacitated by another bout of vomiting and when it had finally subsided I felt that my arms had been unlocked and my legs were free. Dickson helped me sit up and I clung to him feebly. 'What took you so long?' was all I managed to say before spewing up my guts onto the floor.

Dickson helped me stand up and led me gently out. The brightness struck my eyes and as I held up my hand, I could make out that we were in the living room of a house overlooking the beach on the far side. The blinds had now been raised and there was a clear view across the ocean. In the corner I could see Ansaar and No-Fingers strapped to chairs with cable ties. They looked across at me impassively, but said nothing.

Another bout of coughing made me stop. 'You see,' I said to them when I'd recovered, 'I told you I wasn't bluffing. I wouldn't come to a place like Zanzibar without backup and Dickson here is one of the best.' Ansaar scowled at me but I thought it was still worth keeping up my cover. 'Despite not getting off to the best start, I'm still interested in doing business, so keep my card.' I looked across at Dickson. 'Are we finished here?' I asked and then turned back to Ansaar. 'Now perhaps you'd like to give us back our tracker.'

'Your tracker?' he asked, confused.

'Yes. I think you'll find it in your pocket.' It almost made it all worthwhile as the realisation slowly dawned upon him. Dickson walked over and reached inside his jacket and brought out the tracker unit. Shaking his head, he handed it to me.

Back in the car, Dickson pulled out his phone. 'I suppose we'd better get them picked up, though I'm not sure what they can be charged with. Even if I did, the Zanzibar authorities aren't going to like it much – they try to look after their own. I think we'd get them released, though it's tempting to leave them there.' He spoke rapidly in Swahili and then hung up. 'Aren't you pleased to have someone clear up your mess for you?'

'It's better than the alternative,' I said, although I was still finding it difficult to breathe properly. 'I might have been that mess. I think he was moving onto a demonstration of how he lost his fingers.'

Dickson drove us back to the Africa House. 'We've still got a trace on the shipment heading to the mainland,' he said as we got back to our room. He threw the car keys onto a nearby table.

First I went into the bathroom to clean up and change. A sudden coughing fit paralysed me, but my guts were empty and I could bring up nothing more.

Back in my room, I went to my bag and brought out my Truscan equipment. 'It's so frustrating. I was right on them, but I still only managed to get samples of one of the batches of Oxaban. The other one was close to the door leading out to the beach for loading so I suspect that was the fake. I hope this was what they'd separated out from the main consignment.'

I set the equipment on the table, took the packet from my pocket and removed one of the tablets and put it in the scanner. After reading off the report on the first batch, it confirmed 100 percent purity. 'If only I'd got a sample from the other batch that would have proved it. But I still think that this is where they're separating out the genuine from the fake – it's got to be a parallel operation.'

'You think the fake drugs were sent out in the same consignment as the real ones and are being split up here in Zanzibar?'

'That's my theory. And the real ones are then sent onto Mombasa. If I could only work out where they're made and I still feel that I've seen the answer – that it was right in front of me but somehow I missed it.'

Dickson put down the Truscan and crossed to the balcony and opened the patio doors. 'Shall we find out where that boat has got to?'

'There's no point. It's dark now and if they've gone in behind Wasini Island then the extrapolation of the track won't work. Have you got any messages from your office?'

Dickson pulled out his phone. 'No. Nothing. I hope they got there before it got dark.'

'Give them a call and find out.' Once again I listened to Dickson's rapid Swahili and waited impatiently for him to finish.

He finally snapped shut his phone. 'They got there before the dhow arrived,' he told me. 'But it was getting dark and as far as they could tell, she anchored somewhere between the island and the mainland. They think they're probably waiting for daylight before unloading. He can see a faint anchor light south of the ferry dock.'

'We'll have to get back to Mombasa. When's the first flight?'

'I think it's eight, but what about Ansaar?'

'They'll have to wait; it's more important that we follow the consignment. They clearly didn't believe my cover, but the main thing is that we've thrown up enough aerial clutter for them not to know who we really are. With any luck that will mean that they'll continue with their operation here. We can follow it up again later.'

We caught the early morning flight to Mombasa and as we walked across the tarmac to the arrivals hall, I noticed a fleet of planes with unusual livery.

'They belong to various aid agencies and NGOs,' Dickson said. They're always flying supplies and staff around the continent. We joke that it's like a private airline.'

Outside, we picked up the hire car that Dickson had booked and headed south towards the border. 'My colleague Juma is watching them. He went down last night but they didn't raise their anchor until first light this morning and then went a little way down the coast. He can't see them clearly but the office is tracking them and they seem to have run the boat up on the shore. They're mainly hidden by the mangroves but there appears to be a faint path through them and he's staking it out. I've got his position on my phone – I reckon it'll take us about another half hour. He'll meet us there.'

We took the turn-off to Shimoni and headed slowly down the rutted road where we saw the thin line of casuarina trees fringing the beach ahead. Dickson indicated the man waiting under the shade of a palm tree. 'That's Juma, we'd better pull in here.'

Juma came over and pointed down the narrow track which was barely more than a footpath. 'This doesn't go anywhere. It peters out a couple of kilometres further along in the mud flats.'

I looked down the track. 'Have you any idea what they're doing down there?'

'I went earlier this morning. They're unloading the dhow onto the back of a truck. From the look of it there're going to be several trips – there's quite a lot to unload.'

'We've only got to follow them once. They've got to come out this way so let's get back in the car and wait.'

They must have started unloading at first light because we didn't have to wait long before an anonymous truck with no markings drove up and turned east along the road to Shimoni.

We left Juma behind with his own car. I let Dickson drive and he pulled out a long way behind and kept his distance. 'There's only one way this road goes,' he said, 'so we'll keep following until they turn off. They're not expecting any company, so we should be okay.'

We must have driven halfway back to Mombasa before we could see the truck turn off up ahead. We were in a small settlement – it could hardly be called a village – and the track led back east towards the coast. We passed through sugar cane plantations and a large processing plant before reaching the tourist beaches on Kenya's east coast. We stopped well back as we saw the truck turn off the road and head towards a large single-storey building behind the sand dunes that lined the coast.

'I suppose it's good camouflage,' I said. 'No one would think of looking at a building that's surrounded by tourists.'

'That *used* to be,' Dickson added. 'With the Al-Shabaab problem, numbers are less than half what they were.'

We watched as the pickup left a dusty trail to the building. 'This must be it,' I said. 'They're unloading. If you wanted to hide something you couldn't do much better than here. It's anonymous, close to Mombasa and unremarkable. This has got to be it. Let's go and have a look.'

Leaving the car, we walked along the road towards the warehouse. I suppose we must have looked conspicuous but I couldn't see we had any choice. I hoped that anyone who saw us would think that I was a tourist looking for the beach. There was no sign outside as we passed the building's entrance and there was nothing attached to the building itself which indicated what the company was. I saw that further back, we'd passed a roadside fruit and snack stall. I pointed it out to Dickson. 'Go and ask him if he knows who the building belongs to. You could also ask how often they make deliveries.'

I watched as Dickson went ahead and spoke to the stallholder.

After a while, he reached into his pocket and passed over some change. In return, he was given a hand of bananas – I hoped he was getting more than bananas for his money. I waited. I'd followed these fake medicines halfway around the world and I must now be getting close to their final destination – final that is except for the poor people who were going to be treated and perhaps poisoned with them.

I could see that Dickson was making a call, so I assumed he must have a lead of some kind, but the call was brief and he snapped shut his phone and came back to me holding out a banana. I took it while he peeled one for himself. He was obviously going to spin this out for dramatic effect but I refused to rush him and took a bite without saying anything. It tasted surprisingly good.

'He says he doesn't know,' Dickson said. I managed to control myself and wait until he was ready to tell me. 'But he's here every day so he notices what goes in and out.' I could tell Dickson was about to get discursive again when he added, 'Not that he's got much else to do here since the tourists left.'

'So did he tell you anything useful or do I have to let you give it a big build-up?'

'I'm getting there,' Dickson said infuriatingly. 'He said that it was unusual for a factory not to advertise what it was, so that's made it a source of curiosity among the locals. That's what made him look more closely at who came and went. It's funny, isn't it, that trying to be anonymous can have the opposite effect?'

'Spare me your philosophy, Dickson, just tell me what he said.'

'He said that he's seen the same truck a few times. It had "Khalid Pharmaceuticals" written on the side, with an address in Mombasa.'

'I don't suppose he made a note of the address?' I said without hope.

'He didn't need to,' Dickson said and he was now smiling broadly at me with an expression I can only describe as smug. 'I phoned the office and they checked their files. Khalid

Pharmaceuticals is one of the Bakaar companies – it's a sister company to Tau Pharmaceuticals.'

'That fits.' It was starting to make some sense at last. 'The container of pharmaceuticals that we'd tracked leaving the Bakaar facility in India had been hijacked in Zanzibar, rearranged in some way and then sent on here to Kenya in what was obviously an operation that was meant to be secret.'

'Looks like it but we still can't be sure. Should I organise a raid on the warehouse?'

'All we'd find would be the real thing; they would have got rid of the counterfeits – too risky to store them here.' I sighed in frustration. 'We've got to trace where the fakes are coming from before they start mass inoculations.'

Back in Dickson's office near Mombasa's Consulate, I booked a call to update Ken Maxwell using their secure line, but first I wanted to go over what we'd found which made little sense to me. 'If Ansaar is to be believed then they've never heard of Comar Logistics so it's not them who are supplying the fakes.'

'Assuming they are fakes,' Dickson said. 'We haven't established that for certain.'

He could be annoyingly difficult at times – especially when he might be right. 'We know that Comar delivered fakes to pharmacies in Mumbai so it seems reasonable to assume that they're also involved with overseas consignments. We know that the container they offloaded in Zanzibar contained genuine Oxaban as well as fakes.'

'If we can't organise a raid then we could try breaking into the warehouse by the beach.'

'Thanks, Dickson. It was only because of you that I managed to survive my last effort. I'm not about to risk it again – next time you might not be there to rescue me.' Credit where it was due, I thought.

It was time for my call to London and when I got hold of him, Ken appeared to be impressed with the progress I'd made even though I couldn't tell him where it was leading. 'I think it's time to look into the Bakaar family,' he said. 'Try making an appointment to see Jamaal using your International Pharmaceutical identity.'

I told him that it was an interesting suggestion and that I only wish I'd thought of it myself. It was my weakness that sarcasm was often my first resort.

The truth was that I was anxious to get back home. I thought I'd taken this matter as far as I reasonably could and I should be able to leave it to Ken Maxwell and the FDA. In addition, I'd had several messages from Sayed so I was becoming increasingly worried about his situation. I'd replied several times saying that I was abroad but would meet Sayed as soon as I got back to the UK but none of them had been acknowledged. In the past, I knew he had only contacted me when he had something to say so I hoped that his silence meant that there should be nothing to worry about.

In the meantime, Jamaal Bakaar was based here in Mombasa and the trail seemed to lead to him, even if I couldn't work out why. While I was here, I didn't have anything to lose by wheeling out my fake identity as a dealer in pharmaceuticals and it would be passing up a straightforward opportunity if I didn't try to meet him. I thought if Dickson tried to make the appointment it would look as though I had a local support team, but Dickson found it tough going.

'The Bakaar family is like royalty,' he told me. 'Although the father's based in India, they have tentacles spreading through Africa, particularly East Africa. Jamaal might be the youngest of his sons but he holds court like a Mughal emperor of old. He has a team of people around him to protect him. In the publicity I've read about him he describes himself as a strategist so he's unlikely to want to get involved with the sordid business of selling. We'll have to think of another way in.'

'Ahmed Bashara in Mumbai.' I clicked my fingers. 'He's some kind of cousin. He went out of his way to help me and he might make an introduction. Can we find his number somewhere?'

I checked my phone, but all the arrangements had been made using Ranish's phone. 'It shouldn't be difficult, try Googling it.' I didn't know why I was giving instructions about something I could do quite easily myself but I felt on edge at the prospect of facing Jamaal Bakaar with such a flimsy back-up story. At least Bashara might add some degree of assurance.

After going through a succession of Bakaar employees who appeared to guard Bashara like the Crown jewels, I finally spoke to someone who remembered my visits and put me through to the man himself. If it was this difficult speaking to Bashara, then it would be much worse trying to get through to Jamaal Bakaar.

After wading through the polite introductions without which Indian businessmen would feel you were being exceptionally rude, I finally got to the point and told him that I was in Mombasa and wanted an introduction to Jamaal Bakaar. At this, he hesitated until I reminded him of the large orders I was considering placing with his company. He finally told me he would do what he could and gave me a name to ring. 'But wait a couple of hours so that I can speak to him,' he added before we hung up.

I turned to Dickson and gave him the name Bashara had given me and told him to try it. 'Jamaal Bakaar is a busy man. That means he expects anyone who deals with him to have a personal assistant and I'm afraid today you're it. Make out that I'm also extremely busy, with very limited time in Kenya and many demands on me. With an introduction from his cousin in Mumbai, I can't see how he can refuse to meet me so it's worth a try. I'm going back to my hotel so let me know how it goes. Good luck.'

As I left, I could hear that Dickson had decided not to wait and was on the phone trying to penetrate Bakaar's protective cordon, constantly switching between English and Swahili.

Chapter Nineteen

I was in my room later that afternoon catching up on emails when Dickson phoned saying that by judicious lying and deceit, not to mention blatant misrepresentation, he'd managed to get an appointment for the following morning. The bad news was that it was with Jamaal's personal assistant, but I had to agree that this was better than nothing so the next morning found me outside what they called the executive estate on the outskirts of Mombasa.

I'd gone past the impressive Bakaar Kenyan headquarters downtown and it made me wonder what their main HQ in Mumbai might look like. But it seemed that Jamaal Bakaar preferred to work from his own home. I use the word "home" loosely since anywhere else it would be regarded as a small village. The complex occupied an entire block on the outskirts of the city and from a distance looked like a well-frequented oasis with clumps of tall swaying palms towering over the adjacent properties.

I signed in at reception and drove through the extravagantly planted avenue with smaller buildings artfully concealed behind the trees – it looked more like a botanical garden than it did an industrialist's base. Eventually, I came to a sprawling edifice where a woman was standing waiting on the steps. I parked the car and went over to her.

'You are alone?' Her expression indicated that it might be regarded as her fault if there was a visitor missing. 'I thought there were going to be two of you.'

'No, it's just me, I'm afraid. Is Mr Bakaar free to see me?'

She frowned again which might have been her default expression. 'No, you are seeing his personal assistant, Mr Halim. It's this way.'

I followed her through the entrance. On either side were fragments of Islamic art displayed on the walls with subdued but effective lighting. 'Does Mr Bakaar collect these?' I asked my guide. 'They look very old.'

She glanced at the walls. 'He has a large collection – this is only part of it. The more delicate items are kept away from the light. Some of them are from the first millennium. Jamaal Bakaar is a very devout Muslim and believes that our heritage should be protected.'

The passageway led into a large courtyard where the only sound was of the water running into an oval lily pond – it was so peaceful that I realised why Jamaal preferred to work here. Who wouldn't? Even the frogs perching on the lilies seemed relaxed.

Jamaal's personal assistant was a young man who couldn't have been much over thirty, but then Jamaal himself was only a few years older. He greeted me with elaborate courtesy and asked if I would mind staying outside in the shade of one of the porticos surrounding the lily pond. As we sat, someone brought a tray of coffee and Halim poured out a cup and offered it to me. 'Ahmed Bashara tells us that you're trying to set up a new pharmaceutical distribution operation in West Africa. That's a very difficult place to do business.'

'But with many opportunities,' I said, sipping the coffee. 'This is excellent. Where do you get it from?'

'The group includes a coffee plantation in the Aberdare Highlands. It's one of our many perks that we get the choice of the crop.'

'Jamaal Bakaar likes to live well.' I indicated the villa.

'He can afford to and he has very good taste. But back to business. I think we would need to know more about the details of your proposals before we could decide to supply you. We already have an existing network of customers through our local distributors and we don't want to upset them by supplying someone who might be setting up in competition with them.'

'I realise that,' I said. 'But we want to reach new markets not merely compete with existing ones. There would be no point otherwise and I understand that your distribution operation here in Mombasa can supply everything that your facility in Mumbai can make?'

'Within reason, yes, but the volume has to be there.'

'But you have more than one distributor in Kenya?' I thought it time to raise the stakes.

'What do you mean, more than one? We only have a small warehouse in Mombasa, a couple of miles from here. It's only used for overflows or special consignments.'

'But I've been told that you have another place over near the coast.' I was all in now.

Halim's poise seemed to be deserting him. 'I'm telling you,' he said, tapping the table for emphasis, 'they only use the one warehouse in Kenya and that's supplied almost exclusively from our plants in India.'

Why would he lie? What were they covering up? 'Do you have much problem with counterfeits?' I decided to take a chance on it and lead in another suit.

Halim appeared to be struggling to control himself, as if realising that banging the table in a place like this wasn't the done thing. 'I don't know why you're asking me these questions. You've seen our operation in Mumbai and Mr Bashara showed you the lengths we go to to ensure consistent quality. We don't deal in fakes.'

'I wasn't suggesting that there was any problem with your own product.' I hoped my reassurance was sufficiently smooth. 'I was asking whether you have a problem with competing counterfeits undercutting your own product.'

'Counterfeits don't concern us,' he repeated and stood up. 'I think we've covered everything.'

And got nowhere, I thought, although I sensed there was something not right about his response. He wouldn't have reacted so violently if there was nothing to hide. As I stood up I saw an elegantly dressed man walk out from an archway behind me and into the sunlight of the courtyard. From Halim's reaction, I realised that this must be Jamaal Bakaar and it wasn't an opportunity to miss.

I stepped down to cut him off and held out my hand. He was a tall man but I had an inch on him and it was difficult for him to ignore me. Despite his height, he was slim and had the emaciated look of an ascetic and I wondered whether this was associated with his researches into ancient Islamic art.

He looked at me with annoyance which he quickly concealed and, since he had little choice if he wasn't going to walk over me, he also held out his hand. 'You must be the man from International Pharmaceuticals. I heard you were visiting us and I'm sorry I didn't have the time to meet you personally. I hope Halim here has looked after you and answered all your questions.'

He started to walk on but I stepped in front of him. 'I quite understand that you're too busy at the moment,' I said. 'But I'm planning to return to Kenya shortly so perhaps you would be free before then?'

He stopped and looked at me with an expression of such contempt that seemed to me to be beyond normal annoyance at an unwelcome interruption. I sensed danger in his presence.

'It's Mr Hennessey, isn't it?' he said menacingly. 'I thought it was easier to continue this charade for you to speak with my assistant, but I see that you persevere with it.' He snapped his fingers arrogantly and Halim rushed up. 'Show this man out.' Jamaal Bakaar turned back to me and snarled: 'I'd hoped that the message of the driver in Mumbai would have got to you. You will gain nothing by such persistence.'

I grabbed his arm as he turned, and he shook it off impatiently. 'Mr Bakaar,' I said, 'I know you're involved with supplying counterfeit drugs. I haven't yet worked out how, but I will and then I'll come looking for you.'

He shook his head. 'We should have killed the driver, then you might have understood.' He stepped to one side and snarled at Halim, 'Now show him out!' And with that he went through the archway and into one of the offices surrounding the courtyard.

Halim had been trying ineffectually to lead me out of the building, and after Jamaal had gone, Halim took my elbow and directed me towards the entrance foyer. He was now in a state of near panic at the prospect that he would be held responsible for allowing his boss to be jumped upon like that and he couldn't get rid of me fast enough.

Back in London, Ken Maxwell told me that the successful bidder for the vaccination programme was Tau Pharmaceuticals and I realised that this meant there was a strong likelihood of the vaccines being fakes. I fumed at not having found the source of the counterfeit drugs but my phone ringing me reminded me that Sayed's operation was still running. I'd left it on silent but had programmed in certain numbers to ring through and this was Sayed. I'd been trying to get hold of him since I'd returned but he hadn't answered any of my messages. As I looked at the screen of my mobile, I realised that it was decision time.

'Can we meet?' Sayed didn't waste time on pleasantries. 'I've got some news.'

'Where? In the park, or do you want to come to the boat again?'

'Better make it the boat. Crossing London on the Underground I can check if I'm being followed.'

'Fine. When?'

'Make it this afternoon at around four.'

'Is it okay if I ask Ali along,' I asked, 'now you've met him and know you can trust him?'

'If you must. Although I'm not very keen on the idea.'

I disconnected the phone and immediately called Ali and told him that I thought it was about time I met with MI5 myself at Thames House. Not for the first time I wondered why the security services congregated along the waterfront, but eventually concluded cynically that it probably helped them to deal with any leaks. Perhaps there was something about the shifting nature of intelligence that when they looked out over the swirling, muddy River Thames, they were looking at something that mirrored themselves and the murky eddies they operated in.

But this time it was MI5 at Thames House, along the Embankment from the Houses of Parliament that I was visiting. These were the people who were supposed to be keeping us safe in our own homes, as opposed to MI6 who were keeping us safe from other people's homes and had the entire globe as their canvas.

I'd given a call to Jeff Masters, the contact Ali had given me. I'd occasionally dealt with him when our work had overlapped – which hadn't been often. We were always made to feel as though we were treading on their toes whenever we had any contacts in common, and they treated us with the patronising disdain that an uncle might treat an eager but rather dim nephew. But I couldn't see how I could keep them out of this. I didn't have to tell Sayed that they were involved – although, knowing him, he'd probably already guessed that his mosque was likely already under surveillance.

Jeff met me at reception and thought my security clearance at least enabled me to go up to their canteen, even if it didn't allow me any deeper within their organisation. In order to discourage operatives from leaving the premises over lunchtime and run the risk of their conversations being overheard, the MI5 management had gone out of its way to make the staff canteen as attractive as possible. And certainly the view from the top floor was worth staying in for.

Jeff ordered two coffees and we took them to a table by the window, overlooking the river. I realised that he didn't want to take me to his own office since he still regarded me as a possible security risk. I thought this was ironic because I was giving them information, rather than the other way around, but I understood I couldn't be allowed to contaminate the inner workings of the agency. I'd only been up here once before and the riverside views and contemporary décor couldn't have been further removed from the image given in a John Le Carré novel. Perhaps down in the basement they kept the frumpy middle-aged woman with a cigarette dangling from the side of her mouth spreading ash like a nuclear cloud behind her. Up here was more in keeping with the postmodernism of the offices of their brothers further down the river.

Jeff sat down opposite me and sneezed. 'Sorry, a bit of hay fever.'

'I thought you people were supposed to be tough.'

'You're confusing us with Military Intelligence. It's you people who're the tough ones. All that training out on the Scottish moors with only a thimbleful of water to keep you going for a week.'

'It's good to know we have such a reputation. Though in my case I always used to take a hip flask.'

'And I bet it didn't have water in it.'

'No, but it went well with the dew from the heather. The Scottish equivalent of Bourbon and branch water.'

Jeff sighed, and frankly I couldn't blame him. 'Let's get to the point, shall we? How can I help?'

I'd tried to work out the best way of introducing the subject of Khazim's possible recruitment without bringing Sayed into it, but there was no way it could be done. All I could do was to be slightly economical with the truth. 'As Ali told you, I picked up an informant in Afghanistan. He was brought here as a refugee and we've stayed in touch. He's living in Harrow and attends a local mosque.' I could see that Jeff was frowning and I knew why. 'I know we were supposed to register contacts but at first he was adamant that he wouldn't speak to anyone else. He reluctantly agreed to share his information with Ali, but since then he's been rather quiet.'

'Ali registered this information with us. So what's the latest position?'

'Sayed – that's my informant – is meeting me this afternoon, so I assume he must have more information.'

'So where did he develop this loyalty to Philip Hennessey, rather than coming straight to us?'

'It was in Afghanistan. I promised his mother that I'd track him down and, as I say, I traced him here to north London and we've kept in touch. He told me he was grateful for my help and agreed to let me know if he came across anyone being radicalised.'

'And did he?'

'He told me he was suspicious of this other refugee – called Khazim. Apparently Khazim was going on residential Koranic study courses, and you know what that could mean. Presumably you monitor these things?'

Jeff looked at me for a while without saying anything. Eventually, he shook his head. 'I know you had this reputation for working outside the rules, but I thought at least you would know what the rules are. From what you've told me you appear to have been acting as a one-man counter-intelligence agency. Don't you have any concept of teamwork?'

'I always thought that teamwork was getting everyone doing what I wanted them to do.'

'But you never could, could you?'

'Look, Jeff. Cut it out, will you? I'm here now and I'm giving you this lead, aren't I?'

'Are you? I bet you're going to take a mortgage over it – keep ultimate ownership.'

I was getting irritated. I didn't come here to have my failings analysed. 'Do you know about this place? It must have figured somewhere on your radar.'

Jeff realised that whatever he thought about it, I'd brought it to him like a cat with a mouse and dropped it on his mat. He sighed and pulled out a laptop and entered his password details. I waited as he navigated his way through to whatever intelligence they had on the north London activists. 'You say the names are Sayed Alam and someone called Khazim?' I nodded and he carried on with his search. After a while, he brought out his cell phone and dialled a number. 'Giles, would you mind coming up for a moment?'

Jeff put the phone down and turned to me. 'As it happens we do know about this group. Giles Hathaway is the case officer dealing with it. He's been monitoring it for the past year. Ah, Giles.'

I stood up as Giles approached the table. He was a young man – probably not yet thirty – with dark wavy hair and a suntan that I didn't think he'd picked up in north London.

Jeff introduced us and explained about my contact with Sayed and I could see the surprise on Hathaway's face.

'So he's your informant, is he? We had no idea he was in contact with anyone else, but are you sure he's genuine?'

I explained again the background about how I'd tracked him down for his mother and how he'd kept in touch and told me his concerns about Khazim.

'I suppose that makes sense,' Hathaway said. 'We've been keeping an eye on the people there in Harrow. We know about Sayed and Khazim and there are several others we think are involved. We were expecting movement, and have various bugs in place, but you say something might be on very soon?'

'From what little Sayed said on the phone, my guess is that things are coming to a head. He doesn't usually contact me unless he has something to say.'

'And he says that it's Khazim who's going to be running the project?' I nodded. 'That's probably quite likely. It's something they often give to the new boys. Checking them out for more important things.'

'So what have you got on file about Sayed?' I asked. 'Did you know about his background?'

'You know I can't give you any detail. You're no longer security-cleared.' I was getting used to these brush-offs. If he wanted to rub my nose in what it felt like to be on the outside, he couldn't have done much better. He looked up and, as though reading my mind, he added, 'This is a one-way street you realise? You tell us what you know, and we tell you nothing in return.'

'That might normally be the case,' I said evenly, 'but I'm afraid you're not going to get far with my informant if you try to take him over. He's made that quite clear.'

'And your informant, Sayed, what exactly is he going to give you that you're now so eager to share with us even though you've waited all this time to tell us about it?'

'I'm not eager to share it with you, as you put it. I realised that if things are starting to move then you need to know and I don't know any more than I've told you. He thinks this young man, Khazim, is being groomed and, as I say, he promised to keep track of it and keep me informed.'

'So what are we supposed to do with that information?'

I was getting angry but knew where that could lead. 'First you criticise me for not telling you about this informant and now you're making out that you're not interested. You can't have it both ways.' I took a deep breath. 'I came here because Sayed has asked to meet me later this afternoon and I thought it was time to get you people involved.'

'This afternoon? Can we come along and see what he has to say?'

'That wouldn't work. It was difficult enough getting him to talk to Ali, bringing in anyone else would scare him off, but I can call you after he's been and let you know what he says. We can then judge if it's worth following up.'

'We, you say? I think that's something you'll have to leave to us.' He reached into his pocket and pulled out another mobile phone. 'Here, you'd better have this. It's a burner and isn't registered to anyone so can't be hacked. You can give Sayed the number. It's written here.' He handed me a piece of paper. I wondered how many phones he kept to hand and doled out like candy. 'In future, if you want to phone me use that and not your own.' He reached into his pocket again and brought out a small box. 'A tracking device. More accurate than tracing a phone.'

I took the phone, the tracker and the paper, and put them in my pocket without looking at them. I think I was being dismissed but I wanted to look as though I was leaving when I wanted to and not when he wanted me to. I stood up. 'I'll call you after I've spoken to Sayed.'

Ken Maxwell now insisted upon a full debrief and so I went on down to River House for a meeting. I'd already given them an outline of my meeting with Jamaal but thought they ought to understand what it meant.

'He knew who I was,' I told them. 'He knew about the driver in Mumbai and he probably told them to do it.'

'That's not possible,' said Ken. 'How could he? I admit your cover wasn't fool-proof, but it made sense. You were there to buy supplies for the UK.'

'He must have heard what happened in Zanzibar, with Ansaar. They realised that I wasn't an ordinary pharmaceutical buyer.'

'Perhaps not an ordinary one, but in my experience such people have to be pretty resourceful.'

'I don't think they usually waterboard buyers who turn up on their doorstep. It wouldn't be good for business. A card is usually sufficient.' I was annoyed that they couldn't see how things had changed. 'They'll be watching me now. They know I'm not who I said and they know that Ansaar's operation has been compromised.'

'Maybe,' Ken said. 'But perhaps they won't have enough time to set up an alternative route.'

'It's obviously a well-established supply route,' I told them. 'We only followed the boat that supplied southern Kenya, but there were other boats loading up there and we have no idea where they were going.'

'I can guess,' Ken said with a trace of bitterness. 'They could be supplying all of East Africa. Can you estimate the volume that goes through there?'

'Not since we don't yet know how they're doing. I think there could be other similar warehouses on Zanzibar or even Pemba. If you think about it, it took them a day to strip down a container, take out the fakes and send the real ones on.'

'It's a pity you weren't able to find out where they're going – a consignment note or something.'

I thought this was pushing it a bit. 'I'm sorry about that but I was a bit tied up at the time,' I said a touch austerely. 'We can't be 100 percent sure, but nothing else would explain the operation which, as far as we could tell, was pretty well organised. Your satellite equipment seems to be effective, can't you set up a surveillance operation?'

'We looked into that, but there's too much that could go wrong. We could follow the boats that left the warehouse, but we can't track them at night or once they hit the shore and the cargo's offloaded into trucks.'

'Perhaps not, but you could find out what countries they're going to. It might give you an idea of how big this operation is.'

I could see that Ken Maxwell was working through this. 'I suppose we could get the Kenyan and Tanzanian office to follow this up,' he said. 'They might be able to get someone to track it once it's unloaded.'

'That's only if you can trace it back to the original source. So far we've been lucky in tracing this consignment but we can't follow them all.'

'I wouldn't call it luck. But the real problem is that we don't know who's producing them.'

Once again, we got back to the essence of the problem. 'I've been racking my brains,' I said, 'and I have this feeling that it's right under my nose; that I saw it but somehow missed it. All we know for sure is that it's got to be somewhere in or around Mumbai. How else could it have been loaded onto the container?'

'So that's all right, then,' Ken said, laconically. 'Only around twenty million people to search.'

'Let's look at it the other way,' I said. 'Follow the trail backwards from the point of delivery.'

'What?' Ken looked at me in disbelief. 'You mean go around every market stall, every pharmacy in East Africa – every doctor's surgery?'

'No.' I was disappointed by Ken's immediate reaction. 'Couldn't we set up some kind of sting?'

'A bit risky, but I could talk it over with Brent, see what he thinks about it. If it worked we could sit tight and let them bring the drugs to us.'

I'm not sure that Ken could consider that any idea that didn't come from within his own service could ever be considered a good one, but he affected to think about it. 'What do you think?' I prompted.

'We'll work on it but now that your cover's blown I don't think we can risk you getting involved further, so I think it's probably time to say goodbye.' He stood up and held out his hand. 'Brent says to tell you that we've been really grateful for your help. You've done a great job but I think we can take it on from here.'

I took his hand and shook it. To be honest, I was a bit taken aback. I hadn't expected my services to be dispensed with quite so brusquely but I was thinking ahead to my meeting with Sayed.

I knew we'd reach this situation eventually, just didn't expect it to be quite so soon. But a tactical withdrawal now would allow me to open a second front at a later date. I said goodbye and let their operative escort me to the street. It was getting to be a bit of a habit.

Chapter Twenty

I'd arranged to meet Greta that evening after I'd seen Sayed and, following the weekend I'd spent with her on the south coast, I was looking forward to it. But I was still concerned about what Ken Maxwell and his team were going to make of the intelligence I'd given them. One of the worst things anyone can say to you is "Thanks, we can take it from here". And I didn't really intend to be brushed aside as though my contribution was at an end. For the time being, I couldn't really see what I could do about it and I thought an evening with Greta would take my mind off it and perhaps I'd wake up with some ideas the next day.

I thought it time for something a bit more modern, so I brought out my Ottolenghi cookbook but since he didn't have a recipe that used fewer than seventeen ingredients there was no way I could find them all in my local shop. Instead I went through my other books to find something that combined enough complication to impress but without it taking all afternoon in preparation. I didn't want her to think that I'd shot my bolt with beef stroganoff.

I didn't have time to go to the main market so had to make do with what the local shop had in stock and as I walked down the aisles I marvelled again at the sheer quantity of crisps, sweets and snacks that must have taken up at least half the store. They did, however, have some frozen lamb so I had to make do with that, along with some red peppers and olives to make a reasonable stew and took them back to the boat and started cooking.

Some people need narcotics to go into a trance, music will do it for others. For me, it was cooking and it must have been over an hour later, when I finally had everything ready, that I got to open the bottle of Meursault someone had brought me – though knowing my friends they probably thought it was an ordinary plonk. I'd been saving it up for a special occasion and given what had happened to me over the past couple of months, I couldn't think of an occasion more special than a quiet night in with Greta. I was trying unsuccessfully to kid myself that this time I didn't want her to stay overnight. I picked up the wine and sniffed it. If anything would do it, the Meursault would.

Ali had told me that he didn't know whether he could make it but that I should go ahead without him. In a funny sort of way I hoped that Sayed wouldn't have anything of importance to tell me because I wasn't sure how I'd be able to handle it, but there was no point worrying about it until it happened.

When he arrived, Sayed seemed quite cheerful compared to his previous visit. He climbed up the gangplank into the saloon and was still enthusing over his visit back home. I didn't try to interrupt – he'd get around to telling me what he'd come for in his own time. I made the usual mug of tea and handed it to him. Despite his increasingly western outlook, he still wouldn't touch alcohol. He took it and sat down looking out at the city through the saloon windows. I couldn't begin to work out what he saw when he looked at his adoptive city – I hoped it was another home. I sat down and waited for him to finish.

'Sorry,' he said. 'You want to hear the latest. I'm making progress with Khazim although he still doesn't trust me completely, I think he sees me as being on the same side as him.'

'And which side is that?'

Sayed shrugged. 'If you look at all this,' he said indicating the sweep of the river and the towering offices that bordered it, 'how can someone like Khazim think that we Muslims have been dealt a fair hand? Think how it looks to him when he compares it with where he came from.'

I sipped my tea and said nothing. I'd sometimes made these comparisons myself and had given up trying to reconcile them.

If it was difficult for me it must have been even worse for Sayed – and I'd seen the place where he grew up.

'Khazim has been given a project.' I still said nothing. "Project" was what they called a planned operation – a euphemism for possible carnage.

'How do you know?' I thought it was time to try to pin him down. 'Do they talk to you about it?'

'Not directly, but they're used to having me around. I think they assume that I'm one of them.'

'Haven't they tried to recruit you?'

Sayed laughed. 'Of course they have – especially because I know about pharmacy. But you've got to understand what the atmosphere is like in these places. Everyone is a convert, everyone is a fighter for Islam and they think I'm one of them. I try to defuse the situation – I don't say that I'm with them, but I don't say that I'm not. I tell them how much I admire them but hint that I don't think I'm yet ready for it. I tell them I'm still working on my Koranic studies and hoping to reach enlightenment soon and that seems to satisfy them.' This time Sayed's laugh was bitter. 'You can get away with most things if you bring in the Koran. They're so convinced of themselves they don't realise that the Koran is not seen in the same way by everyone. They say the Koran says this, or the Koran says that and it doesn't occur to them that others might have a different view.'

At that moment, there was a knocking on the saloon door and I saw that Ali had managed to get there. I waved him in and he shook hands with Sayed – rather formally, I thought, which was probably no bad thing.

'Sayed thinks that Khazim is on a project,' I told Ali as he walked in. I turned back to Sayed. 'So what do you know about it?'

'It's an arms shipment. It's taking place tomorrow, but I'm not quite sure where.'

'Can you find out?' I asked. 'Perhaps get a bit closer to them?'

'I've been thinking about that, but if I try to get closer I'm afraid they're going to suck me in and once in, they're not going to allow me to leave.'

'I could probably arrange protection,' Ali said.

'Perhaps.' I could tell that Sayed wasn't entirely convinced and I wasn't sure that I was either. 'Couldn't I tip you off when I think they've started to move and then you take it from there?'

'It's going to be a bit difficult if we don't know what they're doing or where they're doing it. We need more information. You've got this far, couldn't you go that bit further?' I realised that although it sounded simple, it was a lot to ask. These people don't take prisoners.

'There seem to be different levels in the group. The foot soldiers start at the bottom and work their way up. After a while, they leave the group and we don't see them again.'

Unless it's on the news, I thought bitterly. *A photograph of them posted onto a website – taken before the attack while they were still alive.*

'So you think this is Khazim's test?' Ali asked.

'If it's what I think it is, then yes. But it's important. They're talking about a large cache of arms. I think they're coming in by boat and Khazim's going to take delivery. He was talking to me about the money they've given him to buy a van. About how he's afraid he might buy the wrong one.' Sayed laughed. 'Khazim is not very practical, but they've told him which one he has to buy so that it can't be traced back to them.'

'Can you get me the registration number when he buys it?' Ali asked, but I thought this was ridiculously over-optimistic. If they regarded an arms shipment as a "simple" test, paving the way to more important things, then it was an indication of how important they considered the next stage to be. I thought of the attacks in France where rapid-fire automatic weapons had sprayed death indiscriminately. If the terrorists were prepared to die, it could create more carnage even than a well-placed bomb and the photographs of the killers would be on front pages around the world.

'There's another meeting tomorrow morning, with a visiting preacher who's quite well known. He's quite a… a…,' Sayed was searching for the word, 'a rabble-rouser. Is that right?'

'Yes, quite right.' His English had made remarkable progress and he now had barely an accent.

'I think it's a sort of code. They advertise that this preacher is coming and it seems innocent to most people but it's a signal for the other people involved that the project is about to start. Once Khazim's bought the van they'll tell him where to take it.'

'You really think it will be tomorrow?' Ali asked, although I couldn't see how we could do much in such a short timescale.

'I think everyone's ready for it, so yes, I think it'll be tomorrow, but there's just one thing.' Here Sayed became hesitant. 'I think that your security services might have already infiltrated the cell. Do you know anything about that?'

I knew that Jeff Masters had told me they had a file on Sayed and Khazim, but that wasn't the same as an infiltration. 'What makes you think that?' I asked, stalling.

'It's a guess, really. I've seen people in odd sorts of places. Khazim says he thinks he was followed once and I think I might have been. You see someone reflected in a shop window and think you've seen him before. Sort of shadows.'

I suddenly had the feeling that I was being used; that Masters knew all along about this cell and was using me as a possible inside source, without telling me that they were already aware of most of what was going on. I looked across at Ali. 'What do you think?'

'Leave that with me,' he said. 'I'll check with my contacts and see. But you shouldn't have to worry about it. I've already told them about you and they understand that you're helping us.'

'I hope they do,' Sayed said, which for him was quite a change. 'If they are watching us then I don't want to get picked up by mistake.' At least he was being realistic.

'Phone me on this number,' I said handing him the paper Jeff Masters had given me. 'It's more secure. Or text me if you can't talk. I'll be nearby.'

'What? No. You can't be. If anyone sees you…'

'They won't. I said I'd be nearby, not next door. You remember that anonymous café we walked past the time before last? I said it might be useful as a meeting place? It's close enough to the mosque in case they take off and we lose them. Oh, I forgot.' I went over to the sideboard. 'They gave me this tracker device. We can track you through your phone, but this is more accurate. Keep it on you.'

Sayed put it in his pocket along with the phone number, but he looked undecided.

'So can you go there tomorrow?' I asked in encouragement.

'Yes. I'll go tomorrow, but I'll… I'll… play it by ear?' Sayed looked at me questioningly, as if hoping he'd got the right phrase.

'That's right,' I said. 'Play it by ear.'

I followed him out on deck and watched him down the pontoon before returning to Ali who was looking at his phone. 'What do you think?' I asked.

He said nothing, apparently reading some of his messages, but I thought this was a pretence to avoid talking to me. He looked up. 'At least this time you've got Thames House involved. Perhaps you've finally realised that the rules might apply to you as well.' He put away his phone and stood up. 'I'll let you update Giles Hathaway. Tell him I'll be in touch about tomorrow.'

He walked out of the saloon without another word and I shook my head as I watched him go. It was clear that the grit that had entered our friendship was working its way into something much more serious.

I sighed as I realised that there wasn't much I could do about it. Ali had always had an outlook that was difficult to change. Instead I brought out the MI5 phone and updated Hathaway with what Sayed had told me.

'Yes,' he said. 'That accords with our own intelligence.'

I didn't like the sound of that. It seemed to confirm Sayed's suspicions. 'So you already know about this operation?'

'I told you, we keep track of most of what's going on in that part of north London. We're getting a team together and can watch the meeting room and hopefully you can tell us if Sayed manages to get a message to you. If this preacher is the excuse for them all to get together, then we want to move fast if your Sayed can tell us where they're headed.'

'According to Sayed it'll just be Khazim. He thinks Khazim's getting a van and is driving to the coast to pick up a consignment of drugs.'

'Coast? You said coast.'

'Did I?' I thought back to our conversation. 'Sayed said the drugs are coming in by boat so it must be somewhere on the coast.'

'Probably Kent,' Hathaway said. 'There aren't so many boats around on the east coast and there are any number of inlets in the Thames estuary where they can simply run the boat up into the creeks and unload. There are plenty of lonely anchorages around there.'

'You can't stake them all out, so we'll have to go with whatever Sayed is able to tell us.' I hoped he would remember that he still needed my help.

I thought it was finally time I turned off, so I made myself a gin and tonic and took it up on deck and relaxed by watching the river's events, which was better than most soap operas. I'd heard that the owner might be planning to come back, so I wasn't going to have much more time to enjoy this privileged position in the heart of the city.

As I clinked the ice around in my glass I thought back to the trail of the counterfeit drugs – the scale of it was industrial and everything Ken and Brent had told me made sense. Fakes administered as the real thing must have been causing countless fatalities.

As I looked out on the river, I could see a lifeboat rush by with its blue light flashing. Until recently it hadn't occurred to many people that a rescue service was needed on the Thames but since establishing it a couple of decades earlier, it had turned into the country's busiest.

'Visitor!' My thoughts were interrupted by my neighbour shouting across from his boat. He obviously didn't seem to understand that I was perfectly able to see my visitors myself and thought he should act as a sort of early warning. Of course that was being charitable – the truth was that he was simply nosy.

I stood up and watched as Greta came along the pontoon. She stopped and waved and once again I admired the light in her golden hair. *Let my neighbour watch*, I thought, *let him be jealous*.

I made Greta a drink and took her back up on deck to watch the evening display. There was something about the river at this time in the evening that was quite magical – a circus couldn't have put on a better show. There was even a tourist boat called Duck Tours which seemed to me to involve the dangers of a high-wire act but transposed to a few inches above the fast running tide. They boasted that they hadn't lost anyone yet, but it seemed only a matter of time. We didn't say much as we watched the show around us, but eventually I stood up and suggested dinner and Greta followed me down to the saloon. I'd made an effort with the new lighting I'd installed and had to agree with myself that it was looking pretty inviting.

I sat Greta at the table and brought her some olives that I'd left marinating.

'These are good,' she said, helping herself to more. 'Sally really lost out when you two split up. She's cooked for me a couple of times and she's really not very good at it – not that I told her so, of course.'

'You didn't need to. Sally is well aware of her limitations, though I hope she finds someone else soon.'

'She works too hard,' Greta said. 'After you separated, I think she married her work. A bit like you.'

'Perhaps I do get a bit obsessed. But I'm not giving up. I can't help thinking there's a simple solution to this and that it was in front of me, but somehow, I missed it. I'll have to go and sit in a darkened room until it comes to me.'

'Not before you've cooked me dinner. Perhaps we can think about darkened rooms afterwards?'

I glanced across at Greta and thought I saw faint signs of blushing, but I let it go – there was no point rushing these things.

I stood up. 'I can take a hint. I'll start cooking. Most of it is already prepared so it shouldn't take long.'

First, I retrieved the Meursault from the fridge and poured out a glass and took it to her. 'We don't normally stretch to white Burgundies but this should be good.'

She took the glass and sipped. 'It is good,' she said and sat down. 'Have you discovered where the fakes are coming from yet?'

'Not yet, but I will. When you first asked me to help I didn't realise it would uncover anything like this.'

'So what's going to happen about the vaccination programme Sally talked about?'

'The SIS people seem to have taken it over and told me they don't need me anymore, but I hope I'm going to find my way back in again. When they said goodbye to me, they clearly didn't mean *au revoir*.'

'But you're still going to see it through?'

'I always need to see everything through.' I turned off the gas and laid out the plates. 'Dinner's served,' I said and we sat down facing each other.

'Tell me about your travels.'

'I did manage to get myself locked up for a while.' I couldn't see any harm in injecting a little drama into my travels.

'What happened?' I could see that Greta wasn't quite sure whether to believe me or not.

'After being tied up in wrapping tape, I managed to escape by posting myself through a nearby letter box.' As I said it I could see that Greta didn't really appreciate such flippancy. 'The partner I was with rescued me so it was all very unheroic,' I added dismissively, which was true but didn't exactly show me in the light that I would have preferred. I told her a bit about No-Fingers which went some way to restoring my image, but I had to admit it hadn't been my finest hour and I was still no nearer to tracking the source of the counterfeits.

Chapter Twenty-One

I'd arranged with Ali that he and Giles Hathaway would keep in touch by phone when staking out the meeting house, rather than meeting nearby. I assumed they were somewhere around, but to their credit I couldn't tell where, although I'd heard a helicopter go past earlier and wondered whether it was anything to do with them. I'd already told Sayed that I was going to hide in public – I'd put on my dirtiest jeans – I had a wide choice after working on *Salacia* – and was sitting in the workman's café that we'd agreed upon. I took along the *Daily Star* as camouflage and was flicking through it when the phone buzzed.

'Have you heard anything from Sayed?' It was Ali. 'I'm with Hathaway and we're ready to follow as soon as you tell us.'

'Not yet.' I was surprised at his impatience – I'd told him I'd contact him as soon as I heard anything. 'Can we keep this line open?' I pulled out my smartphone and checked the map to see where Sayed's GPS tracker was and it hadn't moved from outside the meeting hall down the road. I checked the position of his phone to make sure, but it confirmed it from the tracker.

I went back to my newspaper and the fascinating story of why celebs like dressing up in latex but didn't think I could be blamed for my attention wandering and I almost missed the low buzzing of a received message. It was a vehicle registration number – presumably of the van that Khazim was going to drive. I forwarded it onto Hathaway and Ali without comment. They could call Swansea and find out what type of vehicle it was – assuming that they weren't false plates.

It was a frustrating wait for the next message which finally arrived after about twenty minutes. I was worried that people might be getting suspicious of anyone who could spend that long reading the *Daily Star*. The message said simply: "Meet me outside". Again, I forwarded it to Hathaway but added that I assumed he meant outside the café. I folded my newspaper but kept hold of it in case I needed it again, and walked out and tried to look nonchalant as I waited on the pavement. I was just a workman waiting to be picked up by a workmate and taken to a job. I didn't understand why Sayed couldn't phone and tell me what was happening, but assumed that sending a message was safer, but it made me nervous not having direct contact.

After about five minutes, a van pulled up at the kerb next to me. I could see that Sayed was driving but what I hadn't counted on was that the registration number was the one he'd texted me. This was the van he was telling me to follow and he was driving it himself. He leant over and opened the door and I got in. I started to ask what was going on, but he silenced me and pointed to the phone on the dashboard.

After a while, a voice came through giving him directions. It was in a guttural, heavily accented English and I had difficulty understanding what he was saying.

Eventually, Sayed nodded at me and reached over and turned off the phone. 'Sorry about that. We can talk now. I hope your car's going to be safe wherever you left it.'

'Car?' I asked dumbly before I remembered that I hadn't told him anything about the team from MI5 but I realised that I would have to tell him if I was to keep his trust. 'You were right about being watched,' I said and tried to see his reaction but he was concentrating on the road. 'When I told them about you, they said that arrangements were already in hand to watch the meeting and follow Khazim when he left.'

'I thought so,' Sayed said. 'I told you I was worried about it.' He stopped at some traffic lights and turned to me. 'Is that true, or did you bring them in yourself even though I asked you not to?'

'I told you I couldn't keep it to myself. That's why I brought Ali in. But they were following you anyway.'

A car behind hooted as the lights turned to green and Sayed started off again. 'I suppose it's too late now. Whether you brought them in or they were already watching doesn't make much difference.'

I was relieved that he seemed to be taking it philosophically. 'Why did you give me the number of the car you're driving?' I thought it was a very simple question. 'We don't need to follow you if you can tell us where you're going. Where *are* we going, incidentally?'

'I'm sorry. There was a last-minute change of plans. I think they were also suspicious that there might be a leak. They didn't give me a choice, they gave me the keys to Khazim's van and told me to drive it. They said they'd give me instructions as I went along – as you heard.'

'So where's Khazim? Is he still supposed to be collecting this drugs shipment, or are we going to do it just the two of us?'

'They left him standing there,' Sayed said. 'He was distraught. After all the effort he'd put in sucking up to them and they pull him back at the last moment and get me to make the collection.'

'They must have thought you were one of them after all.'

'They didn't give me any time to think about it. They took the keys from Khazim and handed them to me and told me to get on with it. Poor Khazim. I wonder if he'll speak to me again.'

'So do you know where we're going?'

'Not yet. I've got to wait for further instructions. They told me to go over the Queen Elizabeth Bridge over the Thames and then they'd give me a postcode to find.'

I called Hathaway to let him know of the switch but before I could say anything he interrupted. 'We're tracking the car. It's a white Ford. He's stopped to pick someone up.'

I hesitated before replying because I knew he wasn't going to like what I had to say. 'That was me.' I thought I'd break it to him gently.

'What? What are you talking about?'

'It seems there was a change of plan. Instead of Khazim making the collection, they told Sayed to do it and I'm in the van with him now.'

'Sayed? I thought you said he was your informant.'

'He is, but they don't know that. They think he's one of them.'

'Shit! Are you sure? What about Khazim – are you sure Sayed's not just a decoy?'

'Not unless they've got another van for him to drive,' I said. 'Perhaps they suspected that you'd made Khazim so they decided at the last moment to give it to someone else.'

'They'd certainly have a surprise if they discovered that you were following Sayed from inside the van.'

'Yes – ironic, isn't it? But you're still following?'

'We'll stay with you,' Giles said. 'If your Sayed is going to make a collection you'll probably need backup.'

'Okay. Stay with us.' I put the phone back in my pocket. 'So where are we going then?' I asked Sayed.

'I told you, I don't know. I have to wait for them to phone with the next set of directions.'

At that moment his phone rang and he gestured me to shut up and put it on loud speaker. Once again the guttural tones of his controller came through and I could just make out that we were being directed south across the Thames and then east towards Kent – Jeff Masters' guess had proved right.

At the end of his instructions, Sayed's controller said something I didn't understand. I could see Sayed glance across to me before saying simply '*Sama da*' and reach over and disconnect the call. But my Pashtun wasn't up to understanding what he'd said "okay" to.

There wasn't much I could do now, so I made myself as comfortable as I could and settled down for the ride. I still couldn't decide whether Sayed was really on my side or whether he was simply diverting me from the real shipment.

I was dozing lightly when an abrupt change in the road noise woke me. I looked around groggily. We'd turned off the motorway and were heading towards Sittingbourne. I pulled out my phone and called Hathaway but he didn't answer so I texted him "Still there?" and waited for his reply.

"Still with you," he texted back after a few minutes although I couldn't understand quite why he hadn't answered the phone and told me that.

'Do you have new instructions?' I asked Sayed.

'They sent me a postcode. I've put it into my phone and we're heading there. It's about fifteen miles away. A place called Sheppey Island.'

'The Isle of Sheppey,' I corrected him. So Giles Hathaway was right in his guess. I'd sailed around these waters but it had been quite a while ago and I couldn't say I knew them well. There were plenty of creeks where a boat with short keels could be run up at high water and sit in the mud quite happily as the tide went out.

Sayed's phone went again, but this time he picked it up and held it to his ear. Despite this, I could hear the same voice giving further instructions. Sayed listened and said nothing and then hung up the phone and put it back on the dashboard.

'Well?'

'You'll see,' Sayed said and I looked at him in surprise. And he didn't look his usual controlled self.

'What do you mean?'

'I mean that we still haven't been given our final instructions yet, so we don't know what's going to happen. We go to this postcode and wait.'

I thought this an odd answer but let it go. I brought up my phone and checked the map of where we were heading. Much of the island was a nature reserve and there was little else to justify the high-level bridge they'd built over the Swale River, but this was a popular inshore route for yachts so they, at least, were grateful they could still pass underneath. The railway track alongside had an ancient lifting bridge which added character – although it didn't look as though it could always be relied on to work.

As we left the outskirts of the town, the buildings were thinning out. I called Ali and suggested that they back off.

'Nice to be told how to suck eggs,' he said. 'We're going to take the road up to Sheerness and let you both go on ahead.'

'What about me?' I asked. 'I'm not going to be able to do much on my own.'

'Don't worry. Tell us where you are when you get there. We'll get someone to you.' He didn't say how.

We were now moving into open fields and Sayed stopped and picked up his phone and studied it carefully. 'I know the place,' he said. 'I think I've been here before.'

I couldn't imagine the circumstances under which he could have been there before, but said nothing. He put the phone down and headed off again. The road got narrower and rougher until he came to a stop. 'I think this is far enough. Before we go any further let's check out what's ahead.'

The sky had that grey, flat look that you see on the east coast, as though it couldn't be bothered to put on a show if there was no one out there to watch. Fortunately, the recent dry weather meant that the path wasn't waterlogged as I imagined it often was. We walked up a small mound and ahead could see the narrow River Swale and the Thames estuary beyond it, but it was difficult to see where the sky ended, and the grey water took over. The mud seemed to stretch out until it reached the sky. There was a ramshackle old hut by the side of the path with the remains of fishing nets and a string of cork floats hanging outside. It had to be years since anyone used cork as floats and it could have been years since anyone used this shack, although it wasn't bad as a disguise.

We stopped behind the mound and found a clump of bushes and hid behind them. As far as I could tell it was nearing high tide but still a lot of the mud remained uncovered. I cursed myself for not checking the tides before setting out, but I'd find out soon enough. The path led beyond the shack to a dilapidated wooden jetty but when I looked more closely through the binoculars, I could see some signs that the cross-braces had been reinforced with new bearers attached as splints, although the new timbers seemed to have been covered with mud to conceal the work. This was definitely looking promising. I called Ali again – they'd followed our progress to the coast but had now dropped back. I told him that there was nothing to see and that it was likely to be a long wait. Sayed told me that he'd better take his van down and park it next to the shack – this was where the pick-up was supposed to be and they'd be expecting someone to be there when they arrived.

I was uneasy about the situation – there was something that didn't seem quite right, but perhaps it was the effect of this desolate place. These were the marshes of Charles Dickens' *Great Expectations* and I was expecting Abel Magwitch to come crawling out of the mud at any moment. I searched the mouth of the creek for any signs of a boat, but there was nothing. I looked around at the ring of seaweed indicating the recent high tide mark. From what I could tell there could be another two hours until high tide and the boat wasn't likely to come until it could get right up to the jetty.

I thought about the probable cargo. It was only a 15cwt van so that seemed to confirm that they weren't waiting for anything too heavy. It certainly could be drugs of some sort, though by now I realised they came in many different styles.

Across the mud flats, I could see the shipping in the river beyond. A few distant white triangles were visible, although the wind was light and sailing boats would be unlikely to be making any headway if they were sailing against the tide. This seemed such an unprepossessing place given the history that it had seen over the centuries. This was once the main artery of a huge empire and yet it looked like a grey backwater that was home to nothing more threatening than the occasional polluted oyster.

I found myself daydreaming again until I realised that a small motorboat was heading towards the entrance of the river. It was too far away to tell what it was, but it looked to be about forty-seven feet. Its almost insignificant wake suggested that it was capable of much more speed and as it closed, I could see that it was an elderly motor yacht with a small mizzen mast at its stern. If this was the boat that was bringing in drugs then it looked as though it might have brought them from the evacuation of Dunkirk.

Sayed had finally picked out the boat and opened the rear doors of the van and then walked to the edge of the jetty. The water had now risen up the supports making it accessible to shallow draft boats and I imagined that the approaching motorboat wouldn't draw much more than a couple of feet. I called Ali and told him to keep out of sight – which I realised was unnecessary but I felt a strange reassurance in having him and Giles Hathaway as backup. I didn't know whether they could track the elderly boat with their satellite system but presumably they had to identify it first and after they'd unloaded, it might be too late. Assuming this was our target, that is. But as they approached it became clearer that they were heading for the jetty. A man came out of the cabin and stood on the foredeck with a line which he tossed to Sayed as the boat gunned its engines to push it through the last of the mud and bring it to rest alongside. Sayed tied the rope off as though accustomed to dealing with boats, which seemed unlikely coming from the heart of Afghanistan.

The crewman walked aft and hinged up the two leaves of a deck hatch which covered much of the stern deck. Another man came out of the cabin to help, and together they lifted out boxes and put them on deck.

When they'd got a pile of them, they climbed out and started unloading them over the side onto the jetty. Although they were bulky, they didn't seem to be particularly heavy and they moved them easily. Eventually they had a pile of boxes and I wondered whether they were all going to fit in the van. Sayed went over and reversed the truck down to the jetty and they started loading but from what I could see, they'd hardly addressed any words to him.

When they'd finished, Sayed shut the doors of the van and pulled out his mobile phone. From what he'd told me, he'd have no idea where he was supposed to be taking them and I guessed he was waiting for a call to give him directions.

Meanwhile, I phoned Ali to see if he'd seen the transfer. 'We'll stay with Sayed,' he told me. 'Can you go with him?'

I thought about that. 'No. I think I'll stay here. There's something not quite right about this. It's too easy.'

'Go with him, otherwise you'd be wasting your time. Go back with Sayed and we can find out where he's taking them and then set up surveillance. Why stay?'

To be honest, I couldn't really answer that question, I had a nasty feeling that things weren't quite as they appeared and I wanted to see if anything else happened. 'Sayed can ring me when he knows where he's going, and you're following him anyway. I need you to send someone to collect me. When it's all over.'

'It *is* all over. Jeff and I will come and pick you up.'

'No. I want to see what happens.'

'If you do, you'll have to find your own way home and there aren't any passing taxis at this time of night.'

I checked my phone. 'I've got a couple of bars, I can call a taxi.' I couldn't see why he was so keen that I left with Sayed.

'I thought you trusted him. Do you think he might be setting you up?'

I wasn't going to tell him that the tide had turned and the old wooden cruiser wasn't going anywhere now for at least eight hours. 'We'll see when this is all over,' I said, although I wasn't sure we would recognise the end when we saw it. If what we had seen this afternoon was indeed the start of a new campaign then it might not be over for a very long time.

I watched as Sayed got into the van and drove it back up the track and out of sight behind a training bank.

Hathaway gave me a quick call to say they were following. 'A textbook operation. Couldn't have gone better. He's not going to get away from us now – we've got four cars following, but it always helps to have someone on the inside. We'll let you know how it pans out.'

Four cars? And they couldn't even spare one for me. Glumly, I hunkered down into the hollow I'd made by the bush and checked out the boat through my binoculars. There was little sign of life – both men had gone back inside the cabin and I couldn't see in through the windows. By now, the boat had settled into the mud and was listing at a slight angle. I went over the events in my mind trying to pinpoint why I had this feeling that it wasn't quite over. Whoever was controlling them must have rumbled that Khazim might be under surveillance – people like that are professionally suspicious and switching drivers at the last moment could have been a natural precaution. Switching drivers? I realised it probably wasn't just the drivers they switched, it could have been the vans as well since Giles and Ali couldn't have checked out which driver they were using.

The more I thought about it the more I realised I must have been right. There was a second van and Khazim was driving it. Why else would the boat still be here? They had enough time after unloading to pull themselves out of the mud and motor back out to sea. The way they'd arrived at precisely the right tide suggested that they'd checked this out before and would have known exactly how long they had before they got stuck.

What was it Sayed had said? Decoy? Did they suddenly decide to use him as a decoy? It would explain why they hadn't bothered to give him details of what he was supposed to be doing. As I thought about it, I became even more certain that they hadn't finished here but the question also raised itself – did Sayed know about this? Had he been stringing me along all this time? Perhaps someone knew we were onto them and decided to switch drivers at the last moment. But all that would have to wait – if I was right I had to tell Ali to get Hathaway and his team back here. I looked at my watch – the light was already starting to fade and it would be dark shortly. I brought out my phone and texted him: "Sayed probably decoy. Real delivery later today. Send backup." I looked across at the motorboat. They'd turned on the saloon lights and I could see silhouettes moving about the cabin, but there was nothing more I could do. I felt sure that Khazim would be here soon – perhaps they'd arranged it for darkness.

Chapter Twenty-Two

It must have been nearly an hour later that I saw the jetty lit up by someone opening the cabin door. I could make out the two men going back to the deck hatch and open it up again. This time they brought out some more cases and moved them across to the wooden walkway as before. As they closed the hatch, a beam of headlights travelled across the marshes behind me and I instinctively crouched down. Lights approached down the path as another white 15cwt van pulled up. A young man got out – it must have been Khazim – he reversed down to the jetty and got out and opened the rear doors. He shook hands with the crew and together they carried the boxes into the back of the van. By this time it was almost dark and there wasn't much I could see outside of the cabin lights.

It took them over an hour to load the van and they exchanged few words before Khazim returned to the van and drove off. I watched the red lights disappear up the path and they were finally lost in the darkness.

Back at the boat, the men had gone inside and I could see a new light through a lower porthole. It seemed they might be getting some rest before setting off on the next tide. If they were really concerned that they had been watched then they knew that it would be dark when they left and no satellite could follow them out.

At that moment my phone vibrated. I pulled it out and read the message from Ali: "There's no point waiting. Come back to the main road, we'll pick you up there." Casting one last glance at the boat, I could see that nothing had changed so I stood up and stretched. Fortunately, there was enough moon for me to find my way back up the path. They'd obviously timed it for a spring tide and the more I thought about it the more I realised how carefully planned this operation had been. All we had to do now was follow Khazim, but I guessed they'd already lost him in the darkness.

As I reached the junction with the main road, a car flashed its lights and I walked over and got in. It must have been nearly three hours since they'd left to follow Sayed. There were now two vans on the road and we still didn't know what was in them.

As we drove off, I tried phoning Sayed but it went to voicemail. I left a message asking him to phone me, which was a bit pointless since he'd know that I was trying to contact him but at least it made me feel a bit better. I told the driver to head back to London and tried Ali but that too wasn't answered. I hoped they hadn't lost Sayed – since they couldn't spare one of their four cars they wouldn't have much by way of excuse if they had.

It was frustrating to think that we'd been following the wrong van and even more so that I couldn't decide whether Sayed was in on it and had been deliberately misleading me, or whether someone else had been laying a false trail. If it had been Sayed, he'd done a pretty good job since it had never occurred to me to doubt him, but as I thought back there were numerous little things that might have told me someone had been trying to mislead us. My thoughts were interrupted by the phone – I checked and it was Hathaway's number. At least he was keeping me informed even if I had sent him off following the wrong person.

I answered the phone but it was Ali. 'It's all been unloaded. Hathaway's watching from around the corner. It's a small trading estate in east London – anonymous and like dozens of others. We'll set up observation to see who comes and collects it.'

'I don't think anyone will. Didn't you get my message? You've been following the wrong van.'

'What! What are you talking about?'

I explained that Khazim had arrived with a second van and loaded up with new crates. 'That must be the real consignment. My guess is that the crates Sayed's delivered are probably empty.'

'No chance. They wouldn't go to all this trouble if it wasn't the real shipment. I think you're wasting your time.'

'We'll see. Sayed doesn't necessarily know that Khazim was given a second van nor that the crates he collected are empty – assuming they are, that is.'

'So if he was the decoy, where's Khazim with the real goods?'

I took a deep breath. I hadn't had much of a reputation before this but now I'd set up what looked as though it was going to be a fiasco, no one would be in the least interested in what I had to say. 'I don't know,' I said finally. 'By the time I caught up with the car you'd sent, Khazim was long gone.'

'And could be anywhere?'

'And could be anywhere,' I agreed although I didn't like the hint of triumph in Ali's voice. 'Where are you, anyway?'

Ali gave me a postcode which I keyed into my phone. By now we weren't that far away but there didn't seem much point joining them. My phone buzzed with a second incoming call – it was Sayed. If he was phoning me after all that had gone on, he was either innocent or had the nerves of a fighter. Or both, I thought as Sayed told me where he was. I checked the postcode and it was the same place.

'You've dropped off the cases?'

'Yes. Were they still following? Have they found the place?'

'You mean the industrial estate? Yes, they've found it.'

'And they're watching it?'

'Yes, but I don't think they'll be much to see. I think those cases were empty and that you were called in as a decoy at the last moment. Either there was a leak or you knew about it from the beginning.'

The silence was long enough for me to start to think that we'd been disconnected. 'Was it Khazim?' Sayed asked eventually. 'If you say that I was the decoy then did Khazim make the real collection?'

'You don't know?' I asked bitterly. 'Weren't you in on this all along? Didn't you lead us into a cul de sac while Khazim took the real guns?'

Sayed laughed, although I couldn't see anything funny in the situation. 'I wondered about that. I was a bit suspicious when they suddenly gave me the keys to another van, while Khazim still kept the one they'd bought him. I wondered why we needed two vans.'

'That's not much help. We've lost Khazim and he could be anywhere by now.' Sayed laughed again, but before I could say anything he explained what he'd done, and this time I laughed as well. I should never have doubted him.

I immediately redialled Hathaway and this time he answered. 'Have you still got your tracking equipment with you?' I asked. 'If you have, I suggest you turn it on and locate the tracker you gave me. Sayed told me that before he left, he managed to fix it onto Khazim's van. You can find out where he is by following that.'

I woke up suddenly the following morning, convinced that I'd failed to stop a terrorist attack. But as I slowly gained consciousness, I remembered that despite my suspicions, Sayed had proved reliable – although there must have been times when he doubted that the side he'd chosen was the right one. What I couldn't work out was why they switched drivers at the last moment. But this was a distraction from the imminent vaccination programme and Sally had promised to get me more detailed information about the vaccines but more importantly the timetable for delivery. She'd be at her surgery that morning but I called and left a message asking her to contact me urgently. I wondered how many messages she received were seen as urgent.

Sally returned my call and agreed to come over for a quick lunch on her way from the surgery in south London to the aid agency's offices in Westminster.

Sitting later on deck drinking a morning coffee, I considered my position. I'd been given the brush-off first by Ken Maxwell and then finally, last night, by Giles Hathaway who now seemed to be working closely with Ali. At least they'd managed to track the final destination of the second consignment to another industrial unit in north London and made sure their surveillance was as solid as it was inconspicuous. He told me that they'd also sent a team to track the boat when it finally left the jetty on the next tide.

I'd prepared a selection of simple salads which I took up on deck to the cockpit table. Sally arrived, as usual in a rush, sat at the table and took out a package from her bag. 'These are the details of the immunisation programme. The contract has already been let, but I'll tell you about that later. I'm starving.' I put a plate down in front of her and she reached out and helped herself to the salads. 'Simple but delicious,' she said. 'I see you haven't lost your touch.'

'I wanted you to know what you're missing,' I said, admittedly a bit smugly.

'So how are you and Greta making out?' Sally asked between mouthfuls. 'She told me she's still seeing you.'

'I think we're getting on well.' I said it warily. I still wasn't sure of what Sally thought about my friendship with Greta but I was concerned at what she would think if it got any further than that.

'She's not right for you, you know. She wouldn't put up with you the way I did.'

'But you didn't put up with me, did you? You always wanted too much and I couldn't ever match up to your ideals.'

Sally laughed. 'For all your confidence, you don't know yourself very well, do you? What are you spending so much time on this vaccination programme for if it's not idealism?'

'It's not idealism, I want to see things through once I've started.'

'Same thing – it's still aiming for an ideal and Greta's going to find that very wearing. I have warned her.'

'Do I detect a note of jealousy?' I noticed her blushing so added quickly, 'But at least this time I'm doing something tangible. In the army I often felt as though I was continuing a job started centuries ago which wouldn't be finished for centuries more. An endless treadmill where it was difficult to see what good you were doing.'

'You didn't say that when you were in the army. You seemed to enjoy most things about it.'

'Most things, yes. But ultimately it's no different from you – you want to make a difference and that's difficult in such a large organisation.'

'Being a doctor isn't all it's cracked up to be. It's still more an art than a science and we can't get everything right. But I try.'

I laughed. 'You can say that again. When we were married, you did little else but try. There wasn't much room left for me. But Greta's not like that. She's not competitive like you, she takes things much as she finds them. You always wanted to change things.'

'And you didn't? I sometimes felt like looking out of the window to see if you'd arrived on a white charger. Anyway, don't be fooled by Greta. She can be very tough when she needs to be. She's not as easy-going as she appears. That's why I don't think the two of you are going to make it. I think you should pull out before you get too committed.'

I hesitated. I didn't want to look too sure of myself. 'We'll see. Shall we get on with this?' I picked up the package and leafed through it. There were pages of technical specifications which I didn't understand, along with a timetable that had to be met. Although I couldn't really judge, the bulk of the documents themselves indicated the size and scope of the programme. The list of participating organisations alone ran to almost a page. I picked at my salad as I skimmed the documents. 'It all looks very thorough.'

'It should be.' Sally helped herself to more salad. She'd always had a hearty appetite. 'It's supposed to be a flagship programme and they've got great hopes that it will become the model for future projects.'

I flipped through the pages until I came to the name of the contractor. 'I already knew it was Tau Pharmaceuticals – it's where we first found the fake Oxaban.' I thought about this for a moment. 'But why would they give this contract to a business that's already under suspicion?'

'Probably because they put in the lowest tender. These are public organisations running the programme and they need pretty good reasons if they're not going to accept the lowest tender.

If they're planning to send fakes instead then their costs are minimal and they can undercut everyone.'

'But Tau doesn't manufacture. They buy everything in from Bakaar and we still don't know how the fakes are made. What would happen if vaccinations were counterfeits?'

'I've been thinking about that ever since you told me about this.' Sally hesitated and looked down at her plate before continuing. 'I don't like to admit this but looking at the way the programme is organised it's quite possible we wouldn't even know it was happening. We might only find out about it some years afterwards – when patients died – and by then it would be too late.' She looked up at me and I thought I saw her eyes water. 'I'm afraid that if the vaccines were fakes then whoever supplies them is likely to get away with it and make a fortune. This is one of the largest vaccination programmes ever organised. It simply doesn't bear thinking about if it should go wrong. You have to do something.'

'How much time do you think we have?'

'It's imminent.' Sally put her fork down and took a sip at her water. 'Whoever's supplying the contract will probably have to work around the clock to meet that deadline. Have you any idea what you can do next?'

'Do?' I said it absently. The thought that had been nagging me for the past week was nearing the surface. 'What did you say?'

'I asked how you were going to follow it up.'

'No. No, before that. You said something about meeting deadlines.'

Sally looked at me strangely. 'I only said that they will have to work around the clock to meet the deadlines.'

I stood up suddenly, knocking over her glass of water. 'That's it! I've got it! They work around the clock! It's got to be the night shift!'

'What is it? What's the night shift?' Sally was mopping up the water I'd spilled. 'What's got into you?'

I pulled out my phone and dialled Ken Maxwell's number. 'Ken? It's me. I've realised it's the night shift. The counterfeits are made by the night shift. I'm coming over now.'

Chapter Twenty-Three

I grabbed the folder. 'Sorry – I've got to go, can you leave the keys in the post box?' I didn't give Sally time to argue and ran down the pontoon. Luckily, a taxi was cruising by and I told him to go to River House at Vauxhall Cross, and jumped in.

I was half way there when Ken rang back.

'I got your message,' he said. 'I didn't expect to hear from you so soon.'

'Never mind about that. I've worked out how they do it. I'm on my way to see you now.'

'You say it's the night shift? What's the night shift?'

'I'll tell you when I get there. Tell the desk to expect me. If you can get hold of Brent so much the better. Tell him it's urgent.' With that, I hung up before he could ask any more questions. I needed to get things clear in my mind before I told MI6 about it. I looked back over my conversations in India, and became even more convinced that I had to be right.

The journey to Vauxhall Cross was across London and I resigned myself to the inevitable traffic. By the time I got there, I had my theories all worked out.

'What's the rush?' Ken Maxwell said, as he led me up to his office. 'I was in the middle of a meeting when you phoned. I don't know why you should expect me to drop everything just for you.'

'It's not for me, it's for what I've got to tell you. I've finally worked out how they do it.' Ken opened the door and I followed him into the office and sat down. 'Is Brent coming?'

'He told me he was on his way. He's not convinced it will be worth it, but at least he's giving you the benefit of the doubt. Me? I'll reserve judgement.'

'It's the night shift. In the Mumbai factory, they have a separate night shift. The manager, Ahmed Bashara, told me that they only run a night shift when there's something urgent but that it's a separate operation. I remember thinking at the time that sounded a bit odd. They have a different night manager and different staff. It's the perfect cover: where can you hide the illegal manufacture of fake pharmaceuticals if not in a pharmaceutical factory?'

Just then the phone rang. 'It's Brent,' Ken said. 'Let's wait until he gets here.'

I was too impatient to stop. 'We couldn't work out where the fake drugs were coming from. I thought it was through the logistics company, Comar, but now I realise why Ansaar had never heard of them.'

The door opened and Brent was shown in by one of the runners from the front desk. 'This better be good,' he said, sitting down next to me. 'Okay, run it up the flagpole.'

I brought out the folder that Sally had given me. 'This has the details for the inoculation programme. Vaccinations against malaria, measles and meningitis. If I'm right then I think whoever is responsible for the night shift at Mumbai will be gearing up to supply this.'

'Night shift?' Brent asked, taking the documents. 'You dragged me here to tell me they're working overtime?'

'Philip thinks that the fakes are produced in the same Bakaar factory in Mumbai but by a separate team operating a night shift. It seems a bit far-fetched to me.'

Brent flipped through the pages. 'Perhaps you're not so stupid after all,' he said finally. 'It's been known before but generally in smaller production facilities. Not one as big and sophisticated as Bakaar's Mumbai operation.'

'That's the beauty of it,' I said. 'They told me that their machines could make almost anything and to the highest standards.

They can produce antimalarials containing only what they want to put in. With no active ingredients, the cost to make them is virtually nothing while they can sell it for millions in profit.'

'So what about the distribution?' Ken Maxwell asked. 'How does that work?'

'We saw that they'd set up a parallel distribution operation. What I didn't realise was that there was a parallel manufacturing operation as well. That's why both the genuine and the fakes were made in the same factory and collected by the same transport company and put in the same shipping container for export. It was the perfect cover – nobody could have worked that out. There was no sign of anything wrong. We only got to find out about it when we tracked that consignment and discovered that it was effectively hijacked in Zanzibar. They took the container off the plane, removed the counterfeits and sent the rest on its way.'

'It still seems a bit far-fetched,' Ken Maxwell said. 'Knocking off substandard copies at night of products they make properly during the day.'

'If you think about what you've just said, it makes perfect sense. Where better to make fakes than in a factory that makes the real thing?'

'That still doesn't explain how they're ultimately distributed.' Brent put down the papers. 'What's your great theory saying about that?'

I ignored his habitual sarcasm. 'That's why they need the Ansaar operation, because it supplies the whole of East Africa, not just Kenya. The supplies sent from the Mumbai factory to Kenya and then to the Tau facility in Mombasa are completely clean. If anyone carries out an investigation they're not going to find anything wrong. The fakes have to be sent in the same shipment so that no one knows they exist.

'I went round that factory myself and investigated the transport company. They knew they were being investigated and tried to warn us off by beating up the driver. We realised that we'd stumbled on something but I couldn't work out how they were doing it. It was the perfect cover. By diverting them to Zanzibar they can operate in near secrecy and there's no danger of getting them mixed up. The real drugs have been laundered and are sent on clean while the fakes are offloaded in Zanzibar and then sent onto wherever they're going on the mainland. It's almost fool proof and they can carry on doing it for weeks – or even months – until the vaccination programme is finished.'

'Maybe.' Maxwell was still making heavy weather of this. 'But why couldn't they separate them out in Mumbai and send the fakes directly to a wholesaler on mainland Africa?'

'Because of the risk of discovery. They're concealing the independent night shift, because the despatches are collected by the same company and are sent as a single shipment. No one would think to look into the Mumbai operation and by the time the consignments reach Mombasa they're still clean. It's the diversion to Zanzibar where the switch takes place – they keep back the fakes while sending on the genuine ones.'

'You still haven't answered me,' said Brent impatiently. 'How does the Zanzibar operation distribute them?'

'I haven't worked out all the details yet, but I suspect that it's another parallel operation once it reaches the mainland. The fakes are taken by dhow to various points on the east coast and then to warehouses in Kenya, Tanzania and probably Mozambique as well. But if you study the documents detailing this new programme, the vaccines have to be delivered directly to the local clinics so they wouldn't even get to the warehouses. No one would find out. Even if they were delivered to local distribution points they probably keep supplies of the genuine article so if they're tested they'll pass. My guess is that, if you look into it, you could find this is the result of Jamaal Bakaar's fanaticism.'

'That's absurd.' Ken Maxwell was shaking his head. 'The Bakaar family is one of the most respected families in India. There's no way that Ajmal Bakaar would get involved in this. Apart from anything else, he doesn't need to – he's got more money than he could ever want.'

'I don't think Ajmal Bakaar knows anything about this. I don't think his cousin Ahmed Bashara knows anything either, even though he's running the Mumbai operation. When I asked him he didn't know anything about this vaccination programme which I thought was odd. I think there must be someone above him who's organised this second night shift. Someone closely associated with Jamaal Bakaar.'

'But Jamaal Bakaar is a pillar of the Kenyan establishment.'

'That's a cover. I've met him and he's a dangerous man – he had the driver half killed in Mumbai.' I turned to Brent. 'If I'm right, then that programme would be too good for them to miss. There aren't many people who are able to supply a contract this big so my guess is that Jamaal Bakaar sets up a fake company to put in in a high bid, leaving the field open for him to submit a lower tender price to win the contract. They then source the contract from the fakes made by the night shift in Mumbai that have cost virtually nothing. He not only cleans up with a huge profit but furthers his warped view of *jihad*.'

'But why should they need to take such a huge risk? If they got found out it would be the end of them.'

'Not necessarily. They would simply blame it on some of their more junior managers, which I think is probably the case with the Mumbai operation. You're also assuming that they might get found out, but there's no reason why they should. Once the vaccines are sent out and used, no one would be any the wiser. Until now there's been no suspicion that there could be anything wrong. We've only found out ourselves by accident. From their point of view, it probably seems safe.'

'Even so, why would Jamaal Bakaar be involved in anything like that?' Maxwell was clearly not going to accept my theories without a fight. 'The family's got all that money. Why would he get involved in something criminal?'

Brent turned to Ken. 'You know, the kid could be right but don't let it go to his head. After he told us about his meeting with Jamaal, I had him looked into in more detail. We've had reports that Jamaal might be an Islamic activist – albeit behind the scenes. There've been reports that he might have been bankrolling some of the Al-Shabaab units.'

'That would make sense,' I interjected. 'I introduced myself when I went to his compound in Mombasa and he brushed me off. I saw some of his collection of Islamic art and some of it must be priceless.'

'Just because he collects Islamic art doesn't make him a supporter of terrorism,' Maxwell said.

'But it puts him pretty close to them,' I countered. 'He's a noted ascetic and told me he disapproves of much of the West's influence. He thinks we should go back to simpler ways.'

'Like Sharia law?'

I couldn't tell whether Maxwell was being sarcastic. 'Why not? It's not so far-fetched. It's possible, isn't it, Brent?'

'This is your show, but I think Phil could be right,' he said and once again I winced, but said nothing. 'We haven't got anything concrete on Jamaal but it adds up. What worries me though, is this.' He held up the tender documents. 'According to the date on these, deliveries have to be started in the next few days. Let me make a call to my office. They keep a register of all these programmes.' He brought out his phone, and started to dial.

'That won't work in here,' Ken said. 'All non-service mobiles are screened. You'll have to use the landline.' He reached over to his phone and dialled a code. 'Here. You can dial now.'

Brent took the phone and checked the number from his mobile. After being transferred a few times, he read out the reference number of the vaccination programme and waited. 'They're checking it,' he said to us with his hand over the mouthpiece. We all waited. 'Yes,' he said into the phone. He made a few notes on the pad. 'Okay, got that. Thanks.' He hung up and looked at us. 'Looks like the kid might have hit the bullseye. They're running behind schedule and they're due to make their first deliveries any time now.'

Ken Maxwell wouldn't give up. 'But I still can't believe that someone in Jamaal Bakaar's position could be involved in this.

Why would he be instrumental in putting potentially thousands of children at risk by supplying worthless vaccinations? Why would he do it?'

'One of the reports I read was from a rare interview he gave some years back,' Brent said. 'He suggested that immunisation was some kind of western plot to influence people. But when the interviewer asked him to repeat it, he waved it away as though he'd said more than he meant to.'

I thought we were starting to wander from the point. 'Whatever crazy views he has, we have to put the Bakaar facility under surveillance. Ken, you need to get hold of Ranish in Mumbai. He knows the place and the set-up with the transport company. If you explain that it's the night shift he should be looking at then we might get some notice if they're sending anything out.'

'Why don't we raid the Tau warehouse in Kenya?' asked Ken Maxwell.

'Firstly, because they haven't delivered the drugs for this immunisation programme yet. They haven't had time. Secondly, the tender states that the vaccinations have to be split up into individual packs for delivery directly to each of the immunisation stations and there are dozens of those and we can't track them all.' I looked across at Ken and it was clear that he still wasn't convinced. 'What have we got to lose?'

Finally he nodded and picked up the phone. 'Get me Ranish in Mumbai.'

Brent turned to me. 'Did you work all this out yourself? I wondered about you at the outset, but you seem to have come good.'

That was unusual praise from Brent, but I'd learnt not to take him at face value. 'So now I can come back on board and return to Zanzibar.' I said. 'There isn't enough time to brief anyone else.'

'I don't know about that,' Brent said. 'If you're right, then Jamaal Bakaar will have you in his sights. Last time it was the driver, but this time it would be you he'd go after.'

'I'd be going in and out fast. He wouldn't have time to do anything.'

'You didn't do too well with Ansaar, did you, kid?' Brent said. 'Not your finest hour. The cavalry had to rescue you.'

Ken came off the phone. 'Okay. That's sorted. Ranish will set up surveillance and keep us informed. I told him to pay special attention to any early morning collections by Comar, which are likely to be the fakes and that was the one he should follow.'

'Meanwhile I'd better get out to Zanzibar,' I said quickly, hoping they'd see it as the next logical step.

'There's plenty of time,' Ken said. 'It takes at least a week by sea to Zanzibar.'

'That's if they send it by sea,' I said. 'They didn't last time. But however they send them, we can't afford to wait. My guess is that they'll still send them via Zanzibar because they haven't had time to set up an alternative. I think I need to get out there.'

'It's getting dangerous now,' Brent said. 'Jamaal Bakaar is ruthless and if he's really Al-Shabaab then they don't take prisoners.'

I sensed they were trying to head me off. 'Look, I've called it right most times so far. Work it out for yourselves. Apart from the fact it's on the way to Kenya, they need to separate the fakes from the full-strength deliveries. My bet is that they'll still send a small consignment of full-strength drugs so that they can show them to anyone who investigates. Meanwhile, the much bigger consignment is being diverted to Zanzibar and I think with a contract this big they won't need to take them to the Kenyan warehouse; they'll make them up into individual packages for each inoculation station. Once they're landed in Kenya, we'd never find them.'

'Why don't we go to the vaccination stations and check them there?' This was Maxwell again.

'From what I read about this programme, the whole point is that they're being taken to the individual villages, rather than asking people to go into the towns. It's difficult enough to persuade people to take the injections without asking them to travel for a day to the nearest town. Programmes often fail because people simply refuse to go that far and so this time the programme's being dispersed to each village.'

'Can't they test them first?' This time it was Brent who appeared to be doubting my plan.

'They're always supposed to test a trial, but from what my ex-wife told me, most of these local health centres don't have the right equipment and even if they do, they don't necessarily know how to use it.' I stopped and looked at both of them, but they finally seemed to have run out of questions. 'Can I go now?'

Ken Maxwell sighed. 'Okay, but I'll send Dickson out to look after you.'

I went back to the boat to throw a few things into an overnight case, but as I was about to step onto the gangplank I realised that something was wrong. I looked over the boat carefully. At first I couldn't see anything different, and then I realised that the forward hatch was open. Perhaps Sally had opened it before leaving but that didn't seem likely – she'd locked up and left the keys in the mail box. Anyone who'd been watching would see where to get the key so I shouldn't have been surprised that someone had got on board – the question was: who?

I took a lump of wood from my wood pile and instead of taking the gangplank, I used a foothold on the bows to swing myself up. Fortunately the heavy boat barely moved as I climbed on board. I waited for a moment and listened out for any sound, but beyond the rushing of the water past the hull there was nothing. I hoped it would cover any noise I made as I carefully lowered myself down the forehatch. There was a drop of about a foot down to the lower deck but that would make too much noise so I swung myself across and jumped onto a foam mattress, irrationally holding my breath.

At that moment there was a thump against the hull – probably a piece of driftwood, but I heard the saloon door open and hoped they had gone to take a look. It meant one less to deal with.

I reached down and took off my shoes and padded quietly along the companionway and pushed the door slightly open so I could look in. A man was standing with his back to me looking up to where I saw the shadow of another man out on deck. This had to be my moment. I pushed open the door and ran at him swing my bock of wood up at his head. If it had been cricket, the ball would have cleared the stadium roof. He fell into a rumpled heap at my feet and I stepped over him and went out on deck.

The other man heard me and turned back to face me and immediately went into a crouch, balancing lightly on the balls of his feet and watching me warily. I realised that these weren't simple thieves, they looked and acted like professionals. I feinted to his left and he tried to hit me with his right hand but I stepped back and prodded him with the wooden club. He backed away against the saloon windows, leaving him nowhere to go. We sized each other up and then I feinted again but this time pulled back and as he parried the air, I rammed the wood into his stomach. He gasped and tried to grab it but I pulled away.

'You want to tell me who sent you?' I didn't expect an answer and didn't get one. Instead he launched himself at me suddenly and his weight pushed me over onto my back. He jumped on top of me and immediately grappled for the club. I kneed him in the groin and managed to roll away but caught my foot on a stanchion and lost my balance and he jumped on me again but I held the club in both hands in front of me and jabbed at his throat. He grunted again – obviously a man of few words – but I was able to get to my knees and swing the club at him. He backed off and I stood up facing him again. This had gone on too long.

I kept prodding him and he backed off again until he was against the railings. 'Can you swim?' I asked him. He glanced backwards and I took the moment to ram him again in the stomach and as his head came forward, I hit the side of his head as hard as I could and he fell onto the deck unconscious.

I didn't have much time and ran to my rope cupboard and managed to get both of them trussed up before they regained consciousness. I debated whether to phone Ken Maxwell, thinking it would only make him more concerned about sending me out there, but I couldn't see I had any choice. Nor could I work out how they'd found me so quickly until I remembered that I hadn't used my burner phone to call. I kicked myself for my stupidity – they must have hacked it which explained why they got here so quickly.

I pulled out my burner and called Ken and asked him to get some of his heavies over and I stood guard until they arrived.

They carried both of them ashore and if they were surprised at the state of them, they didn't show it. I rang Ken again and told him to keep them both in isolation. 'We don't want them reporting back to whoever sent them. If it's really Jamaal who wanted me out of the way, then we don't want him to find out what happened.'

Chapter Twenty-Four

Dickson was supposed to meet me at Zanzibar Airport but didn't show. After the attack on me in Wapping, I feared that someone had got to him and I knew that I was now being watched. I had intended to go back to Africa House, but realised that it would be too dangerous; still, I took a taxi to the hotel but when he stopped outside I asked him to pick me up from around the back. To make sure, I told him I'd pay him double and took my bag out and walked through the hotel and out through the kitchens. At first I couldn't see the taxi but eventually he pulled around the corner and I got in and directed him to the city beach where Dickson had found a boat before. After haggling with one of the ferries, I agreed on a price which I realised was probably twice what it was worth, but at least I was away from the main town and heading for Grave Island.

As I landed on the island, Ariana saw me and came over. 'Back again? Still staking out the place opposite? I hope my island is going to feature in a film about it.'

'Not if I can help it. I need to hire a motorboat and thought you could help. The only boats I can see around here are dhows and that wouldn't be fast enough.'

Her usual amusement turned to outright laughter, throaty and uninhibited. 'The design might be many hundreds of years old, but that's because they go faster and further on the monsoon wind and it's why you'll find them everywhere along this coast. They're fantastic designs and I take one out whenever I can. We use Nazeem's boat when we want to take parties on trips to the other islands. I'll give him a call.' She brought out her cell phone and checked the signal before dialling.

'Yes,' she said after a rapid conversation. 'He's free for the next few days. You'll like his boat – it's got a long history of smuggling around the coast but hopefully those days are over – though you never know with Nazeem. I don't like motorboats, but even if I did, I wouldn't recommend one if you're following another boat, it would be too conspicuous. With a dhow it would be one amongst hundreds and no one would notice you.'

We walked back to the reception area and she pointed across to a dhow that was picking up a line from a mooring buoy. 'That's Nazeem, I'll take you out there.'

I followed her down to the small jetty on the beach where we got into a flat-bottom dinghy and she started up the outboard and we headed out.

Once on deck, she introduced me to the skipper who greeted me with an almost toothless smile. His already dark skin had been weathered into a deep teak texture by decades out in the tropical sun, making it impossible to even guess at his age.

There were three other men lounging around on deck, and a boy, who couldn't have been much older than twelve – perhaps Nazeem's son. Perhaps they were all Nazeem's sons – even grandsons. Ariana started speaking to Nazeem in English but then changed to rapid Swahili and after a while, she turned back to me. 'That's all arranged. He pretends he doesn't speak English but he's fluent when he wants to be. He's going to take the boat back to Stone Town and fill up with diesel, then they'll come back and wait for you here.'

'Diesel?' I repeated. 'It has an engine?'

Ariana laughed – I was starting to warm to her infectious good humour. 'An auxiliary engine. It won't push her along as fast as the monsoon wind, but it's useful in calms or when manoeuvring. It's rather old, but I think it should be reliable. It works more from habit than anything else, and it also means that you've got 12-volt power. And there's another thing,' she added, pointing to a post fixed behind the wheelhouse. 'It's got a small radar unit. I made him install it before we allowed him to take our visitors. It's not very powerful, but it lets you see where you're going. If you're going to be following a boat at night then you'll probably find it useful.'

I went with her back to the reception desk and checked my satellite phone but there were no new messages. I was getting increasingly worried about Dickson and I called London to see if they'd heard anything. They'd gone into full alert in Nairobi and a team was being flown out to look for him. Ranish in Mumbai had reported that a large consignment had been collected from the Bakaar night shift and taken straight to the airport and should arrive in Zanzibar that morning. With the tight programme imposed by the vaccination contract, I should have realised that airfreight was the only way they could meet the timescale. Given how long it had taken me to get here from London, the consignment could already have landed and be on its way to the Ansaar warehouse.

I debated whether to stay on the island but decided that the dhow would be safer – that way I could see anyone who came near. It had refuelled and was now lying on a mooring off the island. Ariana's boatman took me out and I could see the Ansaar warehouse from the boat's stern where a large dhow had been brought up on the shore and people were loading it with small insulated boxes. I didn't know whether the vaccines were supposed to be refrigerated, but I supposed that if they were fakes, it wouldn't make much difference.

But there was still no news of Dickson – they'd traced him on the flight to Zanzibar but after that they'd heard nothing. From what I had seen of him, he was able to look after himself but this wasn't his home ground and anything could have happened. I was in a fever of impatience but also of anxiety. If they'd got Dickson then they'd certainly be looking for me. I hoped that it wouldn't occur to them to look for me on Grave Island, let alone out on the dhow.

Finally, at high tide, I watched as the dhow was pushed out to deeper water off the warehouse which indicated that they were getting ready to head off before the next tide, which made it later that afternoon. I'd brought my satellite phone and tracking computer and set them up in the shade of the dhow's doghouse, using a transformer to connect to the dhow's 12-volt batteries. I called Ken Maxwell so that he could monitor our progress back in London.

The sun was low behind Stone Town when I saw the last package being put on board. I watched as a tall man came out and called across to the boat. It must have been Ansaar himself sending them off and a figure at the prow start to pull up the anchor, and then the old dhow manoeuvred into the channel and hoisted their sail. I nodded to Nazeem, but he was already watching the boat closely. I saw the dim glow as he fired up the radar. There were boats all over the place even as darkness was falling and it was difficult to see the one we were following. I could make out the small light at the boat's stern and went over to the wheelhouse and pointed to a target on the radar. Nazeem nodded and handed the wheel over to one of his crew with some sharp instructions that didn't need translating.

As we sailed further away from Zanzibar Island, the other boats disappeared into the night, leaving the faint light of the dhow ahead of us, but even that was soon extinguished – presumably they thought the risk of collision was negligible away from the land. The sky was overcast and only a few stars were visible and the darkness was impenetrable. As I peered ahead, someone tapped me on the shoulder and I turned and saw one of the crew holding out a plate. I followed him forwards to a small cuddy where I was astonished to find a small oven lit by charcoal. The cook showed me what looked like goat's meat cooking on a skewer which he served me with some rice from a boiling pot. I took it forward and sat down and found it surprisingly good. I ate slowly watching the bow wave cream through the water, scattering sparks of phosphorescence into the air as the boat ploughed through the black sea. There was no sign of a light up ahead but I'd checked the track on the computer and could see the target on the antiquated radar unit. On our current course we were heading further south to the commercial port of Tanga. Although this was in Tanzania rather than Kenya, the border wasn't that far away to the north.

I tried to sleep but in spite of the gentle rocking of the boat, my head was swirling with anxiety at whether we might lose them in the darkness. What had started as a chance discovery of mislabelled drugs had turned into a desperate race to prevent what could be a major tragedy. I went back mentally through the steps we'd taken, but couldn't see where I'd ever had an alternative. This had to be the end of it.

I came to, suddenly aware that Nazeem was calling to me. I managed to get to my feet as he beckoned me to follow him back to the wheelhouse and the radar. We looked at the screen which was glowing a dull grey. 'No radar, no course,' Nazeem said.

I looked across to my computer which was linked to my satphone but all it could tell me was where we'd been heading before darkness made it lose the picture. 'Hold this course. They're not going to change it in the middle of the night unless they think they're being followed and I don't see how they could have spotted us amongst all those boats off Zanzibar.'

'No radar, no course,' Nazeem insisted. 'We go back.' With that he turned the wheel and the boat leaned into a curving turn heading back where we came from.

'Let me look at it.'

'No, it doesn't matter,' Nazeem said. 'Leave it.'

I ignored him and went to the radar set and fiddled with the connections at the back. It didn't take me long to see that the scanner unit had been unplugged, leaving the screen display an unhelpful grey. I glanced across at Nazeem who was watching me intently. He turned to one of his crew and spat out a command and I could sense the atmosphere change suddenly.

I heard the two crew members close up behind me but I tried to ignore them and went back to the computer screen. 'We can pick them up again when it gets light,' I said. 'We don't need the radar.' I hoped they wouldn't see me hit the redial button on the satphone. I turned to face the crewmen behind me. One of them was carrying a club and swinging it menacingly. He stepped towards me but on another sharp command from Nazeem, he stopped. I looked from them to Nazeem, but there were too many of them.

Nazeem smiled and spat over the side. 'You want the hard way?' he sighed. 'You should have left the radar alone.'

'You unplugged it yourself,' I said.

Nazeem shrugged. 'Perhaps. But we can't take you back now – I always wanted this to be easy. What's that?' he added, as he heard the satphone. One of the crew went over and picked it up. I couldn't hear if there was anyone on the other end, but Nazeem looked at me and shook his head. 'You won't need this,' he said and unplugged it and threw it overboard. 'You can dive for it but it's half a mile deep here. 'Search him,' he said and repeated it in Swahili.

I held up my arms – I had nothing to hide. 'Why are you doing this? If it's money, I can pay you whatever you want.'

'With people like you it's always money. There are more important things you wouldn't understand.' Nazeem said something rapidly in Swahili and two of the crewmen grabbed me under the arms. 'So what shall we do with you? I think it's better if you simply disappear we'll let the sharks deal with you.' He nodded to the men holding me. 'Kwaheri,' he said and I was pulled to the side of the boat and thrown in.

The shock of hitting the water made me gasp and I nearly took a lungful of seawater which would have finished it there.

When I'd orientated myself, I tried to swim back to the boat to hang on, but I heard them start the engine and watched helplessly as the boat disappeared into the darkness. The sky had now cleared and with just a sliver of a moon the stars were almost bright enough to see the horizon. Almost. The light wind left small waves which glistened with phosphorescence and in any other circumstances it would have been magical. I kicked off my shoes to give me more buoyancy and floated on my back.

The faint lights of the dhow were gone and there was nothing to see except a small disturbance on the surface a dozen metres away.

I watched as a trail of phosphorescence approached and then felt a nudge on my back and then a swirl of water washed over me. I forced myself to stay calm and treaded water as I looked around. My brain told me that I had nothing to fear, that I was only an object of curiosity and not a meal. But my guts told me otherwise and with difficulty I managed to stay quiet. I heard the swish of a tail behind me and turned to see a dorsal fin coming towards me. I moved onto my back and bent my knees.

When I felt the snout brush against me, I kicked out as hard as I could and there was a threshing of water and the fin disappeared into the blackness. Of course there were probably others, but I reassured myself that it was curiosity, rather than hunger, which made the shark approach. I lay on my back and floated – at least the tropical sea was warm and there was hardly a wind to ruffle the surface.

The nearest land was half a mile away – vertically down – otherwise we were twenty miles from Tanga and only the slightest possibility of a boat finding me before the sharks attacked again. I realised that not only was I going to be dead very shortly, but that I hadn't stopped the fake drugs which were on their way to the mainland. I'd failed.

I must have blacked out because I suddenly awoke and saw that the sun had come up and the reflection low over the water was blinding me. I looked around but there was nothing. I was sure that I'd heard something. I listened intently and then heard it again – it was the distinctive sound of rotor blades – a helicopter. I couldn't think what they could be doing out here unless they were looking for me.

I searched the sky but the reflections made it difficult and then suddenly a strobe blinded me as the blades of the helicopter flew across the sun. I couldn't think how I could attracted their attention until I realised that with the sea so calm they wouldn't see anything unless I started splashing. Splashing might attract the sharks, but I had no choice and I cupped my hands and scooped them across the surface of the sea making as much disturbance as I could.

I cried out but realised that nothing could be heard above the noise of the engine. I kept banging the sea but couldn't make out where the helicopter was headed but there was nothing else around me disturbing the surface. It was then that I heard a sort of klaxon and the sound of the rotors changed. I held up my hand against the sun, but there was no doubt that it was heading for me.

The downdraft of the rotor blades started to create turbulence in the water, making it difficult to hold my head above the waves but as I coughed out yet more seawater I saw above me a figure being lowered. As he reached me, he held out a sling and indicated that I should put it around me and when he was satisfied that it was secure, he signalled up to the winchman and I was raised up to the helicopter's cabin.

I managed to grab the side of the bulkhead and looked inside where Brent Hillman was grinning at me complacently. 'You can always rely on the US cavalry. Come on in.' he said and laughed.

Chapter Twenty-Five

'We'll go straight to Tanga,' Brent said. That's where they were heading. 'Got you some dry clothes. Thought you might need them.'

I took the clothes and removed my wet ones. 'What kept you?'

'Is that what you Limeys call gratitude?' Brent said, handing me a towel. 'You think I had nothing better to do than fly around the Indian Ocean looking for a minnow in a shark tank?'

I was starting to recover. 'Now that you mention it, I can't think of anything you could have done better. How did you find me?'

'Where else would you be, kid? Your satellite phone call gave me a bit of a clue, although I would probably have worked it out eventually.'

'My satphone?'

'When you called me, I couldn't hear what was going on but it gave me your position and then it went dead. I'd already flown down to our correspondent's bureau in Mombasa to see what was going on so I got their boys to take me out. You okay?'

I was shivering uncontrollably and my teeth were chattering. I rubbed myself hard with the towel to get back some circulation. To vomit some of the seawater, I retched helplessly.

'Over the side, kid. Don't want to mess up the chopper.' Brent watched unsympathetically and handed me a plastic bag.

'Where are we going?' I managed to ask before retching again. 'Need to get to Tanga.'

'We're on it. That's where you were heading when we lost contact. We've got your people waiting – a guy called Juma is there.'

I suddenly remembered my missing contact. 'Have you found Dickson yet?' I managed to croak.

'You Brits are working on that. They think they might have located him in Zanzibar.'

I said nothing while I got into the dry clothes and tried to get back some control over my limbs and what was left of my brain cells. The helicopter had its nose down and as far as I could tell was heading west where I could see the ribbon of low-lying land that had to be Tanga.

'Take it easy, kid,' Brent said in what, for him, passed as sympathy. 'We've got things under control.'

'We've got to meet Ansaar's boat. It must be there by now. It's got the fakes on board.'

'Easy. We'll be there soon and you can show us. Just take time to recover.'

I took the bag and retched some more but I was starting to feel better and I wanted to be ready for whatever we found in Tanga so I didn't want to show weakness. We were close to the land and I could see the long quay with several ships moored alongside, as well as a couple of dhows.

As if reading my thoughts, Brent said, 'Don't worry, your team was going to meet the dhow when it arrived. Skipper, can you put us down over there?'

The helicopter swayed as the pilot brought it down and landed gently. I followed Brent onto the quay and recognised Juma walking towards us. 'Have they found Dickson yet?' I asked – for some reason I felt responsible for him.

'Yes, a few hours ago. They raided Ansaar's house on the beach and found him locked up in some kind of cell. There were signs of torture that they'd carried out there but fortunately he was okay. They hadn't started on him.'

'Thank God for that.' I remembered my brief stay there. 'Now, which is the dhow we were following?'

'We worked out it must be this one. We extrapolated from the track it was on, although it turned up several hours after we expected it. And there was a truck at the entrance waiting to get in.'

'Only the one?' I asked. 'That's odd. There's supposed to be a small fleet of vans taking them directly to the inoculation stations. Have you looked on board yet?'

'No, we were waiting for you two, but are you sure this is the right consignment?' Juma asked. 'They haven't shown any signs of unloading yet.'

'Let's get on board and find out,' I said to Brent. 'But my Truscan is still on Nazeem's dhow, so it's going to be difficult to check them.'

'Relax, kid. We brought our own equipment with us.' He reached behind his seat in the helicopter and brought out a small box. 'Here we are,' he said, removing the machine and I saw it was very similar to the one I'd brought. 'This is even more accurate,' Brent said, unable to resist breast thumping. 'Made in the US of A.'

I wasn't going to argue with him and nodded to Juma who signalled to his people and jumped on board. Most of the crew were on deck and the skipper came to the side and asked what we wanted. Juma held out his identification and I followed him on board with Brent. I thought I recognised some of the boxes from the Ansaar warehouse but checked the manifest that the skipper was holding.

I moved further along the deck, matching the cases with the list until I came upon the boxes marked as malaria vaccines. I felt a new surge of excitement that I'd finally tracked them down and indicated the boxes to Brent. 'These are some of the ones from Zanzibar. Let's check them out.'

Brent took out a knife, opened the carton and took out a package of vaccines and handed me his measuring equipment. I called out to Juma to come and watch as I set it down and turned it on.

'Look at the printout here.' I pointed to the miniature screen. I placed some of the vaccine into the tray and set it working. The chromatograph profile of what the sample should look like appeared along the top and slowly a graph was drawn below it and as it worked its way to the end it became clear that they were the same.

'These aren't the fakes,' I said, shaking my head. 'We must have been following the wrong consignment. Are you sure it's the same boat?' All dhows looked pretty much the same to me.

Brent looked at the printout and shook his head. 'It must be the same boat. Just not the same cargo.'

'How did that happen? They were heading directly for Tanga.' Reluctantly, I climbed off the boat onto the quay and looked up as the van drove up to the dhow to start unloading. I paced up and down the quay, mentally retracing our steps.

Finally, I stopped in front of Juma. 'You say they arrived several hours late. That could have given them enough time to offload the cargo onto another boat. But are you sure this is the same boat?'

Juma stayed quiet, as if he didn't think it necessary to repeat himself and I thought about our chase. I couldn't see how Nazeem would have had time to report back, but since they'd got hold of Dickson, Ansaar must already know we might be onto them. He could have sent another boat and they transferred the cargo during the night knowing that we'd still be tracking the dhow to Tanga. Which meant that they could still be following their original plan and taking the vaccines to Shimoni. 'How far away is Wasini Island? If they did offload then the logical thing would be for them to take it onto Shimoni.'

'By sea it's just over thirty miles, but it's much longer by road. If they've gone to Shimoni, they'll be way ahead of us by now.'

'Yes, but there's only one road from the coast to the main Mombasa road, so that might give us time to cut them off.' I turned to Brent. 'Can we take the chopper? Fly across to Shimoni?'

'I can call Mombasa,' Juma said. 'They can cut them off on the road from Shimoni.' Then he added, 'Assuming that's where they've gone.'

'Where else would they go? Tanga's not far out of their way. They've got to be there and with the helicopter we could get there at about the same time.' I realised that I sounded more confident than I felt, but couldn't see what choice we had. We walked back to the helicopter and I showed the pilot the route to Wasini Island and he fired up the engines. As the rotor blades started, the crew of the Ansaar dhow rushed to the guardrail and looked on in alarm.

'Look at them. They thought we'd been fooled.' As I said it, I saw the skipper bring out his mobile phone and shouted out to Juma. 'Stop him! He's going to warn the other boat.'

Juma leaped athletically onto the dhow and took the phone from the skipper's hands. He gestured to one of the Tanzanian police and told him to round up their cell phones and keep them under observation.

'That was close,' I said to Brent as we climbed into the helicopter and Juma followed behind. I put on the headphones. 'All set,' I said to the pilot and buckled myself in.

We saw Wasini Island from some miles away and I told the pilot to circle. With the noise we were making, our arrival couldn't be called stealthy, and it certainly got their attention. We could see the entire scene laid out below us and a small dhow had been pulled up amongst the mangroves. There appeared to be a line of people starting to unload and already we could see a small pile of boxes building up on the roadway beside them. A line of vans was drawn up amongst the mangroves but the drivers were looking up at us and hopefully realising that they wouldn't be going anywhere.

I finally felt a slight relaxation in tension; this *had* to be the shipment from Zanzibar. The pilot put us down on the road and Juma rushed past me and started corralling the drivers into a group. I was afraid he might be outnumbered but at that moment reinforcements arrived from Mombasa.

All I needed to do was check the strength of the product. I took the Truscan and went over and opened one of the boxes and selected a sample to analyse.

After a few minutes, we had the result. Bingo! 'Virtually no active ingredients,' I said and turned to Brent.

'Okay, kid,' he said, 'You seem to have hit the bullseye again.'

'Only "seem"? Look at the print-out – that shows I'm right.'

'We could let them get through and follow them. This can only be part of the total programme. There are stations throughout the rest of East Africa which need deliveries. If we stop them now, the rest might get through.'

'Have you contacted Ranish in Mumbai? Are they still running a night shift and making collections early in the morning?'

'As far as I know.'

'We'll tell him to round up the Indian police and mount a raid on the Bakaar factory. Now we know they're fakes tell him to go to the airport and stop the next consignment to Zanzibar.'

'What are you going to do now?' Brent asked.

I laughed. 'I think I'll take the helicopter you've kindly lent and pay a visit on Jamaal Bakaar.'

'You'd better take me with you.'

'I'll drop you off in Mombasa but I've got to see Jamaal Bakaar on my own. This has become personal.'

After dropping Brent off at the airport, I told the helicopter pilot to fly directly to the Bakaar compound in Mombasa. They had plenty of room and I thought it would add sufficient drama to our arrival for even Jamaal Bakaar to take notice. I could see his assistant, Halim, running into the courtyard and trying ineffectually to wave us away. As the helicopter landed and rotors slowed, I jumped out and pushed past him, heading for the archway that I had seen Jamaal go through on my earlier visit.

It was dark inside the office – if it could be called an office – it looked more like a museum with dimly lit display cases along the walls, interspersed with exquisite tapestries tastefully lit with hidden lighting. As my eyes adjusted to the gloom, I could see Jamaal Bakaar sitting at a glass desk at the far end of the room. He said nothing as I approached and once again I felt that there was something about his stillness and his lack of emotion that was chilling. I sat down opposite him.

'We managed to stop it in time,' I said and waited for a response but still he said nothing. 'I worked out how you were doing it. You managed to produce the counterfeits right underneath our noses – it was very clever.'

Finally, Jamaal sighed. 'I suppose you wouldn't believe me if I told you that I didn't know what you're talking about?'

'Who else could have organised it? You can't hide behind the fake companies you set up. The vaccination contract might be in Tau's name, but it was Bakaar who supplied the counterfeits. It was you who arranged it.'

Jamaal gave a thin smile. 'You would have some difficulty proving that.'

'I don't think so. Now we know that you had a night shift producing counterfeit pharmaceuticals in your Mumbai factory, I don't think it would be too difficult to trace it back to you.'

'I would deny it and there would be nothing anyone could do. I carry quite a lot of respect here, so I would be careful what you say in public.'

'Ah yes. Your reputation for asceticism and piety. I don't think you'll be able to hide behind that when people discover the scale of the operation you've been running.'

'*I've* been running? I haven't been running anything.'

I found his impenetrable smugness infuriating and couldn't see how to get through to him. 'We know you have links with Al-Shabaab. That you finance some of their operations.'

'So now I'm a member of Al-Shabaab as well as a counterfeiter of pharmaceuticals? As I say, you can't prove any of this.'

'But you are sympathetic to them?'

'I've made no secret of my dedication to the Prophet. The influence of the western world on traditional Muslim culture here in East Africa is something I regret.'

'And so you're prepared to put thousands of lives at risk for your beliefs?'

'My beliefs!' He stood up and pointed his finger at me – he was shaking with anger. 'What do you know about my beliefs?

I made some enquiries about you and found that you were fighting in Afghanistan so you're the last person to talk about my beliefs. You mention thousands of deaths. What's the difference between that and what you were doing in Helmand?'

'How did you know I was in Helmand?' But as soon as I said it I felt I'd fallen into a trap.

'You're not the only one with intelligence resources. You were part of yet another western effort to interfere in a place you should have left alone.'

'Unlike you I was trying to do good over there. Trying to prevent the killing, not add to it.'

'There are things worth dying for,' he said immediately, and again I was struck by his conviction. There was no hesitation and his comments were made with an adamantine certainty.

'You think that killing children with adulterated vaccines can be justified? That children are a legitimate target?'

'There's always going to be collateral damage. It's unavoidable in war.'

I was so taken aback that for a moment I couldn't say anything. 'You think this is a war? And dead children just collateral damage? What kind of person are you?'

'I'm not someone who is to be judged by you,' he said and he was almost shouting. 'So, you think you've intercepted a consignment of counterfeit pharmaceuticals?'

'I don't think, I know they're counterfeit. I checked them myself.'

'But unimportant when set against the rest of the world,' he said and pounded the desk with his fist. 'We can't win every battle, but eventually we will win the war against the Western corruption that infects us. There are other battlegrounds apart from Kenya and East Africa. While you've been chasing your tail here you'll discover that your own Helmand is not immune.'

I was about to respond but then realised what he'd just said. 'What do you mean about Helmand? What's Afghanistan got to do with this?'

Jamaal said nothing, perhaps realising that he'd said too much. He sat down and stared at his desk. He was obviously making an effort to control himself.

Eventually he looked up. Once again, I got his thin smile which I wanted to scrape off with a razor. 'You will find out soon enough,' he said, and looked at me, his eyes burning with hatred. 'I think we're finished here, aren't we? You can't arrest me so I think you should leave.' He nodded through the window at the helicopter. 'And take that machine with you.'

I realised he was right, but as I left, I ran through what he had said in my mind. What did he mean about fighting more battles? I'd been so preoccupied with the deliveries to East Africa that I hadn't thought about anywhere else, but why should they limit themselves? I'd read enough about counterfeits to know that few places were safe and the most vulnerable were always going to be those with weak governments. Afghanistan! Was he hinting that there were other vaccination programmes, perhaps even as important as this one?

Chapter Twenty-Six

I ran to the helicopter but shook my head at the pilot. I wouldn't hear myself speak if he started the engines. I pulled out my phone and scrolled through to find Sayed's number. Since his last visit to Afghanistan, he'd made contacts with various pharmacies so if anyone knew about what was going on there it should be him. The phone rang and rang and I was about to give up when I heard his voice answering.

'Sayed, can you hear me?' There was a gurgling on the phone but finally I could hear him clearly. 'It's Philip and it's urgent. Can you contact the pharmacy in Chorjah?' At first he didn't understand what I was talking about, but then I realised that my call had come out of the blue and couldn't have made much sense to him. I hurriedly explained the situation and he finally said he would ring me back.

I told the pilot to drop me off back at the airport and anxiously watched my phone for Sayed's call but it took him over an hour before he finally came back to me. 'How did you know?' he started. 'Have you got a sixth sense or what?'

I thought it best not to tell him that it was Jamaal Bakaar himself who'd given me the clue. 'They told me they're part of the programme and are expecting their first deliveries any day now. They're excited that at last there's a peace dividend that will help.'

I thought back to Sayed's village and his excitement and pride when he told me about the restored clinic. Was all that effort in trying to bring peace and progress going to be wasted? 'Tell them not to do anything if it arrives before me. Tell them I'm coming out there.'

Next I called Brent. 'Thanks for the chopper. Now can you get me a plane?' After I'd listen to him expostulating for a while I cut in. 'I've seen the fleets some of these agencies have, there must be something leaving here. When I was in Afghanistan there were always one of your flights coming in or out.'

As I hung up I realised that even if I got to Afghanistan I would have problems in tracking and shipments. Most of our regiment had left and I didn't know any of the people who had replaced us. Although I was reluctant to try, I realised that my only chance lay with Ali. I tried his number and hoped that he wouldn't see it was me calling and refuse to answer. I gave up after several minutes and instead called James in the Whitehall office knowing that he was usually chained to his desk. I told him I needed to speak to Ali urgently and to get him to call me back. As I hung up, I realised that I hadn't eaten since throwing up half the Indian Ocean, so I went in search of the airport cafe where I ordered myself a quick snack, while looking anxiously at my phone.

Finally, Ali called and I snatched it up. 'Ali. It's me. I'm in Kenya and I need your help.' Ali grunted something unintelligible which I ignored. 'I told you about the possibility that they were supplying counterfeit drugs to the huge vaccination programme in East Africa? We've tracked them down and they were fakes.'

'So what are you ringing for? Congratulations?'

'No, listen. I could be wrong but there's a strong suggestion that while we've been chasing the shipments here, another delivery has already been sent to Afghanistan. There's a similar programme there so I need you to check with your contacts and find out where they're likely to be bringing it into the country. The chances are they're counterfeits as well.'

The pause before he answered made me think we had got cut off and I was going to ring again, when he answered. 'Not asking much, are you? How do you expect me to track a single shipment of pharmaceuticals in a country the size of Afghanistan while I'm here in the UK? I hadn't realised you had such a high opinion of me.'

'We can narrow it down. Get in touch with Brent Hillman at the FDA – he's here in Mombasa and I'll tell him to expect your call. He'll be able to find out where the deliveries are supposed to be made and you've got enough contacts out there to be able to intercept it.' I could sense his doubts so I added, 'There are thousands of lives at risk here. We've got to stop it and I don't know who else to ask. You're still in army intelligence and they'll listen to you.'

There was another pause. 'All right.' He said it reluctantly. 'I'll see what I can do. Give me contact details for this Brent person. I'll see if he knows where this shipment is being sent. What is it, by the way?'

'Malaria and measles mainly. Apparently some polio.' I read off Brent's number and told Ali to keep in touch. The triumph I'd felt a few hours earlier had disappeared. Instead, I realised that I'd been too close to the chase to step back and look at it objectively. I, of all people, particularly after my time in Afghanistan, should have known that East Africa was only one battleground and Jamaal had been right about the war being fought on a larger canvas.

But this was a different war with different battles to his. His saw only death and destruction as the objective and life-saving drugs as western interference that had to be stopped. There was no place for the simple things of life in his warped view of the world: bringing up families in peace and security and seeing them live to adulthood; a society which was not controlled by fanatics and which might finally liberate its women. My fight in Afghanistan might have changed little but I'd been on the right side. Jamaal was fighting for oppression, while we had been fighting for at least some kind of freedom.

My thoughts were interrupted by Brent on my mobile phone. He told me that there was a flight leaving for Islamabad in Pakistan and that I should be able to get an onward flight from there. Juma was still mopping up in Shimoni and there wasn't anything more he could do in Mombasa. Meanwhile, I went to track down the aid agency and introduce myself as an additional passenger on the Pakistan flight.

The transport plane had no outside communication beyond the local traffic controllers, so when we finally touched down at Bost Airfield in Lashkar Gah, I was in a state of frustrated excitement. I glared at my phone willing the bars to emerge to tell me I had a signal and as soon as it did so I dialled Brent's number. I'd been out of touch for nearly twenty-four hours – time in which the vaccines could have been distributed and even, perhaps, used.

Nobody stopped me as I walked through the customs area, waiting for Brent to answer. I had no idea where – or even whether – the vaccines had been delivered and until Brent gave me a lead I couldn't see what I could do. Frustratingly, my call eventually went to his voicemail and I left another message. I looked around me. If the goods had been sent airfreight then this was one of the airports they would have used, so I went over to the customs office to ask. As I did so I heard my name called out and turned. 'Ali! What on earth are you doing here?' He was the last person I expected to see.

'When you told me there was a problem with the vaccines, I made some enquiries and found a flight coming out here, so I decided I'd jump on and see what I could find out.'

'And what have you found out?' I asked, although I was still trying to understand why he was here. He'd never shown any interest in the Afghanistan health programmes before.

'I made contact with the FDA man as you suggested and he'd managed to track down the main delivery to Kabul Airport. I told him that I'd go there myself and get the authorities to hold it back.'

'So what are you doing here?'

'When I got to Kabul it seemed that one onward shipment had been made here to Bost Airport, so I came to check it out.'

'And have you been able to locate it yet?' There was something about his explanation that didn't quite ring true.

'Yes, they're looking after it back in the customs shed.'

'Show me. I've got the Truscan equipment and can test it.' I followed him back inside and recognised the boxes containing the vaccines which I had seen in Shimoni.

It took me a few minutes to test a sample with the same result. 'Identical to the consignment we stopped in Kenya. These drugs are lethal. Did you manage to stop them all?'

'All except a batch that's been sent onto the clinic at Chorjah. I was arranging transport so I could follow it down there and then you turned up. I wasn't expecting you.'

'I wasn't expecting to come either, but you've managed to hold back the vaccines?'

'There are still army liaison officers at the major airports. I contacted them and told them to hold onto the vaccines until we arrived. I've got a vehicle outside but we need to hurry if we're going to catch them.'

'Where's your car?'

'I've borrowed a Land Rover – it's parked outside. But we've got to hurry.'

I looked him up and down. 'You're not armed? If we meet trouble we might need some firepower. I'm a civilian now, I can't carry guns.'

'That's okay. Don't worry about it.'

'Great! Give me a few minutes. I've been travelling all night and I need to clean up a bit.'

'We have to leave now,' he insisted. 'I can go ahead on my own and you can follow.'

'A few minutes isn't going to make any difference. We can easily catch up with them.' I went back into the customs area to have a look around and tried Brent one more time. He answered and I relayed what Ali had told me and listened carefully to his response before going back to the customs shed and talking to the security guards there.

'Where've you been?' Ali asked as I joined him in the Land Rover a little while later.

'I told you I needed to clean up first. We'll be okay.'

Ali put the car into gear and was about to drive off when I stopped him. 'The customs officer needs some kind of authority to hold back the vaccinations. I told him he could use my name but he said he needed a signature from someone in authority so there wouldn't be a comeback if it all went wrong. They know who you are so can you go and sign his wretched clipboard?'

'I told them myself,' he snapped. 'I don't need to tell them a second time.'

'Apparently, you do. It's only a signature.'

Ali put the car back into neutral and swore loudly.

'It'll only take a few minutes,' I said encouragingly. 'We'll soon catch up with them.'

Ali looked at me and swore again. 'Stay there. Don't wander off.'

I watched him go back inside the terminal and then climbed out to check what he had in the back.

As Ali drove through the dusty roads, I looked around at the familiar landscape and wondered about warfare. There were many different types of weapon. When I'd been here it was the gun, the landmine and the bomb, but now things were more sophisticated – if that was the right word. There didn't seem to me to be anything sophisticated about attacking children by denying them the protection of modern medicine. To me it seemed positively medieval. The stakes were raised at every stage and the deceptive monochrome landscape around me hid even more horrors than it had before. This apparently anodyne, featureless terrain was once again hiding an even greater hatred and opposing it with ever more desperate measures. Bombs or mines could kill only a few dozen, adulterated vaccines could affect thousands.

I was brought up suddenly in my reveries when the car swerved off the road and pulled to a halt at the edge of a bluff overlooking the long valley beneath. As the dust settled around us, I realised that the time had finally come.

'Wait here,' Ali said and went around to the back and opened up his case. 'I think this, as they say, is where you get off.' I looked across as he came back with a gun pointing at me. 'Get out.'

Under the circumstances I couldn't see any reason not to. 'I was hoping it wouldn't come to this,' I said. 'But that was never very likely, was it? It all started here for you, didn't it?'

'I have no idea what you're talking about. Move over there.' He gestured with the gun. 'No one will ever find you here. In a few days the dust will cover you and no one will know.'

'This is it, then? You're going to shoot me here?'

Ali looked around and shrugged. 'It's as good a place as any. It's probably something I should have done a long time ago.'

'When we were both here together, you mean? When you first saw the light at the head of your twisted road?'

'What are you talking about?'

'You know what I'm talking about. When you were here you were turned, weren't you? All that professing to be done with religious dogma, being modern and forward-looking? I have to say you hid it well; there were only a few clues.'

A look of doubt crossed Ali's face. 'Clues? What clues?'

'I should have realised when you had everyone following Sayed's van – everyone except me, that is. You almost got away with it, didn't you?'

'We don't have to win all the battles,' he said defiantly. 'But this is one I'm about to win. Now move over there.' He waved his gun towards the cliff edge.

At that moment, we heard the low growl of a diesel truck which was labouring up the incline behind us. Ali glanced at it. 'Get back into the car. Back into the passenger seat, until the truck's gone past.'

I wanted to see this through, so I perched on the seat while we watched the truck. I looked back at Ali who appeared increasingly nervous and when the truck had gone he snapped at me to stand up.

I stood up, but kept my hands by my side. 'I can't believe that with your education these people were able to corrupt you. What were you thinking of? You must know they're fanatics.'

Ali waved his gun again. 'Over there. Stand on the edge and look down. It'll be the last thing you see.'

'Can't you answer? How do you justify the warped ideology that you seem to be following? What you're doing is crazy.'

'No. What the West is doing is crazy. You don't think I haven't wrestled with this? But in the end, you made it easy for me.'

'Me? How?'

'That time in Chorjah, it all became clear to me. People like you shouldn't be allowed to tell other countries how they should behave. When you shot at that boy it was like a mist lifting.'

'But I aimed to miss him, you must know that. Anyway, isn't it you who's telling others how they should behave?'

'It's the Koran that tells them, not me.' He waved the gun again. 'Now get over there.'

I realised it was pointless reasoning with him and moved closer to the edge. 'You planted the files, didn't you? It was you who got me sacked, but why? I thought we were friends.'

'We had no business in places like Chorjah. You shouldn't have been there – *we* shouldn't have been there.'

'So you think it will make it all right if you manage to get these counterfeit drugs through? They're fakes – you watched me test them back at the airport, but you already knew that, didn't you?'

He nodded. 'After you'd rung me from Kenya I made some enquiries through my handlers and they told me about it. That's why I flew out here. I knew you might try to stop them and so I had to stop you.'

'But you've made one mistake too many, haven't you?'

Ali moved closer towards me. 'I don't think so. I think it's you who made the mistake by coming out here.'

I shook my head. 'It's one of the first lessons we're taught, isn't it? We're told to look out for the sign. You even told Sayed about it.'

'What sign?' Ali waved his gun again.

'It's a giveaway. The make-up.'

Involuntarily, he reached up and wiped his finger across his forehead.

'You see?' I said. 'You know exactly what I'm talking about. You hoped the mark wouldn't show. You've been praying, haven't you? Praying quite hard by the look of it. Every time you push your head to the ground it leaves a mark.'

Ali took his hand away. 'Okay, so now you know, but it's too late to do you much good where you're going.'

'I think I should tell you that I spoke to the FDA man Brent and he brought in his people who spoke to the customs people at Bost. The signature they asked for was show, the vaccines aren't going anywhere and they've all been held at the other locations. This is a battle you haven't won.' I could see that Ali was trying to work out where exactly he'd gone wrong. 'What is it about people like you?' I asked. 'Why do you want to run other people's lives for them? Why don't you leave them to bring up their families in peace? Why do you think you know better than them?'

'Don't try and make out you know about me. People like you can never know what the real truth is.'

'You turn everything upside down. For you the real truth is lies. For you, death is life while dealing with the sick is to let them die. How many people will suffer if they don't get proper medicines? Think about Shamir Alam – Sayed's brother with polio. Having the right vaccines could have prevented that. Why do you want to hurt them?'

'Because it's the will of Allah, but you wouldn't understand that, would you?'

'Just as it's the will of Allah to kill me?'

'You're insignificant, you count for nothing; less than a grain of sand.' He raised the gun, cocked it and pulled the trigger. I couldn't help flinching.

'I told you, the attempt at make-up gave you away.' I reached into my pocket and held out the bullets. 'You don't think I was going to leave you with a loaded gun, did you? I took them out when you went back to the customs shed. So now what?'

Ali screamed in fury, hurled his gun at me and threw himself forward but I was ready for him and sidestepped quickly and crouched low to trip him. As he fell, he managed to grab at a tree root and hang on, but the root slowly started to pull out of the ground. He stared up at me, an expression of pure hatred on his face, but he said nothing as he slowly slipped and then fell down the cliff. His body bounced a couple of times but then lay still. I left him there. After a few days the dust would cover him and he would be just another anonymous casualty of this never-ending war.

I drove on slowly to Chorjah.

As Sayed had reported, the clinic had been restored and the village was looking, if not yet prosperous, at least peaceful – a peace that people like Ali wanted to destroy.

At the rear of the clinic I found the driver unloading the vaccines and I told him to take them back to the airport. I looked inside his truck where more neat boxes of blister-packed drugs were waiting to be unloaded. Something that was designed to help cure people had instead been sabotaged to try to kill them. They looked so innocent, but they'd been turned into yet another weapon. Things in this war were rarely as they seemed.

When I'd left the last time I'd been a soldier; now I was back and all I'd done was to substitute one kind of fighting for another.

I watched the driver put back the boxes and drive off and as the swirling dust gradually settled behind him, I thought that although there had been times when I'd nearly given up, at least this had been one battle we'd won.

Epilogue

'The owner was supposed to be coming back next week, but his contract has been extended so I can stay.' Greta and I had finished dinner and were sitting up on deck drinking coffee. The river was putting on its usual performance, with the office lights high in the sky competing with the stars. The floodlit Tower Bridge was looking particularly splendid as a flotilla of tourist boats passed underneath with the flashes of their cameras looking like distant gunfire. 'I suppose that means that I've got to get around to completing all the outstanding work, but I've been a bit busy.'

Greta laughed. 'A bit. So what are you going to do now?'

'Apart from finishing the barge, you mean? I had a funny conversation with Ken Maxwell when we got back to London. He kept talking around the subject, but I think he was asking whether I wanted a job with them. These people never come out with a straightforward offer – they have to sort of dangle the prospect in front of you for a few days to see if you bite and ask them for a job.'

'And will you? Bite, I mean.'

'It's funny that. I walked out into the street with Brent and I think he was offering me a job as well. A sort of roving trouble-shooter for drug enforcement. Sounded quite interesting. You know that when they added up all the fake drugs they seized in Kenya, Zanzibar, Mumbai and Afghanistan it added up to nearly twenty million dollars' worth. Perhaps if the FDA were to put me on commission it might be interesting. But he told me that there would be some kind of reward from the big pharmaceutical companies, so that's a bonus. It should mean that I won't have to make any decisions for the time being.'

'So when they arrested everyone in the Kenyan operation, everything they were unloading was fake?'

'We stopped them unloading and got them to put everything back. They went into the hold and sampled a few of the packages with a Truscan unit and got almost zero readings for the active ingredients. So I suggested that they impound the dhow and take it straight to Mombasa where they could destroy them. It was clear that the drivers of the pickups hadn't a clue about what they were supposed to be collecting, although being there at sunrise in a secluded mangrove swamp should have given some of them an idea that what they were doing was at least dubious. It would have been difficult to prove anything against them so we let them go. Kenyan customs, with a bit of help from the FDA, raided Tau's operation and found a complete range of counterfeits – everything from anti-HIV treatments to blood-pressure medications – the lot.'

'But what about Afghanistan?'

'We were just in time. The FDA managed to hold them back at the airports before they were used.'

'And the Bakaar family?'

'Ajmal Bakaar hired a hotshot firm of public relations consultants to firefight for him. You can imagine the damage this has done to his reputation but I believe him when he said he knew nothing about it.'

'But from what you say, they were running a production line of fake drugs in one of his main factories. How could he not know about it?'

'It's only one of the things they do. They've got interests all over the place and Ajmal can't be expected to know everything. But I think they'll be cleaning out their stables after this. I heard that his son Jamaal has been removed as head of the East African division, which is a pretty good indication of guilt, even if nothing can be proved.'

'But what's going to happen to the immunisation programme?'

'That's the good news. Ajmal Bakaar has offered to supply them with the drugs at no charge by way of compensation – I suppose that's the advice the PR company gave him. It certainly made him look good and the cost of it is nothing compared with the potential damage. If he hadn't made the offer, he might have been forced to pay up anyway, so it's not really that generous.'

'Perhaps.' Greta seemed preoccupied and I realised how tough things had been for her while I was away.

'I'm sorry, Greta, I haven't asked how you've been. It must have been difficult with all the… the arrangements. I was sorry I couldn't get to the funeral – how did it go?'

'It was my father's funeral – how do you think it went?' Greta stopped suddenly and stared into the distance.

'I'm sorry, I didn't mean that,' she said after a while. 'It hasn't been a good time and then to discover that the drugs that killed him might have killed thousands more made it very difficult.'

Finally she turned back to me. 'But what happened to the IHG hospital? It was their drugs that killed my father. Isn't anything happening to them?'

I shook my head. 'It was a tragic accident. They were running two operations in parallel in Mumbai, the genuine and the counterfeit and I think someone made a mistake and they got mixed up. Like so many things I think it was a cock-up.'

'So they kill my father and get off scot-free?'

'Ed Carpenter told me they didn't have enough evidence. He was with me when we found they'd cleared their shelves of the fakes so they didn't have much to go on. They had your father's prescription but it wasn't enough. He says that they've made it clear to the top IHG management that they know what happened and insisted they introduce new safeguards.'

'Safeguards? Is that what they're called? Excuses, more like.'

I reached out and took her hand. 'If we hadn't discovered it thousands could have died, so good did come of it.'

'I suppose so,' she said reluctantly. 'Bit I miss him so much. I still find myself wanting to tell him something and picking up the phone to call him.'

I said nothing and she took her hand back. I left her alone with her memories and went below to get some cognac. I brought it topside and held it out to her. 'It's VSOP.' Greta nodded and I poured her out a glass. 'More coffee?'

'No thanks,' she said and sipped her brandy. 'It's a difficult world out there and sometimes I want to shut it out and retreat into my shell.' She said nothing and looked across at the lights. 'This is a pretty good shell to retreat to. To a perfect host – the meal was wonderful.' She held up her glass in a toast.

'To the perfect guest,' I said, and we clinked glasses. 'And I can't imagine anyone I'd prefer to spend the evening with.'

'And the night?' Greta said with welcome shamelessness.

'Especially the night.' I raised my glass again.

We sipped our brandies without saying anything, recognising that we had stepped over a threshold.

'But you still haven't told me who planted the files,' Greta said.

I hadn't told her about my final meeting with Ali and didn't intend to just yet. There would be time for that in the future. 'That all seems so long ago,' I lied. 'I'd almost forgotten about it.'

'You were pretty sore at the time.'

'I suppose I was, but once I'd worked out who'd done it, I sort of lost interest.'

Greta sat up in her chair. 'So who was it?'

'It was Ali. No one else had access to the files and to my quarters.'

'But Ali was your best friend. Why would he do anything like that?'

'I thought he was but I found out otherwise.' I thought back to the enveloping dust of Afghanistan. 'I'm not sure it matters now. If it hadn't been for him, you would never have come looking for my help, so that makes it all worthwhile.'

'If it hadn't been for him, you wouldn't have spent the past few weeks travelling the world like a knight on a charger.'

'That's me; a knight in armour putting right wrongs and rescuing the damsel from a fate worse than death.' I put down my glass and stood up and held out my hand to her. 'When I've finished working on the boat, what do you say to a holiday together? I know a very special island, fringed with palm trees with the Indian Ocean lapping its beaches.'

I'd let her find out about the bats when we got there.